THE PIRATE

Sir Walter Scott

Nothing in him—,
But doth suffer a sea-change.
THE TEMPEST

THE ROOST OF SUMBURGH

With a foreword by
Andrew Wawn

The Shetland Times Ltd.
Lerwick
1996

This edition published 1996 and printed by
The Shetland Times Ltd., Prince Alfred Street,
Lerwick, Shetland, ZE1 0EP.

Reprinted from the text of the 1871 Centenary edition published by
Adam and Charles Black, Edinburgh.

ISBN 1 898852 17 0

Cover design by The Stafford Partnership, Shetland.

The publisher acknowledges subsidy from

THE SCOTTISH **ARTS** COUNCIL

towards the publication of this volume.

CONTENTS

FOREWORD

I

'Who has not read the *Pirate*?' asks an enthusiastic anonymous columnist in the *New York Herald* in 1887. The nineteenth-century response would be that countless readers all over the English-speaking world *had* read and enjoyed Sir Walter Scott's novel of life, love and old lore set in seventeenth-century Orkney and Shetland. Published in December 1821, the work remained readily available for a hundred years, either as an individual novel or in successive Victorian and Edwardian reprintings and repackagings of the complete set of 'Waverley novels'. The Library of Congress catalogue lists well over sixty entries (many of them American) for the novel up to 1925 – and, just as strikingly, not a single entry after that date. *The Pirate* was also imitated, illustrated, epitomised, excerpted for children, set to music, dramatised on the London stage within three weeks of publication,[1] and translated for readers in Germany, Spain and (eventually and appropriately) Iceland; its many poems took their place amongst the light musical fare of fashionable soirées, and its characters were frequently referred to in Victorian travel books about Iceland with a familiarity nowadays reserved for soap-opera favourites. Indeed the sometimes hazy distinction between historical fact and popular fiction finally dissolved in the 1887 *New York Herald* article, re-published in a Shetland newspaper, when readers were informed that the former Miss Rae, a young Orcadian woman whose father had escorted 'the author of *Waverley*' (then newly published) round the island sites during his brief 1814 visit,[2] and on whom the character of Brenda in the novel is supposedly based, was still alive and well and living as an elderly widow in Hamilton, Ontario. Indeed she was sprightly enough to be able to pick up her well-thumbed copy of the novel, and read out to the duly deferential journalist 'the description of the two lovely daughters of "Magnus Troil"'.[3]

The nature and extent of nineteenth-century enthusiasm for *The Pirate* must surprise even the most committed twentieth-century follower of Scott. No modern admirer has seen fit to follow the example of an Icelandic acquaintance of Sir Walter, a formidable and irascible Edinburgh-based philologist called Þorleifur Guðmundsson Repp, who invariably referred to 'the Author of *Waverley*' as 'the author of *The Pirate*'.[4] It is hard to imagine a late twentieth-century exchange between a highly esteemed modern novelist and an enthusiastic reader equivalent to that between Scott and a Dr Yelloly of Carrow Abbey in June 1831. The doctor claims with ponderous lightheartedness to be a descendant of the novel's Yorkshire-born, St Andrews University

I

educated 'projector' and technocrat Triptolemus Yellowley,[5] and requests that he and his family be received at Abbotsford.[6] It is even harder to imagine a modern scholar of Old Icelandic literature and folklore following the example of the great nineteenth-century Oxford-based scholar Guðbrandur Vigfússon, who annotated his copy of Jón Árnason's collection of Icelandic folktales with references to Orkney and Shetland folk customs derived from *The Pirate*.[7]

The melancholy but honest current answer to the question 'Who has not read *The Pirate*?' must be 'virtually everyone'. To the 'common reader' the novel remains in every sense a closed book; and even amongst Scott *aficionados*, few seem familiar with – and fewer enthusiastic about – this atmospheric family drama narrative of confused identities set against a backdrop of misty northern antiquity. *The Pirate* never gained entry into the tiny ring-fenced canon of Scott's works which, even during his post-war fall from favour, enjoyed the protection afforded either by Examination Board syllabus, or colourful Hollywood transformation: *The Pirate* is no *Ivanhoe*; and Clement Cleveland is no Robin Hood. BBC producers have delighted prime ministers by resurrecting Trollope's cathedral closes for the small screen; Scott's windswept glens have not been so fortunate. Nor, during those dog-days of scholarly disregard, did *The Pirate* attract any of the academic scrutiny assigned, for example, to *Waverley*, as a significant staging post in the evolution of the historical novel in English. More recently, as the academic study of literature in the English-speaking world began its improbable infatuation with new theoretical approaches born in the mandarin academies of France, the outlook for *The Pirate* seemed at first sight no brighter. Scott may refer disarmingly to 'our wandering narrative' (269),[8] but it remains a story with a beginning, a middle and an ending, and thus offers no easy pickings to devotees of postmodernist narrative fracture and dislocation. Worse still, *The Pirate* is the work of a once canonical novelist – and he a dead, white, European male to boot: sins enough, it might be thought, to banish the novel to the darkest recesses of university library stacks. And, though supporters of the novel might draw attention to its popularity amongst writers as spectacularly dissimilar as Rudyard Kipling (Stalky and his chums could quote from it), John Cowper Powys[9] and George Bernard Shaw, it is not clear that the terms of Shaw's praise, at least, would commend the novel to a feminist audience seventy years later. Writing to a young actress while staying in Thurso in the summer of 1925, Shaw says that he has been not just 'reading' but '*re*- [my emphasis] reading' *The Pirate* while waiting for the boat to ferry him to Kirkwall: 'as a story teller and entertainer he [Scott] beats hollow all the fearfully clever modern women whose books made one miserable.'[10]

Yet, in the last decade or so, in spite of – or perhaps, indeed, because of – new theoretical approaches within the multinational industry that is modern literary scholarship, Shavian levels of enthusiasm towards Sir Walter Scott's virtues as a novelist have shown signs of re-emerging. The vigorous overall revival of his fortunes – the launch of a major new project to re-edit all the novels, a new biography, several book-length critical studies, and a steady stream of articles in the learned journals — has helped to float even *The Pirate* off the rocks of neglect. Scott, Shaw's merry 'story teller and entertainer', has been replaced by Scott the shrewd chronicler and probing philosopher. It is possible to reflect on the novel's clash between patriarchal benevolence (Magnus Troil) and individualistic capitalism (Triptolemus); its shrewd exploration of gender roles and sibling rivalries (Brenda vs Minna; Clement vs Mordaunt); the universalising force of the text's multiple historical layerings (prehistoric monuments, Viking-age sea-kings, medieval Norse saints, seventeenth-century poets, eighteenth-century pirates, and, proleptically, nineteenth-century ploughs); its concern with what defines nation and nationhood (Shetland vs Orkney; Shetland and Orkney vs Scotland; Shetland, Orkney and Scotland vs England); its fascination with cultural margins as well as centres (the North Atlantic islands vs mainland Britain; pirate ships vs the Royal Navy; witchcraft and the supernatural vs scientific rationalism); its diffused gothicism (Norna of the Fitful Head and her Dunrossness eyrie; the eerie Stones of Stenness; the shadowy aisles of the St Magnus Cathedral at Kirkwall; the 'dreadful' storms and 'hideous combustions of the elements'); its unusual (for 1822) philological and antiquarian depth in both text and notes (from Þormóður Torfason to Thomas Gray; from Bartholinus to Barry's *History of the Orkneys*); its dialectal and idiolectal alertness (from the manipulative Bryce Snailsfoot to the miserly Mistress Barbara Yellowley; from Captain Goffe to Lady Glowrowrum). Nor is the drama of *The Pirate* confined within its narrative frame; the history of the novel's publication, as recently revealed,[11] offers striking evidence of the sometimes bumpy journey of a nineteenth-century novel from script to print.

Some commentators remain to be convinced, however. Perhaps J. G. Lockhart's tales of the breezily uncomplicated nature of his father-in-law's *furor poeticus* while writing *The Pirate* may not have helped the novel's cause in an age unduly impressed by careworn creativity: with Scott it was the quick breakfast, the dash to the dressing room to spin off the next chapter of one or other of the two novels on the needles at that time (*The Pirate* and *The Fortunes of Nigel*), the request that this or that guest might care to flick through the morning's work, the task of parcelling up the pages and catching the next post to the publisher in Edinburgh — and then, with some relief, the trek to wherever on the estate the builders or foresters were busily at work. Scott's 'cracking on well' progress was delayed only by a missing book or an absent well-informed friend.[12] Certainly some modern comments and criticisms resemble uncannily those published within months of the novel's first appearance. We find the *Gentleman's Magazine* critic in 1821 complaining that *The Pirate* was not so much a novel but more 'an essay on the topography of the island of Zetland and the manners and customs of the inhabitants'; whilst over a hundred years later Agnes Mure Mackenzie claimed that 'it is a good guide book, but pure tushery as fiction'.[13] More recently, in his stimulating and irreverent new biography of Scott, John Sutherland strums on a sceptical string:[14] *The Pirate* is a work produced during an 'increasingly superficial' phase in the novelist's creative life, 'dashed off' after 'a day trip to the culture' of Orkney and Shetland, and with an undernourished narrative padded out with ill-digested antiquarian ballast.[15] This recalls Scott's oft-quoted remark that, in *The Pirate*, he was 'making my bricks out of a very limited amount of straw';[16] whilst an early reviewer noted wryly that 'he gives us one volume for ourselves and two volumes for himself'.[17]

The critical debate is, thus, joined anew; and, as ever, readers will want to make up their own minds – but this has been hard to do without ready access to a text of the novel, and *The Pirate* has long been virtually unattainable. No new edition of *The Pirate* has appeared since the 1920s; and even in those second-hand bookshops whose shelves groan under the weight of unsold and incomplete old sets of Scott's novels, copies of *The Pirate* are, in the present writer's experience, as seldom seen as white ravens. The present reprint of the 1871 Centenary edition text allows the novel to regain its rightful place within the public domain.

II

Furnished with a text, readers may well enjoy comparing their own responses with those of earlier generations of critics. One factor which helped to establish a framework for the initial reception of Scott's novel was the (then) current taste for tales about piracy and the sea.[18] While the late twentieth-century mindset has to make do with distant memories of Captain Pugwash, or *The Pirates of Penzance*, or skull-and-crossbones figures from Legoland, early nineteenth-century readers (and theatregoers) of all ages were spoilt for choice. Dozens of swash-buckling heroes fought for their attention, from C. F. Barrett, *The Corsican Pirate; or, the Grand Master of Malta; A Neopolitan Romance* (1805) to *Black Beard the Pirate; or, The Captive Princess: A Drama* (1822); and from [anon], *The Robber of the Wood, and the Russian Pirate: Shewing how the Former came to Life after being broken on the Wheel* (c. 1820; published by the Religious Tract Society – clearly the devil was not to have all the best piratical tunes) to William Bayle Bernard, *The Freebooter's Bride; or, The Black Pirate of the Mediter-ranean: including the Mystery of the Morescoes; a Romance* (1829). To this list we should add James Fenimore Cooper's *The Pilot* (1823), a title and publication date sufficiently close to Scott's work to suggest influence, or even pastiche; this Orkney- and Shetland-related tale has a transatlantic piratical element, with the notorious John Paul Jones, no less, as the shadowy and manipulative eponymous hero.

Clearly, then, if Scott's *The Pirate* was going to make any headway in such a crowded market, the piracy needed some fresh spin on it. Scott had found some of the elements he was looking for – a big theme and an old lore context – whilst working on his earlier narrative poem 'Harold the Dauntless' (1817).[19] The poem tells of Harold, fiery young

IV

son of the Norse King Witikind who, much to his son's disgust, resolved to receive Christian baptism at the end of his life in return for a grant of lands from the Church. Harold, distraught at his father's betrayal of Viking ideals, leaves home. On his travels he encounters and declares his intention to marry the princess Metelill who is already betrothed to the English Lord William. Wulfstane, the girl's father, is appalled by the pagan wildness of this prospective rival son-in-law. Meanwhile the Church authorities scheme to disinherit Harold; he responds violently, but is persuaded into undertaking a knightly quest, during which he hears a ghostly presence (Witikind) lamenting his own fate — condemned to wander as a restless spirit for as long as his unrepentant son is on the rampage. Chancing upon the princess's wedding procession, Harold kills her father and had it not been for the intervention of the Danish warrior's servant Gunnarr, would have killed the bridegroom also. Reaching the destination of his quest, a castle, Harold is tormented by a further nightmarish vision— the region of death, with those confined there making eager preparations for Harold's arrival. He finally confronts and destroys the Odinic spirit ruling over the region, rescues his young companion Gunnarr from Óðinn's malign embrace; Gunnarr (somewhat improbably) turns out to be Eivir, a desirable Danish maiden. Harold announces that he intends to be baptised and wed to Eivir on the same day; the troubled spirit of his father may now rest in peace.

There are several features of the poem which anticipate elements in *The Pirate*. In terms of the work's literary form we have the inset songs and the diversity of mood they help to create, and the supernatural infrastructure (visits to sacrificial shrines, fateful visions, talking trees, bizarre transformations); in terms of character and type-scene we have a wild-eyed sibyl, a diminutive but loyal retainer, and a celebratory feast; and as for themes we may note the clash between romantic individualism and patriarchal authority (both secular and sacred), and between indigenous and invasive cultural values — and there is a rite of passage element in the form of a semi-allegorical battle for the soul of an adolescent infatuated with the berserker values of the Viking age. The hero's stumbling progress towards a more other-centred maturity in Christian marriage is the controlling idea of the poem.

When Scott came to put novelistic flesh on the bones of his pirate story, these were amongst the elements which he sought to recycle and deploy. They provided him with a substantial and original narrative platform on which he could recreate the world of John Gow (or Goffe), a notorious early eighteenth-century pirate. And when to these narrative possibilities were added Scott's shrewd rejection of sultry South Seas exoticism in favour of bleak northern localism; and his vivid sense of north Atlantic island history; and his eagerness to dramatise and debate cultural tensions on several levels; and, not least, his vivid pictorial sense — such raw materials, in Scott's hands, added up to a good deal more than just another formulaic pirate story.

V

If we reflect on some of these distinctive features which Scott wove into his novel, it is the pictorial element which immediately catches the modern eye as we turn the pages of the often lavishly illustrated nineteenth-century editions of *The Pirate*.[20] It was no random figment of George Eliot's novelistic imagination when, in *The Mill on the Floss* (1860), Maggie Tulliver's friend and suitor Philip Wakem arrives one day with the second of three volumes of *The Pirate* in his hand — he was 'studying a scene for a picture'.[21] Several of the pictures which recur in nineteenth-century editions derive from a set of five engravings published in a lavish volume for members of the Royal Association for the Promotion of the Fine Arts in Scotland in 1871.[22] We observe first the sturdy domesticity of Magnus Troil in his comfortable living room along with his daughters Brenda (representing devoted sense) and Minna (disruptive sensibility) — the former seated next to her father and clasping a sheet of music (betokening, no doubt, the cultivation of appropriately womanly arts and virtues), whilst her sister's dreamy, far away look as she stands by the hearth hints at less decorous visions of Viking rovers in their dragon-beaked barques; then there is the foamy wildness of the storm and shipwreck from which Clement Cleveland is rescued; there is the prickly altercation between the uniformed and dignified Cleveland and the pedlar Bryce Snailsfoot, the latter all rhymes, ribbons and native wit; there is the scene aboard the pirate ship in which the temporarily captive Minna receives a pistol with which to defend herself from the cheery and cultivated brigand Bunce (who once trod the boards of Drury Lane), her firm resolve to secure safe passage ashore contrasting with Brenda's terror-struck prostration; and, lastly, every artist's favourite subject, there is the gothic frenzy of Norna of the Fitful Head, in her bleak headland home, performing her curative spells over and around an inert Minna — the sinister sibyl, looking rather younger than one might have imagined her, appears with dark dishevelled hair, dagger in belt, runic markings on skirt, and Norse-style clasps on cloak. In 'The Fatal Sisters' (published 1768), one of Thomas Gray's pair of seductive and much imitated verse paraphrases of Old Norse poems,[23] which found its way into Scott's novel and notes (122, 345-6), the Valkyries 'weave the web of death' for warriors at the bloody Battle of Clontarf; in the 1871 picture, Norna seeks rather to weave the web of life, looking, for all the world, like a saga-age Lady of Shalott, windswept, wild-eyed, and in every sense weird.

If pen and brush played their part in popularising *The Pirate*, so, too, did music and song, and from a very early date. In the 1822 *Quarterly Review*, the novel's very first reviewer claims that 'the poetry is below our author's standard'; and so some of it is when set beside 'The Lay of the Last Minstrel', or even 'Harold the Dauntless'. The shifting moods of the novel nevertheless find telling expression in several of the short lyric pieces: the ancient Viking martial spirit distilled in Claud Halcro's 'Song of Harold Harfager' (122); Bryce Snailsfoot's artful rhymes of self-promotion (263); Cleveland's surprisingly tender love lyrics (195); the hauntingly effective counterpoint between Norna and her transfixed audience in the splendid, saga-derived prophecy scene in Chapter 21

VI

(172-81); Norna's own haunting 'Song of the Reim-Kennar' (51) delivered, as always, in her 'slow, sad, almost ... unearthly accent'; and several boisterous pirate songs such as the 'Robin Rover' fragment (268), singled out for praise by the same *Quarterly Review* critic —'[it] has infinite spirit. You fancy you hear its triumphant chorus as they gallantly bend to their oars. It has a spark of fire carelessly struck out by a powerful hand'.[24] These poems enjoyed a life of their own in editions of Scott's verse, and even on occasions as songs in private performance. In London, in May 1828, a Mrs Arkwrignt entertained Scott and some friends at a small gathering — the great man asked admiringly if the verses sung were by Lord Byron, only to be told that they were by Scott himself, all taken straight from *The Pirate*. This intelligence gratified the great novelist at first — and then depressed him, as he brooded over his failing powers of memory in the last years of his life.[25]

III

Along with the pictures and the songs, Orcadian and Shetlandic actualities have long figured prominently in readers' responses to *The Pirate*. As with Shaw, it was (and surely ought still to be) a case of read the novel and then visit the scenes; or vice versa. With the rain beating down on and the wind whistling outside (if not through) guest-house windows or sailing-ship portholes, *The Pirate* has long offered and offers still bracing companionship for the Orkney and Shetland island traveller in search of 'the genius of the place'. So it is that we find the anonymous *A Walk in Shetland by Two Eccentrics* (Edinburgh, 1831), whose subtitle describes its contents as follows: 'An "Excellent Leetel" Harmless Quiz upon the Funny Shetlanders; and Sketches of "Things in General," from their Bogs and Pig-Styes, to their Geese and Claud Halcro; Being a Companion to The "Pirate," without Sir Walter Scott's Leave'. The eccentrics claim to have found amongst the 'funny Shetlanders' several Magnus Troil types, as well as 'the real original of Claud Halcro'.[26] Some Orkney and Shetland travellers were en route to Iceland, and the published accounts of their journeys sometimes exhibit a powerful engagement with the people and places in Scott's pirate tale. Thus the Reverend Frederick Metcalfe, most fervent of Victorian Icelandophiles, notes that Shetlanders use only the oil from whales, even when they are starving, and might with advantage eat the meat as well; he remarks that 'If Claud Halcro were still in the flesh, and had grown wiser with age, he would doubtless say with Glorious John [Dryden], "'Take the good the Gods provide thee,' and don't starve in the midst of plenty."'[27] So, too, when Metcalfe's imagination animates the medieval Icelandic *alþingi*, the crowded annual assembly on the plains at Þingvellir — we read of pedlars making their profitable way from booth to tent, 'the Bryce Snailsfoots of those times, with silver ornaments, and cloths fine and coarse'.[28] For Metcalfe, to visit the sites of northern antiquity, whether Iceland by ship or Shetland by novel, was more than an act of passive antiquarian curiosity; there is a flash of excitement as contact is renewed with the spiritual roots of the nation: 'all the great names ... of that Scandinavian breed, to which, and not to the Saxon, England owes her pluck, her dash, and her freedom.'[29]

The same pulse is discernible in C. W. G. Lock's 1879 Iceland travel book. Disturbance of his summer sailing schedule in 1875 had meant that the planned route for his voyage to Iceland would no longer include a stop-over at Lerwick. Lock expresses his disappointment at some length – his mind's-eye, *Pirate*-derived vision of Shetland was not to be nourished by first-hand exploration:

> It was here especially that the old Norse sea-kings halted on their western voyages in search of a new home. Here many remained, and built dwellings and gave pure old Norse names to every salient feature of the landscape, names on which a thousand years have had so little corruptible effect that in Iceland alone we can find their rivals for unsullied purity. What feelings would not have been created by visiting the scenes where the inimitable Sir Walter Scott laid his story of 'The Pirate;' how vivid the realizations of the life and surroundings of the old Udaller at Burgh Westra (Icelandic, *Vestriborg*, Western burg), and of the eccentric tenant of Jarlshof (Icelandic, *Járlshof*, Earl's Court). Even the names of the persons occurring in the tale are Norse; Swertha would be called *Svarta* (Black) in Icelandic, a reminder that nicknames are no modern growth; while Sweyn Erickson (Icelandic, *Sveinn [Eiríksson]*) is a name common in Iceland to this hour; and further, the drink *bland* is nought but the *blanda* of Ultima Thule, which I have often drunk, and the expression *jarto*, which the great novelist translates 'my dear,' is assuredly the Icelandic *hjarta* (heart), with scarcely an appreciable difference of pronunciation, the latter remaining still in everyday usage.[30]

Lock's delight in the philological continuities between Iceland and Britain's most northerly islands was no isolated phenomenon. It was shared by people of far greater political weight and moment, such as George Webbe Dasent, a magisterial figure amongst the ranks of saga translators and, more important in terms of influence, for several decades assistant editor of *The Times*. Dasent found the very idea of the Vikings as intoxicating as Minna Troil had done:

> [They possessed] an element of progress, a dash and energy wedded to an endurance and perseverance which no other European race possessed ... Everywhere ... in western and central Europe, where there was traffic to be driven or plunder to be got, where a keel could float or an anchor hold, where winds blew and billows rolled, these dauntless rovers showed their fair, but terrible features.[31]

And Dasent believed that ancient Viking blood still coursed in modern Victorian veins:

They [the Vikings] were like England in the nineteenth
century: fifty years before all the rest of the world with her
manufactories and firms — and twenty years before them
with her railways. They were foremost in the race of
civilisation and progress; well started before all the rest
had thought of running. No wonder therefore that both
won.[32]

There was, thus, a sense in which the images of Viking antiquity which
Scott's colourful piratical romance promoted and popularised so
successfully during the nineteenth century could be appropriated and
recast by some sections of mid-Victorian Britain in such a way as to
explain the spiritual origins and mercantile strengths of Queen
Victoria's vast empire on which the sun, as in an Icelandic summer, never
set.

If Minna Troil's dreams found an echo in the thunderings of *Times*
editors and editorials, there is a more specialised nineteenth-century
political context reflected in another of the novel's characters, Magnus
Troil, the udaller. During the 1880s a group of London-based Orcadians
and Shetlanders founded the Udal League, whose constitution sought to
'promote and encourage a general revival and assertion of the Teutonic
or Norse characteristics of the British nation — straightforwardness, and
obedience to Constitutional law and government'. This latter phrase was
a coded attack on the more interventionist side of Queen Victoria's
monarchical practice, so different from the ideal of constitutional
monarchy and participatory democracy promoted in Victorian readings
of the Icelandic historian Snorri Sturluson's *Heimskringla*, or 'The
Chronicles of the Norse Kings' as the work became known in Samuel
Laing's pioneering and immensely influential 1844 English translation.
Laing's trenchant introductory dissertation celebrates modern udaller
values (notably peasant proprietorship, and the inalienable nature of
traditionally free udal lands), and draws attention to their ancient
representation in Snorri's masterwork. Small wonder that Laing himself,
a frustrated parliamentary candidate for Orkney and Shetland in 1832,
published three pamphlets during the 1846 general election — all of
them under the pseudonym Magnus Troil.[33] And no prizes for guessing
which character in Scott's novel proved most sympathetic to the Udal
Leaguers.

The Pirate had a different readership with different socio-political
agendas in Scott's Edinburgh. It had been an Icelander, Grímur Jónsson
Thorkelín, who had urged John Jamieson to undertake his pioneering
An Etymological Dictionary of the Scottish Language (1808); and it was
another Icelander, Þorleifur Repp, drawing on Jamieson's example, who
lost no opportunity to convince his Edinburgh readers, lecture
audiences and pupils that the Scots language was not some degenerate
form of English, but had its origins rather in a quite separate
Scandinavian linguistic tradition: for Repp, for instance, the familiar
rhyme 'Hogmanay, Trollalay' could be derived from the Icelandic
'Haugmenn æ, Tröll á læ' [(good) elves for ever, evil spirits into the sea],

IX

rather than from the words of a French New Year's greeting.[34] Scott, like most learned folk at the time, owned a copy of Jamieson's *Dictionary*, and the pages of *The Pirate* (including Scott's surprisingly inadequate glossary) bear witness to the novelist's awareness of the philological links (some of them rather eccentrically promoted) between the old Scandinavian and modern Scottish north. Such an awareness was a powerful literary weapon in Scott's novel. It meant that even the small-scale verbal texture of the work supported the twin narrative themes of pride in cultural continuity of the ancient north, and the inevitability and desirability of cultural evolution – change need not mean degeneracy; nostalgic pig-headedness certainly could do. The linguistic theories of Jamieson and Repp could be seen as offering encouragement to Scots of a separatist disposition: for the same philology, which highlighted links with the ancient north, asserted difference from the modern south (that is, England). Philology could thus keep distinct what politics had united by the Act of Union in 1707. But though the philological depth of *The Pirate* is a great narrative strength, its politics offer little encouragement to the forces of defiant separatism. Minna's Viking dreams disintegrate when confronted with piratical reality. And whatever other spirited assertions of localism find their voice within the novel – notably Magnus Troil's irritation with 'Southren' interference (whether in relation to customary law or commercial practice or ploughing equipment), we note that it is the authorities in Kirkwall, supported by the Royal Navy, who restore ultimate order in the community. Indeed it is the Navy which absorbs Clement Cleveland himself. To have reached the condition dramatised in the novel the northern island communities, and their language, had undergone several centuries of evolutionary development. In seeking to turn the clock back, the danger was (as Minna found out) that it would strike thirteen. The *Quarterly Review* critic discerned in *The Pirate* Scott's 'usual pursuit of national, as well as individual, contrast';[35] but in achieving its ultimate sense of harmony out of contrast, *The Pirate* lies comfortably along the grain of Scott's sense of one nationhood, as expressed in the 1707 union.

IV

Enough of politics and philology. It is clear that the novel's earliest readers were drawn more to its atmospherics and antiquities than to its treatment of marginal cultures and communities. It is hard, for example, not to identify some direct influence from *The Pirate* in the spirit of the following lines by Daniel Vedder published in the *Edinburgh Literary Gazette* in 1829:

> Land of the dark – the Runic rhyme
> The mystic ring – the cavern hoar
> The Scandinavian seer – sublime
> In legendary lore:
> Land of a thousand sea kings' graves,

> — Those tameless spirits of the past,
> Fierce as their subject Arctic waves,
> Or hyperborean blast.[36]

The stanza reads like one of Scott's deftly chosen chapter-head verses. The ghosts of Norna and Minna hover overhead: the runes and the rhymes; Minna's dissolving vision of the ancient sea-kings; Norna the sublime seer and mistress of lore; the cave in which Mordaunt was nursed; the hyperborean blasts in which Cleveland's ship foundered; and, not least, the 'mystic ring', surely a reference to the mysterious circle of standing stones at Stenness amidst which Scott sets the final memorable scene of his novel (could this not have been the inspiration behind Thomas Hardy's similar use of the Stonehenge setting at the end of *Tess of the D'Urbevilles*?). Enlightenment travellers had sketched and pondered over the phenomenon: was the circle a random whim of primeval geology — 'so much more than human art and labour could produce';[37] or a Druidical place of ritual worship; or a Viking-age site of judgement or sacrifice? Curiosity was intensified in the wake of a much paraphrased and painted scene from James Macpherson's haunting Ossianic poem *Carric-Thura* (1765) in which, within this same circle of stones, the valiant warrior prince Fingal destroys the malign Odinic spirit of Loda with a stroke of his sword, despatching that monstrous presence from Orkney in a sulphurous cloud and with a fearsome, island-shaking, ocean-stilling shriek.[38] The destruction of a similar Odinic spirit in 'Harold the Dauntless' owes much to this scene. Scott's notes at the end of *The Pirate* which tell of the Stenness stones, the Dwarfie stane and other antiquities may have been produced in hasty response to his publisher's urgent request for material to flesh out the novel's final volume, but they were addressing the real curiosities of actual readers.

Authenticating atmospherics went deeper than those created by the singular features of the local landscape, important though these were. Scott worked hard to achieve a solidly three-dimensional quality to his interior settings and cultural markers. The novel is set in the late seventeenth century, when Claude Halcro's memories of John Dryden and the London coffee-houses were still fresh in his mind (rather too much so for many readers), but 'Glorious John' has to compete for the limelight against an array of sights and sounds assembled from the medieval Norse past. These parade before the reader constantly: in the Valkyrie-like presence of the ubiquitous Norna, weaving her fateful and (ultimately) futile webs; in Minna's 'promises of Odin' and in the string of oaths sworn to St Ronald (Rögnvaldr kali, Orkney jarl, warrior, poet, administrator, d. 1158) and St Olaf (Óláfr Haraldsson, King of Norway, d. 1030) and St Magnus the martyr (Magnús Erlendsson, Orkney jarl, friend of the poor, scourge of plundering Vikings, d. 1117); in the prophetic dreams, and rowing chants, and drinking songs; in the ancient Norse coins unearthed, and the rune-sticks; and, at greater length, in the sword dance which forms the heart of Magnus Troil's lavish feast, and from which the previously popular Mordaunt Mertoun found himself so hurtfully excluded. Such elements find themselves enclosed within larger-scale structures of old northern literary origin. Two examples make the point. First, as Scott confirms in a note (354-6), the scene with Norna and her fortune-telling rhymes is based on the prophecies of Þorbjörg the Sibyl, as dramatised so richly in *Eiríks saga rauða* (The Saga of Erik the Red).[39] This was a scene which Scott had first encountered in another of his Abbotsford volumes – the lengthy and influential treatise of old northern attitudes to death compiled by the seventeenth-century Danish antiquarian Thomas Bartholinus. Secondly, later in the novel, the scene (212-13) in which Norna seeks a piece of metal from the buried coffin of a Norse ancestor of Magnus Troil bears a striking resemblance (not mentioned by Scott – nor, to the best of my knowledge, by anyone else) to a scene in the Icelandic *Hervarar saga*, in which the warlike maiden Hervor makes a nocturnal visit to the grave of her father in order to retrieve a fateful ancestral sword, yielded with much paternal reluctance.[40] Hervor's heroism became widely known in late eighteenth-century Britain through the popularity of 'The Waking of Angantyr',[41] one of the *Five Pieces of Runic Poetry* (1763) which Bishop Thomas Percy offered to the British public in the immediate wake of their first period of Minna Troil-like infatuation with the poetry of the legendary figure of Ossian. For Scott the 'Angantyr' poem had become oppressively popular. There is evidence that he had intended to prepare a précis of *Hervarar saga* as his contribution to a pioneering volume of old northern texts published in Edinburgh in 1814;[42] but so frequently and hamfistedly had Angantyr been woken by third-rate paraphrasers[43] since the 1760s that Scott transferred his loyalties to *Eyrbyggja saga*, which itself became a source of old lore within *The Pirate* (471).

There is one additional feature worthy of comment, hinted at already, relating to Scott's deployment of old northern atmospherics and antiquities in his novel. Some of his knowledge in this area derived from a short period spent looking, listening and note-taking in Orkney and Shetland during his 1814 visit; some was plundered from patient and well-informed friends; but Scott's deepest grounding came from a lifetime of sporadic browsing in one of the best-stocked Scandinavian libraries in Britain – that is, Scott's own library in Abbotsford. John Buchan once accused Scott of creating the character of Minna half from *The Young Ladies Companion* and half from 'a lexicon of Northern antiquities'.[44] Other readers may be tempted to ask: what is wrong with that? Certainly there were 'Northern lexicons' aplenty to consult in Abbotsford. The 1838 catalogue of this library[45] reveals just how formidably extensive the accumulated holdings in Old Icelandic prose and poetry, and related works were. On the shelves were well over a hundred such volumes, many of them notoriously difficult to obtain in Britain at this time, several of them presentation copies from learned Scandinavian scholars well aware of Scott's sympathetic engagement with their ancestral culture. Several of the Abbotsford volumes were published in English in Britain,[46] the fruits of a burgeoning and multi-faceted interest in the ancient and modern north (in particular Iceland) fostered by travel, Ossianic poetry, the sublimities of early gothicism and romanticism, geological curiosity, agrarian improvement, medical research, Whiggish politics, and anti-Napoleonic diplomacy.[47] Scott's library assembled the published results of half a century's old northern enthusiasms; and a novel like *The Pirate* helped in its turn to promote modern northern curiosities still further. So it is that John Sutherland's disapproving remark, quoted earlier, about Scott's 'day trip to the culture' of the ancient Norse kingdoms of Orkney and Shetland begins itself to look 'increasingly superficial'. Many trips to that culture were possible for Scott's animated imagination without his ever leaving Abbotsford.

But what did or does *The Pirate* offer those readers, whether of the first Victorian or second Elizabethan ages, who have no interest in either Victorian politics and philology or northern antiquities and atmospherics? Three nineteenth-century readers offer some guidelines. First, we have the figure of George Eliot's Maggie Tulliver, living a life of ascetic withdrawal from the world, and pondering the volume of *The Pirate* which, as we noted earlier, an admirer had brought with him. Our heroine was not impressed:

> "'The Pirate,'" she said, taking the book from Philip's hands. 'O, I began that at once; I read to where Minna is walking with Cleveland, and I could never get to read the rest. I went on with it in my own head, and I made several endings; but they were all unhappy. I could never make a happy ending out of that beginning. Poor Minna! I wonder what is the real end. For a long while I couldn't get my mind away from the Shetland Isles — I used to feel the wind blowing on me from the rough sea.'
>
> Maggie spoke rapidly, with glistening eyes.
>
> 'Take that volume home with you, Maggie,' said Philip, watching her with delight. 'I don't want it now ... it would make me in love with this world again, as I used to be — it would make me long to see and know many things — it would make me long for a full life.'[48]

Maggie Tulliver reminds us that most readers, whether in real-life or in fiction, judge a book if not by its cover then at least by its characters. With *The Pirate*, however, there was no unanimity amongst early readers as to which characters to judge, if the evidence of unofficial subtitles is to be believed. The fictional Maggie Tulliver liked just Minna; the real-life Sarah Scudgell Wilkinson liked both sisters, in her *The Pirate, or the Sisters of Burgh Westra: A Tale of the Islands of Shetland and Orkney, Epitomized from the Celebrated Novel* (London, 1822) and so did the anonymous author of *The Pirate: or, Minna and Brenda, a Drama* (Edinburgh, [c. 1823]); then again, in an anonymous London publication of 1823, we find Minna forced to share top billing with Norna and Cleveland — *The Pirate, or the Witch of the Winds, with the Adventures of Captain Cleveland and Minna Troil.*

The dark-haired and solitary Maggie's fascination with the dark-haired and solitary Minna ('I want to avenge Rebecca and Flora MacIvor and Minna and all the rest of the dark unhappy ones')[49] has certainly been shared by many readers and critics since. Was Minna's early

XIII

fascination with Viking values naïve; was her abandonment of the reformed Cleveland cruel; was her eventual unmarried status bleakly unsatisfying? 'Reader, she *was* happy' (343) insists Scott at the end of the novel, defending his fiction against the 'sceptic and the scorner'; yet Maggie's inability to imagine any happy ending for Minna is perhaps closer to many people's reading experience – whether from some feminist standpoint (a novel in which empowerment-seeking women such as Norna and Minna are marginalised, demonised and defeated; a novel which validates the patriarchal authority of Magnus Troil), or from a resolutely unreconstructed perspective (both sisters needed a good husband and both Cleveland and Mordaunt needed a good wife, and only Brenda and Mordaunt found one; Minna is condemned to the role of a devoted housebound carer). At the very least, if Minna '*was* happy', having learnt to 'exchange the visions of wild enthusiasm which had exerted and misled her imagination, for a truer and purer connection with the world beyond us' (343), it is hard to see how Brenda, as Mrs Mordaunt Mertoun, now would be any less truly and purely connected to 'the world beyond us', and it is easy to imagine her as a good deal happier in the world around us.

Maggie was afraid to finish the novel, though, not because she couldn't find a happy ending for Minna, but because she thought that the story as a whole might provoke unwanted life-affirming feelings in her – and so indeed the overall process of the novel could have done. There is so much to be cheerful about: the feasting and festivities; the beauty of the deserted voes, the bustle of festive Kirkwall; the banter of the rude mechanics on land and at sea; the Mordaunt marriage; Cleveland's heroic death whilst loyally serving the Royal Navy; Bunce, the chirpy ex-Thespian, also saved from the pirate's gangplank; Triptolemus learning to graft a measure of tact onto the overly rigid root-stock of modern technology; and both Norna and Basil Mertoun being brought to a true understanding of their interlocking lives and fates.

Something of Maggie's mixed response is discernible in that first *Quarterly Review* article already referred to, and can serve as evidence for a second nineteenth-century reader's reaction to the novel.[50] This was an essay which won the approval of Lockhart, Scott's son-in-law ('the manly heartiness of his sympathy ... the honest acuteness of his censure').[51] The judgements are crisp and uncompromising. As a novel, we are told, *The Pirate* would have raised high the reputation of an untried author, but has rather lowered that of 'the author of *Waverley*'. The reviewer sees the plunder on the beach as 'in our author's happiest manner'; he likes the Magnus Troil feast and sword-dance scene; the secret meeting between Brenda and Mertoun is 'delightfully managed'; but fault is found with the nocturnal meeting when Norna meets the two sisters at Kirkwall ('more effort than merit'); and Norna's earlier sibylline prophesy scene is deemed an 'unfortunate blemish' which does 'wanton injury to the interest of the story', and which displays Scott's 'weak powers of self-restraint' (the present writer finds this a baffling judgement). The lengthy beach conversation between Minna and Cleveland during which they examine their fraught situation is 'exquisite', unlike the 'egregious failure' of the scene in which Norna is asked to cure Minna's melancholy; and the coolness which develops between Magnus and Mordaunt could have been 'better accounted for' (as most readers would surely confirm). As regards individual characters, the reviewer writes with great perception on Magnus Troil, clearly a favourite with him; Goffe and the other pirates are 'bold and vigorous' almost to excess; Mordaunt is merely 'insipid'; Triptolemus is 'tiresome'; and the relentlessly jolly Claud Halcro is 'our peculiar aversion'; (it is hard to avoid the conclusion that, having edited the complete works of 'Glorious John' Dryden in eighteen volumes in 1808, Scott was determined to squeeze every last drop from the sponge of his editorial labours). Norna is viewed as generally tedious, a retread of Meg Merrilies, though, with lofty disdain, the reviewer suspects that 'she may please our transatlantic brethren'; and as for Cleveland's rapid transformation from swaggering pirate to loyal patriot, this 'sudden alteration of his destiny ... disposition and conduct ... must, we think, have been an afterthought'. Overall, the reviewer sees *The Pirate* as an over-hasty production, marked by 'inconsistencies ... lame and impotent conclusions'. Its virtues ('full of interest ... activity') are matched by its vices ('confusion, negligence, and improbability'). Its major problems are structural: 'The gentlest, the most confiding reader must be startled at the triple recognition, at the recurrence, in three distinct instances, of the same combination of events, a combination as unusual in real life, as it is trite in fiction.'

In the *London Magazine* a few months later, William Hazlitt is a good deal less censorious, and much more in line with Lockhart's positive view of the novel and its early reception — 'splendid Romance ... the wild freshness of its atmosphere, the beautiful contrast of Brenda and Minna, and the exquisitely drawn character of Captain Cleveland found the reception which they deserved.'[52] It is striking that the structural problems which so exercise the writer in the *Quarterly Review* find few echoes south of the border:

> This is not the best, nor is it the worst (the worst is good enough for us) of the Scotch novels. There is a story in it, an interest excited almost from the first, a clue which you get hold of and wish to follow out; a mystery to be developed, and which does not disappoint you at last. After you once get into the stream you read on with eagerness, and have only to complain of the number of impediments and diversions thrown in your way.[53]

The reviewer suspects that there is some antiquarian padding which Scott has failed fully to digest and integrate, but this and the other 'diversions' need not be a major problem for any reader prepared to:

> travel with him [the novelist], stop when he stops, and turn out of the road as often as he pleases. He dallies with your impatience, and smiles in your face, but you cannot, and dare not be angry with him, while with his giant-hand

he plays at push-pin with the reader, and sweeps the rich stakes from the table.

As for the characters, they are 'not quite so highly wrought up', nor 'so crowded together, so thickly sown' as Scott enthusiasts might have hoped and expected; there are disappointingly few sea scenes and only one fully fledged pirate and even he undergoes a sea-change on Scott's *Tempest*-like island; the reviewer disapproves of Minna deserting Cleveland; unlike his *Quarterly Review* colleague, he relishes Norna's weirdness; he dislikes the 'modern cant and philosophical scepticism' of Triptolemus; Halcro with his 'pribble, prabble' is a bore; the list of characters rewritten from earlier Scott novels is extended (Minna is Effie Deans; Magnus Troil is Baron Bradwardine), but Hazlitt judges them none the worse for that. The overall verdict is positive, bordering on reverential: 'we are true and liege subjects' and are happy to show 'ultra-fealty'. If the novel's structure does not meet the demands of Coleridgean unity, asserts Hazlitt, then that is just too bad for Coleridgean unity. The overall execution of the novel is inferior only when compared with Scott's earlier successes: 'whatever he touches, we see the hand of a master ... [he is] the most popular writer living ... Nature's Secretary'. Only at the end of this paean of praise does the reviewer list with a scowl a handful of examples of what he regards as slovenly use of English.[54]

V

The late twentieth century has not been an age noticeably concerned with slovenly linguistic usage and would look askance at the *London Magazine* critic's strictures. But there is another aspect of early nineteenth-century responses to the novel – the inclination to read it as a romance – which the modern reader may find illuminating to reflect on and develop. Several American editions of *The Pirate* from the 1820s add the subtitle 'a romance' to Scott's main title, and it is, we may recall, as a 'splendid Romance' that Lockhart recalls the novel in his *Memoirs*. Attention has properly been drawn to the links between Scott's novel and Shakespeare's late romance *The Tempest* – the island setting, the sea-changes, the contrast between indigenous and outsider cultures.[55] There is also something to be said for reading the novel alongside some pre-Shakespearean romances – the medieval English tales of which Sir Walter Scott was a great champion by the time of the novel's composition. *The Pirate* bears many of the marks of a medieval bridal-quest romance such as the charming early fourteenth-century English tale *Sir Degaré*, one of the many romances which Scott had come to know through his first-hand familiarity with the contents of the fourteenth-century Auchinleck manuscript in the Advocates' Library in Edinburgh.[56] It tells of a young man who needed to learn who and where his parents were before he could go off and win a wife of his own. The young hero, son of a wandering princess and a passing fair knight, is brought up by humble foster-parents. The knight left behind a tipless sword, intended in due course to assist Degaré in finding his father; and a pair of gloves with the instructions that he is to love no woman until he has found the one whose hands fit the gloves – she will be his mother. The baby boy is left in his cradle at a hermit's homestead along with the gloves, the sword, some silver and an explanatory letter. The young child grows up to be an exemplary young man, and wins the right to marry a king's daughter; arriving at the altar on his wedding day, he remembers the glove test and duly tries them on his bride-to-be, and finds to his horror that they fit – Degaré was, thus, about to marry his mother. Saved from this fate worse than death, he then sets off in search of further adventure, and after performing assorted deeds of chivalric derring-do rescuing princesses in distress, he fights a 'dou3ti kni3t' who, noticing the young man's tipless sword, identifies himself as the young hero's father, a claim duly confirmed when he produces the severed tip out of his wallet. Sir Degaré is able to reunite his parents; as his name implies, he and they were once lost and are now found; and there is every reason for the reader to believe that Sir Degaré's next visit to the altar will not prove as abortive as was his first.

In his illuminating book *Symbolic Stories*, Derek Brewer, drawing on Bruno Bettelheim's influential (and controversial) analysis of fairy tales in *The Uses of Enchantment*[57] reads *Sir Degaré* as a romance of family drama – unreal and yet true.[58] It is marked by improbabilities at every point on the narrative surface and yet full of truths at its latent level and in its deeper structures. Both Bettelheim and Brewer argue that many traditional tales investigate symbolically the unchanging patterns of the age-old, real-life family drama – sibling rivalry, relationships with parents or step-parents, leaving home, finding an appropriate mate, and all the other stages of adolescent rites of passage. Liberated from neo-classical demands for surface narrative verisimilitude – the unities of time, place and action – these symbolic stories can generate many variations on a single standard theme. The point of *Sir Degaré*, Brewer argues, is that a young man can only undertake a successful rite of passage leading to the identification of a desirable sexual partner (of his own age, outside his own family circle) when he has identified all the principal members of that first family circle. He must identify his mother in order not to marry her; he must find (and defeat) his father in order to assume the role and responsibilities of male adulthood – the tipless (and by this stage deeply symbolic) sword must be made whole and the transfer of ownership confirmed. It is this logical latent level of signification which drives the improbable surface narrative.

Brewer's methodology for the analysis of traditional tale and medieval romance proves no less telling when he directs it towards more realistic narratives such as *Mansfield Park* and *Great Expectations*. He sees such novels as rationalised (at least in part) fairy tales. *The Pirate* lends itself very well to such a reading, with the family drama pattern subject to intriguing variations and complications. There are several characters in the novel who, like Sir Degaré, have discoveries to make about the identity of their parents before their lives can proceed in more fruitful directions. Cleveland, the potential but ultimately aborted hero, who is washed ashore like a shipwrecked traveller in *The Tempest*, discovers both his mother (Norna), his father (Bertram Mertoun) and his half-brother (Mordaunt); he then abandons his self-centred, adolescent, piratical ways, and lives the remainder of his life in selfless naval service. Before he can complete this transformation, however, he finds himself locked in a classic sibling rivalry situation with his half-brother Mordaunt; the rivalry had begun before they realised that they were half-brothers — but is given psychological underpinning by the revelation. As so often in medieval romance, the two brothers can be seen as representing conflicting sides of an initially warring but eventually unified personality — each element develops some of the characteristics of the other (the wandering Cleveland becomes more responsible and other-centred, but is eventually jettisoned; the home-loving Mordaunt is eventually released from the potentially regressive gravitational pull of his home and father). The maturation of Mordaunt is signalled by the departure and eventual death of Cleveland, and by the disappearance of his father. One can, indeed, also identify a split father-figure — the benevolent side represented by Magnus Troil, and the ascetic and self-lacerating aspect embodied in Bertram Mertoun whose eventual disappearance, his fierce asperity reduced to mere pathos, seems strange on the surface level of narration, but makes perfect 'family drama' sense at the latent level, for it coincides with Mordaunt himself achieving full maturity in marriage. The sibling split between Minna and Brenda is more obvious, and is resolved differently. Brenda changes hardly at all, and, for all her domesticity, finds her link with the imaginative world of the north through Mordaunt her husband; Minna is left to abandon her imaginary links between the longship heroes and their piratical successors, and then to shrivel and die in loyal service to her ageing parent — her rite of passage incomplete, her departure from home never successfully achieved. In the underlying narrative logic of the story, Brenda deserves a husband because she took more initiatives to get one — notably by being disobedient to her father in her secret meeting with Mordaunt at the feast. In *Waverley* Scott's heart may have been with young Edward in the Highlands, but his head saw what the romance of Highland separatism led to — the bloody field at Preston-pans. So, in *The Pirate*, romantic dreams ultimately run into the sand unless allied with some sense of practical futurity; though happily here there is no bloodshed, and it is only a single life, albeit one central to the novel, which is allowed to wither. The future of Orkney and Shetland and their worthy udal values lies with Mertoun and Brenda, that is, with a still proud Norse localism tempered by practical domesticity and some prospect of agrarian progress.

As we noted with Magnus and Bertram Mertoun, the family drama patterns identifiable amongst the siblings are also to be found in refracted form amongst the parents. Norna needed to be rid of her father (albeit by accidental death) in order to achieve the emotional freedom to reject the bridegroom chosen for her (Magnus Troil) and make her own choice (Bertram Mertoun/Vaughan), unhappy as that proved to be. The trouble with parents is that they are not always wrong. In *Sir Degaré* there is the promise of a happy reunion for the princess's parents; in *The Pirate* the reunion is brief and fruitless. But in family drama narratives this scarcely matters — parents are like giant rockets lifting a satellite; once the projectile (the child) is launched, the rockets can fall to earth and burn up in the atmosphere, their fate of little importance, save when the separating mechanism has failed to release, and the satellite/child is dragged back down to earth, destroyed by its intended source of liberation.

We may recall the words of censure from the *Quarterly Review* about the structure of *The Pirate*: 'the gentlest, the most confiding reader must be startled at the triple recognition, at the recurrence, in three distinct instances, of the same combination of events, a combination as unusual in real life, as it is trite in fiction'. The modern gentle and confiding reader need not be so startled, nor, by implication, so disapproving. The dramas played out in Scott's novel, in all their multiple and refracted forms, are, when decoded, nourished by the same narrative life-blood which animates most traditional tales, a surprising number of nineteenth-century novels, and perhaps, for what it is worth, real life — whatever that is. Their deployment in *The Pirate* need seem no more 'trite' than the recurrence of multiply reworked traditional tunes in the works of an accomplished composer. It would be idle to pretend that *The Pirate* has the epic breadth, range of human sympathy, or unforgettable characters of the greatest works by the greatest European novelists; but it has an attractive diversity of mood, plenty of memorable scenes, an unusually supple way with speech and conversation, and a good deal more intellectual and emotional complexity than first meets the eye. Moreover, in addition to some good one-liners from the novel's agreeably wry and urbane narrator, we are in Scott's debt for Triptolemus's impatient dismissal of *Piers Plowman* when he discovers to his chagrin that it is not a book about farming (32-3) — this remains the only really good joke at the expense of William Langland's masterwork in six hundred years of English literature.

So George Bernard Shaw may be forgiven a long lifetime's literary cantankerousness when we recall his sturdy good sense in sitting in his armchair in his Thurso hotel in 1925 re-reading *The Pirate* whilst waiting for the ferry across the Pentland Firth. Seventy years later his admirable example can now happily be imitated by armchair readers at all latitudes.

ANDREW WAWN
1996

[anon]. 1821-2. Review of *The Pirate, Quarterly Review*, 26, 454-74.

Brewer, Derek. 1988. *Symbolic Stories: Traditional Narratives of the Family Drama in English Literature*. London.

Cockshut, A. O. J. 1969. *The Achievement of Sir Walter Scott*. London.

Hartveit, Lars. 1993. 'A Reading of *The Pirate* in the Light of Scott's Views on the Craft of Fiction', in Alexander J. H. and David Hewitt (eds), *Scott in Carnival*, pp. 332-44. Aberdeen.

[Hazlitt, William]. 1822. Review of *The Pirate, London Magazine*, 25, 80-9.

Johnson, Edgar. 1970. *Sir Walter Scott: The Great Unknown*. 2 vols. London.

Kidd, Colin. 1995. 'Teutonist Ethnology and Scottish Nationalist Inhibition, 1780-1880', *Scottish Historical Review*, 74, 45-68.

Laughlan, William F. (ed.). 1982. *Northern Lights, or A Voyage in the Lighthouse Yacht to Nova Zembla and the Lord knows where in the Summer of 1814*. Hawick.

McMaster, Graham. 1981. *Scott and Society*. Cambridge.

McMullin, B. J. 1989. 'The Publication of Scott's *The Pirate*', *The Bibliothek*, 16, 1-29.

Orr, Marilyn. 1990. 'Repetition, Reversal and the Gothic: *The Pirate* and *St. Ronan's Well*', *English Studies in Canada*, 26, 187-99.

Sells, A. Lytton. 1946. 'The Return of Cleveland: Some Observations on *The Pirate*', *Durham University Journal*, 38/3, 69-78.

Simpson, John M. 1983. 'The Discovery of Shetland from *The Pirate* to the Tourist Board', in Withrington 1983.

Sutherland, John. 1995. *Walter Scott. A Critical Biography*. Oxford.

Wawn, Andrew. 1994. 'Shrieks at the Stones: The Vikings, the Orkneys and the Scottish Enlightenment', in Colleen Batey, Judith Jesch and Christopher Morris (eds), *The Viking Age in Caithness, Orkney and the North Atlantic: Select Papers from the Proceedings of the Eleventh Viking Congress, Thurso and Kirkwall, 22 August - 1 September 1989*, 408-22. Edinburgh.

Welsh, Alexander. 1968. *The Hero of the Waverley Novels*. New York.

Wilt, Judith. 1985. *Secret Leaves: The Novels of Walter Scott*. Chicago.

Withrington, Donald (ed.). 1983. *Shetland and the Outside World 1469-1969*. Oxford.

1   Henry Adelbert White, *Sir Walter Scott's Novels on the Stage* (New Haven and London, 1927), pp. 162-5. See, for instance, T. J. Dibdin, *The Pirate, a Melodramatic Romance, Taken from the Novel* (London, 1822).

2   Scott's account of his island travels, including his meeting with the Rae family, can be followed in William F. Laghlan (ed.), *Northern Lights, or A Voyage in the Lighthouse Yacht to Nova Zembla and the Lord knows where in the Summer of 1814* (Hawick, 1982).

3 [unsigned], 'One of Scott's Characters still living: An Interview with "Brenda"', Shetland Archive ref. D.1/135, p. 273. I am particularly grateful to Brian Smith, Shetland Archivist, for drawing my attention to this and many other valuable early references to the novel: see below, notes 9, 26, 33. Both he and Professor Peter Jorgensen did me the kindness of reading and commenting most helpfully on an earlier draft of this essay.

4 Andrew Wawn, *The Anglo Man. Þorleifur Repp, Philology and Nineteenth-Century Britain.* Studia Islandica, 49 (Reykjavík, 1991), p. 135.

5 On Scott's debt to Sterne's *Tristram Shandy* in his portrayal of Triptolemus, see Jana Davis, 'Scott's *The Pirate*', *Explicator*, 45/3 (1987), 20-2.

6 Wilfred Partington, *Sir Walter's Post-Bag* (London, 1930), pp. 305-6.

7 Guðbrandur's copy of Jón Árnason, *Íslenzkar Þjóðsögur og æfintýri*, 2 vols (Leipzig, 1862-4), is amongst the volumes in the Turville-Petre Icelandic Collection in the English Faculty Library in Oxford. Guðbrandur's flyleaf annotation notes the contrast between the Icelandic popular superstition that rescuing a drowning man means good fortune for the rescuer, and the notion, central to Scott's *The Pirate*, that such a rescue represents bad luck (65).

8 All page references are to the text in the present volume.

9 Rudyard Kipling, 'Propagation of Knowledge' (1926) in *The Complete Stalky and Co.* (Oxford, 1987), p. 229; John Cowper Powys, *Autobiography* (1934; reprinted London, 1967), p. 66.

10 Peter Tompkins (ed.), *To a Young Actress: The Letters of Bernard Shaw to Molly Tompkins* (London, 1960), p. 86, letter dated 9 August 1925.

11 Jane Millgate, *Scott's Last Edition: A Study in Publishing History* (Edinburgh, 1987), pp. 23-4, 73-4; B. J. McMullin, 'The Publication of Scott's *The Pirate*', *The Bibliothek*, 16 (1989), 1-29; James H. Hanford, 'The Manuscript of Scott's *The Pirate*', *Princeton University Library Chronicle*, 18/4 (1957), 215-22.

12 J. G. Lockhart, *Memoirs of the Life of Sir Walter Scott*, 4 vols (Paris, 1838), III, 75, 88; H. J. C. Grierson (ed.), *The Letters of Sir Walter Scott 1787-1832*, 11 vols (London, 1932-6), VI, 16.

13 Both judgements quoted in John Simpson, 'The Discovery of Shetland from *The Pirate* to the Tourist Board', in Donald Withrington (ed.), *Shetland and the Outside World 1469-1969* (Oxford, 1983), p. 138.

14 John Sutherland, *The Life of Walter Scott: A Critical Biography* (Oxford, 1995), pp. 250-2.

15 Evidence of Scott's amplificatory labours can be seen in Iain Gordon Brown (ed.), *Scott's Interleaved Waverley Novels. The 'Magnum Opus': National Library of Scotland MSS 23001-41* (Edinburgh, 1987), pp. 101-3.

16 Grierson (ed.), *Letters*, VII, 12: 1822 letter to William Erskine, his valued source of information about 'the Locale of Zetland'.

17 William Hazlitt in *London Magazine*, 25/5 (1822), 80-9, at 81.

18 See David Cordingley, *Life among the Pirates: The Romance and Reality* (London, 1995).

19 J. Logue Robertson (ed.), *Scott: Poetical Works* (London, 1904), pp. 517-52.

20 Illustrations could also take more elliptical form; Iain Gordon Brown (ed.), *The Todholes of Aisle* (Edinburgh, 1994), offers an 1844 set of character sketches and portraits, including (pp. 90-1) 'Minna' and 'Brenda', daughters of an Alderman Tod.

21 Anthea Bell (ed.), George Eliot, *The Mill on The Floss* (London, 1960), pp. 405-6 (Book V, Chapter 3).

22 [anon], *Portrait of Sir Walter Scott and Fine Engravings in Illustration of* The Pirate *for Members of the Royal Association for the Promotion of Fine Arts in Scotland* (Edinburgh, 1871).

23 Gray's 'The Fatal Sisters' is based on the poem 'Darraðarljóð' from the Icelandic *Brennu-Njáls saga* (Ch. 157); it was later accessible in Þormóður Torfason's *Orcades* (Copenhagen, 1697), and also, in the context of the novel, via the oral traditions of 'some old persons' in eighteenth-century Norn-speaking North Ronaldsay. Scott (230) also refers briefly to 'The Descent of Odin', Gray's other paraphrastic version of an Eddic poem.

24 Review of *The Pirate* in *Quarterly Review,* 26 (1821-2), 454-74, at 474. A list of the early reviews of the novel can be found in J. C. Corson (ed.), *A Bibliography of Sir Walter Scott ... 1797-1940* (1943; reprinted New York, 1968), pp. 245-7.

25 Lockhart, *Memoirs,* IV, 171, note.

26 Second edition, Edinburgh, 1831, p. 16. The Shetland Museum copy of the work has an illuminating marginal note alongside the unflattering Claude Halcro reference on p. 16; the annotator (Harry Cheyne, a mid-nineteenth-century Shetland solicitor) writes 'Dr A— E—dm—s—', an allusion to Dr Arthur Edmondston, whose *A View of the Past and Present State of the Zetland Islands* (Edinburgh, 1809) was amongst the works plundered by Scott whilst he was writing *The Pirate.*

27 *The Oxonian in Iceland; or, Notes of Travel in that Island in the Summer of 1860* (London, 1861), p. 37.

28 Ibid, p. 70.

29 Ibid.

30 *The Home of the Eddas* (London, 1879), pp. 74-5.

31 George Webbe Dasent, *The Norsemen in Iceland* (Oxford, 1858), pp. 166, 176.

32 George Webbe Dasent, *Jest and Earnest,* 2 vols (London, 1873), I, 247.

33 See P. N. Sutherland Graeme, 'The Parliamentary Representation of Orkney and Shetland, 1754-1900', *Orkney Miscellany,* 1 (1953), 64-104, at 82-3. On Laing, Snorri Sturluson and udal values, see Andrew Wawn, 'Samuel Laing, *Heimskringla*, and the "Berserker School"', forthcoming in *Scandinavica* (1995). See also Knut Robberstad, 'Udal Law' in Donald Withrington (ed.), *Shetland and the Outside World 1469-1969* (Oxford, 1983), pp. 49-68; William P. L. Thomson, 'The Udal League', *Orkney View,* 2 (1985), 15-17; J. A. B. Townsend,

'The Viking Society: A Centenary History', *Saga-Book*, 23/4 (1992), 180-212, at 180-94; and Andrew Wawn, 'The Cult of "Stalwart Frith-thjof" in Victorian Britain', in Wawn (ed.), *Northern Antiquity: The Post-Medieval Reception of Edda and Saga* (Enfield Lock, 1994), pp. 211-54, at 243.

34 Þorleifur Repp, 'On the Scottish formula of congratulations on the New Year's Eve, "Hogmanay, Trollalay"', *Archaeologica Scotica*, 4 (1831), 202-12; see also Wawn, *The Anglo Man* (1991), pp. 109-15.

35 *Quarterly Review*, 26 (1821-2), 454-74, at 456.

36 14 November 1829, p. 509.

37 A phrase from John Thomas Stanley's account of the Stones of Stenness; he stayed in Orkney on his way to Iceland in 1789: see Wawn, 'Shrieks at the Stones' (1994), 409-10.

38 Wawn, Ibid, 410-14.

39 This can be read conveniently in Gwyn Jones (trans.), *Eirik the Red and Other Sagas* (London, 1961), pp. 134-7.

40 E. O. G. Turville-Petre (ed.), *Hervarar saga og Heiðreks* (London, 1956), pp. 10-23. Scott's Abbotsford library had a text of P. F. Suhm's 1785 edition, published in Copenhagen as part of the hugely influential saga text series promoted by the Árni Magnússon Commission, each volume with a facing-page Latin translation which rendered the saga accessible to any educated reader throughout Enlightenment Europe.

41 Chapter 7, pp. 49-77 in Suhm's edition.

41 [Henry Weber, Robert Jamieson, Walter Scott], *Illustrations of Northern Antiquities from the Earlier Teutonic and Scandinavian Romances; Being an Abstract of the Book of Heroes, and Nibelungen Lay; with a Translation of Metrical Tales, from the Old German, Danish, Swedish, and Icelandic Languages; with Notes and Dissertations* (Edinburgh, 1814).

43 See Margaret Omberg, *Scandinavian Themes in English Poetry, 1760-1800* (Uppsala, 1976).

44 John Buchan, *Sir Walter Scott* (London, 1932), p. 244.

45 [John Cochrane], *Catalogue of the Library of Abbotsford* (Edinburgh, 1838); see especially pp. 63-4, 98-9, but there are isolated items of Scandinavian interest scattered throughout the catalogue.

46 Amongst them William Herbert, *Select Icelandic Poetry* (London, 1806); Sir George Mackenzie, *Travels in the Island of Iceland in the Summer of the Year MDCCCX* (Edinburgh, 1811).

47 Discussed passim in Andrew Wawn, 'John Thomas Stanley and Iceland: the Sense and Sensibility of an Eighteenth-Century Explorer', *Scandinavian Studies*, 53 (1981), 52-76; and (ed.), *The Iceland Journal of Henry Holland* (London, 1987), 1-67.

48 *The Mill on the Floss,* book 5, chapter I.

49 Ibid.

50 *Quarterly Review,* 26 (1821-2), 454-74.

51 Lockhart, *Memoirs,* III, 92.

52 Ibid.

53 *London Magazine,* 25/5 (1822), 80-9, at p. 80.

54 In revising the novel for re-publication in the *magnum opus* edition, Scott was principally concerned with occasional stylistic fine-tunings; there are very few alterations of substance.

55 Graham McMaster, *Scott and Society* (Cambridge, 1981), pp. 182-92.

56 See Jerome Mitchell, *Scott, Chaucer and Medieval Romance* (Lexington, Kentucky, 1987), pp. 3, 12, 25.

57 Bruno Bettelheim, *The Uses of Enchantment* (Harmondsworth, 1976).

58 Derek Brewer, *Symbolic Stories. Traditional Narratives of the Family Drama in English Literature* (Cambridge, 1980; reissued London, 1988), pp. 66-71.

INTRODUCTION

"Quoth he, there was a ship."

THIS brief preface may begin like the tale of the Ancient Mariner, since it was on shipboard that the Author acquired the very moderate degree of local knowledge and information, both of the people and scenery, which he had endeavoured to embody in the romance of the Pirate.

In the summer and autumn of 1814, the Author was invited to join a party of Commissioners for the Northern Lighthouse Service, who proposed making a voyage round the coast of Scotland, and through its various groups of islands, chiefly for the purpose of seeing the condition of the many lighthouses under their direction,—edifices so important, whether regarding them as benevolent or political institutions. Among the commissioners who manage this important public concern, the sheriff of each county of Scotland which borders on the sea holds ex officio a place at the Board. These gentlemen act in every respect gratuitously, but have the use of an armed yacht, well found and fitted up, when they choose to visit the lighthouses. An excellent engineer, Mr Robert Stevenson, is attached to the Board, to afford the benefit of his professional advice. The Author accompanied this expedition as a guest; for Selkirkshire, though it calls him Sheriff, has not, like the kingdom of Bohemia in Corporal Trim's story, a seaport in its circuit, nor its magistrate, of course, any place at the Board of Commissioners,—a circumstance of little consequence where all were old and intimate friends, bred to the same profession, and disposed to accommodate each other in every possible manner.

1

The nature of the important business which was the principal purpose of the voyage, was connected with the amusement of visiting the leading objects of a traveller's curiosity; for the wild cape, or formidable shelf, which requires to be marked out by a lighthouse, is generally at no great distance from the most magnificent scenery of rocks, caves, and billows. Our time, too, was at our own disposal, and, as most of us were fresh-water sailors, we could at any time make a fair wind out of a foul one, and run before the gale in quest of some object or curiosity which lay under our lee. **

With these purposes of public utility and some personal amusement in view, we left the port of Leith on the 26th July 1814, ran along the east coast of Scotland, viewing its different curiosities, stood over to Zetland and Orkney, where we were some time detained by the wonders of a country which displayed so much that was new to us; and, having seen what was curious in the Ultima Thule of the ancients, where the sun hardly thought it worth while to go to bed, since his rising was at this season so early, we doubled the extreme northern termination of Scotland, and took a rapid survey of the Hebrides, where we found many kind friends. There, that our little expedition might not want the dignity of danger, we were favoured with a distant glimpse of what was said to be an American cruiser, and had opportunity to consider what a pretty figure we should have made had the voyage ended in our being carried captive to the United States. After visiting the romantic shores of Morven, and the vicinity of Oban, we made a run to the coast of Ireland, and visited the Giant's Causeway, that we might compare it with Staffa, which we had surveyed in our course. At length, about the middle of September, we ended our voyage in the Clyde, at the port of Greenock.

And thus terminated our pleasant tour, to which our equipment gave unusual facilities, as the ship's company could form a good boat's crew, independent of those who might be left on board the vessel, which permitted us the freedom to land wherever our curiosity carried us. Let me add, while reviewing for a moment a sunny portion of my life, that among the six or seven friends who performed this voyage together, some of them doubtless of different tastes and pursuits, and remaining for several weeks on board a small vessel, there never occurred the slightest dispute or disagreement, each seeming anxious to submit his own particular wishes to those of his friends. By this mutual accommodation all the purposes of our little expedition were obtained, while for a time we might have adopted the lines of Allan Cunningham's fine sea-song,

> *"The world of waters was our home,*
> *And merry men were we!"*

But sorrow mixes her memorials with the purest remembrances of pleasure. On returning from the voyage which had proved so satisfactory, I found that fate had deprived her country most unexpectedly of a lady, qualified to adorn the high rank which she held, and who had long admitted me to a share of her friendship.† The subsequent loss of one of those comrades who made up the party, and he

---

* [See the Lighthouse Diary in *Scott's Memoirs* by Lockhart.]
† [Harriet Katherine, Duchess of Buccleuch, died 24th August 1814.]

the most intimate friend I had in the world, casts also its shade on recollections which, but for these imbitterments, would be otherwise so satisfactory.*

I may here briefly observe, that my business in this voyage, so far as I could be said to have any, was to endeavour to discover some localities which might be useful in the "Lord of the Isles", a poem with which I was then threatening the public, and which was afterwards printed without attaining remarkable success. But as at the same time the anonymous novel of "Waverley" was making its way to popularity, I already argued the possibility of a second effort in this department of literature, and I saw much in the wild islands of the Orkneys and Zetland, which I judged might be made in the highest degree interesting, should these isles ever become the scene of a narrative of fictitious events. I learned the history of Gow the pirate from an old sibyl (the subject of Note E, end of this volume), whose principal subsistence was by a trade in favourable winds, which she sold to mariners at Stromness. Nothing could be more interesting than the kindness and hospitality of the gentlemen of Zetland, which was to me the more affecting, as several of them had been friends and correspondents of my father.†

I was induced to go a generation or two farther back, to find materials from which I might trace the features of the old Norwegian Udaller, the Scottish gentry having in general occupied the place of that primitive race, and their language and peculiarities of manner having entirely disappeared. The only difference now to be observed betwixt the gentry of these islands and those of Scotland in general is, that the wealth and property is more equally divided among our more northern countrymen, and that there exist among the resident proprietors no men of very great wealth, whose display of its luxuries might render the others discontented with their own lot. From the same cause of general equality of fortunes, and the cheapness of living, which is its natural consequence, I found the officers of a veteran regiment who had maintained the garrison at Fort Charlotte, in Lerwick, discomposed at the idea of being recalled from a country where their pay, however inadequate to the expenses of a capital, was fully adequate to their wants, and it was singular to hear natives of merry England herself regretting their approaching departure from the melancholy isles of the Ultima Thule.

Such are the trivial particulars attending the origin of that publication which took place several years later than the agreeable journey in which it took its rise.

The state of manners which I have introduced in the romance was necessarily in a great degree imaginary, though founded in some

* [Note A. William Erskine of Kinedder.]

† ["I have been told," says Mr Lockhart, "by one of the companions of this voyage, that heartily as Sir Walter entered throughout into their social enjoyments, they all perceived him, when inspecting for the first time scenes of remarkable grandeur, to be in such an abstracted and excited mood, that they felt it would be the kindest and discreetest plan to leave him to himself. "I often," said Lord Kinedder, "on coming up from the cabin at night, found him pacing the deck rapidly, muttering to himself—and went to the forecastle, lest my presence should disturb him. I remember that at Loch Corriskin in particular he seemed quite overwhelmed with his feelings."]

3

measure on slight hints, which, showing what was, seemed to give reasonable indication of what must once have been, the tone of the society in these sequestered but interesting islands.

In one respect I was judged somewhat hastily, perhaps, when the character of Norna was pronounced by the critics a mere copy of Meg Merrilies. That I had fallen short of what I wished and desired to express is unquestionable, otherwise my object could not have been so widely mistaken ; nor can I yet think that any person who will take the trouble of reading the Pirate with some attention, can fail to trace in Norna,—the victim of remorse and insanity, and the dupe of her own imposture, her mind too, flooded with all the wild literature and extravagant superstitions of the north,—something distinct from the Dumfriesshire gipsy, whose pretensions to supernatural powers are not beyond those of a Norwood prophetess. The foundations of such a character may be perhaps traced, though it be too true that the necessary superstructure cannot have been raised upon them, otherwise the remark would have been unnecessary. There is also great improbability in the statement of Norna possessing power and opportunity to impress on others that belief in her supernatural powers which distracted her own mind. Yet, amid a very credulous and ignorant population, it is astonishing what success may be attained by an impostor, who is, at the same time, an enthusiast. It is such as to remind us of the couplet which assures us that

> "The pleasure is as great
> Of being cheated as to cheat."

Indeed, as I have observed elsewhere, the professed explanation of a tale, where appearances or incidents of a supernatural character are explained on natural causes, has often, in the winding up of the story, a degree of improbability almost equal to an absolute goblin tale. Even the genius of Mrs Radcliffe could not always surmount this difficulty.

ABBOTSFORD, 1st May 1831

4

ADVERTISEMENT TO THE FIRST EDITION
December 1821

THE *purpose of the following Narrative is to give a detailed and accurate account of certain remarkable incidents which took place in the Orkney Islands, concerning which the more imperfect traditions and mutilated records of the country only tell us the following erroneous particulars :—*

In the month of January 1724-5 a vessel, called the Revenge, bearing twenty large guns, and six smaller, commanded by John Gow or Goffe, or Smith, came to the Orkney Islands, and was discovered to be a pirate, by various acts of insolence and villainy committed by the crew. These were for some time submitted to, the inhabitants of these remote islands not possessing arms nor means of resistance ; and so bold was the Captain of these banditti, that he not only came ashore, and gave dancing parties in the village of Stromness, but, before his real character was discovered, engaged the affections, and received the troth-plight of a young lady possessed of some property. A patriotic individual, James Fea, younger of Clestron, formed the plan of securing the buccanier, which he effected by a mixture of courage and address, in consequence chiefly of Gow's vessel having gone on shore near the harbour of Calfsound, on the Island of Eda, not far distant from a house then inhabited by Mr Fea. In the various stratagems by which Mr Fea contrived finally, at the peril of his life (they being well armed and desperate) to make the whole pirates his prisoners, he was much aided by Mr James Laing, the grandfather of the late Malcolm Laing, Esq., the acute and ingenious historian of Scotland during the 17th century. *

Gow, and others of the crew, suffered, by sentence of the High Court of Admiralty, the punishment their crimes had long deserved.

He conducted himself with great audacity when before the Court ; and, from an account of the matter, by an eyewitness, seems to have been subjected to some unusual severities, in order to compel him to plead. The words are these : "John Gow would not plead, for which he was brought to the bar, and the Judge ordered that his thumbs should be squeezed by two men with a whip-cord, till it did break; and then it should be doubled, till it did again break, and then laid threefold, and that the executioners should pull with their whole strength ; which sentence Gow endured with a great deal of boldness." *The next morning (27th May 1725), when he had seen the terrible preparations for pressing him to death, his courage gave way, and he told the Marshal of Court, that he would not have given so much trouble, had he been assured of not being hanged in chains. He was then tried, condemned, and executed, with others of his crew.*

---

* [This gentleman was called to the Scotch Bar in the year 1784, but the infirm state of his health induced him, in 1810, to leave the profession, and to reside on his paternal property near Kirkwall, devoting himself to agricultural pursuits. He died in November 1818, aged 55, and was interred in the nave of St. Magnus's Cathedral.]

It is said, that the lady whose affections Gow had engaged, went up to London to see him before his death, and that, arriving too late, she had the courage to request a sight of his dead body ; and then, touching the hand of the corpse, she formally resumed the troth-plight which she had bestowed. Without going through this ceremony, she could not, according to the superstition of the country, have escaped a visit from the ghost of her departed lover, in the event of her bestowing upon any living suitor the faith which she had plighted to the dead. This part of the legend may serve as a curious commentary on the fine Scottish ballad, which begins,

"There came a ghost to Margaret's door," etc*

The common account of this incident farther bears, that Mr Fea, the spirited individual by whose exertions Gow's career of iniquity was cut short, was so far from receiving any reward from Government, that he could not obtain even countenance enough to protect him against a variety of sham suits, raised against him by Newgate solicitors, who acted in the name of Gow, and others of the pirate crew; and the various expenses, vexatious prosecutions; and other legal consequences, in which his gallant exploit involved him, utterly ruined his fortune, and his family ; making his memory a notable example to all who shall in future take pirates on their own authority.

It is to be supposed, for the honour of George the First's Government, that the last circumstance, as well as the dates, and other particulars of the commonly received story, are inaccurate, since they will be found totally irreconcilable with the following veracious narrative, compiled from materials to which he himself alone has had access, by

THE AUTHOR OF WAVERLEY

---

* [This ballad of "Willie's Ghost" is printed in Herd's *Collection*, vol. i. p. 76. It is not so well known as Mallet's version, "Willie and Margaret," which begins, *'Twas at the fearful midnight hour.'*]

THE PIRATE

CHAPTER I.

The storm had ceased its wintry roar,
   Hoarse dash the billows of the sea ;
But who on Thule's desert shore,
   Cries, Have I burnt my harp for thee ?

                         MACNIEL

THAT long, narrow, and irregular island, usually called the Mainland of Zetland, because it is by far the largest of that Archipelago, terminates, as it is well known to the mariners who navigate the stormy seas which surround the Thule of the ancients, in a cliff of immense height, entitled Sumburgh Head, which presents its bare scalp and naked sides to the weight of a tremendous surge, forming the extreme point of the isle to the south-east. This lofty promontory is constantly exposed to the current of a strong and furious tide, which, setting in betwixt the Orkney and Zetland Islands, and running with force only inferior to that of the Pentland Firth, takes its name from the headland we have mentioned, and is called the Roost of Sumburgh ; "roost" being the phrase assigned in these isles to currents of this description.

On the land side the promontory is covered with short grass, and slopes steeply down to a little isthmus, upon which the sea has encroached in creeks, which, advancing from either side of the island, gradually work their way forward, and seem as if in a short time they would form a junction, and altogether insulate Sumburgh Head, when what is now a cape will become a lonely mountain islet, severed from the mainland, of which it is at present the terminating extremity.

Man, however, had in former days considered this as a remote or unlikely event; for a Norwegian chief of other times, or as accounts said, and as the name of Yarlshof seemed to imply, an ancient Earl of the Orkneys had selected this neck of land as the place for establishing a mansion-house. It has been long entirely deserted, and the vestiges only can be discerned with difficulty; for the loose sand, borne on the tempestuous gales of those stormy regions, has overblown, and almost buried, the ruins of the buildings ; but in the end of the seventeenth century a part of the Earl's mansion was still entire and habitable. It was a rude building of rough stone, with nothing about it to gratify the eye, or to excite the imagination ; a large old-fashioned narrow house, with a very steep roof, covered with flags composed of grey sandstone, would perhaps convey the best idea of the place to a modern reader. The windows were few, very small in size, and distributed up and down the building with utter contempt of regularity. Against the main structure has rested, in former times, certain smaller compartments of the mansion-house, containing offices or subordinate apartments, necessary for the Earl's retainers and menials. But these had become ruinous ; and the rafters had been taken down for firewood, or for other purposes; the walls had given way in many places ; and, to complete the devastation, the sand had already drifted amongst the ruins, and filled up what had been once the chambers they contained, to the depth of two or three feet.

Amid this desolation, the inhabitants of Yarlshof had contrived, by constant labour and attention, to keep in order a few roods of land, which had been enclosed as a garden, and which, sheltered by the walls of the house itself from the relentless sea-blast, produced such vegetables as the climate could bring forth, or rather as the sea-gale would permit to grow ; for these islands experience even less of the rigour of cold than is encountered on the mainland of Scotland ; but, unsheltered by a wall of some sort, it is scarce possible to raise even the most ordinary culinary vegetables ; and as for shrubs or trees, they are entirely out of the question, such is the force of the sweeping sea-blast.

At a short distance from the mansion, and near to the sea-beach, just where the creek forms a sort of imperfect harbour, in which lay three or four fishing-boats, there were a few most wretched cottages for the inhabitants and tenants of the township of Yarlshof, who held the whole district of the landlord upon such terms as were in those days usually granted to persons of this description, and which, of course, were hard enough. The landlord himself resided upon an estate which he possessed in a more eligible situation, in a different part of the island, and seldom visited his possessions at Sumburgh Head. He was an honest, plain Zetland gentleman, somewhat passionate, the necessary result of being surrounded by dependants ; and somewhat over-convivial in his habits, the consequence, perhaps, of having too much time at his disposal ; but frank-tempered and generous to his people, and kind and hospitable to strangers. He was descended also of an old and noble Norwegian family ; a circumstance which rendered him dearer to the lower orders, most of whom are of the same race ; while the lairds, or proprietors, are generally of Scottish extraction, who, at that early period, were still considered as strangers and intruders. Magnus Troil, who deduced his descent from the very Earl who was supposed to have founded Yarlshof, was peculiarly of this opinion.

The present inhabitants of Yarlshof had experienced, on several occasions, the kindness and good will of the proprietor of the territory. When Mr. Mertoun—such was the name of the present inhabitant of the old mansion—first arrived in Zetland, some years before the story commences, he had been received at the house of Mr. Troil with that warm and cordial hospitality for which the islands are distinguished. No one asked him whence he came, where he was going, what was his purpose in visiting so remote a corner of the empire, or what was likely to be the term of his stay. He arrived a perfect stranger ; yet was instantly overpowered by a succession of invitations ; and in each house which he visited, he found a home as long as he chose to accept it, and lived as one of the family, unnoticed and unnoticing, until he thought proper to remove to some other dwelling. This apparent indifference to the rank, character and qualities of their guest, did not arise from apathy on the part of his kind hosts, for the islanders had their full share of natural curiosity ; but their delicacy deemed it would be an infringement upon the laws of hospitality, to ask questions which their guest might have found it difficult or unpleasing to answer ; and instead of endeavouring, as is usual in other countries, to wring out of Mr. Mertoun such communications as he might find it agreeable to withhold, the considerate Zetlanders contented themselves with eagerly gathering up such scraps of information as could be collected in the course of conversation.

But the rock in an Arabian desert is not more reluctant to afford water, than Mr. Basil Mertoun was niggard in imparting his confidence, even incidentally ; and certainly the politeness of the gentry of Thule was never put to a more severe test than when they felt that good-breeding enjoined them to abstain from inquiring into the situation of so mysterious a personage.

All that was actually known of him was easily summed up. Mr. Mertoun had come to Lerwick, then rising into some importance, but not yet acknowledged as the principal town of the island, in a Dutch vessel, accompanied only by his son, a handsome boy of about fourteen years old. His own age might exceed forty. The Dutch skipper introduced him to some of the very good friends with whom he used to barter gin and gingerbread for little Zetland bullocks, smoked geese, and stockings of lamb's-wool ; and although Meinheer could only say, that "Meinheer Mertoun hab bay his bassage like one gentlemans, and hab given a Kreitzdollar beside to the crew," this introduction served to establish the Dutchman's passenger in a respectable circle of acquaintances, which gradually enlarged, as it appeared that the stranger was a man of considerable acquirements.

This discovery was made almost *per force* ; for Mertoun was as unwilling to speak upon general subjects, as upon his own affairs. But he was sometimes led into discussions, which showed, as it were in spite of himself, the scholar and the man of the world ; and, at other times, as if in requital of the hospitality which he experienced, he seemed to compel himself, against his fixed nature, to enter into the society of those around him, especially when it assumed the grave, melancholy, or satirical cast, which best suited the temper of his own mind. Upon such occasions, the Zetlanders were universally of opinion that he must have had an excellent education, neglected only in one striking particular, namely, that Mr. Mertoun scarce knew the stem of a ship from the stern; and in the management of a boat, a cow could not be more ignorant. It seemed astonishing such gross ignorance of the most necessary art of life (in the Zetland Isles at least) should subsist along with his accomplishments in other respects; but so it was.

Unless called forth in the manner we have mentioned, the habits of Basil Mertoun were retired and gloomy. From loud mirth he instantly fled; and even the moderated cheerfulness of a friendly party had the invariable effect of throwing him into deeper dejection than even his usual demeanour indicated.

Women are always particularly desirous of investigating mystery, and of alleviating melancholy, especially when these circumstances are united in a handsome man about the prime of life. It is possible, therefore, that amongst the fair-haired and blue-eyed daughters of Thule this mysterious and pensive stranger might have found some one to take upon herself the task of consolation, had he shown any willingness to accept such kindly offices; but, far from doing so, he seemed even to shun the presence of the sex, to which in our distresses, whether of mind or body, we generally apply for pity and comfort.

To these peculiarities Mr. Mertoun added another, which was particularly disagreeable to his host and principal patron, Magnus Troil. This magnate of Zetland, descended by the father's side, as we have already said, from an ancient Norwegian family by the marriage of its representative with a Danish lady, held the devout opinion that a cup of Geneva or Nantz was specific against all cares and afflictions whatever. These were remedies to which Mr Mertoun never applied; his drink was water, and water alone, and no persuasion or entreaties could induce him to taste any stronger beverage than was afforded by the pure stream. Now this Magnus Troil could not tolerate; it was a defiance to the ancient northern laws of conviviality, which, for his own part, he had so rigidly observed, that although he was wont to assert that he had never in his life gone to bed drunk (that is, in his own sense of the word), it would have been impossible to prove that he had ever resigned himself to slumber in a state of actual and absolute sobriety. It may be therefore asked, What did this stranger bring into society to compensate the displeasure given by his austere and abstemious habits? He had, in the first place, that manner and self-importance which mark a person of some consequence; and although it was conjectured that he could not be rich, yet it was certainly known by his expenditure that neither was he absolutely poor. He had, besides, some powers of conversation, when, as we have already hinted, he chose to exert them, and his misanthropy or aversion to the business and intercourse of ordinary life, was often expressed in an antithetical manner, which often passed for

10

wit, when better was not to be had. Above all, Mr. Mertoun's secret seemed impenetrable, and his presence had all the interest of a riddle, which men love to read over and over, because they cannot find out the meaning of it.

Notwithstanding these recommendations, Mertoun differed in so many material points from his host, that after he had been for some time a guest at his principal residence, Magnus Troil was agreeably surprised when, one evening after they had sat two hours in absolute silence, drinking brandy and water—that is, Magnus drinking the alcohol, and Mertoun the element,—the guest asked his host's permission to occupy, as his tenant, this deserted mansion of Yarlshof, at the extremity of the territory called Dunrossness, and situated just beneath Sumburgh Head. "I shall be handsomely rid of him," quoth Magnus to himself, "and his kill-joy visage will never again stop the bottle in its round. His departure will ruin me in lemons, however, for his mere look was quite sufficient to sour a whole ocean of punch."

Yet the kind-hearted Zetlander generously and disinterestedly remonstrated with Mr. Mertoun on the solitude and inconveniences to which he was about to subject himself. "There were scarcely," he said, "even the most necessary articles of furniture in the old house—there was no society within many miles—for provisions, the principal article of food would be sour sillocks, and his only company gulls and gannets."

"My good friend," replied Mertoun, "if you could have named a circumstance which would render the residence more eligible to me than any other, it is that there would be neither human luxury nor human society near the place of my retreat ; a shelter from the weather for my own head, and for the boy's is all I seek for. So name your rent, Mr. Troil, and let me be your tenant at Yarlshof."

"Rent ?" answered the Zetlander ; "why, no great rent for an old house which no one has lived in since my mother's time—God rest her !—and as for shelter, the old walls are thick enough, and will bear many a bang yet. But, Heaven love you, Mr. Mertoun, think what you are purposing. For one of us to live at Yarlshof were a wild scheme enough ; but you, who are from another country, whether English, Scotch, or Irish, no one can tell."

"Nor does it greatly matter," said Mertoun, somewhat abruptly.

"Not a herring's scale," answered the Laird ; "only that I like you the better for being no Scot, as I trust you are not one. Hither they have come like the clack-geese—every chamberlain has brought over a flock of his own, and his own name, and his own hatching, for what I know, and here they roost for ever—catch them returning to their own barren Highlands or Lowlands, when once they have tasted our Zetland beef, and seen our bonny *voes* and lochs. No, sir (here Magnus proceeded with great animation, sipping from time to time the half-diluted spirit, which at the same time animated his resentment against the intruders, and enabled him to endure the mortifying reflection which it suggested),—"No, sir, the ancient days and the genuine manners of these Islands are no more ; for our ancient possessors—our Patersons, our Feas, our Schlagbrenners, our Thorbiorns, have given place to Giffords,

11

Scotts, Mouats, men whose names bespeak them or their ancestors strangers to the soil which we the Troils have inhabited long before the days of Turf-Einar, who first taught these Isles the mystery of burning peat for fuel, and who has been handed down to a grateful posterity by a name which records the discovery."

This was a subject upon which the potentate of Yarlshof was usually very diffuse, and Mertoun saw him enter upon it with pleasure, because he knew he should not be called upon to contribute any aid to the conversation, and might therefore indulge his own saturnine humour while the Norwegian Zetlander declaimed on the change of times and inhabitants. But just as Magnus had arrived at the melancholy conclusion, "how probably it was, that in another century scarce a *merk*–scarce even an *ure* of land, would be in the possession of the Norse inhabitants, the true Udallers* of Zetland," he recollected the circumstances of his guest, and stopped suddenly short. "I do not say all this," he added, interrupting himself, "as if I were unwilling that you should settle on my estate, Mr. Mertoun–But for Yarlshof–the place is a wild one–Come from where you will, I warrant you will say, like other travellers, you came from a better climate than ours, for so say you all. And yet you think of a retreat which the very natives run away from. Will you not take your glass ?–(This was to be considered as interjectional),–"then here's to you."

"My good sir," answered Mertoun, "I am indifferent to climate ; if there is but air enough to fill my lungs, I care not if it be the breath of Arabia or of Lapland."

"Air enough you may have," answered Magnus, "no lack of that–somewhat damp, strangers allege it to be, but we know a corrective for that–Here's to you, Mr. Mertoun – You must learn to *do so*, and to smoke a pipe ; and then, as you say, you will find the air of Zetland equal to that of Arabia. But have you seen Yarlshof ?"

The stranger intimated that he had not.

"Then," replied Magnus, "you have no idea of your undertaking. If you think it a comfortable roadstead like this, with the house situated on the side on an inland voe,† that brings the herrings up to your door, you are mistaken, my heart. At Yarlshof you will see nought but the wild waves tumbling on the bare rocks, and the Roost of Sumburgh running at the rate of fifteen knots an hour."

"I shall see nothing at least of the current of human passions," replied Mertoun.

"You will hear nothing but the clanging and screaming of scarts, sheer-waters, and sea-gulls, from daybreak till sunset."

"I will compound, my friend," replied the stranger, "so that I do not hear the chattering of women's tongues."

"Ah," said the Norman, "that is because you hear just now my little Minna and Brenda singing in the garden with your Mordaunt. Now, I would rather listen to their little voices, than the skylark which I once

* The Udallers are the *allodial* possessors of Zetland who hold their possessions under the old Norwegian law, instead of the feudal tenures introduced among them from Scotland.
† Salt-water lake.

12

heard in Caithness, or the nightingale that I have read of. What will the girls do for want of their playmate Mordaunt ?"

"They will shift for themselves," answered Mertoun ; "younger or elder they will find playmates or dupes. But the question is, Mr. Troil, will you let to me, as your tenant, this old mansion of Yarlshof ?"

"Gladly, since you make it your option to live in a spot so desolate."

"And as for the rent ?" continued Mertoun.

"The rent ?" replied Magnus ; "hum—why, you must have the bit of *plantie cruive,** which they once called a garden, and a right in the *scathold,* and a sixpenny merk of land, that the tenants may fish for you ; eight *lispunds*† of butter, and eight shillings sterling yearly is not too much ?"

Mr. Mertoun agreed to terms so moderate, and from thenceforward resided chiefly at the solitary mansion which we have described in the beginning of this chapter, conforming not only without complaint, but, as it seemed, with a sullen pleasure, to all the privations which so wild and desolate a situation necessarily imposed on its inhabitant.

CHAPTER SECOND

'Tis not alone the scene—the man, Anselmo,
The man finds sympathies in these wild wastes,
And roughly tumbling seas, which fairer views
And smoother waves deny him.

ANCIENT DRAMA

THE few inhabitants of the township of Yarlshof had at first heard with alarm, that a person of rank superior to their own was come to reside in the ruinous tenement, which they still called the Castle. In those days (for the present times are greatly altered for the better) the presence of a superior, in such a situation was almost certain to be attended with additional burdens and exactions, for which, under one pretext or another, feudal customs furnished a thousand apologies. By each of these, a part of the tenants' hard-won and precarious profits was diverted for the use of their powerful neighbour and superior, the tacksman, as he was called. But the sub-tenants speedily found that no oppression of this kind was to be apprehended at the hands of Basil Mertoun. His own means, whether large or small, were at least fully adequate to his expenses, which, so far as regarded his habits of life, were of the most frugal description. The luxuries of a few books, and some philosophical instruments, with which he was supplied from London as occasion offered, seemed to indicate a degree of wealth unusual in these islands ; but, on the other hand, the table and the accommodations at Yarlshof did not exceed what was maintained by a Zetland proprietor of the most inferior description.

* Note B. Plantie cruive.
† A lispund is about thirty pounds English, and the value is averaged by Dr. Edmonston at ten shillings sterling.

13

The tenants of the hamlet troubled themselves very little about the quality of their superior, as soon as they found that their situation was rather to be mended than rendered worse by his presence ; and, once relieved from the apprehension of his tyrannising over them, they laid their heads together to make the most of him by various petty tricks of overcharge and extortion, which for a while the stranger submitted to with the most philosophic indifference. An incident, however, occurred, which put his character in a new light, and effectively checked all future efforts at extravagant imposition.

A dispute arose in the kitchen of the Castle betwixt an old governante, who acted as housekeeper to Mr. Mertoun, and Sweyn Erickson, as good a Zetlander as ever rowed a boat to the *haaf* fishing ;* which dispute, as is usual in such cases, was maintained with such increasing heat and vociferation as to reach the ears of the master (as he was called), who, secluded in a solitary turret, was deeply employed in examining the contents of a new package of books from London, which, after long expectation, had found its way to Hull, from thence by a whaling vessel to Lerwick, and so to Yarlshof. With more than the usual thrill of indignation which indolent people always feel when roused into action on some unpleasant occasion, Mertoun descended to the scene of contest, and so suddenly, peremptorily, and strictly, inquired the cause of dispute, that the parties, not withstanding every evasion which they attempted, became unable to disguise from him that their difference respected the several interests to which the honest governante, and no less honest fisherman, were respectively entitled, in an overcharge of about one hundred per cent on a bargain of rock-cod, purchased by the former from the latter, for the use of the family at Yarlshof.

When this was fairly ascertained and confessed, Mr. Mertoun stood looking upon the culprits with eyes in which the utmost scorn seemed to contend with awakening passion. "Hark you, ye old hag," said he at length to the housekeeper, "avoid my house this instant ! And know that I dismiss you, not for being a liar, a thief, and an ungrateful quean,—for these are qualities as proper to you as your name of woman,—but for daring in my house, to scold above your breath. And for you, you rascal, who suppose you may cheat a stranger as you would *flinch*† a whale, know that I am well acquainted with the rights which, by delegation from your master, Magnus Troil, I can exercise over you if I will. Provoke me to a certain pitch, and you shall learn, to your cost, I can break your rest as easily as you can interrupt my leisure. I know the meaning of *scat,* and *wattle,* and *hawkhen,* and *hagalef,* and every other exaction by which your lords, in ancient and modern days, have wrung your withers ; nor is there one of you that shall not rue the day that you could not be content with robbing me of my money, but must also break in on my leisure with your atrocious northern clamour, that rivals in discord the screaming of a flight of Arctic gulls."

Nothing better occurred to Sweyn, in answer to this objurgation,

* *i.e.* The deep-sea fishing, in distinction to that which is practised along shore.
† The operation of slicing the blubber from the bones of the whale, is called, technically, *flinching.*

14

than the preferring a humble request that his honour would be pleased to keep the cod-fish without payment, and say no more about the matter ; but by this time Mr. Mertoun had worked up his passions into an ungovernable rage, and with one hand he threw the money at the fisherman's head, while with the other he pelted him out of the apartment with his own fish, which he finally flung out of doors after him.

There was so much of appalling and tyrannic fury in the stranger's manner on this occasion, that Sweyn neither stopped to collect the money nor take back his commodity, but fled at a precipitate rate to the small hamlet, to tell his comrades that if they provoked Master Mertoun any farther, he would turn an absolute Pate Stewart* on their hand, and head and hang without any judgement or mercy.

Hither also came the discarded housekeeper, to consult with her neighbours and kindred (for she too was a native of the village) what she should do to regain the desirable situation from which she had been so suddenly expelled. The old Ranzellaar of the village, who had the voice most potential in the deliberations of the township, after hearing what had happened, pronounced that Sweyn Erickson had gone too far in raising the market upon Mr. Mertoun ; and that whatever pretext the tacksman might assume for thus giving way to his anger, the real grievance must have been the charging the rock cod-fish at a penny instead of a halfpenny a-pound ; he therefore exhorted all the community never to raise their exactions in future beyond the proportion of threepence upon the shilling, at which rate their master at the Castle could not reasonably be expected to grumble, since, as he was disposed to do them no harm, it was reasonable to think that, in a moderate way, he had no objection to do them good. "And three upon twelve," said the experienced Ranzellaar, "is a decent and moderate profit, and will bring with it God's blessing and Saint Ronald's."

Proceeding upon the tariff thus judiciously recommended to them, the inhabitants of Yarlshof cheated Mertoun in future only to the moderate extent of twenty-five per cent ; a rate to which all nabobs, army-contractors, speculators in the funds, and others, whom recent and rapid success has enabled to settle in the country upon a great scale, ought to submit, as very reasonable treatment at the hand of their rustic neighbours. Mertoun at least seemed of that opinion, for he gave himself no farther trouble upon the subject of his household expenses.

The conscript fathers of Yarlshof, having settled their own matters, took next under their consideration the case of Swertha, the banished matron who had been expelled from the Castle, whom, as an experienced and useful ally, they were highly desirous to restore to her office of housekeeper, should that be found possible. But as their wisdom here failed them, Swertha, in despair, had recourse to the good offices of Mordaunt Mertoun, with whom she had acquired some favour by her knowledge in old Norwegian ballads, and dismal tales

* Meaning, probably, Patrick Stewart, Earl of Orkney, executed for tyranny and oppression practised on the inhabitants of these remote islands in the beginning of the seventeenth century. [His father, Lord Robert Stewart, was a natural son of James V.]

15

concerning the Trows or Drows (the dwarfs of the Scalds), with whom superstitious eld had peopled many a lonely cavern and brown dale in Dunrossness, as in every other district of Zetland. "Swertha," said the youth, "I can do but little for you, but you may do something for yourself. My father's passion resembles the fury of those ancient champions, those Berserkars, you sing songs about."

"Ay, ay, fish of my heart," replied the old woman, with a pathetic whine ; "the Berserkars were champions who lived before the blessed days of Saint Olàve and who used to run like madmen on swords, and spears, and harpoons, and muskets, and snap them all into pieces, as a finner* would go through a herring-net, and then, when the fury went off, they were as weak and unstable as water."†

"That's the very thing, Swertha," said Mordaunt. "Now, my father never likes to think of his passion after it is over, and is so much of a Berserkar, that, let him be desperate as he will to-day, he will not care about it to-morrow. Therefore, he has not filled up your place in the household at the Castle, and not a mouthful of warm food has been dressed there since you went away, not a morsel of bread baked, but we have lived just upon whatever cold thing came to hand. Now, Swertha, I will be your warrant, that if you boldly go up to the Castle and enter upon the discharge of your duties as usual, you will never hear a single word from him."

Swertha hesitated at first to obey this bold counsel. She said, "to her thinking, Mr. Mertoun, when he was angry, looked more like a fiend than any Berserkar of them all ; that the fire flashed from his eyes, and the foam flew from his lips ; and that it would be plain tempting of Providence to put herself again in such a venture."

But, on the encouragement which she received from the son she determined at length once more to face the parent ; and, dressing herself in her ordinary household attire, for so Mordaunt particularly recommended, she slipped into the Castle, and presently resuming the various and numerous occupations which devolved on her, seemed as deeply engaged in household cares as if she had never been out of office.

The first day of her return to her duty, Swertha made no appearance in presence of her master, but trusted that, after his three days' diet on cold meat, a hot dish, dressed with the best of her simple skill, might introduce her favourably to his recollection. When Mordaunt had reported that his father had taken no notice of this change of diet, and when she herself observed that, in passing and repassing him occasionally, her appearance produced no effect upon her singular master, she began to imagine that the whole affair had escaped Mr. Mertoun's memory, and was active in her duty as usual. Neither was she convinced of the contrary until one day, when, happening somewhat to

* Finner, small whale.
† The sagas of the Scalds are full of descriptions of these champions, and do not permit us to doubt that the Berserkars, so called from fighting without armour, used some physical means of working themselves into a frenzy, during which they possessed the strength and energy of madness. The Indian warriors are well known to do the same by dint of opium and bang.

16

elevate her tone in a dispute with the other maid-servant, her master, who at that time passed the place of contest, eyed her with a strong glance, and pronounced the single word, *Remember!* in a tone which taught Swertha the government of her tongue for many weeks after.

If Mertoun was whimsical in his mode of governing his household, he seemed no less so in his plan of educating his son. He showed the youth but few symptoms of parental affection ; yet, in his ordinary state of mind, the improvement of Mordaunt's education seemed to be the utmost object in his life. He had both books and information sufficient to discharge the task of tutor in the ordinary branches of knowledge ; and in this capacity was regular, calm, and strict, not to say severe, in exacting from his pupil the attention necessary for his profiting. But in the perusal of history, to which their attention was frequently turned, as well as in the study of classic authors, there often occurred facts or sentiments which produced an instant effect upon Mertoun's mind, and brought on him suddenly what Swertha, Sweyn, and even Mordaunt came to distinguish by the name of his dark hour. He was aware, in the usual case, of its approach, and retreated to an inner apartment, into which he never permitted even Mordaunt to enter. Here he would abide in seclusion for days, and even weeks, only coming out at uncertain times, to take food as they had taken care to leave within his reach, which he used in wonderfully small quantities. At other times, and especially during the winter solstice, when almost every person spends the gloomy time within doors in feasting and merriment, this unhappy man would wrap himself in a dark-coloured sea-cloak, and wander out along the stormy beach, or upon the desolate heath, indulging his own gloomy and wayward reveries under the inclement sky, the rather that he was then most sure to wander unencountered and unobserved.

As Mordaunt grew older, he learned to note the particular signs which preceded these fits of gloomy despondency, and to direct such precautions as might insure his unfortunate parent from ill-timed interruption (which had always the effect of driving him to fury), while, at the same time, full provision was made for his subsistence. Mordaunt perceived that at such periods the melancholy fit of his father was greatly prolonged, if he chanced to present himself to his eyes while the dark hour was upon him. Out of respect, therefore, to his parent, as well as to indulge the love of active exercise and of amusement natural to his period of life, Mordaunt used often to absent himself altogether from the mansion of Yarlshof, and even from the district, secure that his father, if the dark hour passed away in his absence, would be little inclined to inquire how his son had disposed of his leisure, so that he was sure he had not watched his own weak moments ; that being the subject on which he entertained the utmost jealousy.

At such times, therefore, all the sources of amusement which the country afforded, were open to the younger Mertoun, who, in these intervals of his education, had an opportunity to give full scope to the energies of a bold, active, and daring character. He was often engaged with the youth of the hamlet in those desperate sports, to which the "dreadful trade of the samphire-gatherer" is like a walk upon level ground—often joined those midnight excursions upon the face of the giddy cliffs, to secure the eggs or the young of the sea-fowl ; and in these daring adventures displayed an address, presence of mind, and activity, which, in one so young, and not a native of the country, astonished the oldest fowlers.*

At other times, Mordaunt accompanied Sweyn and other fishermen in their long and perilous expeditions to the distant and deep sea, learning under their direction the management of the boat, in which they equal, or excel, perhaps, any natives of the British empire. This exercise had charms for Mordaunt, independently of the fishing alone.

At this time, the old Norwegian sagas were much remembered, and often rehearsed, by the fishermen, who still preserved among themselves the ancient Norse tongue, which was the speech of their forefathers. In the dark romance of those Scandinavian tales lay much that was captivating to a youthful ear ; and the classic fables of antiquity were rivalled at least, if not excelled in Mordaunt's opinion, by the strange legends of Berserkars, of Sea-kings, of dwarfs, giants, and sorcerers, which he heard from the native Zetlanders. Often the scenes around him were assigned as the localities of wild poems, which, half recited, half chanted, by voices as hoarse, if not so loud, as the waves over which they floated, pointed out the very bay on which they sailed as the scene of a bloody sea fight ; the scarce-seen heap of stones that bristled over the projecting cape, as the dun, or castle, of some potent earl or noted pirate ; the distant and solitary grey stone on the lonely moor, as marking the grave of a hero ; the wild cavern, up which the sea rolled in heavy, broad, and unbroken billows, as the dwelling of some noted sorceress.†

The ocean also had its mysteries, the effect of which was aided by the dim twilight, through which it was imperfectly seen for more than half the year. Its bottomless depths and secret caves contained, according to the account of Sweyn and others, skilled in legendary lore, such wonders as modern navigators reject with disdain.

In the quiet moonlight bay, where the waves came rippling to the shore, upon a bed of smooth sand intermingled with shells, the mermaid was still seen to glide along the waters by moonlight, and, mingling her voice with the sighing breeze, was often heard to sing of subterranean wonders, or to chant prophecies of future events. The kraken, the hugest of living things, was still supposed to cumber in the recesses of the Northern Ocean ; and often, when some fog-bank covered the sea at a distance, the eye of the experienced boatman saw the horns of the monstrous leviathan welking and waving amidst the wreaths of mist, and bore away with all press of oar and sail, lest the sudden suction, occasioned by the sinking of the monstrous mass to the

---

* Fatal accidents, however, sometimes happen. When I visited the Fair Isle in 1814, a poor lad of fourteen had been killed by a fall from the rocks about a fortnight before our arrival. The accident happened almost within sight of his mother, who was casting peats at no great distance. The body fell into the sea and was seen no more. But the islanders account this an honourable mode of death ; and as the children begin the practice of climbing very early, fewer accidents occur than might be expected.

† Note C. Norse Fragments.

bottom, should drag within the grasp of its multifarious feelers his own frail skiff. The sea-snake was also known, which, arising out of the depths of ocean, stretches to the skies his enormous neck covered with a mane like that of a war-horse, and with his broad glittering eyes, raised mast-head high, looks out, as it seems, for plunder or for victims.

Many prodigious stories of these marine monsters, and of many others less known, were then universally received among the Zetlanders, whose descendants have not as yet by any means abandoned faith in them.*

Such legends are, indeed, everywhere current amongst the vulgar ; but the imagination is far more powerfully affected by them on the deep and dangerous seas of the north, amidst precipices and headlands, many hundreds of feet in height—amid perilous straits, and currents, and eddies—long sunken reefs of rock, over which the vivid ocean foams and boils—dark caverns, to whose extremities neither man nor skiff has ever ventured—lonely, and often uninhabited isles—and occasionally the ruins of ancient northern fastnesses dimly seen by the feeble light of the Arctic winter. To Mordaunt, who had much of romance in his disposition, these superstitions formed a pleasing and interesting exercise of the imagination, while, half doubting, half inclined to believe, he listened to the tales chanted concerning these wonders of nature, and creatures of credulous belief, told in the rude but energetic language of the ancient Scalds.

But there wanted not softer and lighter amusement, that might seem better to Mordaunt's age, than the wild tales and rude exercises which we have already mentioned. The season of winter, when, from the shortness of the daylight, labour becomes impossible, is in Zetland the time of revel, feasting and merriment. Whatever the fisherman has been able to acquire during summer, was expended, and often wasted, in maintaining the mirth and hospitality of his hearth during this period ; while the landlords and gentlemen of the island gave double loose to their convivial and hospitable dispositions, thronged their homes with guests, and drove away the rigour of the season with jest, glee, and song, the dance, and the wine-cup.

Amid the revels of this merry, though rigorous season, no youth added more spirit to the dance, or glee to the revel, than the young stranger, Mordaunt Mertoun. When his father's state of mind permitted, or indeed required, his absence, he wandered from house to house a welcome guest wherever he came, and lent his willing voice to the song, and his foot to the revel. A boat, or, if the weather, as was often the case, permitted not that convenience, one of the numerous ponies, which, straying in hordes about the extensive moors, may be said to be at any man's command who can catch them, conveyed him from the mansion of one hospitable Zetlander to that of another. None excelled him in performing the warlike sword-dance, a species of amusement which had been derived from the habits of the ancient Norsemen. He could play upon the *gue,* and upon the common violin, the melancholy and pathetic tunes peculiar to the country ; and with great spirit and

* Note D. Monsters of the Northern Seas.

19

execution could relieve their monotony with the livelier airs of the North of Scotland. When a party set forth as maskers, or, as they are called in Scotland, *guizards,* to visit some neighbouring Laird, or rich Udaller, it augured well of the expedition if Mordaunt Mertoun could be prevailed upon to undertake the office of *skudler,* or leader of the band. Upon these occasions, full of fun and frolic, he led his retinue from house to house, bring mirth where he went, and leaving regrets when he departed. Mordaunt became thus generally known, and beloved, as generally, through most of the houses composing the patriarchal community of the Main Isle ; but his visits were most frequently and most willingly paid at the mansion of his father's landlord and protector, Magnus Troil.

It was not entirely the hearty and sincere welcome of the worthy old Magnate, nor the sense that he was in effect his father's patron, which occasioned these frequent visits. The hand of welcome was indeed received as eagerly as it was sincerely given, while the ancient Udaller, raising himself in his huge chair, whereof the inside was lined with well-dressed sealskins, and the outside composed of massive oak, carved by the rude graving-tool of some Hamburgh carpenter, shouted forth his welcome in a tone, which might, in ancient times, have hailed the return of *Ioul,* the highest festival of the Goths. There was metal yet more attractive, and younger hearts, whose welcome, if less loud, was as sincere as that of the jolly Udaller. But it is matter which ought not to be discussed at the conclusion of a chapter.

CHAPTER THIRD

"Oh, Bessy Bell and Mary Gray,
    They were twa bonnie lasses ;
They bigged a house on yon burn-brae,
    And theeked it ower wi' rashes.

"Fair Bessy Bell I looed yestreen,
    And thought I ne'er could alter ;
But Mary Gray's twa pawky een
    Have garr'd my fancy falter."

                                    SCOTS SONG

WE have already mentioned Minna and Brenda, the daughters of Magnus Troil. Their mother had been dead for many years, and they were now two beautiful girls, the eldest only eighteen, which might be a year or two younger than Mordaunt Mertoun, the second about seventeen. They were the joy of their father's heart, and the light of his old eyes ; and although indulged to a degree which might have endangered his comfort and their own, they repaid his affection with a love into which even blind indulgence had not introduced slight regards, or feminine caprice. The difference of their tempers and of their

20

complexions was singularly striking, although combined, as is usual, with a certain degree of family resemblance.

The mother of these maidens had been a Scottish lady from the Highlands of Sutherland, the orphan of a noble chief, who, driven from his own country during the feuds of the seventeenth century, had found shelter in those peaceful islands, which, amidst poverty and seclusion, were thus far happy, that they remained unvexed by discord and unstained by civil broil. The father (his name was Saint Clair) pined for his native glen, his feudal tower, his clansmen and his fallen authority, and died not long after his arrival in Zetland. The beauty of his orphan daughter, despite her Scottish lineage, melted the stout heart of Magnus Troil. He sued and was listened to, and she became his bride ; but dying in the fifth year of their union, left him to mourn his brief period of domestic happiness.

From her mother, Minna inherited the stately form and dark eyes, the raven locks and finely-pencilled brows, which showed she was, on one side at least, a stranger to the blood of Thule. Her cheek—

"Oh call it fair, not pale !"

was so slightly and delicately tinged with the rose, that many thought the lily had an undue proportion in her complexion. But in that predominance of the paler flower, there was nothing sickly or languid ; it was the true natural colour of health, and corresponded in a peculiar degree with features, which seemed calculated to express a contemplative and high-minded character. When Minna Troil heard a tale of woe or injustice, it was then her blood rushed to her cheeks, and showed plainly how warm it beat, notwithstanding the generally serious, composed, and retiring disposition, which her countenance and demeanour seemed to exhibit. If strangers sometimes conceived that these fine features were clouded by melancholy, for which her age and situation could scarce have given occasion, they were soon satisfied, upon farther acquaintance, that the placid, mild quietude of her disposition, and the mental energy of a character which was but little interested in ordinary and trivial occurrences, was the real cause of her gravity ; and most men, when they knew that her melancholy had no ground in real sorrow, and was only the aspiration of a soul bent on more important objects than those by which she was surrounded, might have wished her whatever could add to her happiness, but could scarce have desired that, graceful as she was in her natural and unaffected seriousness, she should change that deportment for one more gay. In short, notwithstanding our wish to have avoided that hackneyed simile of an angel, we cannot avoid saying there was something in the serious beauty of her aspect, in the measured, yet graceful ease of her motions, in the music of her voice, and the serene purity of her eye, that seemed as if Minna Troil belonged naturally to some higher and better sphere, and was only the chance visitant of a world that was not worthy of her.

The scarcely less beautiful, equally lovely, and equally innocent Brenda, was of a complexion as differing from her sister, as they differed in character, taste and expression. Her profuse locks were of that paly brown which receives from the passing sunbeam a tinge of gold, but darkens again when the ray has passed from it. Her eye, her mouth, the beautiful row of teeth, which in her innocent vivacity were frequently disclosed, tinging a skin like the drifted snow, spoke her genuine Scandinavian descent. A fairy form, less tall than that of Minna, but still more finely moulded into symmetry—a careless, and almost childish lightness of step—an eye that seemed to look on every object with pleasure, from a natural and serene cheerfulness of disposition, attracted even more general admiration than the charms of her sister, though perhaps that which Minna did excite, might be of a more intense as well as a more reverential character.

The dispositions of these lovely sisters were not less different than their complexions. In the kindly affections neither could be said to excel the other, so much were they attached to their father and to each other. But the cheerfulness of Brenda mixed itself with the everyday business of life, and seemed inexhaustible in its profusion. The less buoyant spirit of her sister appeared to bring to society a contented wish to be interested and pleased with what was going forward, but was rather placidly carried along with the stream of mirth and pleasure, than disposed to aid its progress by any efforts of her own. She endured mirth, rather than enjoyed it ; and the pleasures in which she most delighted were those of a graver and more solitary cast. The knowledge which is derived from books was beyond her reach. Zetland afforded few opportunities, in those day, of studying the lessons, bequeathed

"By dead men to their kind ;"

and Magnus Troil, such as we have described him, was not a person within whose mansion the means of such knowledge were to be acquired. But the book of nature was before Minna, that noblest of volumes, where we are ever called to wonder and to admire, even when we cannot understand. The plants of those wild regions, the shells on the shores, and the long list of feathered clans which haunt their cliffs and eyries, were as well known to Minna Troil as to the most experienced fowlers. Her powers of observation were wonderful, and little interrupted by other tones of feeling. The information which she acquired by habits of patient attention was indelibly riveted in a naturally powerful memory. She had also a high feeling for the solitary and melancholy grandeur of the scenes in which she was placed. The ocean in all its varied forms of sublimity and terror—the tremendous cliffs that resound to the ceaseless roar of the billows, and the clang of the seafowl, had for Minna a charm in almost every state in which the changing seasons exhibited them. With the enthusiastic feelings proper to the romantic race from which her mother descended, the love of natural objects was to her a passion capable not only of occupying, but at times of agitating, her mind. Scenes upon which her sister looked with a sense of transient awe or emotion, which vanished on her return from witnessing them, continued long to fill Minna's imagination, not only in solitude, and in the silence of the night, but in the hours of society. So that sometimes when she sat like a beautiful statue, a present member of

22

the domestic circle, her thoughts were far absent, wandering on the wild sea-shore, and among the yet wilder mountains of her native isles. And yet when recalled to conversation, and mingling in it with interest, there were few to whom her friends were more indebted for enhancing its enjoyments; and although something in her manners claimed deference (not withstanding her early youth) as well as affection, even her gay, lovely, and amiable sister was not more generally beloved than the more retired and pensive Minna.

Indeed the two lovely sisters were not only the delight of their friends but the pride of those islands, where the inhabitants of a certain rank were blended, by the remoteness of their situation and the general hospitality of their habits, into one friendly community. A wandering poet and parcel-musician, who, after going through various fortunes, had returned to end his days as he could in his native islands, had celebrated the daughters of Magnus in a poem, which he entitled Night and Day; and in his description of Minna, might almost be thought to have anticipated, though only in a rude outline, the exquisite lines of Lord Byron—

> "She walks in beauty, like the night
>   Of cloudless climes and starry skies;
> And all that's best of dark and bright
>   Meet in her aspect and her eyes:
> Thus mellow'd to that tender light
>   Which heaven to gaudy day denies.

Their father loved the maidens both so well, that it might be difficult to say which he loved best; saving that, perchance, he liked his graver damsel better in the walk without doors, and his merry maiden better by the fireside; that he more desired the society of Minna when he was sad, and that of Brenda when he was mirthful; and, what was nearly the same thing, preferred Minna before noon, and Brenda after the glass had circulated in the evening.

But it was still more extraordinary, that the affections of Mordaunt Mertoun seemed to hover with the same impartiality as those of their father betwixt the two lovely sisters. From his boyhood, as we have noticed, he had been a frequent inmate of the residence of Magnus at Burgh Westra, although it lay nearly twenty miles distant from Yarlshof. The impassable character of the country betwixt these places, extending over hills covered with loose and quaking bog, and frequently intersected by the creeks and arms of the sea, which indent the island on either side, as well as by fresh-water streams and lakes, rendered the journey difficult, and even dangerous, in the dark season; yet, as soon as the state of his father's mind warned him to absent himself, Mordaunt, at every risk, and under every difficulty, was pretty sure to be found the next day at Burgh Westra, having achieved his journey is less time than would have been employed perhaps by the most active native.

He was of course set down as a wooer of one of the daughters of Magnus, by the public of Zetland; and when the old Udaller's great partiality to the youth was considered, nobody doubted that he might aspire to the hand of either of those distinguished beauties, with as large a share of islets, rocky moorland, and shore-fishings, as might be the fitting portion of a favoured child, and with the presumptive prospect of possessing half the domains of the ancient house of Troil, when their present owner should be no more. This seemed all a reasonable speculation, and, in theory at least, better constructed than many than are current through the world as unquestionable facts. But alas ! All that sharpness of observation which could be applied to the conduct of the parties, failed to determine the main point, to which of the young persons, namely, the attentions of Mordaunt were peculiarly devoted. He seemed, in general, to treat them as an affectionate and attached brother might have treated two sisters, so equally dear to him that a breath would have turned the scale of attention. Or if at any time, which often happened, the one maiden appeared the more especial object of his attention, it seemed only to be because circumstances called her peculiar talents and disposition into more particular and immediate exercise.

Both the sisters were accomplished in the simple music of the north, and Mordaunt, who was their assistant, and sometimes their preceptor, when they were practising this delightful art, might be now seen assisting Minna in the acquisition of those wild, solemn, and simple airs, to which scalds and harpers sung of old the deeds of heroes, and presently found equally active in teaching Brenda the more lively and complicated music, which their father's affection caused to be brought from the English or Scottish capital for the use of his daughters. And while conversing with them, Mordaunt, who mingled a strain of deep and ardent enthusiasm with the gay and ungovernable spirits of youth, was equally ready to enter into the wild and poetical visions of Minna, or into the lively and often humorous chat of her gayer sister. In short, so little did he seem to attach himself to either damsel exclusively, that he was sometimes heard to say, that Minna never looked so lovely, as when her light-hearted sister had induced her, for the time, to forget her habitual gravity ; or Brenda so interesting, as when she sat listening, a subdued and affected partaker of the deep pathos of her sister Minna.

The public of the mainland were, therefore, to use the hunter's phrase, at fault in their farther conclusions, and could but determine, after long vacillating betwixt the maidens, that the young man was positively to marry one of them, but which of the two could only be determined when his approaching manhood, or the interference of stout old Magnus, the father, should teach Master Mordaunt Mertoun to know his own mind. "It was a pretty thing, indeed," they usually concluded, "that he, no native born, and possessed no visible means of subsistence that is known to any one, should presume to hesitate, or affect to have the power of selection and choice, betwixt the two most distinguished beauties of Zetland. If they were Magnus Troil, they would soon be at the bottom of the matter," and so forth. All which remarks were only whispered, for the hasty disposition of the Udaller had too much of the old Norse fire about it to render it safe for any one to become an unauthorised intermeddler with his family affairs ; and thus stood the relation of Mordaunt Mertoun to the family of Mr. Troil of Burgh Westra, when the following incidents took place.

CHAPTER FOURTH

This is no pilgrim's morning—yon grey mist
Lies upon hill, and dale, and field, and forest,
Like the dun wimple of a new-made widow ;
And, by my faith, although my heart be soft,
I'd rather hear that widow weep and sigh,
And tell the virtues of the dear departed,
Than, when the tempest sends his voice abroad,
Be subject to its fury.

THE DOUBLE NUPTIALS

THE spring was far advanced, when, after a week spent in sport and festivity at Burgh Westra, Mordaunt Mertoun bade adieu to the family, pleading the necessity of his return to Yarlshof. The proposal was combated by the maidens, and more decidedly by Magnus himself. He saw no occasion whatever for Mordaunt returning to Yarlshof. If his father desired to see him, which, by the way, Magnus did not believe, Mr Mertoun had only to throw himself into the stern of Sweyn's boat, or betake himself to a pony, if he liked a land journey better, and he would see not only his son, but twenty folk besides, who would be most happy to find that he had not lost the use of his tongue entirely during his long solitude ; "although I must own," added the worthy Udaller, "that when he lived among us, nobody ever made less use of it."

Mordaunt acquiesced both in what respected his father's taciturnity, and his dislike of general society ; but suggested, at the same time, that the first circumstance rendered his own immediate return more necessary, as he was the usual channel of communication betwixt his father and others ; and that the second corroborated the same necessity, since Mr. Mertoun's having no other society whatever, seemed a weighty reason why his son should be restored to him without loss of time. As to his father's coming to Burgh Westra, "they might as well," he said, "expect to see Sumburgh Cape come thither."

"And that would be a cumbrous guest," said Magnus. "But you will stop for our dinner today ? There are the families of Muness, Quendale, Thorslivoe, and I know not who else, are expected ; and, besides the thirty that were in house this blessed night, we shall have as many more as chamber and bower, and barn and boat-house, can furnish with beds, or with barley-straw—and you will leave all this behind you !"

"And the blithe dance at night," added Brenda, in a tone betwixt reproach and vexation ; "and the young men from the Isle of Paba that are to dance the sword-dance, whom shall we find to match them, for the honour of the Main ?"

"There is many a merry dancer on the mainland, Brenda," replied Mordaunt, "even if I should never rise on tiptoe again. And where good

25

dancers are found, Brenda Troil will always find the best partner. I must trip it tonight through the Wastes of Dunrossness."

"Do not say so, Mordaunt," said Minna, who, during this conversation had been looking from the window something anxiously ; "go not, today at least, through the Wastes of Dunrossness."

"And why not today, Minna," said Mordaunt, laughing, "any more than tomorrow ?"

"Oh, the morning mist lies heavy upon yonder chain of isles, nor has it permitted us since day-break even a single glimpse of Fitful Head, the lofty cape that concludes yon splendid range of mountains. The fowl are winging their way to the shore, and the shelldrake seems, through the mist, as large as the scart.* See, the very sheerwaters and bonxies are making to the cliffs for shelter."

"And they will ride out a gale against a king's frigate," said her father ; "there is foul weather when they cut and run."

"Stay, then, with us," said Minna to her friend ; "the storm will be dreadful, yet it will be grand to see it from Burgh Westra, if we have no friend exposed to its fury. See, the air is close and sultry, though the season is yet so early, and the day so calm, that not a windlestraw moves on the heath. Stay with us, Mordaunt : the storm which these signs announce will be a dreadful one."

"I must be gone the sooner," was the conclusion of Mordaunt, who could not deny the signs, which had not escaped his own quick observation. "If the storm be too fierce, I will abide for the night at Stourburgh."

"What !" said Magnus ; "will you leave us for the new chamberlain's new Scotch tacksman, who is to teach all us Zetland savages new ways ? Take your own gate, my lad, if that is the song you sing."

"Nay," said Mordaunt ; "I had only some curiosity to see the new implements he has brought."

"Ay, ay, ferlies make fools fain. I would like to know if his new plough will bear against a Zetland rock ?" answered Magnus.

"I must not pass Stourburgh on the journey," said the youth, deferring to his patron's prejudice against innovation, "if this boding weather bring on tempest ; but if it only break in rain, as is most probably, I am not likely to be melted in the wetting."

"It will not soften into rain alone," said Minna ; "see how much heavier the clouds fall every moment, and see these weather-gaws that streak the lead-coloured mass with partial gleams of faded red and purple."

"I see them all," said Mordaunt ; "but they only tell me I have no time to tarry here. Adieu, Minna ; I will send you the eagle's feathers, if an eagle can be found on Fair Isle or Foulah. And fare-thee-well, my pretty Brenda, and keep a thought for me, should the Paba men dance ever so well."

"Take care of yourself, since go you will," said both sisters, together.

* The cormorant ; which may be seen frequently dashing in wild flight along the roosts and tides of Zetland, and yet more often drawn up in ranks on some ledge of rock, like a body of the Black Brunswickers in 1815.

W. Collins, R. A.

View of the Orkney Islands

From Thurso Bay Headland, "The Man of Hoy"

R. Brandard

W. Collins, R. A.

Scalloway Bay and Castle

ZETLAND.

R. Brandard

Old Magnus scolded them formally for supposing there was any danger to an active young fellow from a spring gale, whether by sea or land ; yet ended by giving his own caution also to Mordaunt, advising him seriously to delay his journey, or at least to stop at Stourburgh. "For," said he, "second thoughts are best ; and as the Scottishman's howf lies right under your lee, why, take any port in a storm. But do not be assured to find the door on the latch, let the storm blow ever so hard ; there are such matters as bolts and bars in Scotland, though, thanks to Saint Ronald, they are unknown here, save the great lock on the old Castle of Scalloway, that all men run to see—may be they make part of this man's improvements. But go, Mordaunt, since go you will. You should drink a stirrup-cup now, were you three years older, but boys should never drink, excepting after dinner ; I will drink it for you, that good customs may not be broken, or bad luck come of it. Here is your bonally, my lad." And so saying, he quaffed a rummer glass of brandy with as much impunity as if it had been spring water. Thus regretted and cautioned on all hands, Mordaunt took leave of the hospitable household, and looking back at the comforts with which it was surrounded, as the dense smoke that rolled upwards from its chimneys, he first recollected the guestless and solitary desolation of Yarlshof, then compared with the sullen and moody melancholy of his father's temper the warm kindness of those whom he was leaving, and could not refrain from a sigh at the thoughts which forced them on his imagination.

The signs of the tempest did not dishonour the predictions of Minna. Mordaunt had not advanced three hours on his journey, before the wind, which had been so deadly still in the morning, began at first to wail and sigh, as if bemoaning beforehand the evils which it might perpetrate in its fury, like a madman in the gloomy state of dejection which precedes his fit of violence, with the full fury of a northern storm. It was accompanied by showers of rain mixed with hail, that dashed with the most unrelenting rage against the hills and rocks with which the traveller was surrounded, distracting his attention, in spite of his utmost exertions, and rendering it very difficult for him to keep the direction of his journey in a country where there is neither road, nor even the slightest track, to direct the steps of the wanderer, and where he is often interrupted by brooks as well as large pools of water, lakes, and lagoons. All these inland waters were now lashed into sheets of tumbling foam, much of which, carried off by the fury of the whirlwind, was mingled with the gale, and transported far from the waves of which it had lately made a part ; while the salt relish of the drift which was pelted against his face, showed Mordaunt that the spray of the more distant ocean, disturbed to frenzy by the storm, was mingled with that of the inland lakes and streams.

Amidst this hideous combustion of the elements, Mordaunt Mertoun struggled forward as one to whom such elemental war was familiar, and who regarded the exertions which it required to withstand its fury, but as a mark of resolution and manhood. He felt even, as happens usually to those who endure great hardships, that the exertion necessary to subdue them, is in itself a kind of elevating triumph. To see and distinguish his path when the cattle were driven from the hill and the very fowls from the firmament, was but the stronger proof of his own superiority. "They shall not hear of me at Burgh Westra," said he to himself, "as they heard of old doited Ringan Ewenson's boat, that foundered betwixt roadstead and key. I am more of a cragsman than to mind fire or water, wave by sea, or quagmire by land." Thus he struggled on, buffeting with the storm, supplying the want of the usual signs by which travellers directed their progress (for rock, mountain, and headland were shrouded in mist and darkness), by the instinctive sagacity with which long acquaintance with these wilds had taught him to mark every minute object, which could serve in such circumstances to regulate his course. Thus, we repeat, he struggled onward, occasionally standing still, or even lying down, when the gust was most impetuous ; making way against it when it was somewhat lulled, by a rapid and bold advance even in its very current ; or when this was impossible, by a movement resembling that of a vessel working to windward by short tacks, but never yielding one inch of the way which he had fought so hard to gain.

Yet, notwithstanding Mordaunt's experience and resolution, his situation was sufficiently uncomfortable, and even precarious ; not because his sailor's jacket and trousers, the common dress of young men through these isles when on a journey, were thoroughly wet, for that might have taken place within the same brief time, in any ordinary day, in this watery climate ; but the real danger was, that, notwithstanding his utmost exertions, he made very slow way through brooks that were sending their waters all abroad, through morasses drowned in double deluges of moisture, which rendered all the ordinary passes more than usually dangerous, and repeatedly obliged the traveller to perform a considerable circuit, which in the usual case was unnecessary. Thus repeatedly baffled, notwithstanding his youth and strength, Mordaunt, after maintaining a dogged conflict with wind, rain, and the fatigue of a prolonged journey, was truly happy, when, not without having been more than once mistaken in his road, he at length found himself within sight of the house of Stourburgh, or Harfra ; for the names were indifferently given to the residence of Mr Triptolemus Yellowley, who was the chosen missionary of the Chamberlain of Orkney and Zetland, a speculative person, who designed through the medium of Triptolemus, to introduce into the *Ultima Thule* of the Romans, a spirit of improvement, which at that early period was scarce known to exist in Scotland itself.

At length, and with much difficulty, Mordaunt reached the house of this worthy agriculturist, the only refuge from the relentless storm which he could hope to meet with for several miles ; and going straight to the door with the most undoubting confidence of instant admission, he was not a little surprised to find it not merely latched, which the weather might excuse, but even bolted, a thing which, as Magnus Troil has already intimated, was almost unknown in the Archipelago. To knock, to call, and finally to batter the door with staff and stones, were the natural resources of the youth, who was rendered alike impatient by the pelting of the storm, and by encountering such most unexpected and unusual obstacles to instant admission. As he was suffered, however, for many minutes to exhaust his impatience in noise and clamour, without receiving any reply, we will employ them in informing the reader who Triptolemus Yellowley was, and how he came by a name so singular.

Old Jasper Yellowley, the father of Triptolemus (though born at the foot of Roseberry Topping, had been *come over* by a certain noble Scottish Earl, who, proving too far north for canny Yorkshire, had persuaded him to accept of a farm in the Mearns, where, it is unnecessary to add, he found matters very different from what he had expected. It was in vain that the stout farmer set manfully to work, to counterbalance, by superior skill, the inconveniences arising from a cold soil and a weeping climate. These might have been probably overcome ; but his neighbourhood to the Grampians exposed him eternally to that species of visitation from the plaided gentry who dwelt within their skirts, which made young Norval a warrior and a hero, but only converted Jasper Yellowley into a poor man. This was, indeed, balanced in some sort by the impression which his ruddy cheek and robust form had the fortune to make upon Miss Barbara Clinkscale, daughter of the umquhile, and sister to the then existing, Clinkscale of that Ilk.

This was thought a horrid and unnatural union in the neighbourhood, considering that the house of Clinkscale had at least as great a share of Scottish pride as of Scottish parsimony, and was amply endowed with both. But Miss Babie had her handsome fortune of two thousand marks at her own disposal, was a woman of spirit who had been *major* and *sui juris* (as the writer who drew the contract assured her), for full twenty years ; so she set consequences and commentaries alike at defiance, and wedded the hearty Yorkshire yeoman. Her brother and her more wealthy kinsmen drew off in disgust, and almost disowned their degraded relative. But the house of Clinkscale was allied (like every other family in Scotland at the time) to a set of relations who were not so nice — tenth and sixteenth cousins, who not only acknowledged their kinswoman Babie after her marriage with Yellowley, but even condescended to eat beans and bacon (though the latter was then the abomination of the Scotch as much as of the Jews) with her husband, and would willingly have cemented the friendship by borrowing a little cash from him, had not his good lady (who understood trap as well as any woman in the Mearns) put a negative on this advance to intimacy. Indeed she knew how to make young Deilbelicket, old Dougald Baresword, the Laird of Bandybrawl, and others, pay for the hospitality which she did not think proper to deny them, by rendering them useful in her negotiations with the lighthanded lads beyond the Cairn, who, finding their late object of plunder was now allied to "kend folks, and owned by them at kirk and market," became satisfied, on a moderate yearly composition, to desist from their depredations.

This eminent success reconciled Jasper to the dominion which his wife began to assume over him ; and what is the prettiest mode of expressing it ? — in the family way. On this occasion, Mrs. Yellowley had a remarkable dream, as is the usual practice of teeming mothers previous to the birth of an illustrious offspring. She "was a dreamed", as her husband expressed it, that she was safely delivered of a plough, drawn by three yoke of Angus-shire oxen ; and being a mighty investigator into such portents, she sat herself down with her gossips to consider what the thing might mean. Honest Jasper ventured, with much hesitation, to intimate his own opinion, that the vision had reference rather to things past him than things future, and might have been occasioned by his wife's nerves having been a little startled by meeting in the loan above the house his own great plough with the six oxen, which were the pride of his heart. But the good *cummers** raised such a hue and cry against this exposition, that Jasper was fain to put his fingers in his ears and to run out of the apartment.

"Hear to him," said an old whigamore carline, "hear to him, wi' his owsen, that are as an idol to him, even as the calf of Bethel ! Na, na — it's nae pleugh of the flesh that the bonny lad-bairn — for a lad it sall be — sall e'er striddle between the stilts o' — it's the pleugh of the spirit — and I trust myself to see him wag the head o' him in a pu'pit ; or, what's better, on a hill-side."

"Now the deil's in your whiggery," said the old lady Glenprosing ; "wad ye hae our cummer's bonny lad-bairn wag the head aff his shouthers like your godly Mess James Guthrie,† that ye hald such a clavering about ? Na, na, he sall walk a mair siccar path, and be a dainty curate— and say he should live to be a bishop, what the waur wad he be ?"

This gauntlet, thus fairly flung down by one sibyl, was caught up by another, and the controversy between presbytery and episcopacy raged, roared, or rather screamed, a round of cinnamon-water serving only like oil to the flame, till Jasper entered with the plough-staff ; and by awe of his presence, and the shame of misbehaving "before the stranger man" imposed some conditions of silence upon the disputants.

I do not know whether it was impatience to give to the light a being destined to such high and doubtful fates, or whether poor Dame Yellowley was rather frightened at the hurly-burly which had taken place in her presence, but she was taken suddenly ill ; and, contrary to the formula in such cases used and provided, was soon reported to be "a good deal worse than was to be expected." She took the opportunity (having still all her wits about her) to extract from her sympathetic husband two promises ; first, that he would christen the child, whose birth was like to cost her so dear, by a name indicative of the vision with which she had been favoured ; and next, that he would educate him for the ministry. The canny Yorkshireman, thinking she had a good title at present to dictate in such matters, subscribed to all she required. A man-child was accordingly born under these conditions, but the state of the mother did not permit her for many days to inquire how far they had been complied with. When she was in some degree convalescent, she

* i.e. Gossips
† [Mr James Guthrie, minister of Stirling, and author of the *Causes of God's Wrath*, 1653, was executed at Edinburgh in 1661, and his head affixed on the Netherbow Port or Gate.]

was informed, that as it was thought fit the child should be immediately christened, it had received the name of Triptolemus ; the Curate, who was a man of some classical skill, conceiving that this epithet contained a handsome and classical allusion to the visionary plough, with its triple yoke of oxen. Mrs. Yellowley was not much delighted with the manner in which her request had been complied with ; but grumbling being to as little purpose as in the celebrated case of Tristram Shandy, she e'en sat down contented with the heathenish name, and endeavoured to counteract the effects it might produce upon the taste and feelings of the nominee, by such an education as might put him above the slightest thought of sacks, coulters, stilts, mould-boards, or any thing connected with the servile drudgery of the plough.

Jasper, sage Yorkshire man, smiled slyly in his sleeve, conceiving that young Trippie was likely to prove a chip off the old block, and would rather take after the jolly Yorkshire yeoman, than the gentle but somewhat *aigre* blood of the house of Clinkscale. He remarked with suppressed glee, that the tune which best answered the purpose of a lullaby was the *Ploughman's Whistle*, and the first words the infant learned to stammer were the names of the oxen ; moreover, that the "bern" preferred home-brewed ale to Scotch twopenny, and never quitted hold of the tankard with so much reluctance as when there had been, by some manoeuvre of Jasper's own device, a double straik of malt allowed to the brewing, above that which was sanctioned by the most liberal recipe of which his dame's household thrift admitted. Besides this, when no other means could be fallen upon to divert an occasional fit of squalling, his father observed that Trip could be always silenced by jingling a bridle at his ear. From all which symptoms he used to swear in private, that the boy would prove true Yorkshire, and mother and mother's kin would have small share of him.

Meanwhile, and within a year after the birth of Triptolemus, Mrs. Yellowley bore a daughter, named after herself Barbara, who, even in earliest infancy, exhibited the pinched nose and thin lips by which the Clinkscale family were distinguished amongst the inhabitants of the Mearns ; and as her childhood advanced, the readiness with which she seized, and the tenacity wherewith she detained, the playthings of Triptolemus, besides a desire to bite, pinch, and scratch, on slight, or no provocation, were all considered by attentive observers as proofs, that Miss Baby would prove "her mother over again". Malicious people did not stick to say, that the acrimony of the Clinkscale blood had not, on this occasion, been cooled and sweetened by that of Old England ; that young Deilbelicket was much about the house, and they could not but think it odd that Mrs. Yellowley, who, as the whole world knew, gave nothing for nothing, should be so uncommonly attentive to heap the trencher, and to fill the caup, of an idle blackguard ne'er-do-weel. But when folk had once looked upon the austere and awfully virtuous countenance of Mrs. Yellowley, they did full justice to her propriety of conduct, and Deilbelicket's delicacy of taste.

Meantime young Triptolemus, having received such instructions as the Curate could give him (for though Dame Yellowley adhered to the persecuted remnant, her jolly husband, edified by the black gown and prayer-book, still conformed to the church as by law established) was, in due process of time, sent to Saint Andrews to prosecute his studies. He went, it is true, but with an eye turned back with sad remembrances on his father's plough, his father's pancakes, and his father's ale, for which the small beer of the college, commonly there termed "thorough-go-nimble," furnished a poor substitute. Yet he advanced in his learning, being found, however, to show a particular favour to such authors of antiquity as had made the improvement of the soil the object of their researches. He endured the Bucolics of Virgil — the Georgics he had by heart — but the Æneid he could not away with ; and he was particularly severe upon the celebrated line expressing a charge of cavalry, because, as he understood the word *putrem*,* he opined that the combatants, in their inconsiderate ardour, galloped over a new-manured ploughed field. Cato, the Roman Censor, was his favourite among classical heroes and philosophers, not on account of the strictness of his morals, but because of his treatise *de Re Rustica.* He had ever in his mouth the phrase of Cicero, *Jam neminem antepones Catoni.* He thought well of Palladius, and of Terentius Varro, but Columella was his pocket-companion. To these ancient worthies, he added the more modern Tusser, Hartlib, and other writers on rural economics, not forgetting the lucubrations of the Shepherd of Salisbury Plain, and such of the better-informed Philomaths, who, instead of loading their almanacs with vain predictions of political events, pretended to see what seeds would grow, and what would not, and direct the attention of their readers to that course of cultivation from which the production of good crops may be safely predicted ; modest sages, in fine, who, careless of the rise and downfall of empires, content themselves with pointing out the fit seasons to reap and sow, with a fair guess at the weather which each month will be likely to present ; as, for example, that if Heaven pleases, we shall have snow in January, and the author will stake his reputation that July proves, on the whole, a month of sunshine. Now, although the Rector of Saint Leonard's was greatly pleased, in general, with the quiet, laborious, and studious bent of Triptolemus Yellowley, and deemed him in so far, worthy of a name of four syllables having a Latin termination, yet he relished not, by any means, his exclusive attention to his favourite authors. It savoured of the earth, he said, if not of something worse, to have a man's mind always grovelling in mould, stercorated or unstercorated ; and he pointed out, but in vain, history, and poetry, and divinity, as more elevating subjects of occupation. Triptolemus Yellowley was obstinate in his own course. Of the battle of Pharsalia, he though not as it affected the freedom of the world, but dwelt on the rich crop which the Emathian fields were likely to produce the next season. In vernacular poetry, Triptolemus could scarce be prevailed upon to read a single couplet, excepting old Tusser, as aforesaid, whose *Hundred Points of Good Husbandry* he had got by heart ; and excepting also *Piers Ploughman's Vision,* which, charmed with the title, he bought with avidity from a packman, but after reading the two first pages, flung it

* Quadrupedumque putrem sonitu quatit ungula campum.

into the fire as an impudent and misnamed political libel. As to divinity, he summed that matter up by reminding his instructors, that to labour the earth and win his bread with the toil of his body and sweat of his brow, was the lot imposed upon fallen man ; and, for his part, he was resolved to discharge, to the best of his abilities, a task so obviously necessary to existence, leaving others to speculate as much as they would upon the more recondite mysteries of theology.

With a spirit so much narrowed and limited to the concerns of rural life, it may be doubted whether the proficiency of Triptolemus in learning, or the use he was like to make of his acquisitions, would have much gratified the ambitious hope of his affectionate mother. It is true, he expressed no reluctance to embrace the profession of a clergyman, which suited well enough with the habitual personal indolence which sometimes attaches to speculative dispositions. He had views, to speak plainly (I wish they were peculiar to himself), of cultivating the *glebe* six days in the week, preaching on the seventh with due regularity, and dining with some fat franklin or country laird, with whom he could smoke a pipe and drink a tankard after dinner, and mix in secret conference on the exhaustless subject,

Quid faciat lætas segetes.

Now, this plan, besides that it indicated nothing of what was then called the root of the matter, implied necessarily the possession of a manse ; and the possession of a manse inferred compliance with the doctrines of prelacy, and other enormities of the time. There was some question how far manse and glebe, stipend, both victual and money, might have outbalanced the good lady's predisposition towards Presbytery ; but her zeal was not put to so severe a trial. She died before her son had completed his studies, leaving her afflicted spouse just as disconsolate as was to be expected. The first act of old Jasper's undivided administration was to recall his son from Saint Andrews, in order to obtain his assistance in his domestic labours. And here it might have been supposed that our Triptolemus, summoned to carry into practice what he so fondly studied in theory, must have been, to use a simile which *he* would have thought lively, like a cow entering upon a clover park. Alas, mistaken thoughts, and deceitful hopes of mankind !

A laughing philosopher, the Democritus of our day, once, in a moral lecture, compared human life to a table pierced with a number of holes, each of which has a pin made exactly to fit it, but which pins being stuck in hastily, and without selection, chance leads inevitably to the most awkward mistakes. "For, how often do we see," the orator pathetically concluded, "how often, I say, do we see the round man stuck into the three cornered hole !" This new illustration of the vagaries of fortune set every one present into convulsions of laughter, excepting one fat alderman, who seemed to make the case his own, and insisted that it was no jesting matter. To take up the simile, however, which is an excellent one, it is plain that Triptolemus Yellowley had been shaken out of the bag at least a hundred years too soon. If he had come on the stage in our own time, that is, if he had flourished at any time within these thirty or forty years, he could not have missed to have held the office of vice-president of some eminent agricultural society, and to have transacted all the business thereof under the auspices of some noble duke or lord, who, as the matter might happen, either knew, or did not know, the difference between a horse and a cart, and a cart-horse. He could not have missed such preferment, for he was exceedingly learned in all those particulars, which, being of no consequence in actual practice, go, of course, a great way to constitute the character of a connoisseur in any art, but especially in agriculture. But, alas ! Triptolemus Yellowley had, as we already have hinted, come into the world at least a century too soon ; for, instead of sitting in an armchair, with a hammer in his hand, and a bumper of port before him, giving forth the toast — "To breeding, in all its branches," his father planted him betwixt the stilts of a plough, and invited him to guide the oxen, on whose beauties he would, in our day, have descanted, and whose rumps he would not have goaded, but have carved. Old Jasper complained, that although no one talked so well of common and several, wheat and rape, fallow and lea, as his learned son (whom he always called Tolimus), yet, "dang it," added the Seneca, "nought thrives wi' un — nought thrives wi' un !" It was still worse, when Jasper, becoming frail and ancient, was obliged, as happened, in the course of a few years, gradually to yield up the reins of government to the academical neophyte.

As if Nature had meant him a spite, he had got one of the *dourest* and most intractable farms in the Mearns, to try conclusions withal, a place which seemed to yield everything but what the agriculturist wanted ; for there were plenty of thistles, which indicated dry land ; and store of fern, which is said to intimate deep land ; and nettles, which show where lime hath been applied ; and deep furrows in the most unlikely spots, which intimated that it had been cultivated in former days by the Peghts, as popular tradition bore. There was also enough of stones to keep the ground warm, according to the creed of some farmers, and great abundance of springs to render it cool and sappy, according to the theory of others. It was in vain that, acting alternately on these opinions, poor Triptolemus endeavoured to avail himself of the supposed capabilities of the soil. No kind of butter that might be churned could be made to stick upon his own bread, any more than on that of poor Tusser, whose *Hundred Points of Good Husbandry,** so useful to others of his day, were never to himself worth as many pennies.†

In fact, excepting an hundred acres of infield, to which old Jasper had early seen the necessity of limiting his labours, there was not a corner of the farm fit for anything but to break plough-graith, and kill cattle. And then, as for the part which was really tilled with some profit, the expense of the farming establishment of Triptolemus, and his

* [The title of this work, published 1557, was afterwards changed to *Five Hundred Points of Good Husbandry*, and passed through many editions.]
† This is admitted by the English agriculturist:—

"My music since has been the plough,
Entangled with some care among ;
The gain not great, the pain enough,
Hath made me sing another song."

34

disposition to experiment, soon got rid of any good arising from the cultivation of it. "The carles and the cart-avers," he confessed, with a sigh, speaking of his farm-servants and horses, "make it all, and the carles and cart-avers eat it all ;" a conclusion which might sum up the year-book of many a gentleman-farmer.

Matters would have soon been brought to a close with Triptolemus in the present day. He would have got a bank-credit, manœuvred with wind bills, dashed out upon a large scale, and soon have seen his crop and stock sequestered by the Sheriff ; but in those days a man could not ruin himself so easily. The whole Scottish tenantry stood upon the same level flat of poverty, so that it was extremely difficult to find any vantage ground, by climbing up to which a man might have an opportunity of actually breaking his neck with some éclat. They were pretty much in the situation of people, who, being totally without credit, may indeed suffer from indigence, but cannot possibly become bankrupt. Besides notwithstanding the failure of Triptolemus's projects, there were to be balanced against the expenditure which they occasioned, all the savings which the extreme economy of his sister Barbara could effect ; and in truth her exertions were wonderful. She might have realised, if any one could, the idea of the learned philosopher, who pronounced that sleeping was a fancy, and eating but a habit, and who appeared to the world to have renounced both, until it was unhappily discovered that he had an intrigue with the cook-maid of the family, who indemnified him for his privations by giving him private entrée to the pantry, and to a share of her own couch. But no such deceptions were practised by Barbara Yellowley. She was up early, and down late, and seemed, to her over-watched, and over-tasked maidens, to be as *wakerife* as the cat herself. Then, for eating, it appeared that the air was a banquet to her, and she would have made it so to her retinue. Her brother who, besides being lazy in his person, was somewhat luxurious in his appetite, would willingly now and then have tasted a mouthful of animal food, were it but to know how his sheep were fed off ; but a proposal to eat a child could not have startled Mistress Barbara more ; and, being of a compliant and easy disposition, Triptolemus reconciled himself to the necessity of a perpetual Lent, too happy when he could get a scrap of butter to his oaten cake, or (as they lived on the banks of the Esk) escape the daily necessity of eating salmon, whether in or out of season, six days out of the seven.

But although Mrs. Barbara brought faithfully to the joint stock all savings which her awful powers of economy accomplished to scrape together, and although the dower of their mother was by degrees expended, or nearly so, in aiding them upon extreme occasions, the term at length approached when it seemed impossible that they could sustain the conflict any longer against the evil star of his absurd speculations, as it was termed by others. Luckily at this sad crisis, a god jumped down to their relief out of a machine. In plain English, the noble lord, who owned their farm, arrived at his mansion-house in their neighbourhood, with his coach and six and his running footmen, in the full splendour of the seventeenth century.

This person of quality was the son of the nobleman who had brought the ancient Jasper into the country from Yorkshire, and he was, like his father, a fanciful and scheming man.* He had schemed well for himself, however, amid the mutations of the time, having obtained, for a certain period of years, the administration of the remote islands of Orkney and Zetland, for payment of a certain rent, with the right of making the most of whatever was the property or revenue of the crown in these districts, under the title of Lord Chamberlain. Now, his lordship had become possessed with a notion, in itself a very true one, that much might be done to render this grant available, by improving the culture of the crown lands, both in Orkney and Zetland ; and then, having some acquaintance with our friend Triptolemus, he thought (rather less happily) that he might prove a person capable of furthering his schemes. He sent for him to the great Hall-house, and was so much edified by the way in which our friend laid down the law upon every given subject relating to rural economy, that he lost no time in securing the co-operation of so valuable an assistant, the first step being to release him from his present unprofitable farm.

The terms were arranged much to the mind of Triptolemus, who had already been taught, by many years' experience, a dark sort of notion, that without undervaluing or doubting for a moment his own skill, it would be quite as well that almost all the trouble and risk should be at the expense of his employer. Indeed, the hopes of advantage which he held out to his patron were so considerable, that the Lord Chamberlain dropped every idea of admitting this dependant into any share of the expected profits ; for, rude as the arts of agriculture were in Scotland, they were far superior to those known and practised in the regions of Thule, and Triptolemus Yellowley conceived himself to be possessed of a degree of insight into these mysteries, far superior to what was possessed or practised even in the Mearns. The improvement, therefore which was to be expected, would bear a double proportion, and the Lord Chamberlain was to reap all the profit, deducting a handsome salary for his steward Yellowley, together with the accommodation of a house and domestic farm, for the support of his family. Joy seized the heart of Mistress Barbara, at hearing this happy termination of what threatened to be so very bad an affair as their lease of Cauldacres.

"If we cannot," she said, "provide for our own house, when all is coming on, and nothing going out, surely we must be worse than infidels !"

Triptolemus was a busy man for some time, huffing and puffing, and eating and drinking in every changehouse, while he ordered and collected together proper implements of agriculture, to be used by the natives of these devoted islands, whose destinies were menaced with this formidable change. Singular tools these would seem, if presented

* At the period supposed, the Earl of Morton held the Islands of Orkney and Zetland, originally granted in 1643, confirmed in 1707, and rendered absolute in 1742. This gave the family much property and influence, which they usually exercised by factors, named chamberlains. In 1766 this property was sold by the then Earl of Morton to Sir Lawrence Dundas, by whose son, Lord Dundas, it is now held. [Thomas Lord Dundas, of Aske in Yorkshire, was created Earl of Zetland in 1838.]

before a modern agricultural society ; but everything is relative, nor could the heavy cartload of timber, called the old Scots plough, seem less strange to a Scottish farmer of this present day, than the corselets and casques of the soldiers of Cortés might seem to a regiment of our own army. Yet the latter conquered Mexico, and undoubtedly the former would have been a splendid improvement on the state of agriculture in Thule.

We have never been able to learn why Triptolemus preferred fixing his residence in Zetland to becoming an inhabitant of the Orkneys. Perhaps he thought the inhabitants of the latter Archipelago the more simple and docile of the two kindred tribes ; or perhaps he preferred the situation of the house and farm he himself was to occupy (which was indeed a tolerable one), as preferable to that which he had it in his power to have obtained upon Pomona (so the main island of the Orkneys is entitled). At Harfa, or, as it was sometimes called, Stourburgh, from the remains of a Pictish fort, which was almost close to the mansion-house, the factor settled himself, in the plenitude of his authority ; determined to honour the name he bore by his exertions, in precept and example, to civilise the Zetlanders, and improve their very confined knowledge in the primary arts of human life.

CHAPTER FIFTH

The wind blew keen frae north and east ;
   It blew upon the floor,
Quo' our goodman to our goodwife,
   "Get up and bar the door."

"My hand is in my housewife-skep,
   Goodman, as ye may see ;
If it shouldna be barr'd this hundred years,
   It's no be barr'd for me !"

OLD SONG

WE can only hope that the gentle reader has not found the latter part of the last chapter extremely tedious ; but, at any rate, his impatience will scarce equal that of young Mordaunt Mertoun, who, while the lightning came flash after flash, while the wind, veering and shifting from point to point, blew with all the fury of a hurricane, and while the rain was dashed against him in deluges, stood hammering, calling, and roaring at the door of the old Place at Harfra, impatient for admittance, and at a loss to conceive any position of existing circumstances, which could occasion the exclusion of a stranger, especially during such horrible weather. At length, finding his noise and vociferation were equally in vain, he fell back so far from the front of the house, as was necessary to enable him to reconnoitre the chimneys ; and amidst "storm and shade", could discover to the increase of his dismay, that though noon, then the dinner hour of these islands, was now nearly arrived, there was no smoke proceeding from the tunnels of the vents to give any note of preparation within.

Mordaunt's wrathful impatience was now changed into sympathy and alarm ; for, so long accustomed to the exuberant hospitality of the Zetland islands, he was immediately induced to suppose some strange and unaccountable disaster had befallen the family ; and forthwith set himself to discover some place at which he could make forcible entry, in order to ascertain the situation of the inmates, as much as to obtain shelter from the still increasing storm. His present anxiety was, however, as much thrown away as his late clamorous importunities for admittance had been. Triptolemus and his sister had heard the whole alarm without, and had already had a sharp dispute on the propriety of opening the door.

Mrs. Baby, as we have described her, was no willing renderer of the rites of hospitality. In their farm of Cauldacres, in the Mearns, she had been the dread and abhorrence of all gaberlunzie men, and travelling packmen, gipsies, long remembered beggars, and so forth, nor was there one of them so wily, as she used to boast, as could ever say they had heard the clink of her sneck. In Zetland, where the new settlers were yet strangers to the extreme hospitality and simplicity of all classes, suspicion and fear joined with frugality in her desire to exclude all wandering guests of uncertain character ; and the second of these motives had its effect on Triptolemus himself, who, though neither suspicious nor penurious, knew good people were scarce, good farmers scarcer, and had a reasonable share of that wisdom which looks towards self-preservation as the first law of nature. These hints may serve as a commentary on the following dialogue which took place betwixt the brother and sister.

"Now, good be gracious to us," said Triptolemus, as he sat thumbing his old school-copy of Virgil, "here is a pure day for the bear seed ! — Well spoke the wise Mantuan — *ventis surgentibus* — and then the groans of the mountains, and the long-resounding shores — but where's the woods, Baby ? tell me, I say, where we shall find the *nemorum murmur,* sister Baby, in these new seats of ours ?"

"What's your foolish will ?" said Baby, popping her head from out of a dark recess in the kitchen, where she was busy about some nameless deed of housewifery.

Her brother, who had addressed himself to her more from habit than intention, no sooner saw her bleak red nose, keen grey eyes, with the sharp features thereunto conforming, shaded by the flaps of the loose *toy* which depended on each side of her eager face, than he bethought himself that his query was likely to find little acceptation from her, and therefore stood another volley before he would resume the topic.

"I say, Mr Yellowley," said sister Baby, coming into the middle of the room, "what are ye crying on me, and me in the midst of my housewife-skep ?"

"Nay, for nothing at all, Baby," answered Triptolemus, "saving that I was saying to myself, that here we had the sea, and the wind, and the

38

rain, sufficient enough, but where's the wood? Where's the wood, Baby, answer me that?"

"The wood?" answered Baby. "Were I no to take better care of the wood than you, brother, there would soon be no more wood about the town than the barber's block that's on your own shoulders, Triptolemus. If ye be thinking of the wreck-wood that the callants brought in yesterday, there was six ounces of it gaed to boil your parritch this morning; though, I trow, a carefu' man wad have ta'en drammock, if breakfast he behoved to have, rather than waste baith meltith and fuel in the same morning."

"That is to say, Baby," replied Triptolemus, who was somewhat of a dry joker in his way, "that when we have fire we are not to have food, and when we have food we are not to have fire, these being too great blessings to enjoy both on the same day. Good luck, you do not propose we should starve with cold and starve with hunger *unico contextu*. But, to tell you the truth, I could never away with raw oatmeal, slockened with water, in all my life. Call it drammock or crowdie, or just what ye list, my vivers must thole fire and water."

"The mair gowk you," said Baby; "can ye not make your brose on the Sunday, and sup them cauld on the Monday, since ye're sae dainty? Mony is the fairer face than yours that has licked the lip after such a cogfu'."

"Mercy on us, sister!" said Triptolemus; "at this rate, it's a finished field with me — I must unyoke the pleugh, and lie down to wait for the deadthraw. Here is that in this house wad hold all Zetland in meal for a twelvemonth, and ye grudge a cogfu' of warm parritch to me that has sic a charge!"

"Whist — hold your silly clavering tongue," said Baby, looking round with apprehension — ye are a wise man to speak of what is in the house, and a fitting man to have the charge of it. Hark, as I live by bread I hear a tapping at the outer yett!"

"Go and open it then, Baby" said her brother, glad at anything that promised to interrupt the dispute.

"Go and open it, said he!" echoed Baby, half angry, half frightened, and half triumphant at the superiority of her understanding over that of her brother — "Go and open it said you, indeed! — is it to lend robbers a chance to take all that is in the house?"

"Robbers!" echoed Triptolemus, in his turn; "there are no more robbers in this country than there are lambs at Yule. I tell you, as I have told you an hundred times, there are no Highlandmen to harry us here. This is a land of quiet and honesty. *O fortunati nimium!*"

"And what good is Saint Rinian to do ye, Tolemus?" said his sister, mistaking the quotation for a Catholic invocation. "Besides, if there be no Highlandmen, there may be as bad. I saw sax or seven as ill-looking chields gang past the Place yesterday, as ever came frae beyont Clochna-ben; ill-fa'red tools they had in their hands, whaaling knives they ca'ed them, but they looked as like dirks and whingers as ae bit airn can look like anither. There is nae honest men carry siccan tools."

Here the knocking and shouts of Mordaunt were very audible

betwixt every swell of the horrible blast which was careering without. The brother and sister looked at each other in real perplexity and fear. "If they have heard of the siller," said Baby, her very nose changing with terror from red to blue, "we are but gane folk !"

"Who speaks now, when they should hold their tongue ?" said Triptolemus. "Go to the shot-window instantly, and see how many there are of them, while I load the old Spanish-barrelled duck-gun — go as if you were stepping on new-laid eggs."

Baby crept to the window, and reported that she saw only "one young chield, clattering and roaring as gin he were daft. How many there might be out of sight, she could not say."

"Out of sight ! Nonsense," said Triptolemus, laying aside the ramrod with which he was loading the piece, with a trembling hand. "I will warrant them out of sight and hearing both — this is some poor fellow catched in the tempest, wants the shelter of our roof, and a little refreshment. Open the door, Baby, it's a Christian deed."

"But is it a Christian deed of him to come in at the window, then ?" said Baby, setting up a most doleful shriek, as Mordaunt Mertoun, who had forced open one of the windows, leaped down into the apartment, dripping water like a river god. Triptolemus, in great tribulation, presented the gun which he had not yet loaded, while the intruder exclaimed, "Hold, hold — what the devil mean you by keeping your doors bolted in weather like this, and levelling your gun at folk's heads as you would at a sealgh's ?"

"And who are you, friend, and what want you ?" said Triptolemus, lowering the butt of his gun to the floor as he spoke, and so recovering his arms.

"What do I want !" said Mordaunt ; " I want everything — I want meat, drink, and fire, a bed for the night, and a sheltie for to-morrow morning, to carry me to Yarlshof."

"And ye said there were nae caterans or sorners here ?" said Baby to the agriculturist reproachfully. "Heard ye ever a breekless loon frae Lochaber tell his mind and her errand mair deftly ? Come, come, friend," she added, addressing herself to Mordaunt, "put up your pipes and gang your gate ; this is the house of his Lordship's factor, and no place of reset for thiggers or sorners."

Mordaunt laughed in her face at the simplicity of the request. "Leave built walls," he said, "and in such a tempest as this ? What take you me for ? — a gannet or a scart do you think I am, that your clapping your hands and skirling at me like a mad-woman should drive me from the shelter into the storm ?"

"And so you propose, young man," said Triptolemus, gravely, "to stay in my house, *volens nolens* — that is, whether we will or no ?"

"Will !" said Mordaunt ; "what right have you to will anything about it ? Do you not hear the thunder ? Do you not hear the rain ? Do you not see the lightning ? And do you not know this is the only house within I wot not how many miles ? Come, my good master and dame, this may be Scottish jesting, but it sounds strange in Zetland ears. You have let out the

40

fire, too, and my teeth are dancing a jig in my head with cold, but I'll soon put that to rights."

He seized the fire-tongs, raked together the embers upon the hearth, broke up into life the gathering peat, which the hostess had calculated should have preserved the seeds of fire, without giving them forth, for many hours ; then casting his eye round, saw in a corner the stock of drift-wood, which Mistress Baby had served forth by ounces, and transferred two or three logs of it at once to the hearth, which, conscious of such unwonted supply, began to transmit to the chimney such a smoke as had not issued from the Place of Harfra for many a day.

While their uninvited guest was thus making himself at home, Baby kept edging and jogging the factor to turn out the intruder. But for this undertaking, Triptolemus Yellowley felt neither courage nor zeal, nor did circumstances seem at all to warrant the favourable conclusion of any fray into which he might enter with the young stranger. The sinewy limbs and graceful form of Mordaunt Mertoun were seen to great advantage in his simple sea-dress ; and with his dark sparkling eye, finely formed head, animated features, close curled dark hair, and bold free looks, the stranger formed a very strong contrast with the host on whom he had intruded himself. Triptolemus was a short, clumsy, duck-legged disciple of Ceres, whose bottle-nose, turned up and handsomely coppered at the extremity, seemed to intimate something of an occasional treaty with Bacchus. It was like to be no equal mellay betwixt persons of such unequal form and strength ; and the difference betwixt twenty and fifty years was nothing in favour of the weaker party. Besides, the factor was an honest good-natured fellow at bottom, and being soon satisfied that his guest had no other views than those of obtaining refuge from the storm, it would, despite his sister's instigations, have been his last act to deny a boon so reasonable and necessary to a youth whose exterior was so prepossessing. He stood, therefore, considering how he could most gracefully glide into the character of his hospitable landlord, out of that of the churlish defender of his domestic castle against an unauthorised intrusion, when Baby, who had stood appalled at the extreme familiarity of the stranger's address and demeanour, now spoke up for herself.

"My troth, lad," said she to Mordaunt, "ye are no blate, to light on at that rate, and the best of wood, too – nane of your sharney peats, but good aik timber, nae less maun serve ye !"

"You come lightly by it, dame," said Mordaunt, carelessly ; "and you should not grudge the fire what the sea gives you for nothing. These good ribs of oak did their last duty upon earth and ocean, when they could hold no longer together under the brave hearts than manned the bark."

"And that's true, too," said the old woman, softening – "this maun be awsome weather by sea. Sit down and warm ye, since the sticks are a-low."

"Ay, ay," said Triptolemus, "It is a pleasure to see siccan a bonny bleeze. I havena seen the like o't since I left Cauldacres."

"And shallna see the like o't again in a hurry," said Baby, "unless the house take fire, or there suld be a coal-heugh found out."

"And wherefore should not there be a coal-heugh found out ?" said the factor triumphantly — "I say, wherefore should not a coal-heugh be found out in Zetland, as well as in Fife, now that the Chamberlain has a far-sighted and discreet man upon the spot to make the necessary perquisitions ? They are baith fishing stations, I trow ?"

"I tell you what it is, Tolemus Yellowley," answered his sister, who had practical reasons to fear her brother's opening upon any false scent, "if you promise my Lord sae mony of these bonnie-wallies we'll no be weel hafted here before we are found out and set a-trotting again. If ane was to speak to you about a gold mine, I ken well wha wad promise he suld have Portugal pieces clinking in his pouch before the year gaed by."

"And why suld I not ?" said Triptolemus — "maybe your head does not know there is a land in Orkney called Ophir, or something very like it ; and wherefore might not Solomon, the wise King of the Jews, have sent thither his ships and his servants for four hundred and fifty talents ? I trow he knew best where to go or send, and I hope you believe in your Bible, Baby ?"

Baby was silenced by an appeal to Scripture, however *mal à propos*, and only answered by an articulate *humph* of incredulity or scorn, while her brother went on addressing Mordaunt — "Yes, you shall all of you see what a change shall coin introduce, even into such an unpropitious country as yours. Ye have not heard of copper, I warrant, or of iron-stone, in these islands, neither ?" Mordaunt said he had heard there was copper neat the Cliffs of Konigsburgh. "Ay, and a copper scum is found on the Loch of Swana, too, young man. But the youngest of you, doubtless, thinks himself a match for such as I am."

Baby, who during all this while had been closely and accurately reconnoitring the youth's person, now interposed in a manner by her brother totally unexpected. "Ye had mair need, Mr. Yellowley, to give the young man some dry clothes, and to see about getting something for him to eat, than to sit there bleezing away with your lang tales, as if the weather were not windy eneuch without your help ; and maybe the lad would drink some *bland*, or siclike, if ye had the grace to ask him."

While Triptolemus looked astonished at such a proposal, considering the quarter it had come from, Mordaunt answered, "he should be very glad to have dry clothes, but begged to be excused from drinking until he had eaten somewhat."

Triptolemus accordingly conducted him into another apartment, and accommodating him with a change of dress, left him to his arrangements, while he himself returned to the kitchen, much puzzled to account for his sister's unusual fit of hospitality. "She must be *fey*,"* he said, "and in that case has not long to live, and though I fall heir to her tocher-good, I am sorry for it ; for she has held the house-gear together

* When a person changes his condition suddenly, as when a miser becomes liberal, or a churl good-humoured, he is said, in Scotch, to be *fey* ; that is, predestined to speedy death, of which such mutations of humour are received as a sure indication.

— drawn the girth over tight it may be now and then, but the saddle sits the better."

When Triptolemus returned to the kitchen, he found his suspicions confirmed ; for his sister was in the desperate act of consigning to the pot a smoked goose, which, with others of the same tribe, had long hung in the large chimney, muttering to herself at the same time, "It maun be eaten sune or syne, and what for no by the puir callant ?"

"What is this of it, sister ?" said Triptolemus. "You have on the girdle and the pot at ance. What day is this wi' you ?"

"E'en such a day as the Israelites had beside the flesh-pots of Egypt, billie Triptolemus: but ye little ken wha ye have in your house this blessed day."

"Troth and little do I ken," said Triptolemus, "as little as I would ken the naig I never saw before. I would take the lad for a *yagger*,* but he has rather ower good havings, and has no pack."

"Ye ken as little as ane of your ain bits of nowt, man," retorted sister Baby ; "if ye ken na him, do ye ken Tronda Dronsdaughter ?"

"Tronda Dronsdaughter !" echoed Triptolemus — "how should I but ken her, when I pay her twal pennies Scots by the day, for working in the house here ? I trow she works as if the things burned her fingers. I had better give a Scots lass a groat of English siller."

"And that's the maist sensible word ye have said this blessed morning. Weel, but Tronda kens this lad weel, and she has often spoke to me about him. They call his father the Silent Man of Sumburgh, and they say he's uncanny."

"Hout, hout — nonsense, nonsense — they are aye at sic trash as that," said the brother, "when you want a day's wark out of them — they have stepped ower the tangs, or they have met an uncanny body, or they have turned about the boat against the sun, and then there's nought to be done that day."

"Weel, weel, brother, ye are so wise," said Baby, "because ye knapped Latin at Saint Andrews ; and can your lair tell me, then, what the lad has round his halse ?"

"A Barcelona napkin, as wet as a dishclout, and I have just lent him one of my own overlays," says Triptolemus.

"A Barcelona napkin !" said Baby, elevating her voice, and then suddenly lowering it, as from apprehension of being overheard — "I say a gold chain !"

"A gold chain !" said Triptolemus.

"In troth is it, hinny ; and how like you that ? The folk say here, as Tronda tells me, that the King of the Drows gave it to his father, the Silent Man of Sumburgh."

I wish you would speak sense, or be the silent woman," said Triptolemus. "The upshot of it all is, then, that this lad is the rich stranger's son, and that you are giving him the goose you were to keep till Michaelmas ?"

"Troth, brother, we maun do something for God's sake, and to make

* A pedlar.

43

friends ; and the lad," added Baby (for even she was not altogether above the prejudices of her sex in favour of outward form), "the lad has a fair face of his ain."

"Ye would have let mony a fair face," said Triptolemus, "pass the door pining, if it had not been for the gold chain."

"Nae doubt, nae doubt," replied Barbara ; "ye wad not have me waste our substance on every thigger or sorner that has the luck to come by the door in a wet day ? But this lad has a fair and a wide name in the country, and Tronda says he is to be married to a daughter of the rich Udaller, Magnus Troil, and the marriage-day is to be fixed whenever he makes his choice (set him up !) between the twa lasses ; and so it wad be as much as our good name is worth, and our quiet forby, to let him sit unserved, although he does come unsent for."

"The best reason in life," said Triptolemus, "for letting a man into the house is, that you dare not bid him go by. However, since there is a man of quality amongst them, I will let him know whom he has to do with, in my person." Then advancing to the door, he exclaimed, *"Heus tibi, Dave !"*

"Adsum," answered the youth, entering the apartment.

"Hem !" said the erudite Triptolemus, "not altogether deficient in his humanities, I see. I will try him farther. Canst thou aught of husbandry, young gentleman ?"

"Troth, sir, not I," answered Mordaunt ; "I have been trained to plough upon the sea, and to reap upon the crag."

"Plough the sea !" said Triptolemus ; "that's a furrow requires small harrowing ; and for your harvest on the crag, I suppose you mean these *scowries*, or whatever you call them. It is a sort of ingathering which the Ranzelman* should stop by the law ; nothing more likely to break an honest man's bones. I profess I cannot see the pleasure men propose by dangling in a rope's-end betwixt earth and heaven. In my case, I had as lief the other end of the rope were fastened to the gibbet ; I should be sure of not falling, at least."

"Now, I would only advise you to try it," replied Mordaunt. "Trust me, the world has few grander sensations than when one is perched in mid-air between a high-browed cliff and a roaring ocean, the rope by which you are sustained seeming scarce stronger than a silken thread, and the stone on which you have one foot steadied, affording such a breadth as the kittywake might rest upon – to feel and know all this, with the full confidence that your own agility of limb, and strength of head, can bring you as safe off as if you had the wing of the gosshawk – this is indeed being almost independent of the earth you tread on !"

Triptolemus stared at this enthusiastic description of an amusement which had so few charms for him ; and his sister, looking at the glancing eye and elevated bearing of the young adventurer, answered, by ejaculating, "My certie, lad, but ye are a brave chield !"

"A brave chield ?" returned Yellowley, "I say a brave goose, to be flichtering and fleeing in the wind when he might abide upon *terra*

* [The Constable.]

44

firma ; but come, here's a goose that is more to the purpose, when once it is well boiled. Get us trenchers and salt, Baby — but in truth it will prove salt enough — a tasty morsel it is ; but I think the Zetlanders be the only folk in the world that think of running such risks to catch geese, and then boiling them when they have done."

"To be sure," replied his sister (it was the only word they had agreed in that day), "it would be an unco thing to bid ony gudewife in Angus or a' the Mearns boil a goose, while there was sic things as spits in the world. But wha's this neist ?" she added, looking towards the entrance with great indignation. "My certie, open doors, and dogs come in — and wha opened the door to him ?"

"I did, to be sure," replied Mordaunt ; "you would not have a poor devil stand beating your deaf door-cheeks in weather like this ? — Here goes something, though, to help the fire," he added, drawing out the sliding bar of oak with which the door had been secured, and throwing it on the hearth, whence it was snatched by Dame Baby in great wrath, she exclaiming at the same time, "It's sea-borne timber, as there's little else here and be dings it about as if it were a fir-clog ! And who be you, an it please you ?" she added, turning to the stranger, "a very hallanshaker loon, as ever crossed my twa een !"

"I am a yagger, if it like your ladyship," replied the uninvited guest, a stout, vulgar little man, who had indeed the humble appearance of a pedlar, called yagger in these islands, "never travelled in a waur day, or was more willing to get to harbourage. Heaven be praised for fire and house-room !"

So saying, he drew a stool to the fire, and sat down without farther ceremony. Dame Baby stared "wild as grey gosshawk," and was meditating how to express her indignation in something warmer than words, for which the boiling pot seemed to offer a convenient hint, when an old half-starved serving woman — the Tronda already mentioned — the sharer of Barbara's domestic cares, who had been as yet in some remote corner of the mansion, now hobbled into the room, and broke out into exclamations which indicated some new cause of alarm.

"O master !" and "O mistress !" were the only sounds she could for some time articulate, and then followed them up with, "The best in the house — the best in the house — set a' on the board, and a' will be little eneugh. There is auld Norna of Fitful Head, the most fearful woman in all the isles !"

"Where can she have been wandering ?" said Mordaunt, not without some apparent sympathy with the surprise, if not with the alarm, of the old domestic ; "but it is needless to ask — the worse the weather, the more likely is she to be a traveller."

"What new tramper is this ?" echoed the distracted Baby, whom the quick succession of guests had driven well-nigh crazy with vexation. "I'll soon settle her wandering, I sall warrant, if my brother has but the soul of a man in him, or if there be a pair of jougs at Scalloway."

"The iron was never forged on stithy that would hald her," said the old maid servant. "She comes — she comes —God's sake speak her fair and canny, or we will have a ravelled hasp on the yarn-windles !"

As she spoke, a woman, tall enough almost to touch the top of the door with her cap, stepped into the room, signing the cross as she entered, and pronouncing, with a solemn voice, "The blessing of God and Saint Ronald on the open door, and their broad malison and mine upon close-handed churls !"

"And wha are ye, that are sae bauld wi' your blessing and banning in other folk's houses ? What kind of country is this, that folk cannot sit quiet for an hour, and serve Heaven, and keep their bit gear thegither, without gangrel men and women coming thigging and sorning ane after another, like a string of wild geese ?"

This speech the understanding reader will easily saddle on Mistress Baby, and what effects it might have produced on the last stranger can only be a matter of conjecture ; for the old servant and Mordaunt applied themselves at once to the party addressed, in order to deprecate her resentment ; the former speaking to her some words of Norse, in a tone of intercession, and Mordaunt saying in English, "They are strangers, Norna, and know not your name or qualities ; they are unacquainted, too, with the ways of this country, and therefore we must hold them excused for their lack of hospitality."

"I lack no hospitality, young man," said Triptolemus, "*miseris succurrere disco* — the goose that was destined to roost in the chimney till Michaelmas, is boiling in the pot for you ; but if we had twenty geese, I see we are like to find mouths to eat them every feather — this must be amended."

"What must be amended, sordid slave ?" said the stranger Norna, turning at once upon him with an emphasis that made him start — "What must be amended ? Bring hither, if thou wilt, thy new-fangled coulters, spades, and harrows, alter the implements of our fathers from the ploughshare to the mouse-trap ; but know thou art in the land that was won of old by the flaxen-haired Kempions of the North, and leave us their hospitality at least, to show we come of what was once noble and generous. I say to you beware — while Norna looks forth at the measureless waters, from the crest of Fitful Head, something is yet left that resembles power of defence. If the men of Thule have ceased to be champions, and to spread the banquet for the raven, the women have not forgotten the arts that lifted them of yore into queens and prophetesses."

The woman who pronounced this singular tirade was as striking in appearance as extravagantly lofty in her pretensions and in her language. She might well have represented on the stage, so far as features, voice, and stature were concerned, the Bonduca or Boadicea of the Britons, or the sage Velleda, Aurinia, or any other fated Pythoness, who ever led to battle a tribe of the ancient Goths. Her features were high and well formed, and would have been handsome, but for the ravages of time and the effects of exposure to the severe weather of her country. Age, and perhaps sorrow, had quenched, in some degree, the fire of a dark-blue eye, whose hue almost approached to black, and had sprinkled snow on such parts of her tresses as had escaped from under her cap, and were dishevelled by the rigour of the storm. Her upper garment, which dropped with water, was of a coarse dark-coloured stuff, called wadmaal, then much used in the Zetland Islands, as also in Iceland and Norway. But as she threw this cloak back from her shoulders, a short jacket, of dark-blue velvet, stamped with figures, became visible, and the vest, which corresponded to it, was of a crimson colour, and embroidered with tarnished silver. Her girdle was plated with silver ornaments, cut into the shape of planetary signs — her blue apron was embroidered with similar devices, and covered a petticoat of crimson cloth. Strong thick enduring shoes, of the half-dressed leather of the country, were tied with straps like those of the Roman buskins, over her scarlet stockings. She wore in her belt an ambiguous-looking weapon, which might pass for a sacrificing knife or dagger, as the imagination of the spectator chose to assign to the wearer the character of a priestess or of a sorceress. In her hand she held a staff, squared on all sides, and engraved with Runic characters and figures, forming one of those portable and perpetual calendars which were used among the ancient natives of Scandinavia, and which, to a superstitious eye, might have passed for a divining rod.

Such were the appearance, features, and attire, of Norna of the Fitful Head, upon whom many of the inhabitants of the island looked with observance, many with fear, and almost all with a sort of veneration. Less pregnant circumstances of suspicion, would, in any other part of Scotland, have exposed her to the investigation of those cruel inquisitors, who were then often invested with the delegated authority of the Privy Council, for the purpose of persecuting, torturing, and finally consigning to the flames, those who were accused of witchcraft or sorcery. But superstitions of this nature pass through two stages ere they become entirely obsolete. Those supposed to be possessed of supernatural powers are venerated in the earlier stages of society. As religion and knowledge increase, they are first held in hatred and horror, and are finally regarded as impostors. Scotland was in the second state — the fear of witchcraft was great, and the hatred against those suspected of it intense. Zetland was as yet a little world by itself, where, among the lower and ruder classes, so much of the ancient northern superstition remained, as cherished the original veneration for those affecting supernatural knowledge, and power over the elements, which made a constituent part of the ancient Scandinavian creed. At least if the natives of Thule admitted that one class of magicians performed their feats by their alliance with Satan, they devoutly believed that others dealt with spirits of a different and less odious class — the ancient Dwarfs, called, in Zetland, Trows, or Drows, the modern fairies, and so forth.

Among those who were supposed to be in league with disembodied spirits, this Norna, descended from and representative of a family, which had long pretended to such gifts, was so eminent, that the name assigned to her, which signifies one of those fatal sisters who weave the web of human fate, has been conferred in honour of her supernatural powers. The name by which she had been actually christened was carefully concealed by herself and her parents ; for to its discovery they superstitiously annexed some fatal consequences. In those times, the doubt only occurred whether her supposed powers were acquired by lawful means. In our days, it would have been questioned whether she was an impostor, or whether her imagination was so deeply impressed with the mysteries of her supposed art, that she might be in some degree a believer in her own pretensions to supernatural knowledge. Certain it is, that she performed her part with such undoubting confidence, and such striking dignity of look and action, and evinced, at the same time, such strength of language, and energy of purpose, that it would have been difficult for the greatest sceptic to have doubted the reality of her enthusiasm, though he might smile at the pretensions to which it gave rise.

CHAPTER SIXTH

— If, by your art, you have
Put the wild waters in this roar, allay them.
                                                TEMPEST

THE storm had somewhat relaxed its rigour just before the entrance of Norna, otherwise she must have found it impossible to travel during the extremity of its fury. But she had hardly added herself so unexpectedly to the party whom chance had assembled at the dwelling of Triptolemus Yellowley, when the tempest suddenly resumed its former vehemence, and raged around the building with a fury which made the inmates insensible to anything except the risk that the old mansion was about to fall above their heads.

Mistress Baby gave vent to her fears in loud exclamations of "The Lord guide us—this is surely the last day—what kind of a country of guisards and gyre-carlines is this ?—and you, ye fool carle," she added, turning on her brother (for all her passions had a touch of acidity in them), "to quit the bonny Mearns land to come here, where there is naething but sturdy beggars and gaberlunzies within ane's house, and Heaven's anger on the outside on't !"

"I tell you, sister Baby," answered the insulted agriculturist, "that all shall be reformed and amended—excepting," he added, betwixt his teeth, "the scalding humours of an ill-natured jaud, that can add bitterness to the very storm."

The old domestic and the pedlar meanwhile exhausted themselves in entreaties to Norna, of which, as they were couched in the Norse language, the master of the house understood nothing.

She listened to them with a haughty and unmoved air, and replied at length aloud, and in English, "I will not. What if this house be strewed in ruins before morning—where would be the world's want in the crazed projector, and the niggardly pinch-commons, by which it is inhabited ?

48

They will needs come to reform Zetland customs, let them try how they like a Zetland storm.—You that would not perish quit this house!"

The pedlar seized on his little knapsack, and began hastily to brace it on his back; the old maid-servant cast her cloak about her shoulders, and both seemed to be in the act of leaving the house as fast as they could.

Triptolemus Yellowley, somewhat commoved by these appearances, asked Mordaunt, with a voice which faltered with apprehension, whether he thought there was any, that is, so very much danger?

"I cannot tell," answered the youth; "I have scarce ever seen such a storm. Norna can tell us better than any one when it will abate; for no one in these islands can judge of the weather like her."

"And is that all thou thinkest Norna can do?" said the sibyl; "thou shalt know her powers are not bounded within such a narrow space. Hear me, Mordaunt, youth of a foreign land, but of a friendly heart—Dost thou quit this doomed mansion with those who now prepare to leave it?"

"I do not—I will not, Norna," replied Mordaunt; "I know not your motive for desiring me to remove, and I will not leave upon these dark threats, the house in which I have been kindly received in such a tempest as this. If the owners are unaccustomed to our practice of unlimited hospitality, I am the more obliged to them that they have relaxed their usages, and opened their doors in my behalf."

"He is a brave lad," said Mistress Baby, whose superstitious feelings had been daunted by the threats of the supposed sorceress, and who, amidst her eager, narrow, and repining disposition, had, like all who possess marked character, some sparks of higher feeling, which made her sympathise with generous sentiments, though she thought it too expensive to entertain them at her own cost—"He is a brave lad," she again repeated, "and worthy of ten geese, if I had them to boil for him, or roast either. I'll warrant him a gentleman's son, and no churl's blood."

"Hear me, young Mordaunt," said Norna, "and depart from this house. Fate has high views on you—you shall not remain in this hovel to be crushed amid its worthless ruins, with the relics of its more worthless inhabitants, whose life is as little to the world as the vegetation of the house-leek, which now grows on their thatch, and which shall soon be crushed amongst their mangled limbs."

"I—I—I will go forth," said Yellowley, who, despite of his bearing himself scholarly and wisely, was beginning to be terrified for the issue of the adventure; for the house was old and the walls rocked formidably to the blast.

"To what purpose?" said his sister. "I trust the Prince of the power of the air has not yet such like power over those that are made in God's image, that a good house should fall about our heads, because a randy quean" (here she darted a fierce glance at the Pythoness) "should boast us with her glamour, as it we were sae mony dogs to crouch at her bidding!"

"I was only wanting," said Triptolemus, ashamed of his motion, "to look at the bear-braird, which must be sair laid wi' this tempest ; but if this honest woman like to bide wi' us, I think it were best to let us a' sit doun canny thegither, till it's working weather again."

"Honest woman ! " echoed Baby—"Foul warlock thief !—Aroint ye, ye limmer !" she added, addressing Norna directly, "out of an honest house, or, shame fa' me, but I'll take the bittle* to you !"

Norna cast on her a look of supreme contempt; then, stepping to the window, seemed engaged in deep contemplation of the heavens, while the old maid-servant, Tronda, drawing close to her mistress, implored, for the sake of all that was dear to man or woman, "Do not provoke Norna of Fitful Head ! You have no sic woman on the mainland of Scotland—she can ride on one of these clouds as easily as man ever rode on a sheltie."

"I shall live to see her ride on the reek of a fat tar-barrel," said Mistress Baby ; "and that will be a fit pacing palfrey for her."

Again Norna regarded the enraged Mrs. Baby Yellowley with a look of that unutterable scorn which her haughty features could so well express, and moving to the window which looked to the north-west, from which quarter the gale seemed at present to blow, she stood for some time with her arms crossed, looking out upon the leaden-coloured sky, obscured as it was by the thick drift, which, coming on in successive gusts of tempest, left ever and anon sad and dreary intervals of expectation betwixt the dying and the reviving blast.

Norna regarded this war of the elements as one to whom their strife was familiar ; yet the stern serenity of her features had in it a cast of awe, and at the same time of authority, as the cabalist may be supposed to look upon the spirit he has evoked, and which, though he knows how to subject him to his spell, bears still an aspect appalling to flesh and blood. The attendants stood by in different attitudes, expressive of their various feelings. Mordaunt, though not indifferent to the risk in which they stood, was more curious than alarmed. He had heard of Norna's alleged power over the elements, and now expected an opportunity of judging for himself of its reality. Triptolemus Yellowley was confounded at what seemed to be far beyond the bounds of his philosophy ; and, if the truth must be spoken, the worthy agriculturist was greatly more frightened than inquisitive. His sister was not in the least curious on the subject; but it was difficult to say whether anger or fear predominated in her sharp eyes and thin compressed lips. The pedlar and old Tronda, confident that the house would never fall while the redoubted Norna was beneath its roof, held themselves ready for a start the instant she should take her departure.

Having looked on the sky for some time in a fixed attitude, and with the most profound silence, Norna at once, yet with a slow and elevated gesture, extended her staff of black oak towards that part of the heavens from which the blast came hardest, and in the midst of its fury chanted

* The beetle with which the Scottish housewives used to perform the office of the modern mangle, by beating newly-washed linen on a smooth stone for the purpose, called the beetling-stone.

50

a Norwegian invocation, still preserved in the Island of Uist, under the name of the Song of the Reim-kennar, though some call it the Song of the Tempest. The following is a free translation, it being impossible to render literally many of the elliptical and metaphorical terms of expression, peculiar to the ancient Northern poetry :—

1

Stern eagle of the far north-west,
Thou that bearest in thy grasp the thunderbolt,
Thou whose rushing pinions stir ocean to madness,
Thou the destroyer of herds, thou the scatterer of navies,
Thou the breaker down of towers,
Amidst the scream of thy rage,
Amidst the rushing of thy onward wings,
Though thy scream be loud as the cry of a perishing nation,
Though the rushing of they wings be like the roaring of ten thousand waves,
Yet hear, in thine ire and thy haste,
Hear thou the voice of the Reim-kennar.

2

Thou hast met the pine trees of Drontheim,
Their dark-green heads lie prostrate beside their uprooted stems ;
Thou hast met the rider of the ocean,
The tall, the strong bark of the fearless rover,
And she has struck to thee the topsail
That she had not veil'd to a royal armada ;
Thou hast met the tower that bears its crest among the clouds,
The battled massive tower of the Yarl of former days,
And the cope-stone of the turret
Is lying upon its hospitable hearth ;
But thou too shall stoop, proud compeller of clouds,
When thou hearest the voice of the Reim-kennar.

3

There are verses that can stop the stag in the forest,
Ay, and when the dark-colour'd dog is opening on his track ;
There are verses can make the wild hawk pause on his wing,
Like the falcon that wears the hood and the jesses,
And who knows the shrill whistle of the fowler.
Thou who canst mock at the scream of the drowning mariner,
And the crash of the ravaged forest,
And the groan of the overwhelm'd crowds,
When the church hath fallen in the moment of prayer,
There are sounds which thou also must list,
When they are chanted by the voice of the Reim-kennar.

4

Enough of woe hast thou wrought on the ocean,
The widows wring their hands on the beach ;
Enough of woe hast thou wrought on the land,
The husbandman folds his arms in despair;
Cease thou the waving of thy pinions,
Let the ocean repose in her dark strength ;
Cease thou the flashing of thine eye,
Let the thunderbolt sleep in the armoury of Odin ;
Be thou still at my bidding, viewless racer of the north-western heaven,
Sleep thou at the voice of Norna the Reim-kennar !

51

We have said that Mordaunt was naturally fond of romantic poetry and romantic situation ; it is not therefore surprising that he listened with interest to the wild address thus uttered to the wildest wind of the compass, in a tone of such dauntless enthusiasm. But though he had heard so much of the Runic rhyme and of the northern spell, in the country where he had so long dwelt, he was not on this occasion so credulous as to believe that the tempest, which had raged so lately, and which was now beginning to decline, was subdued before the charmed verse of Norna. Certain it was, that the blast seemed passing away, and the apprehended danger was already over ; but it was not improbable that this issue had been for some time foreseen by the Pythoness, through signs of the weather imperceptible to those who had not dwelt long in the country, or had not bestowed on the meteorological phenomena the attention of a strict and close observer. Of Norna's experience he had no doubt, and that went a far way to explain what seemed supernatural in her demeanour. Yet still the noble countenance, half-shaded by dishevelled tresses, the air of majesty with which, in a tone of menace as well as of command, she addressed the viewless spirit of the tempest, gave him a strong inclination to believe in the ascendency of the occult arts over the powers of nature ; for, if a woman ever moved on earth to whom such authority over the laws of the universe could belong, Norna of Fitful Head, judging from bearing, figure, and face, was born to that high destiny.

The rest of the company were less slow in receiving conviction. To Tronda and the yagger none was necessary ; they had long believed in the full extent of Norna's authority over the elements. But Triptolemus and his sister gazed at each other with wondering and alarmed looks, especially when the wind began perceptibly to decline, as was remarkably visible during the pauses which Norna made betwixt the strophes of her incantation. A long silence followed the last verse, until Norna resumed her chant, but with a changed and more soothing modulation of voice and tune.

Eagle of the far north-western waters,
Thou hast heard the voice of the Reim-kennar,
Thou hast closed thy wide sails at her bidding,
And folded them in peace by thy side.
My blessing be on thy retiring path !
When thou stoopest from thy place on high,
Soft be thy slumbers in the caverns of the unknown ocean.
Rest till destiny shall again awaken thee ;
Eagle of the north-west, thou hast heard the voice of the Reim-kennar !

"A pretty sang that would be to keep the corn from shaking in har'st," whispered the agriculturist to his sister; "we must speak her fair, Baby—she will maybe part with the secret for a hundred punds Scots."

"An hundred fules' heads !" replied Baby—"bid her five marks of ready siller. I never knew a witch in my life but she was as poor as Job."

Norna turned towards them as if she had guessed their thoughts ; it may be that she did so. She passed them with a look of the most sovereign contempt, and walking to the table on which the preparations for Mrs. Barbara's frugal meal were already disposed, she filled a small wooden quaigh from an earthen pitcher which contained bland, a subacid liquor made out of the serous part of the milk. She broke a single morsel from a barley-cake, and having eaten and drunk, returned towards the churlish hosts. "I give you no thanks," she said, "for my refreshment, for you bid me not welcome to it; and thanks bestowed on a churl are like the dew of heaven on the cliffs of Foulah, where it finds nought that can be refreshed by its influences. I give you no thanks," she said again, but drawing from her pocket a leathern purse that seemed large and heavy, she added, "I pay you with what you will value more than the gratitude of the whole inhabitants of Hialtland. Say not that Norna of Fitful Head hath eaten of your bread and drunk of your cup, and left you sorrowing for the charge to which she hath put your house." So saying, she laid on the table a small piece of antique gold coin, bearing the rude and half-defaced effigies of some ancient northern king.

Triptolemus and his sister exclaimed against this liberality with vehemence ; the first, protesting that he kept no public, and the other exclaiming, "Is the carline made ? Heard ye ever of ony of the gentle house of Clinkscale that gave meat for siller ?"

"Or for love either ?" muttered her brother ; "haud to that, tittie."

"What are ye whittie-whattieing about, ye gowk ?" said his gentle sister, who suspected the tenor of his murmurs ; "gie the lady back her bonnie die there, and be blithe to be sae rid on't—it will be a sclate-stane the morn, if not something worse."

The honest factor lifted the money to return it, yet could not help being struck when he saw the impression, and his hand trembled as he handed it to his sister.

"Yes," said the Pythoness again, as if she read the thoughts of the astonished pair, "you have seen that coin before—beware how you use it! It thrives not with the sordid or the mean-souled—it was won with honourable danger, and must be expended with honourable liberality. The treasure which lies under a cold hearth will one day, like the hidden talent, bear witness against its avaricious possessors."

This last obscure intimation seemed to raise the alarm and the wonder of Mrs. Baby and her brother to the uttermost. The latter tried to stammer out something like an invitation to Norna to tarry with them all night, or at least to take share of the "dinner," so he at first called it; but looking at the company, and remembering the limited contents of the pot, he corrected the phrase, and hoped she would take some part of the "snack, which would be on the table ere a man could loose a pleugh."

"I eat not here—I sleep not here," replied Norna— "nay, I relieve you not only of my own presence, but I will dismiss your unwelcome guests.—Mordaunt," she added, addressing the young Mertoun, "the dark fit is past, and your father looks for you this evening."

"Do you return in that direction ?" said Mordaunt. "I will but eat a morsel, and give you my aid, good mother, on the road. The brooks must be out, and the journey perilous."

"Our ways lie different," answered the Sibyl, " and Norna needs not mortal arm to aid her on the way. I am summoned far to the east, by those who know well how to smooth my passage.—For thee, Bryce Snailsfoot," she continued, speaking to the pedlar, "speed thee on to Sumburgh—the Roost will afford thee a gallant harvest, and worthy the gathering in. Much goodly ware will ere now be seeking a new owner, and the careful skipper will sleep still enough in the deep haaf, and care not that bale and kist are dashing against the shores."

"Na, na, good mother," answered Snailsfoot, "I desire no man's life for my private advantage, and am just grateful for the blessing of Providence on my sma' trade. But doubtless one man's loss is another's gain ; and as these storms destroy a' thing on land, it is but fair they suld send us something by sea. Sae, taking the freedom, like yoursell, mother, to borrow a lump of barley-bread, and a draught of bland, I will bid good day, and thank you, to this good gentleman and lady, and e'en go on my way to Yarlshof, as you advise."

"Ay," replied the Pythoness, "where the slaughter is, the eagles will be gathered ; and where the wreck is on the shore, the yagger is as busy to purchase spoil as the shark to gorge upon the dead."

This rebuke, if it was intended as such, seemed above the comprehension of the travelling merchant, who, bent upon gain, assumed the knapsack and ellwand, and asked Mordaunt, with the familiarity permitted in a wild country, whether he would not take company along with him ?

"I wait to eat some dinner with Mr. Yellowley and Mrs. Baby," answered the youth, "and will set forward in half-an-hour."

"Then I'll just take my piece in my hand," said the pedlar. Accordingly he muttered a benediction, and, without more ceremony, helped himself to what, in Mrs. Baby's covetous eyes, appeared to be two-thirds of the bread, took a long pull at the jug of bland, seized on a handful of the small fish called sillocks, which the domestic was just placing on the board, and left the room without farther ceremony.

"My certie," said the despoiled Mrs. Baby, "there is the chapman's drouth* and his hunger baith, as folk say ! If the laws against vagrants be executed this gate—It's no that I wad shut the door against decent folk," she said, looking to Mordaunt, "more especially in such judgment-weather. But I see the goose is dished, poor thing."

This she spoke in a tone of affection for the smoked goose, which, though it had long been an inanimate inhabitant of her chimney, was far more interesting to Mrs. Baby in that state, than when it screamed amongst the clouds. Mordaunt laughed and took his seat, then turned to look for Norna ; but she had glided from the apartment during the discussion with the pedlar.

"I am glad she is gane, the dour carline," said Mrs. Baby, "though she has left that piece of gowd to be an everlasting shame to us."

"Whisht, mistress, for the love of heaven !" said Tronda

* The chapman's drouth, that is, the pedlar's thirst, is proverbial in Scotland, because these pedestrian traders were in the use of modestly asking only for a drink of water, when, in fact, they were desirous of food.

54

Dronsdaughter; "wha kens where she may be at this moment ?—we are no sure but she may hear us, though we cannot see her."

Mrs. Baby cast a startled eye around, and, instantly recovering herself, for she was naturally courageous as well as violent, said, "I bade her aroint before, and I bid her aroint again, whether she sees me or hears me, or whether she's ower the cairn and awa.—And you, ye silly sumph," she said to poor Yellowley, "what do ye stand glowering there for ?—*You* a Saunt Andrews student !—*you* studied lair and Latin humanities, as ye ca' them, and daunted wi' the clavers of an auld randie wife ! Say your best college grace, man, and witch or nae witch, we'll eat our dinner and defy her. And for the value of the gowden piece, it shall never be said I pouched her siller. I will gie it to some poor body—that is I will test* upon it at my death, and keep it for a purse-penny till that day comes, and that's no using it in the way of spending-siller. Say your best college grace, man, and let us eat and drink in the meantime."

"Ye had muckle better say an *oraamus* to Saint Ronald, and fling a saxpence ower your left shouther, master," said Tronda.†

"That ye may pick it up, ye jaud," said the implacable Mistress Baby ; "it will be lang or ye win the worth of it ony other gate.—Sit down, Triptolemus, and mindna the words of a daft wife."

"Daft or wise," replied Yellowley, very much disconcerted, "she kens more than I would wish she kend. It was awfu' to see sic a wind fa' at the voice of flesh and blood like oursells—and then yon about the hearth-stane—I cannot but think—"

"If ye cannot but think," said Mrs. Baby, very sharply, "at least ye can haud your tongue ?"

The agriculturist made no reply, but sate down to their scanty meal, and did the honours of it with unusual heartiness to his new guest, the first of the intruders who had arrived, and the last who left them. The sillocks speedily disappeared, and the smoked goose, with its appendages, took wing so effectually, that Tronda, to whom the polishing of the bones had been destined, found the task accomplished, or nearly so, to her hand. After dinner, the host produced his bottle of brandy ; but Mordaunt, whose general habits were as sober almost as those of his father, laid a very light tax upon this unusual exertion of hospitality.

During the meal, they learned so much of young Mordaunt, and of his father, and pressed him (at the risk of an expensive supper being added to the charges of the day) to tarry with them till the next morning. But what Norna had said excited the youth's wish to reach home, nor, however far the hospitality of Stourburgh was extended in his behalf, did the house present any particular temptations to induce him to remain there longer. He therefore accepted the loan of the factor's clothes, promising to return them, and send for his own ; and took a civil leave

* Test upon it, i.e. leave it in my will; a mode of bestowing charity, to which many are partial as well as the good dame in the text.

† Although the Zetlanders were early reconciled to the reformed faith, some ancient practices of Catholic superstition survived long among them. In very stormy weather a fisher would vow an *oramus* to Saint Ronald, and acquitted himself of the obligation by throwing a small piece of money in at the window of a ruinous chapel.

55

of his host and Mistress Baby, the latter of whom, however affected by the loss of her goose, could not but think the cost well bestowed (since it was to be expended at all) upon so handsome and cheerful a youth.

CHAPTER SEVENTH

She does no work by halves, yon raving ocean;
Engulphing those she strangles, her wild womb
Affords the mariners whom she hath dealt on,
Their death at once, and sepulchre.

OLD PLAY

THERE were ten "lang Scots miles" betwixt Stourburgh and Yarlshof ; and though the pedestrian did not number all the impediments which crossed Tam o' Shanter's path—for, in a country where there are neither hedges nor stone enclosures, there can be neither "slaps nor stiles"—yet the number and nature of the "mosses and waters" which he had to cross in his peregrination, were fully sufficient to balance the account, and to render his journey as toilsome and dangerous as Tam o' Shanter's celebrated retreat from Ayr. Neither witch nor warlock crossed Mordaunt's path, however. The length of the day was already considerable, and he arrived safe at Yarlshof by eleven o'clock at night. All was still and dark round the mansion, and it was not till he had whistled twice or thrice beneath Swertha's window, that she replied to the signal.

At the first sound, Swertha fell into an agreeable dream of a young whale-fisher, who some forty years since used to make such a signal beneath the window of her hut ; at the second, she waked to remember that Johnnie Fea had slept sound among the frozen waves of Greenland for this many a year, and that she was Mr. Mertoun's governante at Yarlshof ; at the third, she arose and opened the window.

"Whae is that," she demanded, "at sic an hour of the night ?"

"It is I," said the youth.

"And what for comena ye in ? The door's on the latch, and there is a gathering peat on the kitchen fire, and a spunk beside it—ye can light your ain candle."

"All well," replied Mordaunt ; "but I want to know how my father is."

"Just in his ordinary, gude gentleman—asking for you, Maister Mordaunt ; ye are ower far and ower late in your walks, young gentleman."

"Then the dark hour has passed, Swertha ?"

"In troth has it, Maister Mordaunt," answered the governante ; "and your father is very reasonably good-natured for him, poor gentleman. I spoke to him twice yesterday without his speaking first; and the first time he answered me as civil as you could do, and the neist time he bade me no plague him ; and then, thought I, three times were aye canny, so I

56

spake to him again for luck's sake, and he called me a chattering old devil ; but it was quite and clean in a civil sort of way."

"Enough, enough, Swertha," answered Mordaunt; "and now get up, and find me something to eat, for I have dined but poorly."

"Then you have been at the new folk's at Stourburgh ? For there is no another house in a' the Isles but they wad hae gi'en ye the best share of the best they had. Saw ye aught of Norna of the Fitful Head ? She went to Stourburgh this morning, and returned to the town at night."

"Returned !—then she is here ? How could she travel three leagues and better in so short a time ?"

"Wha kens how she travels ?" replied Swertha ; "but I heard her tell the Ranzelman wi' my ain lugs, that she intended that day to have gone on to Burgh Westra, to speak with Minna Troil, but she had seen that at Stourburgh (indeed she said at Harfra, for she never calls it by the other name of Stourburgh), that sent her back to our town. But gang your ways round, and ye shall have plenty of supper—ours is nae toom pantry, and still less a locked ane, though my master be a stranger, and no just that tight in the upper rigging, as the Ranzelman says."

Mordaunt walked round to the kitchen accordingly, where Swertha's care speedily accommodated him with a plentiful, though coarse meal, which indemnified him for the scanty hospitality he had experienced at Stourburgh.

In the morning, some feelings of fatigue made young Mertoun later than usual in leaving his bed ; so that, contrary to what was the ordinary case, he found his father in the apartment where they ate, and which served them indeed for every common purpose, save that of a bedchamber or of a kitchen. The son greeted the father in mute reverence, and waited until he should address him.

"You were absent yesterday, Mordaunt ?" said his father. Mordaunt's absence had lasted a week and more ; but he had often observed that his father never seemed to notice how time passed during the period when he was affected with his sullen vapours. He assented to what the elder Mr. Mertoun had said.

"And you were at Burgh Westra, as I think ?" continued his father.

"Yes, sir," replied Mordaunt.

The elder Mertoun was then silent for some time, and paced the floor in deep silence, with an air of sombre reflection, which seemed as if he were about to lapse into his moody fit. Suddenly turning to his son, however, he observed, in the tone of a query, "Magnus Troil has two daughters—they must be now young women ; they are thought handsome, of course ?"

"Very generally, sir," answered Mordaunt, rather surprised to hear his father making any inquiries about the individuals of a sex which he usually thought so light of, a surprise which was much increased by the next question, put as abruptly as the former.

"Which think you the handsomest ?"

"I, sir ?" replied his son with some wonder, but without embarrassment—"I am really no judge—I never considered which was absolutely the handsomest. They are both very pretty young women."

57

"You evade my question, Mordaunt ; perhaps I have some very particular reason for my wish to be acquainted with your taste in this matter. I am not used to waste words for no purpose. I ask you again, which of Magnus Troil's daughters you think most handsome ?"

"Really, sir," replied Mordaunt—"but you only jest in asking me such a question."

"Young man," replied Mertoun, with eyes which began to roll and sparkle with impatience, "I *never* jest. I desire an answer to my question."

"Then upon my word, sir," said Mordaunt, "it is not in my power to form a judgment betwixt the young ladies—they are both very pretty, but by no means like each other. Minna is dark-haired, and more grave than her sister—more serious, but by no means either dull or sullen."

"Um," replied his father ; "you have been gravely brought up, and this Minna, I suppose, pleases you most ?"

"No, sir, really I can give her no preference over her sister Brenda, who is as gay as a lamb in a spring morning—less tall than her sister, but so well formed, and so excellent a dancer"—

"That she is best qualified to amuse the young man who has a dull home and a moody father ?" said Mr. Mertoun.

Nothing in his father's conduct had ever surprised Mordaunt so much as the obstinacy with which he seemed to pursue a theme so foreign to his general train of thought and habits of conversation ; but he contented himself with answering once more, "that both the young ladies were highly admirable, but he had never thought of them with the wish to do either injustice, by ranking her lower than her sister—that others would probably decide between them, as they happened to be partial to a grave or a gay disposition, or to a dark or fair complexion ; but that he could see no excellent quality in the one that was not balanced by something equally captivating in the other."

It is possible that even the coolness with which Mordaunt made this explanation might not have satisfied his father concerning the subject of investigation ; but Swertha at this moment entered with breakfast, and the youth, notwithstanding his late supper, engaged in that meal with an air which satisfied Mertoun that he held it matter of more grave importance than the conversation which they had just had, and that he had nothing more to say upon the subject explanatory of the answers he had already given. He shaded his brow with his hand, and looked long fixedly upon the young man as he was busied with his morning meal. There was neither abstraction nor a sense of being observed in any of his motions ; all was frank, natural, and open.

"He is fancy-free," muttered Mertoun to himself—"so young, so lively, and so imaginative, so handsome and so attractive in face and person, strange, that at his age, and in his circumstances, he should have avoided the meshes which catch all the world beside !"

When the breakfast was over, the elder Mertoun, instead of proposing, as usual, that his son, who awaited his commands, should betake himself to one branch or other of his studies, assumed his hat and staff, and desired that Mordaunt should accompany him to the top of the cliff, called Sumburgh Head, and from thence look out upon the state of the ocean, agitated as it must still be by the tempest of the preceding day. Mordaunt was at the age when young men willingly exchange sedentary pursuits for active exercise, and started up with alacrity to comply with his father's request ; and in the course of a few minutes they were mounting together the hill, which, ascending from the land side in a long, steep and grassy slope, sinks at once from the summit into the sea in an abrupt and tremendous precipice.

The day was delightful ; there was just so much motion in the air as to disturb the little fleecy clouds which were scattered on the horizon, and by floating them occasionally over the sun, to chequer the landscape with that variety of light and shade which often gives to a bare and unenclosed scene, for the time at least, a species of charm approaching to the varieties of a cultivated and planted country. A thousand flitting hues of light and shade played over the expanse of wild moor, rocks, and inlets, which, as they climbed higher and higher, spread in wide and wider circuit around them.

The elder Mertoun often paused and looked around upon the scene, and for some time his son supposed that he halted to enjoy its beauties ; but as they ascended still higher up the hill, he remarked his shortened breath and his uncertain and toilsome step, and became assured, with some feelings of alarm, that his father's strength was, for the moment, exhausted, and that he found the ascent more toilsome and fatiguing than usual. To draw close to his side, and offer him in silence the assistance of his arm, was an act of youthful deference to advanced age, as well as of filial reverence ; and Mertoun seemed at first so to receive it, for he took in silence the advantage of the aid thus afforded him.

It was but for two or three minutes, however, that the father availed himself of his son's support. They had not ascended fifty yards farther, ere he pushed Mordaunt suddenly, if not rudely, from him ; and, as if stung into exertion by some sudden recollection, began to mount the acclivity with such long and quick steps, that Mordaunt, in his turn, was obliged to exert himself to keep pace with him. He knew his father's peculiarity of disposition ; he was aware from many slight circumstances, that he loved him not even while he took much pains with his education, and while he seemed to be the sole object of his care upon earth. But the conviction had never been more strongly or more powerfully forced upon him than by the hasty churlishness with which Mertoun rejected from a son that assistance, which most elderly men are willing to receive from youths with whom they are but slightly connected, as a tribute which it is alike graceful to yield and pleasing to receive. Mertoun, however, did not seem to perceive the effect which his unkindness had produced upon his son's feelings. He paused upon a sort of level terrace which they had now attained, and addressed his son with an indifferent tone, which seemed in some degree affected.

"Since you have so few inducements, Mordaunt, to remain in these wild islands, I suppose you sometimes wish to look a little more abroad into the world ?"

"By my word, sir," replied Mordaunt, "I cannot say I ever have thought on such a subject."

"And why not, young man ?" demanded his father; "it were but natural, I think, at your age. At your age, the fair and varied breadth of Britain could not gratify me, much less the compass of a sea-girdled peat-moss."

"I have never thought of leaving Zetland, sir," relied the son. "I am happy here, and have friends. You yourself, sir, would miss me, unless indeed"—

"Why, thou wouldst not persuade me," said his father, somewhat hastily, "that you stay here, or desire to stay here, for the love of me ?"

"Why should I not, sir ?" answered Mordaunt, mildly; "it is my duty, and I hope I have hitherto performed it."

"Oh, ay," repeated Mertoun, in the same tone, "your duty—your duty. So it is the duty of the dog to follow the groom that feeds him."

"And does he not do so, sir ?" said Mordaunt.

"Ay," said his father, turning his head aside ; "but he fawns only on those who caress him."

"I hope, sir," replied Mordaunt, "I have not been found deficient?"

"Say no more on't—say no more on't," said Mertoun, abruptly, "we have both done enough by each other—we must soon part.—Let that be our comfort—if separation should require comfort."

"I shall be ready to obey your wishes," said Mordaunt, not altogether displeased at what promised him an opportunity of looking farther abroad into the world. "I presume it will be your pleasure that I commence my travels with a season at the whale-fishing."

"Whale-fishing !" replied Mertoun ; "that were a mode indeed of seeing the world ! But thou speakest but as thou hast learned. Enough of this for the present. Tell me where you had shelter from the storm yesterday ?"

"At Stourburgh, the house of the new factor from Scotland."

"A pedantic, fantastic, visionary schemer," said Mertoun—"and whom saw you there ?"

"His sister, sir," replied Mordaunt, "and old Norna of the Fitful Head."

"What ! the mistress of the potent spell," answered Mertoun, with a sneer — "she who can change the wind by pulling her curch on one side, as King Erick used to do by turning his cap ? The dame journey far from home—how fares she ? Does she get rich by selling favourable winds to those who are port-bound ?"*

"I really do not know, sir," said Mordaunt, whom certain recollections prevented from freely entering into his father's humour.

"You think the matter too serious to be jested with, or perhaps esteem her merchandise too light to be cared after," continued Mertoun, in the same sarcastic tone, which was the nearest approach he ever made to cheerfulness ; "but consider it more deeply. Everything in the universe is bought and sold, and why not wind, if the merchant can find purchasers ? The earth is rented, from its surface down to its most central mines;—the fire, and the means of feeding it, are currently bought and sold—and the wretches that sweep the boisterous ocean with their nets,

* Note E. Sale of Winds.

pay ransom for the privilege of being drowned in it. What title has the air to be exempted from the universal course of traffic. All above the earth, under the earth, and around the earth, has its price, its sellers, and its purchasers. In many countries the priests will sell you a portion of heaven—in all countries, men are willing to buy, in exchange for health, wealth, and peace of conscience, a full allowance of hell. Why should not Norna pursue her traffic ?"

"Nay, I know no reason against it," replied Mordaunt ; "only I wish she would part with the commodity in smaller quantities. Yesterday she was a wholesale dealer—whoever treated with her had too good a pennyworth."

"It is even so," said the father, pausing on the verge of the wild promontory which they had attained, where the huge precipice sinks abruptly down on the wide and tempestuous ocean, "and the effects are still visible."

The face of that lofty cape is composed of the soft and crumbling stone called sand-flag, which gradually becomes decomposed, and yields to the action of the atmosphere, and is split into large masses, that hang loose upon the verge of the precipice, and, detached from it by the fury of the tempests, often descend with great fury into the vexed abyss which lashes the foot of the rock. Numbers of these huge fragments lie strewed beneath the rocks from which they have fallen, and amongst these the tide foams and rages with a fury peculiar to these latitudes.

At the period when Mertoun and his son looked from the verge of the precipice, the wide sea still heaved and swelled with the agitation of yesterday's storm, which had been far too violent in its effects on the ocean to subside speedily. The tide therefore poured on the headland with a fury deafening to the ear, and dizzying to the eye, threatening instant destruction to whatever might be at the time involved in its current. The sight of Nature, in her magnificence, or in her beauty, or in her terror, has at all times an overpowering interest, which even habit cannot greatly weaken ; and both father and son sat themselves down on the cliff to look out upon that unbounded war of waters, which rolled in their wrath to the foot of the precipice.

At once Mordaunt, whose eyes were sharper, and probably his attention more alert than that of his father, started up, and exclaimed, "God in heaven ! there is a vessel in the Roost."

Mertoun looked to the north-westward, and an object was visible amid the rolling tide. "She shows no sail," he observed ; and immediately added, after looking at the object through his spy-glass, "She is dismasted, and lies a sheer hulk upon the water."

"And is drifting on the Sumburgh Head," exclaimed Mordaunt, struck with horror, "without the slightest means of weathering the cape !"

She makes no effort," answered his father ; "she is probably deserted by her crew."

"And in such a day as yesterday," replied Mordaunt, "when no open boat could live were she manned with the best men ever handled an oar—all must have perished."

"It is most probable," said his father, with stern composure ; "and one

61

day, sooner or later, all must have perished. What signifies whether the Fowler, whom nothing escapes, caught them up at one swoop from yonder shattered deck, or whether he clutched them individually, as chance gave them to his grasp ? What signifies it ? — the deck, the battlefield, are scarce more fatal to us than our table and our bed ; and we are saved from the one, merely to drag out a heartless and wearisome existence, till we perish at the other. Would the hour were come—that hour which reason would teach us to wish for, were it not that nature has implanted the fear of it so strongly within us ! You wonder at such a reflection, because life is yet new to you. Ere you have attained my age, it will be the familiar companion of your thoughts."

"Surely, sir," replied Mordaunt, "such distaste to life is not the necessary consequence of advanced age ?"

"To all who have sense to estimate that which it is really worth," said Mertoun. "Those who, like Magnus Troil, possess so much of the animal impulse about them, as to derive pleasure from sensual gratification, may perhaps, like the animals, feel pleasure in mere existence."

Mordaunt liked neither the doctrine nor the example. He thought a man who discharged his duties towards others as well as the good old Udaller, had a better right to have the sun shine fair on his setting, than that which he might derive from mere insensibility. But he let the subject drop; for to dispute with his father, had always the effect of irritating him; and again he adverted to the condition of the wreck.

The hulk, for it was little better, was not in the very midst of the current, and drifting at a great rate towards the foot of the precipice, upon whose verge they were placed. Yet it was a long while ere they had a distinct view of the object which they had at first seen as a black speck amongst the waters, and then, at a nearer distance, like a whale, which now scarce shows its back-fin above the waves, now throws to view its large black side. Now, however, they could more distinctly observe the appearance of the ship, for the huge swelling waves which bore her forward to the shore, heaved her alternately high upon the surface, and then plunged her into the trough or furrow of the sea. She seemed a vessel of two or three hundred tons, fitted up for defence, for they could see her port-holes. She had been dismasted, probably in the gale of the preceding day, and lay water-logged on the waves, a prey to their violence. It appeared certain, that the crew, finding themselves unable either to direct the vessel's course, or to relieve her by pumping, had taken to their boats, and left her to her fate. All apprehensions were therefore unnecessary, so far as the immediate loss of human lives was concerned ; and yet it was not without a feeling of breathless awe that Mordaunt and his father beheld the vessel—that rare masterpiece by which human genius aspires to surmount the waves, and contend with the winds—upon the point of falling a prey to them.

Onward, she came, the large black hull seeming larger at every fathom's length. She came nearer, until she bestrode the summit of one tremendous billow, which rolled on with her unbroken, till the wave and its burden were precipitated against the rock, and then the triumph of the elements over the work of human hands was at once completed.

One wave, we have said, made the wrecked vessel completely manifest in her whole bulk, as it raised her and bore her onward against the face of the precipice. But when that wave receded from the foot of the rock, the ship had ceased to exist ; and the retiring billow only bore back a quantity of beams, planks, casks, and similar objects, which swept out to the offing, to be brought in again by the next wave, and again precipitated upon the face of the rock.

It was at this moment that Mordaunt conceived he saw a man floating on a plank or water-cask, which, drifting away from the main current, seemed about to go ashore upon a small spot of sand, where the water was shallow, and the waves broke more smoothly. To see the danger, and to exclaim, "He lives, and may yet be saved !" was the first impulse of the fearless Mordaunt. The next was, after one rapid glance at the front of the cliff, to precipitate himself—such seemed the rapidity of his movement—from the verge, and to commence, by means of slight fissures, projections, and crevices in the rock, a descent, which, to a spectator, appeared little else than an act of absolute insanity.

"Stop, I command you, rash boy !" said his father ; "the attempt is death. Stop, and take the safer path to the left." But Mordaunt was already completely engaged in his perilous enterprise.

"Why should I prevent him ?" said his father, checking his anxiety with the stern and unfeeling philosophy whose principles he had adopted. "Should he die now, full of generous and high feeling, eager in the cause of humanity, happy in the exertion of his own conscious activity and youthful strength—should he die now, will he not escape misanthropy, and remorse, and age, and the consciousness of decaying powers, both of body and mind ?—I will not look upon it, however—I will not—I cannot behold this young light so suddenly quenched."

He turned from the precipice accordingly, and hastening to the left for more than a quarter of a mile, he proceeded towards a *riva*, or cleft in the rock, containing a path, called Erick's Steps, neither safe, indeed, nor easy, but the only one by which the inhabitants of Yarlshof were wont, for any purpose, to seek access to the foot of the precipice.

But long ere Mertoun had reached even the upper end of the pass, his adventurous and active son had accomplished his more desperate enterprise. He had been in vain turned aside from the direct line of descent, by the intervention of difficulties which he had not seen from above—his route became only more circuitous, but could not be interrupted. More than once, large fragments to which he was about to entrust his weight, gave way before him, and thundered down into the tormented ocean ; and in one or two instances, such detached pieces of rock rushed after him, as if to bear him headlong in their course. A courageous heart, a steady eye, a tenacious hand, and a firm foot, carried him through his desperate attempt ; and in the space of seven minutes, he stood at the bottom of the cliff, from the verge of which he had achieved his perilous descent.

The place which he now occupied was the small projecting spot of stones, sand and gravel, that extended a little way into the sea, which on the right hand lashed the very bottom of the precipice, and on the left, was scarce divided from it by a small wave-worn portion of beach that extended as far as the foot of the rent in the rocks called Erick's Steps, by which Mordaunt's father proposed to descend.

When the vessel split and went to pieces, all was swallowed up in the ocean, which had, after the first shock, been seen to float upon the waves, excepting only a few pieces of wreck, casks, chests, and the like, which a strong eddy, formed by the reflux of the waves, had landed, or at least grounded, upon the shallow where Mordaunt now stood. Amongst there, his eager eye discovered the object that had at first engaged his attention, and which now, seen at nigher distance, proved to be in truth a man, and in a most precarious state. His arms were still wrapt with a close and convulsive grasp round the plank to which he had clung in the moment of the shock, but sense and the power of motion were fled; and, from the situation in which the plank lay, partly grounded upon the beach, partly floating in the sea, there was every chance that it might be again washed off shore, in which case death was inevitable. Just as he had made himself aware of these circumstances, Mordaunt beheld a huge wave advancing, and hastened to interpose his aid ere it burst, aware that the reflux might probably sweep away the sufferer.

He rushed into the surf, and fastened on the body, with the same tenacity, though under a different impulse, with that wherewith the hound seizes its prey. The strength of the retiring wave proved even stronger than he had expected, and it was not without a struggle for his own life, as well as for that of the stranger, that Mordaunt resisted being swept off with the receding billow, when, though an adroit swimmer, the strength of the tide must either have dashed him against the rocks, or hurried him out to sea. He stood his ground, however, and ere another such billow had returned, he drew up, upon the small slip of dry sand, both the body of the stranger, and the plank to which he continued firmly attached. But how to save and to recall the means of ebbing life and strength, and how to remove into a place of greater safety the sufferer, who was incapable of giving any assistance towards his own preservation, were questions which Mordaunt asked himself eagerly, but in vain.

He looked to the summit of the cliff on which he had left his father, and shouted to him for assistance; but his eye could not distinguish his form, and his voice was only answered by the scream of the sea birds. He gazed again on the sufferer. A dress richly laced, according to the fashion of the times, fine linen, and rings upon his fingers, evinced he was a man of superior rank; and his features showed youth and comeliness, notwithstanding they were pallid and disfigured. He still breathed, but so feebly, that his respiration was almost imperceptible, and life seemed to keep such slight hold of his frame, that there was every reason to fear it would become altogether extinguished, unless it were speedily reinforced. To loosen the handkerchief from his neck, to raise him with his face towards the breeze, to support him with his arms, was all that Mordaunt could do for his assistance, whilst he anxiously looked for someone who might lend his aid in dragging the unfortunate to a more safe situation.

At this moment he beheld a man advancing slowly and cautiously along the beach. He was in hopes, at first, it was his father, but instantly recollected that he had not had time to come round by the circuitous descent, to which he must necessarily have recourse, and besides, he saw that the man who approached him was shorter in nature.

As he came nearer, Mordaunt was at no loss to recognise the pedlar whom the day before he had met with at Harfra, and who was known to him before upon many occasions. He shouted as loud as he could, "Bryce, hollo ! Bryce, come hither " But the merchant, intent upon picking up some of the spoils of the wreck, and upon dragging them out of reach of the tide, paid for some time little attention to his shouts.

When he did at length approach Mordaunt, it was not to lend him his aid, but to remonstrate with him on his rashness in undertaking the charitable office. "Are you mad ?" said he ; "you that have lived sae lang in Zetland, to risk the saving of a drowning man ? Wot ye not, if you bring him to life again, he will be sure to do you some capital injury ?*—Come, Master Mordaunt, bear a hand to what's mair to the purpose. Help me to get ane or twa of these kists ashore before anybody else comes, and we shall share, like good Christians, what God sends us, and be thankful."

Mordaunt was indeed no stranger to this inhuman superstition, current at a former period among the lower orders of the Zetlanders, and the more generally adopted, perhaps, that it served as an apology for refusing assistance to the unfortunate victims of shipwreck, while they made plunder of their goods. At any rate, the opinion, that to save a drowning man was to run the risk of future injury from him, formed a strange contradiction in the character of these islanders ; who, hospitable, generous, and disinterested, on all other occasions, were sometimes, nevertheless, induced by this superstition to refuse their aid in those mortal emergencies, which were so common upon their rocky and stormy coasts. We are happy to add, that the exhortation and example of the proprietors have eradicated even the traces of this inhuman belief, of which there might be some observed within the memory of those now alive. It is strange that the minds of men should have ever been hardened towards those involved in a distress to which they themselves were so constantly exposed ; but perhaps the frequent sight and consciousness of such danger tends to blunt the feelings to its consequences, whether affecting ourselves or others.

Bryce was remarkably tenacious of this ancient belief ; the more so, perhaps, that the mounting of his pack depended less upon the warehouses of Lerwick or Kirkwall, than on the consequences of such a north-western gale as that of the day preceding ; for which (being a man who, in his own way, professed great devotion) he seldom failed to express his grateful thanks to Heaven. It was indeed said of him, that if he had spent the same time in assisting the wrecked seaman, which he had employed in rifling their bales and boxes, he would have saved

* Note F. Reluctance to save drowning men.

many lives, and lost much linen. He paid no sort of attention to the repeated entreaties of Mordaunt, although he was now upon the same slip of sand with him. It was well known to Bryce as a place on which the eddy was likely to land such spoils as the ocean disgorged ; and to improve the favourable moment, he occupied himself exclusively in securing and appropriating whatever seemed most portable, and of greatest value. At length Mordaunt saw the honest pedlar fix his views upon a strong sea-chest framed of some Indian wood, well secured by brass plates, and seeming to be of a foreign construction. The stout lock resisted all Bryce's efforts to open it, until, with great composure, he plucked from his pocket a very neat hammer and chisel, and began forcing the hinges.

Incensed beyond patience at his assurance, Mordaunt caught up a wooden stretcher which lay near him, and laying his charge softly on the sand, approached Bryce with a menacing gesture, and exclaimed, "You cold-blooded, inhuman rascal ! either get up instantly and lend me your assistance to recover this man and bear him out of danger from the surf, or I will not only beat you to a mummy on the spot, but inform Magnus Troil of your thievery, that he may have you flogged till your bones are bare, and then banish you from the mainland !"

The lid of the chest had just sprung open as this rough address saluted Bryce's ears, and the inside presented a tempting view of wearing apparel for sea and land ; shirts, plain and with lace ruffles, a silver compass, a silver-hilted sword, and other valuable articles, which the pedlar well knew to be such as stir in the trade. He was half-disposed to start up, draw the sword, which was a cut-and-thrust, and "darraign battaile", as Spenser says, rather than quit his prize, or brook interruption. Being, though short, a stout square-made personage, and not much past the prime of life, having besides the better weapon, he might have given Mordaunt more trouble than his benevolent knight-errantry deserved.

Already, as with vehemence he repeated his injunctions that Bryce should forbear his plunder, and come to the assistance of the dying man, the pedlar retorted with a voice of defiance, "Dinna swear, sir ; dinna swear, sir—I will endure no swearing in my presence ; and if you lay a finger on me, that am taking the lawful spoil of the Egyptians, I will give ye a lesson ye shall remember from this day to Yule !"

Mordaunt would speedily have put the pedlar's courage to the test, but a voice behind him suddenly said, "Forbear !" It was the voice of Norna of the Fitful Head, who, during the heat of their altercation, had approached them unobserved. "Forbear !" she repeated ; "and Bryce, do thou render Mordaunt the assistance he requires. It shall avail thee more, and it is I who say the word, than all that you could earn today besides."

"It is se'enteen hundred linen," said the pedlar, giving a tweak to one of the shirts, in that knowing manner with which matrons and judges ascertain the texture of the loom ;—"it's se'enteen hundred linen, and as strong as an it were dowlas. Nevertheless, mother, your bidding is to be done ; and I would have done Mr. Mordaunt's bidding too," he added, relaxing from his note of defiance into the deferential whining tone with which he cajoled his customers, "if he hadna made use of profane oaths which made my very flesh grow, and caused me, in some sort, to forget myself."

He then took a flask from his pocket, and approached the shipwrecked man. "It's the best of brandy," he said ; "and if that doesna cure him, I ken nought that will." So saying, he took a preliminary gulp himself, as if to show the quality of the liquor, and was about to put it to the man's mouth, when, suddenly, withholding his hand, he looked at Norna—"You ensure me against all risk of evil from him, if I am to render him my help ?—Ye ken yoursell what folk say, mother."

For all other answer, Norna took the bottle from the pedlar's hand, and began to chafe the temples and throat of the shipwrecked man; directing Mordaunt how to hold his head, so as to afford him the means of disgorging the sea-water which he had swallowed during his immersion.

The pedlar looked on inactive for a moment, and then said, "To be sure there is not the same risk in helping him, now he is out of the water, and lying high and dry on the beach; and to be sure, the principal danger is to those who first touch him ; and, to be sure, it is a world's pity to see how these rings are pinching the puir creature's swalled fingers—they make his hand as blue as a partan's back before boiling." So saying, he seized one of the man's cold hands, which had just, by a tremulous motion, indicated the return of life, and began his charitable work of removing the rings, which seemed to be of some value.

"As you love your life forbear," said Norna, sternly, "or I will lay that on you which shall spoil your travels through the isles."

"Now, for mercy's sake, mother, say nae mair about it," said the pedlar, "and I'll e'en do your pleasure in your ain way ! I *did* feel a rheumatize in my back-spauld yestreen ; and it wad be a sair thing for the like of me to be debarred my quiet walk round the country in the way of trade — making the honest penny, and helping myself with what Providence sends on our coasts."

"Peace, then," said the woman.—"Peace, as thou wouldst not rue it ; and take this man on thy broad shoulders. His life is of value, and you will be rewarded."

"I had muckle need," said the pedlar, pensively looking at the lidless chest, and the other matters which strewed the sand ; "for he has comed between me and as muckle spreicherie as wad hae made a man of me for the rest of my life ; and now it maun lie here till the next tide sweep it a' doun the Roost, after them that aught it yesterday morning."

"Fear not," said Norna, "it will come to man's use. See, there come carrion-crows, of scent as keen as thine own."

She spoke truly ; for several of the people from the hamlet of Yarlshof were now hastening along the beach, to have their share in the spoil. The pedlar beheld them approach with a deep groan. "Ay, ay," he said, "the folk of Yarlshof, they will make clean wark ; they are kend for that far and wide ; they winna leave the value of a rotten ratlin ; and what's waur, there isna ane o' them has mense or sense eneugh to give thanks for the mercies when they have gotten them. There is the auld

Ranzelman, Neil Ronaldson, that canna walk a mile to hear the minister, but he will hirple ten if he hears of a ship embayed."

Norna, however, seemed to possess over him so complete an ascendency, that he no longer hesitated to take the man, who now gave strong symptoms of reviving existence, upon his shoulders; and, assisted by Mordaunt, trudged along the sea-beach with his burden, without farther remonstrance. Ere he was borne off, the stranger pointed to the chest, and attempted to mutter something, to which Norna replied, "Enough. It shall be secured."

Advancing towards the passage called Erick's Steps, by which they were to ascend the cliffs, they met the people from Yarlshof hastening in the opposite directions. Man and woman, as they passed, reverently made room for Norna, and saluted her — not without an expression of fear upon some of their faces. She passed them a few paces, and then turning back, called aloud to the Ranzelman, who (though the practice was more common than legal) was attending the rest of the hamlet upon this plundering expedition. "Neil Ronaldson," she said, "mark my words. There stands yonder a chest, from which the lid has been just prized off. Look it be brought down to your own house at Yarlshof, just as it is now. Beware of moving or touching the slightest article. He were better in his grave, that so much as looks at the contents. I speak for nought, nor in aught will I be disobeyed."

"Your pleasure shall be done, mother," said Ronaldson. "I warrant we will not break bulk, since sic is your bidding."

Far behind the rest of the villagers followed an old woman, talking to herself, and cursing her own decrepitude, which kept her the last of the party, yet pressing forward with all her might to get her share of the spoil.

When they met her, Mordaunt was astonished to recognise his father's old housekeeper. "How now," he said, "Swertha, what make you so far from home ?"

"Just e'en daikering out to look after my auld master and your honour," replied Swertha, who felt like a criminal caught in the manner ; for on more occasions than one, Mr. Mertoun had intimated his high disapprobation of such excursions as she was at present engaged in.

But Mordaunt was too much engaged with his own thoughts to take much notice of her delinquency. "Have you seen my father ?" he said.

"And that I have," replied Swertha—"The gude gentleman was ganging to hirsel himsell doun Erick's Steps, whilk would have been the ending of him, that is in no way a cragsman. Sae I e'en gat him wiled away hame—and I was just seeking you that you may gang after him to the hall-house, for, to my thought, he is far frae weel."

"My father unwell ?" said Mordaunt, remembering the faintness he had exhibited at the commencement of that morning's walk.

"Far frae weel—far frae weel," groaned Swertha, with a piteous shake of the head—"white o' the gills—white o' the gills—and him to think of coming down the riva !"

"Return home, Mordaunt," said Norna, who was listening to what had passed. "I will see all that is necessary done for this man's relief, and you will find him at the Ranzelman's, when you list to inquire. You cannot help him more than you already have done."

Mordaunt felt this was true, and, commanding Swertha to follow him instantly, betook himself to the path homeward.

Swertha hobbled reluctantly after her young master in the same direction, until she lost sight of him on his entering the cleft of the rock; then instantly turned about, muttering to herself, "Haste home, in good sooth ?—haste home, and lose the best chance of getting a new rokelay and owerlay that I have had these ten years ? by my certie, na—It's seldom sic rich godsends come on our shore—no since Jenny and James came ashore in King Charlie's time."

So saying, she mended her pace as well as she could, and a willing mind making amends for frail limbs, posted on with wonderful despatch to put in for her share of the spoil. She soon reached the beach, where the Ranzelman, stuffing his own pouches all the while, was exhorting the rest to part things fair, and be neighbourly, and to give to the auld and helpless a share of what was going, which, he charitably remarked, would bring a blessing on the shore, and send them "mair wrecks ere winter."*

CHAPTER EIGHTH

He was a lovely youth I guess ;
The panther in the wilderness
  Was no so fair as he.
And when he chose to sport and play,
No dolphin ever was so gay
  Upon the tropic sea.
WORDSWORTH

THE light foot of Mordaunt Mertoun was not long of bearing him to Yarlshof. He entered the house hastily, for what he himself had observed that morning corresponded in some degree with the ideas which Swertha's tale was calculated to excite. He found his father, however, in the inner apartment, reposing himself after his fatigue ; and his first question satisfied him that the good dame had practised a little imposition to get rid of them both.

"Where is this dying man, whom you have so wisely ventured your own neck to relieve ?" said the elder Mertoun to the younger.

"Norna, sir," replied Mordaunt, "has taken him under her charge ; she understands such matters."

"And is quack as well as witch ?" said the elder Mertoun. "With all my heart—it is a trouble saved. But I hasted home, on Swertha's hint, to look out for lint and bandages ; for her speech was of broken bones."

Mordaunt kept silence, well knowing his father would not persevere in his inquiries upon such a matter, and not willing either to prejudice the old governante, or to excite his father to one of those excesses of

* Note G. Mair wrecks ere winter.

passion into which he was apt to burst, when, contrary to his wont, he thought proper to correct the conduct of his domestic.

It was late in the day ere old Swertha returned from her expedition, heartily fatigued, and bearing with her a bundle of some bulk, containing, it would seem, her share of the spoil. Mordaunt instantly sought her out, to charge her with the deceits she had practised on both his father and himself; but the accused matron lacked not her reply.

"By her troth," she said, "she thought it was time to bid Mr. Mertoun gang hame and get bandages, when she had seen, with her ain twa een, Mordaunt ganging down the cliff like a wild-cat—it was to be thought broken bones would be the end, and lucky if bandages wad do any good;—and, by her troth, she might weel tell Mordaunt his father was puirly, and him looking sae white in the gills (whilk, she wad die upon it, was the very word she used), and it was a thing that couldna be denied by man at this very moment."

"But, Swertha," said Mordaunt, as soon as her clamorous defence gave him time to speak in reply, "how came you, that should have been busy with your housewifery and your spinning, to be out this morning at Erick's Steps, in order to take all this unnecessary care of my father and me ? And what is in that bundle, Swertha, for I fear, Swertha, you have been transgressing the law, and have been out upon the wrecking system."

"Fair fa' your sonsy face, and the blessing of Saint Ronald upon you !" said Swertha, in a tone betwixt coaxing and jesting ; "would you keep a puir body mending hersell, and sae muckle gear lying on the loose sand for the lifting ? Hout, Maister Mordaunt, a ship ashore is a sight to wile the minister out of his very pu'pit in the middle of his preaching, muckle mair a puir auld ignorant wife frae her rock and her tow. And little did I get for my day's wark—just some rags o' cambric things, and a bit or twa of coorse claith, and sic like—the strong and the hearty get a'thing in this warld."

"Yes, Swertha," replied Mertoun, "and that is rather hard, as you must have your share of punishment in this world and the next, for robbing the poor mariners."

"Hout, callant, wha wid punish an auld wife like me for a wheen duds ? Folk speak muckle black ill of Earl Patrick ; but he was a freend to the shore, and made wise laws against ony body helping vessels that were like to gang on the breakers."* And the mariners, I have heard Bryce Yagger say, lose their right frae the time keel touches sand; and, moreover, they are dead and gane, poor souls—dead and gane, and care little about warld's wealth now—Nay, nae mair than the great Yarls and Sea-kings, in the Norse days, did about the treasures that they buried in the tombs and sepulchres auld langsyne. Did I ever tell you the sang, Maister Mordaunt, how Olaf Tryguasson garr'd hide five gold crouns in the same grave with him ?"

"No, Swertha," said Mordaunt, who took pleasure in tormenting the cunning old plunderer—"you never told me that ; but I tell you, that the

* This was literally true.

70

stranger whom Norna has taken down to the town, will be well enough to-morrow, to ask where you have hidden the goods that you have stolen from the wreck."

"But wha will tell him a word about it, hinnie ?" said Swertha, looking slyly up in her young master's face—"The mair by token, since I maun tell ye, that I have a bonny remnant of silk amang the lave, that will make a dainty waistcoat to yourself, the first merry-making ye gang to."

Mordaunt could no longer forbear laughing at the cunning with which the old dame proposed to bribe off his evidence by imparting a portion of her plunder; and, desiring her to get ready what provision she had made for dinner, he returned to his father, whom he found still sitting in the same place, and nearly in the same posture, in which he had left him.

When their hasty and frugal meal was finished, Mordaunt announced to his father his purpose of going down to the town, or hamlet, to look after the shipwrecked sailor.

The elder Mertoun assented with a nod.

"He must be ill accommodated there, sir" added his son—a hint which only produced another nod of assent. "He seemed from his appearance," pursued Mordaunt, "to be of very good rank – and admitting these poor people do their best to receive him, in his present weak state, yet"—

"I know what you would say," said his father, interrupting him ; "we, you think, ought to do something towards assisting him. Go to him, then—if he lacks money, let him name the sum, and he shall have it; but, for lodging the stranger here, and holding intercourse with him, I neither can nor will do so. I have retired to this farthest extremity of the British Isles, to avoid new friends, and new faces, and none such shall intrude on me either their happiness or their misery. When you have known the world half a score of years longer, your early friends will have given you reason to remember them, and to avoid new ones for the rest of your life. Go then—why do you stop ?—rid the country of the man—let me see no one about me but those vulgar countenances, the extent and character of whose petty knavery I know, and can submit to, as to an evil too trifling to cause irritation." He then threw his purse to his son, and signed to him to depart with all speed.

Mordaunt was not long before he reached the village. In the dark abode of Neil Ronaldson, the Ranzelman, he found the stranger seated by the peat-fire, upon the very chest which had excited the cupidity of the devout Bryce Snailsfoot, the pedlar. The Ranzelman himself was absent, dividing, with all due impartiality, the spoils of the wrecked vessel amongst the natives of the community ; listening to and redressing their complaints of equality ; and (if the matter in hand had not been, from beginning to end, utterly unjust and indefensible) discharging the part of a wise and prudent magistrate, in all the details. For at this time, and probably until a much later period, the lower orders of the islands entertained an opinion, common to barbarians also in the same situation, that whatever was cast on their shores became their indisputable property.

Margery Bimbister, the worthy spouse of the Ranzelman, was in the charge of the house, and introduced Mordaunt to her guest, saying, with no great ceremony, "This is the young tacksman—You will maybe tell him your name, though you will not tell it to us. If it had not been for his four quarters, it's but little you would have said to onybody, sae lang as life lasted."

The stranger arose, and shook Mordaunt by the hand, observing, he understood that he had been the means of saving his life and his chest. "The rest of the property," he said, "is, I see, walking the plank ; for they are as busy as the devil in a gale of wind."

"And what was the use of your seamanship, then," said Margery, "that you couldna keep off the Sumburgh Head ? It would have been lang ere Sumburgh Head had come to you."

"Leave us for a moment, good Margery Bimbister," said Mordaunt ; "I wish to have some private conversation with this gentleman."

"Gentleman !" said Margery, with an emphasis ; "not but the man is well enough to look at," she added, again surveying him, "but I doubt if there is muckle of the gentleman about him."

Mordaunt looked at the stranger, and was of a different opinion. He was rather above the middle size, and formed handsomely as well as strongly. Mordaunt's intercourse with society was not extensive ; but he thought his new acquaintance, to a bold sunburnt handsome countenance, which seemed to have faced various climates, added the frank and open manners of a sailor. He answered cheerfully the inquiries which Mordaunt made after his health ; and maintained that one night's rest would relieve him from all the effects of the disaster he had sustained. But he spoke with bitterness of the avarice and curiosity of the Ranzelman and his spouse.

"That chattering old woman," said the stranger, "has persecuted me the whole day for the name of the ship. I think she might be contented with the share she has had of it. I was the principal owner of the vessel that was lost yonder, and they have left me nothing but my wearing apparel. Is there no magistrate, or justice of the peace, in this wild country, that would lend a hand to help one when he is among the breakers ?"

Mordaunt mentioned Magnus Troil, the principal proprietor, as well as the Fowd, or provincial judge, of the district, as the person from whom he was most likely to obtain redress ; and regretted that his own youth, and his father's situation as a retired stranger, should put it out of their power to afford him the protection he required.

"Nay, for your part you have done enough," said the sailor ; "but if I had five out of the forty brave fellows that are fishes' food by this time, the devil a man would I ask to do me the right that I could do for myself !"

"Forty hands !" said Mordaunt; "you were well manned for the size of your ship."

"Not so well as we needed to be. We mounted ten guns, besides chasers; but our cruise on the main had thinned us of men, and lumbered us up with goods. Six of our guns were in ballast—Hands ! if I had enough of hands, we would never have miscarried so infernally. The people were knocked up with working the pumps, and so took to the boats, and left me with the vessel, to sink or swim. But the dogs had their pay, and I can afford to pardon them. The boats swamped in the current—all were lost—and here am I."

"You had come north about then, from the West Indies ?" said Mordaunt.

"Ay, ay ; the vessel was the Good Hope of Bristol, a letter of marque. She had fine luck down on the Spanish main, both with commerce and privateering, but the luck's ended with her now. My name is Clement Cleveland, captain, and part owner, as I said before—I am a Bristol man born—my father was well known on the Tollsell—old Clem Cleveland of the College Green."

Mordaunt had no right to inquire farther, and yet it seemed to him as if his own mind was but half satisfied. There was an affection of bluntness, a sort of defiance, in the manner of the stranger, for which circumstances afforded no occasion. Captain Cleveland had suffered injustice from the islanders, but from Mordaunt he had only received kindness and protection ; yet he seemed as if he involved all the neighbourhood in the wrongs he complained of. Mordaunt looked down and was silent, doubting whether it would be better to take his leave, or to proceed father in his offers of assistance. Cleveland seemed to guess at his thoughts, for he immediately added, in a conciliating manner,—"I am a plain man, Master Mertoun, for that I understand is your name ; and I am a ruined man to boot, and that does not mend one's good manners. But you have done a kind and friendly part by me, and it may be I think as much of it as if I thanked you more. And so before I leave this place, I'll give you my fowling-piece ; she will put a hundred swan-shot through a Dutchman's cap at eighty paces—she will carry ball too—I have hit a wild bull within a hundred and fifty yards—but I have two pieces that are as good, or better, so you may keep this for my sake."

"That would be to take my share of the wreck," answered Mordaunt, laughing.

"No such matter," said Cleveland, undoing a case which contained several guns and pistols—"you see I have saved my private arm-chest, as well as my clothes—that the tall old woman in the dark rigging managed for me. And, between ourselves, it is worth all I have lost ; for," he added, lowering his voice, and looking round, "when I speak of being ruined in the hearing of these land-sharks, I do not mean ruined stock and block. No, here is something will do more than shoot sea-fowl." So saying, he pulled out a great ammunition-pouch marked *Swan-shot*, and showed Mordaunt, hastily, that it was full of Spanish pistoles and Portagues (as the broad Portugal pieces were then called). "No, no," he added, with a smile, "I have ballast enough to trim the vessel again ; and now, will you take the piece ?"

"Since you are willing to give it to me," said Mordaunt, laughing, "with all my heart. I was just going to ask you, in my father's name," he added, showing his purse, "whether you wanted any of that same ballast."

"Thanks, but you see I am provided—take my old acquaintance, and may she serve you as well as she has served me ; but you will never make so good a voyage with her. You can shoot, I suppose ?"

"Tolerably well," said Mordaunt, admiring the piece, which was a beautiful Spanish-barrel gun, inlaid with gold, small in the bore, and of unusual length, such as is chiefly used for shooting sea-fowl, and for ball practice.

"With slugs," continued the donor, "never gun shot closer ; and with single ball, you may kill a seal two hundred yards at sea from the top of the highest peak of this iron-bound coast of yours. But I tell you again that the old rattler will never do you the service she has done me."

"I shall not use her so dexterously, perhaps," said Mordaunt.

"Umph !—perhaps not," replied Cleveland ; "but that is not the question. What say you to shooting the man at the wheel, just as we run aboard of a Spaniard ? So the Don was taken aback, and we laid him athwart the hawse, and carried her cutlass in hand ; and worth the while she was—stout brigantine—El Santo Francisco—bound for Porto Bello, with gold and negroes. That little bit of lead was worth twenty thousand pistoles."

"I have shot at no such game as yet," said Mordaunt.

"Well, all in good time; we cannot weigh till the tide makes. But you are a tight, handsome, active young man. What is to ail you to take a trip after some of this stuff ?" laying his hand on the bag of gold.

"My father talks of my travelling soon," replied Mordaunt, who, born to hold men-of-wars-men in great respect, felt flattered by this invitation from one who appeared a thoroughbred seaman.

"I respect him for the thought," said the Captain ; "and I will visit him before I weigh anchor. I have a consort off these islands, and be cursed to her. She'll find me out somewhere, though she parted company in the bit of a squall, unless she is gone to Davy Jones too.—Well, she was better found than we, and not so deep loaded—she must have weathered it. We'll have a hammock slung for you aboard, and make a sailor and a man of you in the same trip."

"I should like it well enough," said Mordaunt, who eagerly longed to see more of the world than his lonely situation had hitherto permitted; "but then my father must decide."

"Your father ? pooh !" said Captain Cleveland ;— "but you are very right," he added, checking himself ; "Gad, I have lived so long at sea, that I cannot think anybody has a right to think except the captain and the master. But you are very right. I will go up to the old gentleman this instant, and speak to him myself. He lives in that handsome, modern-looking building, I suppose, that I see a quarter of a mile off ?"

"In that old half-ruined house," said Mordaunt, "he does indeed live ; but he will see no visitors."

"Then you must drive the point yourself, for I can't stay in this latitude. Since your father is no magistrate, I must go to see this same Magnus—how call you him ?—who is not justice of peace, but something else that will do the turn as well. These fellows have got two or three things that I must and will have back—let them keep the rest, and be d—d to them. Will you give me a letter to him, just by way of commission ?"

"It is scarce needful," said Mordaunt. "It is enough that you are shipwrecked, and need his help ;—but yet I may as well furnish you with a letter of introduction."

"There," said the sailor, producing a writing-case from his chest, "are your writing-tools.—Meantime, since bulk has been broken, I will nail down the hatches, and make sure of the cargo."

While Mordaunt, accordingly, was engaged in writing to Magnus Troil a letter, setting forth the circumstances in which Captain Cleveland had been thrown upon their coast, the Captain, having first selected and laid aside some wearing apparel and necessaries enough to fill a knapsack, took in hand hammer and nails, employed himself in securing the lid of his sea-chest, by fastening it down in a workman-like manner, and then added the corroborating security of a cord, twisted and knotted with nautical dexterity. "I leave this in your charge," he said, "all except this," showing the bag of gold, "and these," pointing to a cutlass and pistols, "which may prevent all farther risk of my parting company with my Portagues."

"You will find no occasion for weapons in this country, Captain Cleveland," replied Mordaunt ; "a child might travel with a purse of gold from Sumburgh Head to the Scaw of Unst, and no soul would injure him."

"And that's pretty boldly said, young gentleman, considering what is going on without doors at this moment."

"Oh," replied Mordaunt, a little confused, "what comes on land with the tide, they reckon their lawful property. One would think they had studied under Sir Arthegal, who pronounces—

> For equal right in equal things doth stand,
>> And what the mighty sea hath once possess'd,
> And plucked quite from all possessors' hands,
>> Or else by wrecks that wretches have distress'd,
> He may dispose, by his resistless might,
>> As things at random left, to whom he list.[*]

"I shall think the better of plays and ballads as long as I live, for these very words," said Captain Cleveland ; "and yet I have loved them well enough in my day. But this is good doctrine, and more men than one may trim their sails to such a breeze. What the sea sends is ours, that's sure enough. However, in case that your good folks should think the land as well as the sea may present them with waiffs and strays, I will make bold to take my cutlass and pistols.—Will you cause my chest to be secured in your own house till you hear from me, and use your influence to procure me a guide to show me the way, and to carry my kit ?"

"Will you go by sea or land ?" said Mordaunt, in reply.

"By sea !" exclaimed Cleveland. "What—in one of these cockleshells,

[*] [Spenser's *Faerie Queene*, Book iv. Canto vi.]

75

and a cracked cockleshell to boot ? No, no—land, land, unless I knew my crew, my vessel, and my voyage."

They parted accordingly, Captain Cleveland being supplied with a guide to conduct him to Burgh Westra, and his chest being carefully removed to the mansion-house at Yarlshof.

CHAPTER NINTH

This is a gentle trader, and a prudent.
He's no Autolycus, to blear your eye
With quips of worldly gauds and gamesomeness ;
But seasons all his glittering merchandise
With wholesome doctrines suited to the use,
As men sauce goose with sage and rosemary.

OLD PLAY

ON the subsequent morning, Mordaunt, in answer to his father's inquiries, began to give him some account of the shipwrecked mariner, whom he had rescued from the waves. But he had not proceeded far in recapitulating the particulars which Cleveland had communicated, when Mr. Mertoun's looks became disturbed—he arose hastily, and, after pacing twice or thrice across the room, he retired into the inner chamber to which he usually confined himself while under the influence of his mental malady. In the evening he re-appeared, without any traces of his disorder, but it may be easily supposed that his son avoided recurring to the subject which had affected him.

Mordaunt Mertoun was thus left without assistance, to form at his leisure his own opinion, respecting the new acquaintance which the sea had sent him ; and, upon the whole, he was himself surprised to find the result less favourable to the stranger than he could well account for. There seemed to Mordaunt to be a sort of repelling influence about the man. True, he was a handsome man, of a frank and prepossessing manner, but there was an assumption of superiority about him which Mordaunt did not quite so much like. Although he was so keen a sportsman as to be delighted with his acquisition of the Spanish-barrelled gun, and accordingly mounted and dismounted it with great interest, paying the utmost attention to the most minute parts about the lock and ornaments, yet he was, upon the whole, inclined to have some scruples about the mode in which he had acquired it.

"I should not have accepted it," he thought ; "perhaps Captain Cleveland might give it me as a sort of payment for the trifling service I did him ; and yet it would have been churlish to refuse it in the way it was offered. I wish he had looked more like a man whom one would have chosen to be obliged to."

But a successful day's shooting reconciled him to his gun, and he became assured, like most young sportsmen in similar circumstances, that all other pieces were but pop-guns in comparison. But then, to be doomed to shoot gulls and seals when there were Frenchmen and

Spaniards to be come at—when there were ships to be boarded, and steersmen to be marked off, seemed but a dull and contemptible destiny. His father had mentioned his leaving these islands, and no other mode of occupation occurred to his inexperience save that of the sea, with which he had been conversant from his infancy. His ambition had formerly aimed no higher than at sharing the fatigues and dangers of a Greenland fishing expedition ; for it was in that scene that the Zetlanders laid most of their perilous adventures. But war was again raging, the history of Sir Francis Drake, Captain Morgan, and other bold adventurers, an account of whose exploits he had purchased from Bryce Snailsfoot, had made much impression on his mind, and the offer of Captain Cleveland to take him to sea frequently recurred to him, although the pleasure of such a project was somewhat damped by a doubt, whether, in the long run, he should not find many objections to his proposed commander. Thus much he already saw, that he was opinionative, and might probably prove arbitrary ; and that, since even kindness was mingled with an assumption of superiority, his occasional displeasure might contain a great deal more of that disagreeable ingredient than could be palatable to those who sailed under him. And yet, after counting all risks, could his father's consent but be obtained, with what pleasure, he thought, would he embark in quest of new scenes and strange adventures, in which he proposed to himself to achieve such deeds as should be the theme of many a tale to the lovely sisters of Burgh Westra—tales at which Minna should weep and Brenda should smile, and both should marvel ! And this was to be the reward of his labours and his dangers ; for the hearth of Magnus Troil had a magnetic influence over his thoughts, and however they might traverse amid his day-dreams, it was the point where they finally settled.

There were times when Mordaunt thought of mentioning to his father the conversation he had held with Captain Cleveland and the seaman's proposal to him ; but the very short and general account which he had given of that person's history, upon the morning after his departure from the hamlet, had produced a sinister effect on Mr. Mertoun's mind, and discouraged him from speaking farther on any subject connected with it. It would be time enough, he thought, to mention Captain Cleveland's proposal when his consort should arrive, and when he should repeat his offer in a more formal manner ; and these he supposed events likely very soon to happen.

But days grew to weeks, and weeks were numbered into months, and he heard nothing from Cleveland ; and only learned by an occasional visit from Bryce Snailsfoot, that the Captain was residing at Burgh Westra as one of the family. Mordaunt was somewhat surprised at this, although the unlimited hospitality of the islands, which Magnus Troil, both from fortune and disposition, carried to the utmost extent, made it almost a matter of course that he should remain in the family until he disposed of himself otherwise. Still it seemed strange he had not gone to some of the northern isles to inquire after his consort; or that he did not rather choose to make Lerwick his residence, where fishing vessels often brought news from the coasts and ports of Scotland and

Holland. Again, why did he not send for the chest he had deposited at Yarlshof ? and still farther, Mordaunt thought it would have been but polite if the stranger had sent him some sort of message in token of remembrance.

These subjects of reflection were connected with another still more unpleasant, and more difficult to account for. Until the arrival of this person, scarce a week had passed without bringing him some kind greeting or token of recollection from Burgh Westra ; and pretences were scarce ever wanting for maintaining a constant intercourse. Minna wanted the words of a Norse ballad ; or desired to have, for her various collections, feathers, or eggs, or shells, or specimens of the rarer sea-weeds ; or Brenda sent a riddle to be resolved, or a song to be learned ; or the honest old Udaller—in a rude manuscript, which might have passed for an ancient Runic inscription—sent his hearty greetings to his good young friend, with a present of something to make good cheer, and an earnest request he would come to Burgh Westra as soon, and stay there as long as possible. These kindly tokens of remembrance were often sent by special message ; besides which, there was never a passenger or a traveller who crossed from the one mansion to the other who did not bring to Mordaunt some friendly greeting from the Udaller and his family. Of late, this intercourse had become more and more infrequent ; and no messenger from Burgh Westra had visited Yarlshof for several weeks. Mordaunt both observed and felt this alteration, and it dwelt on his mind while he questioned Bryce as closely as pride and prudence would permit, to ascertain, if possible, the cause of the change. Yet he endeavoured to assume an indifferent air while he asked the yagger whether there were no news in the country.

"Great news," the yagger replied ; "and a gey mony of them. That crackbrained carle, the new factor, is for making a change in the *bismars* and the *lispunds ;* * and our worthy Fowd, Magnus Troil, has sworn that, sooner than change them for the still-yard or aught-else, he'll fling Factor Yellowley from Brassa Craig."

"Is that all ?" said Mordaunt, very little interested.

"All ! and eneugh, I think," replied the pedlar. "How are folks to buy and sell if the weights are changed on them ?"

"Very true," replied Mordaunt ; "but have you heard of no strange vessels on the coast ?"

"Six Dutch doggers off Brassa ; and, as I hear, a high-quartered galliot thing, with a gaff mainsail, lying in Scalloway Bay. She will be from Norway."

"No ships of war or sloops ?"

"None," replied the pedlar, "since the Kite Tender sailed with the impress men. If it was His will, and our men were out of her, I wish the deep sea had her !"

"Were there no news at Burgh Westra ? Were the family all well ?"

"A' weel, and weel to do—out-taken, it may be, something ower muckle daffing and laughing—dancing ilk night, they say, wi' the

* These are weights of Norwegian origin, still used in Zetland.

stranger captain that's living there—him that was ashore on Sumburgh Head the tother day—less daffing served him then."

"Daffing! dancing every night!" said Mordaunt, not particularly well satisfied—"Whom does Captain Cleveland dance with?"

"Ony body he likes, I fancy," said the yagger; "at onyrate he gars a' body yonder dance after his fiddle. But I ken little about it, for I am no free in conscience to look upon thae flinging fancies. Folk should mind that life is made but of rotten yarn."

"I fancy that it is to keep them in mind of that wholesome truth that you deal in such tender wares, Bryce," replied Mordaunt, dissatisfied as well with the tenor of the reply as with the affected scruples of the respondent.

"That's as muckle as to say, that I suld hae minded you was a flinger and a fiddler yoursell, Maister Mordaunt; but I am an auld man, and maun unburden my conscience. But ye will be for the dance, I sall warrant that's to be at Burgh Westra on John's Even (*Saunt* John's, as the blinded creatures ca' him), and nae doubt ye will be for some warldly braws—hose, waistcoats, or sic like? I hae pieces frae Flanders"—With that he placed his movable warehouse on the table, and began to unlock it.

"Dance!" repeated Mordaunt—"Dance on St. John's Even?—Were you desired to bid me to it, Bryce?"

"Na—but ye ken well eneugh ye wad be welcome, bidden or no bidden. This captain—how-ca'-ye-him—is to be skudler, as they ca't—the first of the gang, like."

"The devil take him!" said Mordaunt in impatient surprise.

"A' in gude time," replied the yagger; "hurry no man's cattle—the devil will hae his due, I warrant ye, or it winna be for lack of seeking. But it's true I'm telling you, for a' ye stare like a wild cat; and this same Captain—I-wat-na-his-name—bought ane of the very waistcoats that I am ganging to show ye—purple, wi' a gowd binding, and bonnily broidered; and I have a piece for you, the neighbour of it, wi' a green grund; and if ye mean to streek yoursell up beside him, ye maun e'en buy it, for it's gowd that glances in the lasses' een now-a-days. See—look till't," he added, displaying the pattern in various points of view; "look till *it* through the light, and till the light through *it*—wi' the grain, and *against* the grain—it shows ony gate—cam frae Antwerp a' the gate—four dollars is the price; and yon captain was sae weel pleased that he flang down a twenty shilling Jacobus, and bade me keep the change and be d—d!—poor silly profane creature, I pity him."

Without inquiring whether the pedlar bestowed his compassion on the worldly imprudence or the religious deficiencies of Captain Cleveland, Mordaunt turned from him, folded his arms, and paced the apartment, muttering to himself, "Not asked—A stranger to be king of the feast!"—Words which he repeated so earnestly, that Bryce caught a part of their import.

"As for asking, I am almaist bauld to say, that ye will be asked, Maister Mordaunt."

"Did they mention my name, then?" said Mordaunt.

"I canna preceesley say that," said Bryce Snailsfoot ; "but ye needna turn away your head sae sourly, like a sealgh when he leaves the shore ; for, do you see, I heard distinctly that a' the revellers about are to be there ; and is't to be thought they would leave you out, an auld kend freend, and the lightest foot at sic frolics (Heaven send you a better praise in His ain gude time !) that ever flang at a fiddle-squeak between this and Unst ? Sae I consider ye altogether the same as invited—and ye had best provide yourself wi' a waistcoat, for brave and brisk will every man be that's there—the Lord pity them !"

He thus continued to follow with his green glazen eyes the motions of young Mordaunt Mertoun, who was pacing the room in a very pensive manner, which the yagger probably misinterpreted, as he thought, like Claudio, that if a man is sad, it must needs be because he lacks money. Bryce, therefore, after another pause, thus accosted him. "Ye needna be sad about the matter, Maister Mordaunt ; for although I got the just price of the article from the captain-man, yet I maun deal freendly wi' you, as a kend freend and customer, and bring the price, as they say, within your purse-mouth—or it's the same to me to let it lie ower till Martinmas, or e'en to Candlemas. I am decent in the warld, Maister Mordaunt—forbid that I should hurry onybody, far mair a freend that has paid me siller afore now. Or I wad be content to swap the garment for the value in feathers or sea-otters' skins, or ony kind of peltrie—nane kens better that yoursell how to come by sic ware—and I am sure I hae furnished you wi' the primest o' powder. I dinna ken if I tell'd ye it was out o' the kist of Captain Plunket, that perished on the Scaw of Unst, wi' the armed brig Mary, sax years syne. He was a prime fowler himself, and luck it was that the kist came ashore dry. I sell that to nane but gude marksmen. And so, I was saying, if ye had ony wares ye liked to coup* for the waistcoat, I wad be ready to trock wi' you, for assuredly ye will be wanted at Burgh Westra on Saint John's Even ; and ye wadna like to look waur than the Captain—that wadna be setting."

"I will be there, at least, whether wanted or not," said Mordaunt, stopping short in his walk, and taking the waistcoat-piece hastily out of the pedlar's hand ; "and, as you say, will not disgrace them."

"Haud a care—haud a care, Maister Mordaunt," exclaimed the pedlar ; "ye handle it as it were a bale of coarse wadmaal—ye'll fray't to bits—ye might well say my ware is tender—and ye'll mind the price is four dollars—Sall I put ye in my book for it ?"

"No," said Mordaunt, hastily ; and, taking out his purse, he flung down the money.

"Grace to ye to wear the garment," said the joyous pedlar, "and to me to guide the siller ; and protect us from earthly vanities and earthly covetousness ; and send you the white linen raiment, whilk is mair to be desired than the muslins, and cambrics, and lawns, and silks of this world ; and send me the talents which avail more than much fine Spanish gold, or Dutch dollars either—and—but God guide the callant, what for is he wrapping the silk up that gate, like a wisp of hay ?"

* Barter.

At this moment, old Swertha, the housekeeper, entered, to whom, as if eager to get rid of the subject, Mordaunt threw his purchase, with something like careless disdain ; and, telling her to put it aside, snatched his gun, which stood in the corner, threw his shooting accoutrements about him, and, without noticing Bryce's attempt to enter into conversation upon the "braw sealskin, as saft as doe-leather," which made the sling and cover of his fowling-piece, he left the apartment abruptly.

The yagger, with those green, goggling, and gain-descrying kind of optics, which we have already described, continued gazing for an instant after the customer, who treated his wares with such irreverence.

Swertha also looked after him with some surprise. "The callant's in a creel," quoth she.

"In a creel !" echoed the pedlar ; "he will be as wowf as ever his father was. To guide in that gate a bargain that cost him four dollars !—very, very Fifish, as the east-country fisher-folk say."

"Four dollars for that green rag !" said Swertha, catching at the words which the yagger had unwarily suffered to escape—"that was a bargain indeed ! I wonder whether he is the greater fule, or you the mair rogue, Bryce Snailsfoot."

"I didna say it cost him preceesely four dollars," said Snailsfoot ; "but if it had, the lad's siller his ain, I hope ; and he is auld eneugh to make his ain bargains. Mair by token the gudes are weel worth the money, and mair."

"Mair by token," said Swertha, coolly, "I will see what his father thinks about it."

"Ye'll no be sae ill natured, Mistress Swertha," said the yagger ; "that will be but cauld thanks for the bonny owerlay that I hae brought you a' the way frae Lerwick."

"And a bonny price ye'll be setting on't," said Swertha ; "for that's the gate your good deeds end."

"Ye sall hae the fixing of the price yoursell ; or it may lie ower till ye're buying something for the house, or for your master, and it can make a' ae count."

"Troth and that's true, Bryce Snailsfoot ; I am thinking we'll want some napery sune—for it's no to be thought we can spin, and the like, as if there was a mistress in the house ; and sae we make nane at hame."

"And that's what I ca' walking by the word," said the yagger. "'Go unto those that buy and sell ;' there's muckle profit in that text."

"There's a pleasure in dealing with a discreet man, that can make profit of onything," said Swertha ; "and now that I take another look at that daft callant's waistcoat-piece, I think it *is* honestly worth four dollars."

CHAPTER TENTH

I have possessed the regulation of the weather and the distribution of the seasons. The sun has listened to my dictates, and passed from tropic to tropic by my direction ; the clouds, at my command, have poured forth their waters.   RASSELAS

ANY sudden cause for anxious and mortifying reflection, which, in advanced age, occasions sullen and pensive inactivity, stimulates youth to eager and active exertion ; as if, like the hurt deer, they endeavoured to drown the pain of the shaft by the rapidity of motion. When Mordaunt caught up his gun, and rushed out of the house at Yarlshof, he walked on with great activity over waste and wild, without any determined purpose, except that of escaping, if possible, from the smart of his own irritation. His pride was effectually mortified by the report of the yagger, which coincided exactly with some doubts he had been led to entertain, by the long and unkind silence of his friends at Burgh Westra.

If the fortunes of Cæsar had doomed him, as the poet suggests, to have been

"But the best wrestler on the green,"

it is nevertheless to be presumed, that a foil from a rival, in that rustic exercise, would have mortified him as much as a defeat from a competitor, when he was struggling for the empery of the world. And even so Mordaunt Mertoun, degraded in his own eyes from the height which he had occupied as the chief amongst the youth of the island, felt vexed and irritated, as well as humbled. The two beautiful sisters, also, whose smiles all were so desirous of acquiring, with whom he had lived on terms of such familiar affection, that, with the same ease and innocence, there was unconsciously mixed a shade of deeper though undefined tenderness than characterises fraternal love—they also seemed to have forgotten him. He could not be ignorant, that, in the universal opinion of all Dunrossness, nay, of the whole Mainland, he might have had every chance of being the favoured lover of either ; and now at once, and without any failure on his part, he was become so little to them, that he had lost even the consequence of an ordinary acquaintance. The old Udaller, too, whose hearty and sincere character should have made him more constant in his friendships, seemed to have been as fickle as his daughters, and poor Mordaunt had at once lost the smiles of the fair, and the favour of the powerful. These were uncomfortable reflections, and he doubled his pace, that he might outstrip them if possible.

Without exactly reflecting upon the route which he pursued, Mordaunt walked briskly on through a country where neither hedge, wall, nor enclosure of any kind, interrupts the steps of the wanderer, until he reached a very solitary spot, where, embosomed among steep heathy hills, which sunk suddenly down on the verge of the water, lay

82

one of those small fresh-water lakes which are common in the Zetland isles, whose outlets form the sources of the small brooks and rivulets by which the country is watered, and serve to drive the little mills which manufacture their grain.

It was a mild summer day ; the beams of the sun, as is not uncommon in Zetland, were moderated and shaded by a silvery haze, which filled the atmosphere, and, destroying the strong contrast of light and shade, gave even to noon the sober livery of the evening twilight. The little lake, not three-quarters of a mile in circuit, lay in profound quiet ; its surface undimpled, save when one of the numerous waterfowl, which glided on its surface, dived for an instant under it. The depth of the water gave the whole that cerulean tint of bluish green, which occasioned its being called the Green Loch ; and at present, it formed so perfect a mirror to the bleak hills by which it was surrounded, and which lay reflected in its bosom, that it was difficult to distinguish the water from the land ; nay, in the shadowy uncertainty occasioned by the thin haze, a stranger could scarce have been sensible that a sheet of water lay before him. A scene of more complete solitude, having all its peculiarities heightened by the extreme serenity of the weather, the quiet grey composed tone of the atmosphere, and the perfect silence of the elements, could hardly be imagined. The very aquatic birds, who frequented the spot in great numbers, forbore their usual flight and screams, and floated in profound tranquillity upon the silent water.

Without taking any determined aim—without having any determined purpose—almost without thinking what he was about, Mordaunt presented his fowling-piece, and fired across the lake. The large swan-shot dimpled its surface like a partial shower of hail—the hills took up the noise of the report, and repeated it again, and again, and again, to all their echoes ; the water-fowl took to wing in eddying and confused wheel, answering the echoes with a thousand varying screams, from the deep note of the swabie, or swartback, to the querulous cry of the tirracke and kittiewake.

Mordaunt looked for a moment on the clamorous crowd with a feeling of resentment, which he felt disposed at the moment to apply to all nature, and all her objects, animate or inanimate, however little concerned with the cause of his internal mortification.

"Ay, ay," he said, "wheel, dive, scream, and clamour as you will, and all because you have seen a strange sight, and heard an unusual sound. There is many a one like you in this round world. But you, at least, shall learn," he added, as he reloaded his gun, "that strange sights and strange sounds, ay, and strange acquaintances to boot, have sometimes a little shade of danger connected with them.—But why should I wreak my own vexation on these harmless sea-gulls ?" he subjoined, after a moment's pause ; "they have nothing to do with the friends that have forgotten me.—I loved them all so well—and to be so soon given up for the first stranger whom chance threw on the coast !"

As he stood resting upon his gun, and abandoning his mind to the course of these unpleasant reflections, his meditations were unexpectedly interrupted by someone touching his shoulder. He looked around, and saw Norna of Fitful Head, wrapped in her dark and ample mantle. She had seen him from the brow of the hill, and had descended to the lake, through a small ravine which concealed her, until she came with noiseless step so close to him that he turned round at her touch.

Mordaunt Mertoun was by nature neither timorous nor credulous, and a course of reading more extensive than usual had, in some degree, fortified his mind against the attacks of superstition ; but he would have been an actual prodigy, if, living in Zetland in the end of the seventeenth century, he had possessed the philosophy which did not exist in Scotland generally until at least two generations later. He doubted in his own mind the extent, nay, the very existence, of Norna's supernatural attributes, which was a high flight of incredulity in the country where they were universally received ; but still his incredulity went no farther than doubts. She was unquestionably an extraordinary woman, gifted with an energy above others, acting upon motives peculiar to herself, and apparently independent of mere earthly considerations. Impressed with these ideas, which he had imbibed from his youth, it was not without something like alarm that he beheld this mysterious female standing on a sudden so close beside him, and looking upon him with such sad and severe eyes, as those with which the Fatal Virgins, who, according to northern mythology, were called the *Valkyriur,* or "Choosers of the Slain," were supposed to regard the young champions whom they selected to share the banquet of Odin.

It was, indeed, reckoned unlucky, to say the least, to meet with Norna suddenly alone, and in a place remote from witnesses ; and she was supposed, on such occasions, to have been usually a prophetess of evil, as well as an omen of misfortune, to those who had such a rencontre. There were few or none of the islanders, however familiarised with her occasional appearance in society, that would not have trembled to meet her on the solitary banks of the Green Loch.

"I bring you no evil, Mordaunt Mertoun," she said, reading perhaps something of this superstitious feeling in the looks of the young man. "Evil from me you never felt, and never will."

"Nor do I fear any," said Mordaunt, exerting himself to throw aside an apprehension which he felt to be unmanly. "Why should I, mother ? You have been ever my friend."

"Yet, Mordaunt, thou art not of our region ; but to none of Zetland blood, no, not even to those who sit around the hearthstone of Magnus Troil, the noble descendants of the ancient Yarls of Orkney, am I more a well-wisher, than I am to thee, thou kind and brave-hearted boy. When I hung around thy neck that gifted chain, which all in our isles know was wrought by no earthly artist, but by the Drows,* in the secret recesses of their caverns, thou wert then but fifteen years old ; yet thy foot had been on the Maiden-skerrie of Northmaven, known before but to the webbed sole of the swartback, and thy skiff had been in the deepest cavern of Brinnastir, where the *haaf-fish* † had before slumbered in dark obscurity.

* Note H. The Drows.
† The larger seal, or sea-calf, which seeks the most solitary recesses for its abode. See Dr. Edmonston's *Zetland*, vol. ii. p. 294.

Therefore I gave thee that noble gift ; and well thou knowest, that since that day, every eye in these isles has looked on thee as a son, or as a brother, endowed beyond other youths, and the favoured of those whose hour of power is when the night meets with the day."

"Alas ! mother," said Mordaunt, "your kind gift may have given me favour, but it has not been able to keep it for me, or I have not been able to keep it for myself.—What matters it ? I shall learn to set as little by others as they do by me. My father says that I shall soon leave these islands, and therefore, Mother Norna, I will return to you your fairy gift, that it may bring more lasting luck to some other than it has done to me."

"Despise not the gift of the nameless race," said Norna, frowning ; then suddenly changing her tone of displeasure to that of mournful solemnity, she added,—"Despise them not, but O Mordaunt, court them not ! Sit down on that grey stone—thou art the son of my adoption, and I will doff, as far as I may, those attributes that sever me from the common mass of humanity, and speak with you as a parent with a child."

There was a tremulous tone of grief which mingled with the loftiness of her language and carriage, and was calculated to excite sympathy, as well as to attract attention. Mordaunt sat down on the rock which she pointed out, a fragment which, with many others that lay scattered around, had been torn by some winter storm from the precipice at the foot of which it lay, upon the very verge of the water. Norna took her own seat on a stone at about three feet distance, adjusted her mantle so that little more than her forehead, her eyes, and a single lock of her grey hair, were seen from beneath the shade of her dark wadmaal cloak, and then proceeded in a tone in which the imaginary consequence and importance so often assumed by lunacy, seemed to contend against the deep workings of some extraordinary and deeply-rooted mental affliction.

"I was not always," she said, "that which I now am. I was not always the wise, the powerful, the commanding, before whom the young stand abashed, and the old uncover their grey heads. There was a time when my appearance did not silence mirth, when I sympathised with human passion, and had my own share in human joy or sorrow. It was a time of helplessness—it was a time of folly—it was a time of idle and unfruitful laughter—it was a time of causeless and senseless tears ;—and yet, with its follies, and its sorrows, and its weaknesses, what would Norna of Fitful Head give to be again the unmarked and happy maiden that she was in her early days ! Hear me, Mordaunt, and bear with me ; for you heard me utter complaints which have never sounded in mortal ears, and which in mortal ears shall never sound again. I will be what I ought," she continued, starting up and extending her lean and withered arm, "the queen and protectress of these wild and neglected isles,—I will be her whose foot the wave wets not, save by her permission ; ay, even though its rage be at its wildest madness—whose robe the whirlwind respects, when it rends the house-rigging from the roof-tree. Bear me witness, Mordaunt Mertoun,—you heard my words at Harfra—you saw the tempest sink before them—Speak, bear me witness !"

To have contradicted her in this strain of high-toned enthusiasm, would have been cruel and unavailing, even had Mordaunt been more decidedly convinced than he was, that an insane woman, not one of supernatural power, stood before him.

"I heard you sing," he replied, "and I saw the tempest abate."

"Abate !" exclaimed Norna, striking the ground impatiently with her staff of black oak ; "thou speakest it but half—it sunk at once—sunk in shorted space than the child that is hushed to silence by the nurse.— Enough, you know my power—but you know not—mortal man knows not, and never shall know — the price which I paid to attain it. No, Mordaunt, never for the widest sway that the ancient Norsemen boasted, when their banners waved victorious from Bergen to Palestine—never, for all that the round world contains, do thou barter thy peace of mind for such greatness as Norna's." She resumed her seat upon the rock, drew the mantle over her face, rested her head upon her hands, and by the convulsive motion which agitated her bosom, appeared to be weeping bitterly.

"Good Norna," said Mordaunt, and paused, scarce knowing what to say that might console the unhappy woman—"Good Norna," he again resumed, "if there be aught in your mind that troubles it, were you not best to go to the worthy minister at Dunrossness ? Men say you have not for many years been in a Christian congregation—that cannot be well, or right. You are yourself well known as a healer of bodily disease ; but when the mind is sick, we should draw to the Physician of our souls."

Norna had raised her person slowly from the stooping posture in which she sat ; but at length she started up on her feet, threw back her mantle, extended her arm, and while her lip foamed, and her eye sparkled, exclaimed in a tone resembling a scream,—"Me did you speak— me did you bid seek out a priest !—Would you kill the good man with horror ?—Me in a Christian congregation !—Would you have the roof to fall on the sackless assembly, and mingle their blood with their worship ! I—I seek to the good Physician !—Would you have the fiend claim his prey openly before God and man ?"

The extreme agitation of the unhappy speaker naturally led Mordaunt to the conclusion, which was generally adopted and accredited in that superstitious country and period. "Wretched woman," he said, "if indeed thou hast leagued thyself with the Powers of Evil, why should you not seek even yet for repentance ? But do as thou wilt, I cannot, dare not, as a Christian abide longer with you ; and take again your gift," he said, offering back the chain, "good can never come of it, if indeed evil hath not come already."

"Be still and hear me, thou foolish boy," said Norna, calmly, as if she had been restored to reason by the alarm and horror which she perceived in Mordaunt's countenance ; "hear me, I say. I am not of those who have leagued themselves with the Enemy of Mankind, or derive skill or power from his ministry. And although the unearthly powers *were* propitiated by a sacrifice which human tongue can never utter, yet, God knows, my guilt in that offering was no more than that of the blind man who falls from the precipice which he could neither see nor shun. Oh, leave me not—shun me not—in this hour of weakness ! Remain with

86

me till the temptation be passed, or I will plunge myself into that lake, and rid myself at once of my power and my wretchedness !"

Mordaunt, who had always looked up to this singular woman with a sort of affection, occasioned no doubt by the early kindness and distinction which she had shown to him, was readily induced to resume his seat, and listen to what she had farther to say, in hopes that she would gradually overcome the violence of her agitation. It was not long ere she seemed to have gained the victory her companion expected, for she addressed him in her usual steady and authoritative manner.

"It was not of myself, Mordaunt, that I proposed to speak, when I beheld you from the summit of yonder grey rock, and came down the path to meet with you. My fortunes are fixed beyond change, be it for weal or for woe. For myself I have ceased to feel much ; but for those whom she loves, Norna of the Fitful Head has still those feelings which link her to her kind. Mark me. There is an eagle, the noblest that builds in these airy precipices, and into that eagle's nest there has crept an adder—wilt thou lend thy aid to crush the reptile, and to save the noble brood of the lord of the north sky ?"

"You must speak more plainly, Norna," said Mordaunt, "if you would have me understand or answer you. I am no guesser of riddles."

"In plain language, then, you know well the family of Burgh Westra—the lovely daughters of the generous old Udaller, Magnus Troil,—Minna and Brenda, I mean ! You know them, and you love them !"

"I have known them, mother," replied Mordaunt, "and I have loved them—none knows it better than yourself."

"To know them once," said Norna, emphatically, "is to know them always. To love them once, is to love them for ever."

"To have loved them once is to wish them well for ever," replied the youth ; "but it is nothing more. To be plain with you, Norna, the family at Burgh Westra have of late totally neglected me. But show me the means of serving them, I will convince you how much I have remembered old kindness, how little I resent late coldness."

"It is well spoken, and I will put your purpose to the proof," replied Norna. "Magnus Troil has taken a serpent into his bosom—his lovely daughters are delivered up to the machinations of a villain."

"You mean the stranger, Cleveland ?" said Mordaunt.

"The stranger who so calls himself," replied Norna—"the same whom we found flung ashore, like a waste heap of seaweed, at the foot of the Sumburgh Cape. I felt that within me, that would have prompted me to let him lie till the tide floated him off, as it had floated him on shore. I repent me I gave not way to it."

"But," said Mordaunt, "I cannot repent that I did my duty as a Christian man. And what right have I to wish otherwise ? If Minna, Brenda, Magnus, and the rest, like the stranger better than me, I have no title to be offended ; nay, I might well be laughed at for bringing myself into comparison."

"It is well, and I trust they merit thy unselfish friendship."

"But I cannot perceive," said Mordaunt, "in what you can propose that I should serve them. I have but just learned by Bryce the yagger, that this Captain Cleveland is all in all with the ladies at Burgh Westra, and with the Udaller himself. I would like ill to intrude myself where I am not welcome, or to place my home-bred merit in comparison with Captain Cleveland's. He can tell them of battles, when I can only speak of birds' nests—can speak of shooting Frenchmen, when I can only tell of shooting seals—he wears gay clothes, and bears a brave countenance ; I am plainly dressed, and plainly nurtured. Such gay gallants as he can noose the hearts of those he lives with, as the fowler nooses the guillemot with his rod and line."

"You do wrong to yourself," replied Norna, "wrong to yourself, and greater wrong to Minna and Brenda. And trust not the reports of Bryce— he is like the greedy chaffer-whale, that will change his course and dive for the most petty coin which a fisher can cast at him. Certain it is, that if you have been lessened in the opinion of Magnus Troil, that sordid fellow hath had some share in it. But let him count his vantage, for my eye is upon him."

"And why, mother," said Mordaunt, "do you not tell to Magnus what you have told to me ?"

"Because," replied Norna, "they who wax wise in their own conceit must be taught a bitter lesson by experience. It was but yesterday that I spoke with Magnus, and what was his reply ?—'Good Norna, you grow old.' And this was spoken by one bounden to me by so many and such close ties—by the descendant of the ancient Norse earls—this was from Magnus Troil to me ; and it was said in behalf of one, whom the sea flung forth as wreck-weed ! Since he despises the counsel of the aged, he shall be taught by that of the young ; and well that he is not left to his own folly. Go, therefore, to Burgh Westra, as usual upon the Baptist's festival."

"I have had no invitation," said Mordaunt ; "I am not wanted, not wished for, not thought of—perhaps I shall not be acknowledged if I go thither ; and yet, mother, to confess the truth, thither I had thought to go."

"It was a good thought, and to be cherished," replied Norna ; "we seek our friends when they are sick in health, why not when they are sick in mind, and surfeited with prosperity ? Do not fail to go—it may be, we shall meet there. Meanwhile our roads lie different. Farewell, and speak not of this meeting."

They parted, and Mordaunt remained standing by the lake, with his eyes fixed on Norna, until her tall dark form became invisible among the windings of the valley down which she wandered, and Mordaunt returned to his father's mansion, determined to follow counsel which coincided so well with his own wishes.

CHAPTER ELEVENTH

—All your ancient customs,
And long-descended usages, I'll change.
Ye shall not eat, nor drink, nor speak, nor move,
Think, look, or walk, as ye were wont to do.
Even your marriage-beds shall know mutation ;
The bride shall have the stock, the groom the wall
For all old practice will I turn and change,
And call it reformation—marry, will I !
'TIS EVEN THAT WE'RE AT ODDS

THE festal day approached, and still no invitation arrived for that guest,
without whom, but a little space since, no feast could have been held in
the island ; while on the other hand, such reports as reached them on
every side spoke highly of the favour which Captain Cleveland enjoyed
in the family of the old Udaller of Burgh Westra. Swertha and the old
Ranzelman shook their heads at these mutations, and reminded
Mordaunt, by many a half-hint and innuendo, that he had incurred this
eclipse by being so imprudently active to secure the safety of the
stranger, when he lay at the mercy of the next wave beneath the cliffs of
Sumburgh Head. "It is best to let saut water take its gate," said Swertha ;
"luck never came of crossing it."

"In troth," said the Ranzelman, "they are wise folks that let wave and
withy haud their ain—luck never came of a half-drowned man, or a half-
hanged ane either. Who was't shot Will Paterson off the Noss !*—the
Dutchman that he saved from sinking, I trow. To fling a drowning man a
plank or a tow, may be the part of a Christian ; but I say, keep hands aff
him, if ye wad live and thrive free frae his danger."

"Ye are a wise man, Ranzelman, and a worthy," echoed Swertha, with
a groan, "and ken how and whan to help a neighbour, as weel as ony
man that ever drew a net."

"In troth, I have seen length of days," answered the Ranzelman, "and
I have heard what the auld folk said to each other anent sic matters ; and
nae man in Zetland shall go farther than I will in any Christian service to
a man on firm land ; but if he cry 'Help !' out of the saut waves, that's
another story."

"And yet to think of this lad Cleveland standing in our Maister
Mordaunt's light," said Swertha, "and with Magnus Troil, that thought
him the flower of the island but on Whitsunday last, and Magnus, too,
that's both held (when he's fresh, honest man) the wisest and wealthiest
of Zetland !"

* [This is an immensely high cape, called by the islanders the Noup of Noss, but by
sailors Hang Cliff, from its having a projecting appearance. Its height has never been
measured : but I should judge it exceeds 600 feet. Our steersman, however, had often
descended this precipitous rock, having only the occasional assistance of a rope, one end
of which he secured from time to time round some projecting cliff."—From the Author's
Lighthouse Diary.]

89

"He canna win by it," said the Ranzelman, with a look of the deepest sagacity. "There's whiles, Swertha, that the wisest of us (as I am sure I humbly confess mysell not to be) may be little better than gulls, and can no more win by doing deeds of folly than I can step over Sumburgh Head. It has been my own case once or twice in my life. But we shall see soon what ill is to come of all this, for good there cannot come."

And Swertha answered, with the same tone of prophetic wisdom, "Na, na, gude can never come on it, and that is ower truly said."

These doleful predictions, repeated from time to time, had some effect upon Mordaunt. He did not indeed suppose, that the charitable action of relieving a drowning man had subjected him, as a necessary and fatal consequence, to the unpleasant circumstances in which he was placed ; yet he felt as if a sort of spell were drawn around him, of which he neither understood the nature nor the extent ;–that some power, in short, beyond his own control, was acting upon his destiny, and, as it seemed, with no friendly influence. His curiosity, as well as his anxiety, was highly excited, and he continued determined, at all events, to make his appearance at the approaching festival, when he was impressed with the belief that something uncommon was necessarily to take place, which should determine his future views and prospects in life.

As the elder Mertoun was at this time in his ordinary state of health, it became necessary that his son should intimate to him his intended visit to Burgh Westra. He did so ; and his father desired to know the especial reason of his going thither at this particular time.

"It is a time of merry-making," replied the youth, "and all the country are assembled."

"And you are doubtless impatient to add another fool to the number.–Go–but beware how you walk in the path which you are about to tread– a fall from the cliffs of Foula were not more fatal."

"May I ask the reason of your caution, sir ?" replied Mordaunt, breaking through the reserve which ordinarily subsisted betwixt him and his singular parent.

"Magnus Troil," said the elder Mertoun, "has two daughters–you are of the age when men look upon such gauds with eyes of affection, that they may afterwards learn to curse the day that first opened their eyes upon heaven ! I bid you beware of them ; for, as sure as that death and sin came into the world by woman, so sure are their soft words, and softer looks, the utter destruction and ruin of all who put faith in them."

Mordaunt had sometimes observed his father's marked dislike to the female sex, but had never before heard him give vent to it in terms so determined and precise. He replied, that the daughters of Magnus Troil were no more to him than any other females in the islands ; "they were even of less importance," he said, "for they had broken off their friendship with him without assigning any cause."

"And you go to seek the renewal of it ?" answered the father. "Silly moth, that hast once escaped the taper without singeing thy wings, are you not contented with the safe obscurity of these wilds, but must hasten back to the flame, which is sure at length to consume thee ? But why should I waste arguments in deterring thee from thy inevitable fate ?—Go where thy destiny calls thee."

On the succeeding day, which was the eve of the great festival, Mordaunt set forth on his road to Burgh Westra, pondering alternately on the injunctions of Norna—on the ominous words of his father—on the inauspicious auguries of Swertha and the Ranzelman of Yarlshof—and not without experiencing that gloom with which so many concurring circumstances of ill omen combined to oppress his mind.

"It bodes me but a cold reception at Burgh Westra," said he ; "but my stay shall be the shorter. I will but find out whether they have been deceived by this seafaring stranger, or whether they have acted out of pure caprice of temper, and love of change of company. If the first be the case, I will vindicate my character, and let Captain Cleveland look to himself ;—if the latter, why, then, good-night to Burgh Westra and all its inmates."

As he mentally meditated this last alternative, hurt pride, and a return of fondness for those to whom he supposed he was bidding farewell for ever, brought a tear into his eye, which he dashed off hastily and indignantly, as, mending his pace, he continued on his journey.

The weather being now serene and undisturbed, Mordaunt made his way with an ease that formed a striking contrast to the difficulties which he had encountered when he last travelled the same route ; yet there was a less pleasing subject for comparison within his own mind.

"My breast," he said to himself, "was then against the wind, but my heart within was serene and happy. I would I had now the same careless feelings, were they to be bought by battling with the severest storm that ever blew across these lonely hills !"

With such thoughts, he arrived about noon at Harfra, the habitation, as the reader may remember, of the ingenious Mr. Yellowley. Our traveller had, upon the present occasion, taken care to be quite independent of the niggardly hospitality of this mansion, which was now become infamous on that account through the whole island, by bringing with him, in his small knapsack, such provisions as might have sufficed for a longer journey. In courtesy, however, or rather, perhaps, to get rid of his own disquieting thoughts, Mordaunt did not fail to call at the mansion, which he found in singular commotion. Triptolemus himself, invested with a pair or large jack-boots, went clattering up and down stairs, screaming out questions to his sister and his serving-woman Tronda, who replied with shriller and more complicated screeches. At length, Mrs. Baby herself made her appearance, her venerable person endued with what was then called a Joseph, an ample garment, which had once been green, but now, betwixt stains and patches, had become like the vesture of the patriarch whose name it bore—a garment of divers colours. A steeple-crowned hat, the purchase of some long-past moment, in which vanity had got the better of avarice, with a feather which had stood as much wind and rain as if it had been part of a sea-mew's wing, made up her equipment, save that in her hand she held a silver-mounted whip of antique fashion. This attire, as well as an air of determined bustle in the gait and appearance of Mrs. Barbara Yellowley, seemed to bespeak that she was prepared to take a journey, and cared not, as the saying goes, who knew that such was her determination.

She was the first that observed Mordaunt on his arrival, and she greeted him with a degree of mingled emotion. "Be good to us !" she exclaimed, "if there is not the canty callant that wears yon thing about his neck, and that snapped up our goose as light as if it had been a sandie-lavrock !" The admiration of the gold chain, which had formerly made so deep an impression on her mind, was marked in the first part of her speech, the recollection of the untimely fate of the smoked goose was commemorated in the second clause. "I will lay the burden of my life," she instantly added, "that he is ganging our gate."

"I am bound for Burgh Westra, Mrs. Yellowley," said Mordaunt.

"And blithe will we be of your company," she added—"it's early day to eat ; but if you liked a barley scone and a drink of bland—nathless, it is ill travelling on a full stomach, besides quelling your appetite for the feast that is biding you this day ; for all sort of prodigality there will doubtless be."

Mordaunt produced his own stores, and, explaining that he did not love to be burdensome to them on this second occasion, invited them to partake of the provisions he had to offer. Poor Triptolemus, who seldom saw half so good a dinner as his guest's luncheon, threw himself upon the good cheer, like Sancho on the scum of Camacho's kettle, and even the lady herself could not resist the temptation, though she gave way to it with more moderation, and with something like a sense of shame. "She had let the fire out," she said, "for it was a pity wasting fuel in so cold a country, and so she had not thought of getting anything ready, as they were to set out so soon ; and so she could not but say, that the young gentleman's *nacket* looked very good ; and besides, she had some curiosity to see whether the folks in that country cured their beef in the same way they did in the north of Scotland." Under which combined considerations, Dame Baby made a hearty experiment on the refreshments which thus unexpectedly presented themselves.

When their extemporary repast was finished, the factor became solicitous to take the road ; and now Mordaunt discovered that the alacrity with which he had been received by Mistress Baby was not altogether disinterested. Neither she nor the learned Triptolemus felt much disposed to commit themselves to the wilds of Zetland, without the assistance of a guide ; and although they could have commanded the assistance of one of their own labouring folks, yet the cautious agriculturist observed that it would be losing at least one day's work ; and his sister multiplied his apprehensions by echoing back, "One day's work—ye may weel say twenty—for, set ane of their noses within the smell of a kail-pot, and their lugs within the sound of a fiddle, and whistle them back if you can !"

Now the fortunate arrival of Mordaunt, in the very nick of time, not to mention the good cheer which be brought with him, made him as welcome as any one could possibly be to a threshold, which on all ordinary occasions abhorred the passage of a guest ; nor was Mr. Yellowley altogether insensible of the pleasure he promised himself in detailing his plans of improvement to his young companion, and enjoying, what his fate seldom assigned him—the company of a patient and admiring listener.

As the factor and his sister were to prosecute their journey on horseback, it only remained to mount their guide and companion ; a thing easily accomplished, where there are such number of shaggy, long-backed, short-legged ponies, running wild upon the extensive moors, which are the common pasturage for the cattle of every township, where shelties, geese, swine, goats, sheep, and little Zetland cows, are turned out promiscuously, and often in numbers which can obtain but precarious subsistence from the niggard vegetation. There is, indeed, a right of individual property in all these animals, which are branded or tattooed by each owner with his own peculiar mark ; but when any passenger has occasional use for a pony, he never scruples to lay hold of the first which he can catch, puts on a halter, and, having rode him as far as he finds convenient, turns the animal loose to find his way back again as he best can—a matter in which the ponies are sufficiently sagacious.

Although this general exercise of property was one of the enormities which in due time the factor intended to abolish, yet, like a wise man, he scrupled not, in the meantime, to avail himself of so general a practice, which, he condescended to allow, was particularly convenient for those who (as chanced to be his own present case) had no ponies of their own on which their neighbours could retaliate. Three shelties, therefore, were procured from the hill—little shagged animals, more resembling wild bears than anything of the horse tribe, yet possessed of no small degree of strength and spirit, and able to endure as much fatigue and indifferent usage as any creatures in the world.

Two of these horses were already provided and fully accoutred for the journey. One of them, destined to bear the fair person of Mistress Baby, was decorated with a huge side-saddle of venerable antiquity—a mass, as it were, of cushion and padding, from which depended, on all sides, a housing of ancient tapestry, which having been originally intended for a horse of ordinary size, covered up the diminutive palfrey over which it was spread, from the ears to the tail, and from the shoulder to the fetlock, leaving nothing visible but its head, which looked fiercely out from these enfoldments, like the heraldic representation of a lion looking out of a bush. Mordaunt gallantly lifted up the fair Mistress Yellowley, and, at the expense of very slight exertion, placed her upon the summit of her mountainous saddle. It is probable, that, on feeling herself thus squired and attended upon, and experiencing the long unwonted consciousness that she was attired in her best array, some thoughts dawned upon Mistress Baby's mind, which checkered for an instant those habitual ideas about thrift, that formed the daily and all-engrossing occupation of her soul. She glanced her eye upon her faded Joseph, and on the long housings of her saddle, as she observed, with a smile, to Mordaunt, that "travelling was a pleasant thing in fine weather and agreeable company, if," she added, glancing a look at a place where the embroidery was somewhat frayed and tattered, "it was not sae wasteful to ane's horse-furniture."

93

Meanwhile, her brother stepped stoutly to his steed ; and as he chose, notwithstanding the serenity of the weather, to throw a long red cloak over his other garments, his pony was even more completely enveloped in drapery than that of his sister. It happened, moreover, to be an animal of a high and contumacious spirit, bouncing and curvetting occasionally under the weight of Triptolemus, with a vivacity which, notwithstanding his Yorkshire descent, rather deranged him in the saddle ; gambols which, as the palfrey itself was not visible, except upon the strictest inspection, had, at a little distance, an effect as if they were the voluntary movements of the cloaked cavalier, without the assistance of any other legs than those with which nature had provided him ; and, to any who had viewed Triptolemus under such a persuasion, the gravity, and even distress, announced in his countenance, must have made a ridiculous contrast to the vivacious caprioles with which he piaffed along the moor.

Mordaunt kept up with this worthy couple, mounted, according to the simplicity of the time and country, on the first and readiest pony which they had been able to press into the service, with no other accoutrement of any kind than the halter which served to guide him ; while Mr. Yellowley, seeing with pleasure his guide thus readily provided with a steed, privately resolved that this rude custom of helping travellers to horses, without leave of the proprietor, should not be abated in Zetland, until he came to possess a herd of ponies belonging in property to himself, and exposed to suffer in the way of retaliation.

But to other uses or abuses of the country, Triptolemus Yellowley showed himself less tolerant. Long and wearisome were the discourses he held with Mordaunt, or (to speak much more correctly) the harangues which he inflicted upon him, concerning the changes which his own advent in these isles was about to occasion. Unskilled as he was in the modern arts by which an estate may be improved to such a high degree that it shall altogether slip through the proprietor's fingers, Triptolemus had at least the zeal, if not the knowledge, of a whole agricultural society in his own person ; nor was he surpassed by any one who has followed him, in that noble spirit which scorns to balance profit against outlay, but holds the glory of effecting a great change on the face of the land to be like virtue, in a great degree its own reward.

No part of the wild and mountainous region over which Mordaunt guided him, but what suggested to his active imagination some scheme of improvement and alteration. He would make a road through yon scarce passable glen, where at present nothing but the sure-footed creatures on which they were mounted could tread with any safety. He would substitute better houses for the skeoes, or sheds built of dry stones, in which the inhabitants cured or manufactured their fish—they should brew good ale instead of bland—they should plant forests where tree never grew, and find mines of treasure where a Danish skilling was accounted a coin of a most respectable denomination. All these mutations, with many others, did the worthy factor resolve upon, speaking at the same time with the utmost confidence of the

94

countenance and assistance which he was to receive from the higher classes, and especially from Magnus Troil.

"I will impart some of my ideas to the poor man," he said, "before we are both many hours older ; and you will mark how grateful he will be to the instructor who brings him knowledge, which is better than wealth."

"I would not have you build too strongly on that," said Mordaunt, by way of caution ; "Magnus Troil's boat is kittle to trim—he likes his own ways, and his country-ways, and you will as soon teach your sheltie to dive like a sealgh, as bring Magnus to take a Scottish fashion in the place of a Norse one—and yet, if he is steady to his old customs, he may perhaps be as changeable as another in his old friendships."

"*Heus, tu inepte !*" said the scholar of Saint Andrews, "steady or unsteady, what can it matter ?—am not I here in point of trust, and in point of power ? and shall a Fowd, by which barbarous appellative this Magnus Troil still calls himself, presume to measure judgment and weigh reasons with me, who represent the full dignity of the Chamberlain of the islands of Orkney and Zetland ?"

"Still," said Mordaunt, "I would advise you not to advance too rashly upon his prejudices. Magnus Troil, from the hour of his birth to this day, never saw a greater man than himself, and it is difficult to bridle an old horse for the first time. Besides, he has at no time in his life been a patient listener to long explanations, so it is possible that he may quarrel with your proposed reformation, before you can convince him of its advantages."

"How mean you, young man ?" said the factor. "Is there one who dwells in these islands, who is so wretchedly blind as not to be sensible of their deplorable defects ? Can a man," he added, rising into the enthusiasm as he spoke, "or a beast, look at that thing there, which they have the impudence to call a corn-mill,* without trembling to think that corn should be intrusted to such a miserable molendinary ? The wretches are obliged to have at least fifty in each parish, each trundling away upon its paltry mill-stone, under the thatch of a roof no bigger than a bee-skep, instead of a noble and seemly baron's mill, of which you would hear the clack through the haill country, and that casts the meal through the mill-eye by forpits at a time !"

"Ay, ay, brother," said his sister, "that's spoken like your wise sell. The mair cost the mair honour—that's your word ever mair. Can it no creep into your wise head, man, that ilka body grinds their ain neivefu' of meal in this country, without plaguing themsells about baron's mills, and thirls, and sucken, and the like trade ? How mony a time have I heard you bell-the-cat with auld Edie Netherstane, the miller at Grindleburn, and wi' his very knave too, about-in-town and out-town multures—lock, gowpen, and knaveship, and a' the lave o't ; and now naething less will serve you than to bring in the very same fashery on a wheen puir bodies, that big ilk ane a mill for themselves, sic as it is ?"

"Dinna tell me of gowpen and knaveship !" exclaimed the indignant agriculturist ; "better pay the half of the grist to the miller, to have the rest

* Note I. Zetland corn-mills.

grund in a Christian manner, than put good grain into a bairn's whirligig. Look at it for a moment, Baby—Bide still, ye cursed imp ! This interjection was applied to his pony, which began to be extremely impatient, while its rider interrupted his journey, to point out all the weak points of the Zetland mill—"Look at it, I say—it's just one degree better than a hand-quern—it has neither wheel nor trindle—neither cog nor happer—Bide still, there's a canny beast—it canna grind a bickerfu' of meal in a quarter of an hour, and that will be mair like a mash for horse than a meltith for man's use—Wherefore—Bide still, I say—wherefore—wherefore—The deil's in the beast, and nae good, I think !"

As he uttered the last words, the shelty, which had pranced and curvetted for some time with much impatience, at length got its head betwixt its legs, and at once canted its rider into the little rivulet, which served to drive the depreciated engine he was surveying ; then emancipating itself from the folds of the cloak, fled back towards its own wilderness, neighing in scorn, and flinging out its heels at every five yards.

Laughing heartily at his disaster, Mordaunt helped the old man to arise ; while his sister sarcastically congratulated him on having fallen rather into the shallows of a Zetland rivulet than the depths of a Scottish mill-pond. Disdaining to reply to this sarcasm, Triptolemus, so soon as he had recovered his legs, shaken his ears, and found that the folds of his cloak had saved him from being much wet in the scanty streamlet, exclaimed aloud, "I will have cussers from Lanarkshire—brood mares from Ayrshire—I will not have one of these cursed abortions left on the islands, to break honest folk's necks—I say, Baby, I will rid the land of them."

"Ye had better wring your ain cloak, Triptolemus," answered Baby.

Mordaunt meanwhile was employed in catching another pony, from a herd which strayed at some distance ; and, having made a halter out of twisted rushes, he seated the dismayed agriculturist in safety upon a more quiet, though less active steed, than that which he had at first bestrode.

But Mr. Yellowley's fall had operated as a considerable sedative upon his spirits, and, for the full space of five miles' travel, he said scarce a word, leaving full course to the melancholy aspirations and lamentations which his sister Baby bestowed on the old bridle, which the pony had carried off in its flight, and which, she observed, after having lasted for eighteen years come Martinmas, might now be considered as a castaway thing. Finding she had thus the field to herself, the old lady launched forth into a lecture upon economy, according to her own idea of that virtue, which seemed to include a system of privations, which, though observed with the sole purpose of saving money, might, if undertaken upon other principles, have ranked high in the history of a religious ascetic.

She was but little interrupted by Mordaunt, who, conscious he was now on the eve of approaching Burgh Westra, employed himself rather in the task of anticipating the nature of the reception he was about to meet with there from two beautiful young women, than with the

W. Collins   W. Richardson

View in Zetland, in the Valley of Tingwall on the road from Scalloway to Lerwick.

A ZETLAND MILL.

Sir G. Kneller   J. Horsbrugh

John Dryden

prosing of an old one, however wisely she might prove that small-beer was more wholesome than strong ale, and that if her brother had bruised his ankle-bone in his tumble, cumfrey and butter was better to bring him round again, than all the doctors' drugs in the world.

But now, the dreary moorlands, over which their path had hitherto lain, were exchanged for a more pleasant prospect, opening on a salt-water lake, or arm of the sea, which ran up far inland, and was surrounded by flat and fertile ground, producing crops better than the experienced eye of Triptolemus Yellowley had as yet witnessed in Zetland. In the midst of this Goshen stood the mansion of Burgh Westra, screened from the north and east by a ridge of healthy hills which lay behind it, and commanding an interesting prospect of the lake and its parent ocean, as well as the islands and more distant mountains. From the mansion itself, as well as from almost every cottage in the adjacent hamlet, arose such a rich cloud of vapoury smoke, as showed that the preparations for the festival were not confined to the principal residence of Magnus himself, but extended through the whole vicinage.

"My certie," said Mrs. Baby Yellowley, "ane wad think the haill town was on fire !" The very hill-side smells of their wastefulness, and a hungry heart wad scarce seek better kitchen* to a barley scone, than just to waft in the reek that's rising out of yon lums."

CHAPTER TWELFTH

— Thou hast described
A hot friend cooling. Ever note, Lucilius,
When love begins to sicken and decay,
It useth an enforced ceremony.
There are no tricks in plain and simple faith.
JULIUS CÆSAR

IF the smell which was wafted from the chimneys of Burgh Westra up to the barren hills by which the mansion was surrounded, could, as Mistress Barbara opined, have refreshed the hungry, the noise which proceeded from thence might have given hearing to the deaf. It was a medley of all sounds, and all connected with jollity and kind welcome. Nor were the sights associated with them less animating.

Troops of friends were seen in the act of arriving—their dispersed ponies flying to the moors in every direction, to recover their own pastures in the best way they could ;—such, as we have already said, being the usual mode of discharging the cavalry which had been levied for a day's service. At a small but commodious harbour, connected with the house and hamlet, those visitors were landing from their boats, who, living in distant islands, and along the coast, had preferred making their journey by sea. Mordaunt and his companions might see each party pausing frequently to greet each other, and strolling on successively to

* What is eaten by way of relish to dry bread is called *kitchen* in Scotland, as cheese, dried fish, or the like relishing morsels.

the house, whose ever open gate received them alternately in such numbers, that it seemed the extent of the mansion, though suited to the opulence and hospitality of the owner, was scarce, on this occasion, sufficient for the guests.

Among the confused sounds of mirth and welcome which arose at the entrance of each new company, Mordaunt thought he could distinguish the loud laugh and hearty salutation of the Sire of the mansion, and began to feel more deeply than before, the anxious doubt, whether that cordial reception, which was distributed so freely to all others, would be on this occasion extended to him. As they came on, they heard the voluntary scrapings and bravura effusions of the gallant fiddlers, who impatiently flung already from their bows those sounds with which they were to animate the evening. The clamour of the cook's assistants, and the loud scolding tones of the cook himself, were also to be heard—sounds of dissonance at any other time, but which, subdued with others, and by certain happy associations, form no disagreeable part of the full chorus which always precedes a rural feast.

Meanwhile, the guests advanced, each full of their own thoughts. Mordaunt's we have already noticed. Baby was wrapt up in the melancholy grief and surprise excited by the positive conviction that so much victuals had been cooked at once as were necessary to feed all the mouths which were clamouring around her—an enormity of expense, which, though she was no way concerned in bearing it, affected her nerves, as the beholding a massacre would touch those of the most indifferent spectator, however well assured of his own personal safety. She sickened, in short, at the sight of so much extravagance, like Abyssinian Bruce, when he saw the luckless minstrels of Gondar hacked to pieces by the order of Ras Michael. As for her brother, they being now arrived where the rude and antique instruments of Zetland agriculture lay scattered in the usual confusion of a Scottish barn-yard, his thoughts were at once engrossed in the deficiencies of the one-stilted plough—of the *twiscar*, with which they dig peats—of the sledges, on which they transport commodities—of all and every thing, in short, in which the usages of the islands differed from those of the mainland of Scotland. The sight of these imperfect instruments stirred the blood of Triptolemus Yellowley, as that of the bold warrior rises at seeing the arms and insignia of the enemy he is about to combat ; and, faithful to his high emprise, he thought less of the hunger which his journey had occasioned, although about to be satisfied by such a dinner as rarely fell to his lot, than upon the task which he had undertaken, of civilising the manners, and improving the cultivation, of Zetland.

"*Jacta est alea,*" he muttered to himself ; "this very day shall prove whether the Zetlanders are worthy of our labours, or whether their minds are as incapable of cultivation as their peat-mosses. Yet let us be cautious, and watch the soft time of speech. I feel, by my own experience, that it were best to let the body, in its present state, take the place of the mind. A mouthful of that same roast-beef, which smells so delicately, will form an apt introduction to my grand plan for improving the breed of stock."

By this time the visitors had reached the low but ample front of Magnus Troil's residence, which seemed of various dates, with large and ill-imagined additions, hastily adapted to the original building, as the increasing estate, or enlarged family, of successive proprietors, appeared to each to demand. Beneath a low, broad, and large porch, supported by two huge carved posts, once the head ornaments of vessels which had found shipwreck upon the coast, stood Magnus himself, intent on the hospitable toil of receiving and welcoming the numerous guests who successively approached. His strong portly figure was well adapted to the dress which he wore—a blue coat of an antique cut, lined with scarlet, and laced and looped with gold down the seams and button-holes, and along the ample cuffs. Strong and masculine features, rendered ruddy and brown by frequent exposure to severe weather—a quantity of most venerable silver hair, which fell in unshorn profusion from under his gold-laced hat, and was carelessly tied with a ribbon behind, expressed at once his advanced age, his hasty, yet well-conditioned temper, and his robust constitution. As our travellers approached him, a shade of displeasure seemed to cross his brow, and to interrupt for an instant the honest and hearty burst of hilarity with which he had been in the act of greeting all prior arrivals. When he approached Triptolemus Yellowley, he drew himself up, so as to mix, as it were, some share of the stately importance of the opulent Udaller with the welcome afforded by the frank and hospitable landlord.

"You are welcome, Mr. Yellowley," was his address to the factor ; "you are welcome to Westra—the wind has blown you on a rough coast, and we that are the natives must be kind to you as we can. This, I believe, is your sister—Mistress Barbara Yellowley, permit me the honour of a neighbourly salute."— And so saying, with a daring and self-devoted courtesy, which would find no equal in our degenerate days, he actually ventured to salute the withered cheek of the spinstress, who relaxed so much of her usual peevishness of expression as to receive the courtesy with something which approached to a smile. He then looked full at Mordaunt Mertoun, and, without offering his hand, said, in a tone somewhat broken by suppressed agitation, "You too are welcome, Master Mordaunt."

"Did I not think so," said Mordaunt, naturally offended by the coldness of his host's manner, "I had not been here—and it is not yet too late to turn back."

"Young man," replied Magnus, "you know better than most, that from these doors no man can turn, without an offence to their owner. I pray you, disturb not my guests by your ill-timed scruples. When Magnus Troil says welcome, all are welcome who are within hearing of his voice, and it is an indifferent loud one.—Walk on, my worthy guests, and let us see what cheer my lasses can make you within doors."

So saying, and taking care to make his manner so general to the whole party, that Mordaunt should not be able to appropriate any particular portion of the welcome to himself, nor yet to complain of being excluded from all share in it, the Udaller ushered the guests into the house, where two large outer rooms, which, on the present occasion, served the purpose of a modern saloon, were already crowded with guests of every description.

The furniture was sufficiently simple, and had a character peculiar to the situation of these stormy islands. Magnus Troil was, indeed, like most of the higher class of Zetland proprietors, a friend to the distressed traveller, whether by sea or land, and had repeatedly exerted his whole authority in protecting the property and persons of shipwrecked mariners ; yet so frequent were wrecks upon that tremendous coast, and so many unappropriated articles were constantly flung ashore, that the interior of the house bore sufficient witness to the ravages of the ocean, and to the exercise of those rights which the lawyers term *Flotsome and Jetsome*. The chairs, which were arranged around the walls, were such as are used in cabins, and many of them were of foreign construction ; the mirrors and cabinets, which were placed against the walls for ornament or convenience, had, it was plain from their form, been constructed for ship-board, and one or two of the latter were of strange and unknown wood. Even the partition which separated the two apartments seemed constructed out of the bulk-heads of some large vessel, clumsily adapted to the service which it at present performed, by the labour of some native joiner. To a stranger, these evident marks and tokens of human misery might, at the first glance, form a contrast with the scene of mirth with which they were now associated ; but the association was so familiar to the natives, that it did not for a moment interrupt the course of their glee.

To the younger part of these revellers the presence of Mordaunt was like a fresh charm of enjoyment. All came around him to marvel at his absence, and all, by their repeated inquiries, plainly showed that they conceived it had been entirely voluntary on his side. The youth felt that this general acceptation relieved his anxiety on one painful point. Whatever prejudice the family of Burgh Westra might have adopted respecting him, it must be of a private nature ; and at least he had not the additional pain of finding that he was depreciated in the eyes of society at large ; and his vindication, when he found opportunity to make one, would not require to be extended beyond the circle of a single family. This was consoling ; though his heart still throbbed with anxiety at the thought of meeting with his estranged, but still beloved friends. Laying the excuse of his absence on his father's state of health, he made his way through the various groups of friends and guests, each of whom seemed willing to detain him as long as possible, and having, by presenting them to one or two families of consequence, got rid of his travelling companions, who at first stuck fast as burs, he reached at length the door of a small apartment, which, opening from one of the large exterior rooms we have mentioned, Minna and Brenda had been permitted to fit up after their own taste, and to call their peculiar property.

Mordaunt had contributed no small share of the invention and mechanical execution in fitting up this favourite apartment, and in disposing its ornaments. It was, indeed, during his last residence at Burgh Westra, as free to this entrance and occupation, as to its proper mistress. But now, so much were times altered, that he remained with his finger on the latch, uncertain whether he should take the freedom to draw it, until Brenda's voice pronounced the words, "Come in, then," in the tone of one who is interrupted by an unwelcome disturber, who is to be heard and despatched with all the speed possible.

At this signal Mertoun entered the fanciful cabinet of the sisters, which by the additions of many ornaments, including some articles of considerable value, had been fitted up for the approaching festival. The daughters of Magnus, at the moment of Mordaunt's entrance, were seated in deep consultation with the stranger Cleveland, and with a little slight-made old man, whose eye retained all the vivacity of spirit, which had supported him under the thousand vicissitudes of a changeful and precarious life, and which, accompanying him in his old age, rendered his grey hairs less awfully reverend perhaps, but not less beloved, than would a more grave and less imaginative expression of countenance and character. There was even a penetrating shrewdness mingled in the look of curiosity, with which, as he stepped for an instant aside, he seemed to watch the meeting of Mordaunt with the two lovely sisters.

The reception the youth met with resembled, in general character, that which he had experienced from Magnus himself ; but the maidens could not so well cover their sense of the change of circumstances under which they met. Both blushed, as, rising, and without extending the hand, far less offering the cheek, as the fashion of the times permitted, and almost exacted, they paid to Mordaunt the salutation due to an ordinary acquaintance. But the blush of the older was one of those transient evidences of flitting emotion, that vanish as fast as the passing thought which excites them. In an instant she stood before the youth calm and cold, returning, with guarded and cautious courtesy, the usual civilities, which, with a faltering voice, Mordaunt endeavoured to present to her. The emotion of Brenda bore, externally at least, a deeper and more agitating character. Her blush extended over every part of her beautiful skin which her dress permitted to be visible, including her slender neck, and the upper region of a finely-formed bosom. Neither did she even attempt to reply to what share of his confused compliment Mordaunt addressed to her in particular, but regarded him with eyes, in which displeasure was evidently mingled with feelings of regret, and recollections of former times. Mordaunt felt, as it were, assured upon the instant, that the regard of Minna was extinguished, but that it might be yet possible to recover that of the milder Brenda ; and such is the waywardness of human fancy, that though he had never hitherto made any distinct difference betwixt these two beautiful and interesting girls, the favour of her, which seemed most absolutely withdrawn, became at the moment the most interesting in his eyes.

He was disturbed in these hasty reflections by Cleveland, who advanced with military frankness, to pay his compliments to his preserver, having only delayed long enough to permit the exchange of the ordinary salutation betwixt the visitor and the ladies of the family. He made his approach with so good a grace, that it was impossible for Mordaunt, although he dated his loss of favour at Burgh Westra from the stranger's appearance on the coast and domestication in the family, to do less than return his advances as courtesy demanded, accept his thanks with an appearance of satisfaction, and hope that his time had passed pleasantly since their last meeting.

Cleveland was about to answer, but he was anticipated by the little old man, formerly noticed, who now thrusting himself forward, and seizing Mordaunt's hand, kissed him on the forehead ; "How passes time at Burgh Westra ? Was it you that asked it, my prince of the cliff and of the scaur ? How should it pass, but with all the wings that beauty and joy can add to help its flight !"

"And wit and song, too, my good old friend," said Mordaunt, half-serious, half-jesting, as he shook the old man cordially by the hand.— "These cannot be wanting, where Claud Halcro comes !"

"Jeer me not, Mordaunt, my good lad," replied the old man ; "when your foot is as slow as mine, your wit frozen, and your song out of tune"—

"How can you belie yourself, my good master ?" answered Mordaunt, who was not unwilling to avail himself of his old friend's peculiarities to introduce something like conversation, break the awkwardness of this singular meeting, and gain time for observation, ere requiring an explanation of the change of conduct which the family seemed to have adopted towards him. "Say not so," he continued. "Time, my old friend, lays his hand lightly on the bard. Have I not heard you say, the poet partakes the immortality of his song ? and surely the great English poet, you used to tell us of, was elder than yourself when he pulled the bow-oar among all the wits of London."

This alluded to a story which was, as the French term it, Halcro's *cheval de bataille*, and any allusion to which was certain at once to place him in the saddle, and to push his hobby-horse into full career.

His laughing eye kindled with a sort of enthusiasm, which the ordinary folk of this world might have called crazed, while he dashed into the subject which he best loved to talk upon. "Alas, alas ! my dear Mordaunt Mertoun, silver is silver, and waxes not dim by use—and pewter is pewter, and grows the longer the duller. It is not for poor Claud Halcro to name himself in the same twelvemonth with the immortal John Dryden. True it is, as I may have told you before, that I have seen that great man, nay, I have been in the Wits' Coffeehouse, as it was then called, and had once a pinch out of his own very snuff-box. I must have told you all how it happened, but here is Captain Cleveland who never heard it.—I lodged, you must know, in Russel Street—I question not but you know Russel Street, Covent Garden, Captain Cleveland ?

"I should know its latitude pretty well, Mr. Halcro," said the Captain, smiling ; "but I believe you mentioned the circumstance yesterday, and besides we have the day's duty in hand—you must play us this song which we are to study."

"It will not serve the turn now," said Halcro ; "we must think of something that will take in our dear Mordaunt, the first voice in the island, whether for a part or solo. I will never be he will touch a string to you, unless Mordaunt Mertoun is to help us out.—What say you, my fairest Night ?—what think you, my sweet Dawn of Day ?" he added, addressing the young women, upon whom, as we have said elsewhere, he had long before bestowed these allegorical names.

"Mr. Mordaunt Mertoun," said Minna, "has come too late to be of our band on this occasion—it is misfortune, but it cannot be helped."

"How ? what ?" said Halcro hastily—"too late—and you have practised together all your lives ? take my word, my bonny lasses, that old tunes are sweetest, and old friends surest. Mr. Cleveland has a fine bass, that must be allowed ; but I would have you trust for the first effect to one of the twenty fine airs you can sing, where Mordaunt's tenor joins so well with your own witchery—here is my lovely Day approves the change in her heart."

"You were never in your life more mistaken, father Halcro," said Brenda, her cheeks again reddening, more with displeasure, it seemed, than with shame.

"Nay, but how is this ?" said the old man, pausing, and looking at them alternately. "What have we got here ?—a cloudy night and a red morning ?—that betokens rough weather.—What means all this, young women ?—where lies the offence ?—In me, I fear ; for the blame is always laid upon the oldest when young folks like you go by the ears."

"The blame is not with you, father Halcro," said Minna, rising and taking her sister by the arm, "if indeed there be blame anywhere."

"I should fear then, Minna," said Mordaunt, endeavouring to soften his tone into one of indifferent pleasantry, "that the newcomer has brought the offence along with him."

"When no offence is taken," replied Minna, with her usual gravity, "it matters not by whom such may have been offered."

"Is it possible, Minna !" exclaimed Mordaunt, "and is it you who speak thus to me !—And you too, Brenda, can you too judge so harshly of me, yet without permitting me one moment of honest and frank explanation ?"

"Those who should know best," answered Brenda, in a low but decisive tone of voice, "have told us their pleasure, and it must be done.— Sister, I think we have stayed too long here, and shall be wanted elsewhere.—Mr. Mertoun will excuse us on so busy a day."

The sisters linked their arms together. Halcro in vain endeavoured to stop them, making, at the same time, a theatrical gesture, and exclaiming,

"Now, Day and Night, but this is wondrous strange !"

Then turned to Mordaunt Mertoun, and added—"The girls are possessed with the spirit of mutability, showing, as our Master Spenser well saith, that

'Among all living creatures, more or lesse
Change still doth reign, and keep the greater sway.'

Captain Cleveland," he continued, "know you anything that has happened to put these two juvenile Graces out of tune ?"

"He will lose his reckoning," answered Cleveland, "that spends time in inquiring why the wind shifts a point, or why a woman changes her mind. Were I Mr. Mordaunt, I would not ask the proud wenches another question on such a subject."

"It is a friendly advice, Captain Cleveland," replied Mordaunt, "and I will not hold it the less so that it has been given unasked. Allow me to inquire if you are yourself as indifferent to the opinion of your female friends, as it seems you would have me to be ?"

"Who, I ?" said the Captain, with an air of frank indifference ; "I never thought upon such a subject. I never saw a woman worth thinking twice about after the anchor was a-peak—on shore it is another thing ; and I will laugh, sing, dance, and make love, if they like it, with twenty girls, were they but half so pretty as those who have left us, and make them heartily welcome to change their course in the sound of a boatswain's whistle. It will be odds but I wear as fast as they can."

A patient is seldom pleased with that sort of consolation which is founded on holding light the malady of which he complains ; and Mordaunt felt disposed to be offended with Captain Cleveland, both for taking notice of his embarrassment, and intruding upon him his own opinion ; and he replied, therefore, somewhat sharply, "that Captain Cleveland's sentiments were only suited to such as had the art to become universal favourites wherever chance happened to throw them, and who could not lose in one place more than their merit was sure to gain for them in another."

This was spoken ironically ; but there was, to confess the truth, a superior knowledge of the world, and a consciousness of external merit at least, about the man, which rendered his interference doubly disagreeable. As Sir Lucius O'Trigger says, there was an air of success about Captain Cleveland which was mighty provoking. Young, handsome, and well assured, his air of nautical bluntness sat naturally and easily upon him, and was perhaps particularly well fitted to the simple manners of the remote country in which he found himself ; and where, even in the best families, a greater degree of refinement might have rendered his conversation rather less acceptable. He was contented, in the present instance, to smile good-humouredly at the obvious discontent of Mordaunt Mertoun, and replied, "You are angry with me, my good friend, but you cannot make me angry with you. The fair hands of all the pretty women I ever saw in my life would never have fished me up out of the Roost of Sumburgh. So, pray, do not quarrel with me ; for here is Mr. Halcro witness that I have struck both jack and topsail, and should you fire a broadside into me, cannot return a single shot."

"Ay, ay," said Halcro, "you must be friends with Captain Cleveland, Mordaunt. Never quarrel with your friend because a woman is whimsical. Why, man, if they kept one humour, how the devil could we make so many songs on them as we do ?" Even old Dryden himself, glorious old John, could have said little about a girl that was always of one mind—as well write verses upon a mill-pond. It is your tides and your roosts, and your currents and eddies, that come and go, and ebb and flow (by Heaven ! I run into rhyme when I so much as think upon them), that smile one day, rage the next, flatter and devour, delight and ruin us, and so forth—it is these that give the real soul of poetry. Did you never hear my Adieu to the Lass of Northmaven—that was poor Bet Stimbister, whom I call Mary for the sound's sake, as I call myself Hacon after my great ancestor Hacon Goldemund, or Haco with the golden mouth, who came to the island with Harold Harfager, and was his chief Scald ?—Well, but where was I ?—Oh ay—poor Bet Stimbister, she (and partly some debt) was the cause of my leaving the isles of Hjaltland (better so called than Shetland, or Zetland even), and taking to the broad world. I have had a tramp of it since that time—I have battled my way through the world, Captain, as a man of mold may, that has a light head, a light purse, and a heart as light as them both—fought my way, and paid my way—that is, either with money or wit—have seen kings changed and deposed, as you would turn a tenant out of a scathold—knew all the wits of the age, and especially the glorious John Dryden—what man in the islands can say as much, barring lying ?—I had a pinch out of his own snuff-box—I will tell you how I came by such promotion."

"But the song, Mr. Halcro," said Captain Cleveland.

"The song ?" answered Halcro, seizing the Captain by the button,—for he was too much accustomed to have his audience escape from him during recitation, not to put in practice all the usual means of prevention,—"The song ? Why I gave a copy of it, with fifteen others, to the immortal John. You shall hear them all, if you will but stand still a moment ; and you too, my dear boy, Mordaunt Mertoun, I have scarce heard a word from your mouth these six months, and now you are running away from me." So saying, he secured him with his other hand.

"Nay, now he has got us both in tow," said the seaman, "there is nothing for it but hearing him out, though he spins as tough a yarn as ever an old man-of-war's-man twisted on the watch at midnight."

"Nay, now, be silent, and let one of us speak at once," said the poet, imperatively ; while Cleveland and Mordaunt, looking at each other with a ludicrous expression of resignation to their fate, waited in submission for the well-known and inevitable tale. "I will tell you all about it," continued Halcro. "I was knocked about the world like other young fellows, doing this, that and t'other, for a livelihood ; for, thank God, I could turn my hand to anything—but loving still the Muses as much as if the ungrateful jades had found me, like so many blockheads, in my own coach-and-six. However, I held out till my cousin, old Lawrence Linkletter, died and left me the bit of an island yonder ; although, by the way, Cultmalindie was as near to him as I was ; but Lawrence loved wit, though he had little of his own. Well, he left me the wee bit island—it is as barren as Parnassus itself. When then ?—I have a penny to spend, a penny to keep in my purse, a penny to give to the poor—ay, and a bed and a bottle for a friend, as you shall know, boys, if you will go back with me when this merriment is over.—But where was I in my story ?"

"Near port, I hope," answered Cleveland ; but Halcro was too determined a narrator to be interrupted by the broadest hint.

"Oh, ay," he resumed, with the self-satisfied air of one who has recovered the thread of a story, "I was in my old lodgings in Russel Street, with old Timothy Thimblethwaite, the Master Fashioner, then the best-known man about town. He made for all the wits, and for the dull boobies of fortune besides, and made the one pay for the other. He never denied a wit credit save in jest, or for the sake of getting a repartee ; and he was in correspondence with all that was worth knowing about town. He had letters from Crowne, and Tate, and Prior, and Tom Brown, and all the famous fellows of the time, with such pellets of wit, that there was no reading them without laughing ready to die, and all ending with craving a farther term for payment."

"I should have thought the tailor would have found that jest rather serious," said Mordaunt.

"Not a bit—not a bit," replied the eulogist ; "Tim Thimblethwaite (he was a Cumberland man by birth) had the soul of a prince—ay, and died with the fortune of one ; for woe betide the custard-gorged alderman that came under Tim's goose after he had got one of those letters—egad, he was sure to pay the kain ! Why, Thimblethwaite was thought to be the original of little Tom Bibber, in glorious John's comedy of the Wild Gallant ; and I know that he has trusted, ay, and lent John money to boot out of his own pocket, at a time when all his fine court friends blew cold enough. He trusted me too, and I have been two months on the score at a time for my upper room. To be sure, I was obliging in his way—not that I exactly could shape or sew, nor would that have been decorous for a gentleman of good descent ; but I—eh, eh—I drew bills—summed up the books"—

"Carried home the clothes of the wits and aldermen, and got lodging for your labour," interrupted Cleveland.

"No, no—damn it, no," replied Halcro ; "no such thing—you put me out in my story—where was I ?"

"Nay, the devil help you to the latitude," said the Captain, extricating his button from the grip of the unmerciful bard's finger and thumb, "for I have no time to take an observation." So saying, he bolted from the room.

"A silly, ill-bred, conceited fool," said Halcro, looking after him ; "with as little manners as wit in his empty coxcomb. I wonder what Magnus and these silly wenches can see in him— he tells such damnable long-winded stories, too, about his adventures and sea-fights—every second word a lie, I doubt not. Mordaunt, my dear boy, take example by that man—that is, take warning by him—never tell long stories about yourself. You are sometimes given to talk too much about your own exploits on crags and skerries, and the like, which only breaks conversation, and prevents other folk from being heard. Now I see you are impatient to hear out what I was saying—Stop, whereabouts was I ?"

"I fear we must put if off, Mr. Halcro, until after dinner," said Mordaunt, who also meditated his escape, though desirous of effecting it with more delicacy towards his old acquaintance than Captain Cleveland had thought it necessary to use.

"Nay, my dear boy," said Halcro, seeing himself about to be utterly deserted, "do not you leave me too—never take so bad an example as to set light by old acquaintance, Mordaunt. I have wandered many a weary step in my day ; but they were always lightened when I could get hold of the arm of an old friend like yourself."

So saying, he quitted the youth's coat, and, sliding his hand gently under his arm, grappled him more effectually ; to which Mordaunt submitted, a little moved by the poet's observation upon the kindness of old acquaintances, under which he himself was an immediate sufferer. But when Halcro renewed his formidable question, "Whereabouts was I ?" Mordaunt, preferring his poetry to his prose, reminded him of the song which he said he had written upon his first leaving Zetland,—a song to which, indeed, the inquirer was no stranger, but which, as it must be new to the reader, we shall here insert as a favourable specimen of the poetical powers of this tuneful descendant of Haco the Golden-mouthed ; for, in the opinion of many tolerable judges, he held a respectable rank among the inditers of madrigals of the period, and was as well qualified to give immortality to his Nancies of the hills or dales, as many a gentle sonnetteer of wit and pleasure about town. He was something of a musician also, and on the present occasion seized upon a sort of lute, and, quitting his victim, prepared the instrument for an accompaniment, speaking all the while that he might lose no time.

"I learned the lute," he said, "from the same man who taught honest Shadwell—plump Tom, as they used to call him—somewhat roughly treated by the glorious John, you remember—Mordaunt, you remember—

> Methinks I see the new Arion sail,
> The lute still trembling underneath thy nail ;
> At thy well-sharpen'd thumb, from shore to shore,
> The trebles squeak for fear, the basses roar.

Come, I am indifferently in tune now—what was it to be ?—ay, I remember—nay, The Lass of Northmaven is the ditty—poor Bet Stimbister ! I have called her Mary in the verses. Betsy does well for an English song ; but Mary is more natural here." So saying, after a short prelude, he sung, with a tolerable voice and some taste, the following verses :—

Mary

Farewell to Northmaven,
  Grey Hillswicke, farewell !
To the calms of thy haven,
  The storms on thy fell—
To each breeze that can vary
  The mood of thy main,
And to thee, bonny Mary !
  We meet not again.

Farewell the wild ferry,
  Which Hacon could brave,
When the peaks of the Skerry
  Were white in the wave.
There's a maid may look over
  These wild waves in vain—
For the skiff of her lover—
  He comes not again.

The vows thou hast broke,
  On the wild currents fling them ;
On the quicksand and rock
  Let the mermaidens sing them.
New sweetness they'll give her
  Bewildering strain ;
But there's one who will never
  Believe them again.

Oh were there an island,
  Though ever so wild,
Where woman could smile, and
  No man be beguiled—
Too tempting a snare
  To poor mortals were given,
And the hope would fix there,
  That should anchor on heaven !

"I see you are softened, my young friend," said Halcro, when he had finished his song ; "so are most who hear that same ditty. Words and music both mine own ; and without saying much of the wit of it, there is a sort of eh–eh–simplicity and truth about it, which gets its way to most folk's heart. Even your father cannot resist it–and he has a heart as impenetrable to poetry and song as Apollo himself could draw an arrow against. But then he has had some ill luck in his time with the women-folk, as is plain from his owing them such a grudge.–Ay, ay, there the charm lies–none of us but has felt the same sore in our day. But come, my dear boy, they are mustering in the hall, men and women both– plagues as they are, we should get on ill without them–but before we go, only mark the last turn–

'And the hope would fix there,'–

that is, in the supposed island–a place which neither was nor will be–

'That should anchor on heaven.'

Now you see, my good young man, there are here none of your heathenish rants, which Rochester, Etheridge, and these wild fellows, used to string together. A parson might sing the song, and his clerk bear the burden–but there is the confounded bell–we must go now–but never mind–we'll get into a quiet corner at night, and I'll tell you all about it."

CHAPTER THIRTEENTH

Full in the midst the polish'd table shines,
And the bright goblets, rich with generous wines ;
Now each partakes the feast, the wine prepares,
Portions the food, and each the portion shares ;
Nor till the rage of thirst and hunger ceased,
To the high host approach'd the sagacious guest.
ODYSSEY

THE hospitable profusion of Magnus Troil's board, the number of guests who feasted in the hall, the much greater number of retainers, attendants, humble friends, and domestics of every possible description, who revelled without, with the multitude of the still poorer and less honoured assistants, who came from every hamlet or township within twenty miles round, to share the bounty of the munificent Udaller, were such as altogether astonished Triptolemus Yellowley, and made him internally doubt whether it would be prudent in him at this time, and amid the full glow of his hospitality, to propose to the host who presided over such a splendid banquet, a radical change in the whole customs and usages of this country.

True, the sagacious Triptolemus felt conscious that he possessed in his own person wisdom far superior to that of all the assembled feasters, to say nothing of the landlord, against whose prudence the very extent of his hospitality formed, in Yellowley's opinion, sufficient evidence. But yet the Amphitryon with whom one dines, holds, for the time at least, an influence over the minds of his most distinguished guests ; and if the dinner be in good style, and the wines of the right quality, it is humbling to see that neither art nor wisdom, scarce external rank itself, can assume their natural and wonted superiority over the distributor of these good things, until coffee has been brought in.

Triptolemus felt the full weight of this temporary superiority, yet he was desirous to do something that might vindicate the vaunts he had made to his sister and his fellow-traveller, and he stole a look at them from time to time, to mark whether he was not sinking in their esteem from postponing his promised lecture on the enormities of Zetland.

But Mrs. Barbara was busily engaged in noting and registering the waste material incurred in such an entertainment as she had probably never before looked upon, and in admiring the host's indifference to, and the guests' absolute negligence of, those rules of civility in which her youth had been brought up. The feasters desired to be helped from a dish which was unbroken, and might have figured at supper, with as much freedom as if it had undergone the ravages of half-a-dozen guests ; and no one seemed to care—the landlord himself least of all—whether those dishes only were consumed, which, from their nature, were incapable of re-appearance, or whether the assault was extended to the substantial rounds of beef, pasties, and so forth, which, by the rules of good housewifery, were destined to stand two attacks, and which, therefore, according to Mrs. Barbara's ideas of politeness, ought not to have been annihilated by the guests upon the first outset, but spared, like Outis in the cave of Polyphemus, to be devoured the last. Lost in the meditations to which these breaches of convivial discipline gave rise, and in the contemplation of an ideal larder of cold meat which she could have saved out of the wreck of roast, boiled, and baked, sufficient to have supplied her cupboard for at least a twelvemonth, Mrs. Barbara cared very little whether or not her brother supported in its extent the character which he had calculated upon assuming.

Mordaunt Mertoun also was conversant with far other thoughts than those which regarded the proposed reformer of Zetland enormities. His seat was betwixt two blithe maidens of Thule, who, not taking scorn that he had upon other occasions given preference to the daughters of the Udaller, were glad of the chance which assigned to them the attentions of so distinguished a gallant, who, as being their squire at the feast, might in all probability become their partner in the subsequent dance. But, whilst rendering to his fair neighbours all the usual attentions which society required, Mordaunt kept up a covert, but accurate and close observation, upon his estranged friends, Minna and Brenda. The Udaller himself had a share of his attention ; but in him he could remark nothing, except the usual tone of hearty and somewhat boisterous hospitality, with which he was accustomed to animate the banquet upon all such occasions of general festivity. But in the differing mien of the two maidens there was much more room for painful remark.

Captain Cleveland sat betwixt the sisters, was sedulous in his attentions to both, and Mordaunt was so placed, that he could observe all, and hear a great deal, of what passed between them. But Cleveland's peculiar regard seemed devoted to the elder sister. Of this the younger was perhaps conscious, for more than once her eye glanced towards Mordaunt, and, as he thought, with something in it which resembled regret for the interruption of their intercourse, and a sad remembrance of former and more friendly times ; while Minna was exclusively engrossed by the attentions of her neighbour ; and that it should be so, filled Mordaunt with surprise and resentment.

Minna, the serious, the prudent, the reserved, whose countenance and manners indicated so much elevation of character—Minna, the lover of solitude, and of those paths of knowledge in which men walk best without company—the enemy of light mirth, the friend of musing melancholy, and the frequenter of fountain-heads and pathless glens— she whose character seemed, in short, the very reverse of that which might be captivated by the bold, coarse, and daring gallantry of such a man as this Captain Cleveland, gave, nevertheless, her eye and ear to him, as he sat beside her at table, with an interest and a graciousness of attention, which, to Mordaunt, who well know how to judge of her feelings by her manner, intimated a degree of the highest favour. He observed this, and his heart rose against the favourite by whom he had been thus superseded, as well as against Minna's indiscreet departure from her own character.

"What is there about the man," he said within himself, "more than the bold and daring assumption of importance which is derived from success in petty enterprises, and the exercise of petty despotism over a ship's crew ?—His very language is more professional than is used by the superior officers of the British navy ; and the wit which has excited so many smiles, seems to me such as Minna would not formerly have endured for an instant. Even Brenda seems less taken with his gallantry than Minna, whom it should have suited so little."

Mordaunt was doubly mistaken in these his angry speculations. In the first place, with an eye which was, in some respects, that of a rival, he criticised far too severely the manners and behaviour of Captain Cleveland. They were unpolished, certainly ; which was of the less consequence in a country inhabited by so plain and simple a race as the ancient Zetlanders. On the other hand, there was an open, naval frankness in Cleveland's bearing—much natural shrewdness—some appropriate humour—an undoubting confidence in himself—and that enterprising hardihood of disposition, which, without any other recommendable quality, very often leads to success with the fair sex. But Mordaunt was farther mistaken, in supposing that Cleveland was likely to be disagreeable to Minna Troil, on account of the opposition of their characters in so many material particulars. Had his knowledge of the world been a little more extensive, he might have observed, that as unions are often formed betwixt couples differing in complexion and stature, they take place more frequently betwixt persons totally differing in feelings, in taste, in pursuits, and in understanding ; and it would not be saying, perhaps, too much, to aver that two-thirds of the marriages around us have been contracted betwixt persons, who, judging *à priori,* we should have thought had scarce any charms for each other.

A moral and primary cause might be easily assigned for these anomalies, in the wise dispensations of Providence, that the general balance of wit, wisdom, and amiable qualities of all kinds, should be kept up through society at large. For, what a world were it, if the wise were to intermarry only with the wise, the learned with the learned, the amiable with the amiable, nay, even the handsome? and, is it not evident, that the degraded castes of the foolish, the ignorant, the brutal, and the deformed (comprehending, by the way, far the greater portion of mankind), must, when condemned to exclusive intercourse with each other, become gradually as much brutalised in person and disposition as so many ourang-outangs? When, therefore, we see the "gentle joined to the rude," we may lament the fate of the suffering individual, but we must not the less admire the mysterious disposition of that wise Providence which thus balances the moral good and evil of life;—which secures for a family, unhappy in the dispositions of one parent, a share of better and sweeter blood, transmitted from the other, and preserves to the offspring the affectionate care and protection of at least one of those from whom it is naturally due. Without the frequent occurrences of such alliances and unions—mis-sorted as they seem at first sight—the world could not be that for which Eternal Wisdom has designed it—a place of mixed good and evil—a place of trial at once, and of suffering, where even the worst ills are checkered with something that renders them tolerable to humble and patient minds, and where the best blessings carry with them a necessary alloy of imbittering depreciation.

When, indeed, we look a little closer on the causes of those unexpected and ill-suited attachments, we have occasion to acknowledge, that the means by which they are produced do not infer that complete departure from, or inconsistency with, the character of the parties, which we might expect when the result alone is contemplated. The wise purposes which Providence appears to have had in view, by permitting such intermixture of dispositions, tempers, and understandings, in the married state, are not accomplished by any mysterious impulse by which, in contradiction to the ordinary laws of nature, men or women are urged to an union with those whom the world see to be unsuitable to them. The freedom of will is permitted to us in the occurrences of ordinary life, as in our moral conduct; and in the former as well as the latter case, is often the means of misguiding those who possess it. Thus it usually happens, more especially to the enthusiastic and imaginative, that, having formed a picture of admiration in their own mind, they too often deceive themselves by some faint resemblance in some existing being, whom their fancy, as speedily as gratuitously, invests with all the attributes necessary to complete the *beau idéal* of mental perfection. No one perhaps, even in the happiest marriage, with an object really beloved, ever discovered by experience all the qualities he expected to possess; but in far too many cases, he finds he has practised a much higher degree of mental deception, and has erected his airy castle of felicity upon some rainbow, which owed its very existence only to the peculiar state of the atmosphere.

Thus, Mordaunt, if better acquainted with life, and with the course of

111

human things, would have been little surprised that such a man as Cleveland, handsome, bold, and animated,—a man who had obviously lived in danger, and who spoke of it as sport, should have been interested, by a girl of Minna's fanciful character, with an extensive share of those qualities, which, in her active imagination, were held to fill up the accomplishments of a heroic character. The plain bluntness of his manner, if remote from courtesy, appeared at least as widely different from deceit ; and, unfashioned as he seemed by forms, he had enough both of natural sense, and natural good-breeding, to support the delusion he had created, at least as far as externals were concerned. It is scarce necessary to add, that these observations apply exclusively to what are called love-matches ; for when either party fix their attachment upon the substantial comforts of a rental, or a jointure, they cannot be disappointed in the acquisition, although they may be cruelly so in their over-estimation of the happiness it was to afford, or in having too slightly anticipated the disadvantages with which it was to be attended.

Having a certain partiality for the dark beauty whom we have described, we have willingly dedicated this digression, in order to account for a line of conduct which we allow to seem absolutely unnatural in such a narrative as the present, though the most common event in ordinary life ; namely, in Minna's appearing to have over-estimated the taste, talent and ability of a handsome young man, who was dedicating to her his whole time and attention, and whose homage rendered her the envy of almost all the other young women of that numerous party. Perhaps, if our fair readers will take the trouble to consult their own bosoms, they will be disposed to allow, that the distinguished good taste exhibited by any individual, who, when his attentions would be agreeable to a whole circle of rivals, selects *one* as their individual object, entitles him, on the footing of reciprocity, if on no other, to a large share of that individual's favourable, and even partial, esteem. At any rate, if the character shall, after all, be deemed inconsistent and unnatural, it concerns not us, who record the facts as we find them, and pretend no privilege for bringing closer to nature those incidents which may seem to diverge from it ; or for reducing to consistence that most inconsistent of all created things,—the heart of a beautiful and admired female.

Necessity, which teaches all the liberal arts, can render us also adept in dissimulation ; and Mordaunt, though a novice, failed not to profit in her school. It was manifest, that, in order to observe the demeanour of those on whom his attention was fixed, he must needs put constraint on his own, and appear, at least, so much engaged with the damsels betwixt whom he sat, that Minna and Brenda should suppose him indifferent to what was passing around him. The ready cheerfulness of Maddie and Clara Groatsetters, who were esteemed considerable fortunes in the island, and were at this moment too happy in feeling themselves seated somewhat beyond the sphere of vigilance influenced by their aunt, the good old Lady Glowrowrum, met and requited the attempts which Mordaunt made to be lively and entertaining ; and they were soon engaged in a gay conversation, to which as usual on such occasions, the gentleman contributed wit, or what passes for such, and the ladies their prompt laughter and liberal applause. But, amidst this seeming mirth, Mordaunt failed not, from time to time, as covertly as he might, to observe the conduct of the two daughters of Magnus ; and still it appeared as if the elder, wrapt up in the conversation of Cleveland, did not cast away a thought on the rest of the company ; and as if Brenda, more openly as she conceived his attention withdrawn from her, looked with an expression both anxious and melancholy towards the group of which he himself formed a part. He was much moved by the diffidence, as well as the trouble, which her looks seemed to convey, and tacitly formed the resolution of seeking a more full explanation with her in the course of the evening. Norna, he remembered, had stated that these two amiable young women were in danger, the nature of which she left unexplained, but which he suspected to arise out of their mistaking the character of this daring and all-engrossing stranger ; and he secretly resolved, that, if possible, he would be the means of detecting Cleveland, and of saving his early friends.

As he revolved these thoughts, his attention to the Miss Groatsetters gradually diminished, and perhaps he might altogether have forgotten the necessity of his appearing an interested spectator of what was passing, had not the signal been given for the ladies retiring from table. Minna, with a native grace, and somewhat of stateliness in her manner, bent her head to the company in general, with a kinder and more particular expression as her eye reached Cleveland. Brenda, with the blush which attended her slightest personal exertion when exposed to the eyes of others, hurried through the same departing salutation with an embarrassment which almost amounted to awkwardness, but which her youth and timidity rendered at once natural and interesting. Again Mordaunt thought that her eye distinguished him amongst the numerous company. For the first time he ventured to encounter and to return the glance ; and the consciousness that he had done so doubled the glow of Brenda's countenance, while something resembling displeasure was blended with her emotion.

When the ladies had retired, the men betook themselves to the deep and serious drinking, which, according to the fashion of the times, preceded the evening exercise of the dance. Old Magnus himself, by precept and example, exhorted them "to make the best use of their time, since the ladies would soon summon them to shake their feet." At the same time giving the signal to a grey-haired domestic, who stood behind him in the dress of a Dantzic skipper, and who added to many other occupations that of butler, "Eric Scambester," he said, "has the good ship the Jolly Mariner of Canton, got her cargo on board ?"

"Chokeful loaded," answered the Ganymede of Burgh Westra, "with good Nantz, Jamaica sugar, Portugal lemons, not to mention nutmeg and toast, and water taken in from the Shellicoat spring."

Loud and long laughed the guests at this stated and regular jest betwixt the Udaller and his butler, which always served as a preface to the introduction of a punch-bowl of enormous size, the gift of the Captain of one of the Honourable East India Company's vessels, which,

113

bound from China homeward, had been driven north-about by stress of weather into Lerwick Bay, and had there contrived to get rid of part of the cargo, without very scrupulously reckoning for the King's duties.

Magnus Troil, having been a large customer, besides otherwise obliging Captain Coolie, had been remunerated, on the departure of the ship, with this splendid vehicle of conviviality, at the very sight of which, as old Eric Scambester bent under its weight, a murmur of applause ran through the company. The good old toasts dedicated to the prosperity of Zetland, were then honoured with flowing bumpers. "Death to the head that never wears hair !" was a sentiment quaffed to the success of the fishing, as proposed by the sonorous voice of the Udaller. Claud Halcro proposed with general applause, "The health of their worthy landmaster, the sweet sister meat-mistresses ; health to man, death to fish, and growth to the produce of the ground." The same recurring sentiment was proposed more concisely by a whiteheaded compeer of Magnus Troil, in the words, "God open the mouth of the grey fish, and keep his hand about the corn !"*

Full opportunity was afforded to all to honour these interesting toasts. Those nearest the capacious Mediterranean of punch, were accommodated by the Udaller with their portions, dispensed in huge rummer glasses by his own hospitable hand, whilst they who sat at a greater distance replenished their cups by means of a rich silver flagon, facetiously called the Pinnace ; which, filled occasionally at the bowl, served to dispense its liquid treasures to the more remote parts of the table, and occasioned many right merry jests on its frequent voyages. The commerce of the Zetlanders with foreign vessels, and homeward-bound West Indiamen, had early served to introduce among them the general use of the generous beverage, with which the Jolly Mariner of Canton was loaded ; nor was there a man in the archipelago of Thule more skilled in combining its rich ingredients, than old Eric Scambester, who indeed was known far and wide through the isles, by the name of the Punch-maker, after the fashion of the ancient Norwegians, who conferred on Rollo the Walker, and other heroes of their strain, epithets expressive of the feats of strength or dexterity in which they excelled all other men.

The good liquor was not slow in performing its office of exhilaration, and, as the revel advanced, some ancient Norse drinking-songs were sung with great effect by the guests, tending to show, that if, from want of exercise, the martial virtues of their ancestors had decayed among the Zetlanders, they could still actively and intensely enjoy so much of the pleasures of Valhalla as consisted in quaffing the oceans of mead and brown ale, which were promised by Odin to those who should share his Scandinavian paradise. At length, excited by the cup and song, the diffident grew bold, and the modest loquacious—all became desirous of talking, and none were willing to listen— each man mounted his own special hobby-horse, and began eagerly to call on his neighbours to witness his agility. Amongst others, the little bard, who had now got next to our friend Mordaunt Mertoun, evinced a positive

* See Hibbert's *Description of the Shetland Islands,* p. 470.

determination to commence and conclude, in all its longitude and latitude, the story of his introduction to glorious John Dryden ; and Triptolemus Yellowley, as his spirits arose, shaking off a feeling of involuntary awe, with which he was impressed by the opulence indicated in all he saw around him, as well as by the respect paid to Magnus Troil by the assembled guests, began to broach, to the astonished and somewhat offended Udaller, some of those projects for ameliorating the islands, which he had boasted of to his fellow-travellers upon their journey of the morning.

But the innovations which he suggested, and the reception which they met at the hand of Magnus Troil, must be told in the next chapter.

CHAPTER FOURTEENTH

We'll keep our customs—what is law itself,
But old establish'd custom ? What religion
(I mean, with one-half of the men that use it),
Save the good use and wont that carries them
To worship how and where their fathers worshipp'd ?
All things resolve in custom—we'll keep ours.
OLD PLAY

WE left the company of Magnus Troil engaged in high wassail and revelry. Mordaunt, who, like his father, shunned the festive cup, did not partake in the cheerfulness which the Ship diffused among the guests as they unloaded it, and the Pinnace, as it circumnavigated the table. But, in low spirits as he seemed, he was the more meet prey for the story-telling Halcro, who had fixed upon him, as in a favourable state to play the part of listener, with something of the same instinct that directs the hooded crow to the sick sheep amongst the flock, which will most patiently suffer itself to be made a prey of. Joyfully did the poet avail himself of the advantages afforded by Mordaunt's absence of mind, and unwillingness to exert himself in measures of active defence. With the unfailing dexterity peculiar to prosers, he contrived to dribble out his tale to double its usual length, by the exercise of the privilege of unlimited digressions ; so that the story, like a horse on the *grand pas*, seemed to be advancing with rapidity, while, in reality, it scarce was progressive at the rate of a yard in the quarter of an hour. At length, however, he had discussed, in all its various bearings and relations, the history of his friendly landlord, the master-fashioner in Russel Street, including a short sketch of five of his relations, and anecdotes of three of his principal rivals, together with some general observations upon the dress and fashion of the period ; and, having marched thus far through the environs and outworks of his story, he arrived at the body of the place, for so the Wits' Coffeehouse might be termed. He paused on the threshold, however, to explain the nature of his landlord's right occasionally to intrude himself into this well-known temple of the Muses.

"It consisted," said Halcro, "in the two principal points, of bearing and forbearing ; for my friend Thimblethwaite was a person of wit himself, and never quarrelled with any jest which the wags who frequented that house were flinging about, like squibs and crackers on a rejoicing night ; and then, though some of the wits—ay, and I daresay the greater number might have had some dealings with him in the way of trade, he never was the person to put any man of genius in unpleasant remembrance of such trifles. And though, my dear young Master Mordaunt, you may think this is but ordinary civility, because in this country it happens seldom that there is either much borrowing or lending, and because, praised be Heaven, there are neither bailiffs nor sheriff-officers to take a poor fellow by the neck, and because there are no prisons to put him into when they have done so, yet, let me tell you, that such a lamb-like forbearance as that of my poor, dear, deceased landlord, Thimblethwaite, is truly uncommon within the London bills of mortality. I could tell you of such things that have happened even to myself, as well as others, with these cursed London tradesmen, as would make your hair stand on end.—But what the devil has put old Magnus into such note ? he shouts as if he were trying his voice against a north-west gale of wind."

Loud indeed was the roar of the old Udaller, as, worn out of patience by the schemes of improvement which the factor was now undauntedly pressing upon his consideration, he answered him (to use an Ossianic phrase), like a wave upon a rock.

"Trees, Sir Factor—talk not to me of trees ! I care not though there never be one on the island, tall enough to hang a coxcomb upon. We will have no trees but those that rise in our havens—the good trees that have yards for boughs, and standing rigging for leaves."

"But touching the draining of the lake of Braebaster, whereof I spoke to you, Master Magnus Troil," answered the persevering agriculturist, "whilk I opine would be of so much consequence, there are two ways,—down the Linklater glen, or by the Scalmester burn. Now, having taken the level of both"—

"There is a third way, Master Yellowley," answered the landlord.

"I profess I can see none," replied Triptolemus, with as much good faith as a joker could desire in the subject of his wit, "in respect that the hill called Braebaster on the south, and ane high bank on the north, of whilk I cannot carry the name rightly in my head"—

"Do not tell us of hills and banks, Master Yellowley—there is a third way of draining the loch, and it is the only way that shall be tried in my day. You say my Lord Chamberlain and I are the joint proprietors—so be it—let each of us start an equal proportion of brandy, lime juice, and sugar, into the loch — a ship's cargo or two will do the job—let us assemble all the jolly Udallers of the country, and in twenty-four hours you shall see dry ground where the loch of Braebaster now is."

A loud laugh of applause, which for a time actually silenced Triptolemus, attended a jest so very well suited to time and place—a jolly toast was given—a merry song was sung—the Ship unloaded her sweets—the Pinnace made its genial rounds—the duet betwixt Magnus and

Triptolemus, which had attracted the attention of the whole company from its superior vehemence, now once more sunk, and merged into the general hum of the convivial table, and the poet Halcro again resumed his usurped possession of the ear of Mordaunt Mertoun.

"Whereabouts was I ?" he said, with a tone which expressed to his weary listener more plainly than words could, how much of his desultory tale yet remained to be told. "Oh, I remember—we were just at the door of the Wits' Coffeehouse—it was set up one by one"—

"Nay, but, my dear Master Halcro," said his hearer, somewhat impatiently, "I am desirous to hear of your meeting with Dryden."

"What, with glorious John ?—true—ay—where was I ? At the Wits' coffeehouse—Well, in at the door we got—the waiters, and so forth, staring at me ; for as to Thimblethwaite, honest fellow, his was a well-known face.—I can tell you a story about that"—

"Nay, but John Dryden," said Mordaunt, in a tone which deprecated father digression.

"Ay, ay, glorious John—where was I ?—Well, as we stood close by the bar, where one fellow sat grinding of coffee, and another putting up tobacco into penny parcels—a pipe and a dish cost just a penny— then and there it was that I had the first peep of him. One Dennis sat near him, who"—

"Nay, but John Dryden—what like was he ?" demanded Mordaunt.

"Like a little fat old man, with his own grey hair, and in a full trimmed black suit, that sat close as a glove. Honest Timblethwaite let no one but himself shape for glorious John, and he had a slashing hand at a sleeve, I promise you—But there is no getting a mouthful of common sense spoken here—d—n that Scotchman, he and old Magnus are at it again !"

It was very true ; and although the interruption did not resemble a thunder-clap, to which the former stentorian exclamation of the Udaller might have been likened, it was a close and clamorous dispute, maintained by question, answer, retort, and repartee, as closely huddled upon each other as the sounds which announce from a distance a close and sustained fire of musketry.

"Hear reason, sir ?" said the Udaller ; "we will hear reason, and speak reason too ; and if reason fall short, we shall have rhyme to boot.—Ha, my little friend Halcro !"

Though cut off in the middle of his best story (if that could be said to have a middle which had neither beginning nor end), the bard bristled up at the summons, like a corps of light infantry, when ordered up to the support of the grenadiers, looked smart, slapped the table with his hand, and denoted his becoming readiness to back his hospitable landlord as becomes a well-entertained guest. Triptolemus was a little daunted at this reinforcement of his adversary ; he paused, like a cautious general, in the sweeping attack which he had commenced on the peculiar usages of Zetland, and spoke not again until the Udaller poked him with the insulting query, "Where is your reason now, Master Yellowley, that you were deafening me with a moment since ?"

"Be but patient, worthy sir," replied the agriculturist ; "what on earth can you or any other man say in defence of that thing you call a plough, in this blinded country ? Why, even the savage Highlandmen, in Caithness and Sunderland, can make more work, and better, with their gascromh, or whatever they call it."

"But what ails you at it, sir ?" said the Udaller ; "let me hear your objections to it. It tills our land, and what would ye more ?"

"It hath but one handle or stilt," replied Triptolemus.

"And who the devil," said the poet, aiming at something smart, "would wish to need a pair of stilts, if he can manage to walk with a single one ?"

"Or tell me," said Magnus Troil, "how it were possible for Neil of Lupness, that lost one arm by his fall from the crag of Nekbreckan, to manage a plough with two handles ?"

"The harness is of raw seal-skin," said Triptolemus.

"It will save dressed leather," answered Magnus Troil.

"It is drawn by four wretched bullocks," said the agriculturist, "that are yoked breast-fashion ; and two women must follow this unhappy instrument, and complete the furrows with a couple of shovels."

"Drink about, Master Yellowley," said the Udaller ; "and, as you say in Scotland, 'never fash your thumb.' Our cattle are too high-spirited to let one go before the other ; our men are too gentle and well-nurtured to take the working-field without the women's company ; our ploughs till our land—our land bears us barley ; we brew our ale, eat our bread, and make strangers welcome to their share of it. Here's to you, Master Yellowley."

This was said in a tone meant to be decisive of the question ; and, accordingly, Halcro whispered to Mordaunt, "That has settled the matter, and now we will get on with glorious John.—There he sat in his suit of full-trimmed black ; two years due was the bill, as mine honest landlord afterwards told me,—and such an eye in his head !—none of your burning, blighting, falcon eyes, which we poets are apt to make a rout about,—but a soft, full, thoughtful, yet penetrating glance—never saw the like of it in my life, unless it were little Stephen Kleancogg's, the fiddler, at Papastow, who"—

"Nay, but John Dryden ?" said Mordaunt, who, for want of better amusement, had begun to take a sort of pleasure in keeping the old gentleman to his narrative, as men herd a restive sheep, when they wish to catch him. He returned to his theme, with his usual phrase of "Ay, true—glorious John—Well, sir, he cast his eye, such as I have described it, on my landlord, and 'Honest Tim,' said he, 'what hast thou got here ? and all the wits, and lords, and gentlemen, that used to crowd round him, like the wenches round a pedlar at a fair, they made way for us, and up we came to the fireside, where he had his own established chair,—I have heard it was carried to the balcony in summer, but it was by the fireside when I saw it,—so up came Tim Thimblethwaite, through the midst of them, as bold as a lion, and I followed with a small parcel under my arm, which I had taken up partly to oblige my landlord, as the shop-porter was not in the way, and partly that I might be thought to have something to do there, for you are to think there was no admittance at the Wits' for

118

strangers who had no business there.—I have heard that Sir Charles Sedley said a good thing about that"—

"Nay, but you forget glorious John," said Mordaunt.

"Ay, glorious you may well call him. They talk of their Blackmore, and Shadwell, and such like,—not fit to tie the latchets of John's shoes—'Well,' he said to my landlord, 'what have you got there ?' and he, bowing, I warrant, lower than he would to a duke, said he had made bold to come and show him the stuff which Lady Elizabeth had chose for her night-gown.—'And which of your geese is that, Tim, who has got it tucked under his wing ?'—'He is an Orkney goose, if it please you, Mr. Dryden,' said Tim, who had wit at will, 'and he hath brought you a copy of verses for your honour to look at.'—'Is he amphibious ?' said glorious John, taking the paper,—and methought I could rather have faced a battery of cannon than the crackle it gave as it opened, though he did not speak in a way to dash one neither ;—and then he looked at the verses, and he was pleased to say, in a very encouraging way indeed, with a sort of good-humoured smile on his face, and certainly, for a fat elderly gentleman,—for I would not compare it to Minna's smile, or Brenda's,—he had the pleasantest smile I ever saw,—'Why, Tim,' he said, 'this goose of yours will prove a swan on our hands.' With that he smiled a little, and they all laughed, and none louder than those who stood too far off to hear the jest ; for every one knew when he smiled there was something worth laughing at, and so took it upon trust ; and the word passed through among the young Templars, and the wits, and the smarts, and there was nothing but question on question who we were ; and one French fellow was trying to tell them it was only Monsieur Tim Thimblethwaite ; but he made such work with his Dumbletate and Timbletate, that I thought his explanation would have lasted"—

"As long as your own story," thought Mordaunt ; but the narrative was at length finally cut short, by the strong and decided voice of the Udaller.

"I will hear no more on it, Mr. Factor," he exclaimed.

"At least let me say something about the breed of horses," said Yellowley, in rather a cry-mercy tone of voice. "Your horses, my dear sir, resemble cats in size, and tigers in devilry !"

"For their size," said Magnus, "they are the easier for us to get off and on them—[as Triptolemus experienced this morning, thought Mordaunt to himself]—and, as for their devilry, let no one mount them that cannot manage them."

A twinge of self-conviction, on the part of the agriculturist, prevented him from reply. He darted a deprecatory glance at Mordaunt, as if for the purpose of imploring secrecy respecting his tumble ; and the Udaller, who saw his advantage, although he was not aware of the cause, pursued it with the high and stern tone proper to one who had all his life been unaccustomed to meet with, and unapt to endure, opposition.

"By the blood of St. Magnus the Martyr," he said, "but you are a fine fellow, Master Factor Yellowley ! You come to us from a strange land, understanding neither our laws, nor our manners, nor our language, and you propose to become governor of the country, and that we should all be your slaves !"

"My pupils, worthy sir, my pupils !" said Yellowley, "and that only for your own proper advantage."

"We are too old to go to school," said the Zetlander. "I tell you once more, we will sow and reap our grain as our fathers did—we will eat what God sends us, with our doors open to the stranger, even as theirs were open. If there is aught imperfect in our practice, we will amend it in time and season ; but the blessed Baptist's holiday was made for light hearts and quick heels. He that speaks a word more of reason, as you call it, or anything that looks like it, shall swallow a pint of sea-water—he shall, by this hand !—and so fill up the good ship, the Jolly Mariner of Canton, once more, for the benefit of those that will stick by her ; and let the rest have a fling with the fiddlers, who have been summoning us this hour. I will warrant every wench is on tiptoe by this time. Come, Mr. Yellowley, no unkindness, man—why, man, thou feelest the rolling of the Jolly Mariner still"—(for, in truth, honest Triptolemus showed a little unsteadiness of motion, as he rose to attend his host)—"but never mind, we shall have thee find thy land-legs to reel it with yonder bonny belles. Come along, Triptolemus—let me grapple thee fast, lest thou *trip*, old Triptolemus—ha, ha, ha !"

So saying, the portly though weatherbeaten hulk of the Udaller sailed off like a man-of-war that had braved a hundred gales, having his guest in tow like a recent prize. The greater part of the revellers followed their leader with loud jubilee, although there were several stanch topers, who, taking the option left them by the Udaller, remained behind to relieve the Jolly Mariner of a fresh cargo, amidst many a pledge to the health of their absent landlord, and to the prosperity of his roof-tree, with whatsoever other wishes of kindness could be devised as an apology for another pint-bumper of noble punch.

The rest soon thronged the dancing-room, an apartment which partook the simplicity of the time and of the country. Drawing-rooms and saloons were then unknown in Scotland, save in the houses of the nobility, and of course absolutely so in Zetland ; but a long, low, anomalous store-room, sometimes used for the deposition of merchandise, sometimes for putting aside lumber, and a thousand other purposes, was well known to all the youth of Dunrossness, and of many a district besides, as the scene of the merry dance, which was sustained with so much glee when Magnus Troil gave his frequent feasts.

The first appearance of this ball-room might have shocked a fashionable party, assembled for the quadrille or the waltz. Low as we have stated the apartment to be, it was but imperfectly illuminated by lamps, candles, ship-lanterns, and a variety of other *candelabra*, which served to throw a dusky light upon the floor, and upon the heaps of merchandise and miscellaneous articles which were piled around ; some of them stores for the winter ; some, goods destined for exportation ; some, the tribute of Neptune, paid at the expense of shipwrecked vessels, whose owners were unknown ; some, articles of barter received by the proprieter, who, like most others at the period, was somewhat of a merchant as well as a landholder, in exchange for the fish, and other articles, the produce of his estate. All these, with the chests, boxes, casks, etc., which contained them, had been drawn aside, and piled one above the other, in order to give room for the dancers, who, light and lively as if they had occupied the most splendid saloon in the parish of St. James's, executed their national dances with equal grace and activity.

The group of old men who looked on, bore no inconsiderable resemblance to a party of aged tritons, engaged in beholding the sports of sea-nymphs; so hard a look had most of them acquired by contending with the elements, and so much did the shaggy hair and beards, which many of them cultivated after the ancient Norwegian fashion, give their heads the character of these supposed natives of the deep. The young people, on the other hand, were uncommonly handsome, tall, well-made, and shapely; the men with long fair hair, and, until broken by the weather, a fresh ruddy complexion, which, in the females, was softened into a bloom of infinite delicacy. Their natural good ear for music qualified them to second to the utmost the exertions of a band, whose strains were by no means contemptible; while the elders, who stood around, or sat quiet upon the old sea-chests, which served for chairs, criticised the dancers, as they compared their execution with their own exertions in former days; or, warmed by the cup and flagon, which continued to circulate among them, snapped their fingers, and beat time with their feet to the music.

Mordaunt looked upon this scene of universal mirth with the painful recollection, that he, thrust aside from his pre-eminence, no longer exercised the important duties of chief of the dancers, or office of leader of the revels, which had been assigned to the stranger Cleveland. Anxious, however, to suppress the feelings of his own disappointment, which he felt it was neither wise to entertain nor manly to display, he approached his fair neighbours to whom he had been so acceptable at table, with the purpose of inviting one of them to become his partner in the dance. But the awfully ancient old lady, even the Lady Glowrowrum, who had only tolerated the exuberance of her nieces' mirth during the time of dinner, because her situation rendered it then impossible for her to interfere, was not disposed to permit the apprehended renewal of the intimacy implied in Mertoun's invitation. She therefore took upon herself, in the name of her two nieces, who sat pouting beside her in displeased silence, to inform Mordaunt, after thanking him for his civility, that the hands of her nieces were engaged for that evening; and, as he continued to watch the party at a little distance, he had an opportunity of being convinced that the alleged engagement was a mere apology to get rid of him, when he saw the two good-humoured sisters join the dance under the auspices of the next young man who asked their hands. Incensed at so marked a slight, and unwilling to expose himself to another, Mordaunt Mertoun drew back from the circle of dancers, shrouded himself amongst the mass of inferior persons who crowded into the bottom of the room as spectators, and there, concealed from the observation of others, digested his own mortification as well as he could—that is to say, very ill—and with all the philosophy of his age—that is to say, with none at all.

CHAPTER FIFTEENTH

A torch for me—let wantons, light of heart,
Tickle the useless rushes with their heels ;
For I am proverb'd with a grandsire phrase—
I'll be a candle-holder and look on.

ROMEO AND JULIET

THE youth, says the moralist Johnson, cares not for the boy's hobby-horse, nor the man for the youth's mistress ; and, therefore the distress of Mordaunt Mertoun, when excluded from the merry dance, may seem trifling to many of my readers, who would, nevertheless, think they did well to be angry if deposed from their usual place in an assembly of a different kind. There lacked not amusement, however, for those whom the dance did not suit, or who were not happy enough to find partners to their liking. Halcro, now completely in his element, had assembled round him an audience, to whom he was declaiming his poetry with all the enthusiasm of glorious John himself, and receiving in return the usual degree of applause allowed to minstrels who recite their own rhymes—so long at least as the author is within hearing of the criticism. Halcro's poetry might indeed have interested the antiquary as well as the admirer of the Muses, for several of his pieces were translations or imitations from the Scaldic sagas, which continued to be sung by the fishermen of these islands even until a very late period ; insomuch, that when Gray's poems first found their way to Orkney, the old people recognised at once, in the ode of the "Fatal Sisters," the runic rhymes which had amused or terrified their infancy under the title of the "Magicians," and which the fishers of North Ronaldshaw, and other remote isles, used still to sing when asked for a Norse ditty.*

Half-listening, half-lost in his own reflections, Mordaunt Mertoun stood near the door of the apartment, and in the outer ring of the little circle formed around old Halcro, while the bard chanted to a low, wild, monotonous air, varied only by the efforts of the singer to give interest and emphasis to particular passages, the following imitation of a northern war-song:—

𝕿𝖍𝖊 𝕾𝖔𝖓𝖌 𝖔𝖋 𝕳𝖆𝖗𝖔𝖑𝖉 𝕳𝖆𝖗𝖋𝖆𝖌𝖊𝖗

The sun is rising dimly red,
The wind is wailing low and dread,
From his cliff the eagle sallies,
Leaves the wolf his darksome valleys ;
In the mist the ravens hover,
Peep the wild-dogs from the cover,
Screaming, croaking, baying, yelling,
Each in his wild accents telling,
"Soon we feast on dead and dying,
Fair-hair'd Harold's flag is flying."

Many a crest in air is streaming,
Many a helmet darkly gleaming,
Many an arm the axe uprears,
Doom'd to hew the wood of spears.
All along the crowded ranks ;
Horses neigh and armour clanks ;
Chiefs are shouting, clarions ringing,
Louder still the bard is singing,
"Gather, footmen—gather, horsemen,
To the field, ye valiant Norsemen !

* See Note C.

122

"Halt ye not for food or slumber,
View not vantage, count not number ;
Jolly reapers, forward still ;
Grow the crop on vale or hill,
Thick or scatter'd, stiff or lithe,
It shall down before the scythe.
Forward with your sickles bright,
Reap the harvest of the fight—
Onward, footmen,—onward, horsemen,
To the charge, ye gallant Norsemen !

"Fatal Choosers of the Slaughter,
O'er you hovers Odin's daughter ;
Hear the choice she spreads before ye,—
Victory, and wealth, and glory ;
Or old Valhalla's roaring hail,
Her ever-circling mead and ale,
Where for eternity unite
The joys of wassail and of fight.
Headlong forward, foot and horsemen,
Charge and fight, and die like
            Norsemen !"

"The poor unhappy blinded heathens !" said Triptolemus, with a sigh deep enough for a groan ; "they speak of their eternal cups of ale, and I question if they kend how to manage a croft land of grain !"

"The cleverer fellows they, neighbour Yellowley," answered the poet, "if they made ale without barley."

"Barley !—alack-a-day !" replied the more accurate agriculturist, "who ever heard of barley in these parts ? Bear, my dearest friend, bear is all they have, and wonderment it is to me that they ever see an awn of it. Ye scart the land with a bit thing ye ca' a pleugh—ye might as weel give it a ritt with the teeth of a redding-kame. Oh, to see the sock, and the heel, and the sole-clout of a real steady Scottish pleugh, with a chield like a Samson between the stilts, laying a weight on them would keep down a mountain ; twa stately owsen, and as many broad-breasted horse in the traces, going through soil and till, and leaving a fur in the ground would carry off water like a causeyed syver ! They that have seen a sight like that, have seen something to crack about in another sort, than those unhappy auld-warld stories of war and slaughter, of which the land has seen ever but too mickle, for a' your singing and soughing awa in praise of such bloodthirsty doings, Master Claud Halcro."

"It is a heresy," said the animated little poet, bridling and drawing himself up as if the whole defence of the Orcadian Archipelago rested on his single arm—"It is a heresy so much as to name one's native country, if a man is not prepared when and how to defend himself—ay, and to annoy another. The time has been, that if we made not good ale and aquavitæ, we knew well enough where to find that which was ready-made to our hand ; but now the descendants of Sea-kings, and Champions and Berserkars, are become as incapable of using their swords, as if they were so many women. Ye may praise them for a strong pull on an oar, or a sure foot on a skerry ; but what else could glorious John himself say of ye, my good Hjaltlanders, that any man would listen to ?"

"Spoken like an angel, most noble poet," said Cleveland, who, during an interval of the dance, stood near the party in which this conversation was held, "The old champions you talked to us about yesternight were the men to make a harp ring—gallant fellows that were friends to the sea, and enemies to all that sailed on it. Their ships, I suppose, were clumsy enough, but if it is true that they went upon the account as far as the Levant, I scarce believe that ever better fellows unloosed a topsail."

"Ay," replied Halcro, "there you spoke them right. In those days none could call their life and means of living their own, unless they dwelt twenty miles out of sight of the blue sea. Why, they had public prayers put up in every church in Europe, for deliverance from the ire of the Northmen. In France and England, ay, and in Scotland too, for as high as they hold their head now-a-days, there was not a bay or a haven, but it was freer to our forefathers than to the poor devils of natives ; and now we cannot, forsooth, so much as grow our own barley without Scottish help"—(here he darted a sarcastic glance at the factor)—"I would I saw the time we were to measure arms with them again."

"Spoken like a hero once more," said Cleveland.

"Ah !" continued the little bard, "I would it were possible to see our barks, once the water-dragons of the world, swimming with the black raven standard waving at the topmast, and their decks glimmering with arms, instead of being heaped up with stockfish—winning with our fearless hands what the niggard soil denies—paying back all old scorn and modern injury—reaping where we never sowed, and felling what we never planted—living and laughing through the world, and smiling when we were summoned to quit it !"

So spoke Claud Halcro, in no serious, or at least most certainly in no sober mood, his brain (never the more stable) whizzing under the influence of fifty well remembered sagas, besides five bumpers of usquebaugh and brandy ; and Cleveland, between jest and earnest, clapped him on the shoulder, and again repeated, "Spoken like a hero !"

"Spoken like a fool, I think, " said Magnus Troil, whose attention had been also attracted by the vehemence of the little bard—"where would you cruise upon, or against whom ?—we are all subjects of one realm, I trow, and I would have you to remember that your voyage may bring up at Execution-dock. I like not the Scots—no offence, Mr Yellowley—that is, I would like them well enough if they would stay quiet in their own land, and leave us at peace with our own people, and manners, and fashions ; and if they would but abide there till I went to harry them like a mad old Berserkar, I would leave them in peace till the day of judgment. With what the sea sends us, and the land lends us, as the proverb says, and a set of honest neighbourly folks to help us to consume it, so help me, Saint Magnus, as I think we are even but too happy !"

"I know what war is," said an old man, "and I would as soon sail through Sumburgh Roost in a cockleshell, or in a worse loom, as I would venture there again."

"And pray, what wars knew your valour ?" said Halcro, who, though forbearing to contradict his landlord from a sense of respect, was not a whit inclined to abandon his argument to any meaner authority.

"I was pressed," answered the old Triton, "to serve under Montrose, when he came here about the sixteen hundred and fifty-one, and carried a sort of us off, will ye nill ye, to get our throats cut in the wilds of Strathnavern*—I shall never forget it—we had been hard put to it for victuals—what would I have given for a luncheon of Burgh Westra beef— ay, or a mess of sour sillocks ?— When our Highlandmen brought in a dainty drove of kyloes, much ceremony there was not, for we shot and

124

felled, and flayed, and roasted, and broiled, as it came to every man's hand ; till, just as our beards were at the greasiest, we heard—God preserve us— a tramp of horse, then twa or three drapping shots,—then came a full salvo, —and then, when the officers were crying on us to stand, and maist of us looking which way we might run away, down they broke, horse and foot, with old John Urry, or Hurry,† or whatever they call him—he hurried us that day, and worried us to boot—and we began to fall as thick as the stots that we were felling five minutes before."

"And Montrose," said the soft voice of the graceful Minna ; "what became of Montrose, or how looked he ?"

"Like a lion with the hunters before him," answered the old gentleman ; "but I looked not twice his way, for my own lay right over the hill."

"And so you left him ?" said Minna, in a tone of the deepest contempt.

"It was no fault of mine, Mistress Minna," answered the old man, somewhat out of countenance ; "but I was there with no choice of my own ; and, besides, what good could I have done ?—all the rest were running like sheep, and why should I have stayed ?"

"You might have died with him," said Minna.

"And lived with him to all eternity, in immortal verse !" added Claud Halcro.

"I thank you, Mistress Minna," replied the plain-dealing Zetlander ; "and I thank you, my old friend Claud ;—but I would rather drink both your healths in this good bicker of ale, like a living man as I am, than that you should be making songs in my honour, for having died forty or fifty years agone. But what signified it,—run or fight, 'twas all one ;—they took Montrose, poor fellow, for all his doughty deeds, and they took me, that did no doughty deeds at all ; and they hanged him, poor man, and as for me"—

"I trust in Heaven they flogged and pickled you," said Cleveland, worn out of patience with the dull narrative of the peaceful Zetlander's poltroonery, of which he seemed so wondrous little ashamed.

"Flog horses, and pickle beef," said Magnus ; "why, you have not the vanity to think, that, with all your quarterdeck airs, you will make poor old neighbour Haagen ashamed that he was not killed some scores of years since ? You have looked on death yourself, my doughty young friend, but it was with the eyes of a young man who wishes to be thought of ; but we are a peaceful people,—peaceful, that is, as long as any one should be peaceful, and that is till someone has the impudence to wrong us, or our neighbours ; and then, perhaps, they may not find our northern blood much cooler in our veins than was that of the old Scandinavians that gave us our names and lineage.—Get ye along, get ye along to the sword-dance,* that the strangers that are amongst us may

---

* Montrose, in his last and ill-advised attempt to invade Scotland, augmented his small army of Danes and Scottish Royalists, by some bands of raw troops, hastily levied, or rather pressed into his service, in the Orkney and Zetland Isles, who, having little heart either to the cause or manner of service, behaved but indifferently when they came into action.

† Note J. Sir John Urry.

see that our hands and our weapons are not altogether unacquainted even yet."

A dozen cutlasses, selected hastily from an old arm-chest, and whose rusted hue bespoke how seldom they left the sheath, armed the same number of young Zetlanders, with whom mingled six maidens, led by Minna Troil ; and the minstrelsy instantly commenced a tune appropriate to the ancient Norwegian war-dance, the evolutions of which are perhaps still practised in those remote islands.

The first movement was graceful and majestic, the youths holding their swords erect, and without much gesture ; but the tune, and the corresponding motions of the dancers, became gradually more and more rapid,—they clashed their swords together, in measured time, with a spirit which gave the exercise a dangerous appearance in the eye of the spectator, though the firmness, justice, and accuracy, with which the dancers kept time with the stroke of their weapons, did, in truth, ensure its safety. The most singular part of the exhibition was the courage exhibited by the female performers, who now, surrounded by the swordsmen, seemed like the Sabine maidens in the hands of their Roman lovers ; now, moving under the arch of steel which the young men had formed, by crossing their weapons over the heads of their fair partners, resembled the band of Amazons when they first joined in the Pyrrhic dance with the followers of Theseus. But by far the most striking and appropriate figure was that of Minna Troil, whom Halcro had long since entitled the Queen of Swords, and who, indeed, moved amidst the swordsmen with an air, which seemed to hold all the drawn blades as the proper accompaniments of her person, and the implements of her pleasure. And when the mazes of the dance became more intricate, when the close and continuous clash of the weapons made some of her companions shrink, and show signs of fear, her cheek, her lip, and her eye, seemed rather to announce that, at the moment when the weapons flashed fastest, and rung sharpest around her, she was most completely self-possessed, and in her own element. Last of all, when the music had ceased, and she remained for an instant upon the floor by herself, as the rule of the dance required, the swordsmen and maidens, who departed from around her, seemed the guards and the train of some princess, who, dismissed by her signal, were leaving her for a time to solitude. Her own look and attitude, wrapped, as she probably was, in some vision of the imagination, corresponded admirably with the ideal dignity which the spectators ascribed to her ; but, almost immediately recollecting herself, she blushed, as if conscious she had been, though but for an instant, the object of undivided attention, and gave her hand gracefully to Cleveland, who, though he had not joined in the dance, assumed the duty of conducting her to her seat.

As they passed, Mordaunt Mertoun might observe that Cleveland whispered into Minna's ear, and that her brief reply was accompanied with even more discomposure of countenance than she had manifested when encountering the gaze of the whole assembly. Mordaunt's

* Note K. The sword-dance.

126

suspicions were strongly awakened by what he observed, for he knew Minna's character well, and with what equanimity and indifference she was in the custom of receiving the usual compliments and gallantries with which her beauty and her situation rendered her sufficiently familiar.

"Can it be possible she really loves this stranger ?" was the unpleasant thought that instantly shot across Mordaunt's mind ;—"And if she does, what is my interest in the matter ?" was the second ; and which was quickly followed by the reflection, that though he claimed no interest at any time but as a friend, and though that interest was now withdrawn, he was still, in consideration of their former intimacy, entitled both to be sorry and angry at her for throwing away her affections on one he judged unworthy of her. In this process of reasoning, it is probable that a little mortified vanity, or some indescribable shade of selfish regret, might be endeavouring to assume the disguise of disinterested generosity ; but there is so much of base alloy in our very best (unassisted) thoughts, that it is melancholy work to criticise too closely the motives of our most worthy actions ; at least we would recommend to every one to let those of his neighbours pass current, however narrowly he may examine the purity of his own.

The sword-dance was succeeded by various other specimens of the same exercise, and by songs, to which the singers lent their whole soul, while the audience were sure, as occasion offered, to unite in some favourite chorus. It is upon such occasions that music, though of a simple and even rude character, finds its natural empire over the generous bosom, and produces that strong excitement which cannot be attained by the most learned compositions of the first masters, which are caviare to the common ear, although, doubtless, they afford a delight, exquisite in its kind, to those whose natural capacity and education have enabled them to comprehend and relish those difficult and complicated combinations of harmony.

It was about midnight when a knocking at the door of the mansion, with the sound of the *Gue* and the *Langspiel,** announced, by their tinkling chime, the arrival of fresh revellers, to whom, according to the hospitable custom of the country, the apartments were instantly thrown open.

CHAPTER SIXTEENTH

—My mind misgives,
Some consequence, yet hanging in the stars,
Shall bitterly begin his fearful date,
With this night's revels.

ROMEO AND JULIET

THE new comers were, according to the frequent custom of such frolickers all over the world, disguised in a sort of masquing habits, and

* [Musical instruments formerly used in Shetland,—the latter was a small harp.]

designed to represent the Tritons and Mermaids with whom ancient traditions and popular beliefs have peopled the northern seas. The former, called by Zetlanders of that time, Shoupeltins, were represented by young men grotesquely habited, with false hair, and beards made of flax, and chaplets composed of sea-ware interwoven with shells, and other marine productions, with which also were decorated their light-blue or greenish mantles of wadmaal, repeatedly before mentioned. They had fish-spears, and other emblems of their assumed quality, amongst which the classical taste of Claud Halcro, by whom the masque was arranged, had not forgotten the conch-shells, which were stoutly and hoarsely winded, from time to time, by one or two of the aquatic deities, to the great annoyance of all who stood near them.

The Nereids and Water-nymphs who attended on this occasion, displayed, as usual, a little more taste and ornament than was to be seen amongst their male attendants. Fantastic garments of green silk, and other materials of superior cost and fashion, had been contrived, so as to imitate their idea of the inhabitants of the waters, and, at the same time, to show the shape and features of the fair wearers to the best advantage. The bracelets and shells, which adorned the neck, arms, and ankles of the pretty Mermaidens, were, in some cases, intermixed with real pearls ; and the appearance, upon the whole, was such as might have done no discredit to the court of Amphitrite, especially when the long bright locks, blue eyes, fair complexions, and pleasing features of the maidens of Thule, were taken into consideration. We do not indeed pretend to aver, that any of these seeming Mermaids had so accurately imitated the real siren, as commentators have supposed those attendant on Cleopatra did, who, adopting the fish's train of their original, were able, nevertheless, to make their "bends," or "ends" (said commentators cannot tell which), "adornings."* Indeed, had they not left their extremities in their natural state, it would have been impossible for the Zetland sirens to have executed the very pretty dance, with which they rewarded the company for the ready admission which had been granted to them.

It was soon discovered that these masquers were no strangers, but a part of the guests, who, stealing out a little time before, had thus disguised themselves, in order to give variety to the mirth of the evening. The muse of Claud Halcro, always active on such occasions, had supplied them with an appropriate song, of which we may give the following specimen. The song was alternate betwixt a Nereid or Mermaid, and a Merman or Triton—the males and females on either part forming a semi-chorus, which accompanied and bore burden to the principal singer.

---

* See some admirable discussion on this passage, in the Variorum Shakespeare.

I
MERMAID

Fathoms deep beneath the wave,
  Stringing beads of glistening pearl,
Singing the achievements brave
  Of many an old Norwegian earl ;
Dwelling where the tempest's raving
  Falls as light upon our ear,
As the sigh of lover, craving
  Pity from his lady dear,
Children of wild Thule, we,
From the deep caves of the sea,
As the lark springs from the lea,
Hither come, to share your glee.

II
MERMAN

From reining of the water-horse,
  That bounded till the waves were foaming,
Watching the infant tempest's course,
  Chasing the sea-snake in his roaming ;
From winding charge-notes on the shell,
  When the huge whale and sword-fish duel
Or tolling shroudless seamen's knell,
  When the winds and waves are cruel ;
Children of wild Thule, we
Have plough'd such furrows on the sea,
As the steer draws on the lea,
And hither we come to share your glee.

III
MERMAIDS AND MERMEN

We heard you in our twilight caves,
  A hundred fathoms deep below,
For notes of joy can pierce the waves,
  That drown each sound of war and woe.
Those who dwell beneath the sea
  Love the sons of Thule well
Thus, to aid your mirth, bring we
  Dance, and song, and sounding shell.
Children of dark Thule, know,
Those who dwell by haaf and voe,
Where your daring shallops row,
Come to share the festal show.

The final chorus was borne by the whole voices, excepting those carrying the conch shells, who had been trained to blow them in a sort of rude accompaniment, which had a good effect. The poetry, as well as the performance of the masquers, received great applause from all who pretended to be judges of such matters ; but, above all, from Triptolemus

Yellowley, who, his ear having caught the agricultural sounds of plough and furrow, and his brain being so well drenched that it could only construe the words in their most literal acceptation, declared roundly, and called Mordaunt to bear witness, that, though it was a shame to waste so much good lint as went to form the Tritons' beards, and periwigs, the song contained the only words of common sense which he had heard all that long day.

But Mordaunt had no time to answer the appeal, being engaged in attending with the utmost vigilance to the motions of one of the female masquers, who had given him a private signal as they entered, which induced him, though uncertain who she might prove to be, to expect some communication from her of importance. The siren who had so boldly touched his arm, and had accompanied the gesture with an expression of eye which bespoke his attention, was disguised with a good deal more care than her sister-masquers, her mantle being loose, and wide enough to conceal her shape completely, and her face hidden beneath a silk mask. He observed that she gradually detached herself from the rest of the masquers, and at length placed herself, as if for the advantage of the air, near the door of a chamber which remained open, looked earnestly at him again, and then, taking an opportunity when the attention of the company was fixed upon the rest of her party, she left the apartment.

Mordaunt did not hesitate instantly to follow his mysterious guide, for such we may term the masquer, as she paused to let him see the direction she was about to take, and then walked swiftly towards the shore of the *voe,* or salt-water lake, now lying full before them, its small summer-waves glistening and rippling under the influence of a broad moonlight, which, added to the strong twilight of those regions during the summer solstice, left no reason to regret the absence of the sun, the path of whose setting was still visible on the waves of the west, while the horizon on the east side was already beginning to glimmer with the lights of dawn.

Mordaunt had therefore no difficulty in keeping sight of his disguised guide, as she tripped it over height and hollow to the sea-side, and, winding among the rocks, led the way to the spot where his own labours, during the time of his former intimacy at Burgh Westra, had constructed a sheltered and solitary seat, where the daughters of Magnus were accustomed to spend, when the weather was suitable, a good deal of their time. Here then was to be the place of explanation ; for the masquer stopped, and, after a moment's hesitation, sat down on the rustic settle. But from the lips of whom was he to receive it ? Norna had first occurred to him ; but her tall figure and slow majestic step were entirely different from the size and gait of the more fairy-formed siren, who had preceded him with as light a trip as if she had been a real Nereid, who, having remained too late upon the shore, was, under the dread of Amphitrite's displeasure, hastening to regain her native element. Since it was not Norna, it could be only, he thought, Brenda, who thus singled him out ; and when she had seated herself upon the bench, and taken the mask from her face, Brenda it accordingly proved to be. Mordaunt had certainly done nothing to make him dread her presence ; and yet such is the influence of bashfulness over the ingenuous youth of both sexes, that he experienced all the embarrassment of one who finds himself unexpectedly placed before a person who is justly offended with him. Brenda felt no less embarrassment ; but as she had courted this interview, and was sensible it must be a brief one, she was compelled, in spite of herself, to begin the conversation.

"Mordaunt," she said, with a hesitating voice ; then correcting herself, she proceeded—"You must be surprised, Mr. Mertoun, that I should have taken this uncommon freedom."

"It was not till this morning, Brenda," replied Mordaunt, "that any mark of friendship or intimacy from you or from your sister could have surprised me. I am far more astonished that you should shun me without reason for so many hours, than that you should now allow me an interview. In the name of Heaven, Brenda, in what have I offended you ? or why are we on these unusual terms ?"

"May it not be enough to say," replied Brenda, looking downward, "that it is my father's pleasure ?"

"No, it is not enough," returned Mertoun. "Your father cannot have so suddenly altered his whole thoughts of me, and his whole actions towards me, without acting under the influence of some strong delusion. I ask you but to explain of what nature it is ; for I will be contented to be lower in your esteem than the meanest hind in these islands, if I cannot show that his change of opinion is only grounded upon some infamous deception, or some extraordinary mistake."

"It may be so," said Brenda—"I hope it is so—that I do hope it is so, my desire to see you thus in private may well prove to you. But it is difficult— in short it is impossible for me to explain to you the cause of my father's resentment. Norna has spoken with him concerning it boldly, and I fear they parted in displeasure ; and you well know no light matter could cause that."

"I have observed," said Mordaunt, "that your father is most attentive to Norna's counsel, and more complaisant to her peculiarities than to those of others—this I have observed, though he is no willing believer in the supernatural qualities to which she lays claim."

"They are related distantly," answered Brenda, "and were friends in youth—nay, as I have heard, it was once supposed they would have been married ; but Norna's peculiarities showed themselves immediately on her father's death, and there was an end of that matter, if ever there was anything in it. But it is certain my father regards her with much interest ; and it is, I fear, a sign how deeply his prejudices respecting you must be rooted, since they have in some degree quarrelled on your account."

"Now, blessings upon you, Brenda, that you have called them prejudices," said Mertoun, warmly and hastily—"a thousand blessings on you ! You were ever gentle-hearted—you could not have maintained even the show of unkindness long."

"It was indeed but a show," said Brenda, softening gradually into the familiar tone in which they had conversed from infancy ; "I could never

131

think, Mordaunt,—never, that is, seriously believe, that you could say aught unkind of Minna or of me."

"And who dares to say I have ?" said Mordaunt, giving way to the natural impetuosity of his disposition—"Who dares to say that I have, and ventures at the same time to hope that I will suffer his tongue to remain in safety betwixt his jaws ? By Saint Magnus the Martyr, I will feed the hawks with it !"

"Nay, now," said Brenda, "your anger only terrifies me, and will force me to leave you."

"Leave me," said he, "without telling either the calumny, or the name of the villanous calumniator !"

"Oh, there are more than one," answered Brenda, "that have possessed my father with an opinion—which I cannot myself tell you—but there are more than one who say"—

"Were they hundreds, Brenda, I will do no less to them than I have said—Sacred Martyr !—to accuse me of speaking unkindly of those whom I most respected and valued under Heaven—I will back to the apartment this instant, and your father shall do me right before all the world."

"Do not go, for the love of Heaven !" said Brenda ; "do not go, as you would not render me the most unhappy wretch in existence !"

"Tell me then, at least, if I guess aright," said Mordaunt, "when I name this Cleveland for one of those who have slandered me ?"

"No, no," said Brenda, vehemently, "you run from one error into another more dangerous. You say you are my friend ;— I am willing to be yours :— be still for a moment, and hear what I have to say ;—our interview has lasted but too long already, and every additional moment brings additional danger with it."

"Tell me, then," said Mertoun, much softened by the poor girl's extreme apprehension and distress, "what it is that you require of me ; and believe me, it is impossible for you to ask aught that I will not do my very utmost to comply with."

"Well, then—this Captain," said Brenda, "this Cleveland"—

"I knew it, by Heaven !" said Mordaunt ; "my mind assured me that that fellow was, in one way or other, at the bottom of all this mischief and misunderstanding."

"If you cannot be silent, and patient, for an instant," replied Brenda, "I must instantly quit you : what I meant to say had no relation to you, but to another,—in one word, to my sister Minna. I have nothing to say concerning her dislike to you, but an anxious tale to tell concerning his attention to her."

"It is obvious, striking, and marked," said Mordaunt ; "and, unless my eyes deceive me, it is received as welcome, if, indeed, it is not returned."

"That is the very cause of my fear," said Brenda. "I, too, was struck with the external appearance, frank manners, and romantic conversation of this man."

"His appearance !" said Mordaunt ; "he is stout and well-featured enough, to be sure ; but, as old Sinclair of Quendale said to the Spanish admiral, 'Farcie on his face ! I have seen many a fairer hang on the Borough Moor.'—From his manners, he might be captain of a privateer ;

132

and, by his conversation, the trumpeter to his own puppet-show ; for he speaks of little else than his own exploits."

"You are mistaken," answered Brenda ; "he speaks but too well on all that he has seen and learned ; besides, he has really been in many distant countries, and in many gallant actions, and he can tell them with as much spirit as modesty. You would think you saw the flash and heard the report of the guns. And he has other tones of talking too—about the delightful trees and fruits of distant climates ; and how the people wear no dress, through the whole year, half so warm as our summer gowns, and, indeed, put on little except cambric and muslin."

"Upon my word, Brenda, he does seem to understand the business of amusing young ladies," replied Mordaunt.

"He does indeed," said Brenda, with great simplicity. "I assure you that, at first, I liked him better than Minna did ; and yet, though she is so much cleverer than I am, I know more of the world than she does ; for I have seen more of cities, having been once at Kirkwall ; beside that, I was thrice at Lerwick, when the Dutch ships were there, and so I should not be very easily deceived in people."

"And pray, Brenda," said Mertoun, "what was it that made you think less favourably of the young fellow, who seems to be so captivating ?"

"Why," said Brenda, after a moment's reflection, "at first he was much livelier ; and the stories he told were not quite so melancholy, or so terrible ; and he laughed and danced more."

"And, perhaps, at that time, danced oftener with Brenda than with her sister ?" added Mordaunt.

"No—I am not sure of that," said Brenda ; "and yet, to speak plain, I could have no suspicion of him at all while he was attending equally to us both ; for you know that then he could have been no more to us than yourself, Mordaunt Mertoun, or young Swaraster, or any other young man in the islands."

"But why then," said Mordaunt, "should you not see him, with patience, become acquainted with your sister ?—He is wealthy, or seems to be so at least. You say he is accomplished and pleasant ;—what else would you desire in a lover for Minna ?"

"Mordaunt, you forget who we are," said the maiden, assuming an air of consequence, which sat as gracefully upon her simplicity, as did the different tone in which she had spoken hitherto. "This is a little world of ours, this Zetland, inferior perhaps, in soil and climate, to other parts of the earth, at least so strangers say ; but it is our own little world, and we, the daughters of Magnus Troil, hold a first rank in it. It would, I think, little become us, who are descended from Sea-kings and Yarls, to throw ourselves away upon a stranger, who comes to our coast, like the eider-duck in spring, from we know not whence, and may leave it in autumn, to go we know not where."

"And who may ne'ertheless entice a Zetland golden-eye to accompany his migration," said Mertoun.

"I will hear nothing light on such a subject," replied Brenda indignantly ; "Minna, like myself, is the daughter of Magnus Troil, the friend of strangers, but the Father of Hjaltland. He gives them the hospitality they need ; but let not the proudest of them think that they can, at their pleasure, ally with his house."

She said this in a tone of considerable warmth, which she instantly softened, as she added, "No, Mordaunt, do not suppose that Minna Troil is capable of so far forgetting what she owes to her father and her father's blood, as to think of marrying this Cleveland ; but she may lend an ear to him so long as to destroy her future happiness. She has that sort of mind, into which some feelings sink deeply ;—you remember how Ulla Storlson used to go, day by day, to the top of Vossdale Head, to look for her lover's ship that was never to return ? When I think of her slow step, her pale cheek, her eye that grew dimmer and dimmer, like the lamp that is half-extinguished for lack of oil,—when I remember the fluttered look, of something like hope, with which she ascended the cliff at morning, and the deep dead despair which sat on her forehead when she returned,—when I think on all this, can you wonder that I fear for Minna, whose heart is formed to entertain, with such deep-rooted fidelity, any affection that may be implanted in it ?"

"I do not wonder," said Mordaunt, eagerly sympathising with the poor girl ; for, besides the tremulous expression of her voice, the light could almost show him the tear which trembled in her eye, as she drew the picture to which her fancy had assimilated her sister,—"I do not wonder that you should feel and fear whatever the purest affection can dictate ; and if you can but point out to me in what I can serve your sisterly love, you shall find me as ready to venture my life, if necessary, as I have been to go out on the crag to get you the eggs of the guillemot ; and, believe me, that whatever has been told to your father or yourself, of my entertaining the slightest thougths of disrespect or unkindness, is as false as a fiend could devise."

"I believe it," said Brenda, giving him her hand ; "I believe it, and my bosom is lighter, now I have renewed my confidence in so old a friend. How you can aid us, I know not ; but it was by the advice, I may say by the commands of Norna, that I have ventured to make this communication ; and I almost wonder," she added, as she looked around her, "that I have had courage to carry me through it. At present you know all that I can tell you of the risk in which my sister stands. Look after this Cleveland—beware how you quarrel with him, since you must so surely come by the worst with an experienced soldier."

"I do not exactly understand," said the youth, "how that should so surely be. This I know, that with the good limbs and good heart that God hath given me, ay, and with a good cause to boot—I am little afraid of any quarrel which Cleveland can fix upon me."

"Then, if not for your own sake, for Minna's sake," said Brenda—"for my father's—for mine—for all our sakes, avoid any strife with him, but be contented to watch him, and, if possible, to discover who he is, and what are his intentions towards us. He has talked of going to Orkney, to inquire after the consort with whom he sailed ; but day after day, and week after week, passes, and he goes not ; and while he keeps my father company over the bottle, and tells Minna romantic stories of foreign people, and distant wars, in wild and unknown regions, the time glides on, and the stranger, of whom we know nothing except that he is one, becomes gradually closer and more inseparably intimate in our society.— And now, farewell. Norna hopes to make your peace with my father, and entreats you not to leave Burgh Westra to-morrow, however cold he and my sister may appear towards you. I too," she said, stretching her hand towards him, "must wear a face of cold friendship as towards an unwelcome visitor, but at heart we are still Brenda and Mordaunt. And now separate quickly, for we must not be seen together."

She stretched her hand to him, but withdrew it in some slight confusion, laughing and blushing, when, by a natural impulse, he was about to press it to his lips. He endeavoured for a moment to detain her, for the interview had for him a degree of fascination, which, as often as he had before been alone with Brenda, he had never experienced. But she extricated herself from him, and again signing an adieu, and pointing out to him a path different from that which she was herself about to take, tripped towards the house, and was soon hidden from his view by the acclivity.

Mordaunt stood gazing after her in a state of mind, to which, as yet, he had been a stranger. The dubious neutral ground between love and friendship may be long and safely trodden, until he who stands upon it is suddenly called upon to recognise the authority of one or the other power ; and then it most frequently happens, that the party who for years supposed himself only to be a friend, finds himself at once transformed into a lover. That such a change in Mordaunt's feelings should take place from this date, although he himself was unable exactly to distinguish its nature, was to be expected. He found himself at once received, with the most unsuspicious frankness, into the confidence of a beautiful and fascinating young woman, by whom he had, so short a time before, imagined himself despised and disliked ; and, if anything could make a change, in itself so surprising and pleasing, yet more intoxicating, it was the guileless and open-hearted simplicity of Brenda, that cast an enchantment over everything which she did or said. The scene too might have had its effect, though there was little occasion for its aid. But a fair face looks yet fairer under the light of the moon, and a sweet voice sounds yet sweeter among the whispering sounds of a summer night. Mordaunt, therefore, who had by this time returned to the house, was disposed to listen with unusual patience and complacency to the enthusiastic declamation pronounced upon moonlight by Claud Halcro, whose ecstasies had been awakened on the subject by a short turn in the open air, undertaken to qualify the vapours of the good liquor, which he had not spared during the festival.

"The sun, my boy," he said, "is every wretched labourer's day-lantern—it comes glaring yonder out of the east, to summon up a whole world to labour and to misery ; whereas the merry moon lights all of us to mirth and to love."

"And to madness, or she is much belied," said Mordaunt, by way of saying something.

"Let it be so," answered Halcro, "so she does not turn us melancholy mad.—My dear young friend, the folks of this painstaking world are far

135

too anxious about possessing all their wits, or having them, as they say, about them. At least I know I have been often called half-witted, and I am sure I have gone through the world as well as if I had double the quantity. But stop—where was I ? Oh, touching and concerning the moon—why man, she is the very soul of love and poetry. I question if there was ever a true lover in existence who had not got at least as far as 'O thou,' in a sonnet in her praise."

"The moon," said the factor, who was now beginning to speak very thick, "ripens the corn, at least the old folk said so—and she fills nuts also, whilk is of less matter—*sparge nuces, pueri.*"

"A fine, a fine," said the Udaller, who was now in his altitudes ; "the factor speaks Greek—by the bones of my holy namesake, Saint Magnus, he shall drink off the yawl full of punch, unless he gives us a song on the spot !"

"Too much water drowned the miller," answered Triptolemus. "My brain has more need of draining than of being drenched with more liquor."

"Sing then," said the landlord, "for no one shall speak any other language here, save honest Norse, jolly Dutch, or Danske, or broad Scots, at the least of it. So, Eric Scambester, produce the yawl, and fill it to the brim, as a charge for demurrage."

Ere the vessel could reach the agriculturist, he, seeing it under way, and steering towards him by short tacks (for Scambester himself was by this time not over steady in his course), made a desperate effort, and began to chant, or rather to croak forth, a Yorkshire harvest-home ballad, which his father used to sing when he was a little mellow, and which went to the tune of "Hey Dobbin, away with the waggon." The rueful aspect of the singer, and the desperately discordant tones of his voice, formed so delightful a contrast with the jollity of the words and tune, that honest Triptolemus afforded the same sort of amusement which a reveller might give, by appearing on a festival-day in the holyday coat of his grandfather. The jest concluded the evening, for even the mighty and strong-headed Magnus himself had confessed the influence of the sleepy god. The guests went off as the best might, each to his separate crib and resting-place, and in a short time the mansion, which was of late so noisy, was hushed into perfect silence.

136

CHAPTER SEVENTEENTH

They man their boats, and all the young men arm,
With whatsoever might the monsters harm ;
Pikes, halberds, spits, and darts, that would afar,
The tools of peace and implements of war.
Now was the time for vigorous lads to show
What love or honour could incite them to :—
A goodly theatre, where rocks are round
With reverend age and lovely lasses crown'd.

BATTLE OF THE SUMMER ISLANDS

THE morning which succeeds such a feast as that of Magnus Troil, usually lacks a little of the zest which seasoned the revels of the preceding day, as the fashionable reader may have observed at a public breakfast during the race-week in a country-town ; for, in what is called the best society, these lingering moments are usually spent by the company, each apart in their own dressing-rooms. At Burgh Westra, it will readily be believed, no such space for retirement was afforded ; and the lasses, with their paler cheeks, the elder dames, with many a wink and yawn, were compelled to meet with their male companions (headaches and all) just three hours after they had parted from each other.

Eric Scambester had done all that man could do to supply the full means of diverting the ennui of the morning meal. The board groaned with rounds of hung beef, made after the fashion of Zetland—with pasties—with baked meats—with fish, dressed and cured in every possible manner ; nay, with the foreign delicacies of tea, coffee, and chocolate ; for, as we have already had occasion to remark, the situation of these islands made them early acquainted with various articles of foreign luxury, which were, as yet, but little known in Scotland, where, at a much later period than that we write of, one pound of green tea was dressed like cabbage, and another converted into a vegetable sauce for salt beef, by the ignorance of the good housewives to whom they had been sent as rare presents.

Besides these preparations, the table exhibited whatever mighty portions were resorted to by *bons vivants,* under the facetious name of a "hair of the dog that bit you." There was the potent Irish Usquebaugh—right Nantz—genuine Schiedam—Aquavitæ from Caithness—and golden Wasser from Hamburgh ; there was rum of formidable antiquity, and cordials from the Leeward Islands. After these details, it were needless to mention the stout home-brewed ale—the German mum, and Schwartz-bier—and still more would it be beneath our dignity to dwell upon the innumerable sorts of pottage and flummery, together with the bland, and various preparations of milk, for those who preferred thinner potations.

No wonder that the sight of so much good cheer awakened the appetite and raised the spirits of the fatigued revellers. The young men

137

began immediately to seek out their partners of the preceding evening, and to renew the small talk which had driven the night so merrily away ; while Magnus, with his stout old Norse kindred, encouraged, by precept and example, those of elder days and graver mood, to a substantial flirtation with the good things before them. Still, however, there was a long period to be filled up before dinner ; for the most protracted breakfast cannot well last above an hour ; and it was to be feared that Claud Halcro meditated the occupation of this vacant morning with a formidable recitation of his own verses, besides telling, at its full length, the whole history of his introduction to glorious John Dryden. But fortune relieved the guests of Burgh Westra from this threatened infliction, by sending them means of amusement peculiarly suited to their taste and habits.

Most of the guests were using their toothpicks, some were beginning to talk of what was to be done next, when, with haste in his step, fire in his eye, and a harpoon in his hand, Eric Scambester came to announce to the company, that there was a whale on shore, or nearly so, at the throat of the voe. Then you might have seen such a joyous, boisterous, and universal bustle, as only the love of sport, so deeply implanted in our nature, can possibly inspire. A set of country squires, about to beat for the first woodcocks of the season, were a comparison as petty, in respect to the glee, as in regard to the importance of the object ; the battue, upon a strong cover in Ettrick Forest, for the destruction of the foxes ; the insurrection of the sportsmen of the Lennox, when one of the Duke's deer gets out from Inch-Mirran ; nay, the joyous rally of the fox-chase itself, with all its blithe accompaniments of hound and horn, fall infinitely short of the animation with which the gallant sons of Thule set off to encounter the monster, whom the sea had sent for their amusement at so opportune a conjuncture.

The multifarious stores of Burgh Westra were rummaged hastily for all sorts of arms, which could be used on such an occasion. Harpoons, swords, pikes, and halberds, fell to the lot of some ; others contented themselves with hay-forks, spits and whatever else could be found, that was at once long and sharp. Thus hastily equipped, one division, under the command of Captain Cleveland, hastened to man the boats which lay in the little haven, while the rest of the party hurried by land to the scene of action.

Poor Triptolemus was interrupted in a plan, which he, too, had formed against the patience of the Zetlanders, and which was to have consisted in a lecture upon the agriculture, and the capabilities of the country, by this sudden hubbub, which put an end at once to Halcro's poetry, and to his no less formidable prose. It may be easily imagined, that he took very little interest in the sport which was so suddenly substituted for his lucubrations, and he would not even have deigned to have looked upon the active scene which was about to take place, had he not been stimulated thereunto by the exhortations of Mistress Baby. "Pit yoursell forward, man," said that provident person, "pit yoursell forward—wha kens where a blessing may light ?—they say that a' men share and share equals-aquals in the creature's ulzie, and a pint o't wad be worth siller, to light the cruize in the lang dark nights that they speak of. Pit yoursell forward, man—there's a graip to ye—faint heart never wan fair lady—wha kens but what, when it's fresh, it may eat weel eneugh, and spare butter ?"

What zeal was added to Triptolemus's motions, by the prospect of eating fresh train-oil instead of butter, we know not ; but, as better might not be, he brandished the rural implement (a stable-fork) with which he was armed, and went down to wage battle with the whale.

The situation in which the enemy's ill-fate had placed him was particularly favourable to the enterprise of the islanders. A tide of unusual height had carried the animal over a large bar of sand, into the voe or creek in which he was now lying. So soon as he found the water ebbing, he became sensible of his danger, and had made desperate efforts to get over the shallow water where the waves broke on the bar ; but hitherto he had rather injured than mended his condition, having got himself partly grounded, and lying therefore particularly exposed to the meditated attack. At this moment the enemy came down upon him. The front ranks consisted of the young and hardy, armed in the miscellaneous manner we have described ; while, to witness and animate their efforts, the young women, and the elderly persons of both sexes, took their place among the rocks, which overhung the scene of action.

As the boats had to double a little headland, ere they opened the mouth of the voe, those who came by land to the shores of the inlet had time to make the necessary reconnaissances upon the force and situation of the enemy, on whom they were about to commence a simultaneous attack by land and sea.

This duty the stout-hearted and experienced general, for so the Udaller might be termed, would intrust to no eyes but his own ; and indeed, his external appearance, and his sage conduct, rendered him alike qualified for the command which he enjoyed. His gold-laced hat was exchanged for a bearskin cap, his suit of blue broadcloth, with its scarlet lining, and loops, and frogs of bullion, had given place to a red flannel jacket, with buttons of black horn, over which he wore a seal-skin shirt curiously seamed and plaited on the bosom, such as are used by the Esquimaux, and sometimes by the Greenland whale-fishers. Sea-boots of a formidable size completed his dress, and in his hand he held a large whaling-knife, which he brandished, as if impatient to employ it in the operation of *flinching* the huge animal which lay before them,—that is, the act of separating its flesh from its bones. Upon closer examination, however, he was obliged to confess, that the sport to which he had conducted his friends, however much it corresponded with the magnificent scale of his hospitality, was likely to be attended with its own peculiar dangers and difficulties.

The animal, upwards of sixty feet in length, was lying perfectly still, in a deep part of the voe into which it had weltered, and where it seemed to await the return of tide, of which it was probably assured by instinct. A council of experienced harpooners was instantly called, and it was agreed than an effort should be made to noose the tail of this torpid leviathan, by casting a cable around it, to be made fast by anchors to the shore, and thus to secure against his escape, in case the tide should make before they were able to despatch him. Three boats were destined to this delicate piece of service, one of which the Udaller himself proposed to command, while Cleveland and Mertoun were to direct the two others. This being decided, they sat down on the strand, waiting with impatience until the naval part of the force should arrive in the voe. It was during this interval, that Triptolemus Yellowley, after measuring with his eyes the extraordinary size of the whale, observed, that in his poor mind, "A wain with six owsen, or with sixty owsen either, if they were the owsen of the country, could not drag siccan a huge creature from the water, where it was now lying, to the sea-beach."

Trifling as this remark may seem to the reader, it was connected with a subject which always fired the blood of the old Udaller, who, glancing upon Triptolemus a quick and stern look, asked him what the devil it signified, supposing a hundred oxen could not drag the whale upon the beach ? Mr. Yellowley, though not much liking the tone with which the question was put, felt that his dignity and his profit compelled him to answer as follows:—"Nay, sir—you know yoursell, Master Magnus Troil, and every one knows that knows anything, that whales of siccan size as may not be masterfully dragged on shore by the instrumentality of one wain with six owsen, are the right and property of the Admiral, who is at this time the same noble lord who is, moreover, Chamberlain of these isles."

"And I tell you, Mr. Triptolemus," said the Udaller, "as I would tell your master if he were here, that every man who risks his life to bring that fish ashore, shall have an equal share and partition, according to our ancient and lovable Norse custom and wont ; nay, if there is so much as a woman looking on, that will but touch the cable, she will be partner with us ; ay, and more than all that, if she will but say there is a reason for it, we will assign a portion to the babe that is unborn."

The strict principle of equity which dictated this last arrangement, occasioned laughter among the men, and some slight confusion among the women. The factor, however, thought it shame to be so easily daunted. "*Suum cuique tribuito*," said he ; "I will stand for my lord's right and my own."

"Will you ?" replied Magnus ; "then, by the Martyr's bones, you shall have no law of partition but that of God and Saint Olave, which we had before either factor, or treasurer, or chamberlain was heard of !—All shall share that lend a hand, and never a one else. So you, Master Factor, shall be busy as well as other folk, and think yourself lucky to share like other folk. Jump into that boat" (for the boats had by this time pulled round the headland), "and you, my lads, make way for the factor in the stern-sheets—he shall be the first man this blessed day that shall strike the fish."

The loud, authoritative voice, and the habit of absolute command inferred in the Udaller's whole manner, together with the conscious want of favourers and backers amongst the rest of the company, rendered it difficult for Triptolemus to evade compliance, although he was thus about to be placed in a situation equally novel and perilous. He was still, however, hesitating, and attempting an explanation, with a voice in which anger was qualified by fear, and both thinly disguised under an attempt to be jocular, and to represent the whole as a jest, when he heard the voice of Baby maundering in his ear,—"Wad he lose his share of the ulzie, and the lang Zetland winter coming on, when the lightest day in December is not so clear as a moonless night in the Mearns ?"

This domestic instigation, in addition to those of fear of the Udaller, and shame to seem less courageous than others, so inflamed the agriculturist's spirits, that he shook his *graip* aloft, and entered the boat with the air of Neptune himself, carrying on high his trident.

The three boats destined for this perilous service now approached the dark mass, which lay like an islet in the deepest part of the voe, and suffered them to approach without showing any sign of animation. Silently, and with such precaution as the extreme delicacy of the operation required, the intrepid adventurers, after the failure of their first attempt, and the expenditure of considerable time, succeeded in casting a cable around the body of the torpid monster, and in carrying the ends of it ashore, when an hundred hands were instantly employed in securing them. But ere this was accomplished, the tide began to make fast, and the Udaller informed his assistants, that either the fish must be killed, or at least greatly wounded, ere the depth of water on the bar was sufficient to float him ; or that he was not unlikely to escape from their joint prowess.

"Wherefore," said he, "we must set to work, and the factor shall have the honour to make the first throw."

The valiant Triptolemus caught the word ; and it is necessary to say that the patience of the whale, in suffering himself to be noosed without resistance, had abated his terrors, and very much lowered the creature in his opinion. He protested the fish had no more wit, and scarcely more activity, than a black snail ; and, influenced by this undue contempt of the adversary, he waited neither for a farther signal, nor a better weapon, nor a more suitable position, but, rising in his energy, hurled his graip with all his force against the unfortunate monster. The boats had not yet retreated from him to the distance necessary to ensure safety, when this injudicious commencement of the war took place.

Magnus Troil, who had only jested with the factor, and had reserved the launching of the first spear against the whale to some much more skilful hand, had just time to exclaim, "Mind yourselves, lads, or we are all swamped !" when the monster, roused at once from inactivity by the blow of the factor's missile, blew, with a noise resembling the explosion of a steam-engine, a huge shower of water into the air, and at the same time began to lash the waves with its tail in every direction. The boat in which Magnus presided received the shower of brine which the animal spouted aloft ; and the adventurous Triptolemus, who had a full share of the immersion, was so much astonished and terrified by the consequences of his own valorous deed, that he tumbled backwards amongst the feet of the people, who, too busy to attend to him, were actively engaged in getting the boat into shoal water, out of the whale's reach. Here he lay for some minutes, trampled on by the feet of the boatmen, until they lay on their oars to bale, when the Udaller ordered them to pull to shore, and land this spare hand, who had commenced the fishing so inauspiciously.

While this was doing, the other boats had also pulled off to safer distance, and now, from these as well as from the shore, the unfortunate native of the deep was overwhelmed by all kinds of missiles,—harpoons and spears flew against him on all sides—guns were fired, and each various means of annoyance plied which could excite him to exhaust his strength in useless rage. When the animal found that he was locked in by shallows on all sides, and became sensible, at the same time, of the strain of the cable on his body, the convulsive efforts which he made to escape, accompanied with sounds resembling deep and loud groans, would have moved the compassion of all but a practised whale-fisher. The repeated showers which he spouted into the air began now to be mingled with blood, and the waves which surrounded him assumed the same crimson appearance. Meantime the attempts of the assailants were redoubled ; but Mordaunt Mertoun and Cleveland, in particular, exerted themselves to the uttermost, contending who should display most courage in approaching the monster, so tremendous in its agonies, and should inflict the most deep and deadly wounds upon its huge bulk.

The contest seemed at last pretty well over ; for although the animal continued from time to time to make frantic exertions at liberty, yet its strength appeared so much exhausted, that, even with the assistance of the tide, which had now risen considerably, it was thought it could scarcely extricate itself.

Magnus gave the signal to venture nearer to the whale, calling out at the same time, "Close in, lads, she is not half so mad now—The factor may look for a winter's oil for the two lamps at Harfra—Pull close in, lads."

Ere his orders could be obeyed, the other two boats had anticipated his purpose ; and Mordaunt Mertoun, eager to distinguish himself above Cleveland, had, with the whole strength he possessed, plunged a half-pike into the body of the animal. But the leviathan, like a nation whose resources appear totally exhausted by previous losses and calamities, collected his whole remaining force for an effort, which proved at once desperate and successful. The wound, last received, had probably reached through his external defences of blubber, and attained some very sensitive part of the system ; for he roared aloud, as he sent to the sky a mingled sheet of brine and blood, and snapping the strong cable like a twig, overset Mertoun's boat with a blow of his tail, shot himself, by a mighty effort, over the bar, upon which the tide had now risen considerably, and made out to sea, carrying with him a whole grove of the implements which had been planted in his body, and leaving behind him, on the waters, a dark red trace of his course.

"There goes to sea your cruise of oil, Master Yellowley," said Magnus, "and you must consume mutton suet, or go to bed in the dark."

"*Operam et oleum perdidi,*" muttered Triptolemus ; "but if they catch me whale-fishing again, I will consent that the fish shall swallow me as he did Jonah."

"But where is Mordaunt Mertoun all this while ?" exclaimed Claud Halcro ; and it was instantly perceived that the youth, who had been stunned when his boat was stove, was unable to swim to shore as the other sailors did, and now floated senseless upon the waves.

We have noticed the strange and inhuman prejudice, which rendered the Zetlanders of that period unwilling to assist those whom they saw in the act of drowning, though that is the calamity to which the islanders are most frequently exposed. Three men, however, soared above this superstition. The first was Claud Halcro, who threw himself from a small rock headlong into the waves, forgetting, as he himself afterwards stated, that he could not swim, and, if possessed of the harp of Arion, had no dolphins in attendance. The first plunge which the poet made in deep water, reminding him of these deficiencies, he was fain to cling to the rock from which he had dived, and was at length glad to regain the shore, at the expense of a ducking.

Magnus Troil, whose honest heart forgot his late coolness towards Mordaunt, when he saw the youth's danger, would instantly have brought him more effectual assistance, but Eric Scambester held him fast.

"Hout, sir—hout," exclaimed that faithful attendant—"Captain Cleveland has a grip of Mr. Mordaunt—just let the twa strangers help ilk other, and stand by the upshot. The light of the country is not to be quenched for the like of them. Bide still, sir, I say—Bredness Voe is not a bowl of punch, that a man can be fished out of like a toast with a long spoon."

This sage remonstrance would have been altogether lost upon Magnus, had he not observed that Cleveland had in fact jumped out of the boat, and swam to Mertoun's assistance, and was keeping him afloat till the boat came to the aid of both. As soon as the immediate danger which called so loudly for assistance was thus ended, the honest Udaller's desire to render aid terminated also ; and recollecting the cause of offence which he had, or thought he had, against Mordaunt Mertoun, he shook off his butler's hold, and turning round scornfully from the beach, called Eric an old fool for supposing that he cared whether the young fellow sank or swam.

Still, however, amid his assumed indifference, Magnus could not help peeping over the heads of the circle, which, surrounding Mordaunt as soon as he was brought on shore, were charitably employed in endeavouring to recall him to life ; and he was not able to attain the appearance of absolute unconcern, until the young man sat up on the beach, and showed plainly that the accident had been attended with no material consequences. It was then first that, cursing the assistants for not giving the lad a glass of brandy, he walked sullenly away, as if totally unconcerned in his fate.

The women, always accurate in observing the tell-tale emotions of each other, failed not to remark, that when the sisters of Burgh Westra saw Mordaunt immersed in the waves, Minna grew as pale as death, while Brenda uttered successive shrieks of terror. But though there were some nods, winks, and hints that auld acquaintance were not easily forgot, it was, on the whole, candidly admitted, that less than such marks of interest could scarce have been expected, when they saw the companion of their early youth in the act of perishing before their eyes.

Whatever interest Mordaunt's condition excited while it seemed perilous, began to abate as he recovered himself ; and when his senses were fully restored, only Claud Halcro, with two or three others, was standing by him. About ten paces off stood Cleveland–his hair and clothes dropping water, and his features wearing so peculiar an expression, as immediately to arrest the attention of Mordaunt. There was a suppressed smile on his cheek, and a look of pride in his eye, that implied liberation from a painful restraint, and something resembling gratified scorn. Claud Halcro hastened to intimate to Mordaunt, that he owed his life to Cleveland ; and the youth, rising from the ground, and losing all other feelings in those of gratitude, stepped forward with his hand stretched out, to offer his warmest thanks to his preserver. But he stopped short in surprise, as Cleveland, retreating a pace or two, folded his arms on his breast, and declined to accept his proffered hand. He drew back in turn, and gazed with astonishment at the ungracious manner, and almost insulting look, with which Cleveland, who had formerly rather expressed a frank cordiality, or at least openness of bearing, now, after having thus rendered him a most important service, chose to receive his thanks.

"It is enough," said Cleveland, observing his surprise, "and it is unnecessary to say more about it. I have paid back my debt, and we are now equal."

"You are more than equal with me, Captain Cleveland," answered Mertoun, "because you endangered your life to do for me, what I did for you without the slightest risk ;–besides," he added, trying to give the discourse a more pleasant turn, "I have your rifle-gun to boot."

"Cowards only count danger for any point of the game," said Cleveland. "Danger has been my consort for life, and sailed with me on a thousand worse voyages ;–and for rifles, I have enough of my own, and you may see, when you will, which can use them best."

There was something in the tone with which this was said, that struck Mordaunt strongly ; it was miching malicho, as Hamlet says, and meant mischief. Cleveland saw his surprise, came close up to him, and spoke in a low tone of voice:–"Hark ye, my young brother,–there is a custom amongst us gentlemen of fortune, that when we follow the same chase and take the wind out of each other's sails, we think sixty yards of the sea-beach, and a brace of rifles, are no bad way of making our odds even."

"I do not understand you, Captain Cleveland," said Mordaunt.

"I do not suppose you do,–I did not suppose you would," said the Captain ; and, turning on his heel, with a smile that resembled a sneer, Mordaunt saw him mingle with the guests, and very soon beheld him at the side of Minna, who was talking to him with animated features, that seemed to thank him for his gallant and generous conduct.

"If it were not for Brenda," thought Mordaunt, "I almost wish he had left me in the voe, for no one seems to care whether I am alive or dead.–

144

Two rifles and sixty yards of sea-beach—is that what he points at?—It may come,—but not on the day he has saved my life with risk of his own."

While he was thus musing, Eric Scambester was whispering to Halcro, "If these two lads do not do each other a mischief, there is no faith in freits. Master Mordaunt saves Cleveland,—well.—Cleveland, in requital, has turned all the sunshine of Burgh Westra to his own side of the house ; and think what it is to lose favour in such a house as this, where the punch-kettle is never allowed to cool ! Well, now that Cleveland in his turn has been such a fool as to fish Mordaunt out of the voe, see if he does not give him sour sillocks for stock-fish."

"Pshaw, pshaw !" replied the poet, "that is all old women's fancies, my friend Eric ; for what says glorious Dryden—sainted John,—

"The yellow gall that in your bosom floats,
Engenders all these melancholy thoughts."

"Saint John, or Saint James either, may be mistaken in the matter," said Eric ; "for I think neither of them lived in Zetland. I only say, that if there is faith in old saws, these two lads will do each other a mischief ; and if they do, I trust it will light on Mordaunt Mertoun."

"And why, Eric Scambester," said Halcro hastily and angrily, "should you wish ill to that poor young man, that is worth fifty of the other ?"

"Let every one roose the ford as he find it," replied Eric ; "Master Mordaunt is all for wan water, like his old dog-fish of a father ; now Captain Cleveland, d'ye see, takes his glass, like an honest fellow and a gentleman."

"Rightly reasoned, and in thine own division," said Halcro ; and breaking off their conversation, took his way back to Burgh Westra, to which the guests of Magnus were now returning, discussing as they went, with much animation, the various incidents of their attack upon the whale, and not a little scandalised that it should have baffled all their exertions.

"I hope Captain Donderdrecht of the Eintracht of Rotterdam will never hear of it," said Magnus ; "he would swear, donner and blitzen, we were only fit to fish flounders."*

CHAPTER EIGHTEENTH

And helter-skelter have I rode to thee,
And tidings do I bring, and lucky joys,
And golden times, and happy news of price.
ANCIENT PISTOL

FORTUNE, who seems at times to bear a conscience, owed the hospitable Udaller some amends, and accordingly repaid to Burgh Westra the disappointment occasioned by the unsuccessful whale-fishing, by sending thither, on the evening of the day in which that incident happened, no less a person than the yagger, or travelling merchant, as he styled himself, Bryce Snailsfoot, who arrived in great pomp, himself on

* The contest about the whale will remind the poetical reader of Waller's Battle of the Summer Islands.

one pony, and his pack of goods swelled to nearly double its usual size, forming the burden of another, which was led by a bare-headed, bare-legged boy.

As Bryce announced himself the bearer of important news, he was introduced to the dining-apartment, where (for that primitive age was no respecter of persons) he was permitted to sit down at a side-table, and amply supplied with provisions and good liquor ; while the attentive hospitality of Magnus permitted no questions to be put to him, until, his hunger and thirst appeased, he announced, with the sense of importance attached to distant travels, that he had just yesterday arrived at Lerwick from Kirkwall, the capital of Orkney, and would have been here yesterday, but it blew hard off the Fitful Head.

"We had no wind here," said Magnus.

"There is somebody has not been sleeping then," said the pedlar, "and her name begins with N ; but Heaven is above all."

"But the news from Orkney, Bryce, instead of croaking about a capful of wind ?"

"Such news," replied Bryce, "as has not been heard this thirty years— not since Cromwell's time."

"There is not another Revolution, is there ?" said Halcro ; "King James has not come back as blithe as King Charlie did, has he ?"

"It's news," replied the pedlar, "that are worth twenty kings, and kingdoms to boot of them ; for what good did the revolutions ever do us ? and I dare say we have seen a dozen, great and sma'."

"Are any Indiamen come north about ?" said Magnus Troil.

"Ye are nearer the mark, Fowd," said the yagger ; "but it is nae Indiamen, but a gallant armed vessel, chokeful of merchandise, that they part with so easy that a decent man like mysell can afford to give the country the best pennyworths you ever saw ; and that you will say when I open that pack, for I count to carry it back another sort lighter than when I brought it here."

"Ay, ay, Bryce," said the Udaller, "you must have had good bargains if you can sell cheap ; but what ship was it ?"

"Cannot justly say—I spoke to nobody but the captain, who was a discreet man ; but he had been down on the Spanish Main, for she has silks and satins, and tobacco, I warrant you, and wine, and no lack of sugar, and bonny-wallies baith of silver and gowd, and a bonnie dredging of gold dust into the bargain."

"What was she like ?" said Cleveland, who seemed to give much attention.

"A stout ship," said the itinerant merchant, "schooner-rigger, sails like a dolphin, they say, carried twelve guns, and is pierced for twenty."

"Did you hear the captain's name ?" said Cleveland, speaking rather lower than his usual tone.

"I just ca'd him the Captain," replied Bryce Snailsfoot ; "for I make it a rule never to ask questions of them I deal with in the way of trade ; for there is many an honest captain, begging your pardon, Captain Cleveland, that does not care to have his name tacked to his title; and as long as we ken what bargains we are making, what signifies it wha we are making them wi', ye ken ?"

"Bryce Snailsfoot is a cautious man," said the Udaller, laughing ; "he knows a fool may ask more questions than a wise man cares to answer."

"I have dealt with the fair traders in my day," replied Snailsfoot, "and I ken nae use in blurting braid out with a man's name at every moment ; but I will uphold this gentleman to be a gallant commander—ay, and a kind one too ; for every one of his crew is as brave in apparel as himself nearly—the very foremast-men have their silken scarfs ; I have seen many a lady wear a warse, and think hersell nae sma' drink—and for siller buttons, and buckles, and the lave of sic vanities, there is nae end of them."

"Idiots !" muttered Cleveland between his teeth ; and then added, "I suppose they are often ashore to show all their bravery to the lasses of Kirkwall ?"

"Ne'er a bit of that are they. The Captain will scarce let them stir ashore without the boatswain go in the boat—as rough a tarpaulin as ever swab'd a deck—and you may as weel catch a cat without her claws as him without his cutlass and his double brace of pistols about him ; every man stands as much in awe of him as of the commander himsell."

"That must be Hawkins or the devil," said Cleveland.

"Aweel, Captain," replied the yagger, "be he the tane or the tither, or a wee bit o' baith, mind it is you that gave him these names, and not me."

"Why, Captain Cleveland," said the Udaller, "this may prove the very consort you spoke of."

"They must have had some good luck, then," said Cleveland, "to put them in better plight than when I left them.—Did they speak of having lost their consort, pedlar ?"

"In troth did they," said Bryce ; "that is, they said something about a partner that had gane down to Davie Jones in these seas."

"And did you tell them what you knew of her ?" said the Udaller.

"And wha the deevil wad hae been the fule, then," said the pedlar, "that I suld say sae ? When they kend what came of the ship, the next question wad have been about the cargo—and ye wad not have had me bring down an armed vessel on the coast, to harrie the poor folk about a wheen rags of duds that the sea flung upon their shores ?"

"Besides what might have been found in your own pack, you scoundrel !" said Magnus Troil ; an observation which produced a loud laugh. The Udaller could not help joining in the hilarity which applauded his jest ; but instantly composing his countenance, he said, in an unusually grave tone, "You may laugh, my friends ; but this is a matter which brings both a curse and a shame on the country ; and till we learn to regard the rights of them that suffer by the winds and waves, we shall deserve to be oppressed and hag-ridden, as we have been and are, by the superior strength of the strangers who rule us."

The company hung their heads at the rebuke of Magnus Troil. Perhaps some, even of the better class, might be conscience-struck on their own account ; and all of them were sensible that the appetite for plunder, on the part of the tenants and inferiors, was not at all times

147

restrained with sufficient strictness. But Cleveland made answer gaily, "If these honest fellows be my comrades, I will answer for them that they will never trouble the country about a parcel of chests, hammocks, and such trumpery, that the Roost may have washed ashore out of my poor sloop. What signifies to them whether the trash went to Bryce Snailsfoot, or to the bottom, or to the devil ! So unbuckle thy pack, Bryce, and show the ladies thy cargo, and perhaps we may see something that will please them."

"It cannot be his consort," said Brenda, in a whisper to her sister ; "he would have shown more joy at their appearance."

"It must be the vessel," answered Minna ; "I saw his eye glisten at the thought of being again united to the partner of his dangers."

"Perhaps it glistened," said her sister, still apart, "at the thought of leaving Zetland ; it is difficult to guess the thought of the heart from the glance of the eye."

"Judge not at least unkindly of a friend's thought," said Minna ; "and then, Brenda, if you are mistaken, the fault rests not with you."

During this dialogue, Bryce Snailsfoot was busied in uncoiling the carefully arranged cordage of his pack, which amounted to six good yards of dressed sealskin, curiously complicated and secured by all manner of knots and buckles. He was considerably interrupted in the task by the Udaller and others, who pressed him with questions respecting the stranger vessel.

"Were the officers often ashore ? and how were they received by the people of Kirkwall ?" said Magnus Troil.

"Excellently well," answered Bryce Snailsfoot ; "and the Captain and one or two of his men had been at some of the vanities and dances which went forward in the town ; but there has been some word about customs, or king's duties, or the like, and some of the higher folk, that took upon them as magistrates, or the like, had had words with the Captain, and he refused to satisfy them ; and then it is like he was more coldly looked on, and he spoke of carrying the ship round to Stromness, or the Langhope, for she lay under the guns of the battery at Kirkwall. But he" (Bryce) "thought she wad bide at Kirkwall till the summer-fair was over, for all that."

"The Orkney gentry," said Magnus Troil, "are always in a hurry to draw the Scotch collar tighter round their own necks. Is it not enough that we must pay *scat* and *wattle*,* which were all the public dues under our old Norse government ; but must they come over us with king's dues and customs besides ? It is the part of an honest man to resist these things. I have done so all my life, and will do so to the end of it."

There was a loud jubilee and shout of applause among the guests, who were (some of them at least) better pleased with Magnus Troil's latitudinarian principles with respect to the public revenue (which were extremely natural to those living in so secluded a situation, and subjected to many additional exactions), than they had been with the rigour of his judgment on the subject of wrecked goods. But Minna's inexperienced feelings carried her farther than her father, while she

* There were old Danish taxes, the latter originally for behoof of the church.

W. Collins, R. A.

View on the Coast of Zetland

The Morning after a storm.

W. Miller

W. Collins, R. A.

W. Miller

View on the Coast of Zetland, near the Njols

Moonlight.

whispered to Brenda, not unheard by Cleveland, that the tame spirit of the Orcadians had missed every chance which late incidents had given them to emancipate these islands from the Scottish yoke.

"Why," she said, "should we not, under so many changes as late times have introduced, have seized the opportunity to shake off an allegiance which is not justly due from us, and to return to the protection of Denmark, our parent country? Why should we yet hesitate to do this, but that the gentry of Orkney have mixed families and friendship so much with our invaders, that they have become dead to the throb of the heroic Norse blood, which they derived from their ancestors?"

The latter part of this patriotic speech happened to reach the astonished ears of our friend Triptolemus, who, having a sincere devotion for the Protestant succession, and the Revolution as established, was surprised into the ejaculation, "As the old cock crows the young cock learns—hen I should say, mistress, and I crave your pardon if I say anything amiss in either gender. But it is a happy country where the father declares against the king's customs, and the daughter against the king's crown ; and, in my judgment, it can end in naething but trees and tows."

"Trees are scarce among us," said Magnus ; "and for ropes, we need them for our rigging, and cannot spare them to be shirt collars."

"And whoever," said the Captain, "takes umbrage at what this young lady says, had better keep his ears and tongue for a safer employment than such an adventure."

"Ay, ay," said Triptolemus, "it helps the matter much to speak truths, whilk are as unwelcome to a proud stomach, as wet clover to a cow's, in a land where lads are ready to draw the whittle if a lassie but looks awry. But what manners are to be expected in a country where folk call a pleugh-sock a markal ?"

"Hark ye, Master Yellowley," said the Captain, smiling, "I hope my manners are not among those abuses which you come hither to reform ; any experiment on them may be dangerous."

"As well as difficult," said Triptolemus, drily ; "but fear nothing, Captain Cleveland, from my remonstrances. My labours regard the men and things of the earth, and not the men and things of the sea,—you are not of my element."

"Let us be friends, then, old Clod-compeller," said the Captain.

"Clod-compeller !" said the agriculturist, bethinking himself of the lore of his earlier days ; "Clod-compeller *pro* cloud-compeller Νεφεληγερέτα Ζευς — *Græcum est,*—in which voyage came you by that phrase ?"

"I have travelled books as well as seas in my day," said the Captain ; "but my last voyages have been of a sort to make me forget my early cruises through classic knowledge.—But come here, Bryce—hast cast off the lashing ?—Come all hands, and let us see if he has aught in his cargo that is worth looking upon."

With a proud, and, at the same time, a wily smile, did the crafty pedlar display a collection of wares far superior to those which usually filled his packages, and, in particular, some stuffs and embroideries, of such beauty and curiosity, fringed, flowered, and worked, with such art and magnificence, upon foreign and arabesque patterns, that the sight might have dazzled a far more brilliant company than the simple race of Thule. All beheld and admired, while Mistress Baby Yellowley, holding up her hands, protested it was a sin even to look upon such extravagance, and worse than murder so much as to ask the price of them.

Others, however, were more courageous ; and the prices demanded by the merchant, if they were not, as he himself declared, something just more than nothing—short only of an absolute free gift of his wares, were nevertheless so moderate, as to show that he himself must have made an easy acquisition of the goods, judging by the rate at which he offered to part with them. Accordingly, the cheapness of the articles created a rapid sale ; for in Zetland, as well as elsewhere, wise folk buy more from the prudential desire to secure a good bargain, than from any real occasion for the purchase. The Lady Glowrowrum bought seven petticoats and twelve stomachers on this sole principle, and other matrons present rivalled her in this sagacious species of economy. The Udaller was also a considerable purchaser ; but the principal customer for whatever could please the eye of beauty, was the gallant Captain Cleveland, who rummaged the yagger's stores in selecting presents for the ladies of the party, in which Minna and Brenda Troil were especially remembered.

"I fear," said Magnus Troil, "that the young women are to consider these pretty presents are keepsakes, and that all this liberality is only a sure sign we are soon to lose you ?"

This question seemed to embarrass him to whom it was put.

"I scarce know," he said, with some hesitation, "whether this vessel is my consort or no—I must take a trip to Kirkwall to make sure of that matter, and then I hope to return to Dunrossness to bid you all farewell."

"In that case," said the Udaller, after a moment's pause, "I think I may carry you thither. I should be at the Kirkwall fair, to settle with the merchants I have consigned my fish to, and I have often promised Minna and Brenda that they should see the fair. Perhaps also your consort, or these strangers, whoever they be, may have some merchandise that will suit me. I love to see my rigging-loft well stocked with goods, almost as much as to see it full of dancers. We will go to Orkney in my own brig, and I can offer you a hammock, if you will."

The offer seemed so acceptable to Cleveland, that, after pouring himself forth in thanks, he seemed determined to mark his joy by exhausting Bryce Snailsfoot's treasures in liberality to the company. The contents of a purse of gold were transferred to the yagger, with a facility and indifference on the part of its former owner which argued either the greatest profusion, or consciousness of superior and inexhaustible wealth ; so, that Baby whispered to her brother, that "if he could afford to fling away money at this rate, the lad had made a better voyage in a broken ship, than all the skippers of Dundee had made in their haill anes for a twelvemonth past."

But the angry feeling in which she made this remark was much mollified, when Cleveland, whose object it seemed that evening to be, to buy golden opinions of all sorts of men, approached her with a garment somewhat resembling in shape the Scottish plaid, but woven of a sort of wool so soft, that it felt to the touch as if it were composed of eider down. "This," he said, "was a part of a Spanish lady's dress called a *mantilla*; as it would exactly fit the size of Mrs. Baby Yellowley, and was well suited for the fogs of the climate of Zetland, he entreated her to wear it for his sake." The lady, with as much condescending sweetness as her countenance was able to express, not only consented to receive this mark of gallantry, but permitted the donor to arrange the mantilla upon her projecting and bony shoulder-blades, where, said Claud Halcro, "it hung for all the world, as if it had been stretched betwixt a couple of cloak-pins."

While the Captain was performing this piece of courtesy, much to the entertainment of the company, which, it may be presumed, was his principal object from the beginning, Mordaunt Mertoun made purchase of a small golden chaplet, with the private intention of presenting it to Brenda, when he should find an opportunity. The price was fixed, and the article laid aside. Claud Halcro also showed some desire of possessing a silver box of antique shape, for depositing tobacco, which he was in the habit of using in considerable quantity. But the bard seldom had current coin in promptitude, and, indeed, in his wandering way of life, had little occasion for any; and Bryce, on the other hand, his having been hitherto a ready-money trade, protested, that his very moderate profits upon such rare and choice articles would not allow of his affording credit to the purchaser. Mordaunt gathered the import of this conversation from the mode in which they whispered together, while the bard seemed to advance a wishful finger towards the box in question, and the cautious pedlar detained it with the weight of his whole hand, as if he had been afraid it would literally make itself wings, and fly into Claud Halcro's pocket. Mordaunt Mertoun at this moment, desirous to gratify an old acquaintance, laid the price of the box on the table, and said he would not permit Master Halcro to purchase that box, as he had settled in his own mind to make him a present of it.

"I cannot think of robbing you, my dear young friend," said the poet; "but the truth is, that that same box does remind me strangely of glorious John's, out of which I had the honour to take a pinch at the Wits' Coffeehouse, for which I think more highly of my right-hand finger and thumb than any other part of my body; only you must allow me to pay you back the price when my Urkaster stock-fish come to market."

"Settle that as you like betwixt you," said the yagger, taking up Mordaunt's money; "the box is bought and sold."

"And how dare you sell over again," said Captain Cleveland, suddenly interfering, "what you already have sold to me?"

All were surprised at this interjection, which was hastily made, as Cleveland, having turned from Mistress Baby, had become suddenly, and, as it seemed, not without emotion, aware what articles Bryce Snailsfoot was now disposing of. To this short and fierce question, the yagger, afraid to contradict a customer of his description, answered only by stammering, that the "Lord knew he meant nae offence."

"How, sir ! no offence !" said the seaman, "and dispose of my property ?" extending his hand at the same time to the box and chaplet ; "restore the young gentleman's money, and learn to keep your course on the meridian of honesty."

The yagger, confused and reluctant, pulled out his leathern pouch to repay to Mordaunt the money he had just deposited in it ; but the youth was not to be so satisfied.

"The articles," he said, "were bought and sold—these were your own words, Bryce Snailsfoot, in Master Halcro's hearing ; and I will suffer neither you nor any other to deprive me of my property."

"*Your* property, young man ?" said Cleveland ; "it is mine—I spoke to Bryce respecting them an instant before I turned from the table."

"I—I—I had not just heard distinctly," said Bryce, evidently unwilling to offend any party.

"Come, come," said the Udaller, "we will have no quarrelling about baubles ; we shall be summoned presently to the rigging-loft,"—so he used to call the apartment used as a ball-room,—"and we must all go in good humour. The things shall remain with Bryce for to-night, and to-morrow I will myself settle whom they shall belong to."

The laws of the Udaller in his own house were absolute as those of the Medes. The two young men, regarding each other with looks of sullen displeasure, drew off in different directions.

It is seldom that the second day of a prolonged festival equals the first. The spirits, as well as the limbs, are jaded, and unequal to the renewed expenditure of animation and exertion ; and the dance at Burgh Westra was sustained with much less mirth than on the prèceding evening. It was yet an hour from midnight, when even the reluctant Magnus Troil, after regretting the degeneracy of the times, and wishing he could transfuse into the modern Hjaltlanders some of the vigour which still animated his own frame, found himself compelled to give the signal for general retreat.

Just as this took place, Halcro, leading Mordaunt Mertoun a little aside, said he had a message to him from Captain Cleveland.

"A message !" said Mordaunt, his heart beating somewhat thick as he spoke—"A challenge, I suppose ?"

"A challenge !" repeated Halcro ; "who ever heard of a challenge in our quiet islands ? Do you think that I look like a carrier of challenges, and to you of all men living ?—I am none of those fighting fools, as glorious John calls them ; and it was not quite a message I had to deliver—only thus far—this Captain Cleveland, I find, hath set his heart upon having these articles you looked at."

"He shall not have them, I swear to you," replied Mordaunt Mertoun.

"Nay, but hear me," said Halcro ; "it seems that, by the marks or arms that are upon them, he knows that they were formerly his property. Now, were you to give me the box, as you promised, I fairly tell you, I should give the man back his own."

"And Brenda might do the like," thought Mordaunt to himself, and instantly replied aloud, "I have thought better of it, my friend. Captain

Cleveland shall have the toys he sets such store by, but it is on one sole condition."

"Nay, but you will spoil all with your conditions," said Halcro ; "for as glorious John says, conditions are but"—"

"Hear me, I say, with patience.—My condition is, that he keeps the toys in exchange for the rifle-gun I accepted from him, which will leave no obligation between us on either side."

"I see where you would be—this is Sebastian and Dorax all over. Well, you may let the yagger know he is to deliver the things to Cleveland—I think he is mad to have them—and I will let Cleveland know the conditions annexed, otherwise honest Bryce might come by two payments instead of one ; and I believe his conscience would not choke upon it."

With these words, Halcro went to seek out Cleveland, while Mordaunt, observing Snailsfoot, who, as a sort of privileged person, had thrust himself into the crowd at the bottom of the dancing-room, went up to him, and gave him directions to deliver the disputed articles to Cleveland as soon as he had an opportunity.

"Ye are in the right, Maister Mordaunt," said the yagger ; "ye are a prudent and a sensible lad—a calm answer turneth away wrath—and myself, I sall be willing to please you in ony trifling matters in my sma' way ; for, between the Udaller of Burgh Westra and Captain Cleveland, a man is, as it were, atween the deil and the deep sea ; and it was like that the Udaller in the end would have taken your part in the dispute, for he is a man that loves justice."

"Which apparently you care very little about, Maister Snailsfoot," said Mordaunt, "otherwise there could have been no dispute whatsoever, the right being so clearly on my side, if you had pleased to bear witness according to the dictates of truth."

"Maister Mordaunt," said the yagger, "I must own there was, as it were, a colouring or shadow of justice on your side ; but then, the justice that I meddle with is only justice in the way of trade, to have an ellwand of due length, if it be not something worn out with leaning on it in my lang and painful journeys, and to buy and sell by just weight and measure, twenty-four merks to the lispund ; but I have nothing to do, to do justice betwixt man and man, like a Fowd* or a Law right-man, at a lawting lang syne."

"No one asked you to do so, but only to give evidence according to your conscience," replied Mordaunt, not greatly pleased either with the part the yagger had acted during the dispute, or the construction which he seemed to put on his own motives for yielding up the point.

But Bryce Snailsfoot wanted not his answer : "My conscience," he said, "Maister Mordaunt, is as tender as ony man's in my degree ; but she is something of a timorsome nature, cannot abide angry folk, and can never speak above her breath when there is aught of a fray going forward. Indeed, she hath at all times a small and low voice."

"Which you are not much in the habit of listening to," said Mordaunt.

* Sheriff or judge. See Glossary.

"There is that on your ain breast that proves the contrary," said Bryce resolutely.

"In my breast ?" said Mordaunt, somewhat angrily—"what know I of you ?"

"I said *on* your breast, Maister Mordaunt, and not *in* it. I am sure nae eye that looks on that waistcoat upon your gallant brisket, but will say, that the merchant who sold such a piece for four dollars had justice and conscience, and a kind heart to a customer to the boot of a' that ; sae ye shouldna be sae thrawart wi' me for having spared the breath of my mouth in a fool's quarrel."

"I thrawart !" said Mordaunt ; "pooh, you silly man ! I have no quarrel with you."

"I am glad of it," said the travelling merchant ; "I will quarrel with no man, with my will—least of all with an old customer ; and if you will walk by my advice, you will quarrel nane with Captain Cleveland. He is like one of yon cutters and slashers that have come into Kirkwall, that think as little of slicing a man, as we do flinching a whale—it's their trade to fight, and they live by it ; and they have the advantage of the like of you, that only take it up at your own hand, and in the way of pastime, when you hae nothing better to do."

The company had now almost dispersed ; and, Mordaunt, laughing at the yagger's caution, bade him good-night, and went to his own place of repose, which had been assigned to him by Eric Scambester (who acted the part of chamberlain as well as butler) in a small room or rather closet in one of the out-houses, furnished for the occasion with the hammock of a sailor.

CHAPTER NINETEENTH

I pass like night from land to land,
  I have strange power of speech ;
So soon as e'er his face I see,
I know the man that must hear me,
  To him my tale I teach.
COLERIDGE'S RIME OF THE ANCIENT MARINER

THE daughters of Magnus Troil shared the same bed, in a chamber which had been that of their parents before the death of their mother. Magnus, who suffered grievously under that dispensation of Providence, had become disgusted with the apartment. The nuptial chamber was abandoned to the pledges of his bereaved affection, of whom the eldest was at that period only four years old, or thereabouts ; and having been their nursery in infancy, continued, though now tricked and adorned according to the best fashion of the islands and the taste of the lovely sisters themselves, to be their sleeping-room, or, in the old Norse dialect, their bower.

It had been for many years the scene of the most intimate confidence, if that could be called confidence, where, in truth, there was nothing to be confided—where neither sister had a secret—and where every thought that had birth in the bosom of the one was, without either hesitation or doubt, confided to the other as spontaneously as it had arisen. But since Cleveland abode in the mansion of Burgh Westra, each of the lovely sisters had entertained thoughts which are not lightly or easily communicated, unless she who listens to them has previously assured herself that the confidence will be kindly received. Minna had noticed, what other and less interested observers had been unable to perceive, that Cleveland, namely, held a lower rank in Brenda's opinion than in her own; and Brenda, on her side, thought that Minna had hastily and unjustly joined in the prejudices which had been excited against Mordaunt Mertoun in the mind of their father. Each was sensible that she was no longer the same to her sister; and this conviction was a painful addition to other painful apprehensions which they supposed they had to struggle with. Their manner toward each other was, in outward appearances, and in all the little cares by which affection can be expressed, even more assiduously kind than before, as if both, conscious that their internal reserve was a breach of their sisterly union, strove to atone for it by double assiduity in those external marks of affection, which, at other times, when there was nothing to hide, might be omitted without inferring any consequences.

On the night referred to in particular the sisters felt more especially the decay of the confidence which used to exist betwixt them. The proposed voyage to Kirkwall, and that at the time of the fair, when persons of every degree in these islands repair thither, either for business or amusement, was likely to be an important incident in lives usually so simple and uniform as theirs; and a few months ago Minna and Brenda would have been awake half the night, anticipating, in their talk with each other, all that was likely to happen on so momentous an occasion. But now the subject was just mentioned, and suffered to drop, as if the topic was likely to produce a difference betwixt them, or to call forth a more open display of their several opinions than either was willing to make to the other.

Yet such was their natural openness and gentleness of disposition, that each sister imputed to herself the fault that there was aught like estrangement existing between them; and when, having finished their devotions and betaken themselves to their common couch, they folded each other in their arms, and exchanged a sisterly kiss and a sisterly good-night, they seemed mutually to ask pardon, and to exchange forgiveness, although neither said a word of offence, either offered or received; and both were soon plunged in that light and yet profound repose which is only enjoyed when sleep sinks down on the eyes of youth and innocence.

On the night to which the story relates, both sisters were visited by dreams, which, though varied by the moods and habits of the sleepers, bore yet a strange general resemblance to each other.

Minna dreamed that she was in one of the most lonely recesses of the beach called Swartaster, where the incessant operation of the waves,

155

indenting a calcareous rock, has formed a deep *halier*, which, in the language of the island, means a subterranean cavern, into which the tide ebbs and flows. Many of these run to an extraordinary and unascertained depth under ground, and are the secure retreat of cormorants and seals, which it is neither easy nor safe to pursue to their extreme recesses. Amongst these this halier of Swartaster was accounted peculiarly inaccessible, and shunned both by fowlers and by seamen on account of sharp angles and turnings in the cave itself, as well as the sunken rocks which rendered it very dangerous for skiffs or boats to advance far into it, especially if there was the usual swell of an island tide. From the dark-browed mouth of this cavern it seemed to Minna in her dream that she beheld a mermaid issue, not in the classical dress of a Nereid, as in Claud Halcro's masque of the preceding evening, but with comb and glass in hand, according to popular belief, and lashing the waves with that long scaly train, which, in the traditions of the country, forms so frightful a contrast with the fair face, long tresses, and displayed bosom, of a human and earthly female of surpassing beauty. She seemed to beckon to Minna, while her wild notes rang sadly in her ear, and denounced, in prophetic sounds, calamity and woe.

The vision of Brenda was of a different description, yet equally melancholy. She sat, as she thought, in her favourite bower, surrounded by her father and a party of his most beloved friends, amongst whom Mordaunt Mertoun was not forgotten. She was required to sing ; and she strove to entertain them with a lively ditty, in which she was accounted eminently successful, and which she sung with such simple, yet natural humour, as seldom failed to produce shouts of laughter and applause, while all who could, or who could not sing, were irresistibly compelled to lend their voices to the chorus. But, on this occasion, it seemed as if her own voice refused all its usual duty, and as if, while she felt herself unable to express the words of the well-known air, it assumed, in her own despite, the deep tones and wild and melancholy notes of Norna of Fitful Head, for the purpose of chanting some wild Runic rhyme, resembling those sung by the heathen priests of old, when the victim (too often human) was bound to the fatal altar of Odin or of Thor.

At length the two sisters at once started from sleep, and, uttering a low scream of fear, clasped themselves in each other's arms. For their fancy had not altogether played them false ; the sounds which had suggested their dreams were real, and sung within their apartment. They knew the voice well, indeed, and yet, knowing to whom it belonged, their surprise and fear were scarce the less when they saw the well-known Norna of Fitful Head seated by the chimney of the apartment, which, during the summer season, contained an iron lamp well trimmed, and in winter a fire of wood or of turf.

She was wrapped in her long and ample garment of wadmaal, and moved her body slowly to and fro over the pale flame of the lamp as she sung lines to the following purport, in a slow, sad, almost an unearthly accent:—

For leagues along the watery way,
    Through gulf and stream my course has been ;
The billows know my Runic lay,
    And smooth their crests to silent green.

The billows know my Runic lay,—
    The gulf grows smooth, the stream is still ;
But human hearts, more wild than they,
    Know but the rule of wayward will.

One hour is mine, in all the year,
    To tell my woes—and one alone ;
When gleams this magic lamp, 'tis here,—
    When dies the mystic light, 'tis gone.

Daughters of northern Magnus, hail !
    The lamp is lit, the flame is clear,—
To you I come to tell my tale,
    Awake, arise, my tale to hear !

Norna was well known to the daughters of Troil, but it was not without emotion, although varied by their respective dispositions, that they beheld her so unexpectedly, and at such an hour. Their opinions with respect to the supernatural attributes to which she pretended were extremely different.

Minna, with an unusual intensity of imagination, although superior in talent to her sister, was more apt to listen to, and delight in, every tale of wonder, and was at all times more willing to admit impressions which gave her fancy scope and exercise, without minutely examining their reality. Brenda, on the other hand, had, in her gaiety, a slight propensity to satire, and was often tempted to laugh at the very circumstances upon which Minna founded her imaginative dreams ; and, like all who love the ludicrous, she did not readily suffer herself to be imposed upon, or overawed, by pompous pretensions of any kind whatever. But, as her nerves were weaker and more irritable than those of her sister, she often paid in voluntary homage, by her fears, to ideas which her reason disowned ; and hence Claud Halcro, used to say, in reference to many of the traditionary superstitions around Burgh Westra, that Minna believed them without trembling, and that Brenda trembled without believing them. In our own more enlightened days, there are few whose undoubting mind and native courage have not felt Minna's high-wrought tone of enthusiasm, and perhaps still fewer, who have not, at one time or other, felt, like Brenda, their nerves confess the influence of terrors which their reason disowned and despised.

Under the power of such different feelings, Minna, when the first moment of surprise was over, prepared to spring from her bed, and go to greet Norna, who, she doubted not, had come on some errand fraught with fate ; while Brenda, who only beheld in her a woman partially deranged in her understanding, and who yet, from the extravagance of her claims, regarded her as an undefined object of awe, or rather terror, detained her sister, by an eager and terrified grasp, while she whispered in her ear an anxious entreaty that she would call for assistance. But the soul of Minna was too highly wrought up by the crises at which her fate seemed to have arrived, to permit her to follow the dictates of her sister's fears ; and, extricating herself from Brenda's hold, she hastily threw on a loose night-gown, and, stepping boldly across the apartment, while her heart throbbed rather with high excitement than with fear, she thus addressed her singular visitor:—

"Norna, if your mission regards us, as your words seem to express, there is one of us, at least, who will receive its import with reverence, but without fear."

"Norna, dear Norna," said the tremulous voice of Brenda,— who, feeling no safety in the bed after Minna quitted it, had followed her, as fugitives crowd into the rear of an advancing army, because they dare not remain behind, and who now stood half-concealed by her sister, and holding fast by the skirts of her gown—"Norna, dear Norna," said she, "whatever you are to say, let it be to-morrow. I will call Euphane Fea, the housekeeper, and she will find a bed for you for the night."

"No bed for me !" said their nocturnal visitor ; "no closing of the eyes for me ! They have watched as shelf and stack appeared and disappeared betwixt Burgh Westra and Orkney—they have seen the man of Hoy sink into the sea, and the Peak of Hengcliff arise from it, and yet they have not tasted of slumber ; nor must they slumber now till my task is ended. Sit down then, Minna, and thou, silly trembler, sit down, while I trim my lamp—Don your clothes, for the tale is long, and ere 'tis done, ye will shiver with worse than cold."

"For Heaven's sake, then, put it off till daylight, dear Norna !" said Brenda ; "the dawn cannot be far distant ; and if you are to tell us of anything frightful, let it be by daylight, and not by the dim glimmer of that blue lamp."

"Patience, fool !" said their uninvited guest. "Not by daylight should Norna tell a tale that might blot the sun out of heaven, and blight the hopes of the hundred boats that will leave this shore ere noon, to commence their deep-sea fishing,—ay, and of the hundred families that will await their return. The demon, whom the sounds will not fail to awaken, must shake his dark wings over a shipless and a boatless sea, as he rushes from his mountain to drink the accents of horror he loves so well to listen to."

"Have pity on Brenda's fears, good Norna," said the elder sister, "and at least postpone this frightful communication to another place and hour."

"Maiden, no !" replied Norna, sternly ; "it must be told while that lamp yet burns. Mine is no daylight tale—by that lamp it must be told, which is framed out of the gibbet-irons of the cruel Lord of Wodensvoe, who murdered his brother ; and has for its nourishment—but be that nameless—enough that its food never came either from the fish or from the fruit !—See, it waxes dim and dimmer, nor must my tale last longer than its flame endureth. Sit ye down there, while I sit here opposite to you, and place the lamp betwixt us ; for within the sphere of its light the demon dares not venture."

The sisters obeyed, Minna casting a slow, awe-struck, yet determined look all around, as if to see the Being, who, according to the doubtful words of Norna, hovered in their neighbourhood ; while Brenda's fears were mingled with some share both of anger and of impatience. Norna paid no attention to either, but began her story in the following words:—

"Ye know, my daughters, that your blood is allied to mine, but in what degree ye know not ; for there was early hostility betwixt your grandsire and him who had the misfortune to call me daughter.—Let me term him by his Christian name of Erland, for that which marks our relation I dare not bestow. Your grandsire Olave was the brother of Erland. But when the wide Udal possessions of their father Rolfe Troil, the most rich and well estated of any who descended from the old Norse stock, were divided betwixt the brothers, the Fowd gave to Erland his father's lands in Orkney, and reserved for Olave those of Hjaltland. Discord arose between the brethren ; for Erland held that he was wronged ; and when the Lawting,* with the Raddmen and Lawright men, confirmed the division, he went in wrath to Orkney, cursing Hjaltland and its inhabitants—cursing his brother and his blood.

"But the love of the rock and of the mountain still wrought on Erland's mind, and he fixed his dwelling not on the soft hills of Ophir, or the green plains of Gramesey, but in the wild and mountainous Isle of Hoy, whose summit rises to the sky like the cliffs of Foulah and of Feroe.† He knew,—that unhappy Erland,—whatever of legendary lore Scald and Bard had left behind them ; and to teach me that knowledge, which was to cost us both so dear, was the chief occupation of his old age. I learned to visit each lonely barrow—each lofty cairn—to tell its appropriate tale, and to soothe with rhymes in his praise the spirit of the stern warrior who dwelt within. I knew where the sacrifices were made of yore to Thor and to Odin—on what stones the blood of the victims flowed—where stood the dark browed priest—where the crested chiefs, who consulted the will of the idol—where the most distant crowd of inferior worshippers, who looked on in awe or in terror. The places most shunned by the timid peasants had no terrors for me ; I dared walk in the fairy circle, and sleep by the magic spring.

"But, for my misfortune, I was chiefly fond to linger about the Dwarfie Stone, as it is called, a relic of antiquity, which strangers look on with curiosity, and the natives with awe. It is a huge fragment of a rock, which lies in a broken and rude valley, full of stones and precipices, in the recesses of the Ward Hill of Hoy. The inside of the rock has two couches, hewn by no earthly hand, and having a small passage between them. The doorway is now open to the weather ; but beside it lies a large stone, which, adapted to grooves, still visible in the entrance, once had served to open and to close this extraordinary dwelling, which Trolld, a dwarf famous in the northern Sagas, is said to have framed for his own favourite residence. The lonely shepherd avoids the place, for at sunrise,

* The Lawting was the Comitia, or Supreme Court of the country, being retained both in Orkney and Zetland, and presenting, in their constitution, the rude origin of a parliament.

† And from which hill of Hoy, at midsummer, the sun may be seen, it is said, at midnight. So says the geographer Bleau (1653), although, according to Dr. Wallace, it cannot be the true body of the sun which is visible, but only its image refracted through some watery cloud upon the horizon.

high noon, or sunset, the misshapen form of the necromantic owner may sometimes still be seen sitting by the Dwarfie Stone.* I feared not the apparition, for, Minna, my heart was as bold, and my hand was as innocent as yours. In my childish courage, I was even but too presumptuous, and the thirst after things unattainable led me, like our primitive mother, to desire increase of knowledge, even by prohibited means. I longed to possess the power of the Voluspæ and divining women of our ancient race ; to wield, like them, command over the elements ; and to summon the ghosts of deceased heroes from their caverns, that they might recite their daring deeds, and impart to me their hidden treasures. Often when watching by the Dwarfie Stone, with mine eyes fixed on the Ward Hill, which rises above that gloomy valley, I have distinguished, among the dark rocks, that wonderful carbuncle,† which gleams ruddy as a furnace to them who view it from beneath, but has ever become invisible to him whose daring foot has scaled the precipices from which it darts its splendour. My vain and youthful bosom burned to investigate these and an hundred other mysteries, which the Sagas that I perused, or learned from Erland, rather indicated than explained ; and in my daring mood, I called on the Lord of the Dwarfie Stone to aid me in attaining knowledge inaccessible to mere mortals."

"And the evil spirit heard your summons ?" said Minna, her blood curdling as she listened.

"Hush," said Norna, lowering her voice, "vex him not with reproach—he is with us—he hears us even now."

Brenda started from her seat.—"I will to Euphane Fea's chamber," she said, "and leave you, Minna and Norna, to finish your stories of hobgoblins and of dwarfs at your own leisure ; I care not for them at any time, but I will not endure them at midnight, and by this pale lamplight."

She was accordingly in the act of leaving the room, when her sister detained her.

"Is this the courage," she said, "of her that disbelieves whatever the history of our fathers tells us of supernatural prodigy ? What Norna has to tell us concerns the fate, perhaps, of our father and his house ;—if I can listen to it, trusting that God and my innocence will protect me from all that is malignant, you, Brenda, who believe not in such influence, have surely no cause to tremble. Credit me, that for the guiltless there is no fear."

"There may be no danger," said Brenda, unable to suppress her natural turn for humour, "but as the old jest-book says, there is much fear. However, Minna, I will stay with you ;—the rather," she added, in a whisper, "that I am loath to leave you alone with this frightful woman, and that I have a dark staircase and long passage betwixt and Euphane Fea, else I would have her here ere I were five minutes older."

"Call no one hither, maiden, upon peril of thy life," said Norna, "and interrupt not my tale again ; for it cannot and must not be told after that charmed light has ceased to burn."

* Note L. The Dwarfie Stone.
† Note M. Carbuncle on the Ward Hill.

"And I thank Heaven," said Brenda to herself, "that the oil burns low in the cruize ! I am sorely tempted to lend it a puff, but then Norna would be alone with us in the dark, and that would be worse."

So saying, she submitted to her fate, and sat down, determined to listen, with all the equanimity which she could command to the remaining part of Norna's tale, which went on as follows:—

"It happened on a hot summer day, and just about the hour of noon," continued Norna, "as I sat by the Dwarfie Stone, with my eyes fixed on the Ward Hill, whence the mysterious and ever-burning carbuncle shed its rays more brightly than usual, and repined in my heart at the restricted bounds of human knowledge, that at length I could not help exclaiming, in the words of an ancient Saga—

> Dwellers of the mountain, rise,
> Trolld the powerful, Haims the wise !
> Ye who taught weak woman's tongue
> Words that sway the wise and strong,
> Ye who taught weak woman's hand
> How to wield the magic wand,
> And wake the gales on Foulah's steep,
> Or lull wild Sumburgh's waves to sleep !
> Still are ye yet ?—Not yours the power
> Ye knew in Odin's mightier hour.
> What are ye now but empty names,
> Powerful Trolld, sagacious Haims,
> That, lightly spoken, lightly heard,
> Float on the air like thistle's beard ?

"I had scarce uttered these words," proceeded Norna, "ere the sky, which had been till then unusually clear, grew so suddenly dark around me, that it seemed more like midnight than noon. A single flash of lightning showed me at once the desolate landscape of heath, morass, mountain, and precipice, which lay around ; a single clap of thunder wakened all the echoes of the Ward Hill, which continued so long to repeat the sound, that it seemed some rock, rent by the thunderbolt from the summit, was rolling over cliff and precipice into the valley. Immediately after fell a burst of rain so violent, that I was fain to shun its pelting, by creeping into the interior of the mysterious stone.

"I seated myself on the larger stone couch, which is cut at the farther end of the cavity, and with my eyes fixed on the smaller bed, wearied myself with conjectures respecting the origin and purpose of my singular place of refuge. Had it been really the work of that powerful Trolld, to whom the poetry of the Scalds referred it ? Or was it the tomb of some Scandinavian chief, interred with his arms and his wealth, perhaps also with his immolated wife, that what he loved best in life might not in death be divided from him ? Or was it the abode of penance, chosen by some devoted anchorite of later days ? Or the idle work of some wandering mechanic, whom chance, and whim, and leisure, had thrust upon such an undertaking ? I tell you the thoughts that then floated through my brain, that you may know that what ensued

* Or consecrated mountain, used by the Scandinavian priests for the purposes of their idol-worship.

was not the vision of a prejudiced or prepossessed imagination, but an apparition, as certain as it was awful.

"Sleep had gradually crept on me, amidst my lucubrations, when I was startled from my slumbers by a second clap of thunder ; and, when I awoke, I saw, through the dim light which the upper aperture admitted, the unshapely and indistinct form of Trolld the dwarf, seated opposite me on the lesser couch, which his square and misshaped bulk seemed absolutely to fill up. I was startled, but not affrighted ; for the blood of the ancient race of Lochlin was warm in my veins. He spoke ; and his words were of Norse, so old, that few, save my father, or I myself, could have comprehended their import,–such language as was spoken in these islands ere Olave planted the cross on the ruins of heathenism. His meaning was dark also and obscure, like that which the Pagan priests were wont to deliver, in the name of their idols, to the tribes that assembled at the *Helgafels*.* This was the import,–

A thousand winters dark have flown,
Since o'er the threshold of my Stone
A votaress pass'd, my power to own.
Visitor bold
† Of the mansion of Trolld,
    Maiden haughty of heart,
Who hast hither presumed,–
Ungifted, undoom'd,
    Thou shalt not depart.
The power thou dost covet
    O'er tempest and wave,
Shall be thine, thou proud maiden,
    By beach and by cave,–
By stack† and by skerry‡, by noup§, and by voeʃ,
By airʃʃ, and by wick**, and by helyer†† and gio‡‡,
And by every wild shore which the northern winds know,
    And the northern tides lave.
But though this shall be given thee, thou desperately brave,
I doom thee that never the gift thou shalt have,
    Till thou reave thy life's giver
    Of the gift which he gave.

"I answered him in nearly the same strain ; for the spirit of the ancient Scalds of our race was upon me, and, far from fearing the phantom, with whom I sat cooped within so narrow a space, I felt the impulse of that high courage which thrust the ancient champions and Druidesses upon contests with the invisible world, when they thought that the earth no longer contained enemies worthy to be subdued by them. Therefore did I answer him thus:–

* Or consecrated mountain, used by the Scandinavian priests for the purposes of their idol-worship.
† *Stack.* A precipitous rock rising out of the sea.
‡*Skerry.* A flat insulated rock, not subject to the overflowing of the sea.
§ *Noup.* A round-headed entrance.
ʃ *Voe.* A creek or inlet of the sea.
ʃʃ *Air.* An open sea-beach.
** *Wick.* An open bay.
†† *Helyer.* A cavern into which the tide flows.
‡‡ *Gio.* A deep ravine which admits the sea.

Dark are thy words, and severe,
　　Thou dweller in the stone ;
But trembling and fear
　　To her are unknown,
Who hath sought thee here
　　In thy dwelling lone.
Come what comes soever,
　　The worst I can endure ;
Life is but a short fever,
　　And Death is the cure.

"The Demon scowled at me, as if at once incensed and overawed ; and then, coiling himself up in a thick and sulphureous vapour, he disappeared from his place. I did not, till that moment, feel the influence of fright, but then it seized me. I rushed into the open air, where the tempest had passed away, and all was pure and serene. After a moment's breathless pause, I hasted home, musing by the way on the words of the phantom, which I could not, as often happens, recall so distinctly to memory at the time, as I have been since able to do.

"It may seem strange that such an apparition should, in time, have glided from my mind, like a vision of the night—but so it was. I brought myself to believe it the work of fancy—I thought I had lived too much in solitude, and had given way too much to the feelings inspired by my favourite studies. I abandoned them for a time, and I mixed with the youth of my age. I was upon a visit at Kirkwall when I learned to know your father, whom business had brought thither. He easily found access to the relation with whom I lived, who was anxious to compose, if possible, the feud which divided our families. Your father, maidens, has been rather hardened than changed by years—he had the same manly form, the same old Norse frankness of manner and of heart, the same upright courage and honesty of disposition, with more of the gentle ingenuousness of youth, an eager desire to please, a willingness to be pleased, and a vivacity of spirits which survives not our early years. But though he was thus worthy of love, and though Erland wrote to me, authorising his attachment, there was another—a stranger, Minna, a fatal stranger—full of arts unknown to us, and graces which to the plain manners of your father were unknown. Yes, he walked, indeed, among us like a being of another and of a superior race.—Ye look on me as if it were strange that I should have had attractions for such a lover ; but I present nothing that can remind you that Norna of Fitful Head was once admired and loved as Ulla Troil—the change betwixt the animated body and the corpse after decease, is scarce more awful and absolute than I have sustained, while I yet linger on earth. Look on me, maidens—look on me by this glimmering light—Can ye believe that these haggard and weather-wasted features—these eyes, which have been almost converted to stone, by looking upon sights of terror—these locks, that, mingled with grey, now stream out, the shattered pennons of a sinking vessel—that these, and she to whom they belong, could once be the objects of fond affection ?—But the waning lamp sinks fast, and let it sink while I tell my infamy.—We loved in secret, we met in secret, till I gave the last proof of fatal and of guilty passion !—And now beam out, thou magic

163

glimmer—shine out a little space, thou flame so powerful even in thy feebleness—bid him who hovers near us, keep his dark pinions aloof from the circle thou dost illuminate—live but a little till the worst be told, and then sink when thou wilt into darkness, as black as my guilt and sorrow !"

While she spoke thus, she drew together the remaining nutriment of the lamp, and trimmed its decaying flame ; then again, with a hollow voice, and in broken sentences, pursued her narrative.

"I must waste little time in words. My love was discovered, but not my guilt. Erland came to Pomona in anger, and transported me to our solitary dwelling in Hoy. He commanded me to see my lover no more, and to receive Magnus, in whom he was willing to forgive the offences of his father, as my future husband. Alas ! I no longer deserved his attachment—my only wish was to escape from my father's dwelling, to conceal my shame in my lover's arms. Let me do justice—he was faithful— too, too faithful—his perfidy would have bereft me of my senses ; but the fatal consequences of his fidelity have done me a tenfold injury."

She paused, and then resumed, with the wild tones of insanity, "It has made me the powerful and the despairing Sovereign of the Seas and Winds !"

She paused a second time after this wild exclamation, and resumed her narrative in a more composed manner.

"My lover came in secret to Hoy, to concert measures for my flight, and I agreed to meet him, that we might fix the time when his vessel should come into the Sound. I left the house at midnight."

Here she appeared to gasp with agony, and went on with her tale by broken and interrupted sentences. "I left the house at midnight—I had to pass my father's door, and I perceived it was open—I thought he watched us, and, that the sound of my steps might not break his slumbers, I closed the fatal door—a light and trivial action—but, God in heaven ! what were the consequences !—At noon, the room was full of suffocating vapour— my father was dead—dead through my act—dead through my disobedience—dead through my infamy ! All that follows is mist and darkness—a choking, suffocating, stifling mist envelops all that I said and did, all that was said and done, until I became assured that my doom was accomplished, and walked forth the calm and terrible being you now behold me—the Queen of the Elements—the sharer in the power of those beings to whom man and his passions give such sport as the tortures of the dog-fish afford the fisherman, when he pierces his eyes with thorns, and turns him once more into his native element, to transverse the waves in blindness and agony.* No, maidens, she whom you see before you is impassive to the follies of which your minds are the sport. I am she that made the offering—I am she that bereaved the giver of the gift of life which he gave me—the dark saying has been interpreted by my deed, and I am taken from humanity, to be something pre-eminently powerful, pre-eminently wretched !"

As she spoke thus, the light, which had been long quivering, leaped

* This cruelty is practised by some fishers, out of a vindictive hatred to these ravenous fishes.

164

high for an instant, and seemed about to expire, when Norna, interrupting herself, said hastily, "No more now—he comes—he comes— Enough that ye know me, and the right I have to advise and command you.—Approach now, proud Spirit ! if thou wilt."

So saying, she extinguished the lamp, and passed out of the apartment with her usual loftiness of step, as Minna could observe from its measured cadence.

CHAPTER TWENTIETH

Is all the counsel that we two have shared—
The sisters' vow, the hours that we have spent,
When we have chid the hasty-footed time
For parting us—Oh, and is all forgot ?
                        A MIDSUMMER NIGHT'S DREAM

THE attention of Minna was powerfully arrested by this tale of terror, which accorded with and explained many broken hints respecting Norna which she had heard from her father and other near relations, and she was for a time so lost in surprise, not unmingled with horror, that she did not even attempt to speak to her sister Brenda. When, at length, she called her by her name, she received no answer, and, on touching her hand, she found it cold as ice. Alarmed to the uttermost, she threw open the lattice and the window-shutters, and admitted at once the free air and the pale glimmer of the hyperborean summer night. She then became sensible that her sister was in a swoon. All thoughts concerning Norna, her frightful tale, and her mysterious connection with the invisible world, at once vanished from Minna's thoughts, and she hastily ran to the apartment of the old housekeeper, to summon her aid, without reflecting for a moment what sights she might encounter in the long dark passages which she had to traverse.

The old woman hastened to Brenda's assistance, and instantly applied such remedies as her experience suggested ; but the poor girl's nervous system had been so much agitated by the horrible tale she had just heard, that, when recovered from her swoon, her utmost endeavours to compose her mind could not prevent her falling into a hysterical fit of some duration. This also was subdued by the experience of old Euphane Fea, who was well versed in all the simple pharmacy used by the natives of Zetland, and who, after administering a composing draught, distilled from simples and wild flowers, at length saw her patient resigned to sleep. Minna stretched herself beside her sister, kissed her cheek, and courted slumber in her turn ; but the more she invoked it, the farther it seemed to fly from her eyelids ; and if at times she was disposed to sink into repose the voice of the involuntary parricide seemed again to sound in her ears, and startled her into consciousness.

The early morning hour at which they were accustomed to rise, found the state of the sisters different from what might have been expected. A sound sleep had restored the spirit of Brenda's lightsome eye and the rose on her laughing cheek ; the transient indisposition of the preceding night having left as little trouble on her look, as the fantastic terrors of Norna's tale had been able to impress on her imagination. The looks of Minna, on the contrary, were melancholy, downcast, and apparently exhausted by watching and anxiety. They said at first little to each other, as if afraid of touching a subject so fraught with emotion as the scene of the preceding night. It was not until they had performed together their devotions, as usual, that Brenda, while lacing Minna's bodice (for they rendered the services of the toilet to each other reciprocally), became aware of the paleness of her sister's looks ; and having ascertained by a glance at the mirror, that her own did not wear the same dejection, she kissed Minna's cheek, and said affectionately, "Claud Halcro was right, my dearest sister, when his poetical folly gave us these names of Night and Day."

"And wherefore should you say so now ?" said Minna.

"Because we each are bravest in the season that we take our name from ; I was frightened well-nigh to death, by hearing those things last night, which you endured with courageous firmness ; and now, when it is broad light, I can think of them with composure, while you look as pale as a spirit who is surprised by sunrise."

"You are lucky, Brenda," said her sister, gravely, "who can so soon forget such a tale of wonder and of horror."

"The horror," said Brenda, "is never to be forgotten, unless one could hope that the unfortunate woman's excited imagination, which shows itself so active in conjuring up apparitions, may have fixed on her an imaginary crime."

"You believe nothing, then," said Minna, "of her interview at the Dwarfie Stone, that wondrous place, of which so many tales are told, and which, for so many centuries, has been reverenced as the work of a demon, and as his abode ?"

"I believe," said Brenda, "that our unhappy relative is no impostor,— and therefore I believe that she was at the Dwarfie Stone during a thunderstorm, that she sought shelter in it, and that, during a swoon, or during sleep perhaps, some dream visited her, concerned with the popular traditions with which she was so conversant ; but I cannot easily believe more."

"And yet the event," said Minna, "corresponded to the dark intimations of the vision."

"Pardon me," said Brenda, "I rather think the dream would never have been put into shape, or perhaps remembered at all, but for the event. She told us herself she had nearly forgot the vision, till after her father's dreadful death,—and who shall warrant how much of what she then supposed herself to remember was not the creation of her own fancy, disordered at it naturally was, by the horrid accident ? Had she really seen and conversed with a necromantic dwarf, she was likely to remember the conversation long enough—at least, I am sure I should."

"Brenda," replied Minna, "you have heard the good minister of the Cross Kirk say, that human wisdom was worse than folly, when it applied to mysteries beyond its comprehension ; and that, if we believed no

166

more than we could understand, we should resist the evidence of our senses, which presented us, at every turn, circumstances as certain as they were unintelligible."

"You are too learned yourself, sister," answered Brenda, "to need the assistance of the good minister of Cross Kirk ; but I think his doctrine only related to the mysteries of our religion, which it is our duty to receive without investigation or doubt—but in things occurring in common life, as God has bestowed reason upon us, we cannot act wrong in employing it. But you, my dear Minna, have a warmer fancy than mine, and are willing to receive all those wonderful stories for truth, because you love to think of sorcerers, and dwarfs, and water-spirits, and would like much to have a little trow, or fairy, as the Scotch call them, with a green coat, and a pair of wings as brilliant as the hues of the starling's neck, specially to attend on you."

"It would spare you at least the trouble of lacing my bodice," said Minna, "and of lacing it wrong, too ; for in the heat of your argument you have missed two eyelet-holes."

"That error shall be presently mended," said Brenda ; "and then, as one of our friends might say, I will haul tight and belay—but you draw your breath so deeply, that it will be a difficult matter."

"I only sighed," said Minna, in some confusion, "to think how soon you can trifle with and ridicule the misfortunes of this extraordinary woman."

"I do not ridicule them, God knows !" replied Brenda, somewhat angrily ; "it is you, Minna, who turn all I say in truth and kindness, to something harsh and wicked. I look on Norna as a woman of very extraordinary abilities, which are very often reconciled with a strong cast of insanity ; and I consider her as better skilled in the signs of the weather than any woman in Zetland. But that she has any power over the elements, I no more believe, than I do in the nursery stories of King Erick, who could make the wind blow from the point he set his cap to."

Minna, somewhat nettled with the obstinate incredulity of her sister, replied sharply, "And yet, Brenda, this woman—half-mad woman, and the veriest impostor—is the person by whom you choose to be advised in the matter next to your own heart at this moment !"

"I do not know what you mean," said Brenda, colouring deeply, and shifting to get away from her sister. But, as she was now undergoing the ceremony of being laced in her turn, her sister had the means of holding her fast by the silken string with which she was fastening the bodice, and, tapping her on the neck, which expressed, by its sudden writhe, and sudden change to a scarlet hue, as much pettish confusion as she had desire to provoke, she added, more mildly, "Is it not strange, Brenda, that, used as we have been by the stranger Mordaunt Mertoun, whose assurance has brought him uninvited to a house where his presence is so unacceptable, you should still look on or think of him with favour ? Surely that you do so should be a proof to you that there are such things as spells in the country, and that you yourself labour under them. It is not for nought that Mordaunt wears a chain of elfin gold—look to it, Brenda, and be wise in time."

"I have nothing to do with Mordaunt Mertoun," answered Brenda, hastily, "nor do I know or care what he or any other young man wears about his neck. I could see all the gold chains of all the bailies of Edinburgh, that Lady Glowrowrum speaks so much of, without falling in fancy with one of the wearers." And having thus complied with the female rule of pleading not guilty in general to such an indictment, she immediately resumed, in a different tone, "But to say the truth, Minna, I think you, and all of you, have judged far too hastily about this young friend of ours, who has been so long our most intimate companion. Mind, Mordaunt Mertoun is no more to me than he is to you—who best know how little difference he made betwixt us ; and that, chain or no chain, he lived with us like a brother with two sisters ; and yet you can turn him off at once, because a wandering seaman, of whom we know nothing, and a peddling yagger, whom we know to be a thief, a cheat, and a liar, speak words and carry tales in his disfavour ! I do not believe he ever said he could have his choice of either of us, and only waited to see which was to have Burgh Westra and Brednes Voe—I do not believe he ever spoke such a word, or harboured such a thought, as that of making a choice between us."

"Perhaps," said Minna, coldly, "you may have had reason to know that his choice was already determined."

"I will not endure this," said Brenda, giving way to her natural vivacity, and springing from between her sister's hands ; then turning round and facing her, while her glowing cheek was rivalled in the deepness of its crimson by as much of her neck and bosom as the upper part of the half-laced bodice permitted to be visible,—"Even from you, Minna," she said, "I will not endure this ! You know that all my life I have spoken the truth and that I love the truth ; and I tell you that Mordaunt Mertoun never in his life made distinction betwixt you and me until"—

Here some feeling of consciousness stopped her short, and her sister replied, with a smile, "Until *when*, Brenda ? Methinks your love of truth seems choked with the sentence you were bringing out."

"Until you ceased to do him the justice he deserves," said Brenda, firmly, "since I must speak out. I have little doubt that he will not long throw his friendship on you, who hold it so lightly."

"Be it so," said Minna ; "you are secure from my rivalry, either in his love or friendship. But bethink you better Brenda—this is no scandal of Cleveland's—Cleveland is incapable of slander—no falsehood of Bryce Snailsfoot—not one of our friends or acquaintance but says it has been the common talk of the island, that the daughters of Magnus Troil were patiently awaiting the choice of the nameless and birthless stranger, Mordaunt Mertoun.—Is it fitting that this should be said of us, the descendants of a Norwegian Yarl, and the daughters of the first Udaller in Zetland ? or, would it be modest or maidenly to submit to it unresented, were we the meanest lasses that ever lifted a milk-pail ?"

"The tongues of fools are no reproach," replied Brenda, warmly ; "I will never quit my own thoughts of an innocent friend for the gossip of the island, which can put the worst meaning on the most innocent actions."

168

"Hear but what our friends say," repeated Minna ; "hear but the Lady Glowrowrum ; hear but Maddie and Clara Groatsettar."

"If I were to hear Lady Glowrowrum," said Brenda, steadily, "I should listen to the worst tongue in Zetland ; and as for Maddie and Clara Groatsettar, they were both blithe enough to get Mordaunt to sit betwixt them at dinner the day before yesterday, as you might have observed yourself, but that your ear was better engaged."

"Your eyes, at least, have been but indifferently engaged, Brenda," retorted the elder sister, "since they were fixed on a young man, whom all the world but yourself believes to have talked of us with the most insolent presumption ; and even if he be innocently charged, Lady Glowrowrum says it is unmaidenly and bold of you even to look in the direction where he sits, knowing it must confirm such reports."

"I will look which way I please," said Brenda, growing still warmer ; "Lady Glowrowrum shall neither rule my thoughts, nor my words, nor my eyes. I hold Mordaunt Mertoun to be innocent,—I will look at him as such,—I will speak of him as such ; and if I did not speak to him also, and behave to him as usual, it is in obedience to my father, and not for what Lady Glowrowrum, and all her nieces, had she twenty instead of two, could think, wink, nod, or tattle, about the matter that concerns them not."

"Alas ! Brenda," answered Minna, with calmness, "this vivacity is more than is required for the defence of the character of a mere friend !— Beware—He who ruined Norna's peace for ever, was a stranger, admitted to her affections against the will of her family."

"He was a stranger," replied Brenda, with emphasis, "not only in birth, but in manners. She had not been bred up with him from her youth,—she had not known the gentleness, the frankness, of his disposition, by an intimacy of many years. He was indeed a stranger, in character, temper, birth, manners, and morals,—some wandering adventurer, perhaps, whom chance or tempest had thrown upon the islands, and who knew how to mask a false heart with a frank brow. My good sister, take home your own warning. There are other strangers at Burgh Westra besides this poor Mordaunt Mertoun."

Minna seemed for a moment overwhelmed with the rapidity with which her sister retorted her suspicion and her caution. But her natural loftiness of disposition enabled her to reply with assumed composure.

"Were I to treat you, Brenda, with the want of confidence you show towards me, I might reply, that Cleveland is no more to me than Mordaunt was ; or than young Swaraster, or Lawrence Ericson, or any other favourite guest of my father's, now is. But I scorn to deceive you, or to disguise my thoughts.—I love Clement Cleveland."

"Do not say so, my dearest friend," said Brenda, abandoning at once the air of acrimony with which the conversation had been latterly conducted, and throwing her arms round her sister's neck, with looks, and with a tone of the most earnest affection,—"do not say so, I implore you ! I will renounce Mordaunt Mertoun,—I will swear never to speak to him again ; but do not repeat that you love this Cleveland !"

"And why should I not repeat," said Minna, disengaging herself gently from her sister's grasp, "a sentiment in which I glory ? The boldness, the strength and energy, of his character to which command is natural, and fear unknown,—these very properties, which alarm you for my happiness, are the qualities which ensure it. Remember, Brenda, that when your foot loved the calm smooth sea-beach of the summer sea, mine ever delighted in the summit of the precipice, when the waves were in fury."

"And it is even that which I dread," said Brenda ; "it is even that adventurous disposition which now is urging you to the brink of a precipice more dangerous than ever was washed by a spring-tide. This man,—do not frown, I will say no slander of him,—but is he not, even in your own partial judgment, stern and overbearing ? accustomed, as you say, to command ; but, for that very reason, commanding where he has no right to do so, and leading whom it would most become him to follow ? rushing on danger, rather for its own sake, than for any other object ? And can you think of being yoked with a spirit so unsettled and stormy, whose life has hitherto been led in scenes of death and peril, and who, even while sitting by your side, cannot disguise his impatience again to engage in them ? A lover, methinks, should love his mistress better than his own life ; but yours, my dear Minna, loves her less than the pleasure of inflicting death on others."

"And it is even for that I love him," said Minna. "I am a daughter of the old dames of Norway, who could send their lovers to battle with a smile, and slay them with their own hands, if they returned with dishonour. My lover must scorn the mockeries by which our degraded race strive for distinction, or must practise them only in sport, and in earnest of nobler dangers. No whale-striking, bird-nesting favourite for me ; my lover must be a Sea-king, or what else modern times may give that draws near to that lofty character."

"Alas, my sister !" said Brenda, "it is now that I must in earnest begin to believe the force of spells and of charms. You remember the Spanish story which you took from me long since, because I said, in your admiration of the chivalry of the olden times of Scandinavia, you rivalled the extravagance of the hero. Ah, Minna ! your colour shows that your conscience checks you, and reminds you of the book I mean ;—is it more wise, think you, to mistake a windmill for a giant, or the commander of a paltry corsair for a Kiempe, or a Vi-king ?"

Minna did indeed colour with anger at this insinuation, of which, perhaps, she felt in some degree the truth.

"You have a right," she said, "to insult me, because you are possessed of my secret."

Brenda's soft heart could not resist this charge of unkindness ; she adjured her sister to pardon her, and the natural gentleness of Minna's feelings could not resist her entreaties.

"We are unhappy," she said, as she dried her sister's tears, "that we cannot see with the same eyes—let us not make each other more so by mutual insult and unkindness. You have my secret—It will not, perhaps, long be one, for my father shall have the confidence to which he is entitled, so soon as certain circumstances will permit me to offer it.

Meantime, I repeat, you have my secret, and I more than suspect that I have yours in exchange, though you refuse to own it."

"How, Minna," said Brenda ; "would you have me acknowledge for any one such feelings as you allude to, ere he has said the least word that could justify such a confession ?"

"Surely not ; but a hidden fire may be distinguished by heat as well as flame."

"You understand these signs, Minna," said Brenda, hanging down her head, and in vain endeavouring to suppress the temptation to repartee which her sister's remark offered ; "but I can only say, that if ever I love at all, it shall not be until I have been asked to do so once or twice at least, which has not yet chanced to me. But do not let us renew our quarrel, and rather let us think why Norna should have told us that horrible tale, and to what she expects it should lead."

"It must have been as a caution," replied Minna—"a caution which our situation, and, I will not deny it, which mine in particular, might seem to her to call for ;—but I am alike strong in my own innocence, and in the honour of Cleveland."

Brenda would fain have replied, that she did not confide so absolutely in the latter security as in the first ;—but she was prudent, and, forbearing to awake the former painful discussion, only replied, "It is strange that Norna should have said nothing more of her lover. Surely he could not desert her in the extremity of misery to which he had reduced her ?"

"There may be agonies of distress," said Minna, after a pause, "in which the mind is so much jarred, that it ceases to be responsive even to the feelings which have most engrossed it ;—her sorrow for her lover may have been swallowed up in horror and despair."

"Or he may have fled from the islands, in fear of our father's vengeance," said Brenda.

"If for fear, or faintness of heart," said Minna, looking upwards, "he was capable of flying from the ruin which he had occasioned, I trust he has long ere this sustained the punishment which Heaven reserves for the most base and dastardly of traitors and of cowards. Come, sister, we are ere this expected at the breakfast board."

And they went thither, arm in arm, with much more of confidence than had lately subsisted between them ; the little quarrel which had taken place having served the purpose of a *bourasque*, or sudden squall, which dispels mists and vapours, and leaves fair weather behind it.

On their way to the breakfast apartment, they agreed that it was unnecessary, and might be imprudent, to communicate to their father the circumstance of the nocturnal visit, or to let him observe that they now knew more than formerly of the melancholy history of Norna.

CHAPTER TWENTY-FIRST

But lost to me, for ever lost those joys,
Which reason scatters, and which time destroys.
No more the midnight fairy train I view,
All in the merry moonlight tippling dew.
Even the last lingering fiction of the brain,
The churchyard ghost, is now at rest again.

THE LIBRARY

THE moral bard,* from whom we borrow the motto of this chapter, has touched a theme with which most readers have some feeling that vibrate unconsciously. Superstition, when not arrayed in her full horrors, but laying a gentle hand only on her suppliant's head, had charms which we fail not to regret, even in those stages of society from which her influence is well-nigh banished by the light of reason and general education. At least, in more ignorant periods, her system of ideal terrors had something in them interesting to minds, which had few means of excitement. This is more especially true of those lighter modifications of superstitious feelings and practises which mingle in the amusements of the ruder ages, and are, like the auguries of Hallow-e'en in Scotland, considered partly as a matter of merriment, partly as sad and prophetic earnest. And, with similar feelings, people even of tolerable education have, in our times, sought the cell of a fortune-teller, upon a frolic, as it is termed, and yet not always in a disposition absolutely sceptical towards the responses they receive.

When the sisters of Burgh Westra arrived in the apartment destined for a breakfast as ample as that which we have described on the preceding morning, and had undergone a jocular rebuke from the Udaller for their late attendance, they found the company, most of whom had already breakfasted, engaged in an ancient Norwegian custom, of the character which we have just described.

It seems to have been borrowed from those poems of the Scalds, in which champions and heroines are so often represented as seeking to know their destiny from some sorceress or prophetess, who, as in the legend called by Gray the Descent of Odin, awakens by the force of Runic rhyme the unwilling revealer of the doom of fate, and compels from her answers, often of dubious import, but which were then believed to express some shadow of the events of futurity.

An old sibyl, Euphane Fea, the housekeeper we have already mentioned, was installed in the recess of a large window, studiously darkened by bear-skins and other miscellaneous drapery, so as to give it something the appearance of a Laplander's hut, and accommodated, like a confessional chair, with an aperture, which permitted the person within to hear with ease whatever questions should be put, though not to see the querist. Here seated, the Voluspa, or sibyl, was to listen to the

* Rev. George Crabbe.

172

rhythmical inquiries which should be made to her, and return an extemporaneous answer. The drapery was supposed to prevent her from seeing by what individuals she was consulted, and the intended or accidental reference which the answer given under such circumstances bore to the situation of the person by whom the question was asked, often furnished food for laughter, and sometimes, as it happened, for more serious reflection. The sibyl was usually chosen from her possessing the talent of improvisation in the Norse poetry ; no unusual accomplishment, where the minds of many were stored with old verses, and where the rules of metrical composition are uncommonly simple. The questions were also put in verse ; but as this power of extemporaneous composition, though common, could not be supposed universal, the medium of an interpreter might be used by any querist, which interpreter, holding the consulter of the oracle by the hand, and standing by the place from which the oracles were issued, had the task of rendering into verse the subject of inquiry.

On the present occasion, Claud Halcro was summoned, by the universal voice, to perform the part of interpreter ; and, after shaking his head, and muttering some apology for decay of memory and poetical powers, contradicted at once by his own conscious smile of confidence and by the general shout of the company, the light-hearted old man came forward to play his part in the proposed entertainment.

But just as it was about to commence, the arrangement of parts was singularly altered. Norna of the Fitful Head, whom every one excepting the two sisters believed to be at the distance of many miles, suddenly, and without greeting, entered the apartment, walked majestically up to the bearskin tabernacle, and signed to the female who was there seated to abdicate her sanctuary. The old woman came forth, shaking her head, and looking like one overwhelmed with fear ; nor, indeed, were there many in the company who saw with absolute composure, the sudden appearance of a person, so well known and so generally dreaded as Norna.

She paused a moment at the entrance of the tent ; and, as she raised the skin which formed the entrance, she looked up to the north, as if imploring from that quarter a train of inspiration ; then signing to the surprised guests that they might approach in succession the shrine in which she was about to install herself, she entered the tent, and was shrouded from their sight.

But this was a different sport from what the company had meditated, and to most of them seemed to present so much more of earnest than of game, that there was no alacrity shown to consult the oracle. The character and pretensions of Norna seemed, to almost all present, too serious for the part which she had assumed ; the men whispered to each other, and the women, according to Claud Halcro, realised the description of glorious John Dryden,—

"With horror shuddering, on a heap they ran."

The pause was interrupted by the loud manly voice of the Udaller.

173

"Why does the game stand still, my masters ? Are you afraid because my kinswoman is to play our Voluspa ? It is kindly done in her, to do for us what none in the isles can do so well ; and we will not baulk our sport for it, but rather go on the merrier."

There was still a pause in the company, and Magnus Troil added, "It shall never be said that my kinswoman sat in her bower unhalsed,* as if she were some of the old mountain-giantesses, and all from faint heart. I will speak first myself ; but the rhyme comes worse from my tongue than when I was a score of years younger.—Claud Halcro, you must stand by me."

Hand in hand they approached the shrine of the supposed sibyl, and after a moment's consultation together, Halcro thus expressed the query of his friend and patron. Now, the Udaller, like many persons of consequence in Zetland, who, as Sir Robert Sibbald† has testified for them, had begun thus early to apply both to commerce and navigation, was concerned to some extent in the whale fishery of the season, and the bard had been directed to put into his halting verse an inquiry concerning its success.

CLAUD HALCRO

Mother darksome, Mother dread,
Dweller on the Fitful Head,
Thou canst see what deeds are done
Under the never-setting sun.
Look through sleet, and look through frost,
Look to Greenland's caves and coast,—
By the iceberg is a sail
Chasing of the swarthy whale ;
Mother doubtful, Mother dread,
Tell us, has the good ship sped ?

The jest seemed to turn to earnest, as all, bending their heads around, listened to the voice of Norna, who, without a moment's hesitation, answered from the recesses of the tent in which she was enclosed :—

NORNA

The thought of the aged is ever on gear,
On his fishing, his furrow, his flock, and his steer ;
But thrive may his fishing, flock, furrow, and herd,
While the aged for anguish shall tear his grey beard.

There was a momentary pause, during which Triptolemus had time to whisper, "If ten witches and as many warlocks were to swear it, I will never believe that a decent man will either fash his beard or himself about anything, so long as stock and crop goes as it should do."

But the tone from within the tent resumed its low monotonous tone

---

* Unsaluted.

† The *Description of the Isles of Orkney and Zetland* was published by Sir Robert Sibbald, M.D., Edinburgh, 1711, folio.

of recitation, and, interrupting farther commentary, proceeded as follows :—

NORNA

The ship, well-laden as bark need be,
Lies deep in the furrow of the Iceland sea ;—
The breeze from Zetland blows fair and soft,
And gaily the garland* is fluttering aloft :
Seven good fishes have sprouted their last,
And their jaw-bones are hanging to yard and mast ;†
Two are for Lerwick, and two for Kirkwall,—
And three for Burgh Westra, the choicest of all.

"Now the powers above look down and protect us !" said Bryce Snailsfoot ; "for it is mair than woman's wit that has spaed out that ferly. I saw them at North Ronaldshaw, that had seen the good bark, the Olave of Lerwick, that our worthy patron has such a great share in that she may be called his own in a manner, and they had broomed†† the ship, and, as sure as there are stars in heaven, she answered them for seven fish, exact as Norna has telled us in her rhyme."

"Umph—seven fish exactly ? and you heard it at North Ronaldshaw ?" said Captain Cleveland, "and I suppose told it as a good piece of news when you came hither ?"

"It never crossed my tongue, Captain," answered the pedlar ; "I have kend mony chapmen, travelling merchants, and such like, neglect their goods to carry clashes and clavers up and down, from one country-side to another ; but that is no traffic of mine. I dinna believe I have mentioned the Olave's having made up her cargo to three folks since I crossed to Dunrossness."

"But if one of those three had spoken the news over again, and it is two to one that such a thing happened, the old lady prophesies upon velvet."

Such was the speech of Cleveland, addressed to Magnus Troil, and heard without any applause. The Udaller's respect for his country extended to its superstitions, and so did the interest which he took in his unfortunate kinswoman. If he never rendered a precise assent to her high supernatural pretensions, he was not at least desirous of hearing them disputed by others.

"Norna," he said, "his cousin" (an emphasis on the word), "held no communication with Bryce Snailsfoot, or his acquaintances. He did not pretend to explain how she came by her information ; but he had always remarked that Scotsmen, and indeed strangers in general, when they came to Zetland, were ready to find reasons for things which remained sufficiently obscure to those whose ancestors had dwelt there for ages."

---

* The garland is an artificial coronet, composed of ribbons by those young women who take an interest in a whaling vessel or her crew ; it is always displayed from the rigging and preserved with great care during the voyage.
† The best oil exudes from the jaw-bones of the whale, which, for purposes of collecting it, are suspended to the masts of the vessel.
†† There is established among whalers a sort of telegraphic signal, in which a certain number of motions, made with a broom, express to any other vessel the number of fish which they have caught.

Captain Cleveland took the hint, and bowed, without attempting to defend his own scepticism.

"And now forward, my brave hearts," said the Udaller ; "and may all have as good tidings as I have ! Three whales cannot but yield—let me think, how many hogsheads"—

There was an obvious reluctance on the part of the guests to be the next in consulting the oracle of the tent.

"Gude news are welcome to some folks, if they came frae the deil himself," said Mistress Baby Yellowley, addressing the Lady Glowrowrum,—for a similarity of disposition in some respects had made a sort of intimacy betwixt them—"but I think, my leddy, that this has ower mickle of rank witchcraft in it, to have the countenance of douce Christian folks like you and me, my leddy."

"There may be something in what you say, my dame," replied the good Lady Glowrowrum ; "but we Hjaltlanders are no just like other folks ; and this woman, if she be a witch, being the Fowd's friend and near kinswoman, it will be ill taen if we haena our fortunes spaed like a' the rest of them ; and sae my nieces may e'en step forward in their turn and nae harm dune. They will hae time to repent, ye ken, in the course of nature, if there be onything wrang in it, Mistress Yellowley."

While others remained under similar uncertainty and apprehension, Halcro, who saw by the knitting of the old Udaller's brows, and by a certain impatient shuffle of his right foot, like the motion of a man who with difficulty refrains from stamping, that his patience began to wax rather thin, gallantly declared, that he himself would, in his own person, and not as a procurator for others put the next query to the Pythoness. He paused a minute—collected his rhymes, and thus addressed her.

CLAUD HALCRO

Mother doubtful, Mother dread,
Dweller of the Fitful Head,
Thou hast conn'd full many a rhyme,
That lives upon the surge of time :
Tell me shall my lays be sung,
Like Hacon's of the golden tongue,
Long after Halcro's dead and gone ?
Or, shall Hjaltland's minstrel own
One note to rival glorious John ?

The voice of the sibyl immediately replied from her sanctuary,

NORNA

The infant loves the rattle's noise ;
Age, double childhood, hath its toys ;
But different far the descant rings,
As strikes a different hand the strings.
The eagle mounts the polar sky—
The Imber-goose, unskill'd to fly,
Must be content to glide along,
Where seal and sea-dog list his song.

176

Halcro bit his lip, shrugged his shoulders, and then, instantly recovering his good-humour, and the ready, though slovenly power of extemporaneous composition, with which long habit had invested him, he gallantly rejoined,

CLAUD HALCRO

Be mine the Imber-goose to play,
And haunt lone cave and silent bay ;—
The archer's aim so shall I shun—
So shall I'scape the levell'd gun—
Content my verse's tuneless jingle,
With Thule's sounding tides to mingle,
While, to the ear of wondering wight.
Upon the distant headland's height,
Soften'd by murmur of the sea,
The rude sounds seem like harmony !

As the little bard stepped back, with an alert gait, and satisfied air, general applause followed the spirited manner in which he had acquiesced in the doom which levelled him with an Imber-goose. But his resigned and courageous submission did not even yet encourage any other person to consult the redoubted Norna.

"The coward fools !" said the Udaller. "Are you too afraid, Captain Cleveland, to speak to an old woman ?—Ask her anything—ask her whether the twelve-gun sloop at Kirkwall be your consort or no."

Cleveland looked at Minna, and probably conceiving that she watched with anxiety his answer to her father's question, he collected himself, after a moment's hesitation.

"I was never afraid of man or woman.—Master Halcro, you have heard the question which our host desires me to ask—put it in my name, and in your own way—I pretend to as little skill in poetry as I do in witchcraft."

Halcro did not wait to be invited twice, but, grasping Captain Cleveland's hand in his, according to the form which the game prescribed, he put the query which the Udaller had dictated to the stranger in the following words :—

CLAUD HALCRO

Mother doubtful, Mother dread,
Dweller of the Fitful Head,
A gallant bark from far abroad,
Saint Magnus hath her in his road,
With guns and firelocks not a few—
A silken and a scarlet crew,
Deep stored with precious merchandise,
Of gold, and goods of rare device :
What interest hath our comrade bold
In bark and crew, in goods and gold ?

There was a pause of unusual duration ere the oracle would return any answer ; and when she replied, it was in a lower, though an equally decided tone, with that which she had hitherto employed :—

Gold is ruddy, fair, and free,
Blood is crimson, and dark to see ;—
I look'd out on Saint Magnus Bay.
And I saw a falcon that struck her prey,—
A gobbet of flesh in her beak she bore,
And talons and singles are dripping with gore ;
Let him that asks after them look on his hand,
And if there is blood on't, he's one of their band.

Cleveland smiled scornfully, and held out his hand,—"Few men have been on the Spanish Main as often as I have, without having had to do with the *Guarda Costas* once and again ; but there never was aught like a stain on my hand that a wet towel would not wipe away."

The Udaller added his voice potential—"There is never peace with Spaniards beyond the Line,—I have heard Captain Tragendeck and honest old Commodore Rummelaer say so a hundred times, and they have both been down in the Bay of Honduras and all thereabouts.—I hate all Spaniards, since they came here and reft the Fair Isle men of their vivers in 1588.* I have heard my grandfather speak of it ; and there is an old Dutch history somewhere about the house, that shows what work they made in the Low Countries long since. There is neither mercy nor faith in them."

"True—true, my old friend," said Cleveland ; "they are as jealous of their Indian possessions as an old man of his young bride ; and if they can catch you at disadvantage, the mines for your life is the word,—and so we fight them with our colours nailed to the mast."

"That is the way," shouted the Udaller ; "the old British jack should never down. When I think of the wooden walls, I almost think myself an Englishman, only it would be becoming too like my Scottish neighbours ;—but come, no offence to any here, gentlemen—all are friends, and all are welcome.—Come, Brenda, go on with the play—do you speak next, you have Norse rhymes enough, we all know."

"But none that suit the game we play at, father," said Brenda, drawing back.

"Nonsense !" said her father, pushing her onward, while Halcro seized on her reluctant hand ; "never let mistimed modesty mar honest mirth—Speak for Brenda, Halcro—it is your trade to interpret maidens' thoughts."

The poet bowed to the beautiful young woman, with the devotion of a poet and the gallantry of a traveller, and having, in a whisper, reminded her that she was in no way responsible for the nonsense he was about to speak, he paused, looked upwards, simpered as if he had caught a sudden idea, and at length set off in the following verses :—

* The Admiral of the Spanish Armada was wrecked on the Fair Isle, halfway betwixt the Orkney and Zetland Archipelago. The Duke of Medina Sidonia landed, with some of his people, and pillaged the islanders of their winter stores. These strangers are remembered as having remained on the island by force, and on bad terms with the inhabitants, till spring returned, when they effected their escape.

CLAUD HALCRO

Mother doubtful, Mother dread,
Dweller of the Fitful Head,
Well thou know'st it is thy task
To tell what beauty will not ask ;—
Then steep thy words in wine and milk,
And weave a doom of gold and silk,—
For we would know, shall Brenda prove
In love, and happy in her love ?

The prophetess replied almost immediately from behind her curtain :—

NORNA

Untouch'd by love, the maiden's breast
Is like the snow on Rona's crest,
High seated in the middle sky,
In bright and barren purity ;
But by the sunbeam gently kiss'd,
Scarce by the gazing eye 'tis miss'd,
Ere down the lonely valley stealing,
Fresh grass and growth its course revealing
It cheers the flock, revives the flower,
And decks some happy shepherd's bower.

"A comfortable doctrine, and most justly spoken," said the Udaller, seizing the blushing Brenda, as she was endeavouring to escape—"Never think shame for the matter, my girl. To be the mistress of some honest man's house, and the means of maintaining some old Norse name, making neighbours happy, the poor easy, and relieving strangers, is the most credible lot a young woman can look to, and I heartily wish it to all here. Come, who speaks next ?—good husbands are going—Maddie Groatsetter—my pretty Clara, come and have your share."

The Lady Glowrowrum shook her head, and "could not," she said, "altogether approve"—

"Enough said—enough said," replied Magnus : "no compulsion ; but the play shall go on till we are tired of it. Here, Minna—I have got you at command. Stand forth, my girl—there are plenty of things to be ashamed of besides old-fashioned and innocent pleasantry.—Come, I will speak for you myself—though I am not sure I can remember rhyme enough for it."

There was a slight colour which passed rapidly over Minna's face, but she instantly regained her composure, and stood erect by her father, as one superior to any little jest to which her situation might give rise.

Her father, after some rubbing of his brow, and other mechanical efforts to assist his memory, at length recovered verse sufficient to put the following query, though in less gallant strains than those of Halcro :—

MAGNUS TROIL

Mother, speak, and do not tarry,
Here's a maiden fain would marry.
Shall she marry, ay or not ?
If she marry, what's her lot ?

A deep sigh was uttered within the tabernacle of the soothsayer, as if she compassioned the subject of the doom which she was obliged to pronounce. She then, as usual, returned her response :—

NORNA

Untouch'd by love, the maiden's breast
Is like the snow on Rona's crest ;
So pure, so free from earthly dye,
It seems, whilst leaning on the sky,
Part of the heaven to which 'tis nigh ;
But passion, like the wild March rain,
May soil the wreath with many a stain.
We gaze—the lovely vision's gone—
A torrent fills the bed of stone,
That, hurrying to destruction's shock,
Leaps headlong from the lofty rock.

The Udaller heard this reply with high resentment. "By the bones of the Martyr," he said, his brave visage becoming suddenly ruddy, "this is an abuse of courtesy ! and, were it any but yourself that had classed my daughter's name and the word destruction together, they had better have left the word unspoken. But, come forth of the tent, thou old galdragon,"* he added, with a smile—"I should have known that thou canst not long joy in anything that smacks of mirth, God help thee !" His summons received no answer ; and, after waiting a moment, he again addressed her—"Nay, never be sullen with me, kinswoman, though I did speak a hasty word—thou knowest I bear malice to no one ; least of all to thee—so come forth, and let us shake hands.—Thou mightst have foretold the wreck of my ship and boats, or a bad herring-fishery, and I should have said never a word ; but Minna or Brenda, you know, are things which touch me nearer. But come out, shake hands, and there let be an end on't."

Norna returned no answer whatever to his repeated invocations, and the company began to look upon each other with some surprise, when the Udaller, raising the skin which covered the entrance of the tent, discovered that the interior was empty. The wonder was now general, and not unmixed with fear ; for it seemed impossible that Norna could have, in any manner, escaped from the tabernacle in which she was enclosed, without having been discovered by the company. Gone, however, she was, and the Udaller, after a moment's consideration, dropped the skin curtain again over the entrance of the tent.

"My friends," he said, with a cheerful countenance, "we have long known of my kinswoman and that her ways are not like those of the ordinary folks of this world. But she means well by Hjaltland, and hath the love of a sister for me, and for my house ; and no guest of mine needs either to fear evil, or to take offence, at her hand. I have little doubt she will be with us at dinner-time."

"Now, Heaven forbid !" said Mrs. Baby Yellowley—"for, my gude Leddy Glowrowrum, to tell your ladyship the truth, I likena cummers

* *Galdra Kinna*—The Norse for a sorceress.

that can come and gae like a glance of the sun, or the whisk of a whirlwind."

"Speak lower, speak lower," said the Lady Glowrowrum, "and be thankful that yon carlin hasna ta'en the house-side away wi' her. The like of her have played warse pranks, and so has she hersell, unless she is the sairer lied on."

Similar murmurs ran through the rest of the company, until the Udaller uplifted his stentorian and imperative voice to put them to silence, and invited, or rather commanded, the attendance of his guests to behold the boats set off for the *haaf* or deep-sea fishing.

"The wind has been high since sunrise," he said, "and had kept the boats in the bay ; but now it was favourable, and they would sail immediately."

This sudden alteration of the weather occasioned sundry nods and winks among the guests, who were not indisposed to connect it with Norna's sudden disappearance ; but, without giving vent to observations which could not but be disagreeable to their host, they followed his stately step to the shore, as the herd of deer follows the leading stag, with all manner of respectful observance.*

CHAPTER TWENTY-SECOND

There was a laughing devil in his sneer,
That raised emotions both of rage and fear ;
And where his frown of hatred darkly fell,
Hope withering fled—and Mercy sigh'd farewell.
                                              THE CORSAIR, *Canto* I

THE ling or white fishery is the principal employment of the natives of Zetland, and was formerly that upon which the gentry chiefly depended for their income, and the poor for their subsistence. The fishing season is, therefore, like the harvest of an agricultural country, the busiest and most important, as well as the most animating, period of the year.

The fishermen of each district assemble at particular stations, with their boats and crews, and erect upon the shore small huts, composed of shingle, and covered with turn, for their temporary lodging, and skeos, or drying-houses for the fish ; so that the lonely beach at once assumes the appearance of an Indian town. The banks to which they repair for the Haaf fishing are often many miles distant from the station where the fish is dried ; so that they are always twenty or thirty hours absent, frequently longer ; and under unfavourable circumstances of wind and tide, they remain at sea, with a very small stock of provisions, and in a boat of a construction which seems extremely slender, for two or three days, and are sometimes heard of no more. The departure of the fishers, therefore, on this occupation, has in it a character of danger and of suffering, which renders it dignified, and the anxiety of the females who

* Note N. Fortune-telling rhymes.

remain on the beach, watching the departure of the lessening boat, or anxiously looking out for its return, gives pathos to the scene.*

The scene, therefore, was in busy and anxious animation, when the Udaller and his friends appeared on the beach. The various crews of about thirty boats, amounting each to from three to five or six men, were taking leave of their wives and female relatives, and jumping on board their long Norway skiffs, where their lines and tackle lay ready stowed. Magnus was not an idle spectator of the scene ; he went from one place to another, inquiring into the state of their provisions for the voyage, and their preparations for the fishing—now and then, with a rough Dutch or Norse oath, abusing them for blockheads, for going to sea with their boats indifferently found, but always ending by ordering from his own stores a gallon of gin, a lispund of meal, or some similar essential addition to their sea-stores. The hardy sailors, on receiving such favours, expressed their thanks in the brief gruff manner which their landlord best approved ; but the women were more clamorous in their gratitude, which Magnus was often obliged to silence by cursing all female tongues from Eve's downwards.

At length all were on board and ready, the sails were hoisted, the signal for departure given, the rowers began to pull, and all started from the shore, in strong emulation to get first to the fishing ground, and to have their lines set before the rest ; an exploit to which no little consequence was attached by the boat's crew who should be happy enough to perform it.

While they were yet within hearing of the shore, they chanted an ancient Norse ditty, appropriate to the occasion of which Claud Halcro had executed the following literal translation :—

Farewell, merry maidens, to song and to laugh,
For the brave lads of Westra are bound to the Haaf ;
And we must have labour, and hunger and pain,
Ere we dance with the maids of Dunrossness again.

For now, in our trim boats of Noroway deal,
We must dance on the waves, with the porpoise and seal ;
The breeze it shall pipe, so it pipe not too high,
And the gull be our songstress whene'er she flits by.

Sing on, my brave bird, while we follow, like thee,
By bank, shoal, and quicksand, the swarms of the sea ;
And when twenty-score fishes are straining our line,
Sing louder, brave bird, for their spoils shall be thine.

We'll sing while we bait, and we'll sing when we haul,
For the deeps of the Haaf have enough for us all ;
There is torsk for the gentle, and skate for the carle,
And there's wealth for bold Magnus, the son of the earl.

Huzza ! my brave comrades, give way for the Haaf,
We shall sooner come back to the dance and the laugh ;
For life without mirth is a lamp without oil :
Then, mirth and long life to the bold Magnus Troil !

* Note O. Zetland fisherman.

182

The rude words of the song were soon drowned in the ripple of the waves, but the tune continued long to mingle with the sound of wind and sea, and the boats were like to many black specks on the surface of the ocean, diminishing by degrees as they bore far and farther seaward ; while the ear could distinguish touches of the human voice, almost drowned amid that of the elements.

The fishermen's wives looked their last after the parting sails, and were now departing slowly, with downcast and anxious looks, towards the huts in which they were to make arrangements for preparing and drying the fish, with which they hoped to see their husbands and friends return deeply laden. Here and there an old sibyl displayed the superior importance of her experience, by predicting, from the appearance of the atmosphere, that the wind would be fair or foul, while others recommended a vow to the Kirk of Saint Ninian's, for the safety of their men and boats (an ancient Catholic superstition, not yet wholly abolished), and others, but in a low and timorous tone, regretted to their companions, that Norna of Fitful Head had been suffered to depart in discontent that morning from Burgh Westra, "and, of all days in the year, that they suld have contrived to give her displeasure on the first day of the white-fishing !"

The gentry, guests of Magnus Troil, having whiled away as much time as could be so disposed of, in viewing the little armament set sail, and in conversing with the poor women who had seen their friends embark in it, began now to separate into various groups and parties, which strolled in different directions, as fancy led them, to enjoy what may be called the clair-obscure of a Zetland summer day, which, though without the brilliant sunshine that cheers other countries during the fine season, had a mild and pleasing character of its own, that softens while it saddens landscapes, which, in their own lonely, bare, and monotonous tone, have something in them stern as well as barren.

In one of the loneliest recesses of the coast where a deep indenture of the rocks gave the tide access to the cavern, or, as it is called, the *Helyer* of Swartaster, Minna Troil was walking with Captain Cleveland. They had probably chosen that walk, as being little liable to interruption from others ; for, as the force of the tide rendered the place unfit either for fishing or sailing, so it was not the ordinary resort of walkers, on account of its being the supposed habitation of a Mermaid, a race which Norwegian superstition invests with magical as well as mischievous qualities. Here, therefore, Minna wandered with her lover.

A small spot of milk-white sand, that stretched beneath one of the precipices which walled in the creek on either side, afforded them space for a dry, firm, and pleasant walk of about a hundred yards, terminated at one extremity by a dark stretch of the bay, which, scarce touched by the wind, seemed almost as smooth as glass, and which was seen from between two lofty rocks, the jaws of the creek, or indenture, that approached each other above, as if they wished to meet over the dark tide that separated them. The other end of their promenade was closed by a lofty and almost unscaleable precipice, the abode of hundreds of sea-fowl of different kinds, in the bottom of which the huge helyer, or sea-cave, itself yawned, as if for the purpose of swallowing up the advancing tide, which it seemed to receive into an abyss of immeasurable depth and extent. The entrance to this dismal cavern consisted not in a single arch, as usual, but was divided into two, by a huge pillar of natural rock, which, rising out of the sea, and extending to the top of the cavern, seemed to lend its support to the roof, and thus formed a double portal to the helyer, on which the fishermen and peasants had bestowed the rude name of the Devil's Nostrils. In this wild scene, lonely and undisturbed but by the clang of the sea-fowl, Cleveland had already met with Minna Troil more than once ; for with her it was a favourite walk, as the objects which it presented agreed peculiarly with the love of the wild, with melancholy, and the wonderful. But now the conversation in which she was earnestly engaged, was such as entirely to withdraw her attention, as well as that of her companion, from the scenery around them.

"You cannot deny it," she said : "you have given way to feelings respecting this young man, which indicate prejudice and violence—the prejudice unmerited, as far as you are concerned at least, and the violence equally imprudent and unjustifiable."

"I should have thought," replied Cleveland, "that the service I rendered him yesterday might have freed me from such a charge. I do not talk of my own risk, for I have lived in danger, and love it ; it is not every one, however, would have ventured so near the furious animal to save one with whom they had no connection."

"It is not every one, indeed, who could have saved him," answered Minna, gravely ; "but every one who has courage and generosity would have attempted it. The giddy-brained Claud Halcro would have done as much as you, had his strength been equal to his courage—my father would have as much, though having such just cause of resentment against the young man, for his vain and braggart abuse of our hospitality. Do not, therefore, boast of your exploit too much, my good friend, lest you should make me think that it required too great an effort. I know you love not Mordaunt Mertoun, though you exposed your own life to save his."

"Will you allow nothing, then," said Cleveland, "for the long misery I was made to endure from the common and prevailing report, that this beardless bird-hunter stood betwixt me and what I on earth coveted most—the affections of Minna Troil ?"

He spoke in a tone at once impassioned and insinuating, and his whole language and manner seemed to express a grace and elegance, which formed the most striking contrast with the speech and gesture of the unpolished seaman, which he usually affected or exhibited. But his apology was unsatisfactory to Minna.

"You have known," she said, "perhaps too soon, and too well, how little you had to fear—if you indeed feared—that Mertoun, or any other, had interest with Minna Troil.—Nay, truce to thanks and protestations ; I would accept it as the best proof of gratitude, that you would be reconciled with this youth, or at least avoid every quarrel with him."

"That we should be friends, Minna, is impossible," replied Cleveland ;

"even the love I bear you, the most powerful emotion that my heart ever knew, cannot work that miracle."

"And, why, I pray you ?" said Minna ; "there have been no evil offices between you, but rather an exchange of mutual services ; why can you not be friends ?—I have many reasons to wish it."

"And can you, then, forget the slights which he has cast upon Brenda, and on yourself, and on your father's house ?"

"I can forgive them all," said Minna ;—"can you not say so much, who have in truth received no offence ?"

Cleveland looked down, and paused for an instant ; then raised his head, and replied, "I might easily deceive you, Minna, and promise you what my soul tells me is an impossibility ; but I am forced to use too much deceit with others, and with you I will use none. I cannot be friend to this young man :—there is a natural dislike—an instinctive aversion—something like a principle of repulsion in our mutual nature, which makes us odious to each other. Ask himself—he will tell you he has the same antipathy against me. The obligation he conferred on me was a bridle to my resentment ; but I was so galled by the restraint, that I could have gnawed the curb till my lips were bloody."

"You have worn what you are wont to call your iron mask so long, that your features," replied Minna, "retain the impressions of its rigidity even when it is removed."

"You do me injustice, Minna," replied her lover, "and you are angry with me because I deal with you plainly and honestly. Plainly and honestly, however, will I say that I cannot be Mertoun's friend, but it shall be his own fault, not mine, if I am ever his enemy. I seek not to injure him ; but do not ask me to love him. And of this remain satisfied ; that it would be vain even if I could do so ; for as sure as I attempted any advances towards his confidence, so sure would I be to awaken his disgust and suspicion. Leave us to the exercise of our natural feelings, which, as they will unquestionably keep us as far separate as possible, are most likely to prevent any possible interference with each other.—Does this satisfy you ?"

"It must," said Minna, "since you tell me there is no remedy.—And now tell me why you looked so grave when you heard of your consort's arrival—for that it is she I have no doubt—in the port of Kirkwall ?"

"I fear," replied Cleveland, "the consequences of that vessel's arrival with her crew, as comprehending the ruin of my fondest hopes. I had made some progress in your father's favour, and with time, might have made more, when hither come Hawkins and the rest to blight my prospects for ever. I told you on what terms we parted. I then commanded a vessel braver and better found than their own, with a crew who, at my slightest nod, would have faced fiends armed with their own fiery element ; but I now stand alone, a single man, destitute of all means to overawe or to restrain them ; and they will soon show so plainly the ungovernable license of their habits and dispositions, that ruin to themselves and to me will in all probability be the consequence."

"Do not fear it," said Minna ; "my father can never be so unjust as to hold you liable for the offences of others."

"But what will Magnus Troil say to my own demerits, fair Minna ?" said Cleveland, smiling.

"My father is a Zetlander, or rather a Norwegian," said Minna, "one of an oppressed race, who will not care whether you fought against the Spaniards, who are the tyrants of the New World, or against the Dutch and English, who have succeeded to their usurped dominions. His own ancestors supported and exercised the freedom of the seas in those gallant barks, whose pennons were the dread of all Europe."

"I fear, nevertheless," said Cleveland, "that the descendant of an ancient sea-king will scarce acknowledge a fitting acquaintance in a modern sea-rover. I have not disguised from you that I have reason to dread the English laws ; and Magnus, though a great enemy to taxes, imposts, scat, wattle, and so forth, has no idea of latitude upon points of a more general character ;—he would willingly reeve a rope to the yard-arm for the benefit of an unfortunate bucanier."

"Do not suppose so," said Minna ; "he himself suffers too much oppression from the tyrannical laws of our proud neighbours of Scotland. I trust he will soon be able to rise in resistance against them. The enemy—such I will call them— are now divided amongst themselves, and every vessel from their coast brings intelligence of fresh commotions—the Highlands against the Lowlands—the Williamites against the Jacobites—the Whigs against the Tories, and, to sum the whole, the kingdom of England against that of Scotland. What is there, as Claud Halcro well hinted, to prevent our availing ourselves of the quarrels of these robbers, to assert the independence of which we are deprived ?"

"To hoist the raven standard on the Castle of Scalloway," said Cleveland, in imitation of her tone and manner, "and proclaim your father Earl Magnus the First !"

"Earl Magnus the Seventh, if it please you," replied Minna ; "for six of his ancestors have worn, or were entitled to wear, the coronet before him. You laugh at my ardour—but what *is* there to prevent all this ?"

"Nothing *will* prevent it," replied Cleveland, "because it will never be attempted—Anything *might* prevent it, that is equal in strength to the long-boat of a British man-of-war."

"You treat us with scorn, sir," replied Minna : "yet yourself should know what a few resolved men may perform."

"But they must be armed, Minna," replied Cleveland, "and willing to place their lives upon each desperate adventure.—Think not of such visions. Denmark has been cut down into a second-rate kingdom, incapable of exchanging a single broadside with England ; Norway is a starving wilderness ; and in these islands, the love of independence has been suppressed by a long term of subjection, or shows itself but in a few muttered growls over the bowl and bottle.—And were your men as willing warriors as their ancestors, what could the unarmed crews of a few fishing-boats do against the British navy ?—Think no more of it, sweet Minna—it is a dream, and I must term it so, though it makes your eye so bright, and your step so noble."

"It is indeed a dream !" said Minna, looking down, "and it ill becomes a daughter of Hjaltland to look or to move like a free-woman—Our eye should be on the ground, and our step slow and reluctant, as that of one who obeys a taskmaster."

"There are lands," said Cleveland, "in which the eye may look bright upon groves of the palm and the cocoa, and where the foot may move light as a galley under sail, over fields carpeted with flowers, and savannahs surrounded by aromatic thickets, and where subjection is unknown, except that of the brave to the bravest, and of all to the most beautiful."

Minna paused a moment ere she replied, and then answered, "No, Cleveland. My own rude country has charms for me, even desolate as you think it, and depressed as it surely is, which no other land on earth can offer to me. I endeavour in vain to represent to myself those visions of trees, and of groves, which my eye never saw; but my imagination can conceive no sight in nature more sublime than these waves, when agitated by a storm, or more beautiful, than when they come, as they now do, rolling in calm tranquillity to the shore. Not the fairest scene in a foreign land,—not the brightest sunbeam that ever shone upon the richest landscape, would win my thoughts for a moment from that lofty rock, misty hill, and wide-rolling ocean. Hjaltland is the land of my deceased ancestors, and of my living father; and in Hjaltland will I live and die."

"Then in Hjaltland," answered Cleveland, "will I too live and die. I will not go to Kirkwall,—I will not make my existence known to my comrades, from whom it were else hard for me to escape. Your father loves me, Minna; who knows whether long attention, anxious care, might not bring him to receive me into his family? Who would regard the length of a voyage that was certain to terminate in happiness?"

"Dream not of such an issue," said Minna; "it is impossible. While you live in my father's house—while you receive his assistance, and share his table, you will find him the generous friend, and the hearty host; but touch him on what concerns his name and family, and the frank-hearted Udaller will start up before you the haughty and proud descendant of a Norwegian Yarl. See you,—a moment's suspicion has fallen on Mordaunt Mertoun, and he has banished from his favour the youth whom he so lately loved as a son. No one must ally with his house that is not of untainted northern descent."

"And mine may be so, for aught that is known to me upon the subject," said Cleveland.

"How!" said Minna; "have you any reason to believe yourself of Norse descent?"

"I have told you before," replied Cleveland, "that my family is totally unknown to me. I spent my earliest days upon a solitary plantation in the little island of Tortuga, under the charge of my father, then a different person from what he afterwards became. We were plundered by the Spaniards, and reduced to such extremity of poverty, that my father, in desperation, and in thirst of revenge, took up arms, and having become a chief of a little band, who were in the same circumstances, became a bucanier, as it is called, and cruised against Spain, with various vicissitudes of good and bad fortune, until, while he interfered to check some violence of his companions, he fell by their hands—no uncommon fate among the captains of these rovers. But whence my father came, or what was the place of his birth, I know not, fair Minna, nor have I ever had a curious thought on the subject."

"He was a Briton, at least, your unfortunate father ?" said Minna.

"I have no doubt of it," said Cleveland ; "his name, which I have rendered too formidable to be openly spoken, is an English one ; and his acquaintance with the English language, and even with English literature, together with the pains which he took, in better days, to teach me both, plainly spoke him to be an Englishman. If the rude bearing which I display towards others is not the genuine character of my mind and manners, it is to my father, Minna, that I owe any share of better thoughts and principles, which may render me worthy, in some small degree, of your notice and approbation. And yet it sometimes seems to me, that I have two different characters ; for I cannot bring myself to believe, that I, who now walk this lone beach with the lovely Minna Troil, and am permitted to speak to her of the passion which I have cherished, have ever been the daring leader of the bold band whose name was as terrible as a tornado."

"You had not been permitted," said Minna, "to use that bold language toward the daughter of Magnus Troil, had you *not* been the brave and undaunted leader, who, with so small means, has made his name so formidable. My heart is like that of a maiden of the ancient days, and is to be won, not by fair words, but by gallant deeds."

"Alas ! that heart," said Cleveland ; "and what is it that I may do—what is it that man can do, to win in it the interest which I desire ?"

"Rejoin your friends—pursue your fortunes—leave the rest to destiny," said Minna. "Should you return, the leader of a gallant fleet, who can tell what may befall ?"

"And what shall assure me, that, when I return—if return I ever shall—I may not find Minna Troil a bride or a spouse ?—No, Minna, I will not trust to destiny the only object worth attaining, which my stormy voyage in life has yet offered me."

"Hear me," said Minna. "I will bind myself to you, if you dare accept such an engagement, by the promise of Odin,* the most sacred of our northern rites which are yet practised among us, that I will never favour another, until you resign the pretensions which I have given to you.—Will that satisfy you ?—for more I cannot—more I will not give."

"Then with that," said Cleveland, after a moment's pause, "I must perforce be satisfied ;—but remember, it is yourself that throw me back upon a mode of life which the laws of Britain denounce as criminal, and which the violent passions of the daring men by whom it is pursued, have rendered infamous."

"But I," said Minna, "am superior to such prejudices. In warring with England, I see their laws in no other light than as if you were engaged with an enemy, who, in fulness of pride and power, has declared he will give his antagonist no quarter. A brave man will not fight the worse for

* Note P. Promise of Odin.

this ;—and, for the manners of your comrades, so that they do not infect your own, why should their evil report attach to you ?"

Cleveland gazed on her as she spoke, with a degree of wondering admiration, in which, at the same time, there lurked a smile at her simplicity.

"I could not," he said, "have believed, that such high courage could have been found united with such ignorance of the world, as the world is new wielded. For my manners, they who best know me will readily allow, that I have done my best, at the risk of my popularity, and of my life itself, to mitigate the ferocity of my mates ; but how can you teach humanity to men burning with vengeance against the world by whom they are proscribed, or teach them temperance and moderation in enjoying the pleasures which chance throws in their way, to vary a life which would be otherwise one constant scene of peril and hardship ?— But this promise, Minna—this promise, which is all I am to receive in guerdon for my faithful attachment—let me at least lose no time in claiming that."

"It must not be rendered here, but in Kirkwall.—We must invoke, to witness the engagement, the Spirit which presides over the ancient Circle of Stennis. But perhaps you fear to name the ancient Father of the Slain too, the Severe, the Terrible ?"

Cleveland smiled.

"Do me the justice to think, lovely Minna, that I am little subject to fear real causes of terror ; and for those which are visionary, I have no sympathy whatever."

"You believe not in them, then," said Minna, "and are so far better suited to be Brenda's lover than mine."

"I will believe," replied Cleveland, "in whatever you believe. The whole inhabitants of that Valhalla, about which you converse so much with that fiddling, rhyming fool, Claud Halcro—all these shall become living and existing things to my credulity. But, Minna, do not ask me to fear any of them."

"Fear ! no—not to *fear* them, surely," replied the maiden ; "for, not before Thor or Odin, when they approached in the fulness of their terrors, did the heroes of my dauntless race yield one foot in retreat. Nor do I own them as Deities—a better faith prevents so foul an error. But, in our own conception, they are powerful spirits for good or evil. And when you boast not to fear them, bethink you that you defy an enemy of a kind you have never yet encountered."

"Not in these northern latitudes," said the lover, with a smile, "where hitherto I have seen but angels ; but I have faced, in my time, the demons of the Equinoctial Line, which we rovers suppose to be as powerful, and as malignant, as those of the north."

"Have you, then, witnessed those wonders that are beyond the visible world ?" said Minna, with some degree of awe.

Cleveland composed his countenance, and replied,—"A short while before my father's death, I came, though then very young, into the command of a sloop, manned with thirty as desperate fellows as ever handled a musket. We cruised for a long while with bad success, taking nothing but wretched small-craft, which were destined to catch turtle, or otherwise loaded with coarse and worthless trumpery. I had much ado to prevent my comrades from avenging upon the crews of those baubling shallops the disappointment which they had occasioned to us. At length we grew desperate, and made a descent on a village, where we were told we should intercept the mules of a certain Spanish governor laden with treasure. We succeeded in carrying the place ; but while I endeavoured to save the inhabitants from the fury of my followers, the muleteers, with their precious cargo, escaped into the neighbouring woods. This filled up the measure of my unpopularity. My people, who had been long discontented, became openly mutinous. I was deposed from my command, in solemn council, and condemned, as having too little luck and too much humanity for the profession I had undertaken, to be marooned,* as the phrase goes, on one of those little sandy, bushy islets, which are called in the West Indies, keys, and which are frequented only by turtle and by sea-fowl. Many of them are supposed to be haunted—some by the demons worshipped by the old inhabitants— some by Caciques and others, whom the Spaniard had put to death by torture, to compel them to discover their hidden treasures, and others by the various spectres in which sailors of all nations have implicit faith.† My place of banishment, called Coffin Key, about two leagues and a half to the south-east of Bermudas, was so infamous as the resort of these supernatural inhabitants, that I believe the wealth of Mexico would not have persuaded the bravest of scoundrels who put me ashore there, to have spent an hour on the islet alone, even in broad daylight ; and when they rowed off, they pulled for the sloop like men that dared not cast their eyes behind them. And there they left me, to subsist as I might, on a speck of unproductive sand, surrounded by the boundless Atlantic, and haunted, as they supposed by malignant demons."

"And what was the consequence ?" said Minna, eagerly.

"I supported life," said the adventurer, "at the expense of such sea-fowl, aptly called boobies, as were silly enough to let me approach so near as to knock them down with a stick : and by means of turtle-eggs, when these complaisant birds became better acquainted with the mischievous disposition of the human species, and more shy, of course, of my advances."

"And the demons of whom you spoke ?"—continued Minna.

"I had my secret apprehensions upon their account," said Cleveland : "In open day-light, or in absolute darkness, I did not greatly apprehend their approach ; but in the misty dawn of the morning, or when evening was about to fall, I saw, for the first week of my abode on the key, many a dim and undefined spectre, now resembling a Spaniard, with his capa

* To *maroon* a seaman, signified to abandon him on a desolate coast or island—a piece of cruelty often practised by Pirates and Bucaniers.

† An elder brother, now no more, who was educated in the navy, and had been a midshipman in Rodney's squadron in the West Indies, used to astonish the author's boyhood with tales of those haunted islets. On one of them, called, I believe, Coffin Key, the seamen positively refused to pass the night, and came off every evening while they were engaged in completing the watering of the vessel, returning the following sunrise.

wrapped around him, and his huge sombrero as large as an umbrella, upon his head—now a Dutch sailor, with his rough cap and trunk-hose—and now an Indian Cacique, with his feathery crown and long lance of cane."

"Did you not approach and address them ?" said Minna.

"I always approached them," replied the seamen ; "but—I grieve to disappoint your expectations, my fair friend—whenever I drew near them, the phantom changed into a bush, or a piece of driftwood, or a wreath of mist, or some such cause of deception, until at last I was taught by experience to cheat myself no longer with such visions, and continued a solitary inhabitant of Coffin Key, as little alarmed by visionary terrors, as I ever was in the great cabin of a stout vessel, with a score of companions around me."

"You have cheated me into listening to a tale of nothing," said Minna ; "but how long did you continue on the island ?"

"Four weeks of wretched existence," said Cleveland, "when I was relieved by the crew of a vessel which came thither a-turtling. Yet my miserable seclusion was not entirely useless to me ; for on that spot of barren sand I found, or rather forged, the iron-mask, which has since been my chief security against treason, or mutiny of my followers. It was there I formed the resolution to seem no softer hearted, nor better instructed—no more humane, and no more scrupulous, than those with whom fortune had leagued me. I thought over my former story, and saw that seeming more brave, skilful, and enterprising than others, had gained me command and respect, and that seeming more gently nurtured, and more civilised than they had made them envy and hate me as a being of another species. I bargained with myself, then, that since I could not lay aside my superiority of intellect and education, I could do my best to disguise, and to sink in the rude seaman, all appearance of better feeling and better accomplishments. I foresaw then what has since happened, that, under the appearance of daring obduracy, I should acquire such a habitual command over my followers, that I might use it for the insurance of discipline, and for relieving the distresses of the wretches who fell under our power. I saw, in short, that, to attain authority, I must assume the external semblance, at least, of those over whom it was to be exercised. The tidings of my father's fate, while it excited me to wrath and to revenge, confirmed the resolution I had adopted. He also had fallen a victim to his superiority of mind, morals, and manners, above those whom he commanded. They were wont to call him the Gentleman ; and, unquestionably, they thought he waited some favourable opportunity to reconcile himself, perhaps at their expense, to those existing forms of society his habits seemed best to suit with, and, even therefore, they murdered him. Nature and justice alike called on me for revenge. I was soon at the head of a new body of adventurers, who are so numerous in those islands. I sought not after those by whom I had been myself marooned, but after the wretches who had betrayed my father ; and on them I took a revenge so severe, that it was of itself sufficient to stamp me with the character of that inexorable ferocity which I was desirous to be thought to possess, and which, perhaps, was gradually creeping on my natural disposition in actual earnest. My manner, speech, and conduct, seemed so totally changed, that those who formerly knew me were disposed to ascribe the alteration to my intercourse with the demons who haunted the sands of Coffin Key ; nay, there were some, superstitious enough to believe, that I had actually formed a league with them."

"I tremble to hear the rest !" said Minna ; "did you not become the monster of courage and cruelty whose character you assumed ?"

"If I have escaped being so, it is to you, Minna," replied Cleveland, "that the wonder must be ascribed. It is true, I have always endeavoured to distinguish myself rather by acts of adventurous valour, than by schemes of revenge or of plunder, and that at length I could save lives by a rude jest, and sometimes, by the excess of the measures which I myself proposed, could induce those under me to intercede in favour of prisoners ; so that the seeming severity of my character has better served the cause of humanity, than had I appeared directly devoted to it."

He ceased, and as Minna replied not a word, both remained silent for a little space, when Cleveland again resumed the discourse—

"You are silent," he said, "Miss Troil, and I have injured myself in your opinion by the frankness with which I have laid my character before you. I may truly say, that my natural disposition has been controlled, but not altered, by the untoward circumstances in which I am placed."

"I am uncertain," said Minna, after a moment's consideration, "whether you had been thus candid had you not known I should soon see your comrades and discover from their conversation and their manners what you would otherwise gladly have concealed."

"You do me injustice, Minna, cruel injustice. From the instant that you knew me to be a sailor of fortune, an adventurer, a bucanier, or, if you will have the broad word, a PIRATE, what had you to expect less than what I have told you ?"

"You speak too truly," said Minna—"all this I might have anticipated, and I know not how I should have expected it otherwise. But it seemed to me that a war on the cruel and superstitious Spaniards had in it something ennobling—something that refined the fierce employment to which you have just now given its true and dreaded name. I thought that the independent warriors of the Western Ocean, raised up, as it were, to punish the wrongs of so many murdered and plundered tribes, must have had something of gallant elevation, like that of the Sons of the North, whose long galleys avenged on so many coasts the oppressions of degenerate Rome. This I thought, and this I dreamed—I grieve that I am awakened and undeceived. Yet I blame you not for the erring of my own fancy.—Farewell ; we must now part."

"Say, at least," said Cleveland, "that you do not hold me in horror for having told you the truth."

"I must have time for reflection," said Minna, "time to weigh what you have said, ere I can fully understand my own feelings. This much, however, I can say even now, that he who pursues the wicked purpose by means of blood and cruelty, and who must veil his remains of natural remorse under an affectation of superior profligacy, is not, and cannot be, the lover whom Minna Troil expected to find in Cleveland; and if she still love him, it must be as a penitent, and not as a hero."

So saying, she extricated herself from his grasp (for he still endeavoured to detain her), making an imperative sign to him to forbear from following her.—"She is gone," said Cleveland, looking after her; "wild and fanciful as she is, I expected not this.—She startled not at the name of my perilous course of life, yet seems totally unprepared for the evil which must necessarily attend it; and so all the merit I have gained by my resemblance to a Norse Champion, or King of the Sea, is to be lost at once, because a gang of pirates do not prove to be a choir of saints. I would that Rackam, Hawkins, and the rest, had been at the bottom of the Race of Portland—I would the Pentland Firth had swept them to hell rather than to Orkney! I will not, however, quit the chase of this angel for all that these fiends can do. I will—I must to Orkney before the Udaller makes his voyage thither—our meeting might alarm even his blunt understanding, although, thank Heaven, in this wild country, men know the nature of our trade only by hearsay, through our honest friends the Dutch, who take care never to speak very ill of those they make money by.—Well, if fortune would but stand my friend with this beautiful enthusiast, I would pursue her wheel no farther at sea, but set myself down amongst these rocks, as happy as if they were so many groves of bananas and palmettoes."

With these and such thoughts, half rolling in his bosom, half expressed in indistinct hints and murmurs, the pirate Cleveland returned to the mansion of Burgh Westra.

CHAPTER TWENTY-THIRD

There was shaking of hands, and sorrow of heart,
For the hour was approaching when merry folks must part;
So we call'd for our horses, and ask'd for our way,
While the jolly old landlord said, "Nothing's to pay."
LILLIPUT, A POEM

WE do not dwell upon the festivities of the day, which had nothing in them to interest the reader particularly. The table groaned under the usual plenty, which was disposed of by the guests with the usual appetite—the bowl of punch was filled and emptied with the same celerity as usual—the men quaffed, and the women laughed—Claud Halcro rhymed, punned, and praised John Dryden—the Udaller bumpered and sang choruses—and the evening concluded, as usual, in the rigging-loft, as it was Magnus Troil's pleasure to term the dancing apartment.

It was then and there that Cleveland, approaching Magnus, where he sat betwixt his two daughters, intimated his intention of going to Kirkwall in a small brig, which Bryce Snailsfoot, who had disposed of his goods with unprecedented celerity, had freighted thither to procure a supply.

Magnus heard the sudden proposal of his guest with surprise, not unmingled with displeasure, and demanded sharply of Cleveland how long it was since he had learned to prefer Bryce Snailsfoot's company to his own ? Cleveland answered, with his usual bluntness of manner, that time and tide tarried for no one, and that he had his own particular reasons for making his trip to Kirkwall sooner than the Udaller proposed to set sail—that he hoped to meet with him and his daughters at the great fair, which was now closely approaching, and might perhaps find it possible to return to Zetland along with them.

While he spoke this, Brenda kept her eye as much upon her sister as it was possible to do without exciting general observation. She remarked that Minna's pale cheek became yet paler while Cleveland spoke, and that she seemed, by compressing her lips and slightly knitting her brows, to be in the act of repressing the effects of strong interior emotion. But she spoke not ; and when Cleveland, having bidden adieu to the Udaller, approached to salute her, as was then the custom, she received his farewell without trusting herself to attempt a reply.

Brenda had her own trial approaching ; for Mordaunt Mertoun, once so much loved by her father, was now in the act of making his cold parting from him, without receiving a single look of friendly regard. There was, indeed, sarcasm in the tone with which Magnus wished the youth a good journey, and recommended to him, if he met a bonny lass by the way, not to dream that she was in love because she chanced to jest with him. Mertoun coloured at what he felt as an insult, though it was but half intelligible to him ; but he remembered Brenda, and suppressed every feeling of resentment. He proceeded to take his leave of the sisters. Minna, whose heart was considerably softened towards him, received his farewell with some degree of interest ; but Brenda's grief was so visible in the kindness of her manner and the moisture which gathered in the eye, that it was noticed even by the Udaller, who exclaimed, half angrily, "Why, ay, lass, that may be right enough, for he was an old acquaintance ; but mind ! I have no will that he remain one."

Mertoun, who was slowly leaving the apartment, half overheard this disparaging observation, and half turned round to resent it. But his purpose failed him when he saw that Brenda had been obliged to have recourse to her handkerchief to hide her emotion, and the sense that it was excited by his departure obliterated every thought of her father's unkindness. He retired—the other guests followed his example ; and many of them, like Cleveland and himself, took their leave over-night, with the intention of commencing their homeward journey on the succeeding morning.

That night, the mutual sorrow of Minna and Brenda, if it could not wholly remove the reserve which had estranged the sisters from each other, at least melted all its frozen and unkindly symptoms. They went in each other's arms ; and though neither spoke, yet each became dearer to the other ; because they felt that the grief which called forth these drops had a source common to them both.

It is probable, that though Brenda's tears were most abundant, the grief of Minna was most deeply seated ; for, long after the younger had sobbed herself asleep, like a child, upon her sister's bosom, Minna lay awake, watching the dubious twilight, while tear after tear slowly gathered in her eye, and found a current down her cheek, as soon as it became too heavy to be supported by her long black silken eyelashes. As she lay, bewildered among the sorrowful thoughts which supplied these tears, she was surprised to distinguish, beneath the window, the sounds of music. At first she supposed it was some freak of Claud Halcro, whose fantastic humour sometimes indulged itself in such serenades. But it was not the *gue* of the old minstrel, but the guitar, that she heard ; an instrument which none in the island knew how to touch except Cleveland, who had learned, in his intercourse with the South American Spaniards, to play on it with superior execution. Perhaps it was in these climates also that he had learned the song, which, though he now sung it under the window of a maiden of Thule, had certainly never been composed for the native of a climate so northerly and so severe, since it spoke of productions of the earth and skies which are there unknown.

1
Love wakes and weeps
While Beauty sleeps :
Oh for Music's softest numbers,
To prompt a theme,
For Beauty's dream,
Soft as the pillow of her slumbers !

2
Through groves of palm
Sigh gales of balm
Fire-flies on the air are wheeling :
While through the gloom
Comes soft perfume
The distant beds of flowers revealing.

3
O wake and live,
No dream can give
A shadow'd bliss, the real excelling ;
No longer sleep,
From lattice peep,
And list the tale that Love is telling !

The voice of Cleveland was deep, rich and manly, and accorded well with the Spanish air, to which the words, probably a translation from the same language, had been adapted. His invocation would not probably have been fruitless, could Minna have arisen without awakening her sister. But that was impossible ; for Brenda, who, as we have already mentioned, had wept bitterly before she had sunk into repose, now lay with her face on her sister's neck, and one arm stretched around her, in the attitude of a child which has cried itself asleep in the arms of its nurse. It was impossible for Minna to extricate herself from her grasp without awakening her ; and she could not, therefore, execute her hasty purpose of donning her gown, and approaching the window to speak with Cleveland, who, she had no doubt, had resorted to this contrivance to procure an interview. The restraint was sufficiently provoking, for it was more than probable that her lover came to take his last farewell ; but that Brenda, inimical as she seemed to be of late towards Cleveland, should awake and witness it, was a thought not to be endured.

There was a short pause, in which Minna endeavoured more than once, with as much gentleness as possible, to unclasp Brenda's arm from her neck ; but whenever she attempted it, the slumberer muttered some little pettish sound, like a child disturbed in its sleep, which sufficiently showed that perseverance in the attempt would awaken her fully.

To her great vexation, therefore, Minna was compelled to remain still and silent ; when her lover, as if determined upon gaining her ear by music of another strain, sung the following fragment of a sea-ditty :—

> Farewell ! Farewell ! the voice you hear,
>   Has left its last soft tone with you,—
> Its next must join the seaward cheer,
>   And shout among the shouting crew.
>
> The accents which I scarce could form
>   Beneath your frown's controlling check,
> Must give the word, above the storm,
>   To cut the mast and clear the wreck.
>
> The timid eye I dared not raise,—
>   The hand that shook when press'd to thine,
> Must point the guns upon the chase,—
>   Must bid the deadly cutlass shine.
>
> To all I love, or hope, or fear,—
>   Honour, or own, a long adieu !
> To all that life has soft and dear,
>   Farewell ! save memory of you !*

He was again silent ; and again she, to whom the serenade was addressed, strove in vain to arise without rousing her sister. It was impossible ; and she had nothing before her but the unhappy thought that Cleveland was taking leave in his desolation, without a single glance, or a single word. He, too, whose temper was so fiery, yet who subjected his violent mood with such sedulous attention to her will,— could she but have stolen a moment to say adieu—to caution him against new quarrels with Mertoun—to implore him to detach himself from such comrades as he had described,—could she but have done this, who could say what effect such parting admonitions might have had upon his character—nay, upon the future events of his life ?

Tantalised by such thoughts, Minna was about to make another and decisive effort, when she heard voices beneath the window, and thought she could distinguish that they were those of Cleveland and Mertoun, speaking in a sharp tone, which, at the same time, seemed cautiously suppressed, as if the speakers feared being overheard. Alarm now mingled with her former desire to rise from bed, and she accomplished at once the purpose which she had so often attempted in vain. Brenda's

* I cannot suppress the pride of saying that these lines have been beautifully set to original music by Mrs. Arkwright, Derbyshire.

arm was unloosed from her sister's neck, without the sleeper receiving more alarm than provoked two or three unintelligible murmurs ; while, with equal speed and silence, Minna put on some part of her dress, with the intention to steal to the window. But, ere she could accomplish this, the sound of the voices without was exchanged for that of blows and struggling, which terminated suddenly by a deep groan.

Terrified at this last signal of mischief, Minna sprung to the window, and endeavoured to open it, for the persons were so close under the walls of the house that she could not see them, save by putting her head out of the casement. The iron hasp was stiff and rusted, and, as generally happens, the haste with which she laboured to undo it only rendered the task more difficult. When it was accomplished, and Minna had eagerly thrust her body half out at the casement, those who had created the sounds which alarmed her were become invisible, excepting that she saw a shadow cross the moonlight, the substance of which must have been in the act of turning a corner, which concealed it from her sight. The shadow moved slowly, and seemed that of a man who supported another upon his shoulders ; an indication which put the climax to Minna's agony of mind. The window was not above eight feet from the ground, and she hesitated not to throw herself from it hastily, and to pursue the object which had excited her terror.

But when she came to the corner of the buildings from which the shadow seemed to have been projected, she discovered nothing which could point out the way that the figure had gone ; and, after a moment's consideration, became sensible that all attempts at pursuit would be alike wild and fruitless. Besides all the projections and recesses of the many-angled mansion, and its numerous offices—besides the various cellars, storehouses, stables, and so forth, which defied her solitary search, there was a range of low rocks, stretching down to the haven, and which were, in fact, a continuation of the ridge which formed its pier. These rocks had many indentures, hollows, and caverns, into any one of which the figure to which the shadow belonged might have retired with his fatal burden ; for fatal she feared it was most likely to prove.

A moment's reflection, as we have said, convinced Minna of the folly of farther pursuit. Her next thought was to alarm the family ; but what tale had she to tell, and of whom was that tale to be told ?—on the other hand, the wounded man—if indeed he were wounded—alas, if indeed he were not mortally wounded, might not be past the reach of assistance ; and with this idea, she was about to raise her voice, when she was interrupted by that of Claud Halcro, who was returning apparently from the haven, and singing, in his manner, a scrap of an old Norse ditty, which might run thus in English :—

> And you shall deal the funeral dole ;
> Ay, deal it, mother mine,
> To weary body, and to heavy soul,
> The white bread and the wine.

And you shall deal my horses of pride ;
 Ay, deal them, mother mine ;
And you shall deal my lands so wide,
 And deal my castles nine.

But deal not vengeance for the deed,
 And deal not for the crime ;
The body to its place, and the soul to Heaven's grace,
 And the rest in God's own time.

The singular adaptation of these rhymes to the situation in which she found herself, seemed to Minna like a warning from Heaven. We are speaking of a land of omens and superstitions, and perhaps will scarce be understood by those whose limited imagination cannot conceive how strongly these operate upon the human mind during a certain progress of society. A line of Virgil, turned up casually, was received in the seventeenth century, and in the court of England,* as an intimation of future events ; and no wonder that a maiden of the distant and wild isles of Zetland should have considered as an injunction from Heaven verses which happened to convey a sense analogous to her present situation.

"I will be silent," she muttered—"I will seal my lips—

The body to its place, and the soul to Heaven's grace,
And the rest in God's own time."

"Who speaks there ?" said Claud Halcro, in some alarm ; for he had not, in his travels in foreign parts, been able by any means to rid himself of his native superstitions. In the condition to which fear and horror had reduced her, Minna was at first unable to reply ; and Halcro, fixing his eyes upon the female white figure, which he saw indistinctly (for she stood in the shadow of the house, and the morning was thick and misty), began to conjure her in an ancient rhyme which occurred to him as suited for the occasion, and which had in its gibberish a wild and unearthly sound, which may be lost in the ensuing translation :—

Saint Magnus control thee, that martyr of treason ;
Saint Ronan rebuke thee, with rhyme and with reason ;
By the mass of Saint Martin, the might of Saint Mary,
Be thou gone, or thy weird shall be worse if thou tarry !
 If of good, go hence and hallow thee,—
 If of ill, let the earth swallow thee,—
 If thou'rt of air, let the grey mist fold thee,—
 If of earth, let the swart mine hold thee,—
 If a Pixie, seek thy ring,
 If a Nixie, seek thy spring :—
 If on middle earth thou'st been
 Slave of sorrow, shame, and sin,
 Hast eat the bread of toil and strife,
 And dree'd the lot which men call life,
Begone to thy stone ! for thy coffin is scant of thee,
The worm, thy play-fellow, wails for the want of thee ;—
Hence, houseless ghost ! let the earth hide thee,

* The celebrated Sortes Virgilianæ were resorted to by Charles I and his courtiers, as a mode of prying into futurity.

198

Till Michael shall blow the blast, see that there thou bide thee !
Phantom, fly hence ! take the Cross for a token,
Hence pass till Hallowmass !—my spell is spoken.

"It is I, Halcro," muttered Minna, in a tone so thin and low, that it might have passed for the faint reply of the conjured phantom.

"You !—you !" said Halcro, his tone of alarm changing to one of extreme surprise ; "by this moonlight, which is waning, and so it is !—Who could have thought to find you, my most lovely Night, wandering abroad in your own element !—but you saw them, I reckon, as well as I ?—bold enough in you to follow them, though."

"Saw whom ?—follow whom ?" said Minna, hoping to gain some information on the subject of her fears and her anxiety.

"The corpse-lights which danced at the haven," replied Halcro ; "they bode no good, I promise you—you wot well what the old rhyme says—

Where corpse-light
Dances bright,
Be it day or night,
Be it light or dark,
There shall corpse lie stiff and stark.

I went half as far as the haven to look after them, but they had vanished. I think I saw a boat put off, however—some one bound for the Haaf, I suppose—I would we had good news of this fishing—there was Norna left us in anger—and then these corpse-lights !—Well, God help the while ! I am an old man, and can but wish that all were well over.—But how now, my pretty Minna ? tears in your eyes ?—And, now that I see you in the fair moonlight, barefooted too, by Saint Magnus !—Were there no stockings of Zetland wool soft enough for these pretty feet and ankles, that glance so white in the moonbeam ?—What, silent ?—angry, perhaps," he added, in a more serious tone, "at my nonsense ? For shame, silly maiden !—Remember I am old enough to be your father, and have always loved you as my child."

"I am not angry," said Minna, constraining herself to speak—"but heard you nothing ?—saw you nothing ?—They must have passed you."

"They ?" said Claud Halcro ; "what mean you by they ?—is it the corpse-lights ?—No, they did not pass by me, but I think they have passed by you—and blighted you with their influence, for you are as pale as a spectre.—Come, come, Minna," he added, opening a side-door of the dwelling, "these moonlight walks are fitter for old poets than for young maidens—And so lightly clad as you are ! Maiden, you should take care how you give yourself to the breezes of a Zetland night, for they bring more sleet than odours upon their wings.—But, maiden, go in ; for, as glorious John says—or, as he does not say—for I cannot remember how his verse chimes—but, as I say myself, in a pretty poem, written when my muse was in her teens,—

Menseful maiden ne'er should rise,
Till the first beam tinge the skies ;
Silk-fringed eyelids still should close
Till the sun has kiss'd the rose ;

Maiden's foot we should not view,
Mark'd with tiny print on dew,
Till the opening flowerets spread
Carpet meet for beauty's tread—

Stay, what comes next ?—let me see."

When the spirit of recitation seized on Claud Halcro, he forgot time and place, and might have kept his companion in the cold air for half-an-hour, giving poetical reasons why she ought to have been in bed. But she interrupted him by the question, earnestly pronounced, yet in a voice which was scarcely articulate, holding Halcro, at the same time, with a trembling and convulsive grasp, as if to support herself from falling—"Saw you no one in the boat which put to sea but now ?"

"Nonsense," replied Halcro ; "how could I see any one, when light and distance only enabled me to know that it was a boat, and not a grampus ?"

"But there must have been some one in the boat ?" repeated Minna, scarce conscious of what she said.

"Certainly," answered the poet ; "boats seldom work to windward of their own accord.—But come, this is all folly ; and so, as the Queen says, in an old play, which was revived for the stage by rare Will D'Avenant, 'To bed—to bed—to bed !'"

They separated, and Minna's limbs conveyed her with difficulty, through several devious passages, to her own chamber, where she stretched herself cautiously beside her still sleeping sister, with a mind harassed with the most agonising apprehensions. That she had heard Cleveland, she was positive—the tenor of the songs left her no doubt on that subject. If not equally certain that she had heard young Mertoun's voice in hot quarrel with her lover, the impression to that effect was strong on her mind. The groan, with which the struggle seemed to terminate—the fearful indication from which it seemed that the conqueror had borne off the lifeless body of his victim—all tended to prove that some fatal event had concluded the contest. And which of the unhappy men had fallen ?—which had met a bloody death ?—which had achieved a fatal and a bloody victory ?—These were questions to which the still small voice of interior conviction answered, that her lover Cleveland, from character, temper, and habits, was most likely to have been the survivor of the fray. She received from the reflection an involuntary consolation, which she almost detested herself for admitting, when she recollected that it was at once darkened with her lover's guilt, and imbittered with the destruction of Brenda's happiness for ever.

"Innocent, unhappy sister !" such were her reflections ; "thou that art ten times better than I, because so unpretending—so unassuming in thine excellence ! How is it possible that I should cease to feel a pang, which is only transferred from my bosom to thine ?"

As these cruel thoughts crossed her mind, she could not refrain from straining her sister so close to her bosom, that, after a heavy sigh, Brenda awoke.

"Sister," she said, "is it you ?—I dreamed I lay on one of those monuments which Claud Halcro described to us, where the effigy of the inhabitant beneath lies carved in stone upon the sepulchre. I dreamed such a marble form lay by my side, and that it suddenly acquired enough of life and animation to fold me to its cold, moist bosom—and it is yours, Minna, that is indeed so chilly. You are ill, my dearest Minna ! for God's sake, let me rise and call Euphane Fea.—What ails you ? has Norna been here again ?"

"Call no one hither," said Minna, detaining her ; "nothing ails me for which any one has a remedy—nothing but apprehensions of evil worse than even Norna could prophesy. But God is above all, my dear Brenda ; and let us pray to Him to turn, as he only can, our evil into good."

They did jointly repeat their usual prayer for strength and protection from on high, and again composed themselves to sleep, suffering no word, save "God bless you," to pass betwixt them, when their devotions were finished ; thus scrupulously dedicating to Heaven their last waking words, if human frailty prevented them from commanding their last waking thoughts. Brenda slept first, and Minna, strongly resisting the dark and evil presentiments which again began to crowd themselves upon her imagination, was at last so fortunate as to slumber also.

The storm which Halcro had expected began about day-break,—a squall, heavy with wind and rain, such as is often felt, even during the finest part of the season, in these latitudes. At the whistle of the wind, and the clatter of the rain on the shingle-roofing of the fishers' huts, many a poor woman was awakened, and called on her children to hold up their little hands, and join in prayer for the safety of the dear husband and father, who was even then at the mercy of the disturbed elements. Around the house of Burgh Westra, chimneys howled, and windows clashed. The props and rafters of the higher parts of the building, most of them formed out of wreck-wood, groaned and quivered, as fearing to be again dispersed by the tempest. But the daughters of Magnus Troil continued to sleep as softly and as sweetly as if the hand of Chantrey had formed them out of statuary marble. The squall had passed away, and the sunbeams, dispersing the clouds which drifted to leeward, shone full through the lattice, when Minna first started from the profound sleep into which fatigue and mental exhaustion had lulled her, and raising herself on her arm, began to recall events, which, after this interval of profound repose, seemed almost to resemble the baseless visions of the night. She almost doubted if what she recalled of horror, previous to her starting from her bed, was not indeed the fiction of a dream, suggested, perhaps, by some external sounds.

"I will see Claud Halcro instantly," she said ; "he may know something of these strange noises, as he was stirring at the time."

With that she sprung from bed, but hardly stood upright on the floor, ere her sister exclaimed, "Gracious Heaven ! Minna, what ails your foot—your ankle ?"

She looked down, and saw with surprise, which amounted to agony, that both her feet, but particularly one of them, was stained with dark crimson, resembling the colour of dried blood.

Without attempting to answer Brenda, she rushed to the window, and cast a desperate look on the grass beneath, for there she knew she must have contracted the fatal stain. But the rain, which had fallen there in treble quantity, as well from the heavens, as from the eaves of the house, had washed away that guilty witness, if indeed such had ever existed. All was fresh and fair, and the blades of grass, overcharged and bent with rain-drops, glittered like diamonds in the bright morning sun.

While Minna stared upon the spangled verdure, with her full dark eyes fixed and enlarged to circles by the intensity of her terror, Brenda was hanging about her, and with many an eager inquiry, pressed to know whether or how she had hurt herself ?"

"A piece of glass cut through my shoe," said Minna, bethinking herself that some excuse was necessary to her sister ; "I scarce felt it at the time."

"And yet see how it has bled," said her sister. "Sweet Minna," she added, approaching her with a wetted towel, "let me wipe the blood off— the hurt may be worse than you think of."

But as she approached, Minna, who saw no other way of preventing discovery that the blood with which she was stained had never flowed in her own veins, harshly and hastily repelled the proffered kindness. Poor Brenda, unconscious of any offence which she had given to her sister, drew back two or three paces on finding her service thus unkindly refused, and stood gazing at Minna with looks in which there was more of surprise and mortified affection than of resentment, but which had yet something also of natural displeasure.

"Sister," said she, "I thought we had agreed but last night, that happen to us what might, we would at least love each other."

"Much may happen betwixt night and morning," answered Minna, in words rather wrenched from her by her situation, than flowing forth the voluntary interpreters of her thoughts.

"Much may indeed have happened in a night so stormy," answered Brenda ; "for see where the very wall around Euphane's plant-a-cruive has been blown down ; but neither wind, nor rain, nor aught else, can cool our affection, Minna."

"But that may chance," replied Minna, "which may convert it into"—

The rest of the sentence she muttered in a tone so indistinct, that it could not be apprehended ; while, at the same time, she washed the blood-stains from her feet and left ankle. Brenda, who still remained looking on at some distance, endeavoured in vain to assume some tone which might re-establish kindness and confidence betwixt them.

"You were right," she said, "Minna to suffer no one to help you to dress so simple a scratch—standing where I do, it is scarce visible."

"The most cruel wounds," replied Minna, "are those which make no outward show—Are you sure you see it at all ?"

"Oh yes !" replied Brenda, framing her answer as she thought would best please her sister ; "I see a very slight scratch ; nay, now you draw on the stocking, I can see nothing."

"You do indeed see nothing," answered Minna, somewhat wildly ; "but the time will soon come that all—ay, all—will be seen and known."

So saying, she hastily completed her dress, and led the way to breakfast, where she assumed her place amongst the guests ; but with a countenance so pale and haggard and manners and speech so altered and so bewildered, that it excited the attention of the whole company, and the utmost anxiety on the part of her father, Magnus Troil. Many and various were the conjectures of the guests, concerning a distemperature which seemed rather mental than corporeal. Some hinted that the maiden had been struck with an evil eye, and something they muttered about Norna of the Fitful Head ; some talked of the departure of Captain Cleveland, and murmured, "it was a shame for a young lady to take on so after a landlouper, of whom no one knew anything ;" and this contemptuous epithet was in particular bestowed on the Captain by Mistress Baby Yellowley, while she was in the act of wrapping round her old skinny neck the very handsome owerlay (as she called it) wherewith the said Captain had presented her. The old Lady Glowrowrum had a system of her own, which she hinted to Mistress Yellowley, after thanking God that her own connection with the Burgh Westra family was by the lass's mother, who was a canny Scotswoman, like herself.

"For, as to these Troils, you see, Dame Yellowley, for as high as they hold their heads, they say that ken" (winking sagaciously), "that there is a bee in their bonnet ;—that Norna, as they call her, for it's not her right name neither, is at whiles far beside her right mind,—and they that ken the cause, say the Fowd was some gate or other linked in with it, for he will never hear an ill word of her. But I was in Scotland then, or I might have kend the real cause, as well as other folk. At ony rate, there is a kind of wildness in the blood. Ye ken very well daft folk dinna bide to be contradicted ; and I'll say that for the Fowd—he likes to be contradicted as ill as ony man in Zetland. But it shall never be said that I said ony ill of the house that I am sae nearly connected wi'. Only ye will mind, dame, it is through the Sinclairs that we are akin, not through the Troils, and the Sinclairs are kend far and wide for a wise generation, dame.—But I see there is the stirrup-cup coming round."

"I wonder," said Mistress Baby to her brother, as soon as the Lady Glowrowrum turned from her, "what gars that muckle wife dame, dame, dame, that gate at me ? She might ken the blude of the Clinkscales is as gude as ony Glowrowrum's amang them."

The guests, meanwhile, were fast taking their departure, scarcely noticed by Magnus, who was so much engrossed with Minna's indisposition, that, contrary to his hospitable wont, he suffered them to go away unsaluted. And thus concluded, amidst anxiety and illness, the festival of Saint John, as celebrated on that season at the house of Burgh Westra ; adding another caution to that of the Emperor of Ethiopia,— with how little security man can reckon upon the days which he destines to happiness.

CHAPTER TWENTY-FOURTH

But this sad evil which doth her infest,
Doth course of natural cause far exceed,
And housed is within her hollow brest,
That either seems some cursed witch's deed,
Or evill spright that in her doth such torment breed.
THE FAIRIE QUEENE, *Book III, Canto III*

THE term had now elapsed, by several days, when Mordaunt Mertoun, as he had promised at his departure, should have returned to his father's abode at Yarlshof, but there were no tidings of his arrival. Such delay might, at another time, have excited little curiosity, and no anxiety ; for old Swertha, who took upon her the office of thinking and conjecturing for the little household, would have concluded that he had remained behind the other guests upon some party of sport or pleasure. But she knew that Mordaunt had not been lately in favour with Magnus Troil ; she knew that he proposed his stay at Burgh Westra should be a short one, upon account of his father's health, to whom, notwithstanding the little encouragement which his filial piety received, he paid uniform attention. Swertha knew all this, and she became anxious. She watched the looks of her master, the elder Mertoun ; but wrapt in dark and stern uniformity of composure, his countenance, like the surface of a midnight lake enabled no one to penetrate into what was beneath. His studies, his solitary meals, his lonely walks, succeeded each other in unvaried rotation, and seemed undisturbed by the least thought about Mordaunt's absence.

At length such reports reached Swertha's ear, from various quarters, that she became totally unable to conceal her anxiety, and resolved, at the risk of provoking her master into fury, or perhaps that of losing her place in his household, to force upon his notice the doubts which afflicted her own mind. Mordaunt's good humour and goodly person must indeed have made no small impression on the withered and selfish heart of the poor old woman, to induce her to take a course so desperate and from which her friend the Ranzelman endeavoured in vain to deter her. Still, however, conscious that a miscarriage in the matter, would, like the loss of Trinculo's bottle in the horse-pool, be attended not only with dishonour, but with infinite loss, she determined to proceed on her high emprise with as much caution as was consistent with the attempt.

We have already mentioned, that it seemed a part of the very nature of this reserved and unsociable being, at least since his retreat into the utter solitude of Yarlshof, to endure no one to start a subject of conversation, or to put any question to him, that did not arise out of urgent and pressing emergency. Swertha was sensible, therefore, that, in order to open the discourse favourably which she proposed to hold with her master, she must contrive that it should originate with himself.

To accomplish this purpose, while busied in preparing the table for

Mr. Mertoun's simple and solitary dinner meal, she formally adorned the board with two covers instead of one, and made all her other preparations, as if he was to have a guest or companion at dinner.

The artifice succeeded ; for Mertoun, on coming from his study, no sooner saw the table thus arranged, than he asked Swertha, who, waiting the effect of the stratagem as a fisher watches his ground-baits, was fiddling up and down the room, "Whether Mordaunt was not returned from Burgh Westra ?"

This question was the cue for Swertha, and she answered in a voice of sorrowful anxiety, half real, half affected, "Na, na !—nae sic divot had dunted at their door. It wad be blithe news indeed to ken that young Maister Mordaunt, puir dear bairn, were safe at hame."

"And, if he be not at home, why should you lay a cover for him, you doting fool ?" replied Mertoun, in a tone well calculated to stop the old woman's proceedings. But she replied, boldly, "That indeed, somebody should take thought about Maister Mordaunt ; a' that she could do was to have seat and plate ready for him when he came. But she thought the dear bairn had been ower long awa ; and, if she maun speak out, she had her ain fears when and whether he might ever come hame."

"*Your* fears !" replied Mertoun, his eyes flashing as they usually did when his hour of ungovernable passion approached ; "do you speak of your idle fears to me, who know that all of your sex, that is not fickleness, and folly, and self-conceit, and self-will, is a bundle of idiotical fears, vapours, and tremors ? What are your fears to me, you foolish old hag ?"

It is an admirable quality in womankind, that, when a breach of the laws of natural affection comes under their observation, the whole sex is in arms. Let a rumour arise in a street of a parent that has misused a child, or a child that has insulted a parent,—I say nothing of the case of husband and wife, where the interest may be accounted for in sympathy,—and all the women within hearing will take animated and decided part with the sufferer. Swertha, notwithstanding her greed and avarice, had her share of the generous feeling which does so much honour to her sex, and was, on this occasion, so much carried on by its impulse, that she confronted her master, and upbraided him with his hard-hearted indifference, with a boldness at which she herself was astonished.

"To be sure it wasna her that suld be fearing for her young maister, Maister Mordaunt, even although he was, as she might well say, the very sea-calf of her hert ; but ony other father, but his honour himsell, wad have had speerings made after the poor lad, and him gane this eight days from Burgh Westra, and naebody kend when or where he had gane. There wasna a bairn in the howff but was maining for him ; for he made all their bits of boats with his knife ; there wadna be a dry eye in the parish, if aught worse than weal should befall him,—no, no ane, unless it might be his honour's ain."

Mertoun had been much struck, and even silenced, by the insolent volubility of his insurgent housekeeper ; but, at the last sarcasm, he imposed on her silence in her turn with an audible voice, accompanied with one of the most terrific glances which his dark eye and stern features could express. But Swertha, who, as she afterwards acquainted the Ranzelman, was wonderfully supported during the whole scene, would not be controlled by the loud voice and ferocious look of her master, but proceeded in the same tone as before.

"His honour," she said, "had made an unco wark because a wheen bits of kists and duds, that naebody had use for, had been gathered on the beach by the poor bodies of the township ; and here was the bravest lad in the country lost, and cast away, as it were, before his een, and nae ane asking what was come o' him."

"What should come of him but good, you old fool," answered Mr. Mertoun, "as far, at least, as there can be good in any of the follies he spends his time in ?"

This was spoken rather in a scornful than an angry tone, and Swertha, who had got into the spirit of the dialogue, was resolved not to let it drop, now that the fire of her opponent seemed to slacken.

"O ay, to be sure I am an auld fule,—but if Maister Mordaunt should have settled down in the Roost, as mair than ae boat has been lost in that wearifu' squall the other morning—by good luck it was short as it was sharp, or naething could have lived in it—or if he were drowned in a loch coming hame on foot, or if he were killed by miss of footing on a craig—the haill island kend how venturesome he was—who," said Swertha, "will be the auld fule then ?" And she added a pathetic ejaculation, that "God would protect the poor motherless bairn ! for if he had had a mother, there would have been search made after him before now."

This last sarcasm affected Mertoun powerfully,—his jaw quivered, his face grew pale, and he muttered to Swertha to go into his study (where she was scarcely ever permitted to enter), and fetch him a bottle which stood there.

"O ho !" quoth Swertha to herself, as she hastened on the commission, "my master knows where to find a cup of comfort to qualify his water with upon fitting occasions."

There was indeed a case of such bottles as were usually employed to hold strong waters, but the dust and cobwebs in which they were enveloped showed that they had not been touched for many years. With some difficulty Swertha extracted the cork of one of them, by the help of a fork—for corkscrew there was none at Yarlshof—and having ascertained by smell, and, in case of any mistake, by a moderate mouthful, that it contained wholesome Barbadoes waters, she carried it into the room, where her master still continued to struggle with his faintness. She then began to pour a small quantity into the nearest cup that she could find, wisely judging, that, upon a person so much unaccustomed to the use of spirituous liquors, a little might produce a strong effect. But the patient signed to her impatiently to fill the cup, which might hold more than the third of an English pint measure, up to the very brim, and swallowed it down without hesitation.

"Now the saunts above have a care on us !" said Swertha, "he will be drunk as weel as mad, and wha is to guide him then, I wonder ?"

But Mertoun's breath and colour returned, without the slightest symptom of intoxication ; on the contrary, Swertha afterwards reported, that, "Although she had always had a firm opinion in favour of a dram, yet she never saw one work such miracles—he spoke mair like a man of the middle world, than she had ever heard him do since she had entered his service."

"Swertha," he said, "you are right in this matter, and I was wrong. Go down to the Ranzelman directly, tell him to come and speak with me, without an instant's delay, and bring me special word what boats and people he can command ; I will employ them all in the search, and they shall be plentifully rewarded."

Stimulated by the spur which maketh the old woman proverbially to trot, Swertha posted down to the hamlet, with all the speed of threescore, rejoicing that her sympathetic feelings were likely to achieve their own reward, having given rise to a quest which promised to be so lucrative, and in the profits whereof she was determined to have her share, shouting out as she went, and long before she got within hearing, the names of Niel Ronaldson, Sweyn Erickson, and the other friends and confederates who were interested in her mission. To say the truth, notwithstanding that the good dame really felt a deep interest in Mordaunt Mertoun, and was mentally troubled on account of his absence, perhaps a few things would have disappointed her more than if he had at this moment started up in her path safe and sound, and rendered unnecessary, by his appearance, the expense and the bustle of searching after him.

Soon did Swertha accomplish her business in the village, and adjust with the senators of the township her own little share of percentage upon the profits likely to accrue on her mission ; and speedily did she return to Yarlshof, with Niel Ronaldson by her side, schooling him to the best of her skill in all the peculiarities of her master.

"Aboon a' things," she said, "never make him wait for an answer ; and speak loud and distinct as if you were hailing a boat,—for he downa bide to say the same thing twice over ; and if he asks about distance, ye may make leagues for miles, for he kens naething about the face of the earth that he lives upon ; and if he speak of siller, ye may ask dollars for shillings, for he minds them nae mair than sclate-stanes."

Thus tutored, Niel Ronaldson was introduced into the presence of Mertoun, but was utterly confounded to find that he could not act upon the system of deception which had been projected.—When he attempted, by some exaggeration of distance and peril, to enhance the hire of the boats and of the men (for the search was to be by sea and land), he found himself at once cut short by Mertoun, who showed not only the most perfect knowledge of the country, but of distances, tides, currents, and all belonging to the navigation of those seas, although these were topics with which he had hitherto appeared to be totally unacquainted. The Ranzelman, therefore, trembled when they came to speak of the recompense to be afforded for their exertions in the search ; for it was not more unlikely that Mertoun should be as well informed of what was just and proper upon this head as upon others ; and Niel remembered the storm of his fury, when, at an early period after he had settled at Yarlshof, he drove Swertha and Sweyn Erickson from his

207

presence. As, however, he stood hesitating betwixt the opposite fears of asking too much or too little, Mertoun stopped his mouth, and ended his uncertainty, by promising him a recompense beyond what he dared to have ventured to ask, with an additional gratuity, in case they returned with the pleasing intelligence that his son was safe.

When this great point was settled, Niel Ronaldson, like a man of conscience, began to consider earnestly the various places where search should be made after the young man ; and having undertaken faithfully that the inquiry should be prosecuted at all the houses of the gentry, both in this and the neighbouring islands, he added, that, "after all, if his honour would not be angry, there was ane not far off, that if any body dared speer her a question, and if she liked to answer it, could tell more about Maister Mordaunt than anybody else could.—Ye will ken wha I mean, Swertha ? Her that was down at the haven this morning." Thus he concluded, addressing himself with a mysterious look to the housekeeper, which she answered with a nod and a wink.

"How mean you ?" said Mertoun ; "speak out short and open—whom do you speak off ?"

"It is Norna of the Fitful Head," said Swertha, "that the Ranzelman is thinking about ; for she had gone up to Saint Ringan's Kirk this morning on business of her own."

"And what can this person know of my son ?" said Mertoun ; "she is, I believe, a wandering madwoman, or impostor."

"If she wanders," said Swertha, "it is for nae lack of means at hame, and that is weel known—plenty o a' thing has she of her ain, forby that the Fowd himsell would let her want naething."

"But what is that to my son ?" said Mertoun, impatiently.

"I dinna ken—she took unco pleasure in Maister Mordaunt from the time she saw him, and mony a braw thing she gave him at ae time or another, forby the gowd chain that hangs about his bonny craig—folk say it is of fairy gold—I kenna what gold it is, but Bryce Snailsfoot says, that the value will amount to an hundred punds English, and that is nae deaf nuts."

"Go, Ronaldson," said Mertoun, "or else send some one to seek this woman out—if you think there be a chance of her knowing anything of my son."

"She kens a' thing that happens in thae islands," said Niel Ronaldson, "muckle sooner than other folk, and that is Heaven's truth. But as to going to the kirk, or the kirkyard, to speer after her, there is not a man in Zetland will do it, for meed or for money—and that's Heaven's truth as weel as the other."

"Cowardly, superstitious fools !" said Mertoun,—"But give me my cloak, Swertha.—This woman has been at Burgh Westra—she is related to Troil's family—she may know something of Mordaunt's absence and its cause—I will seek her myself—She is at the Cross Kirk, you say ?"

"No, not at the Cross Kirk, but at the auld Kirk of Saint Ringan's—it's a dowie bit, and far frae being canny ; and if your honour," added Swertha, "wad walk by my rule, I wad wait until she came back, and no trouble her when she may be mair busied wi' the dead, for onything that

208

we ken, than she is wi' the living. The like of her carena to have other folk's een on them when they are, gude sain us ! doing their ain particular turns."

Mertoun made no answer, but throwing his cloak loosely around him (for the day was misty, with passing showers), and leaving the decayed mansion of Yarlshof, he walked at a pace much faster than was usual with him, taking the direction of the ruinous church, which stood, as he well knew, within three or four miles of his dwelling.

The Ranzelman and Swertha stood gazing after him in silence, until he was fairly out of ear-shot, when, looking seriously on each other, and shaking their sagacious heads in the same boding degree of vibration, they uttered their remarks in the same breath.

"Fools are aye fleet and fain," said Swertha.

"Fey folk run fast," added the Ranzelman ; "and the thing that we are born to, we cannot win by.—I have known them that tried to stop folk that were fey. You have heard of Helen Emberson of Camsey, how she stopped all the boles and windows about the house, that her gudeman might not see daylight, and rise to the Haaf-fishing, because she feared foul weather ; and how the boat he should have sailed in was lost in the Roost ; and how she came back, rejoicing in her gudeman's safety—but ne'er may care, for there she found him drowned in his own masking-fat, within the wa's of his ain biggin ; and moreover"—

But here Swertha reminded the Ranzelman that he must go down to the haven to get off the fishing-boats ; "For both that my heart is sair for the bonny lad, and that I am fear'd he cast up of his ain accord before you are at sea ; and as I have often told ye, my master may lead, but he winna drive ; and if ye do not his bidding, and get out to sea, the never a bodle of boat-hire will ye see."

"Weel, weel, good dame," said the Ranzelman, "we will launch as fast as we can ; and by good luck, neither Clawson's boat nor Peter Grot's is out to the Haaf this morning, for a rabbit ran across the path as they were going on board, and they came back like wise men, kenning they wad be called to other wark this day. And a marvel it is to think, Swertha, how few real judicious men are left in this land. There is our great Udaller is weel eneugh when he is fresh, but he makes ower mony voyages in his ship and his yawl to be lang sae ; and now, they say, his daughter, Mistress Minna, is sair out of sorts.—Then there is Norna kens muckle mair than other folk, but wise woman ye cannot call her. Our tacksman here, Maister Mertoun, his wit is sprung in the bowsprit, I doubt—his son is a daft gowk ; and I ken few of consequence hereabouts—excepting always myself, and may be you, Swertha—but what may, in some sense or other, be called fules."

"That may be, Niel Ronaldson," said the dame ; "but if you do not hasten the faster to the shore, you will lose tide ; and, as I said to my master some short time syne, wha will be the fule then ?"

CHAPTER TWENTY-FIFTH

I do love these ancient ruins—
We never tread upon them but we set
Our foot upon some reverend history ;
And, questionless, here, in this open court
(Which now lies naked to the injuries
Of stormy weather), some men lie interr'd,
Loved the Church so well, and gave so largely to it,
They thought it should have canopied their bones
Till doomsday ;—but all things have their end—
Churches and cities, which have diseases like to men,
Must have like death which we have.

THE DUCHESS OF MALFI

THE ruinous church of Saint Ninian had, in its time, enjoyed great celebrity ; for that mighty system of Roman superstition, which spread its roots over all Europe, had not failed to extend them even to this remote archipelago, and Zetland had, in the Catholic times, her saints, her shrines, and her relics, which, though little known elsewhere, attracted the homage, and commanded the observance, of the simple inhabitants of Thule. Their devotion to this church of Saint Ninian, or, as he was provincially termed, Saint Ringan, situated, as the edifice was, close to the sea-beach, and serving, in many points, as a landmark to their boats, was particularly obstinate, and was connected with so much superstitious ceremonial and credulity, that the reformed clergy thought it best, by an order of the Church Courts, to prohibit all spiritual service within its walls, as tending to foster the rooted faith of the simple and rude people around in saint-worship, and other erroneous doctrines of the Romish Church.

After the church of Saint Ninian had been thus denounced as a seat of idolatry, and desecrated of course, the public worship was transferred to another church ; and the roof, with its lead and its rafters, having been stripped from the little rude old Gothic building, it was left in the wilderness to the mercy of the elements. The fury of the uncontrolled winds, which howled along an exposed space, resembling that which we have described at Yarlshof, very soon choked up nave and aisle, and, on the north-west side, which was chiefly exposed to the wind, hid the outside walls more than half-way up with the mounds of drifted sand, over which the gable-ends of the building, with the little belfry, which was built above its eastern angle, arose in ragged and shattered nakedness of ruin.

Yet, deserted as it was, the Kirk of Saint Ringan still retained some semblance of the ancient homage formerly rendered there. The rude and ignorant fishermen of Dunrossness observed a practice, of which they themselves had well nigh forgotten the origin, and from which the Protestant clergy in vain endeavoured to deter them. When their boats were in extreme peril, it was common amongst them to propose to vow

210

an *awmous*, as they termed it, that is, an alms, to Saint Ringan ; and when the danger was over, they never failed to absolve themselves of their vow, by coming singly and secretly to the old church, and putting off their shoes and stockings at the entrance of the churchyard, walked thrice around the ruins, observing that they did so in the course of the sun. When the circuit was accomplished for the third time, the votary dropped his offering, usually a small silver coin, through the mullions of a lanceolated window, which opened into a side aisle, and then retired, avoiding carefully to look behind him till he was beyond the precincts which had once been hallowed ground ; for it was believed that the skeleton of the saint received the offering in his bony hand, and showed his ghastly death's head at the window in which it was thrown.

Indeed, the scene was rendered more appalling to weak and ignorant minds, because the same stormy and eddying winds, which, on the one side of the church threatened to bury the ruins with sand, and had, in fact, heaped it up in huge quantities, so as almost to hide the side-wall with its buttresses, seemed in other places bent on uncovering the graves of those who had been laid to their long rest on the south-eastern quarter ; and after an unusual hard gale, the coffins, and sometimes the very corpses, of those who had been interred without the usual cerements, were discovered, in a ghastly manner, to the eyes of the living.

It was to this desolate place of worship that the elder Mertoun now proceeded, though without any of those religious or superstitious purposes with which the church of Saint Ringan was usually approached. He was totally without the superstitious fears of the country—nay, from the sequestered and sullen manner in which he lived, withdrawing himself from human society, even when assembled for worship, it was the general opinion that he erred on the more fatal side, and believed rather too little than too much of that which the Church receives and enjoins to Christians.

As he entered the little bay, on the shore and almost on the beach of which the ruins are situated, he could not help pausing for an instant, and becoming sensible that the scene, as calculated to operate on human feelings, had been selected with much judgment as the site of a religious house.—In front lay the sea, into which two headlands, which formed the extremities of the bay, projected their gigantic causeways of dark and sable rocks, on the ledges of which the gulls, scouries, and other sea-fowl, appeared like flakes of snow ; while, upon the lower ranges of the cliffs stood whole lines of cormorants, drawn up alongside of each other, like soldiers in their battle array, and other living thing was there none to see. The sea, although not in a tempestuous state, was disturbed enough to rush on these capes with a sound, like distant thunder, and the billows, which rose in sheets of foam half-way up these sable rocks, formed a contrast of colouring equally striking and awful.

Betwixt the extremities or capes of these projecting headlands there rolled, on the day when Mertoun visited the scene, a deep and dense aggregation of clouds, through which no human eye could penetrate, and which, bounding the vision, and excluding all view of the distant ocean, rendered it no unapt representation of the sea in the Vision of Mirza, whose extent was concealed by vapours, and clouds, and storms. The ground, rising steeply from the sea-beach, permitting no view into the interior of the country, appeared a scene of irretrievable barrenness, where scrubby and stunted heath, intermixed with the long bent or coarse grass, which first covers sandy soils, were the only vegetables that could be seen. Upon a natural elevation, which rose above the beach in the very bottom of the bay, and receded a little from the sea, so as to be without reach of the waves, arose the half-buried ruin which we have already described, surrounded by a wasted, half-ruinous, and mouldering wall, which, breached in several places, served still to divide by accident into this solitary bay pretended that the church was occasionally observed to be full of lights, and, from that circumstance, were used to prophesy shipwrecks and deaths by sea.

As Mertoun approached near to the chapel he adopted, insensibly, and perhaps without too much premeditation, measures to avoid being himself seen, until he came close under the walls of the burial-ground, which he approached, as it chanced, on that side where the sand was blowing from the graves, in the manner we have described.

Here, looking through one of the gaps in the wall, which time had made, he beheld the person whom he sought occupied in a manner which assorted well with the ideas popularly entertained of her character, but which was otherwise sufficiently extraordinary.

She was employed beside a rude monument, on one side of which was represented the rough outline of a cavalier or knight on horseback, while on the other appeared a shield, with the armorial bearings so defaced as not to be intelligible ; which escutcheon was suspended by one angle, contrary to the modern custom, which usually places them straight and upright. At the foot of this pillar were believed to repose, as Mertoun had formerly heard, the bones of Ribol Troil, one of the remote ancestors of Magnus, and a man renowned for deeds of valorous emprise in the fifteenth century. From the grave of this warrior Norna of the Fitful Head seemed busied in shovelling the sand, an easy task where it was so light and loose ; so that it seemed plain that she would shortly complete what the rude winds had begun, and made bare the bones which lay there interred. As she laboured, she muttered her magic song ; for without the Runic rhyme no form of northern superstition was ever performed. We have, perhaps, preserved too many examples of these incantations ; but we cannot help attempting to translate that which follows :—

Champion, famed for warlike toil,
Art thou silent, Ribolt Troil ?
Sand, and dust, and pebbly stones,
Are leaving bare thy giant bones.
Who dared touch the wild-bear's skin
Ye slumber'd on while life was in ?
A woman now, or babe, may come
And cast the covering from thy tomb.

Yet be not wrathful, Chief, nor
 blight
Mine eyes or ears with sound or
 sight !
I come not, with unhallow'd tread,
To wake the slumbers of the dead,
Or lay thy giant relics bare ;
But what I seek thou well canst spare.

Be it to my hand allow'd
To shear a merk's weight from thy
  shroud,
Yet leave thee sheeted lead enough
To shield they bones from weather
  rough.

See, I draw my magic knife—
Never while thou wert in life
Laid'st thou still for sloth or fear,
When point and edge were glittering
  near ;
See, the cerements now I sever—
Waken now, or sleep for ever !
Thou wilt not wake ? the deed is
  done !—
The prize I sought is fairly won.

Thanks, Ribolt, thanks—for this the
  sea
Shall smooth its ruffled crest for
  thee—
And while afar its billows foam
Subside to peace near Ribolt's tomb.
Thanks, Ribolt, thanks—for this the
  might
Of wild winds raging at their height,
When to thy place of slumber nigh,
Shall soften to a lullaby.

She, the dame of doubt and dread,
Norna of the Fitful Head,
Mighty in her own despite—
Miserable in her might ;
In despair and frenzy great,
In her greatness desolate ;
Wisest, wickedest who lives,
Well can keep the word she gives !

While Norna chanted the first part of this rhyme, she completed the task of laying bare a part of the leaden coffin of the ancient warrior, and severed from it, with much caution and apparent awe, a portion of the metal. She then reverentially threw back the sand upon the coffin ; and by the time she had finished her song, no trace remained that the secrets of the sepulchre had been violated.

Mertoun remained gazing on her from behind the churchyard wall during the whole ceremony, not from any impression of veneration for her or her employment, but because he conceived that to interrupt a madwoman in her act of madness, was not the best way to obtain from her such intelligence as she might have to impart. Meanwhile he had full time to consider her figure, although her face was obscured by her dishevelled hair, and by the hood of her dark mantle, which permitted no more to be visible than a Druidess would probably have exhibited at the celebration of her mystical rites.

Mertoun had often heard of Norna before ; nay, it is most probable that he might have seen her repeatedly, for she had been in the vicinity of Yarlshof more than once since his residence there. But the absurd stories which were in circulation respecting her, prevented his paying any attention to a person whom he regarded as either an impostor or a madwoman, or a compound of both. Yet, now that his attention was, by circumstances, involuntarily fixed upon her person and deportment, he could not help acknowledging to himself that she was either a complete enthusiast, or rehearsed her part so admirably, that no Pythoness of ancient time could have excelled her. The dignity and solemnity of her gesture,—the sonorous, yet impressive tone of voice with which she addressed the departed spirit whose mortal relics she ventured to disturb, were such as failed not to make an impression upon him, careless and indifferent as he generally appeared to all that went on around him. But no sooner was her singular occupation terminated, than, entering the churchyard with some difficulty, by clambering over the disjointed ruins of the wall, he made Norna aware of his present. Far from starting, or expressing the least surprise at his appearance in a place so solitary, she said, in a tone that seemed to intimate that he had been expected, "So—you have sought me at last?"

"And found you," replied Mertoun, judging he would best introduce the inquiries he had to make, by assuming a tone which corresponded to her own.

"Yes!" she replied, "found me you have, and in the place where all men must meet—amid the tabernacles of the dead."

"Here we must, indeed, meet at last," replied Mertoun, glancing his eyes on the desolate scene around, where headstones, half-covered with sand, and others, from which the same wind had stripped the soil on which they rested, covered with inscriptions, and sculptured with emblems of mortality, were the most conspicuous objects,—"here, as in the house of death, all men must meet at length; and happy those that come soonest to the quiet haven."

"He that dares desire this haven," said Norna, "must have steered a steady course in life. I dare not hope for such quiet harbour. Darest *thou* expect it? or has the course thou hast kept deserved it?"

"It matters not to my present purpose," replied Mertoun; "I have to ask you what tidings you know of my son Mordaunt Mertoun?"

"A father," replied the sibyl, "asks of a stranger what tidings she has of his son! How should I know aught of him? the cormorant says not to the mallard, Where is my brood?"

"Lay aside this useless affectation of mystery," said Mertoun; "with the vulgar and ignorant it has its effect, but upon me it is thrown away. The people of Yarlshof have told me that you do know, or may know, something of Mordaunt Mertoun, who has not returned home from the festival of Saint John's, held in the house of your relative, Magnus Troil. Give me such information, if indeed ye have it to give; and it shall be recompensed, if the means of recompense are in my power."

"The wide round of earth," replied Norna, "holds nothing that I would call a recompense for the slightest word that I throw away upon a living ear. But for thy son, if thou wouldst see him in life, repair to the approaching Fair of Kirkwall, in Orkney."

"And wherefore thither?" said Mertoun; "I know he had no purpose in that direction."

"We drive on the stream of fate," answered Norna, "without oar or rudder. You had no purpose this morning of visiting the Kirk of Saint Ringan, yet you are here;—you had no purpose but a minute hence of being at Kirkwall, and yet you will go thither."

"Not unless the cause is more distinctly explained to me. I am no believer, dame, in those who assert your supernatural powers."

"You shall believe in them ere we part," said Norna. "As yet you know but little of me, nor shall you know more. But I know enough of you, and could convince you with one word that I do so."

"Convince me, then," said Mertoun; "for unless I am so convinced, there is little chance of my following your counsel."

"Mark, then," said Norna, "what I have to say on your son's score, else what I shall say to you on your own will banish every other thought from

214

your memory. You shall go to the approaching Fair at Kirkwall ; and, on the fifth day of the Fair, you shall walk, at the hour of noon, in the outer aisle of the Cathedral of Saint Magnus, and there you shall meet a person who will give you tidings of your son."

"You must speak more distinctly, dame," returned Mertoun, scornfully, "if you hope that I shall follow your counsel. I have been fooled in my time by women, but never so grossly as you seem willing to gull me."

"Hearken then !" said the old woman. "The word which I speak shall touch the nearest secret of thy life, and thrill thee through nerve and bone."

So saying, she whispered a word into Mertoun's ear, the effect of which seemed almost magical. He remained fixed and motionless with surprise, as, waving her arms slowly aloft, with an air of superiority and triumph, Norna glided from him, turned round a corner of the ruins, and was soon out of sight.

Mertoun offered not to follow, or to trace her. "We fly from our fate in vain," he said, as he began to recover himself ; and turning, he left behind him the desolate ruins with their cemetery. As he looked back from the very last point at which the church was visible, he saw the figure of Norna, muffled in her mantle, standing on the very summit of the ruined tower, and stretching out to the sea-breeze something which resembled a white pennon, or flag. A feeling of horror, similar to that excited by her last words, again thrilled through his bosom, and he hastened onwards with unwonted speed, until he had left the church of Saint Ninian, with its bay of sand, far behind him.

Upon his arrival at Yarlshof, the alteration in his countenance was so great, that Swertha conjectured he was about to fall into one of those fits of deep melancholy, which she termed his dark hour.

"And what better could be expected," thought Swertha, "when he must needs go visit Norna of the Fitful Head, when she was in the haunted Kirk of Saint Ringan's ?"

But without testifying any other symptoms of an alienated mind, than that of deep and sullen dejection, her master acquainted her with his intention to go to the Fair of Kirkwall,—a thing so contrary to his usual habits, that the housekeeper well-nigh refused to credit her ears. Shortly after, he heard, with apparent indifference, the accounts returned by the different persons who had been sent out in quest of Mordaunt, by sea and land, who all of them returned without any tidings. The equanimity with which Mertoun heard the report of their bad success, convinced Swertha still more firmly that in his interview with Norna, that issue had been predicted to him by the sibyl whom he had consulted.

The township were yet more surprised, when their tacksman, Mr. Mertoun, as if on some sudden resolution, made preparations to visit Kirkwall during the Fair, although he had hitherto avoided sedulously all such places of public resort. Swertha puzzled herself a good deal, without being able to penetrate this mystery ; and vexed herself still more concerning the fate of her young master. But her concern was much softened by the deposit of a sum of money, seeming, however moderate in itself, a treasure in her eyes, which her master put into her hands, acquainting her, at the same that, that he had taken his passage for Kirkwall, in a small bark belonging to the proprietor of the island of Mousa.

CHAPTER TWENTY-SIXTH

Nae langer she wept,—her tears were a' spent.—
Despair it was come, and she thought it content ;
She thought it content, but her cheek it grew pale,
And she droop'd, like a lily broke down by the hail.[*]
CONTINUATION OF AULD ROBIN GRAY

THE condition of Minna resembled that of the village heroine in Lady Ann Lindsay's beautiful ballad. Her natural firmness of mind prevented her from sinking under the pressure of the horrible secret, which haunted her while awake, and was yet more tormenting during her broken and hurried slumber. There is no grief so dreadful as that which we dare not communicate, and in which we can neither ask nor desire sympathy ; and when to this is added the burden of a guilty mystery to an innocent bosom, there is little wonder that Minna's health should have sunk under the burden.

To the friends around, her habits and manners, nay, her temper, seemed altered to such an extraordinary degree, that it is no wonder that some should have ascribed the change to witchcraft, and some to incipient madness. She became unable to bear the solitude in which she formerly delighted to spend her time ; yet when she hurried into society, it was without either joining in, or attending to, what passed. Generally she appeared wrapped in sad, and even sullen abstraction, until her attention was suddenly roused by some casual mention of the name of Cleveland, or of Mordaunt Mertoun, at which she started with the horror of one who sees the lighted match applied to a charged mine, and expects to be instantly involved in the effects of the explosion. And when she observed that the discovery was not yet made, it was so far from being a consolation, that she almost wished the worst was known, rather than endure the continued agonies of suspense.

Her conduct towards her sister was so variable, yet uniformly so painful to the kind-hearted Brenda, that it seemed to all around one of the strongest features of her malady. Sometimes Minna was impelled to seek her sister's company, as if by the consciousness that they were common sufferers by a misfortune of which she herself alone could grasp the extent ; and then suddenly feeling the injury which Brenda had received through the supposed agency of Cleveland, made her

* It is worthwhile saying, that this motto, and the ascription of the beautiful ballad from which it is taken to the Right Honourable Lady Ann Lindsay, occasioned the ingenious authoress's acknowledgment of the ballad, of which the Editor, on her permission, published a small impression, inscribed to the Bannatyne Club.

unable to bear her presence, and still less to endure the consolation which her sister, mistaking the nature of her malady, vainly endeavoured to administer. Frequently, also, did it happen, that, while Brenda was imploring her sister to take comfort, she incautiously touched upon some subject which thrilled to the very centre of her soul ; so that, unable to conceal her agony, Minna would rush hastily from the apartment. All these different moods, though they too much resembled, to one who knew not their real source, the caprices of unkind estrangement, Brenda endured with such prevailing and unruffled gentleness of disposition, that Minna was frequently moved to shed floods of tears upon her neck ; and, perhaps, the moments in which she did so, though imbittered by the recollection that her fatal secret concerned the destruction of Brenda's happiness as well as her own, were still, softened as they were by sisterly affection, the most endurable moments of this most miserable period of her life.

The effects of the alterations of moping melancholy, fearful agitation, and bursts of nervous feeling, were soon visible on the poor young woman's face and person. She became pale and emaciated ; her eye lost the steady quiet look of happiness and innocence, and was alternately dim and wild, as she was acted upon by a general feeling of her own distressful condition, or by some quicker and more poignant sense of agony. Her very features seemed to change, and become sharp and eager, and her voice, which, in its ordinary tones, was low and placid, now sometimes sunk in indistinct mutterings, and sometimes was raised beyond the natural key, in hasty and abrupt exclamations. When in company with others, she was sullenly silent, and when she ventured into solitude, was observed (for it was now thought very proper to watch her on such occasions) to speak much to herself.

The pharmacy of the islands was in vain resorted to by Minna's anxious father. Sages of both sexes, who knew the virtues of every herb which drinks the dew, and augmented these virtues by words of might, used while they prepared and applied the medicines, were attended with no benefit ; and Magnus, in the utmost anxiety, was at last induced to have recourse to the advice of his kinswoman, Norna of the Fitful Head, although, owing to circumstances, noticed in the course of the story, there was at this time some estrangement between them. His first application was in vain—Norna was then at her usual place of residence, upon the sea-coast, near the headland from which she usually took her designation ; but, although Eric Scambester himself brought the message, she refused positively to see him or return any answer.

Magnus was angry at the slight put upon his messenger and message, but his anxiety on Minna's account, as well as the respect which he had for Norna's real misfortunes and imputed wisdom and power, prevented him from indulging, on the present occasion, his usual irritability of disposition. On the contrary, he determined to make an application to his kinswoman in his own person. He kept his purpose, however, to himself, and only desired his daughters to be in readiness to attend him upon a visit to a relation whom he had not seen for some time, and directed them, at the same time, to carry some provisions along with them, as the journey was distant, and they might perhaps find their friend unprovided.

Unaccustomed to ask explanations of his pleasure, and hoping that exercise and the amusement of such an excursion might be of service to her sister, Brenda, upon whom all household and family charges now devolved, caused the necessary preparations to be made for the expedition ; and on the next morning, they were engaged in tracing the long and tedious course of beach and of moorland, which, only varied by occasional patches of oats and barley, where a little ground had been selected for cultivation, divided Burgh Westra from the north-western extremity of the Mainland (as the principal island is called), which terminates in the cape called Fitful Head, as the south-western point ends in the cape of Sumburgh.

On they went, through wild and over wold, the Udaller bestriding a strong, square-made, well-barrelled palfrey, of Norwegian breed, somewhat taller, and yet as stout, as the ordinary ponies of the country ; while Minna and Brenda, famed, amongst other accomplishments, for their horsemanship, rode two of those hardy animals, which, bred and reared with more pains than is usually bestowed, showed, both by the neatness of their form and their activity, that the race, so much and so carelessly neglected, is capable of being improved into beauty without losing anything of its spirit or vigour. They were attended by two servants on horseback, and two on foot, secure that the last circumstance would be no delay to their journey, because a great part of the way was so rugged, or so marshy, that the horses would only move at a foot pace ; and that, whenever they met with any considerable tract of hard and even ground, they had only to borrow from the nearest herd of ponies the use of a couple for the accommodation of these pedestrians.

The journey was a melancholy one, and little conservation passed, except when the Udaller, pressed by impatience and vexation, urged his pony to a quick pace, and again, recollecting Minna's weak state of health, slackened to a walk, and reiterated inquiries how she felt herself, and whether the fatigue was not too much for her. At noon the party halted, and partook of some refreshment, for which they had made ample provision, beside a pleasant spring, the pureness of whose waters, however, did not suit the Udaller's palate, until qualified by a liberal addition of right Nantz. After he had a second, yea, and a third time, filled a large silver travelling-cup, embossed with a German Cupid smoking a pipe, and a German Bacchus emptying his flask down the throat of a bear, he began to become more talkative than vexation had permitted him to be during the early part of their journey, and thus addressed his daughters :—

"Well, children, we are within a league or two of Norna's dwelling, and we shall soon see how the old spell-mutterer will receive us."

Minna interrupted her father with a faint exclamation, while Brenda, surprised to a great degree, exclaimed, "Is it then to Norna that we are to make this visit ?—Heaven forbid !"

"And wherefore should Heaven forbid ?" said the Udaller, knitting his

218

brows ; "wherefore, I would gladly know, should Heaven forbid me to visit my kinswoman, whose skill may be of use to your sister, if any woman in Zetland, or man either, can be of service to her ?—You are a fool, Brenda,—your sister has more sense.—Cheer up, Minna !—thou wert ever wont to like her songs and stories, and used to hang about her neck, when little Brenda cried and ran from her like a Spanish merchantman from a Dutch caper."*

"I wish she may not frighten me as much to-day, father," replied Brenda, desirous of indulging Minna in her taciturnity, and at the same time to amuse her father by sustaining the conversation ; "I have heard so much of her dwelling, that I am rather alarmed at the thought of going there uninvited."

"Thou art a fool," said Magnus, "to think that a visit from her kinsfolks can ever come amiss to a king, hearty, Hjaltland heart, like my cousin Norna's.—And, now I think on't, I will be sworn that is the reason why she would not receive Eric Scambester !—It is many a long day I have seen her chimney smoke, and I have never carried you thither—She hath indeed some right to call me unkind. But I will tell her the truth—and that is, that though such be the fashion, I do not think it is fair or honest to eat up the substance of lone women-folks, as we do that of our brother Udallers, when we roll about from house to house in the winter season, until we gather like a snowball, and eat up all wherever we come."

"There is no fear of our putting Norna to any distress just now," replied Brenda, "for I have ample provision of every thing that we can possibly need—fish, and bacon, and salted mutton, and dried geese— more than we could eat in a week, besides enough of liquor for you, father."

"Right, right, my girl !" said the Udaller ; "a well-found ship makes a merry voyage—so we shall only want the kindness of Norna's roof, and a little bedding for you ; for, as to myself, my sea-cloak, and honest dry boards of Norway deal, suit me better than your eider-gown cushions and mattresses. So that Norna will have the pleasure of seeing us without having a stiver's worth of trouble."

"I wish she may think it a pleasure, sir," replied Brenda.

"Why, what does the girl mean, in the name of the Martyr ?" replied Magnus Troil ; "dost thou think my kinswoman is a heathen, who will not rejoice to see her own flesh and blood ?—I would I were as sure of a good year's fishing !—No, no ! I only fear we may find her from home at present, for she is often a wanderer, and all with thinking over much on what can never be helped."

Minna sighed deeply as her father spoke, and the Udaller went on :—

"Dost thou sigh at that, my girl ?—why 'tis the fault of half the world— let it never be thine own, Minna."

Another suppressed sigh intimated that the caution came too late.

"I believe you are afraid of my cousin as well as Brenda is," said the Udaller, gazing on her pale countenance ; "if so, speak the word, and we

* A light armed vessel of the seventeenth century, adapted for privateering, and much used by the Dutch.

will return back again as if we had the wind on our quarter, and were running fifteen knots by the line."

"Do, for Heaven's sake, sister, let us return !" said Brenda, imploringly ; "you know—you remember—you must be well aware that Norna can do nought to help you."

"It is but too true," said Minna, in a subdued voice ; "but I know not—she may answer a question—a question that only the miserable may ask of the miserable."

"Nay, my kinswoman is no miser," answered the Udaller, who only heard the beginning of the word ; "a good income she has, both in Orkney and here, and many a fair lispund of butter is paid to her. But the poor have the best share of it, and shame fall the Zetlander who begrudges them ; the rest she spends, I wot not how, in her journeys through the islands. But you will laugh to see her house, and Nick Strumpfer, whom she calls Pacolet—many folks think Nick is the devil ; but he is flesh and blood, like any of us—his father lived in Græmsay.—I shall be glad to see Nick again."

While the Udaller thus ran on, Brenda, who, in recompense for a less portion of imagination than her sister, was gifted with sound common sense, was debating with herself the probable effect of this visit on her sister's health. She came finally to the resolution of speaking with her father aside upon the first occasion which their journey should afford. To him she determined to communicate the whole particulars of their nocturnal interview with Norna,—to which, among other agitating causes, she attributed the depression of Minna's spirits,—and then make himself the judge whether he ought to persist in his visit to a person so singular, and expose his daughter to all the shock which her nerves might possibly receive from the interview.

Just as she had arrived at this conclusion, her father, dashing the crumbs from his laced waistcoat with one hand, and receiving with the other a fourth cup of brandy and water, drank devoutly to the success of their voyage, and ordered all to be in readiness to set forward. Whilst they were saddling their ponies, Brenda, with some difficulty, contrived to make her father understand she wished to speak with him in private—no small surprise to the honest Udaller, who, though secret as the grave in the very few things where he considered secrecy as of importance, was so far from practising mystery in general, that his most important affairs were often discussed by him openly in presence of his whole family, servants included.

But far greater was his astonishment, when, remaining purposely with his daughter Brenda, a little in the wake, as he termed it, of the other riders, he heard the whole account of Norna's visit to Burgh Westra, and of the communication with which she had then astounded his daughters. For a long time he could utter nothing but interjections, and ended with a thousand curses on his kinswoman's folly in telling his daughters such a history of horror.

"I have often heard," said the Udaller, "that she was quite mad, with all her wisdom, and all her knowledge of the seasons ; and, by the bones of my namesake, the Martyr, I begin now to believe it most assuredly ! I know no more how to steer than if I had lost my compass. Had I known this before we set out, I think I had remained at home ; but now that we have come so far, and that Norna expects us"—

"Expects us, father !" said Brenda ; "how can that be possible ?"

"Why, that I know not—but she that can tell how the wind is to blow, can tell which way we are designing to ride. She must not be provoked ;— perhaps she has done my family this ill for the words I had with her about that lad Mordaunt Mertoun, and if so, she can undo it again ;—and so she shall, or I will know the cause wherefore. But I will try fair words first."

Finding it thus settled that they were to go forward, Brenda endeavoured next to learn from her father whether Norna's tale was founded in reality. He shook his head, groaned bitterly, and in a few words acknowledged that the whole, so far as concerned her intrigue with a stranger, and her father's death, of which she became the accidental and most innocent cause, was a matter of sad and indisputable truth. "For her infant," he said, "he could never, by any means learn what became of it."

"Her infant !" exclaimed Brenda ; "she spoke not a word of her infant !"

"Then I wish my tongue had been blistered," said the Udaller, "when I told you of it !—I see that, young and old, a man has no better chance of keeping a secret from you women, than an eel to keep himself in his hold when he is sniggled with a loop of horse-hair—sooner or later the fisher teazes him out of his hole, when he has once the noose round his neck."

"But the infant, my father," said Brenda, still insisting on the particulars of this extraordinary story, "what became of it ?"

"Carried off, I fancy, by the blackguard Vaughan," answered the Udaller, with a gruff accent, which plainly betokened how weary he was of the subject.

"By Vaughan ?" said Brenda, "the lover of poor Norna, doubtless !— what sort of man was he, father ?"

"Why, much like other men, I fancy," answered the Udaller ; "I never saw him in my life.—He kept company with the Scottish families at Kirkwall ; and I with the good old Norse folk—Ah ! if Norna had dwelt always amongst her own kin, and not kept company with her Scottish acquaintance, she would have known nothing of Vaughan, and things might have been otherwise—But then I should have known nothing of your blessed mother, Brenda—and that," he said, his large blue eyes shining with a tear, "would have saved me a short joy and a long sorrow."

"Norna could but ill have supplied my mother's place to you, father, as a companion and a friend—that is, judging from all I have heard," said Brenda, with some hesitation. But Magnus, softened by recollections of his beloved wife, answered her with more indulgence than she expected.

"I would have been content," he said, "to have wedded Norna at one time. It would have been the soldering of an old quarrel—the healing of an old sore. All our blood relations wished it, and, situated as I was, especially not having seen your blessed mother, I had little will to oppose their counsels. You must not judge of Norna or of me by such an appearance as we now present to you—She was young and beautiful, and I gamesome as Highland buck, and little caring what haven I made for, having, as I thought, more than one under my lee. But Norna preferred this man Vaughan, and, as I told you before, it was, perhaps, the best kindness she could have done to me."

"Ah, poor kinswoman !" said Brenda. "But believe you, father, in the high powers which she claims—in the mysterious vision of the dwarf—in the"—

She was interrupted in these questions by Magnus, to whom they were obviously displeasing.

"I believe, Brenda," he said, "according to the belief of my forefathers—I pretend not to be a wiser man than they were in their time,—and they all believed that, in cases of great wordly distress, Providence opened the eyes of the mind, and afforded the sufferers a vision of futurity. It was but a trimming of the boat, with reverence,"— here he touched his hat reverentially ; "and after all the shifting of ballast, poor Norna is as heavily loaded in the bows as ever was an Orkneyman's yawl at the dog-fishing—she has more than affliction enough on board to balance whatever gifts she may have had in the midst of her calamity. They are as painful to her, poor soul, as a crown of thorns would be to her brows, though it were the badge of the empire of Denmark. And do not you, Brenda, seek to be wiser than your fathers. Your sister Minna, before she was so ill, had as much reverence for whatever was produced in Norse, as if it had been in the Pope's bull, which is all written in pure Latin."

"Poor Norna !" repeated Brenda ; "and her child—was it never recovered ?"

"What do I know of her child ?" said the Udaller, more gruffly than before, "except that she was very ill, both before and after the birth, though we kept her as merry as we could with pipe and harp, and so forth ;—the child had come before its time into this bustling world, so it is likely it has been long dead.—But you know nothing of these matters, Brenda ; so get along for a foolish girl, and ask no more questions about what it does not become you to inquire into."

So saying the Udaller gave his sturdy little palfrey the spur, and cantering forward over rough and smooth, while the pony's accuracy and firmness of step put all difficulties of the path at secure defiance, he placed himself soon by the side of the melancholy Minna, and permitted her sister to have no farther share in his conversation than as it was addressed to them jointly. She could but comfort herself with the hope that, as Minna's disease appeared to have its seat in the imagination, the remedies recommended by Norna might have some chance of being effectual, since, in all probability, they would be addressed to the same faculty.

Their way had hitherto held chiefly over moss and moor, varied occasionally by the necessity of making a circuit around the heads of those long lagoons, called voes, which run up into and indent the

222

country in such a manner, that, though the Mainland of Zetland may be thirty miles or more in length, there is, perhaps, no part of it which is more than three miles distant from the salt water. But they had now approached the north-western extremity of the isle, and travelled along the top of an immense ridge of rocks, which had for ages withstood the rage of the Northern Ocean, and of all the winds by which it is buffeted.

At length exclaimed Magnus to his daughters, "There is Norna's dwelling!—Look up, Minna, my love ; for if this does not make you laugh, nothing will.—Saw you ever anything but an osprey that would have made such a nest for herself as that is ?—By my namesake's bones, there is not the like of it that living thing ever dwelt in (having no wings and the use of reason), unless it chanced to be the Frawa Stack off Papa, where the King's daughter or Norway was shut up to keep her from her lovers—and all to little purpose, if the tale be true,* for, maidens, I would have you to wot that it is hard to keep flax from the lowe."†

CHAPTER TWENTY-SEVENTH

Thrice from the cavern's darksome womb
    Her groaning voice arose ;
And come, my daughter, fearless come,
    And fearless tell thy woes !

MEIKLE

THE dwelling of Norna, though none but a native of Zetland, familiar, during his whole life, with every variety of rock-scenery, could have seen anything ludicrous in this situation, was not unaptly compared by Magnus Troil to the eyry of the osprey or sea-eagle. It was very small, and had been fabricated out of one of those dens which are called Burghs and Picts-houses in Zetland, and Duns on the mainland of Scotland and the Hebrides, and which seemed to be the first effort at architecture—the connecting link betwixt a fox's hole in a cairn of loose stones, and an attempt to construct a human habitation out of the same materials, without the use of lime or cement of any kind,—without any timber, so far as can be seen from their remains,—without any knowledge of the arch or of the stair. Such as they are, however, the numerous remains of these dwellings, for there is one found on every headland, islet, or point of vantage, which could afford the inhabitants additional means of defence, tend to prove that the remote people by whom these Burghs were constructed, were a numerous race, and that the islands had then a much greater population, than, from other circumstances, we might have been led to anticipate.

The Burgh of which we at present speak had been altered and repaired at a later period, probably by some petty despot, or sea-rover,

---

* The *Frawa Stack,* or Maiden Rock, an inaccessible cliff, divided by a narrow gulf, from the island of Papa, has on the summit some ruins, concerning which there is a legend similar to that of Danaë.

† *Lowe,* flame.

who, tempted by the security of the situation, which occupied the whole of a projecting point of rock, and was divided from the mainland by a rent or chasm of some depth, had built some additions to it in the rudest style of Gothic defensive architecture ;—had plastered the inside with lime and clay, and broken out windows for the admission of light and air; and finally, by roofing it over, and dividing it into storeys by means of beams of wreck-wood, had converted the whole into a tower, resembling a pyramidical dovecot, formed by a double wall, still containing within its thickness that set of circular galleries, or concentric rings, which is proper to all the forts of this primitive construction, and which seem to have constituted the only shelter which they were originally qualified to afford to their shivering inhabitants.*

This singular habitation, built out of the loose stones which lay scattered around, and exposed for ages to the vicissitudes of the elements, was as grey, weatherbeaten, and wasted, as the rock on which it was founded, and from which it could not easily be distinguished, so completely did it resemble in colour and so little did it differ in regularity of shape from, a pinnacle or fragment of the cliff.

Minna's habitual indifference to all that of late had passed around her, was for a moment suspended by the sight of an abode, which at another and happier period of her life, would have attracted at once her curiosity and her wonder. Even now she seemed to feel interest as she gazed upon this singular retreat, and recollected it was that of certain misery, and probable insanity, connected, as its inhabitant asserted, and Minna's faith admitted, with power over the elements and the capacity of intercourse with the invisible world.

"Our kinswoman," she muttered, "has chosen her dwelling well, with no more of earth than a sea-fowl might rest upon, and all around sightless tempests and raging waves. Despair and magical power could not have a fitter residence."

Brenda, on the other had, shuddered when she looked on the dwelling to which they were advancing, by a difficult, dangerous, and precarious path, which sometimes, to her great terror, approached to the verge of the precipice ; so that, Zetlander as she was, and confident as she had reason to be in the steadiness and sagacity of the sure-footed pony, she could scarce suppress an inclination to giddiness, especially at one point, when, being foremost of the party, and turning a sharp angle of the rock, her feet, as they projected from the side of the pony, hung for an instant sheer over the ledge of the precipice, so that there was nothing save empty space betwixt the sole of her shoe, and the white foam of the vexed ocean, which dashed, howled, and foamed, five hundred feet below. What would have driven a maiden of another country into delirium, gave her but a momentary uneasiness, which was instantly lost in the hope that the impression which the scene appeared to make on her sister's imagination might be favourable to her cure.

She could not help looking back to see how Minna should pass the point of peril, which she herself had just rounded ; and could hear the strong voice of the Udaller, though to him such rough paths were

* Note Q. Pictish Burgh.

familiar as the smooth sea-beach, call in a tone of some anxiety, "Take heed, yarta," as Minna, with an eager look, dropped her bridle, and stretched forward her arms, and even her body, over the precipice, in the attitude of the wild swan, when, balancing itself, and spreading its broad pinions, it prepares to launch from the cliff on the bosom of the winds. Brenda felt, at that instant, a pang of unutterable terror, which left a strong impression on her nerves, even when relieved, as it instantly was, by her sister recovering herself and sitting upright on her saddle, the opportunity and temptation (if she felt it) passing away, as the quiet steady animal which supported her rounded the projecting angle, and turned its patient and firm step from the verge of the precipice.

They now attained a more level and open space of ground, being the flat top of an isthmus of projecting rock, narrowing again towards a point, where it was terminated by the chasm which separated the small peak, or *stack*, occupied by Norna's habitation, from the main ridge of cliff and precipice. This natural fosse, which seemed to have been the work of some convulsion of nature, was deep, dark and irregular, narrower towards the bottom, which could not be distinctly seen, and widest at top, having the appearance as if that part of the cliff occupied by the building had been half rent away from the isthmus which it terminated,—an idea favoured by the angle at which it seemed to recede from the land, and lean towards the sea, with the building which crowned it.

This angle of projection was so considerable, that it required recollection to dispel the idea that the rock, so much removed from the perpendicular, was about to precipitate itself seaward, with its old tower ; and a timorous person would have been afraid to put foot upon it, lest an addition of weight, so inconsiderable as that of the human body, should hasten a catastrophe which seemed at every instant impending.

Without troubling himself about such fantasies, the Udaller rode towards the tower, and there dismounting along with his daughters, gave the ponies in charge to one of their domestics, with directions to disencumber them of their burdens, and turn them out for rest and refreshment upon the nearest heath. This done, they approached the gate, which seemed formerly to have been connected with the land by a rude drawbridge, some of the apparatus of which was still visible. But the rest had been long demolished, and was replaced by a stationary footbridge, formed of barrel-staves covered with turf, very narrow and ledgeless, and supported by a sort of arch, constructed out of the jaw-bones of the whale. Along this "brigg of dread" the Udaller stepped with his usual portly majesty of stride, which threatened its demolition and his own at the same time ; his daughters trod more lightly and more safely after him, and the whole party stood before the low and rugged portal of Norna's habitation.

"If she should be abroad after all," said Magnus, as he plied the black oaken door with repeated blows ;—"but if so, we will at least lie by a day for her return, and make Nick Strumpfer pay the demurrage in bland and brandy."

As he spoke, the door opened, and displayed, to the alarm of Brenda, and the surprise of Minna herself, a square-made dwarf about four feet five inches high, with a head of most portentous size, and features correspondent—namely, a huge mouth, a tremendous nose, with large black nostrils, which seemed to have been slit upwards, blubber lips of an unconscionable size, and huge wall eyes, with which he leered, sneered, grinned, and goggled on the Udaller as an old acquaintance, without uttering a single word. The young women could hardly persuade themselves that they did not see before their eyes the very demon Trolld, who made such a distinguished figure in Norna's legend. Their father went on addressing this uncouth apparition in terms of such condescending friendship as the better sort apply to their inferiors, when they wish, for any immediate purpose, to conciliate or coax them,—a tone, by the by, which generally contains, in its very familiarity, as much offence as the more direct assumption of distance and superiority.

"Ha, Nick ! honest Nick !" said the Udaller, "here you are, lively and lovely as Saint Nicholas your namesake, when he is carved with an axe for the headpiece of a Dutch dogger. How dost thou do, Nick, or Pacolet, if you like that better ? Nicholas, here are my two daughters, nearly as handsome as thyself thou seest."

Nick grinned, and did a clumsy obeisance by way of courtesy, but kept his broad misshapen person firmly placed in the doorway.

"Daughters," continued the Udaller, who seemed to have his reasons for speaking this Cerberus fair, at least according to his own notions of propitiation,—"this is Nick Strumpfer, maidens, whom his mistress calls Pacolet, being a light-limbed dwarf, as you see, like him that wont to fly about, like a *Scourie*, on his wooden hobbyhorse, in the old story-book of Valentine and Orson, that you, Minna, used to read whilst you were a child. I assure you he can keep his mistress's counsel, and never told one of her secrets in his life—ha, ha, ha !"

The ugly dwarf grinned ten times wider than before, and showed the meaning of the Udaller's jest, by opening his immense jaws, and throwing back his head, so as to discover, that in the immense cavity of his mouth there only remained the small shrivelled remnant of a tongue, capable, perhaps, of assisting him in swallowing his food, but unequal to the formation of articulate sounds. Whether this organ had been curtailed by cruelty , or injured by disease, it was impossible to guess ; but that the unfortunate being had not been originally dumb, was evident from his retaining the sense of hearing. Having made this horrible exhibition, he repaid the Udaller's mirth with a loud, horrid, and discordant laugh, which had something in it the more hideous that his mirth seemed to be excited by his own misery. The sisters looked on each other in silence and fear, and even the Udaller appeared disconcerted.

"And how now ?" he proceeded after a minute's pause. "When didst thou wash that throat of thine, that is about the width of the Pentland Firth, with a cup of brandy ? Ha, Nick ! I have that with me which is sound stuff, boy, ha !"

226

The dwarf bent his beetle-brows, shook his misshapen head, and made a quick sharp indication, throwing his right hand up to his shoulder with the thumb pointed backwards.

"What! my kinswoman," said the Udaller, comprehending the signal, "will be angry ? Well, shalt have a flask to carouse when she is from home, old acquaintance ;—lips and throats may swallow, though they cannot speak."

Pacolet grinned a grim assent.

"And now," said the Udaller, "stand out of the way, Pacolet, and let me carry my daughters to see their kinswoman. By the bones of Saint Magnus, it shall be a good turn in thy way—nay, never shake thy head, man ; for if thy mistress be at home, see her we will."

The dwarf again intimated the impossibility of their being admitted, partly by signs, partly by mumbling some uncouth and most disagreeable sounds, and the Udaller's mood began to arise.

"Tittle tattle, man !" said he ; "trouble not me with thy gibberish, but stand out of the way, and the blame, if there be any, shall rest with me."

So saying, Magnus Troil laid his sturdy hand upon the collar of the recusant dwarf's jacket of blue wadmaal, and, with a strong, but not a violent grasp, removed him from the doorway, pushed him gently aside and entered, followed by his two daughters, whom a sense of apprehension, arising out of all which they saw and heard, kept very close to him. A crooked and dusky passage, through which Magnus led the way, was dimly enlightened by a shot-hole, communicating with the interior of the building, and originally intended, doubtless, to command the entrance by a hagbut, or culverin. As they approached nearer, for they walked slowly and with hesitation, the light, imperfect as it was, was suddenly obscured ; and on looking upward to discern the cause, Brenda was startled to observe the pale and obscurely-seen countenance of Norna gazing downward upon them, without speaking a word. There was nothing extraordinary in this, as the mistress of the mansion might be naturally enough looking out to see what guests were thus suddenly and unceremoniously intruding themselves on her presence. Still, however, the natural paleness of her features, exaggerated by the light in which they were at present exhibited,—the immovable sternness of her look, which showed neither kindness nor courtesy of civil reception,—her dead silence, and the singular apperance of everything about her dwelling, augmented the dismay which Brenda had already conceived. Magnus Troil and Minna had walked slowly forward, without observing the apparition of their singular hostess.

CHAPTER TWENTY-EIGHTH

The witch then raised her wither'd arm,
    And waved her wand on high,
And, while she spoke the mutter'd charm,
    Dark lightning fill'd her eye.

MEIKLE

"THIS should be the stair," said the Udaller, blundering in the dark against some steps of irregular ascent—"This should be the stair, unless my memory greatly fail me ; ay, and there she sits," he added, pausing at a half-open door, "with all her tackle about her as usual, and as busy, doubtless, as the devil in a gale of wind."

As he made this irreverent comparison, he entered, followed by his daughters, the darkened apartment in which Norna was seated, amidst a confused collection of books of various languages, parchment scrolls, tablets and stones inscribed with the straight and angular characters of the Runic alphabet, and similar articles, which the vulgar might have connected with the exercise of the forbidden arts. There was also lying in the chamber, or hung over the rude and ill-contrived chimney, an old shirt of mail, with the headpiece, battle-axe, and lance, which had once belonged to it ; and on a shelf were disposed, in great order, several of those curious stone axes, formed of green granite, which are often found in these islands, where they are called thunderbolts by the common people, who usually preserve them as a charm of security against the effects of lightning. There were, moreover, to be seen amid the strange collection, a stone sacrificial knife, used perhaps for immolating human victims, and one or two of the brazen implements called Celts, the purpose of which has troubled the repose of so many antiquaries. A variety of other articles, some of which had neither name nor were capable of description, lay in confusion about the apartment ; and in one corner, on a quantity of withered sea-weed, reposed what seemed, at first view, to be a large unshapely dog, but, when seen more closely, proved to be a tame seal, which it had been Norna's amusement to domesticate.

This uncouth favourite bristled up in its corner upon the arrival of so many strangers, with an alertness similar to that which a terrestrial dog would have displayed on a similar occasion ; but Norna remained motionless, seated behind a table of rough granite, propped up by misshapen feet of the same material, which, besides the old book with which she seemed to be busied, sustained a cake of the coarse unleavened bread, three parts oatmeal, and one the sawdust of fir, which is used by the poor peasants of Norway, beside which stood a jar of water.

Magnus Troil remained a minute in silence gazing upon his kinswoman, while the singularity of her mansion inspired Brenda with

228

much fear, and changed, though but for a moment, the melancholy and abstracted mood of Minna, into a feeling of interest not unmixed with awe. The silence was interrupted by the Udaller, who, unwilling on the one hand to give his kinswoman offence, and desirous on the other to show that he was not daunted by a reception so singular, opened the conversation thus :—

"I give you good e'en, cousin Norna—my daughters and I have come far to see you."

Norna raised her eyes from her volume, looked full at her visitors, then let them quietly sit down on the leaf with which she seemed to be engaged.

"Nay, cousin," said Magnus, "take your own time—our business with you can wait your leisure.—See here, Minna, what a fair prospect here is of the cape, scarce a quarter of a mile off ! you may see the billows breaking on it topmast high. Our kinswoman has got a pretty seal, too,—Here, sealchie, my man, whew, whew !"

The seal took no farther notice of the Udaller's advances to acquaintance, than by uttering a low growl.

"He is not so well trained," continued the Udaller, affecting an air of ease and unconcern, "as Peter MacRaw's, the old piper of Stornoway, who had a seal that flapped its tail to the tune of *Caberfae,* and acknowledged no other whatever.*—Well, cousin," he concluded, observing that Norna closed her book, "are you going to give us a welcome at last, or must we go farther than our blood-relation's house to seek one, and that when the evening is wearing late apace ?"

"Ye dull and hard-hearted generation, as deaf as the adder to the voice of the charmer," answered Norna, addressing them, "why come ye to me ? You have slighted every warning I could give of the coming harm, and now that it hath come upon you, ye seek my counsel when it can avail you nothing."

"Look you, kinswoman," said the Udaller, with his usual frankness, and boldness of manner and accent, "I must needs tell you that your courtesy is something of the coarsest and the coldest. I cannot say that I ever saw an adder, in regard there are none in these parts ; but touching my own thoughts of what such a thing may be, it cannot be termed a suitable comparison to me or to my daughters, and that I would have you to know. For old acquaintance, and certain other reasons, I do not leave your house upon the instant ; but as I came hither in all kindness and civility, so I pray you to receive me with the like, otherwise we will depart, and leave shame on your inhospitable threshold."

"How !" said Norna, "dare you use such bold language in the house of one from whom all men—from whom you yourself—come to solicit counsel and aid ? They who speak to the Reimkennar, must lower their voice to her before whom winds and waves hush both blast and billow."

"Blast and billow may hush themselves if they will," replied the

---

* The MacRaws were followers of the MacKenzies, whose chief has the name of Caberfae, or Buckshead, from the cognisance borne on his standards. Unquestionably the worthy piper trained the seal on the same principle of respect to the clan-term which I have heard has been taught to dogs, who, unused to any other air, dance after their fashion to the tune of Caberfae.

peremptory Udaller, "but that will not I. I speak in the house of my friend as in my own, and strike sail to none."

"And hope ye," said Norna, "by this rudeness to compel me to answer to your interrogatories?

"Kinswoman," replied Magnus Troil, "I know not so much as you of the old Norse sagas; but this I know, that when kempies were wont, long since, to seek the habitations of the gal-dragons and spae-women,* they came with their axes on their shoulders, and their good swords drawn in their hands, and compelled the power whom they invoked to listen to and to answer them, ay, were it Odin himself."

"Kinsman," said Norna, arising from her seat, and coming forward, "thou hast spoken well, and in good time for thyself and thy daughters; for hadst thou turned from my threshold without extorting an answer, morning's sun had never again shone upon you. The spirits who serve me are jealous, and will not be employed in aught that may benefit humanity, unless their service is commanded by the undaunted importunity of the brave and the free. And now speak, what wouldst thou have of me?"

"My daughter's health," replied Magnus, " which no remedies have been able to restore."

"Thy daughter's health?" answered Norna; "and what is the maiden's ailment?"

"The physician," said Troil, "must name the disease. All that I can tell thee of it is"—

"Be silent," said Norna, interrupting him; "I know all that thou canst tell me, and more than thou thyself knowest. Sit down, all of you—and thou, maiden," she said, addressing Minna, "sit thou in that chair," pointing to the place she had just left, "once the seat of Giervada, at whose voice the stars hid their beams, and the moon herself grew pale."

Minna moved with slow and tremulous step towards the rude seat thus indicated to her. It was composed of stone, formed into some semblance of a chair by the rough and unskilful hand of some ancient Gothic artist.

Brenda, creeping as close as possible to her father, seated herself along with him upon a bench at some distance from Minna, and kept her eyes, with a mixture of fear, pity, and anxiety, closely fixed upon her. It would be difficult altogether to decipher the emotions by which this amiable and affectionate girl was agitated at that moment. Deficient in her sister's predominating quality of high imagination, and little credulous, of course, to the marvellous, she could not but entertain some vague and indefinite fears on her own account, concerning the nature of the scene which was soon to take place. But these were in a manner swallowed up in her apprehensions on the score of her sister, who, with a frame so much weakened, spirits so much exhausted, and a mind so susceptible of the impressions which all around her was calculated to excite, now sat pensively resigned to the agency of one, whose treatment might produce the most baneful effects upon such a subject.

* Sorceresses and fortune-tellers.

230

Brenda gazed at Minna, who sat in that rude chair of dark stone, her finely formed shape and limbs making the strongest contrast with its ponderous and irregular angles, her cheek and lips as pale as clay, and her eyes turned upward, and lighted with the mixture of resignation and excited enthusiasm, which belonged to her disease and her character. The younger sister then looked on Norna, who muttered to herself in a low monotonous manner, as, gliding from one place to another, she collected different articles, which she placed one by one on the table. And lastly, Brenda looked anxiously to her father, to gather, if possible, from his countenance, whether he entertained any part of her own fears for the consequences of the scene which was to ensue, considering the state of Minna's health and spirits. But Magnus Troil seemed to have no such apprehensions ; he viewed with stern composure Norna's preparations, and appeared to wait the event with the composure of one, who, confiding in the skill of a medical artist, sees him preparing to enter upon some important and painful operation, in the issue of which he is interested by friendship or by affection.

Norna, meanwhile, went onward with her preparations, until she had placed on the stone table a variety of miscellaneous articles, and among the rest, a small chafing-dish full of charcoal, a crucible, and a piece of thin sheet-lead. She then spoke aloud—"It is well that I was aware of your coming hither—ay, long before you yourself had resolved it—how should I else have been prepared for that which is now to be done ?—Maiden," she continued, addressing Minna, "where lies thy pain ?"

The patient answered, by pressing her hand to the left side of her bosom.

"Even so," replied Norna, "even so—'tis the site of weal or woe.—And you, her father and her sister, think not this the idle speech of one who talks by guess—if I can tell the ill, it may be that I shall be able to render that less severe, which may not, by any aid, be wholly amended.—The heart—ay, the heart—touch that, and the eye grows dim, the pulse fails, the wholesome stream of our blood is choked and troubled, our limbs decay like sapless sea-weed in summer's sun ; our better views of existence are past and gone ; what remains is the dream of lost happiness, or the fear of inevitable evil. But the Reimkennar must to her work—well is it that I have prepared the means."

She threw off her long dark-coloured mantle, and stood before them in her short jacket of light-blue wadmaal, with its skirt of the same stuff, fancifully embroidered with black velvet, and bound at the waist with a chain or girdle of silver, formed into singular devices. Norna next undid the fillet which bound her grizzled hair, and shaking her head wildly, caused it to fall in dishevelled abundance over her face and around her shoulders, so as almost entirely to hide her features. She then placed a small crucible on the chafing-dish already mentioned,—dropped a few drops from a vial on the charcoal below,—pointed towards it her wrinkled forefinger, which she had previously moistened with liquid from another small bottle, and said with a deep voice, "Fire, do thy duty;"—and the words were no sooner spoken, than, probably by some chemical combination of which the spectators were not aware, the charcoal which was under the crucible became slowly ignited ; while Norna, as if impatient of the delay, threw hastily back her disordered tresses, and while her features reflected the sparkles and red light of the fire, and her eyes flashed from amidst her hair like those of a wild animal from its cover, blew fiercely till the whole was in an intense glow. She paused a moment from her toil, and muttering that the elemental spirit must be thanked, recited, in her usual monotonous, yet wild note of chanting, the following verses :—

> Thou so needful, yet so dread,
> With cloudy crest and wing of red ;
> Thou, without whose genial breath
> The North would sleep the sleep of death ;
> Who deign'st to warm the cottage hearth,
> Yet hurl'st proud palaces to earth,—
> Brightest, keenest of the Powers,
> Which form and rule this world of ours,
> With my rhyme of Runic I
> Thank thee for thy agency.

She then severed a portion from the small mass of sheet-lead which lay upon the table, and, placing it in the crucible, subjected it to the action of the lighted charcoal, and, as it melted she sung,

> Old Reimkennar, to thy art
> Mother Hertha sends her part ;
> She, whose gracious bounty gives
> Needful food for all that lives.
> From the deep mine of the North
> Came the mystic metal forth,
> Doom'd amidst disjointed stones,
> Long to cere a champion's bones,
> Disinhumed my charms to aid—
> Mother Earth, my thanks are paid.

She then poured out some water from the jar into a large cup, or goblet, and sung once more, as she slowly stirred it round with the end of her staff :—

> Girdle of our islands dear,
> Element of Water, hear !
> Thou whose power can overwhelm
> Broken mounds and ruin'd realm
>   On the lowly Belgian strand ;
> All thy fiercest rage can never
> Of our soil a furlong sever
>   From our rock-defended land ;
> Play then gently thou thy part,
> To assist old Norna's art.

She then, with a pair of pincers, removed the crucible from the chafing-dish, and poured the lead, now entirely melted, into the bowl of water, repeating at the same time,—

Elements, each other greeting,
Gifts and powers attend your meeting!

The melted lead, spattering as it fell into the water, formed, of course, the usual combination of irregular forms which is familiar to all who in childhood have made the experiment, and from which, according to our childish fancy, we may have selected portions bearing some resemblance to domestic articles—the tools of mechanics, or the like. Norna seemed to busy herself in some such researches, for she examined the mass of lead with scrupulous attention, and detached it into different portions, without apparently being able to find a fragment in the form which she desired.

At length she again muttered, rather as speaking to herself than to her guests, "He, the Viewless, will not be omitted,—he will have his tribute even in the work to which he gives nothing.—Stern compeller of the clouds, thou shalt also hear the voice of the Reimkennar."

Thus speaking, Norna once more threw the lead into the crucible, where, hissing and spattering as the wet metal touched the sides of the red-hot vessel, it was soon again reduced into a state of fusion. The sibyl meantime turned to a corner of the apartment, and opening suddenly a window which looked to the north-west, let in the fitful radiance of the sun, now lying almost level upon a great mass of red clouds, which, boding future tempests, occupied the edge of the horizon, and seemed to brood over the billows of the boundless sea. Turning to this quarter, from which a low hollow moaning breeze then blew, Norna addressed the Spirit of the Winds, in tones which seemed to resemble his own :—

Thou, that over billows dark
Safely send'st the fisher's bark,—
Giving him a path and motion
Through the wilderness of ocean ;
Thou, that when the billows brave ye,
O'er the shelves canst drive the navy,—
Did'st thou chafe as one neglected,
While thy brethren were respected ?
To appease thee, see, I tear
This full grasp of grizzled hair ;
Oft thy breath hath through it sung,
Softening to my magic tongue,—
Now, 'tis thine to bid it fly
Through the wide expanse of sky,
'Mid the countless swarms to sail
Of wild-fowl wheeling on thy gale.
Take thy portion and rejoice,—
Spirit, thou hast heard my voice !

233

Norna accompanied these words with the action which they described, tearing a handful of hair with vehemence from her head, and strewing it upon the wind as she continued her recitation. She then shut the casement, and again involved the chamber in the dubious twilight, which best suited her character and occupation. The melted lead was once more emptied into the water, and the various whimsical comformations which it received from the operation were examined with great care by the sibyl, who at length seemed to intimate, by voice and gesture, that her spell had been successful. She selected from the fused metal a piece about the size of a small nut, bearing in shape a close resemblance to that of the human heart, and approaching Minna, again spoke in song,—

> She who sits by haunted well,
> Is subject to the Nixie's spell ;
> She who walks on lonely beach,
> To the Mermaid's charmed speech ;
>
> She who walks round ring of green,
> Offends the peevish Fairy Queen ;
> And she who takes rest in the Dwarfie's cave,
> A weary weird of woe shall have.
>
> By ring, by spring, by cave, by shore,
> Minna Troil has braved all this and more ;
> And yet hath the root of her sorrow and ill
> A source that's more deep and more mystical still.

Minna, whose attention had been latterly something disturbed by reflections on her own secret sorrow, now suddenly recalled it, and looked eagerly on Norna as if she expected to learn from her rhymes something of deep interest. The northern sibyl, meanwhile, proceeded to pierce the piece of lead, which bore the form of a heart, and to fix in it a piece of gold wire, by which it might be attached to a chain or necklace. She then proceeded in her rhyme,—

> Thou art within a demon's hold,
> More wise than Haims, more strong than Trolld ;
> No siren sings so sweet as he,—
> No fay springs lighter on the lea ;
> No elfin power hath half the art
> To soothe, to move, to wring the heart,—
> Life-blood from the cheek to drain,
> Drench the eye, and dry the vein.
> Maiden, ere we farther go,
> Dost thou note me, ay or no ?

Minna replied in the same rhythmical manner, which, in jest and earnest, was frequently used by the ancient Scandinavians,—

> I mark thee, my mother, both word, look, and sign ;
> Speak on with the riddle—to read it be mine.

"Now, Heaven and every saint be praised !" said Magnus : "They are the first words to the purpose which she hath spoken these many days."

234

"And they are the last which she shall speak for many a month," said Norna, incensed at the interruption, "if you again break the progress of my spell. Turn your faces to the wall, and look not hitherward again, under penalty of my severe displeasure. You, Magnus Troil, from hard-hearted audacity of spirit, and you, Brenda, from wanton and idle disbelief in that which is beyond your bounden comprehension, are unworthy to look on this mystic work ; and the glance of your eyes mingles with, and weakens the spell ; for the powers cannot brook distrust."

Unaccustomed to be addressed in a tone so peremptory, Magnus would have made some angry reply ; but reflecting that the health of Minna was at stake, and considering that she who spoke was a woman of many sorrows, he suppressed his anger, bowed his head, shrugged his shoulders, assumed the prescribed posture, averting his head from the table, and turning towards the wall. Brenda did the same, on receiving a sign from her father, and both remained profoundly silent.

Norna then addressed Minna once more,—

Mark me ! for the word I speak,
Shall bring the colour to thy cheek.
This leaden heart, so light of cost,
The symbol of a treasure lost,
Thou shalt wear in hope and in peace,
That the cause of your sickness and sorrow may cease,
When crimson foot meets crimson hand
In the Martyrs' Aisle, and in Orkney-land.

Minna coloured deeply at the last couplet, intimating, as she failed not to interpret it, that Norna was completely acquainted with the secret cause of her sorrow. The same conviction led the maiden to hope in the favourable issue, which the sibyl seemed to prophesy ; and not venturing to express her feelings in any manner more intelligible, she pressed Norna's withered hand with all the warmth of affection, first to her breast and then to her bosom, bedewing it at the same time with her tears.

With more of human feeling than she usually exhibited, Norna extricated her hand from the grasp of the poor girl, whose tears now flowed freely, and then, with more tenderness of manner than she had yet shown, she knotted the leaden heart to a chain of gold, and hung it around Minna's neck, singing, as she performed that last branch of the spell,—

Be patient, be patient, for Patience hath power,
To ward us in danger, like mantle in shower ;
A fairy gift you best may hold
In a chain of fairy gold ;
The chain and the gift are each a true token,
That not without warrant old Norna hath spoken ;
But thy nearest and dearest must never behold them,
Till time shall accomplish the truths I have told them.

The verses being concluded, Norna carefully arranged the chain around her patient's neck, so as to hide it in her bosom, and thus ended the spell—a spell which, at the moment I record these incidents, it is known, has been lately practised in Zetland, where any decline of health, without apparent cause, is imputed by the lower orders to a demon having stolen the heart from the body of the patient, and where the experiment of supplying the deprivation by a leaden one, prepared in the manner described, has been resorted to within these few years. In a metaphorical sense, the disease may be considered as a general one in all parts of the world ; but, as this simple and original remedy is peculiar to the isles of Thule, it were unpardonable not to preserve it at length, in a narrative connected with Scottish antiquities.*

A second time Norna reminded her patient, that if she showed, or spoke of, the fairy gifts, their virtue would be lost—a belief so common as to be received into the superstitions of all nations. Lastly, unbuttoning the collar which she had just fastened, she showed her a link of the gold chain, which Minna instantly recognised as that formerly given by Norna to Mordaunt Mertoun. This seemed to intimate he was yet alive, and under Norna's protection ; and she gazed on her with the most eager curiosity. But the sibyl imposed her finger on her lips in token of silence, and a second time involved the chain in those folds which modestly and closely veiled one of the most beautiful, as well as one of the kindest, bosoms in the world.

Norna then extinguished the lighted charcoal, and as the water hissed upon the glowing embers, commanded Magnus and Brenda to look around, and behold her task accomplished.

CHAPTER TWENTY-NINTH

See yonder woman, whom our swains revere,
And dread in secret, while they take her counsel
When sweetheart shall be kind, or when cross dame shall die ;
Where lurks the thief who stole the silver tankard,
And how the pestilent murrain may be cured.—
This sage adviser's mad, stark mad, my friend ;
Yet in her madness, hath the art and cunning
To wring fools' secrets from their inmost bosoms,
And pay inquirers with the coin they gave her.

OLD PLAY

IT seemed as if Norna had indeed full right to claim the gratitude of the Udaller for the improved condition of his daughter's health. She once more threw open the windows, and Minna, drying her eyes and advancing with affectionate confidence, threw herself on her father's neck, and asked his forgiveness for the trouble she had of late occasioned to him. It is unnecessary to add, that this was at once granted, with a full, though rough burst of paternal tenderness, and as

* The spells described in this chapter are not altogether imaginary. By this mode of pouring lead into water, and selecting the part which chances to assume a resemblance to the human heart, which must be worn by the patient around her or his neck, the sage persons of Zetland pretend to cure the fatal disorder called the loss of a heart.

many close embraces as if his child had been just rescued from the jaws of death. When Magnus had dismissed Minna from his arms, to throw herself into those of her sister, and express to her, rather by kisses and tears than in words, the regret she entertained for her late wayward conduct, the Udaller thought proper, in the meantime, to pay his thanks to their hostess, whose skill had proved so efficacious. But scarce had he come out with "Much respected kinswoman, I am but a plain old Norseman,"—when she interrupted him, by pressing her finger on her lips.

"There are those around us," she said, "who must hear no mortal voice, witness no sacrifice to mortal feelings—there are times when they even mutiny against me, their sovereign mistress, because I am still shrouded in the flesh of humanity. Fear, therefore, and be silent. I, whose deeds have raised me from the low-sheltered valley of life, where dwell its social wants and common charities—I, who have bereft the Giver of the Gift which he gave, and stand alone on a cliff of immeasurable height, detached from earth, save from the small portion that supports my miserable tread—I alone am fit to cope with these sullen mates. Fear not, therefore, but yet be not too bold, and let this night to you be one of fasting and of prayer."

If the Udaller had not, before the commencement of the operation, been disposed to dispute the commands of the sibyl, it may be well believed he was less so now, that it had terminated to all appearance so fortunately. So he sat down in silence, and seized upon a volume which lay near him, as a sort of desperate effort to divert ennui, for on no other occasion had Magnus been known to have recourse to a book for that purpose. It chanced to be a book much to his mind, being the well-known work of Olaus Magnus, upon the manners of the ancient Northern nations. The book is unluckily in the Latin language, and the Danske or Dutch were, either of them, much more familiar to the Udaller. But then it was the fine edition published in 1555, which contains representations of the war-chariots, fishing exploits, warlike exercises, and domestic employments of the Scandinavians ; and thus the information which the work refused to the understanding, was addressed to the eye, which, as is well known both to old and young, answers the purpose of amusement as well, if not better.

Meanwhile the two sisters, pressed as close to each other as two flowers on the same stalk, sat with their arms reciprocally passed over each other's shoulder, as if they feared some new and unforeseen cause of coldness was about to separate them, and interrupt the sister-like harmony which had been but just restored. Norna sat opposite to them, sometimes revolving the large parchment volume with which they had found her employed at their entrance, and sometimes gazing on the sisters, with a fixed look, in which an interest of a kind unusually tender seemed occasionally to disturb the stern and rigorous solemnity of her countenance. All was still and silent as death, and the subsiding emotions of Brenda had not yet permitted her to wonder whether the remaining hours of the evening were to be passed in the same manner, when the scene of tranquillity was suddenly interrupted by the entrance of the dwarf Pacolet, or, as the Udaller called him, Nicholas Strumpfer.

Norna darted an angry glance on the intruder, who seemed to deprecate her resentment by holding up his hands and uttering a babbling sound ; then instantly resorting to his usual mode of conversation, he expressed himself by a variety of signs made rapidly upon his fingers, and as rapidly answered by his mistress, so that the young women, who had never heard of such an art, and now saw it practised by two beings so singular, almost conceived their mutual intelligence the work of enchantment. When they had ceased their intercourse, Norna turned to Magnus Troil with much haughtiness, and said, "How, my kinsman ! have you so far forgot yourself, as to bring earthly food into the house of the Reimkennar, and make preparations in the dwelling of Power and of Despair, for refection, and wassail, and revelry ?—Speak not—answer not," she said ; "the duration of the cure which was wrought even now, depends on your silence and obedience—bandy but a single look or word with me, and the latter condition of that maiden shall be worse than the first !"

This threat was an effectual charm upon the tongue of the Udaller, though he longed to indulge it in vindication of his conduct.

"Follow me, all of you," said Norna, striding to the door of the apartment, "and see that no one looks backwards—we leave not this apartment empty, though we, the children of mortality, be removed from it."

She went out, and the Udaller signed to his daughters to follow, and to obey her injunctions. The sibyl moved swifter than her guests down the rude descent (such it might rather be termed than a proper staircase), which led to the lower apartment. Magnus and his daughters, when they entered the chamber, found their own attendants aghast at the presence and proceedings of Norna of the Fitful Head.

They had been previously employed in arranging the provisions, which they had brought along with them, so as to present a comfortable cold meal, as soon as the appetite of the Udaller, which was regular as the return of tide, should induce him to desire some refreshment ; and now they stood staring in fear and surprise, while Norna, seizing upon one article after another, and well supported by the zealous activity of Pacolet, flung their whole preparations out of the rude aperture which served for a window, and over the cliff, from which the ancient Burgh arose, into the ocean, which raged and foamed beneath. *Vifda* (dried beef), hams, and pickled pork, flew after each other into empty space, smoked geese were restored to the air, and cured fish to the sea, their native elements indeed, but which they were no longer capable of traversing ; and the devastation proceeded so rapidly, that the Udaller could scarce secure from the wreck his silver drinking cup ; while the large leathern flask of brandy, which was destined to supply his favourite beverage, was sent to follow the rest of the supper, by the hands of Pacolet, who regarded, at the same time, the disappointed Udaller with a malicious grin, as if, notwithstanding his own natural taste for the liquor, he enjoyed the disappointment and surprise of Magnus Troil still more than he would have relished sharing his enjoyment.

The destruction of the brandy-flask exhausted the patience of Magnus, who roared out in a tone of no small displeasure, "Why, kinswoman, this is wasteful madness—where, and on what, would you have us sup ?"

"Where you will," answered Norna, "and on what you will,—but not in my dwelling, and not on the food with which you have profaned it. Vex my spirit no more, but begone every one of you ! You have been here too long for my good, perhaps for your own."

"How, kinswoman !" said Magnus, "would you make outcasts of us at this time of night, when even a Scotchman would not turn a stranger from the door ?—Bethink you, dame, it is shame on our lineage for ever, if this squall of yours should force us to slip cables, and go to sea so scantily provided."

"Be silent, and depart," said Norna ; "let it suffice you have got that for which you came. I have no harbourage for mortal guests, no provision to relieve human wants. There is beneath the cliff a beach of the finest sand, a stream of water as pure as the well of Kildinguie, and the rocks bear dulse as wholesome as that of Guiodin ; and well you wot, that the well of Kildinguie and the dulse of Guiodin will cure all maladies save Black Death."*

"And well I wot," said the Udaller, "that I would eat corrupted sea-weed, like a starling, or salted seal's flesh, like the men of Burraforth, or wilks, buckies, and lampits, like the poor sneaks of Stroma, rather than break wheat bread and drink red wine in a house where it is begrudged me.—And yet," he said, checking himself, "I am wrong, very wrong, my cousin, to speak thus to you, and I should rather thank you for what you have done, than upbraid you for following your own ways. But I see you are impatient—we will be all under way presently. And you, ye knaves," addressing his servants, "that were in such hurry with your sevice before it was lacked, get out of doors with you presently, and manage to catch the ponies ; for I see we must make for another harbour to-night, if we would not sleep with an empty stomach, and on a hard bed."

The domestics of Magnus, already sufficiently alarmed at the violence of Norna's conduct, scarce waited the imperious command of their master to evacuate her dwelling with all despatch ; and the Udaller, with a daughter in each arm, was in the act of following them, when Norna said emphatically, "Stop !" They obeyed, and again turned towards her. She held out her hand to Magnus, which the placable Udaller instantly folded in his own ample palm.

"Magnus," she said, "we part by necessity, but, I trust, not in anger ?"

"Surely not, cousin," said the warm-hearted Udaller, wellnigh stammering in his hasty disclamation of all unkindness,—"most assuredly not. I never bear ill-will to any one, much less to one of my own blood, and who has piloted me with her advice through many a rough tide, as I would pilot a boat betwixt Swona and Stroma, through all the waws, wells, and swelchies of the Pentland Firth."

* So at least says an Orkney proverb.

"Enough," said Norna, "and now farewell, with such a blessing as I dare bestow—not a word more ! Maidens," she added, "draw near, and let me kiss your brows."

The sibyl was obeyed by Minna with awe, and by Brenda with fear ; the one overmastered by the warmth of her imagination, the other by the natural timidity of her constitution. Norna then dismissed them, and in two minutes afterwards they found themselves beyond the bridge, and standing upon the rocky platform in front of the ancient Pictish Burgh, which it was the pleasure of this sequestered female to inhabit. The night, for it was now fallen, was unusally serene. A bright twilight, which glimmered far over the surface of the sea, supplied the brief absence of the summer's sun ; and the waves seemed to sleep under its influence, so faint and slumberous was the sound with which one after another rolled on and burst against the foot of the cliff on which they stood. In front of them stood the rugged fortress, seeming, in the uniform greyness of the atmosphere, as aged, as shapeless, and as massive as the rock on which it was founded. There was neither sight nor sound that indicated human habitation, save that from one rude shot-hole glimmered the flame of the feeble lamp by which the sibyl was probably pursuing her mystical and nocturnal studies, shooting upon the twilight, in which it was soon lost and confounded, a single line of tiny light ; bearing the same proportion to that of the atmosphere, as the aged woman and her serf, the sole inhabitants of that desert, did to the solitude with which they were surrounded.

For several minutes, the party, thus suddenly and unexpectedly expelled from the shelter where they had reckoned upon spending the night, stood in silence, each wrapt in their own separate reflections. Minna, her thoughts fixed on the mystical consolation which she had received, in vain endeavoured to extract from the words of Norna a more distinct and intelligible meaning ; and the Udaller had not yet recovered his surprise at the extrusion to which he had been thus whimsically subjected, under circumstances that prohibited him from resenting as an insult, treatment which, in all other respects, was so shocking to the genial hospitality of his nature, that he still felt like one disposed to be angry, if he but knew how to set about it. Brenda was the first who brought matters to a point, by asking whither they were to go, and how they were to spend the night ? The question, which was asked in a tone, that, amidst its simplicity, had something dolorous in it, entirely changed the train of her father's ideas ; and the unexpected perplexity of their situation now striking him in a comic point of view, he laughed till his very eyes ran over, while every rock around him rung, and the sleeping sea-fowl were startled from their repose, by the loud, hearty explosions of his obstreperous hilarity.

The Udaller's daughters, eagerly representing to their father the risk of displeasing Norna by this unlimited indulgence of his mirth, united their efforts to drag him to a farther distance from her dwelling. Magnus, yielding to their strength, which, feeble as it was, his own fit of laughter rendered him incapable of resisting, suffered himself to be pulled to a considerable distance from the Burgh, and then escaping from their hands, and sitting down, or rather suffering himself to drop, upon a large stone which lay conveniently by the wayside, he again laughed so long and lustily, that his vexed and anxious daughters became afraid that there was something more than natural in these repeated convulsions.

At length his mirth exhausted both itself and the Udaller's strength. He groaned heavily, wiped his eyes, and said, not without feeling some desire to renew his obstreperous cachinnation, "Now, by the bones of Saint Magnus, my ancestor and namesake, one would imagine that being turned out of doors, at this time of night, was nothing short of an absolutely exquisite jest ; for I have shaken my sides at it till they ached. There we sat, made snug for the night, and I made as sure of a good supper and a can as ever I had been of either,—and here we are all taken aback ; and then poor Brenda's doleful voice, and melancholy question, of 'What is to be done, and where are we to sleep ?' In good faith, unless one of those knaves, who must needs torment the poor woman by their trencher-work before it was wanted, can make amends by telling us of some snug port under our lee, we have no other course for it but to steer through the twilight on the bearing of Burgh Westra, and rough it out as well as we can by the way. I am sorry but for you, girls ; for many a cruise have I been upon when we were on shorter allowance than we are like to have now.—I would I had but secured a morsel for you, and a drop for myself ; and then there had been but little to complain of."

Both sisters hastened to assure the Udaller that they felt not the least occasion for food.

"Why, that is well," said Magnus : "and so being the case, I will not complain of my own appetite, though it is sharper than convenient. And the rascal, Nicholas Strumpfer,—what a leer the villain gave me as he started the good Nantz into the salt water ! He grinned, the knave, like a seal on a skerry.—Had it not been for vexing my poor kinswoman, Norna, I would have sent his misbegotten body, and misshapen jolterhead, after my bonny flask, as sure as Saint Magnus lies at Kirkwall !"

By this time the servants returned with the ponies, which they had very soon caught—these sensible animals finding nothing so captivating in the pasture where they had been suffered to stray, as inclined them to resist the invitation again to subject themselves to saddle and bridle. The prospects of the party were also considerably improved by learning that the contents of their sumpter-ponies' burden had not been entirely exhausted,—a small basket having fortunately escaped the rage of Norna and Pacolet, by the rapidity with which one of the servants had caught up and removed it. The same domestic, an alert and ready-witted fellow, had observed upon the beach, not above three miles distant from the Burgh, and about a quarter of a mile off their straight path, a deserted *Skio*, or fisherman's hut, and suggested that they should occupy it for the rest of the night, in order that the ponies might be refreshed, and the young ladies spend the night under cover from the raw evening air.

When we are delivered from great and serious dangers, our mood is, or ought to be, grave, in proportion to the peril we have escaped, and the gratitude due to protecting Providence. But few things raise the spirits more naturally or more harmlessly, than when means of extrication from any of the lesser embarrassments of life are suddenly presented to us ; and such was the case in the present instance. The Udaller, relieved from the apprehensions for his daughters suffering from fatigue, and himself from too much appetite and too little food, carolled Norse ditties, as he spurred Bergen through the twilight, with as much glee and gallantry as if the night-ride had been entirely a matter of his own free choice. Brenda lent her voice to some of his choruses, which were echoed in ruder notes by the servants, who, in that simple state of society, were not considered as guilty of any breach of respect by mingling their voices with the song. Minna, indeed, was as yet unequal to such an effort ; but she compelled herself to assume some share in the general hilarity of the meeting ; and contrary to her conduct since the fatal morning which concluded the Festival of Saint John, she seemed to take her usual interest in what was going on around her, and answered with kindness and readiness the repeated inquiries concerning her health, with which the Udaller every now and then interrupted his carol. And thus they proceeded by night a happier party by far than they had been when they traced the same route on the preceding morning, making light of the difficulties of the way, and promising themselves shelter and a comfortable night's rest in the deserted hut which they were now about to approach, and which they expected to find in a state of darkness and solitude.

But it was the lot of the Udaller that day to be deceived more than once in his calculations.

"And which way lies this cabin of yours, Laurie ?" said the Udaller, addressing the intelligent domestic of whom we just spoke.

"Yonder it should be," said Laurence Scholey, "at the head of the voe—but, by my faith, if it be the place, there are folk there before us— God and Saint Ronan send that they be canny company !"

In truth there was a light in the deserted hut, strong enough to glimmer through every chink of the shingles and wreck-wood of which it was constructed, and to give the whole cabin the appearance of a smithy seen by night. The universal superstition of the Zetlanders seized upon Magnus and his escort.

"They are trows," said one voice.

"They are witches," murmured another.

"They are mermaids," muttered a third ; "only hear their wild singing !"

All stopped ; and, in effect, some notes of music were audible, which Brenda, with a voice that quivered a little, but yet had a turn of arch ridicule in its tone, pronounced to be the sound of a fiddle.

"Fiddle or fiend," said the Udaller, who, if he believed in such nightly apparitions as had struck terror into his retinue, certainly feared them not—"fiddle or fiend, may the devil fetch me if a witch cheats me out of supper to-night for the second time !"

So saying, he dismounted, clenched his trusty truncheon in his hand, and advanced towards the hut, followed by Laurence alone ; the rest of his retinue continuing stationary on the beach beside his daughters and his ponies.

CHAPTER THIRTIETH

What ho, my jovial mates ! come on ! we'll frolic it
Like fairies frisking in the merry moonshine,
Seen by the curtal friar, who, from some christening
Or some blithe bridal, hies belated cell-ward—
He starts, and changes his bold bottle swagger
To churchman's pace professional, and ransacking
His treacherous memory for some holy hymn,
Finds but the roundel of the midnight catch.
                                                                    OLD PLAY

THE stride of the Udaller relaxed nothing of its length or of its firmness
as he approached the glimmering cabin, from which he now heard
distinctly the sound of the fiddle. But if still long and firm, his steps
succeeded each other rather more slowly than usual ; for, like a cautious,
though a brave general, Magnus was willing to reconnoitre his enemy
before assailing him. The trusty Laurence Scholey, who kept close
behind his master, now whispered into his ear, "So help me, sir, as I
believe that the ghaist, if ghaist it be, that plays so bravely on the fiddle,
must be the ghaist of Maister Claud Halcro, or his wraith at least ; for
never was bow drawn across thairm which brought out the gude auld
spring of 'Fair and Lucky,' so like his ain."

Magnus was himself much of the same opinion ; for he knew the
blithe minstrelsy of the spirited little old man, and hailed the hut with a
hearty hilloa, which was immediately replied to by the cheery note of his
ancient messmate, and Halcro himself presently made his appearance
on the beach.

The Udaller now signed to his retinue to come up, while he asked his
friend, after a kind greeting and much shaking of hands, "How the devil
he came to sit there, playing old tunes in so desolate a place, like an owl
whooping to the moon ?"

"And tell me rather, Fowd," said Claud Halcro, "how you came to be
within hearing of me ? ay, by my word, and with your bonny daughters,
too ?—Yarta Minna and Yarta Brenda. I bid you welcome to these yellow
sands—and there shake hands, as glorious John, or some other body,
says, upon the same occasion. And how came you here like two fair
swans, making day out of twilight, and turning all you step upon to
silver ?"

"You shall know all about them presently," answered Magnus ; "but
what messmates have you got in the hut with you ? I think I hear some
one speaking."

"None," replied Claud Halcro, "but that poor creature, the Factor, and
my imp of a boy Giles. I—but come in—come in—here you will find us
starving in comfort—not so much as a mouthful of sour sillocks to be had
for love or money."

"That may be in a small part helped," said the Udaller ; " for though

243

the best of our supper is gone over the Fitful Crags to the sealchies and the dog-fish, yet we have got something in the kit still.—Here, Laurie, bring up the *vifda*."

"*Yokul, yokul !*"* was Laurence's joyful answer ; and he hastened for the basket.

"By the bicker of Saint Magnus,"† said Halcro, "and the burliest bishop that ever quaffed it for luck's sake, there is no finding your locker empty, Magnus ! I believe sincerely that ere a friend wanted, you could, like old Luggie‡ the warlock, fish up boiled and roasted out of the pool of Kibster."

"You are wrong there, Yarto Claud,"§ said Magnus Troil, "for, far from helping me to a supper, the foul fiend, I believe, has carried off great part of mine this blessed evening ; but you are welcome to share and share of what is left." This was said while the party entered the hut.

Here, in a cabin which smelled strongly of dried fish, and whose sides and roof were jet black with smoke, they found the unhappy Triptolemus Yellowley seated beside a fire made of dried sea-weed, mingled with some peats and wreck-wood ; his sole companion a bare-footed, yellow-haired Zetland boy, who acted occasionally as a kind of page to Claud Halcro, bearing his fiddle on his shoulders, saddling his pony, and rendering him similar duties of kindly observance. The disconsolate agriculturist, for such his visage betokened him, displayed little surprise, and less animation, at the arrival of the Udaller and his companions, until, after the party had drawn close to the fire (a neighbourhood which the dampness of the night air rendered far from disagreeable), the pannier was opened, and a tolerable supply of barley-bread and hung-beef, besides a flask of brandy (no doubt smaller than that which the relentless hand of Pacolet had emptied into the ocean), gave assurances of a tolerable supper. Then, indeed, the worthy Factor grinned, chuckled, rubbed his hands, and inquired after all friends at Burgh Westra.

When they had all partaken of this needful refreshment, the Udaller repeated his inquiries of Halcro, and more particularly of the Factor, how they came to be nestled in such a remote corner at such an hour of night.

"Maister Magnus Troil," said Triptolemus, when a second cup had given him spirits to tell his tale of woe, "I would not have you think that it is a little thing that disturbs me. I come of that grain that takes a sair wind to shake it. I have seen many a Martinmas and many a Whitsunday in my day whilk are the times peculiarly grievous to those of my craft,

* *Yokul,* yes sir ; a Norse expression, still in common use.

† The Bicker of Saint Magnus, a vessel of enormous dimensions, was preserved at Kirkwall, and presented to each Bishop of the Orkneys. If the new incumbent was able to quaff it out at one draught, which was a task for Hercules or Rorie Mhor of Dunvegan, the omen boded a crop of unusual fertility.

‡ Luggie, a famous conjuror, was wont, when storms prevented him from going to his usual employment of fishing, to angle over a steep rock, at the place called, from his name, Luggie's Knoll. At other times he drew up dressed food while they were out at sea, of which his comrades partook boldly from natural courage, without caring who stood cook. The poor man was finally condemned and burnt at Scalloway.

§ *Yarto,* dear.

and I could aye bide the bang ; but I think I am like to be dung ower a'thegither in this damned country of yours—Gude forgie me for swearing—but evil communication corrupteth good manners."

"Now, Heaven guide us," said the Udaller, "what is the matter with the man ? Why, man, if you will put your plough into new land, you must set us an example of patience, seeing you came here for our improvement."

"And the deil was in my feet when I did so," said the Factor ; "I had better have set myself to improve the cairn on Clochnaben."

"But what is it, after all," said the Udaller, "that has befallen you ?—what is it that you complain of ?"

"Of everything that has chanced to me since I landed on this island, which I believe was accursed at the very creation," said the agriculturist, "and assigned as a fitting station for sorners, thieves, whores (I beg the ladies' pardon), witches, bitches, and all evil spirits !"

"By my faith, a goodly catalogue !" said Magnus ; "and there has been the day, that if I had heard you give out the half of it, I should have turned improver myself, and have tried to amend your manners with a cudgel."

"Bear with me," said the Factor, "Maister Udaller, or whatever else they may call you, and as you are strong be pitiful, and consider the luckless lot of any inexperienced person who lights upon this earthly paradise of yours. He asks for drink, they bring him sour whey—no disparagement to your brandy, Fowd, which is excellent—You ask for meat, and they bring you sour sillocks that Satan might choke upon—You call your labourers together, and bid them work ; it proves Saint Magnus's day, or Saint Ronan's day, or some infernal saint or other's—or else, perhaps, they have dreamed of a roasted horse—in short, nothing is to be done—Give them a spade, and they work as if it burned their fingers ; but set them to dancing, and see when they will tire of funking and flinging !"

"And why should they, poor bodies," said Claud Halcro, "as long as there are good fiddlers to play to them ?"

"Ay, ay," said Triptolemus, shaking his head, "you are a proper person to uphold them in such a humour. Well, to proceed :—I till a piece of my best ground ; down comes a sturdy beggar that wants a kailyard, or a plant-a-cruive, as you call it, and he claps down an enclosure in the middle of my bit shot of corn, as lightly as if he was baith laird and tenant ; and gainsay him wha likes, there he dibbles in his kail-plants ! I sit down to my sorrowful dinner, thinking to have peace and quietness there at least ; when in comes one, two, three, four, or half-a-dozen of skelping long lads, from some foolery or anither, misca' me for barring my ain door against them, and eat up the best half of what my sister's providence—and she is not over bountiful—has allotted for my dinner ! Then enters a witch, with an ellwand in her hand, and she raises the wind or lays it, whichever she likes, majors up and down my house as if she was mistress of it, and I am bounden to thank Heaven if she carries not the broadside of it away with her !"

"Still," said the Fowd, "this is no answer to my question—how the foul fiend I come to find you at moorings here ?"

245

"Have patience, worthy sir," replied the afflicted Factor, "and listen to what I have to say, for I fancy it will be as well to tell you the whole matter. You must know, I once thought that I had gotten a small godsend, that might have made all these matters easier."

"How ! a godsend ! Do you mean a wreck, Master Factor ?" exclaimed Magnus ; "shame upon you, that should have set example to others !"

"It was no wreck, " said the Factor ; "but if you must needs know, it chanced that as I raised an hearthstane in one of the old chambers at Stourburgh (for my sister is minded that there is little use in mair fireplaces about a house than one, and I wanted the stane to knock bear upon), when, what should I light on but a horn full of old coins, silver the maist feck of them, but wi' a bit sprinkling of gold among them too.* Weel, I thought this was a dainty windfa', and so thought Baby, and we were the mair willing to put up with a place where there were siccan braw nest eggs—and we slade down the stane cannily over the horn, which seemed to me to be the very cornucopia, or horn of abundance ; and for farther security, Baby wad visit the room may be twenty times in the day, and mysell at an orra time, to the boot of a' that."

"On my word, and a very pretty amusement," said Claud Halcro, "to look over a horn of one's own siller. I question if glorious John Dryden ever enjoyed such a pastime in his life—I am very sure I never did."

"Yes, but you forget, Yarto Claud," said the Udaller, "that the Factor was only counting over the money for my Lord the Chamberlain. As he is so keen for his Lordship's rights in whales and wrecks, surely he would not forget him in treasure-trove."

"A-hem ! a-hem ! a-he—he—hem !" ejaculated Triptolemus, seized at the moment with an awkward fit of coughing,—"no doubt, my Lord's right in the matter would have been considered, being in the hand of one, though I say it, as just as can be found in Angusshire, let alone the Mearns. But mark what happened of late ! One day, as I went up to see that all was safe and snug, and just to count out the share that should have been his Lordship's—for surely the labourer, as one may call the finder, is worthy of his hire—nay, some learned men say, that when the finder, in point of trust and in point of power, representeth the *dominus*, or lord superior, he taketh the whole ; but let that pass, as a kittle question *in apicibus juris*, as we wont to say at Saint Andrews—Well, sir and ladies, when I went to the upper chamber, what should I see but an ugsome, ill-shaped, and most uncouth dwarf, that wanted but hoofs and horns to have made an utter devil of him, counting over the very hornful of siller ! I am no timorous man, Master Fowd, but, judging that I should proceed with caution in such a matter—for I had reason to believe that there was devilry in it—I accosted him in Latin (whilk it is maist becoming to speak to aught whilk taketh upon it as a goblin), and conjured him *in nomine*, and so forth, with such words as my poor learning could furnish of a suddenty, whilk, to say truth, were not so many, nor altogether so purely latineezed as might have been, had I not been few years at college, and many at the pleugh. Well, sirs, he started at first, as one that heareth that which he expects not ; but presently

* Note R. Antique coins found in Zetland.

recovering himself, he wawls on me with his grey een, like a wild-cat, and opens his mouth, whilk resembled the mouth of an oven, for the deil a tongue he had in it, that I could spy, and took upon his ugly self altogether the air and bearing of a bull-dog, whilk I have seen loosed at a fair upon a mad staig ;* whereupon I was something daunted, and withdrew myself to call upon sister Baby, who fears neither dog nor devil, when there is in question the little penny siller. And truly she raise to the fray as I hae seen the Lindsays and Ogilvies bristle up, when Donald MacDonnoch, or the like, made a start down frae the Highlands on the braes of Islay. But an auld useless carline, called Tronda Dronsdaughter (they might call her Drone the sell of her, without farther addition), flung herself right in my sister's gate, and yelloched and skirled, that you would have thought her a whole generation of hounds ; whereupon I judged it best to make ae yoking of it, and stop the pleugh until I got my sister's assistance. Whilk when I had done, and we mounted the stair to the apartment in which the said dwarf, devil, or other apparition, was to be seen, dwarf, horn, and siller, were as clean gane as if the cat had lickit the place where I saw them."

Here Triptolemus paused in his extraordinary narration, while the rest of the party looked upon each other in surprise, and the Udaller muttered to Claud Halcro—"By all tokens, this must have been either the devil of Nicholas Strumpfer ; and, if it were him, he is more of a goblin than e'er I gave him credit for, and shall be apt to rate him as such in future." Then, addressing the Factor, he inquired—"Saw ye nought how this dwarf of yours parted company ?"

"As I shall answer it, no," replied Triptolemus, with a cautious look around him, as if daunted by the recollection ; "neither I, nor Baby, who had her wits more about her, not having seen this unseemly vision, could perceive any way by whilk he made evasion. Only Tronda said she saw him flee forth of the window of the west roundel of the auld house, upon a dragon, as she averred. But, as the dragon is held a fabulous animal, I suld pronounce her averment to rest upon *deceptio visus*."

"But, may we not ask farther," said Brenda, stimulated by curiosity to know as much of her cousin Norna's family as was possible, "how all this operated upon Master Yellowley, so as to occasion his being in this place at so unseasonable an hour ?"

"Seasonable it must be, Mistress Brenda, since it brought us into your sweet company," answered Claud Halcro, whose mercurial brain far outstripped the slow conceptions of the agriculturist, and who became impatient of being so long silent. "To say the truth, it was I, Mistress Brenda, who recommended to our friend the Factor, whose house I chanced to call at just after this mischance (and where, by the way, owing doubtless to the hurry of their spirits, I was but poorly received), to make a visit to our other friend at Fitful Head, well judging from certain points of the story, at which my other and more particular friend than either (looking at Magnus) may chance to form a guess, that they who break a head are the best to find a plaster. And as our friend the

* Young unbroken horse.

247

Factor scrupled travelling on horseback,—in respect of some tumbles from our ponies"—

"Which are incarnate devils," said Triptolemus, aloud, muttering under his breath, "like every live thing that I have found in Zetland."

"Well, Fowd," continued Halcro, "I undertook to carry him to Fitful Head in my little boat, which Giles and I can manage as if it were an Admiral's barge full manned ; and Master Triptolemus Yellowley will tell you how seaman-like I piloted him to the little haven within a quarter of a mile of Norna's dwelling."

"I wish to heaven you had brought me as safe back again," said the Factor.

"Why, to be sure," replied the minstrel, "I am, as glorious John says—

A daring pilot in extremity,
Pleased with the danger when the waves go high,
I seek the storm—but, for a calm unfit,
Will steer too near the sands, to show my wit.

"I showed little wit in entrusting myself to your charge," said Triptolemus ; "and you still less when you upset the boat at the throat of the voe, as you call it, when even the poor bairn, that was mair than half drowned, told you that you were carrying too much sail ; and then ye wad fasten the rape to the bit stick on the boat-side, that ye might have time to play on the fiddle."

"What !" said the Udaller, "made fast the sheets to the thwart ? a most unseasonable practice, Claud Halcro."

"And sae came of it," replied the agriculturist ; "for the neist blast (and we are never lang without ane in these parts) whomled us as a gudewife would whomle a bowie, and ne'er a thing wad Maister Halcro save but his fiddle. The puir bairn swam out like a water-spaniel, and I swattered hard for my life, wi' the help of ane of the oars ; and here we are, comfortless creatures, that, till a good wind blew you here, had naething to eat but a mouthful of Norway rusk, that has mair sawdust than ryemeal in it, and tastes liker turpentine than onything else."

"I thought we heard you very merry," said Brenda, "as we came along the beach."

"Ye heard a fiddle, Mistress Brenda," said the Factor, "and maybe ye may think there can be nae dearth, miss, where that is skirling. But then it was Maister Claud Halcro's fiddle, whilk, I am apt to think, wad skirl at his father's death-bed, or at his ain, sae lang as his fingers could pinch the thairm. And it was nae sma' aggravation to my misfortune to have him bumming a' sorts of springs—Norse and Scots, Highland and Lawland, English and Italian—in my lug, as if nothing had happened that was amiss, and we all in such stress and perplexity."

"Why, I told you sorrow would never right the boat, Factor," said the thoughtless minstrel, "and I did my best to make you merry ; if I failed, it was neither my fault nor my fiddle's. I have drawn the bow across it before glorious John Dryden himself."

"I will hear no stories about glorious John Dryden," answered the

Udaller, who dreaded Halcro's narratives as much as Triptolemus did his music,—I will hear nought of him, but one story to every three bowls of punch,—it is our old paction, you know. But tell me, instead, what said Norna to you about your errand ?"

"Ay, there was anither fine upshot," said Master Yellowley. "She wadna look at us, or listen to us ; only she bothered our acquaintance, Master Halcro here, who thought he could have sae much to say wi' her, with about a score of questions about your family and household estate, Master Magnus Troil ; and when she had gotten a' she wanted out of him, I thought she wad hae dung him ower the craig, like an empty peacod."

"And for yourself ?" said the Udaller.

"She wadna listen to my story, nor hear sae much as a word that I had to say," answered Triptolemus ; "and sae much for them that seek to witches and familiar spirits !"

"You needed not to have had recourse to Norna's wisdom, Master Factor," said Minna, not unwilling, perhaps, to stop his railing against the friend who had so lately rendered her service ; "the youngest child in Orkney could have told you, that fairy treasures, if they are not wisely employed for the good of others, as well as of those to whom they are imparted, do not dwell long with their possessors."

"Your humble servant to command, Mistress Minnie," said Triptolemus ; "I thank ye for the hint,—and I am blithe that you have gotten your wits—I beg pardon, I meant your health—into the barn-yard again. For the treasure, I neither used nor abused it—they that live in the house with my sister Baby wad find it hard to do either !—and as for speaking of it, whilk they say muckle offends them whom we in Scotland call Good Neighbours, and you call Drows, the face of the auld Norse kings on the coins themselves might have spoken as much about it as ever I did."

"The Factor," said Claud Halcro, not unwilling to seize the opportunity of revenging himself on Triptolemus, for disgracing his seamanship and disparaging his music,—"The Factor was so scrupulous, as to keep the thing quiet even from his master, the Lord Chamberlain ; but, now that the matter has ta'en wind, he is likely to have to account to his master for that which is no longer in his possession ; for the Lord Chamberlain will be in no hurry, I think, to believe the story of the dwarf. Neither do I think" (winking to the Udaller) "that Norna gave credit to a word of so odd a story ; and I daresay that was the reason that she received us, I must needs say, in a very dry manner. I rather think she knew that Triptolemus, our friend here, had found some other hiding-hole for the money, and that the story of the goblin was all his own invention. For my part, I will never believe there was such a dwarf to be seen as the creature Master Yellowley describes, until I set my own eyes on him."

"Then you may do so at this moment," said the Factor ; "for by—" (he muttered a deep asseveration as he sprung on his feet in great horror), "there the creature is !"

All turned their eyes in the direction in which he pointed, and saw the hideous misshapen figure of Pacolet, with his eyes fixed and glaring at them through the smoke. He had stolen upon their conversation unperceived, until the Factor's eye lighted upon him in the manner we have described. There was something so ghastly in his sudden and unexpected appearance, that even the Udaller, to whom his form was familiar, could not help starting. Neither pleased with himself for having testified this degree of emotion, however slight, nor with the dwarf who had given cause to it, Magnus asked him sharply, what was his business there ? Pacolet replied by producing a letter, which he gave to the Udaller, uttering a sound resembling the word *Shogh.* *

"That is the Highlandman's language," said the Udaller—"didst thou learn that, Nicholas, when you lost your own ?"

Pacolet nodded, and signed to him to read his letter.

"That is no such easy matter by firelight, my good friend," replied the Udaller ; "but it may concern Minna, and we must try."

Brenda offered her assistance, but the Udaller answered, "No, no, my girl,—Norna's letters must be read by those they are written to. Give the knave, Strumpfer, a drop of brandy the while, though he little deserves it at my hands, considering the grin with which he sent the good Nantz down the crag this morning, as if it had been as much ditch-water."

"Will you be this honest gentleman's cup-bearer—his Ganymede, friend Yellowley, or shall I ?" said Claud Halcro aside to the Factor ; while Magnus Troil, having carefully wiped his spectacles, which he produced from a large copper case, had disposed them on his nose, and was studying the epistle of Norna.

"I would not touch him, or go near him, for all the Carse of Gowrie," said the Factor, whose fears were by no means entirely removed, though he saw that the dwarf was received as a creature of flesh and blood by the rest of the company ; "but I pray you ask him what he has done with my horn of coins ?"

The dwarf, who heard the question, threw back his head, and displayed his enormous throat, pointing to it with his finger.

"Nay, if he has swallowed them, there is no more to be said," replied the Factor ; "only I hope he will thrive on them as a cow on wet clover. He is dame Norna's servant, it's like,—such man, such mistress ! But if theft and witchcraft are to go unpunished in this land, my Lord must find another factor ; for I have been used to live in a country where men's worldly gear was keepit from infang and outfang thief, as well as their immortal souls from the claws of the deil and his cummers—sain and save us !"

The agriculturist was perhaps the less reserved in expressing his complaints, that the Udaller was for the present out of hearing, having drawn Claud Halcro apart into another corner of the hut.

"And tell me," said he, "friend Halcro, what errand took thee to Sumburgh, since I reckon it was scarce the mere pleasure of sailing in partnership with yonder barnacle ?"

"In faith, Fowd," said the bard, "and if you will have the truth, I went to speak to Norna on your affairs."

* In Gaelic, *there.*

250

"On my affairs ?" replied the Udaller ; "on what affairs of mine ?"

"Just touching your daughter's health. I heard that Norna refused your message, and would not see Eric Scambester. Now, said I to myself, I have scarce joyed in meat, or drink, or music, or aught else, since Yarta Minna has been so ill ; and I may say, literally as well as figuratively, that my day and night have been made sorrowful to me. In short, I thought I might have some more interest with old Norna than another, as scalds and wise women were always accounted something akin ; and I undertook the journey with the hope to be of some use to my old friend and his lovely daughter."

"And it was most kindly done of you, good warm-hearted Claud," said the Udaller, shaking him warmly by the hand—"I ever said you showed the good old Norse heart amongst all thy fiddling and thy folly.— Tut, man, never wince for the matter, but be blithe that thy heart is better than thy head. Well,—and I warrant you got no answer from Norna ?"

"None to purpose," replied Claud Halcro ; "but she held me close to question about Minna's illness, too,—and I told her how I had met her abroad the other morning in no very good weather, and how her sister Brenda said she had hurt her foot ;—in short, I told her all and everything I knew."

"And something more besides, it would seem," said the Udaller ; "for I, at least, never heard before that Minna had hurt herself."

"Oh, a scratch ! a mere scratch !" said the old man ; "but I was startled about it—terrified lest it had been the bite of a dog, or some hurt from a venomous thing. I told all to Norna however."

"And what," answered the Udaller, "did she say, in the way of reply ?"

"She bade me begone about my business, and told me that the issue would be known at the Kirkwall Fair ; and said just the like to this noodle of a Factor—it was all that either of us got for our labour," said Halcro.

"That is strange," said Magnus. "My kinswoman writes me in this letter not to fail going thither with my daughters. This Fair runs strongly in her head ;—one would think she intended to lead the market, and yet she has nothing to buy or to sell there that I know of. And so you came away as wise as you went, and swamped your boat at the mouth of the voe ?"

"Why, how could I help it ?" said the poet. "I had set the boy to steer, and as the flaw came suddenly off shore, I could not let go the tack and play on the fiddle at the same time. But it is all well enough,—salt water never harmed Zetlander, so as he could get out of it ; and, as Heaven would have it, we were within man's depth of the shore, and chancing to find this skio, we should have done well enough, with shelter and fire, and are much better than well with your good cheer and good company. But it wears late, and Night and Day must be both as sleepy as old Midnight can make them. There is an inner crib here, where the fishers slept,—somewhat fragrant with the smell of their fish, but that is wholesome. They shall bestow themselves there, with the help of what cloaks you have, and then we will have one cup of brandy, and one stave of glorious John, or some little trifle of my own, and so sleep as sound as cobblers."

"Two glasses of brandy, if you please," said the Udaller, "if our stores do not run dry; but not a single stave of glorious John, or of anyone else to-night."

And this being arranged and executed agreeably to the peremptory pleasure of the Udaller, the whole party consigned themselves to slumber for the night, and on the next day departed for their several habitations, Claud Halcro having previously arranged with the Udaller that he would accompany him and his daughters on their proposed visit to Kirkwall.

CHAPTER THIRTY-FIRST

By this hand, thou think'st me as far in the devil's book as thou and
    Falstaff, for obduracy and persistency. Let the end try the man...
    Albeit I could tell to thee (as to one it pleases me, for fault of a
    better, to call my friend), I could be sad, and sad indeed too.
                          HENRY IV, *Part II*

WE must now change the scene from Zetland to Orkney, and request our readers to accompany us to the ruins of an elegant, though ancient structure, called the Earl's Palace. These remains, though much dilapidated, still exist in the neighbourhood of the massive and venerable pile, which Norwegian devotion dedicated to Saint Magnus the Martyr, and, being contiguous to the Bishop's Palace, which is also ruinous, the place is impressive, as exhibiting vestiges of the mutations both in Church and State which have affected Orkney, as well as countries more exposed to such convulsions. Several parts of these ruinous buildings might be selected (under suitable modifications) as the model of a Gothic mansion, provided architects would be contented rather to imitate what is really beautiful in that species of building, than to make a medley of the caprices of the order, confounding the military, ecclesiastical, and domestic styles of all ages at random, with additional fantasies and combinations of their own device, "all formed out of the builder's brain."

The Earl's Palace forms three sides of an oblong square, and has, even in its ruins, the air of an elegant yet massive structure, uniting, as was usual in the residence of feudal princes, the character of a palace and of a castle. A great banqueting-hall, communicating with several large rounds, or projecting turret-rooms, and having at either end an immense chimney, testifies the ancient Northern hospitality of the Earls of Orkney, and communicates, almost in the modern fashion, with a gallery, or withdrawing room, of corresponding dimensions, and having, like the hall, its projecting turrets. The lordly hall itself is lighted by a fine Gothic window of shafted stone at one end, and is entered by a spacious and elegant staircase, consisting of three flights of stone steps. The exterior ornaments and proportions of the ancient building are also very handsome, but, being totally unprotected, this remnant of the pomp and grandeur of Earls, who assumed the license as well as the dignity of petty sovereigns, is now fast crumbling to decay, and has suffered considerably since the date of our story.

With folded arms and downcast looks, the pirate Cleveland was pacing slowly the ruined hall which we have just described ; a place of retirement which he had probably chosen because it was distant from public resort. His dress was considerably altered from that which he usually wore in Zetland, and seemed a sort of uniform, richly laced, and exhibiting no small quantity of embroidery ; a hat with a plume, and a small sword very handsomely mounted, then the constant companion of every one who assumed the rank of a gentleman, showed his pretensions to that character. But if his exterior was so far improved, it seemed to be otherwise with his health and spirits. He was pale, and had lost both the fire of his eyes and the vivacity of his step, and his whole appearance indicated melancholy of mind, or suffering of body, or a combination of both evils.

As Cleveland thus paced these ancient ruins, a young man, of a light and slender form, whose showy dress seemed to have been studied with care, yet exhibited more extravagance than judgment or taste, whose manner was a jaunty affectation of the free and easy rake of the period, and the expression of whose countenance was lively, with a cast of effrontery, tripped up the staircase, entered the hall, and presented himself to Cleveland, who merely nodded to him, and pulling his hat deeper over his brows, resumed his solitary and discontented promenade.

The stranger adjusted his own hat, nodded in return, took snuff, with the air of a *petit maître*, from a richly chased gold box, offered it to Cleveland as he passed, and being repulsed rather coldly, replaced the box in his pocket, folded his arms in his turn, and stood looking with fixed attention on his motions whose solitude he had interrupted. At length Cleveland stopped short, as if impatient of being longer the subject of his observation, and said abruptly, "Why can I not be left alone for half-an-hour, and what the devil is it that you want ?"

"I am glad you spoke first," answered the stranger carelessly ; "I was determined to know whether you were Clement Cleveland, or Cleveland's ghost, and they say ghosts never take the first word, so I now set it down for yourself in life and limb ; and here is a fine old hurly-house you have found out for an owl to hide himself in at midday, or a ghost to revisit the pale glimpses of the moon, as the divine Shakespeare says."

"Well, well," answered Cleveland, abruptly, "your jest is made, and now let us have your earnest."

"In earnest, then, Captain Cleveland," replied his companion, "I think you know me for your friend."

"I am content to suppose so," said Cleveland.

"It is more than supposition," replied the young man ; "I have proved it—proved it both here and elsewhere."

"Well, well," answered Cleveland, "I admit you have been always a friendly fellow—and what then ?"

"Well, well—and what then ?" replied the other ; "this is but a brief way of thanking folk. Look you, Captain, here is Benson, Barlowe, Dick Fletcher, and a few others of us who wished you well, have kept your old comrade Captain Goffe in these seas upon the look-out for you, when he and Hawkins, and the greater part of the ship's company, would fain have been down on the Spanish Main, and at the old trade."

"And I wish to God that you had all gone about your business," said Cleveland, "and left me to my fate."

"Which would have been to be informed against and hanged, Captain, the first time that any of these Dutch or English rascals, whom you have lightened of their cargoes, came to set their eyes upon you ; and no place more likely to meet with seafaring men, than in these islands. And here, to screen you from such a risk, we have been wasting our precious time, till folk are grown very peery ; and when we have no more goods or money to spend amongst them, the fellows will be for grabbing the ship."

"Well, then, why do you not sail off without me ?" said Cleveland— "There has been fair partition, and all have had their share—let all do as they like. I have lost my ship, and having been once a Captain, I will not go to sea under command of Goffe, or any other man. Besides, you know well enough that both Hawkins and he bear me ill-will for keeping them from sinking the Spanish brig, with the poor devils of negroes on board."

"Why, what the foul fiend is the matter with thee ?" said his companion : "Are you Clement Cleveland, our own old true-hearted Clem of the Cleuch, and do you talk of being afraid of Hawkins and Goffe, and a score of such fellows, when you have myself, and Barlowe, and Dick Fletcher at your back ? When was it we deserted you, either in council or in fight, that you should be afraid of our flinching now ? And as for serving under Goffe, I hope it is no new thing for gentlemen of fortune who are going on the account, to change a Captain now and then ? Let us alone for that,—Captain you shall be ; for death rock me asleep if I serve under that fellow Goffe, who is as very a bloodhound as ever sucked bitch ? No, no, I thank you—my Captain must have a little of the gentleman about him, howsoever. Besides, you know, it was you who first dipped my hands in the dirty water, and turned me from a stroller by land, to a rover by sea."

"Alas, poor Bunce !" said Cleveland, "you owe me little thanks for that service."

"That is as you take it," replied Bunce ; "for my part I see no harm in levying contributions on the public either one way or t'other. But I wish you would forget that name of Bunce, and call me Altamont, as I have often desired you to do. I hope a gentleman of the roving trade has as good a right to have an alias as a stroller, and I never stepped on the boards but what I was Altamont at the least."

"Well, then, Jack Altamont," replied Cleveland, "since Altamont is the word"—

"Yes, but, Captain, *Jack* is not the word, though Altamont be so. Jack

Altamont—why, 'tis a velvet coat with paper lace—Let it be Frederick, Captain ; Frederick Altamont is all of a piece."

"Frederick be it then, with all my heart," said Cleveland ; "and pray tell me, which of your names will sound best at the head of the Last Speech, Confession, and Dying Words of John Bunce, *alias* Frederick Altamont, who was this morning hanged at Execution Dock, for the crime of Piracy upon the High Seas ?"

"Faith, I cannot answer that question, without another can of grog, Captain ; so if you will go down with me to Bet Haldane's on the quay, I will bestow some thought on the matter, with the help of a right pipe of Trinidado. We will have the gallon bowl filled with the best stuff you ever tasted, and I know some smart wenches who will help us to drain it. But you shake your head—you're not i' the vein ?—Well, then, I will stay with you ; for by this hand, Clem, you shift me not off. Only I will ferret you out of this burrow of old stones, and carry you into sunshine and fair air.—Where shall we go ?"

"Where you will," said Cleveland, "so that you keep out of the way of our own rascals, and all others."

"Why, then," replied Bunce, "you and I will go up to the Hill of Whitford, which overlooks the town, and walk together as gravely and honestly as a pair of well employed attorneys."

As they proceeded to leave the ruinous castle, Bunce, turning back to look at it, thus addressed his companion :—

"Hark ye, Captain, dost thou know who last inhabited this old cockloft ?"

"An Earl of the Orkneys, they say," replied Cleveland.

"And are you avised what death he died of ?" said Bunce, "for I have heard that it was of a tight neck collar—a hempen fever, or the like."

"The people here do say," replied Cleveland, "that his Lordship, some hundred years ago, had the mishap to become acquainted with the nature of a loop and a leap in the air."

"Why, la ye there now !" said Bunce ; "there was some credit in being hanged in those days, and in such worshipful company. And what might his lordship have done to deserve such promotion ?"

"Plundered the liege subjects, they say," replied Cleveland ; "slain and wounded them, fired upon his Majesty's flag, and so forth."

"Near akin to a gentleman rover, then," said Bunce, making a theatrical bow towards the old building ; "and, therefore, my most potent, grave, and reverend Signior Earl, I crave leave to call you my loving cousin, and bid you most heartily adieu. I leave you in the good company of rats and mice, and so forth, and I carry with me an honest gentleman, who, having of late had no more heart than a mouse, is now desirous to run away from his profession and friends like a rat, and would therefore be a most fitting denizen of your Earlship's palace."

"I would advise you not to speak so loud, my good friend Frederick Altamont, or John Bunce," said Cleveland ; "when you were on the stage, you might safely rant as loud as you listed ; but in your present profession, of which you are so fond, every man speaks under correction of the yard-arm and a running noose."

The comarades left the little town of Kirkwall in silence, and ascended the Hill of Whitford, which raises its brow of dark heath, uninterrupted by enclosures, of cultivation of any kind, to the northward of the ancient Burgh of Saint Magnus. The plain at the foot of the hill was already occupied by numbers of persons who were engaged in making preparations for the Fair of Saint Olla, to be held upon the ensuing day, and which forms a general rendezvous to all the neighbouring islands of Orkney, and is even frequented by many persons from the more distant archipelago of Zetland. It is, in the words of the Proclamation, "a free Mercat and Fair, holden at the good Burgh of Kirkwall on the third of August, being Saint Olla's day," and continuing for an indefinite space thereafter, extending from three days to a week, and upwards. The fair is of great antiquity, and derives its name from Olaus, Olave, Ollaw, the celebrated Monarch of Norway, who, rather by the edge of his sword than any milder argument, introduced Christianity into these isles, and was respected as the patron of Kirkwall some time before he shared that honour with Saint Magnus the Martyr.

It was no part of Cleveland's purpose to mingle in the busy scene which was here going on ; and, turning their route to the left, they soon ascended into undisturbed solitude, save where the grouse, more plentiful in Orkney, perhaps, than in any other part of the British dominions, rose in covey, and went off before them.* Having continued to ascend till they had wellnigh reached the summit of the conical hill, both turned round, as with one consent, to look at and admire the prospect beneath.

The lively bustle which extended between the foot of the hill and the town, gave life and variety to that part of the scene ; then was seen the town itself, out of which arose, like a great mass, superior in proportion as it seemed to the whole burgh, the ancient Cathedral of Saint Magnus, of the heaviest order of Gothic architecture, but grand, solemn, and stately, the work of a distant age, and of a powerful hand. The quay, with the shipping, lent additional vivacity to the scene ; and not only the whole beautiful bay, which lies betwixt the promontories of Inganess and Quanterness, at the bottom of which Kirkwall is situated, but all the sea, so far as visible, and in particular the whole strait betwixt the island of Shapinsha and that called Pomona, or the Mainland, was covered and enlivened by a variety of boats and small vessels, freighted from distant islands to convey passengers of merchandise to the Fair of Saint Olla.

Having attained the point by which this fair and busy prospect was most completely commanded, each of the strangers, in seaman fashion, had recourse to his spy-glass, to assist the naked eye in considering the bay of Kirkwall, and the numerous vessels by which it was traversed. But the attention of the two companions seemed to be arrested by different objects. That of Bunce, or Altamont, as he chose to call himself, was rivetted to the armed sloop, where, conspicuous by her square rigging and length of beam, with the English Jack and pennon, which they had

* It is very curious that the grouse, plenty in Orkney as the text declares, should be totally unknown in the neighbouring archipelago of Zetland, which is only about sixty miles' distance, with the Fair Isle as a step between.

the precaution to keep flying, she lay among the merchant vessels, as distinguished from them by the trim neatness of her appearance, as a trained soldier amongst a crowd of clowns.

"Yonder she lies," said Bunce ; "I wish to God she was in the bay of Honduras—you Captain, on the quarter-deck, I your lieutenant, and Fletcher quarter-master, and fifty stout fellows under us—I should not wish to see these blasted heaths and rocks again for a while !—And Captain you shall soon be. The old brute Goffe gets drunk as a lord every day, swaggers, and shoots, and cuts among the crew ; and besides, he has quarrelled with the people here so damnably, that they will scarce let water or provisions go on board of us, and we expect an open breach every day."

As Bunce received no answer, he turned short round on his companion, and, perceiving his attention otherwise engaged, exclaimed,—"What the devil is the matter with you ? or what can you see in all that trumpery small craft, which is only loaded with stock-fish, and ling, and smoked geese, and tubs of butter that is worse than tallow ?— the cargoes of the whole lumped together would not be worth the flash of a pistol.—No, no, give me such a chase as we might see from the mast-head off the island of Trinidado. Your Don, rolling as deep in the water as a grampus, deep-loaden with rum, sugar, and bales of tobacco, and all the rest ingots, moidores, and gold dust, then set all sail, clear the deck, stand to quarters, up with the Jolly Roger* —we near her—we make her out to be well manned and armed"—

"Twenty guns on her lower deck," said Cleveland.

"Forty, if you will," retorted Bunce, "and we have but ten mounted— never mind. The Don blazes away—never mind yet, my brave lads—run her alongside, and on board with you—to work with your grenadoes, your cutlasses, pole-axes, and pistols—The Don cries Misericordia, and we share the cargo without *co licencio, Seignior.*"

"By my faith," said Cleveland," thou takest so kindly to the trade, that all the world may see that no honest man was spoiled when you were made a pirate. But you shall not prevail on me to go farther in the devil's road with you ; for you know yourself that what is got over his back is spent—you wot how. In a week, or a month at the most, the rum and the sugar are out, the bales of tobacco have become smoke, the moidores, ingots, and gold dust have got out of our hands, into those of the quiet, honest, conscientious folks who dwell at Port Royal and elsewhere— wink hard on our trade as long as we have money, but not a jot beyond. Then we have cold looks, and it may be a hint is given to the Judge Marshal ; for, when our pockets are worth nothing, our honest friends, rather than want, will make money upon our heads. Then comes a high gallows and a short halter, and so dies the Gentleman Rover. I tell thee, I will leave this trade ; and when I turn my glass from one of these barks and boats to another, there is not the worst of them which I would not row for life, rather than continue to be what I have been. These poor men make the sea a means of honest livelihood and friendly

* The pirates gave this name to the black flag, which, with many horrible devices to enhance its terrors, was their favourite ensign.

communication between shore and shore, for the mutual benefit of the inhabitants ; but we have made it a road to the ruin of others, and to our own destruction here and in eternity.—I am determined to turn honest man, and use this life no longer !"

"And where will your honesty take up its abode, if it please you ?" said Bunce.—"You have broken the laws of every nation, and the hand of the law will detect and crush you wherever you may take refuge.— Cleveland, I speak to you more seriously than I am wont to do. I have had my reflections, too, and they have been bad enough, though they have lasted but a few minutes, to spoil me weeks of joviality. But here is the matter,—what can we do but go on as we have done, unless we have a direct purpose of adorning the yard-arm ?"

"We may claim the benefit of the proclamation to those of our sort who come in and surrender," said Cleveland.

"Umph !" answered his companion, drily ; "the date of that day of grace has been for some time over, and they may take the penalty or grant the pardon at their pleasure. Were I you, I would not put my neck in such a venture."

"Why, others have been admitted but lately to favour, and why should not I ?" said Cleveland.

"Ay," replied his associate, "Harry Glasby and some others have been spared ; but Glasby did what was called good service, in betraying his comrades, and retaking the Jolly Fortune ; and that I think you would scorn, even to be revenged of the brute Goffe yonder."

"I would die a thousand times sooner," said Cleveland.

"I will be sworn for it," said Bunce ; "and the others were forecastle fellows—petty larceny rogues, scarce worth the hemp it would have cost to hang them. But your name has stood too high amongst the gentlemen of fortune for you to get off so easily. You are the prime buck of the herd, and will be marked accordingly."

"And why so, I pray you ?" said Cleveland ; "you know well enough my aim, Jack."

"Frederick, if you please," said Bunce.

"The devil take your folly !—Prithee keep thy wit, and let us be grave for a moment."

"For a moment—be it so," said Bunce ; "but I feel the spirit of Altamont coming fast upon me,—I have been a grave man for ten minutes already."

"Be so then for a little longer," said Cleveland ; "I know, Jack, that you really love me ; and, since we have come thus far in this talk, I will trust you entirely. Now tell me, why should I be refused the benefit of this gracious proclamation ? I have borne a rough outside, as thou knowest ; but, in time of need, I can show the number of lives which I have been the means of saving, the property which I have restored to those who owned it, when, without my intercession, it would have been wantonly destroyed. In short, Bunce, I can show"—

"That you were as gentle a thief as Robin Hood himself," said Bunce ; "and for that reason, I Fletcher, and the better sort among us, love you, as one who saves the character of us Gentlemen Rovers from utter

258

reprobation.—Well, suppose your pardon made out, what are you to do next ?—what class in society will receive you ?—with whom will you associate ? Old Drake, in Queen Bess's time, could plunder Peru and Mexico without a line of commission to show for it, and, blessed be her memory ! he was knighted for it on his return. And there was Hal Morgan, the Welshman, nearer our time, in the days of merry King Charles, brought all his gettings home, had his estate and his country-house, and who but he ? But that is all ended now—once a pirate, and an outcast for ever. The poor devil may go and live, shunned and despised by every one, in some obscure seaport, with such part of his guilty earnings as courtiers and clerks leave him—for pardons do not pass the seals for nothing;— and, when he takes his walk along the pier, if a stranger asks, who is the down-looking, swarthy, melancholy man, for whom all make way, as if he brought the plague in his person, the answer shall be, that is such a one, the pardoned pirate !—No honest man will speak to him, no woman of repute will give him her hand."

"Your picture is too highly coloured, Jack," said Cleveland, suddenly interrupting his friend ; "there are women—there is one at least that would be true to her lover, even if he were what you have described."

Bunce was silent for a moment, and looked fixedly at his friend. "By my soul !" he said, at length, "I begin to think myself a conjuror. Unlikely as it all was, I could not help suspecting from the beginning that there was a girl in the case. Why, this is worse than Prince Volscius in love, ha ! ha ! ha !"

"Laugh as you will," said Cleveland, "it is true ;—there is a maiden who is contented to love me, pirate as I am; and I will fairly own to you, Jack, that, though I have often at times detested our roving life, and myself for following it, yet I doubt if I could have found resolution to make the break which I have now resolved on, but for her sake."

"Why, then, God-a-mercy !" replied Bunce, "there is no speaking sense to a madman ; and love in one of your trade, Captain, is little better than lunacy. The girl must be a rare creature, for a wise man to risk hanging for her. But, hark ye, may she not be a little touched, as well as yourself ?—and is it not sympathy that has done it ? She cannot be one of our ordinary cockatrices, but a girl of conduct and character."

"Both are as undoubted as that she is the most beautiful and bewitching creature whom the eye ever opened upon," answered Cleveland.

"And she loves thee, knowing thee, most noble Captain, to be a commander among those gentlemen of fortune, whom the vulgar call pirates ?"

"Even so—I am assured of it," said Cleveland.

"Why, then," answered Bunce, "she is either mad in good earnest, as I said before, or she does not know what a pirate is."

"You are right in the last point," replied Cleveland. "She has been bred in such remote simplicity, and utter ignorance of what is evil, that she compares our occupation with that of the old Norsemen who swept sea and haven with their victorious galleys, established colonies, conquered countries, and took the name of Sea Kings."

"And a better one it is than that of pirate, and comes much to the same purpose, I dare say," said Bunce. But this must be a mettled wench !—why did you not bring her aboard ? methinks it was pity to baulk her fancy."

"And do you think," said Cleveland, "that I could so utterly play the part of a fallen spirit as to avail myself of her enthusiastic error, and bring an angel of beauty and innocence acquainted with such a hell as exists on board of yonder infernal ship of ours ?—I tell you, my friend, that, were all my former sins doubled in weight and in dye, such a villany would have outglared and outweighed them all."

"Why, then, Captain Cleveland," said his confidant, "methinks it was but a fool's part to come hither at all. The news must one day have gone abroad, that the celebrated pirate Captain Cleveland, with his good sloop the Revenge, had been lost on the Mainland of Zetland, and all hands perished ; so you would have remained hid both from friend and enemy, and might have married your pretty Zetlander, and converted your sash and scarf into fishing-nets, and your cutlass into a harpoon, and swept the seas for fish instead of florins."

"And so I had determined," said the Cpatain ; "but a Yagger, as they call them here, like a meddling, peddling thief as he is, brought down intelligence to Zetland of your lying here, and I was fain to set off, to see if you were the consort of whom I had told them, long before I thought of leaving the roving trade."

"Ay," said Bunce, "and so far you judged well. For, as you had heard of our being at Kirkwall, so we should have soon learned that you were at Zetland ; and some of us for friendship, some for hatred, and some for fear of your playing Harry Glasby upon us, would have come down for the purpose of getting you into our company again."

"I suspected as much," said the Captain, "and therefore was fain to decline the courteous offer of a friend, who proposed to bring me here about this time. Besides, Jack, I recollected, that, as you say, my pardon will not pass the seals without money, my own was waxing low—no wonder, thou knowest I was never a churl of it—and so"—

"And so you came for your share of the cobs ?" replied his friend—"It was wisely done ; and we shared honourably—so far Goffe has acted up to articles, it must be allowed. But keep your purpose of leaving him close in your breast, for I dread his playing you some dog's trick or other ; for he certainly thought himself sure of your share, and will hardly forgive your coming alive to disappoint him."

"I fear him not," said Cleveland, "and he knows that well. I would I were as well clear of the consequences of having been his comrade, as I hold myself to be of all those which may attend his ill-will. Another unhappy job I may be troubled with—I hurt a young fellow who has been my plague for some time, in an unhappy brawl that chanced the morning I left Zetland."

"Is he dead ?" asked Bunce ; "it is a more serious question here than it would be on the Grand Caimains or the Bahama Isles, where a brace or two of fellows may be shot in a morning, and no more heard of, or asked about them, than if they were so many wood-pigeons. But here it may be otherwise ; so I hope you have not made your friend immortal."

"I hope not," said the Captain, "though my anger has been fatal to those who have given me less provocation. To say the truth, I was sorry for the lad, notwithstanding, and especially as I was forced to leave him in mad keeping."

"In mad keeping ?" said Bunce, "why, what means that ?"

"You shall hear," replied his friend. "In the first place, you are to know, this young man came suddenly on me while I was trying to gain Minna's ear, for a private interview before I set sail, that I might explain my purpose to her. Now, to be broken in on by the accursed rudeness of this young fellow at such a moment"—

"The interruption deserved death," said Bunce, "by all the laws of love and honour !"

"A truce with your ends of plays, Jack, and listen one moment.—The brisk youth thought proper to retort, when I commanded him to be gone. I am not, thou knowest, very patient, and enforced my commands with a blow, which he returned as roundly. We struggled, till I became desirous that we should part at any rate, which I could only effect by a stroke of my poniard, which, according to old use, I have, thou knowest, always about me. I had scarce done this when I repented ; but there was no time to think of anything save escape and concealment, for if the house rose on me, I was lost ; as the fiery old man, who is head of the family, would have done justice on me had I been his brother. I took the body hastily on my shoulders to carry it down to the sea-shore, with the purpose of throwing it into a *riva*, as they call them, or chasm, of great depth, where it would have been long enough in being discovered. This done, I intended to jump into the boat which I had lying ready, and set sail for Kirkwall. But as I was walking hastily towards the beach with my burden, the poor young fellow groaned, and so apprised me that the wound had not been instantly fatal. I was by this time well concealed amongst the rocks, and, far from desiring to complete my crime, I laid the young man on the ground, and was doing what I could to staunch the blood, when suddenly an old woman stood before me. She was a person whom I had frequently seen while in Zetland, and to whom they ascribe the character of a sorceress, or, as the negroes say, an Obi woman. She demanded the wounded man of me, and I was too much pressed for time to hesitate in complying with her request. More she was about to say to me, when we heard the voice of a silly old man belonging to the family, singing at some distance. She then pressed her finger on her lip as a sign of secrecy, whistled very low, and a shapeless, deformed brute of a dwarf coming to her assistance, they carried the wounded man into one of the caverns with which the place abounds, and I got to my boat and to sea with all expedition. If that old hag be, as they say, connected with the King of the Air, she favoured me that morning with a turn of her calling ; for not even the West Indian tornadoes, which we have weathered together, made a wilder racket than the squall that drove me so far out of our course, that, without a pocket-compass, which I chanced to have about me, I should never have recovered the Fair Isle,

261

for which we ran, and where I found a brig which brought me to this place. But, whether the old woman meant me weal or woe, here we came at length in safety from the sea, and here I remain in doubts and difficulties of more kinds than one."

"Oh, the devil take the Sumburgh Head," said Bunce, "or whatever they call the rock that you knocked our clever little Revenge against !"

"Do not say *I* knocked her on the rock," said Cleveland ; "have I not told you fifty times, if the cowards had not taken to their boat, though I showed them the danger, and told them they would all be swamped, which happened the instant they cast off the painter, she would have been afloat at this moment ? Had they stood by me and the ship, their lives would have been saved ; had I gone with them, mine would have been lost ; who can say which is for the best ?"

"Well," replied his friend, "I know your case now, and can the better help and advise. I will be true to you, Clement, as the blade to the hilt ; but I cannot think that you should leave us. As the old Scottish song says, 'Wae's my heart that we should sunder !'—But come, you will aboard with us to-day, at any rate ?"

"I have no other place of refuge," said Cleveland with a sigh.

He then once more ran his eyes over the bay, directed his spy-glass upon several of the vessels which traversed its surface, in hopes, doubtless, of discerning the vessel of Magnus Troil, and then followed his companion down the hill in silence.

CHAPTER THIRTY-SECOND

I strive like to the vessel in the tide-way,
Which, lacking favouring breeze, hath not the power
To stem the powerful current.—Even so,
Resolving daily to forsake my vices,
Habits, strong circumstance, renew'd temptation,
Sweep me to sea again.—O heavenly breath,
Fill thou my sails, and aid the feeble vessel,
Which ne'er can reach the blessed port without thee !
TIS ODDS WHEN EVENS MEET

CLEVELAND, with his friend Bunce, descended the hill for a time in silence, until at length the latter renewed their conversation.

"You have taken this fellow's wound more on your conscience than you need, Captain—I have known you do more, and think less on't."

"Not on such slight provocation, Jack," replied Cleveland. "Besides, the lad saved my life ; and, say that I requited him the favour, still we should not have met on such evil terms ; but I trust that he may receive aid from that woman, who has certainly strange skill in simples."

"And over simpletons, Captain," said his friend, "in which class I must e'en put you down, if you think more on this subject. That you should be made a fool of by a young woman, why, it is many an honest man's case ;—but to puzzle your pate about the mummeries of an old one, is far

262

too great a folly to indulge a friend in. Talk to me of your Minna, since you so call her, as much as you will ; but you have no title to trouble your faithful squire-errant with your old mumping magician. And now here we are once more amongst the booths and tents, which these good folk are pitching—let us look, and see whether we may not find some fun and frolic amongst them. In merry England, now, you would have seen, on such an occasion, two or three bands of strollers, as many fire-eaters and conjurors, as many shows of wild beasts ; but amongst these grave folks, there is nothing but what savours of business and of commodity—no, not so much as a single squall from my merry gossip Punch and his rib Joan."

As Bunce thus spoke, Cleveland cast his eyes on some very gay clothes, which, with other articles, hung out upon one of the booths, that had a good deal more of ornament and exterior decoration than the rest. There was in front a small sign of canvas painted, announcing the variety of goods which the owner of the booth, Bryce Snailsfoot, had on sale, and the reasonable prices at which he proposed to offer them to the public. For the farther gratification of the spectator, the sign bore on the opposite side an emblematic device, resembling our first parents in their vegetable garments, with this legend—

Poor sinners whom the snake deceives
Are fain to cover them with leaves.
Zetland hath no leaves, 'tis true,
Because that trees are none, or few ;
But we have flax and taits of woo',
For linen cloth, and wadmaal blue ;
And we have many of foreign knacks
Of finer waft than woo' or flax.
Ye gallanty Lambmas lads,* appear,
And bring your Lambmas sisters here.
Bryce Snailsfoot spares not cost or care,
To pleasure every gentle pair.

While Cleveland was perusing these goodly rhymes, which brought to his mind Claud Halcro, to whom, as the poet laureate of the island, ready with his talent alike in the service of the great and small, they probably owed their origin, the worthy proprietor of the booth, having cast his eye upon him, began with hasty and trembling hand to remove some of the garments, which, as the sale did not commence till the ensuing day, he had exposed either for the purpose of airing them, or to excite the admiration of the spectators.

"By my word, Captain," whispered Bunce to Cleveland, "you must have had that fellow under your clutches one day, and he remembers one gripe of your talons and fears another. See how fast he is packing his wares out of sight, so soon as he set eyes on you."

* It was anciently a custom at Saint Olla's Fair at Kirkwall, that the young people of the lower class, and of either sex, associated in pairs for the period of the Fair, during which the couple were termed Lambmas brother and sister. It is easy to conceive that the exclusive familiarity arising out of this custom was liable to abuse, the rather that it is said little scandal was attached to the indiscretions which it occasioned.

"*His* wares !" said Cleveland, on looking more attentively at his proceedings : "by Heaven, they are my clothes which I left in a chest at Yarlshof when the Revenge was lost there—Why, Bryce Snailsfoot, thou thief, dog, and villain, what means this ? Have you not made enough of us by cheap buying and dear selling, that you have seized on my trunk and wearing apparel ?"

Bryce Snailsfoot, who probably would otherwise not have been willing to *see* his friend the Captain, was now, by the vivacity of his attack, obliged to pay attention to him. He first whispered to his little foot-page, by whom, as we have already noticed, he was usually attended, "Run to the town-council-house, yarto, and tell the provost and bailies they maun send some of their officers speedily, for here is like to be wild wark in the fair."

So having said, and having seconded his commands by a push on the shoulder of his messenger, which sent him spinning out of the shop as fast as heels could carry him, Bryce Snailsfoot turned to his old acquaintance, and, with that amplification of words and exaggeration of manner, which in Scotland is called "making a phrase," he ejaculated— "The Lord be gude to us ! the worthy Captain Cleveland, that we were all so grieved about, returned to relieve our hearts again ! Wat have my cheeks been for you" (here Bryce wiped his eyes), "and blithe am I now to see you restored to your sorrowing friends !"

"My sorrowing friends, you rascal !" said Cleveland ; "I will give you better cause for sorrow than ever you had on my account, if you do not tell me instantly where you stole all my clothes."

"Stole !" ejaculated Bryce, casting up his eyes : "now the Powers be gude to us !—the poor gentleman has lost his reason in that weary gale of wind."

"Why, you insolent rascal !" said Cleveland, grasping the cane which he carried, "do you think to bamboozle me with your impudence ? As you would have a whole head on your shoulders, and your bones in a whole skin, one minute longer, tell me where the devil you stole my wearing apparel ?"

Bryce Snailsfoot ejaculated once more a repetition of the word "Stole ! Now Heaven be gude to us !" but at the same time, conscious that the Captain was likely to be sudden in execution, cast an anxious look to the town, to see the loitering aid of the civil power advance to his rescue.

"I insist on an instant answer," said the Captain, with upraised weapon, "or else I will beat you to a mummy, and throw out all your frippery upon the common !"

Meanwhile, Master John Bunce, who considered the whole affair as an excellent good jest and not the worse one that it made Cleveland angry, seized hold of the Captain's arm, and, without any idea of ultimately preventing him from executing his threats, interfered just so much as was necessary to protract a discussion so amusing.

"Nay, let the honest man speak," he said, "messmate ; he has as fine a cozening face as ever stood on a knavish pair of shoulders, and his are the true flourishes of eloquence, in the course of which men snip the cloth an inch too short. Now, I wish you to consider that you are both of a trade—he measures bales by the yard, and you by the sword,—and so I will not have him chopped up till he has had a fair chase."

"You are a fool," said Cleveland, endeavouring to shake his friend off.—"Let me go ! for, by Heaven, I will be foul of him !"

"Hold him fast," said the pedlar, "good dear merry gentleman, hold him fast !"

"Then say something for yourself," said Bunce ; "use your gob-box, man ; patter away, or, by my soul, I will let him loose on you !"

"He says I stole these goods," said Bryce, who now saw himself run so close, that pleading to the charge became inevitable. "Now, how could I steal them, when they are mine by fair and lawful purchase ?"

"Purchase ! you beggarly vagrant !" said Cleveland ; "from whom did you dare to buy my clothes ? or who had the impudence to sell them ?"

"Just that worthy professor, Mrs. Swertha, the housekeeper at Yarlshof, who acted as your executor," said the pedlar ; "and a grieved heart she had."

"And so she was resolved to make a heavy pocket of it, I suppose," said the Captain ; "but how did she dare to sell the things left in her charge ?"

"Why she acted all for the best, good woman !" said the pedlar, anxious to protract the discussion until the arrival of succours ; "and if you will but hear reason, I am ready to account with you for the chest and all that it holds."

"Speak out then, and let us have none of thy damnable evasions," said Captain Cleveland ; "if you show ever so little purpose of being somewhat honest for once in thy life, I will not beat thee."

"Why you see, noble Captain," said the pedlar,—and then muttered to himself, "plague on Pate Paterson's cripple knee, they will be waiting for him, hirpling useless body !" then resumed aloud—"The country, ye see, is in great perplexity,—great perplexity, indeed—much perplexity, truly. There was your honour missing, that was loved by great and small—clean missing—nowhere to be heard of—a lost man—umquhile—dead—defunct !"

"You shall find me alive to your cost, you scoundrel !" said the irritated Captain.

"Weel, but take patience,—ye will not hear a body speak," said the Yagger.— "Then there was the lad Mordaunt Mertoun"—

"Ha !" said the Captain, "what of him ?"

"Cannot be heard of," said the pedlar ; "clean and clear tint,—a gone youth ;—fallen, it is thought, from the craig into the sea—he was aye venturous. I have had dealings with him for furs and feathers, whilk he swapped against powder and shot, and the like ; and now he has worn out from among us—clean retired—utterly vanished, like the last puff of an auld wife's tobacco pipe."

"But what is all this to the Captain's clothes, my dear friend ?" said Bunce ; "I must presently beat you myself unless you come to the point."

"Weel, weel,—patience, patience," said Bryce, waving his hand ; "you will get all time enough. Weel, there are two folks gane, as I said, forbye the distress at Burgh Westra about Mistress Minna's sad ailment"—

"Bring not *her* into your buffoonery, sirrah," said Cleveland, in a tone of anger, not so loud, but far deeper and more concentrated than he had hitherto used ; "for, if you name her with less than reverence, I will crop the ears out of your head, and make you swallow them on the spot !"

"He, he, he !" faintly laughed the Yagger ; "that were a pleasant jest ! you are pleased to be witty. But to say naething of Burgh Westra, there is the carle at Yarlshof, he that was the auld Mertoun, Mordaunt's father, whom men thought as fast bound to be the place he dwelt in as the Sumburgh Head itsell, naething maun serve him but he is lost as weel as the lave about whom I have spoken. And there's Magnus Troil (wi' favour be he named) taking horse ; and there is pleasant Maister Claud Halcro taking boat, whilk he steers worst of any man in Zetland, his head running on rambling rhymes ; and the Factor body is on the stir—the Scots Factor,—him that is aye speaking of dykes and delving, and such unprofitable wark, which has naething of merchandise in it, and he is on the lang trot, too ; so that ye might say, upon a manner, the tae half of the Mainland of Zetland is lost, and the other is running to and fro seeking it—awfu' times !"

Captain Cleveland had subdued his passion, and listened to this tirade of the worthy man of merchandise, with impatience indeed, yet not without the hope of hearing something that might concern him. But his companion was now become impatient in his turn :—"The clothes !" he exclaimed, "the clothes, the clothes, the clothes !" accompanying each repetition of the words with a flourish of his cane, the dexterity of which consisted in coming mighty near the Yagger's ears without actually touching them.

The Yagger, shrinking from each of these demonstrations, continued to exclaim, "Nay, sir—good sir—worthy sir—for the clothes—I found the worthy dame in great distress on account of her old maister, and on account of her young maister, and on account of worthy Captain Cleveland ; and because of the distress of the worthy Fowd's family, and the trouble of the great Fowd himself,—and because of the Factor, and in respect of Claud Halcro, and on other accounts and respects. Also we mingled our sorrows and our tears with a bottle, as the holy text hath it, and called in the Ranzelman to our council, a worthy man, Niel Ronaldson by name, who hath a good reputation."

Here another flourish of the cane came so very near that it partly touched his ear. The Yagger started back, and the truth, or that which he desired should be considered as such, bolted from him without more circumlocution ; as a cork, after much unnecessary buzzing and fizzing, springs forth from a bottle of spruce beer.

"In brief, what the deil mair would you have of it ?—the woman sold me the kist of clothes—they are mine by purchase, and that is what I will live and die upon."

"In other words," said Cleveland, "this greedy old hag had the impudence to sell what was none of hers ; and you, honest Bryce Snailsfoot, had the assurance to be the purchaser ?"

"Ou dear, Captain," said the conscientious pedlar, "what wad ye hae had twa poor folk to do ? There was yoursell gane that aught the things, and Maister Mordaunt was gane that had them in keeping, and the things were but damply put up, where they were rotting with moth and mould, and"—

"And so this old thief sold them, and you bought them, I suppose, just to keep them from spoiling ?" said Cleveland.

"Weel then," said the merchant, "I'm thinking, noble Captain, that wad be just the gate of it."

"Well then, hark ye, you impudent scoundrel," said the Captain. "I do not wish to dirty my fingers with you, or to make any disturbance in this place"—

"Good reason for that, Captain—aha !" said the Yagger, slyly.

"I will break your bones if you speak another word," replied Cleveland. "Take notice—I offer you fair terms—give me back the black leathern pocket-book with the lock upon it, and the purse with the doubloons, with some few of the clothes I want, and keep the rest in the devil's name !"

"Doubloons ! ! !"—exclaimed the Yagger, with an exaltation of voice intended to indicate the utmost extremity of surprise,—"What do I ken of doubloons ? my dealing was for doublets, and not for doubloons—If there were doubloons in the kist, doubtless Swerta will have them for safe keeping for your honour—the damp wouldna harm the gold, ye ken."

"Give me back my pocket-book and my goods, you rascally thief," said Cleveland, "or without a word more I will beat your brains out !"

The wily Yagger, casting eye around him, saw that succour was near, in the shape of a party of officers, six in number ; for several rencontres with the crew of the pirate had taught the magistrates of Kirkwall to strengthen their police parties when these strangers were in question.

"Ye had better keep the *thief* to suit yoursell, honoured Captain," said the Yagger, imboldened by the approach of the civil power ; "for wha kens how a' these fine goods and bonny-dies were come by ?"

"This was uttered with such provoking slyness in look and tone, that Cleveland made no further delay, but seizing upon the Yagger by the collar, dragged him over his temporary counter, which was, with all the goods displayed thereon, over-set in the scuffle ; and, holding him with one hand, inflicted on him with the other a severe beating with his cane. All this was done so suddenly and with such energy, that Bryce Snailsfoot, though rather a stout man, was totally surprised by the vivacity of the attack, and made scarce any other effort at extricating himself than by roaring for assistance like a bull-calf. The "loitering aid" having at length come up, the officers made an effort to seize on Cleveland, and by their united exertions succeeded in compelling him to quit hold of the pedlar, in order to defend himself from their assault. This he did with infinite strength, resolution, and dexterity, being at the same time well seconded by his friend Jack Bunce, who had seen with glee the drubbing sustained by the pedlar, and now combated tightly to save his companion from the consequences. But, as there had been for some time a growing feud between the townspeople and the crew of the Rover, the former, provoked by the insolent deportment of the seamen, had resolved to stand by each other, and to aid the civil power upon such occasions of riot as should occur in future ; and so many assistants came up to the rescue of the constables, that Cleveland, after fighting most manfully, was at length brought to the ground and made prisoner. His more fortunate companion had escaped by speed of foot, as soon as he saw that the day must needs be determined against them.

The proud heart of Cleveland, which,even in its perversion, had in its feelings something of original nobleness, was like to burst, when he felt himself borne down in this unworthy brawl—dragged into the town as a prisoner, and hurried through the streets towards the Council-house, where the magistrates of the burgh were then seated in council. The probability of imprisonment, with all its consequences, rushed also upon his mind, and he cursed a hundred times the folly which had not rather submitted to the pedlar's knavery, than involved him in so perilous an embarrassment.

But, just as they approached the door of the Council-house, which is situated in the middle of the little town, the face of matters was suddenly changed by a new and unexpected incident.

Bunce, who had designed, by his precipitate retreat, to serve as well his friend as himself, had hied him to the haven, where the boat of the Rover was then lying, and called the cockswain and boat's crew to the assistance of Cleveland. They now appeared on the scene—fierce desperadoes, as became their calling, with features bronzed by the tropical sun under which they had pursued it. They rushed at once amongst the crowd, laying about them with their stretchers ; and, forcing their way up to Cleveland, speedily delivered him from the hands of the officers, who were totally unprepared to resist an attack so furious and so sudden, and carried him off in triumph towards the quay, two or three of their number facing about from time to time to keep back the crowd, whose efforts to recover the prisoner were the less violent, that most of the seamen were armed with pistols and cutlasses, as well as with the less lethal weapons which alone they had as yet made use of.

They gained their boat in safety, and jumped into it, carrying along with them Cleveland, to whom circumstances seemed to offer no other refuge, and pushed off for their vessel, singing in chorus to their oars an old ditty, of which the natives of Kirkwall could only hear the first stanza :—

Robin Rover
    Said to his crew
Up with the black flag,
    Down with the blue !—
Fire on the main-top,
    Fire on the bow,
Fire on the gun-deck
    Fire down below!

The wild chorus of their voices was heard long after the words ceased to be intelligible.—And thus was the pirate Cleveland again thrown almost involuntarily amongst those desperate associates, from whom he had so often resolved to detach himself.

CHAPTER THIRTY-THIRD

Parental love, my friend, has power o'er wisdom,
And is the charm, which, like the falconer's lure,
Can bring from heaven the highest soaring spirits.—
So, when famed Prosper doff'd his magic robe,
It was Miranda pluck'd it from his shoulders.

OLD PLAY

OUR wandering narrative must now return to Mordaunt Mertoun.—We left him in the perilous condition of one who has received a severe wound, and we now find him in the situation of a convalescent—pale, indeed, and feeble, from the loss of much blood, and the effects of a fever which had followed the injury, but so far only occasioned a great effusion of blood, without touching any vital part, and was now well-nigh healed ; so efficacious were the vulnerary plants and salves with which it had been treated by the sage Norna of Fitful Head.

The matron and her patient now sat together in a dwelling in a remote island. He had been transported during his illness, and ere he had perfect consciousness, first to her singular habitation near Fitful Head, and thence to her present abode, by one of the fishing boats in the station of Burgh Westra. For such was the command possessed by Norna over the superstitious character of her countrymen, that she never failed to find faithful agents to execute her commands, whatever these happened to be ; and, as her orders were generally given under injunctions of the strictest secrecy, men reciprocally wondered at occurrences, which had in fact been produced by their own agency, and that of their neighbours, and in which, had they communicated freely with each other, no shadow of the marvellous would have remained.

Mordaunt was now seated by the fire, in an apartment indifferently well furnished, having a book in his hand, which he looked upon from time to time with signs of ennui and impatience ; feelings which at length so far overcame him, that flinging the volume on the table, he fixed his eyes on the fire, and assumed the attitude of one who is engaged in unpleasant meditation.

Norna, who sat opposite to him, and appeared busy in the composition of some drug or unguent, anxiously left her seat, and, approaching Mordaunt, felt his pulse, making at the same time the most affectionate inquiries whether he felt any sudden pain, and where it was seated. The manner in which Mordaunt replied to these earnest inquiries, although worded so as to express gratitude for her kindness, while he disclaimed any feeling of indisposition, did not seem to give satisfaction to the Pythoness.

"Ungrateful boy !" she said, "for whom I have done so much ; you whom I have rescued, by my power and skill, from the very gates of death,—are you already so weary of me that you cannot refrain from

269

showing how desirous you are to spend, at a distance from me, the very first intelligent days of the life which I have restored you ?"

"You do me injustice, my kind preserver," replied Mordaunt ; "I am not tired of your society ; but I have duties which recall me to ordinary life."

"Duties !" repeated Norna ; "and what duties can or ought to interfere with the gratitude which you owe to me ?—Duties ! Your thoughts are on the use of your gun, or on clambering among the rocks in quest of sea-fowl. For these exercises your strength doth not yet fit you : and yet these are the duties to which you are so anxious to return !"

"Not so, my good and kind mistress," said Mordaunt.—"To name one duty, out of many, which makes me seek to leave you, now that my strength permits, let me mention that of a son to his father."

"To your father !" said Norna, with a laugh that had something in it almost frantic. "Oh ! you know not how we can, in these islands, at once cancel such duties ! And, for your father," she added, proceeding more calmly, "what has he done for you to deserve the regard and duty you speak of ?—Is he not the same, who, as you have long since told me, left you for so many years poorly nourished among strangers, without inquiring whether you were alive or dead, and only sending, from time to time, supplies in such fashion as men relieve the leprous wretch to whom they fling alms from a distance ? And, in these later years, when he had made you the companion of his misery, he has been by starts your pedagogue, by starts your tormentor, but never, Mordaunt, never your father."

"Something of truth there is in what you say," replied Mordaunt : "My father is not fond ; but he is, and has ever been, effectively kind. Men have not their affections in their power, and it is a child's duty to be grateful for the benefits which he receives, even when coldly bestowed. My father has conferred instruction on me, and I am convinced he loves me. He is unfortunate ; and, even if he loved me not"—

"And he does *not* love you," said Norna, hastily ; "he never loved anything, or any one, save himself. He is unfortunate, but well are his misfortunes deserved.—O Mordaunt, you have one parent only,—one parent, who loves you as the drops of the heart-blood !"

"I know I have but one parent," replied Mordaunt ; "my mother has been long dead.—But your words contradict each other."

"They do not—they do not," said Norna, in a paroxysm of the deepest feeling ; "you have but one parent. Your unhappy mother is not dead—I would to God that she were !—but she is not dead. Thy mother is the only parent that loves thee ; and I—I, Mordaunt," throwing herself on his neck, "am that most unhappy—yet most happy mother."

She closed him in a strict and convulsive embrace ; and tears, the first, perhaps, which she had shed for many years, burst in torrents as she sobbed on his neck. Astonished at what he heard, felt, and saw,—moved by the excess of her agitation, yet disposed to ascribe this burst of passion to insanity,—Mordaunt vainly endeavoured to tranquillise the mind of this extraordinary person.

"Ungrateful boy !" she said, "who but a mother would have watched

270

over thee as I have watched ? From the instant I saw thy father, when he little thought by whom he was observed, a space now many years back, I knew him well ; and, under his charge, I saw you, then a stripling,— while Nature, speaking loud in my bosom, assured me, thou wert blood of my blood, and bone of my bone. Think how often you have wondered to see me, when least expected, in your places of pastime and resort ! Think how often my eye has watched you on the giddy precipices, and muttered those charms which subdue the evil demons, who show themselves to the climber on the giddiest point of his path, and force him to quit his hold! Did I not hang around thy neck, in pledge of thy safety, that chain of gold, which an Elfin King gave to the founder of our race ? Would I have given that dear gift to any but the son of my bosom ?—Mordaunt, my power has done that for thee that a mere mortal mother would dread to think of. I have conjured the Mermaid at midnight, that thy bark might be prosperous on the Haaf ! I have hushed the winds, and navies have flapped their empty sails against the mast in inactivity, that you might safely indulge your sport upon the crags !"

Mordaunt, perceiving that she was growing yet wilder in her talk, endeavoured to frame an answer which should be at once indulgent, soothing, and calculated to allay the rising warmth of her imagination.

"Dear Norna," he said, "I have indeed many reasons to call you mother, who have bestowed so many benefits upon me ; and from me you shall ever receive the affection and duty of a child. But the chain you mentioned, it has vanished from my neck—I have not seen it since the ruffian stabbed me."

"Alas ! and can you think of it at this moment ?" said Norna, in a sorrowful accent.—"But be it so ;—and know, it was I took it from thy neck, and tied it around the neck of her who is dearest to you ; in token that the union betwixt you, which has been the only earthly wish which I have had the power to form, shall yet, even yet, be accomplished—ay, although hell should open to forbid the banns !"

"Alas !" said Mordaunt, with a sigh, "you remember not the difference betwixt our situation—her father is wealthy and of ancient birth."

"Not more wealthy than will be the heir of Norna of Fitful Head," answered the Pythoness—"not of better or more ancient blood than that which flows in thy veins, derived from thy mother, the descendant of the same Yarls and Sea-kings from whom Magnus boasts his origin.—Or dost thou think, like the pedant and fanatic strangers who have come amongst us, that thy blood is dishonoured because my union with thy father did not receive the sanction of a priest ?—Know, that we were wedded after the ancient manner of the Norse—our hands were clasped within the circle of Odin,* with such deep vows of eternal fidelity, as even the laws of usurping Scots would have sanctioned as equivalent to a blessing before the altar. To the offspring of such a union, Magnus has nought to object. It was weak—it was criminal on my part, but it conveyed no infamy to the birth of my son."

The composed and collected manner in which Norna argued these points began to impose upon Mordaunt an incipient belief in the truth

* See an explanation of this promise, Note P.

271

of what she said ; and, indeed, she added so many circumstances, satisfactorily and rationally connected with each other, as seemed to confute the notion that her story was altogether the delusion of that insanity which sometimes showed itself in her speech and actions. A thousand confused ideas rushed upon him, when he supposed it possible that the unhappy person before him might actually have a right to claim from him the respect and affection due to a parent from a son. He could only surmount them by turning his mind to a different, and scarce less interesting topic, resolving within himself to take time for further inquiry and mature consideration, ere he either rejected or admitted the claim which Norna preferred upon his affection and duty. His benefactress, at least, she undoubtedly was, and he could not err in paying her, as such, the respect and attention due from a son to a mother ; and so far, therefore, he might gratify Norna without otherwise standing committed.

"And do you really think, my mother,—since so you bid me term you,"—said Mordaunt, "that the proud Magnus Troil may, by any inducement, be prevailed upon to relinquish the angry feelings which he has of late adopted towards me, and to permit my addresses to his daughter Brenda ?"

"Brenda ?" repeated Norna—"who talks of Brenda ?—It is of Minna that I spoke to you."

"But it was Brenda that I thought," replied Mordaunt, "of her that I now think, and of her alone that I will ever think."

"Impossible, my son !" replied Norna. "You cannot be so dull of heart, so poor of spirit, as to prefer the idle mirth and housewife simplicity of the younger sister, to the deep feeling and high mind of the noble-spirited Minna ? Who would stoop to gather the lowly violet, that might have the rose for stretching out his hand ?"

"Some think the lowliest flowers are the sweetest," replied Mordaunt, "and in that faith will I live and die."

"You dare not tell me so !" answered Norna, fiercely ; then, instantly changing her tone, and taking his hand in the most affectionate manner, she proceeded :—"You must not—you will not tell me so, my dear son— you will not break a mother's heart in the very first hour in which she has embraced her child !—Nay, do not answer, but hear me. You must wed Minna—I have bound around her neck a fatal amulet, on which the happiness of both depends. The labours of my life have for years had this direction. Thus it must be, and not otherwise—Minna must be the bride of my son !"

"But is not Brenda equally near, equally dear to you ?" replied Mordaunt.

"As near in blood," said Norna, "but not so dear, no, not half so dear, in affection. Minna's mild, yet high and contemplative spirit, renders her a companion meet for one, whose ways, like mine, are beyond the ordinary paths of this world. Brenda is a thing of common and ordinary life, an idle laugher and scoffer, who would level art with ignorance, and reduce power to weakness, by disbelieving and turning into ridicule whatever is beyond the grasp of her shallow intellect."

"She is, indeed," answered Mordaunt, "neither superstitious nor enthusiastic, and I love her the better for it. Remember also, my mother, that she returns my affection, and that Minna, if she loves any one, loves the stranger Cleveland."

"She does not—she dares not," answered Norna, "nor dares he pursue her farther. I told him, when first he came to Burgh Westra, that I destined her for you."

"And to that rash annunciation," said Mordaunt, "I owe this man's persevering enmity—my wound, and well-nigh the loss of my life. See, my mother, to what point your intrigues have already conducted us, and, in Heaven's name, prosecute them no farther!"

It semed as if this reproach struck Norna with the force, at once, and vivacity of lightning ; for she struck her forehead with her hand, and seemed about to drop from her seat. Mordaunt, greatly shocked, hastened to catch her in his arms, and, though scarce knowing what to say, attempted to utter some incoherent expressions.

"Spare me, Heaven, spare me !" were the first words which she muttered ; "do not let my crime be avenged by his means !—Yes, young man," she said, after a pause, "you have pressed that upon me, which, if it be truth, I cannot believe, and yet continue to live !"

Mordaunt in vain endeavoured to interrupt her with protestations of his ignorance how he had offended or grieved her, and of his extreme regret that he had unintentionally done either. She proceeded, while her voice trembled wildly, with vehemence.

"Yes ! you have touched on that dark suspicion which poisons the consciousness of my power,—the sole boon which was given me in exchange for innocence and for peace of mind ! Your voice joins that of the demon which, even while the elements confess me their mistress, whispers to me, 'Norna, this is but delusion—your power rests but in the idle belief of the ignorant, supported by a thousand petty artifices of your own.'—This is what Brenda says—this is what you would say ; and false, scandalously false, as it is, there are rebellious thoughts in this wild brain of mine" (touching her forehead with her finger as she spoke), "that, like an insurrection in an invaded country, arise to take part against their distressed sovereign.—Spare me, my son !" she continued in a voice of supplication, "spare me !—the sovereignty of which your words would deprive me, is no enviable exaltation. Few would covet to rule over gibbering ghosts, and howling winds, and raging currents. My throne is a cloud, my sceptre a meteor, my realm is only peopled with fantasies ; but I must either cease to be, or continue to be the mightiest as well as the most miserable of beings !*

"Do not speak thus mournfully, my dear and unhappy benefactress," said Mordaunt, much affected ; "I will think of your power whatever you would have me believe. But, for your own sake, view the matter otherwise. Turn your thoughts from such agitating and mystical studies—from such wild subjects of contemplation, into another and a better channel. Life will again have charms, and religion will have comforts for you."

* Note S. Character of Norna.

She listened to him with some composure, as if she weighed his counsel, and desired to be guided by it ; but, as he ended, she shook her head and exclaimed—

"It cannot be. I must remain the dreaded—the mystical—the Reimkennar—the controller of the elements, or I must be no more ! I have no alternative, no middle station. My post must be high on yon lofty headland, where never stood human foot save mine—or I must sleep at the bottom of the unfathomable ocean, its white billows booming over my senseless corpse. The parricide shall never also be denounced as the impostor !"

"The parricide !" echoed Mordaunt, stepping back in horror.

"Yes, my son !" answered Norna, with a stern composure, even more frightful than her former impetuosity, "within these fatal walls my father met his death by my means. In yonder chamber was he found a livid and lifeless corpse. Beware of filial disobedience, for such are its fruits !"

So saying, she arose and left the apartment, where Mordaunt remained alone to meditate at leisure upon the extraordinary communication which he had received. He himself had been taught by his father a disbelief in the ordinary superstitions of Zetland ; and he now saw that Norna, however ingenious in duping others, could not altogether impose on herself. This was a strong cuircumstance in favour of her sanity of intellect ; but, on the other hand, her imputing to herself the guilt of parricide seemed so wild and improbable, as, in Mordaunt's opinion, to throw much doubt upon her other assertions.

He had leisure enough to make up his mind on these particulars, for no one approached the solitary dwelling, of which Norna, her dwarf, and he himself, were the sole inhabitants. The Hoy island, in which it stood, is rude, bold, and lofty, consisting entirely of three hills—or rather one huge mountain divided into three summits, with the chasms, rents, and valleys, which descend from its summit to the sea, while its crest, rising to great height, and shivered into rocks which seem almost inaccessible, intercepts the mists as they drive from the Atlantic, and, often obscured from the human eye, forms the dark and unmolested retreat of hawks, eagles, and other birds of prey.*

The soil of the island is wet, mossy, cold, and unproductive, presenting a sterile and desolate appearance, excepting where the sides of small rivulets, of mountain ravines, are fringed with dwarf bushes of birch, hazel, and wild currant, some of them so tall as to be denominated trees in that bleak and bare country.

But the view of the sea-beach, which was Mordaunt's favourite walk, when his convalescent state began to permit him to take exercise, had charms which compensated the wild appearance of the interior. A broad and beautiful sound, or strait, divides this lonely and mountainous island from Pomona, and in the centre of that sound lies, like a tablet composed of emerald, the beautiful and verdant little island of Græmsay. On the distant Mainland is seen the town or village of Stromness, the excellence of whose haven is generally evinced by a considerable number of shipping in the roadstead, and, from the bay growing

* Note T. Birds of prey.

274

narrower, and lessening as it recedes, runs inland into Pomona, where its tide fills the fine sheet of water called the Loch of Stennis.

On this beach Mordaunt was wont to wander for hours, with an eye not insensible to the beauties of the view, though his thoughts were agitated with the most embarrassing meditations on his own situation. He was resolved to leave the island as soon as the establishment of his health should permit him to travel ; yet gratitude to Norna, of whom he was at least the adopted, if not the real son, would not allow him to depart without her permission, even if he could obtain means of conveyance, of which he saw little possibility. It was only by importunity that he extorted from his hostess a promise, that, if he would consent to regulate his motions according to her directions, she would herself convey him to the capital of the Orkney Islands, when the approaching Fair of Saint Olla should take place there.

CHAPTER THIRTY-FOURTH

Hark to the insult loud, the bitter sneer,
The fierce threat answering to the brutal jeer ;
Oaths fly like pistol-shots, and vengeful words
Clash with each other like conflicting swords.—
The robber's quarrel by such sounds is shown,
And true men have some chance to gain their own.
CAPTIVITY, A POEM

WHEN Cleveland, borne off in triumph from his assailants in Kirkwall, found himself once more on board the pirate vessel, his arrival was hailed with hearty cheers by a considerable part of the crew, who rushed to shake hands with him, and offer their congratulations on his return ; for the situation of a Bucanier Captain raised him very little above the level with the lowest of his crew, who, in all social intercourse, claimed the privilege of being his equal.

When his faction, for so these clamorous friends might be termed, had expressed their own greetings, they hurried Cleveland forward to the stern, where Goffe, their present commander, was seated on a gun, listening in a sullen and discontented manner to the shout which announced Cleveland's welcome. He was a man betwixt forty and fifty, rather under the middle size, but so very strongly made, that his crew used to compare him to a sixty-four cut down. Black-haired, bull-necked, and beetle-browed, his clumsy strength and ferocious countenance contrasted strongly with the manly figure and open countenance of Cleveland, in which even the practice of his atrocious profession had not been able to eradicate a natural grace of motion and generosity of expression. The two piratical Captains looked upon each other for some time in silence, while the partisans of each gathered around him. The elder part of the crew were the principal adherents of Goffe, while the young fellows, amongst whom Jack Bunce was a principal leader and agitator, were in general attached to Cleveland.

At length Goffe broke silence. "You are welcome aboard, Captain Cleveland.—Smash my taffrail ! I suppose you think yourself commodore yet ! but that was over, by G——, when you lost your ship, and be d—d !"

And here, once for all, we may take notice, that it was the gracious custom of this commander to mix his words and oaths in nearly equal proportions, which he was wont to call *shotting* his discourse. As we delight not, however, in the discharge of such artillery, we shall only indicate by a space like this —— the places in which these expletives occurred ; and thus, if the reader will pardon a very poor pun, we will reduce Captain Goffe's volley of sharp shot into an explosion of blank cartridges. To his insinuations that he was come on board to assume the chief command, Cleveland replied, that he neither desired nor would accept any such promotion, but would only ask Captain Goffe for a cast of the boat, to put him ashore in one of the other islands, as he had no wish either to command Goffe, or to remain in a vessel under his orders.

"And why not under my orders, brother ?" demanded Goffe, very austerely ; "—— —— —— are you too good a man, —— —— —— with your cheese-toaster and your gib there, —— —— to serve under my orders, and be d——d to you, where there are so many gentlemen that are elder and better seamen than yourself ?"

"I wonder which of these capital seamen it was," said Cleveland coolly, "that laid the ship under the fire of yon six-gun battery, that could blow her out of the water, if they had a mind, before you could either cut or slip ? Elder and better sailors than I may like to serve under such a lubber, but I beg to be excused for my own share, Captain—that's all I have got to tell you."

"By G——, I think you are both mad !" said Hawkins the boatswain ; "a meeting with sword and pistol may be devilish good fun in its way, when no better is to be had ; but who the devil that had common sense, amongst a set of gentlemen in our condition, would fall a-quarrelling with each other, to let these duck-winged, web-footed islanders have a chance of knocking us all upon the head ?"

"Well said, old Hawkins !" said Derrick the quarter-master, who was an officer of very considerable importance among these rovers ; "I say, if the two captains won't agree to live together quietly, and club both heart and head to defend the vessel, why, d——n me, depose them both, say I, and choose another in their stead !"

"Meaning yourself, I suppose, Master Quarter-Master !" said Jack Bunce ; "but that cock won't fight. He that is to command gentlemen, should be a gentleman himself, I think ; and I give my vote for Captain Cleveland, as spirited and as gentleman-like a man as ever daffed the world aside, and bid it pass !"

"What ! *you* call yourself a gentleman, I warrant !" retorted Derrick ; "why —— your eyes ! a tailor would make a better out of the worst suit of rags in your strolling wardrobe !—It is a shame for men of spirit to have such a Jack-a-dandy scarecrow on board !"

Jack Bunce was so incensed at these base comparisons, that, without more ado, he laid his hand on his sword. The carpenter, however, and boatswain, interfered, the former brandishing his broad axe, and swearing he would put the skull of the first who should strike a blow past clouting, and the latter reminding them, that by their articles, all quarrelling, striking, or more especially fighting on board, was strictly prohibited ; and that, if any gentlemen had a quarrel to settle, they were to go ashore, and decide it with cutlass and pistol in presence of two of their messmates.

"I have no quarrel with any one, — — — !" said Goffe, sullenly ; "Captain Cleveland has wandered about among the islands here, amusing himself, — — — ! and we have wasted our time and property in waiting for him, when we might have been adding twenty or thirty thousand dollars to the stock-purse. However, if it pleases the rest of the gentlemen-adventurers, — — — ! why, I shall not grumble about it."

"I propose," said the boatswain, "that there should be a general council called in the great cabin, according to our articles, that we may consider what course we are to hold in this matter."

A general assent followed the boatswain's proposal ; for every one found his own account in these general councils, in which each of the rovers had a free vote. By far the greater part of the crew only valued this franchise, as it allowed them, upon such solemn occasions, an unlimited quantity of liquor—a right which they failed not to exercise to the uttermost, by way of aiding their deliberations. But a few amongst the adventurers, who united some degree of judgment with the daring and profligate character of their profession, were wont, at such periods, to limit themselves within the bounds of comparative sobriety, and by these, under the apparent form of a vote of the general council, all things of moment relating to the voyage and undertakings of the pirates were in fact determined. The rest of the crew, when they recovered from their intoxication, were easily persuaded that the resolution adopted had been the legitimate effort of the combined wisdom of the whole senate.

Upon the present occasion the debauch had proceeded until the greater part of the crew were, as usual, displaying inebriation in all its most brutal and disgraceful shapes—swearing empty and unmeaning oaths—venting the most horrid imprecations in the mere gaiety of their heart—singing songs, the ribaldry of which was only equalled by their profaneness ; and, from the middle of this earthly hell, the two captains, together with one or two of their principal adherents, as also the carpenter and boatswain, who always took a lead on such occasions, had drawn together into a pandemonium, or privy council of their own, to consider what was to be done ; for, as the boatswain metaphorically observed, they were in a narrow channel, and behoved to keep sounding the tideway.

When they began their consulatations, the friends of Goffe remarked, to their great displeasure, that he had not observed the wholesome rule to which we have just alluded ; but that, in endeavouring to drown his mortification at the sudden appearance of Cleveland, and the reception he met with from the crew, the elder Captain had not been able to do so without overflowing his reason at the same time. His natural sullen taciturnity had prevented this from being observed until the council began its deliberations, when it proved impossible to hide it.

The first person who spoke was Cleveland, who said, that so far from wishing the command of the vessel, he desired no favour at any one's hand, except to land him upon some island or holm at a distance from Kirkwall, and leave him to shift for himself.

The boatswain remonstrated strongly against this resolution.

"The lads," he said, "all knew Cleveland, and could trust his seamanship, as well as his courage ; besides, he never let the grog get quite uppermost, and was always in proper trim, either to sail the ship, or to fight the ship, whereby she was never without some one to keep her course when he was on board.—And as for the noble Captain Goffe," continued the mediator, "he is as stout a heart as ever broke biscuit, and that I will uphold him ; but then, when he has his grog aboard—I speak to his face—he is so d——d funny with his cranks and his jests, that there is no living with him. You all remember how nigh he had run the ship on that cursed Horse of Copinsha, as they call it, just by way of frolic ; and then you know how he fired off his pistol under the table, when we were at the great council, and shot Jack Jenkins in the knee, and cost the poor devil his leg, with his pleasantry."*

"Jack Jenkins was not a chip the worse," said the carpenter ; "I took the leg off with my saw as well as any loblolly-boy in the land could have done—heated my broad axe, and seared the stump—ay, by—— ! and made a jury-leg that he shambles about with as well as ever he did—for Jack could never cut a feather."†

"You are a clever fellow, carpenter," replied the boatswain, "a d——d clever fellow ! but I had rather you tried your saw and red-hot axe upon the ship's knee timbers than on mine, sink me !—But that here is not the case—The question is, if we shall part with Captain Cleveland here, who is a man of thought and action, whereby it is my belief it would be heaving the pilot overboard when the gale is blowing on a lee-shore. And, I must say, it is not the part of a true heart to leave his mates, who have been here waiting for him till they have missed stays. Our water is wellnigh out, and we have junketed till provisions are low with us. We cannot sail without provisions—we cannot get provisions without the good-will of the Kirkwall folks. If we remain here longer, the Halcyon frigate will be down upon us—she was seen off Peterhead two days since,—and we shall hang up at the yard-arm to be sun-dried. Now, Captain Cleveland will get us out of the hobble, if any can. He can play the gentleman with these Kirkwall folks, and knows how to deal with them on fair terms, and foul, too, if there be occasion for it."

"And so you would turn honest Captain Goffe a-grazing, would ye ?" said an old weatherbeaten pirate, who had but one eye ; "what though he has his humours, and made my eye dowse the glim in his fancies and

* This was really an exploit of the celebrated Avery the pirate, who suddenly and without provocation, fired his pistols under the table where he sat drinking with his messmates, wounded one man severely, and thought the matter a good jest. What is still more extraordinary, his crew regarded it in the same light.

† A ship going fast through the sea is said to cut a feather, alluding to the ripple which she throws off from her bows.

frolics, he is as honest a man as ever walked a quarter-deck, for all that ; and d——n me but I stand by him so long as t'other lantern is lit !"

"Why, you would not hear me out," said Hawkins ; "a man might as well talk to so many negers !—I tell you, I propose that Cleveland shall only be captain from one, *post meridiem*, to five *a.m.*, during which time Goffe is always drunk."

The Captain of whom he last spoke gave sufficient proof of the truth of his words, by uttering an inarticulate growl, and attempting to present a pistol at the mediator Hawkins.

"Why, look ye now !" said Derrick, "there is all the sense he has, to get drunk on council day, like one of these poor silly fellows !"

"Ay," said Bunce, "drunk as Davy's sow, in the face of the field, the fray, and the senate !"

"But, nevertheless," continued Derrick, "it will never do to have two Captains in the same day. I think week about might suit better—and let Cleveland take the first turn."

"There are as good here as any of them," said Hawkins ; "howsomdever, I object nothing to Captain Cleveland, and I think he may help us into deep water as well as another."

"Ay," exclaimed Bunce, "and a better figure he will make at bringing these Kirkwallers to order than his sober predecessor !—So Captain Cleveland for ever !"

"Stop, gentlemen," said Cleveland, who had hitherto been silent ; "I hope you will not choose me captain without my own consent !"

"Ay, by the blue vault of heaven will we," said Bunce, "if it be *pro bono publico !*"

"But hear me, at least," said Cleveland—"I do consent to take command of the vessel, since you wish it, and because I see you will ill get out of the scrape without me."

"Why, then, I say, Cleveland for ever, again !" shouted Bunce.

"Be quiet, prithee, dear Bunce !—honest Altamont !" said Cleveland.— "I undertake the business on this condition ; that, when I have got the ship cleared for her voyage, with provisions, and so forth, you will be content to restore Captain Goffe to the command, as I said before, and put me ashore somewhere to shift for myself—You will then be sure it is impossible I can betray you, since I will remain with you to the last moment."

"Ay, and after the last moment too, by the blue vault ! or I mistake the matter," muttered Bunce to himself.

The matter was now put to the vote ; and so confident were the crew in Cleveland's superior address and management, that the temporary deposition of Goffe found little resistance even among his own partisans, who reasonably enough observed, "He might at least have kept sober to look after his own business—E'en let him put it to rights again himself next morning, if he will."

But when the next morning came, the drunken part of the crew, being informed of the issue of the deliberations of the council, to which they were virtually held to have assented, showed such a superior sense of Cleveland's merits, that Goffe, sulky and malcontent as he was, judged it wisest for the present to suppress his feelings of resentment until a safer opportunity for suffering them to explode, and to submit to the degradation which so frequently took place among a piratical crew.

Cleveland, on his part, resolved to take upon him, with spirit and without loss of time, the task of extricating his ship's company from their perilous situation. For this purpose, he ordered the boat, with the purpose of going ashore in person, carrying with him twelve of the stoutest and best men of the ship's company, all very handsomely appointed (for the success of their nefarious profession had enabled the pirates to assume nearly as gay dresses as their officers), and, above all, each man being sufficiently armed with cutlass and pistols, and several having pole-axes and poniards.

Cleveland himself was gallantly attired in a blue coat, lined with crimson silk, and laced with gold very richly, crimson damask waistcoat and breeches, a velvet cap, richly embroidered, with a white feather, white silk stockings, and red-heeled shoes, which were the extremity of finery among the gallants of the day. He had a gold chain several times folded round his neck, which sustained a whistle of the same metal, the ensign of his authority. Above all, he wore a decoration peculiar to those daring depredators, who, besides one, or perhaps two, brace of pistols at their belt, had usually two additional brace, of the finest mounting and workmanship, suspended over their shoulders in a sort of sling or scarf of crimson ribbon. The hilt and mounting of the Captain's sword corresponded in value to the rest of his appointments, and his natural good mien was so well adapted to the whole equipment, that when he appeared on deck, he was received with a general shout by the crew, who, as in other popular societies, judged a great deal by the eye.

Cleveland took with him in the boat, amongst others, his predecessor in office, Goffe, who was also very richly dressed, but who, not having the advantage of such an exterior as Cleveland's, looked like a boorish clown in the dress of a courtier, or rather like a vulgar-faced footpad decked in the spoils of some one whom he has murdered, and whose claim to the property of his garments is rendered doubtful in the eyes of all who look upon him, by the mixture of awkwardness, remorse, cruelty, and insolence, which clouds his countenance. Cleveland probably chose to take Goffe ashore with him, to prevent his having any opportunity, during his absence, to debauch the crew from their allegiance. In this guise they left the ship, and singing to their oars, while the water foamed higher at the chorus, soon reached the quay of Kirkwall.

The command of the vessel was in the meantime intrusted to Bunce, upon whose allegiance Cleveland knew that he might perfectly depend, and, in private conversation with him of some length, he gave him directions how to act in such emergencies as might occur.

These arrangements being made, and Bunce having been repeatedly charged to stand upon his guard alike against the adherents of Goffe and any attempt from the shore, the boat put off. As she approached the harbour, Cleveland displayed a white flag, and could observe that their appearance seemed to occasion a good deal of bustle and alarm. People were seen running to and fro, and some of them appeared to be getting under arms. The battery was manned hastily, and the English colours displayed. These were alarming symptoms, the rather that Cleveland knew, that, though there were no artillerymen in Kirkwall, yet there were many sailors perfectly competent to the management of great guns, and willing enough to undertake such service in case of need.

Noting these hostile preparations with a heedful eye, but suffering nothing like doubt or anxiety to appear on his countenance, Cleveland ran the boat right for the quay, on which several people, armed with muskets, rifles, and fowling-pieces, and others with half-pikes and whaling-knives, were now assembled, as if to oppose his landing. Apparently, however, they had not positively determined what measures they were to pursue ; for, when the boat reached the quay, those immediately opposite bore back, and suffered Cleveland and his party to leap ashore without hindrance. They immediately drew up on the quay, except two, who, as their Captain had commanded, remained in the boat, which they put off to a little distance ; a manœuvre which, while it placed the boat (the only one belonging to the sloop) out of danger of being seized, indicated a sort of careless confidence in Cleveland and his party, which was calculated to intimidate their opponents.

The Kirkwallers, however, showed the old Northern blood, put a manly face upon the matter, and stood upon the quay, with their arms shouldered, directly opposite to the rovers, and blocking up against them the street which leads to the town.

Cleveland was the first who spoke, as the parties stood thus looking upon each other.—"How is this, gentlemen burghers ?" he said ; "are you Orkney folks turned Highlandmen, that you are all under arms so early this morning ; of have you manned the quay to give me the honour of a salute, upon taking the command of my ship ?"

The burghers looked on each other, and one of them replied to Cleveland—"We do not know who you are ; it was that other man," pointing to Goffe, "who used to come ashore as Captain."

"That other gentleman is my mate, and commands in my absence," said Cleveland ;—"but what is that to the purpose ? I wish to speak with your Lord Mayor, or whatever you call him."

"The Provost is sitting in council with the Magistrates," answered the spokesman.

"So much the better," replied Cleveland.—"Where do their Worships meet ?"

"In the Council-house," answered the other.

"Then make way for us, gentlemen, if you please, for my people and I are going there."

There was a whisper among the townspeople ; but several were unresolved upon engaging in a desperate, and perhaps an unnecessary conflict, with desperate men ; and the more determined citizens formed the hasty reflection that the strangers might be more easily mastered in the house, or perhaps in the narrow streets which they had to traverse, than when they stood drawn up and prepared for battle upon the quay. They suffered them, therefore, to proceed unmolested ; and Cleveland, moving very slowly, keeping his people close together, suffering no one to press upon the flanks of his little detachment, and making four men, who constituted his rear-guard, turn round and face to the rear from time to time, rendered it, by his caution, a very dangerous task to make any attempt upon them.

In this manner they ascended the narrow street, and reached the Council-house, where the Magistrates were actually sitting, as the citizen had informed Cleveland. Here the inhabitants began to press forward, with the purpose of mingling with the pirates, and availing themselves of the crowd in the narrow entrance, to secure as many as they could, without allowing them room for free use of their weapons. But this also had Cleveland foreseen, and, ere entering the council-room, he caused the entrance to be cleared and secured, commanding four of his men to face down the street, and as many to confront the crowd who were thrusting each other from above. The burghers recoiled back from the ferocious, swarthy, and sunburnt countenances, as well as the levelled arms, of these desperadoes, and Cleveland, with the rest of his party, entered the council-room, where the Magistrates were sitting in council, with very little attendance. These gentlemen were thus separated effectually from the citizens, who looked to them for orders, and were perhaps more completely at the mercy of Cleveland than he, with his little handful of men, could be said to be at that of the multitude by whom they were surrounded.

The Magistrates seemed sensible of their danger ; for they looked upon each other in some confusion, when Cleveland thus addressed them :—

"Good morrow, gentlemen,—I hope there is no unkindness betwixt us. I am come to talk with you about getting supplies for my ship yonder in the roadstead—we cannot sail without them."

"Your ship, sir ?" said the Provost, who was a man of sense and spirit,—how do we know that you are her Captain ?"

"Look at me," said Cleveland, "and you will, I think, scarce ask the question again."

The Magistrate looked at him, and accordingly did not think proper to pursue that part of the inquiry, but proceeded to say—"And if you are her Captain, whence comes she, and where is she bound for ? You look too much like a man-of-war's man to be master of a trader, and we know that you do not belong to the British navy."

"There are more men-of-war on the sea than sail under the British flag," replied Cleveland ; "but say that I were commander of a free-trader here, willing to exchange tobacco, brandy, gin, and such like, for cured fish and hides, why, I do not think I deserve so very bad usage from the merchants of Kirkwall as to deny me provisions for my money ?"

"Look you, Captain," said the Town-clerk, "it is not that we are so very strait-laced neither—for, when gentlemen of your cloth come this way, it is as weel, as I tauld the Provost, just to do as the collier did when he met the devil,—and that is, to have naething to say to them, if they have naething to say to us ;—and there is the gentleman," pointing to Goffe "that was Captain before you, and may be Captain after you,"—("The cuckold speaks truth in that," muttered Goffe),— "he knows well how handsomely we entertained him, till he and his men took upon them to run through the town like hellicat devils—I see one of them there !—that was the very fellow that stopped my servant wench on the street, as she carried the lantern home before me, and insulted her before my face !"

"If it please your noble Mayorship's honour and glory," said Derrick, the fellow at whom the Town-clerk pointed, "it was not I that brought-to the bit of a tender that carried the lantern in the poop—it was quite a different sort of person."

"Who was it, then, sir ?" said the Provost.

"Why, please your majesty's worship," said Derrick, making several sea bows, and describing, as nearly as he could, the exterior of the Magistrate himself, "he was an elderly gentleman,—Dutch built, round in the stern, with a white wig and a red nose—very like your majesty, I think ;" then, turning to a comrade, he added, "Jack, don't you think the fellow that wanted to kiss the pretty girl with the lantern t'other night, was very like his worship ?"

"By G——, Tom Derrick," answered the party appealed to. "I believe it is the very man !"

"This is insolence which we can make you repent of, gentlemen !" said the Magistrate, justly irritated at their effrontery ; "you have behaved in this town, as if you were in an Indian village at Madagascar. You yourself, Captain, if captain you be, were at the head of another riot, no longer since than yesterday. We will give you no provisions till we know better whom we are supplying. And do not think to bully us ; when I shake this handkerchief out at the window, which is at my elbow, your ship goes to the bottom. Remember she lies under the guns of our battery."

"And how many of these guns are honeycombed, Mr. Mayor ?" said Cleveland. He put the question by chance ; but instantly perceived, from a sort of confusion which the Provost in vain endeavoured to hide, that the artillery of Kirkwall was not in the best order. "Come, come, Mr. Mayor," he said, "bullying will go down with us as little as with you. Your guns yonder will do more harm to the poor old sailors who are to work them, than to our sloop ; and if we bring a broadside to bear on the town, why, your wives' crockery will be in some danger. And then talk to us of seamen being a little frolicsome ashore, why, when are they otherwise. You have the Greenland whalers playing the devil among you every now and then ; and the very Dutchmen cut capers in the streets of Kirkwall, like porpoises before a gale of wind. I am told you are a man of sense, and I am sure you and I could settle this matter in the course of a five minutes' palaver."

"Well, sir," said the Provost, "I will hear what you have to say, if you will walk this way."

Cleveland accordingly followed him into a small interior apartment, and, when there, addressed the Provost thus :—"I will lay aside my pistols, sir, if you are afraid of them."

"D——n your pistols !" answered the Provost, "I have served the King, and fear the smell of powder as little as you do !"

"So much the better," said Cleveland, "for you will hear me the more coolly.—Now, sir, let us be what perhaps you suspect us, or let us be anything else, what, in the name of Heaven, can you get by keeping us here, but blows and bloodshed ? for which, believe me, we are much better provided than you can pretend to be. The point is a plain one—you are desirous to be rid of us—we desirous to be gone. Let us have the means of departure, and we leave you instantly."

"Look ye, Captain," said the Provost—"I thirst for no man's blood. You are a pretty fellow, as there were many among the bucaniers in my time—but there is no harm in wishing you a better trade. You should have the stores and welcome, for your money, so you would make these seas clear of you. But then here lies the rub. The Halcyon frigate is expected here in these parts immediatiely ; when she hears of you she will be at you ; for there is nothing the white lapelle loves better than a rover—you are seldom without a cargo of dollars. Well, he comes down, gets under his stern"—

"Blows us into the air if you please," said Cleveland.

"Nay, that must be as *you* please, Captain," said the Provost ; "but then, what is to come of the good town of Kirkwall, that has been packing and peeling with the King's enemies ? The burgh will be laid under a round fine, and it may be that the Provost may not come off so easily."

"Well, then," said Cleveland, "I see where your pinch lies. Now, suppose that I run round this island of yours, and get into the roadstead at Stromness ? We could get what we want put on board there, without Kirkwall or the Provost seeming to have any hand in it ; or, if it should be ever questioned, your want of force and our superior strength will make a sufficient apology."

"That may be," said the Provost ; "but if I suffer you to leave your present station, and go elsewhere, I must have some security that you will not do harm to the country."

"And we," said Cleveland, "must have some security on our side, that you will not detain us, by dribbling out our time till the Halcyon is on the coast. Now, I am myself perfectly willing to continue on shore as a hostage, on the one side, provided you will give me your word not to betray me, and send some magistrate, of person of consequence, aboard the sloop, where his safety will be a guarantee for mine."

The Provost shook his head, and intimated it would be difficult to find a person willing to place himself as hostage in such a perilous condition ; but said he would propose the arrangement to such of the council as were fit to be trusted with a matter of such weight.

CHAPTER THIRTY-FIFTH

I left my poor plough to go ploughing the deep !
DIBDIN

WHEN the Provost and Cleveland had returned into the public council-room, the former retired a second time with such of his brethren as he thought proper to advise with ; and while they were engaged in discussing Cleveland's proposal, refreshments were offered to him and his people. These the Captain permitted his people to partake of, but with the greatest precaution against surprisal, one party relieving the guard whilst the others were at their food.

He himself, in the meanwhile, walked up and down the apartment, and conversed upon indifferent subjects with those present, like a person quite at his ease.

Amongst these individuals he saw, somewhat to his surprise, Triptolemus Yellowley, who, chancing to be at Kirkwall, had been summoned by the magistrates as representative, in a certain degree, of the Lord Chamberlain, to attend council on this occasion. Cleveland immediately renewed the acquaintance which he had formed with the agriculturist at Burgh Westra, and asked him his present business in Orkney.

"Just to look after some of my little plans, Captain Cleveland. I am weary of fighting with wild beasts at Ephesus yonder, and I just cam ower to see how my orchard was thriving, whilk I had planted four or five miles from Kirkwall, it may be a year by-gane, and how the bees were thriving, whereof I had imported nine skeps, for the improvement of the country, and for the turning of the heather bloom into wax and honey."

"And they thrive, I hope ?" said Cleveland, who, however little interested in the matter, sustained the conversation, as if to break the chilly and embarrassed silence which hung upon the company assembled.

"Thrive !" replied Triptolemus ; "they thrive like everything else in this country, and that is the backward way."

"Want of care, I suppose ?" said Cleveland.

"The contrary, sir, quite and clean the contrary," replied the Factor ; "they died of ower muckle care, like Lucky Christie's chickens.—I asked to see the skeps, and cunning and joyful did the fallow look who was to have taken care of them—'Had there been onybody in charge but mysell,' he said, 'ye might have seen the skeps, or whatever you ca' them ; but there wad hae been as mony solan geese as flees in them, if it hadna been for my four quarters ; for I watched them so closely, that I saw them a' creeping out at the little holes one sunny morning, and if I had not stopped the leak on the instant with a bit clay, the deil a bee, or flee, or whatever they are, would have been left in the skeps, as ye ca' them !'—

285

In a word, sir, he had clagged up the hives, as if the puir things had had the pestilence, and my bees were as dead as if they had been smeaked—and so ends my hope, *generandi gloria mellis*, as Virgilius hath it."

"There is an end of your mead, then," replied Cleveland ; "but what is your chance of cider ?—How does the orchard thrive ?"

"O, Captain ! this same Solomon of the Orcadian Ophir—I am sure no man need to send hither to fetch either talents of gold or talents of sense !—I say, this wise man had watered the young apple-trees, in his great tenderness, with hot water, and they are perished, root and branch ! But what avails grieving ?—and I wish you would tell me instead what is all the din that these good folks are making about pirates ? and what for are all these ill-looking men, that are armed like so mony Highlandmen, assembled in the judgment chamber ?—for I am just come from the other side of the island, and I have heard nothing distinct about it.—And now I look at you yoursell, Captain, I think you have mair of these foolish pistolets about you than should suffice an honest man in quiet times."

"And so I think, too," said the pacific Triton, old Haagen, who had been an unwilling follower of the daring Montrose ; "if you had been in the Glen of Edderachyllis, when we were sae sair worried by Sir John Worry"—

"You have forgot the whole matter, neighbour Haagen," said the Factor ; "Sir John Urry was on your side, and was ta'en with Montrose ; by the same token, he lost his head."

"Did he ?" said the Triton.—"I believe you may be right ; for he changed sides mair than ance, and wha kens whilk he died for ?—But always he was there, and so was I ;—a fight there was, and I never wish to see another !"

The entrance of the Provost here interrupted their desultory conversation.—"We have determined," he said, "Captain, that your ship shall go round to Stromness, or Scalpa-flow, to take in stores, in order that there may be no more quarrels between the Fair folks and your seamen. And as you wish to stay on shore to see the Fair, we intend to send a respectable gentleman on board your vessel to pilot her round the Mainland, as the navigation is but ticklish."

"Spoken like a quiet and sensible magistrate, Mr. Mayor," said Cleveland, "and no otherwise than as I expected.—And what gentleman is to honour our quarter-deck during my absence ?"

"We have fixed that, too, Captain Cleveland," said the Provost ; "you may be sure we were each more desirous than another to go upon so pleasant a voyage, and in such good company ; but being Fair time, most of us have some affairs in hand—I myself, in respect of my office, cannot be well spared—the eldest Bailie's wife is lying in—the Treasurer does not agree with the sea—two Bailies have the gout—the other two are absent from town—and the other fifteen members of council are all engaged on particular business."

"All that I can tell you, Mr. Mayor," said Cleveland, raising his voice, "is, that I expect"—

"A moment's patience, if you please, Captain," said the Provost, interrupting him—"So that we have come to the resolution that our worthy Mr. Triptolemus Yellowley, who is Factor to the Lord Chamberlain of these islands, shall, in respect of his official situation, be preferred to the honour and pleasure of accompanying you."

"Me !" said the astonished Triptolemus ; "what the devil should I do going on your voyages ?—my business is on dry land !"

"The gentlemen want a pilot," said the Provost, whispering to him, "and there is no eviting to give them one."

"Do they want to go bump on shore, then ?" said the Factor—"how the devil would I pilot them, that never touched rudder in my life ?"

"Hush !—hush !—be silent !" said the Provost ; "if the people of this town heard ye say such a word, your utility, and respect, and rank, and every thing else, is clean gone !—No man is anything with us island folks, unless he can hand, reef, and steer.—Besides, it is but a mere form ; and we will send old Pate Sinclair to help you. You will have nothing to do but to eat, drink, and be merry all day."

"Eat and drink !" said the Factor, not able to comprehend exactly why this piece of duty was pressed upon him so hastily, and yet not very capable of resisting or extricating himself from the toils of the more knowing Provost—"Eat and drink ?—that is all very well ; but, to speak truth, the sea does not agree with me any more than with the Treasurer; and I have always a better appetite for eating and drinking ashore."

"Hush ! hush ! hush !" again said the Provost, in an under tone of earnest expostulation ; " would you actually ruin your character out and out ?—A factor of the High Chamberlain of the Isles of Orkney and Zetland, and not like the sea !—you might as well say you are a Highlander, and do not like whisky !"

"You must settle it somehow, gentlemen," said Captain Cleveland ; "it is time we were under weigh.—Mr. Triptolemus Yellowley, are we to be honoured with your company ?"

"I am sure, Captain Cleveland," stammered the Factor, "I would have no objection to go any where with you—only"—

"He has no objection," said the Provost, catching at the first limb of the sentence, without awaiting the conclusion.

"He has no objection," cried the Treasurer.

"He has no objection," sung out the whole four Bailies together ; and the fifteen Councillors, all catching up the same phrase of assent, repeated it in chorus, with the additions of—"good man"—"public spirited"—"honourable gentleman"—"burgh eternally obliged"—"where will you find such a worthy Factor ?" and so forth.

Astonished and confused at the praises with which he was overwhelmed on all sides, and in no shape understanding the nature of the transaction that was going forward, the astounded and overwhelmed agriculturist became incapable of resisting him, and was delivered up by Captain Cleveland to his party, with the strictest injunctions to treat him with honour and attention. Goffe and his companions began now to lead him off, amid the applause of the whole meeting, after the manner in which the victim of ancient days was garlanded and greeted by shouts when consigned to the priests for the purpose of being led to the altar, and knocked on the head, a sacrifice of the common weal. It was while they thus conducted, and in a manner forced him out of the council-chamber, that poor Triptolemus, much alarmed at finding that Cleveland, in whom he had some confidence, was to remain behind the party, tried, when just going out at the door, the effect of one remonstrating bellow—"Nay, but Provost !—Captain !— Bailies !—Treasurer !—Councillors !—if Captain Cleveland does not go aboard to protect me, it is nae bargain, and go I will not, unless I am trailed with cart-ropes !"

His protest was, however, drowned in the unanimous chorus of the Magistrates and Councillors, returning him thanks for his public spirit—wishing him a good voyage—and praying to Heaven for his happy and speedy return. Stunned and overwhelmed, and thinking, if he had any distinct thoughts at all, that remonstrance was vain, where friends and strangers seemed alike determined to carry the point against him, Triptolemus, without farther resistance, suffered himself to be conducted into the street, where the pirate's boat's crew, assembling around him, began to move slowly towards the quay, many of the town's folk following out of curiosity, but without any attempt at interference or annoyance ; for the pacific compromise which the dexterity of the first Magistrate had achieved, was unanimously approved of as a much better settlement of the disputes betwixt them and the strangers, than might have been attained by the dubious issue of an appeal to arms.

Meanwhile, as they went slowly along, Triptolemus had time to study the appearance, countenance, and dress of those into whose hands he had been thus delivered, and began to imagine that he read in their looks, not only the general expression of a desperate character, but some sinister intentions directed particularly towards himself. He was alarmed by the truculent looks of Goffe, in particular, who, holding his arm with a gripe which resembled in delicacy of touch the compression of a smith's vice, cast on him from the outer corner of his eye oblique glances, like those which the eagle throws upon the prey which she has clutched, ere yet she proceeds, as it is technically called, to plume it. At length Yellowley's fears got so far the better of his prudence, that he fairly asked his terrible conductor, in a sort of crying whisper, "Are you going to murder me, Captain, in the face of the laws baith of God and man ?"

"Hold your peace, if you are wise," said Goffe, who had his own reasons for desiring to increase the panic of his captive ; "we have not murdered a man these three months, and why should you put us in mind of it ?"

"You are but joking, I hope, good worthy Captain," replied Triptolemus. "This is worse than witches, dwarfs, dirking of whales, cowping of cobles, put all together !—this is an away-ganging crop, with a vengeance !—What good, in Heaven's name, would murdering me do to you ?"

"We might have some pleasure in it, at least," said Goffe.—"Look these fellows in the face, and see if you see one among them that would not rather kill a man than let it alone !—But we will speak more of that when

288

you have first had a taste of the bilboes—unless, indeed, you come down with a handsome round handful of Chili boards* for your ransom."

"As I shall live by bread, Captain," answered the Factor, "that misbegotten dwarf has carried off the whole hornful of silver !"

"A cat-and-nine-tails will make you find it again," said Goffe, gruffly ; "flogging and pickling is an excellent recipe to bring a man's wealth into his mind—twisting a bow-string round his skull till the eyes start a little, is a very good remembrancer too !"

"Captain," replied Yellowley, stoutly, "I have no money—seldom can improvers have.—We turn pasture to tillage, and barley into aits, and heather into greensward, and the poor *yarpha*, as the benighted creatures here call their peat-bogs, into baittle grass-land ; but we seldom make anything of it that comes back to our ain pouch.—The carles and the cart-avers make it all, and the carles and the cart-avers eat it all, and the deil clink doun with it !"

"Well, well," said Goffe, "if you be really a poor fellow, as you pretend, I'll stand your friend ;" then, inclining his head so as to reach the ear of the Factor, who stood on tiptoe with anxiety, he said, "If you love your life, do not enter the boat with us."

"But how am I to get away from you, while you hold me so fast by the arm, that I could not get off if the whole year's crop of Scotalnd depended on it ?"

"Hark ye, you gudgeon," said Goffe, "just when you come to the water's edge, and when the fellows are jumping in and taking their oars, slue yourself round suddenly to the larboard—I will let go your arm—and then cut and run for your life !"

Triptolemus did as he was desired, Goffe's willing hand relaxed the grasp as he had promised, the agriculturist trundled off like a football that has just received a strong impulse from the foot of one of the players, and, with celerity which surprised himself as well as all beholders, fled through the town of Kirkwall. Nay, such was the impetus of his retreat, that, as if the grasp of the pirate was still open to pounce upon him, he never stopped till he had traversed the whole town, and attained the open country on the other side. They who had seen him that day—his hat and wig lost in the sudden effort he had made to bolt forward, his cravat awry, and his waistcoat unbuttoned,—and who had an opportunity of comparing his round spherical form and short legs with the portentous speed at which he scoured through the street, might well say, that if Fury ministers arms, Fear confers wings. His very mode of running seemed to be that peculiar to his fleecy care, for, like a ram in the midst of his race, he ever and anon encouraged himself by a great bounding attempt at a leap, though there were no obstacles in his way.

There was no pursuit after the agriculturist ; and though a musket or two were presented, for the purpose of sending a leaden messenger after him, yet Goffe, turning peacemaker for once in his life, so exaggerated the dangers that would attend a breach of the truce with the people of Kirkwall, that he prevailed upon the boat's crew to forbear any active hostilities, and to pull off for their vessel with all despatch.

* Commonly called, by landsmen, Spanish dollars.

The burghers, who regarded the escape of Triptolemus as a triumph on their side, gave the boat three cheers, by way of an insulting farewell; while the Magistrates, on the other hand, entertained great anxiety respecting the probable consequences of this breach of articles between them and the pirates; and, could they have seized upon the fugitive very privately, instead of complimenting him with a civic feast in honour of the agility which he displayed, it is likely they might have delivered the runaway hostage once more into the hands of his foemen. But it was impossible to set their face publicly to such an act of violence, and therefore they contented themselves with closely watching Cleveland, whom they determined to make responsible for any aggression which might be attempted by the pirates. Cleveland, on his part, easily conjectured that the motive which Goffe had for suffering his hostage to escape, was to leave him answerable for all consequences, and, relying more on the attachment and intelligence of his friend and adherent Frederick Altamont, alias Jack Bunce, than on anything else, expected the result with considerable anxiety, since the Magistrates, though they continued to treat him with civility, plainly intimated they would regulate his treatment by the behaviour of the crew, though he no longer commanded them.

It was not, however, without some reason that he reckoned on the devoted fidelity of Bunce; for no sooner did that trusty adherent receive from Goffe, and the boat's crew, the news of the escape of Triptolemus, than he immediately concluded it had been favoured by the late Captain, in order that, Cleveland being either put to death or consigned to hopeless imprisonment, Goffe might be called upon to resume the command of the vessel.

"But the drunken old Boatswain shall miss his mark," said Bunce to his confederate Fletcher; "or else I am contented to quit the name of Altamont, and be called Jack Bunce, or Jack Dunce, if you like it better, to the end of the chapter."

Availing himself accordingly of a sort of nautical eloquence, which his enemies termed slack-jaw, Bunce set before the crew in a most animated manner, the disgrace which they all sustained by their Captain remaining, as he was pleased to term it, in the bilboes without any hostage to answer for his safety; and succeeded so far, that besides exciting a good deal of discontent against Goffe, he brought the crew to the resolution of seizing the first vessel of a tolerable appearance, and declaring that the ship, crew, and cargo should be dealt with according to the usage which Cleveland should receive on shore. It was judged at the same time proper to try the faith of the Orcadians, by removing from the roadstead of Kirkwall, and going round to that of Stromness, where, according to the treaty betwixt Provost Torfe and Captain Cleveland, they were to victual their sloop. They resolved, in the meantime, to intrust the command of the vessel to a council, consisting of Goffe, the boatswain, and Bunce himself, until Cleveland should be in a situation to resume his command. These resolutions having been proposed and acceded to, they weighed anchor, and got their sloop under sail, without experiencing any opposition or annoyance from the battery, which relieved them of one important apprehension incidental to their situation.

CHAPTER THIRTY-SIXTH

Clap on more sail, pursue up with your fights,
Give fire—she is my prize, or ocean whelm them all !

SHAKESPEARE

A VERY handsome brig, which, with several other vessels, was the property of Magnus Troil, the great Zetland Udaller, had received on board that Magnate himself, his two lovely daughters, and the facetious Claud Halcro, who, for friendship's sake chiefly, and the love of beauty proper to his poetical calling, attended them on their journey from Zetland to the capital of Orkney, to which Norna had referred them, as the place where her mystical oracles should at length receive a satisfactory explanation.

They passed, at a distance, the tremendous cliffs of the lonely spot of earth called the Fair Isle, which at an equal distance from either archipelago, lies in the sea which divides Orkney from Zetland ; and at length, after some baffling winds, made the Start of Sanda. Off the headland so named, they became involved in a strong current, well known by those who frequent these seas as the Roost of the Start, which carried them considerably out of their course, and, joined to an adverse wind, forced them to keep on the east side of the island of Stronsa, and finally compelled them to lie by for the night in Papa Sound, since the navigation in dark or thick weather, amongst so many low islands, is neither pleasant nor safe.

On the ensuing morning they resumed their voyage under more favourable auspices ; and coasting along the island of Stronsa, whose flat, verdant, and comparatively fertile shores formed a strong contrast to the dun hills and dark cliffs of their own islands, they doubled the cape called the Lamb Head, and stood away for Kirkwall.

They had scarce opened the beautiful bay betwixt Pomona and Shapinsha, and the sisters were admiring the massive church of Saint Magnus, as it was first seen to rise from amongst the inferior buildings of Kirkwall, when the eyes of Magnus and of Claud Halcro were attracted by an object which they thought more interesting. This was an armed sloop with her sails set, which had just left the anchorage in the bay, and was running before the wind by which the brig of the Udaller was beating in.

"A tight thing that, by my ancestors' bones !" said the old Udaller ; "but I cannot make out of what country, as she shows no colours. Spanish built, I should think her."

"Ay, ay," said Claud Halcro, "she has all the look of it. She runs before the wind that we must battle with, which is the wonted way of the world. As glorious John says—

> With roomy deck, and guns of mighty strength,
>> Whose low-laid mouths each mountain billow laves,
> Deep in her draught, and warlike in her length,
>> She seems a sea-wasp flying on the waves.

Brenda could not help telling Halcro, when he had spouted this stanza with great enthusiasm, "that though the description was more like a first-rate than a sloop, yet the simile of the sea-wasp served but indifferently for either."

"A sea-wasp?" said Magnus, looking with some surprise, as the sloop, shifting her course, suddenly bore down on them—"Egad, I wish she may not show us presently that she has a sting!"

What the Udaller said in jest was fulfilled in earnest ; for, without hoisting colours or hailing, two shots were discharged from the sloop, one of which ran dipping and dancing upon the water, just ahead of the Zetlander's bows, while the other went through his mainsail.

Magnus caught up a speaking-trumpet, and hailed the sloop, to demand what she was, and what was the meaning of this unprovoked aggression. He was only answered by the stern command—"Down topsails instantly, and lay your mainsail to the mast—you shall see who we are presently."

There were no means within the reach of possibility by which obedience could be evaded, where it would instantly have been enforced by a broadside ; and, with much fear on the part of the sisters and Claud Halcro, mixed with anger and astonishment on that of the Udaller, the brig lay-to to await the commands of the captors.

The sloop immediately lowered a boat, with six armed hands, commanded by Jack Bunce, which rowed directly for their prize. As they approached her, Claud Halcro whispered to the Udaller—"If what we hear of bucaniers be true, these men, with their silk scarfs and vests, have the very cut of them."

"My daughters ! my daughters !" muttered Magnus to himself, with such an agony as only a father could feel—"Go down below and hide yourselves, girls, while I"—

He threw down his speaking trumpet and seized on a handspike, while his daughters, more afraid of the consequences of his fiery temper to himself than of anything else, hung round him, and begged him to make no resistance. Claud Halcro united his entreaties, adding, "It were best pacify the fellows with fair words. They might," he said, "be Dunkirkers, or insolent man-of-war's-men on a frolic."

No, no," answered Magnus, "it is the sloop which the yagger told us of. But I will take your advice—I will have patience for these girls' sakes ; yet"—

He had no time to conclude the sentence, for Bunce jumped on board with his party, and drawing his cutlass, struck it upon the companion-ladder, and declared the ship was theirs.

"By what warrant of authority do you stop us on the high seas ?" said Magnus.

"Here are half-a-dozen of warrants," said Bunce, showing the pistols which were hung round him, according to a pirate fashion already mentioned ; "choose which you like, old gentleman, and you shall have the perusal of it presently."

"That is to say, you intend to rob us ?" said Magnus.—"So be it—we have no means to help it—only be civil to the women, and take what you please from the vessel. There is not much, but I will and can make it worth more if you use us well."

"Civil to the women !" said Fletcher, who had also come on board with the gang—"when were we else than civil to them ? ay, and kind to boot ?—Look here, Jack Bunce ! what a trimgoing little thing here is !—By G——, she shall make a cruise with us, come of old Squaretoes what will !"

He seized upon the terrified Brenda with one hand, and insolently pulled back with the other the hood of the mantle in which she had muffled herself.

"Help, father !—help, Minna !" exclaimed the affrighted girl unconscious, at the moment, that they were unable to render her assistance.

Magnus again uplifted the handspike, but Bunce stopped his hand.— "Avast, father !" he said, "or you will make a bad voyage of it presently— And you, Fletcher, let go the girl !"

"And d——n me ! why should I let her go ?" said Fletcher.

"Because I command you, Dick," said the other, "and because I'll make it a quarrel else.—And now let me know, beauties, is there one of you bears that queer heathen name of Minna, for which I have a certain sort of regard ?"

"Gallant sir !" said Halcro, "unquestionably it is because you have some poetry in your heart."

"I have had enough of it in my mouth in my time," answered Bunce ; "but that day is by, old gentleman—however, I shall soon find out which of these girls is Minna.—Throw back your mufflings from your faces, and don't be afraid, my Lindamiras ; no one here shall meddle with you to do you wrong. On my soul, two pretty wenches !–I wish I were at sea in an egg-shell, and a rock under my lee-bow, if I would wish a better leaguer lass than the worst of them !—Hark you, my girls ; which of you would like to swing in a rover's hammock ?—you should have gold for the gathering !"

The terrified maidens clung close together, and grew pale at the bold and familiar language of the desperate libertine.

"Nay, don't be frightened," said he ; "no one shall serve under the noble Altamont but by her own free choice—there is no pressing amongst gentlemen of fortune. And do not look so shy upon me neither, as if I spoke of what you never thought of before. One of you, at least, has heard of Captain Cleveland, the Rover."

Brenda grew still paler, but the blood mounted at once in Minna's cheeks, on hearing the name of her lover thus unexpectedy introduced ; for the scene was in itself so confounding, that the idea of the vessel's being the consort of which Cleveland had spoken at Burgh Westra, had occurred to no one save the Udaller.

"I see how it is," said Bunce, with a familiar nod, "and I will hold my course accordingly.—You need not be afraid of any injury, father," he added, addressing Magnus familiarly ; "and though I have made many a pretty girl pay tribute in my time, yet yours shall go ashore without either wrong or ransom."

"If you will assure me of that," said Magnus, "you are as welcome to the brig and cargo, as ever I made man welcome to a can of punch."

"And it is no bad thing that same can of punch," said Bunce, "if we had any one that could mix it well."

"I will do it," said Halcro, "with any man that ever squeezed lemon— Eric Scambester, the punch-maker of Burgh Westra, being alone excepted."

"And you are within a grapnel's length of him, too," said the Udaller.— "Go down below, my girls," he added, "and send up the rare old man, and the punch-bowl."

"The punch-bowl !" said Fletcher ; "I say, the bucket, d——n me !— Talk of bowls in the cabin of a paltry merchantman, but not to gentlemen strollers—rovers, I would say," correcting himself, as he observed that Bunce looked sour at the mistake.

"And I say, these two pretty girls shall stay on deck, and fill my can," said Bunce ; "I deserve some attendance, at least, for all my generosity."

"And they shall fill mine, too," said Fletcher—"they shall fill it to the brim !—and I will have a kiss for every drop they spill—broil me if I won't !"

"Why, then, I tell you, you shan't !" said Bunce ; "for I'll be d——d if any one shall kiss Minna but one, and that's neither you nor I ; and her other little bit of a consort shall 'scape for company ;—there are plenty of willing wenches in Orkney.—And so, now I think on it, these girls shall go down below, and bolt themselves into the cabin ; and we shall have the punch up here on deck, *al fresco*, as the old gentleman proposes."

"Why, Jack, I wish you knew your own mind," said Fletcher ; " I have been your messmate these two years, and I love you ; and yet flay me like a wild bullock, if you have not as many humours as a monkey !—And what shall we have to make a little fun of, since you have sent the girls down below ?"

"Why, we will have Master Punch-maker here," answered Bunce, "to give us toasts, and sing songs.—And, in the meantime, you there, stand by sheets and tacks, and get her under weigh !—and you, steersman, as you would keep your brains in your skull, keep her under the stern of the sloop.—If you attempt to play us any trick, I will scuttle your sconce as if it were an old calabash !"

The vessel was accordingly got under weigh, and moved slowly on in the wake of the sloop, which, as had been previously agreed upon, held her course, not to return to the Bay of Kirkwall, but for an excellent roadstead called Inganess Bay, formed by a promontory which extends to the eastward two or three miles from the Orcadian metropolis, and where the vessels might conveniently lie at anchor, while the rovers maintained any communication with the Magistrates which the new state of things seemed to require.

Meantime Claud Halcro had exerted his utmost talents in compounding a bucketful of punch for the use of the pirates, which they drank out of large cans ; the ordinary seamen, as well as Bunce and Fletcher, who acted as officers, dipping them into the bucket with very little ceremony, as they came and went upon their duty. Magnus, who was particularly apprehensive that liquor might awaken the brutal passions of these desperadoes, was yet so much astonished at the quantities which he saw them drink, without producing any visible effect upon their reason, that he could not help expressing his surprise to Bunce himself, who, wild as he was, yet appeared by far the most civil and conversable of his party, and whom he was, perhaps, desirous to conciliate, by a compliment of which all boon topers know the value.

"Bones of Saint Magnus !" said the Udaller, "I used to think I took off my can like a gentleman ; but to see your men swallow, Captain, one would think their stomachs were as bottomless as the hole of Laifell in Foula, which I have sounded myself with a line of a hundred fathoms. By my soul, the Bicker of Saint Magnus were but a sip to them !"

"In our way of life, sir," answered Bunce, "there is no stint till duty calls, or the puncheon is drunk out."

"By my word, sir," said Claud Halcro, "I believe there is not one of your people but could drink out the mickle bicker of Scarpa, which was always offered to the bishop of Orkney brimful of the best bummock that ever was brewed."[*]

"If drinking could made them bishops," said Bunce, "I should have a reverend crew of them ; but as they have no other clerical qualities about them, I do not propose that they shall get drunk to-day ; so we will cut our drink with a song."

"And I'll sing it, by ____ !" said or swore Dick Fletcher, and instantly struck up the old ditty—

It was a ship, and a ship of fame,
Launch'd off the stocks, bound for the main.
With an hundred and fifty brisk young men,
All pick'd and chosen every one.

"I would sooner be keel-hauled than hear that song over again," said Bunce ; "and confound your lantern jaws, you can squeeze nothing else out of them !"

"By ____ ____," said Fletcher, "I will sing my song, whether you like it or no ;" and again he sung, with the doleful tone of a north-easter whistling through sheets and shrouds—

Captain Glen was our captain's name ;
A very gallant and brisk young man ;
As bold a sailor as e'er went to sea,
And we were bound for High Barbary.

[*] Liquor brewed for a Christmas treat.

"I tell you again," said Bunce, "we will have none of your screech-owl music here ; and I'll be d——d if you shall sit here and make that infernal noise !"

"Why, then, I'll tell you what," said Fletcher, getting up, "I'll sing when I walk about, and I hope there is no harm in that, Jack Bunce." And so, getting up from his seat, he began to walk up and down the sloop, croaking out his long and disastrous ballad.

"You see how I manage them," said Bunce, with a smile of self-applause—"allow that fellow two strides on his own way, and you make a mutineer of him for life. But I tie him strict up, and he follows me as kindly as a fowler's spaniel after he has got a good beating.—And now your toast and your song, sir," addressing Halcro ; "or rather your song without your toast. I have got a toast for myself. Here is success to all roving blades, and confusion to all honest men !"

"I should be sorry to drink that toast, if I could help it," said Magnus Troil.

"What ! you reckon yourself one of the honest folks, I warrant ?" said Bunce.—"Tell me your trade, and I'll tell you what I think of it. As for the punch-maker here, I knew him at first glance to be a tailor, who has, therefore, no more pretensions to be honest, than he has not to be mangy. But you are some High Dutch skipper, I warrant me, that tramples on the cross when he is in Japan, and denies his religion for a day's gain."

"No," replied the Udaller, "I am a gentleman of Zetland."

"Oh, what !" retorted the satirical Mr. Bunce, "you are come from the happy climate where gin is a groat a bottle, and where there is daylight for ever ?"

"At your service, Captain," said the Udaller, suppressing with much pain some disposition to resent these jests on his country, although under every risk, and at all disadvantage.

"At *my* service !" said Bunce—"Ay, if there was a rope stretched from the wreck to the beach, you would be at my service to cut the hawser, make *floatsome* and *jetsome* of the ship and cargo, and well if you did not give me a rap on the head with the back of the cutty axe ; and you call yourself honest ? But never mind—here goes the aforesaid toast—and do you sing me a song, Mr. Fashioner ; and look it be as good as your punch."

Halcro, internally praying for the powers of a new Timotheus, to turn his strain and check his auditor's pride, as glorious John had it, began a heart-soothing ditty with the following lines :—

Maidens fresh as fairest rose,
Listen to this lay of mine.

"I will hear nothing of maidens or roses," said Bunce : "it puts me in mind what sort of a cargo we have got on board ; and, by ——, I will he true to my messmate and my captain as long as I can !—And now I think on't, I'll have no more punch either—that last cup made innovation, and I am not to play Cassio to-night—and if I drink not, nobody else shall."

So saying, he manfully kicked over the bucket, which, notwithstanding the repeated applications made to it, was still half full, got up from his seat, shook himself a little to rights, as he expressed it, cocked his hat, and, walking the quarter-deck with an air of dignity, gave, by word and signal, the orders for bringing the ships to anchor, which were readily obeyed by both, Goffe being then, in all probability, past any rational state of interference.

The Udaller, in the meantime, condoled with Halcro on their situation. "It is bad enough," said the tough old Norseman ; "for these are rank rogues—and yet, were it not for the girls, I should not fear them. That young vapouring fellow, who seems to command, is not such a born devil as he might have been."

"He has queer humours, though," said Halcro ; "and I wish we were loose from him. To kick down a bucket half full of the best punch ever was made, and to cut me short in the sweetest song I ever wrote,—I promise you, I do not know what he may do next—it is next door to madness."

Meanwhile the ships being brought to anchor, the valiant Lieutenant Bunce called upon Fletcher, and, resuming his seat by his unwilling passengers, he told them they should see what message he was about to send to the wittols of Kirkwall, as they were something concerned in it. "It shall run in Dick's name," he said, "as well as in mine. I love to give the poor young fellow a little countenance now and then—don't I, Dick, you stupid d——d ass ?"

"Why, yes, Jack Bunce," said Dick, "I can't say but as you do—only you are always bullocking one about something or other, too—but howsomdever, d'ye see"—

"Enough said—belay your jaw, Dick," said Bunce, and proceeded to write his epistle, which, being read aloud, proved to be of the following tenor :—"For the Mayor and Aldermen of Kirkwall—Gentlemen, As, contrary to your good faith given, you have not sent us on board a hostage for the safety of our Captain remaining on shore at your request, these come to tell you, we are not thus to be trifled with. We have already in our possession a brig with a family of distinction, its owners and passengers ; and as you deal with our Captain, so will we deal with them in every respect. And as this is the first, so assure yourselves it shall not be the last damage which we will do to your town and trade, if you do not send on board our Captain and supply us with stores according to treaty.

"Given on board the brig Mergoose of Burgh Westra, lying in Inganess Bay. Witness our hands, commanders of the Fortune's Favourite, and gentlemen adventurers."

He then subscribed himself Frederick Altamont, and handed the letter to Fletcher, who read the said subscription with much difficulty ; and admiring the sound of it very much, swore he would have a new name himself, and the rather that Fletcher was the most crabbed word to spell and conster, he believed, in the whole dictionary. He subscribed himself accordingly, Timothy Tugmutton.

"Will you not add a few lines to the coxcombs ?" said Bunce, addressing Magnus.

"Not I," returned the Udaller, stubborn in his ideas of right and wrong, even in so formidable an emergency. "The Magistrates of Kirkwall know their duty, and were I they"— But here the recollection that his daughters were at the mercy of these ruffians, blanked the bold visage of Magnus Troil, and checked the defiance which was just about to issue from his lips.

"D——n me," said Bunce who easily conjectured what was passing in the mind of his prisoner—"that pause would have told well on the stage—it would have brought down pit, box, and gallery, egad, as Bayes has it."

"I will hear nothing of Bayes," said Claud Halcro (himself a little elevated) ; "it is an impudent satire on glorious John ; but he tickled Buckingham off for it.

> In the first rank of these did Zimri stand ;
> A man so various—

"Hold your peace ?" said Bunce, drowning the voice of the admirer of Dryden in louder and more vehement asseveration "the Rehearsal is the best farce ever was written—and I'll make him kiss the gunner's daughter that denies it. D——n me, I was the best Prince Prettyman ever walked the boards—

> Sometimes a fisher's son, sometimes a prince.

But let us to business.—Hark ye, old gentleman" (to Magnus), "you have a sort of sulkiness about you, for which some of my profession would cut your ears out of your head, and broil them for your dinner with red pepper. I have known Goffe do so to a poor devil, for looking sour and dangerous when he saw his sloop go to Davy Jones's locker with his only son on board. But I'm a spirit of another sort ; and if you or the ladies are ill used, it shall be the Kirkwall people's fault, and not mine, and that's fair ; and so you had better let them know your condition and your circumstances, and so forth,—and that's fair too."

Magnus, thus exhorted, took up the pen, and attempted to write ; but his high spirit so struggled with his paternal anxiety, that his hand refused its office. "I cannot help it," he said, after one or two illegible attempts to write—"I cannot form a letter, if all our lives depended upon it."

And he could not, with his utmost efforts, so suppress the convulsive emotions which he experienced, but that they agitated his whole frame. The willow which bends to the tempest, often escapes better than the oak which resists it ; and so, in great calamities, it sometimes happens, that light and frivolous spirits recover their elasticity and presence of mind sooner than those of a loftier character. In the present case Claud Halcro was fortunately able to perform the task which the deeper feelings of his friend and patron refused. He took the pen, and, in as few words as possible, explained the situation in which they were placed, and the cruel risks to which they were exposed, insinuating at the same time, as delicately as he could express it, that, to the magistrates of the country, the life and honour of its citizens should be a dearer object than even the apprehension or punishment of the guilty ; taking care, however, to qualify the last expression as much as possible, for fear of giving umbrage to the pirates.

Bunce read over the letter, which fortunately met his approbation ; and on seeing the name of Claud Halcro at the bottom, he exclaimed, in great surprise, and with more energetic expressions of asseveration than we choose to record—"Why, you are the little fellow that played the fiddle to old Manager Gadabout's company, at Hogs Norton, the first season I came out there ! I thought I knew your catchword of glorious John."

At another time this recognition might not have been very grateful to Halcro's minstrel pride ; but as matters stood with him, the discovery of a golden mine could not have made him more happy. He instantly remembered the very hopeful young performer who came out in Don Sebastian, and judiciously added, that the muse of glorious John had never received such excellent support during the time that he was first (he might have added, and only) violin to Mr. Gadabout's company.

"Why, yes," said Bunce, "I believe you are right—I think I might have shaken the scene as well as Booth or Betterton either. But I was destined to figure on other boards" (striking his foot upon the deck), "and I believe I must stick by them, till I find no board at all to support me. But now, old acquaintance, I will do something for you—slue yourself this way a bit—I would have you solus." They leaned over the taffrail, while Bunce whispered with more seriousness than he usually showed, "I am sorry for this honest old heart of Norway pine—blight me if I am not—and for the daughters, too—besides I have my own reasons for befriending one of them. I can be a wild fellow with a willing lass of the game ; but to such decent and innocent creatures—d——n me, I am Scipio at Numantia, and Alexander in the tent of Darius. You remember how I touch off Alexander ?" (here he started into heroics) :

> Thus from the grave I rise to save my love ;
> All draw your swords, with wings of lightning move.
> When I rush on, sure none will dare to stay—
> 'Tis beauty calls, and glory shows the way.

Claud Halcro failed not to bestow the necessary commendations on his declamation, declaring that, in his opinion as an honest man, he had always thought Mr. Altamont's giving that speech far superior in tone and energy to Betterton.

Bunce, or Altamont, wrung his hand tenderly. "Ah, you flatter me, my dear friend," he said ; "yet, why had not the public some of your judgment !—I should not then have been at this pass. Heaven knows, my dear Mr. Halcro—Heaven knows with what pleasure I could keep you on board with me, just that I might have one friend who loves as much to hear, as I do to recite, the choicest pieces of our finest dramatic authors. The most of us are beasts—and, for the Kirkwall hostage yonder, he uses me, egad, as I use Fletcher, I think, and huffs me the more, the more I do

299

for him. But how delightful would it be in a tropic night, when the ship was hanging on the breeze, with a broad and steady sail, for me to rehearse Alexander, with you for my pit, box and gallery ! Nay (for you are a follower of the muses, as I remember), who knows but you and I might be the means of inspiring, like Orpheus and Eurydice, a pure taste into our companions, and softening their manners, while we excited their better feelings ?"

This was spoken with so much unction, that Claud Halcro began to be afraid he had both made the actual punch over potent, and mixed too many bewitching ingredients in the cup of flattery which he had administered ; and that, under the influence of both potions, the sentimental pirate might detain him by force, merely to realise the scenes which his imagination presented. The conjuncture was, however, too delicate to admit of any active effort on Halcro's part to redeem his blunder, and therefore he only returned the tender pressure of his friend's hand, and uttered the interjection "alas !" in as pathetic a tone as he could.

Bunce immediately resumed : "You are right, my friend, these are but vain visions of felicity, and it remains but for the unhappy Altamont to serve the friend to whom he is now to bid farewell. I have determined to put you and the two girls ashore, with Fletcher for your protection ; and so call up the young women, and let them be gone before the devil get aboard of me, or of some one else. You will carry my letter to the magistrates, and second it with your own eloquence, and assure them, that if they hurt but one hair of Cleveland's head, there will be the devil to pay, and no pitch hot."

Relieved at heart by this unexpected termination of Bunce's harangue, Halcro descended the companion-ladder two steps at a time, and knocking at the cabin door, could scarce find intelligible language enough to say his errand. The sisters, hearing with uexpected joy that they were to be set ashore, muffled themselves in their cloaks, and, when they learned that the boat was hoisted out, came hastily on deck, where they were apprised, for the first time, to their great horror, that their father was still to remain on board of the pirate.

"We will remain with him at every risk," said Minna—"we may be of some assistance to him, were it but for an instant—we will live and die with him !"

"We shall aid him more surely," said Brenda, who comprehended the nature of their situation better then Minna, "by interesting the people of Kirkwall to grant these gentlemen's demands."

"Spoken like an angel of sense and beauty," said Bunce ; "and now away with you ; for, d——n me, if this is not like having a lighted linstock in the powder-room—if you speak another word more, confound me if I know how I shall bring myself to part with you !"

"Go, in God's name, my daughters," said Magnus, "I am in God's hand ; and when you are gone I shall care little for myself—and I shall think and say, as long as I live, that this good gentleman deserves a better trade.—Go—go—away with you !"—for they yet lingered in unwillingness to leave him.

300

"Stay not to kiss," said Bunce, "for fear I be tempted to ask my share. Into the boat with you—yet stop an instant." He drew the three captives apart—"Fletcher," said he, "will answer for the rest of the fellows, and will see you safe off the sea-beach. But how to answer for Fletcher, I know not, except by trusting Mr. Halcro with this little guarantee."

He offered the minstrel a small double-barrelled pistol, which, he said, was loaded with a brace of balls. Minna observed Halcro's hand tremble as he stretched it out to take the weapon. "Give it to me, sir," she said, taking it from the outlaw ; "and trust to me for defending my sister and myself."

"Bravo, bravo !" shouted Bunce. "There spoke a wench worthy of Cleveland, the King of Rovers !"

"Cleveland !" repeated Minna, "do you then know that Cleveland, whom you have twice named ?"

"Know him ! Is there a man alive," said Bunce, "that knows better than I do the best and stoutest fellow ever stepped betwixt stem and stern ? When he is out of the bilboes, as please Heaven he shall soon be, I reckon to see you come on board of us, and reign the queen of every sea we sail over.—You have got the little guardian, I suppose you know how to use it. If Fletcher behaves ill to you, you need only draw up this piece of iron with your thumb, so—and if he persists, it is but crooking your pretty forefinger thus, and I shall lose the most dutiful messmate that ever a man had—though, d——n the dog, he will deserve his death if he disobeys my orders. And now, into the boat—but stay, one kiss for Cleveland's sake."

Brenda, in deadly terror, endured his courtesy, but Minna, stepping back with disdain, offered her hand. Bunce laughed, but kissed, with a theatrical air, the fair hand which she extended as a ransom for her lips, and at length the sisters and Halcro were placed in the boat, which rowed off under Fletcher's command.

Bunce stood on the quarter-deck, soliloquising after the manner of his original profession. "Were this told at Port-Royal now, or at the isle of Providence, or in the Petits Guaves, I wonder what they would say of me ! Why, that I was a good natured milksop—a Jack-a-lent—an ass.—Well, let them. I have done enough of bad to think about it ; it is worth while doing one good action, if it were but for the rarity of the thing, and to put one in good humour with one's-self." Then turning to Magnus Troil, he proceeded—"By —— these are bonarobas, these daughters of yours. The eldest would make her fortune on the London boards. What a dashing attitude the wench had with her, as she seized the pistol !— d——n me, that touch would have brought the house down. What a Roxalana the jade would have made !" (for, in his oratory, Bunce, like Sancho's gossip, Thomas Cecial, was apt to use the most energetic word which came to hand, without accurately considering its propriety). "I would give my whole share of the next prize to hear her spout—

> Away, begone, and give a whirlwind room,
> Or I will blow you up like dust.—Avaunt !
> Madness but meanly represents my rage.

301

And then, again, that soft, shy, tearful trembler, for Statira, to hear her recite—

> He speaks the kindest words, and looks such things,
> Vows with such passion, swears with so much grace,
> That 'tis a kind of heaven to be deluded by him.

What a play we might have run up !—I was a beast not to think of it before I sent them off—I to be Alexander—Claud Halcro Lysimachus—this old gentleman might have made a Clytus, for a pinch. I was an idiot not to think of it !"

There was much in this effusion which might have displeased the Udaller; but, to speak truth, he paid no attention to it. His eye, and finally his spy-glass, was employed in watching the return of his daughters to the shore. He saw them land on the beach, and, accompanied by Halcro and another man (Fletcher, doubtless), he saw them ascend the acclivity and proceed upon the road to Kirkwall, and he could even distinguish that Minna, as if considering herself as the guardian of the party, walked a little aloof from the rest, on the watch, as it seemed, against surprise, and ready to act as occasion should require. At length, as the Udaller was just about to lose sight of them, he had the exquisite satisfaction to see the party halt, and the pirate leave them, after a space just long enough for a civil farewell, and proceed slowly back on his return to the beach. Blessing the Great Being who had thus relieved him from the most agonising fears which a father can feel, the worthy Udaller, from that instant, stood resigned to his own fate, whatever that might be.

CHAPTER THIRTY-SEVENTH

> Over the mountains and under the waves,
> Over the fountains and under the graves,
> Over floods that are deepest,
> Which Neptune obey,
> Over rocks that are steepest,
> Love will find out the way.
>
> OLD SONG

THE parting of Fletcher from Claud Halcro and the sisters of Burgh Westra on the spot where it took place was partly occasioned by a small party of armed men being seen at a distance in the act of advancing from Kirkwall, an apparition hidden from the Udaller's spy-glass by the swell of the ground, but quite visible to the pirate, whom it determined to consult his own safety by a speedy return to his boat. He was just turning away, when Minna occasioned the short delay which her father had observed.

"Stop," she said ; "I command you !—Tell your leader from me that whatever the answer may be from Kirkwall, he shall carry his vessel, nevertheless, round to Stromness ; and being anchored there, let him send a boat ashore for Captain Cleveland when he shall see a smoke on the Bridge of Broisgar."

Fletcher had thought, like his messmate Bunce, of asking a kiss, at least, for the trouble of escorting these beautiful young women ; and, perhaps, neither the terror of the approaching Kirkwall men nor of Minna's weapon might have prevented his being insolent. But the name of his Captain, and still more the unappalled, dignified, and commanding manner of Minna Troil overawed him. He made a sea bow—promised to keep a sharp look-out, and, returning to his boat, went on board with his message.

As Halcro and the sisters advanced towards the party whom they saw on the Kirkwall road, and who, on their part, had halted as if to observe them, Brenda, relieved from the fears of Fletcher's presence, which had hitherto kept her silent, exclaimed, "Merciful Heaven !—Minna, in what hands have we left our dear father ?"

"In the hands of brave men," said Minna steadily—"I fear not for him."

"As brave as you please," said Claud Halcro, "but very dangerous rogues for all that.—I know that fellow Altamont, as he calls himself, though that is not his right name neither, as deboshed a dog as ever made a barn ring with blood and blank verse. He began with Barnwell, and everybody thought he would end with the gallows, like the last scene in Venice Preserved."

"It matters not," said Minna—"the wilder the waves, the more powerful is the voice that rules them. The name alone of Cleveland ruled the mood of the fiercest amongst them."

"I am sorry for Cleveland," said Brenda, "if such are his companions ; but I care little for him in comparison to my father."

"Reserve your compassion for those who need it," said Minna, "and fear nothing for our father.—God knows, every silver hair on his head is to me worth the treasure of an unsunned mine ; but I know that he is safe while in yonder vessel, and I know that he will be soon safe on shore."

"I would I could see it," said Claud Halcro ; "but I fear the Kirkwall people, supposing Cleveland to be such as I dread, will not dare to exchange him against the Udaller. The Scots have very severe laws against theft-boot, as they call it."

"But who are those on the road before us ?" said Brenda ; "and why do they halt there so jealously ?"

"They are a patrol of the militia," answered Halcro. "Glorious John touches them off a little sharply—but then John was a Jacobite—

> Mouths without hands, maintain'd at vast expense,
> In peace a charge, in war a weak defence ;
> Stout once a month, they march, a blustering band,
> And ever, but in time of need, at hand.

I fancy they halted just now, taking us, as they saw us on the brow of the hill, for a party of the sloop's men, and, now they can distinguish that you wear petticoats, they are moving on again."

They came on accordingly, and proved to be, as Claud Halcro had suggested, a patrol sent out to watch the motions of the pirates, and to prevent their attempting descents to damage the country.

They heartily congratulated Claud Halcro, who was well known to more than one of them, upon his escape from captivity ; and the commander of the party, while offering every assistance to the ladies, could not help condoling with them on the circumstances in which their father stood, hinting, though in a delicate and doubtful manner, the difficulties which might be in the way of his liberation.

When they arrived at Kirkwall, and obtained an audience of the Provost and one or two of the Magistrates, these difficulties were more plainly insisted upon.—"The Halcyon frigate is upon the coast," said the Provost ; "she was seen off Duncansbay Head ; and though I have the deepest respect for Mr. Troil of Burgh Westra, yet I shall be answerable to law if I release from prison the captain of his suspicious vessel, on account of the safety of any individual who may be unhappily endangered by his detention. This man is now known to be the heart and soul of these bucaniers, and am I at liberty to send him abroad that he may plunder the country, or perhaps go fight the King's ship ?—for he has impudence enough for anything."

"Courage enough for anything, you mean, Mr. Provost," said Minna, unable to restrain her displeasure.

"Why, you may call it as you please, Miss Troil," said the worthy magistrate ; "but in my opinion, that sort of courage which proposes to fight singly against two, is little better than a kind of practical impudence."

"But our father ?" said Brenda, in a tone of the most earnest entreaty—"our father—the friend, I may say the father, of his country—to whom so many look for kindness, and so many for actual support—whose loss would be the extinction of a beacon in a storm—will you indeed weigh the risk which he runs against such a trifling thing as letting an unfortunate man from prison to seek his unhappy fate elsewhere ?"

"Miss Brenda is right," said Claud Halcro ; "I am for let-a-be for let-a-be, as the boys say ; and never fash about a warrant of liberation, Provost, but just take a fool's counsel, and let the goodman of the jail forget to draw his bolt on the wicket, or leave a chink of a window open, or the like, and we shall be rid of the rover, and have the one best honest fellow in Orkney or Zetland on the lee-side of a bowl of punch with us in five hours."

The Provost replied in nearly the same terms as before, that he had the highest respect for Mr. Magnus Troil of Burgh Westra, but that he could not suffer his consideration for any individual, however respectable, to interfere with the discharge of his duty.

Minna then addressed her sister in a tone of calm and sarcastic displeasure.—"You forget," she said, "Brenda, that you are talking of the safety of a poor insignificant Udaller of Zetland, to no less a person than the Chief Magistrate of the metropolis of Orkney—can you expect so great a person to condescend to such a trifling subject of consideration ? It will be time enough for the Provost to think of complying with the terms sent to him—for comply with them at length he both must and will—when the Church of Saint Magnus is beat down about his ears."

"You may be angry with me, my pretty young lady," said the good-humoured Provost Torfe, "but I cannot be offended with you. The Church of Saint Magnus had stood many a day, and, I think, will outlive both you and me, much more yonder pack of unhanged dogs. And besides that your father is half an Orkneyman, and has both estate and friends among us, I would, I give you my word, do as much for a Zetlander in distresss as I would for any one, excepting one of our own native Kirkwallers, who are doubtless to be preferred. And if you will take up your lodgings here with my wife and myself, we will endeavour to show you," continued he, "that you are as welcome in Kirkwall, as ever you could be in Lerwick or Scalloway."

Minna deigned no reply to this good-humoured invitation, but Brenda declined it in civil terms, pleading the necessity of taking up their abode with a wealthy widow of Kirkwall, a relation, who already expected them.

Halcro made another attempt to move the Provost, but found him inexorable.—"The Collector of the Customs had already threatened," he said, "to inform against him for entering into treaty, or, as he called it, packing and peeling with those strangers, even when it seemed the only means of preventing a bloody affray in the town ; and, should he now forego the advantage afforded by the imprisonment of Cleveland and the escape of the Factor, he might incur something worse than censure." The burden of the whole was, "that he was sorry for the Udaller, he was sorry even for the lad Cleveland, who had some sparks of honour about him ; but his duty was imperious, and must be obeyed." The Provost then precluded farther argument, by observing, that another affair from Zetland called for his immediate attention. A gentleman named Mertoun, residing at Yarlshof, had made complaint against Snailsfoot the Yagger for having assisted a domestic of his in embezzling some valuable articles which had been deposited in his custody, and he was about to take examination on the subject, and cause them to be restored to Mr. Mertoun, who was accountable for them to the right owner.

In all this information, there was nothing which seemed interesting to the sisters excepting the word Mertoun, which went like a dagger to the heart of Minna, when she recollected the circumstances under which Mordaunt Mertoun had disappeared, and which, with an emotion less painful, though still of a melancholy nature, called a faint blush into Brenda's cheek, and a slight degree of moisture into her eye. But it was soon evident that the Magistrate spoke not of Mordaunt, but of his father ; and the daughters of Magnus, little interested in his detail, took leave of the Provost to go to their own lodgings.

When they arrived at their relation's, Minna made it her business to learn, by such inquiries as she could make without exciting suspicion, what was the situation of the unfortunate Cleveland, which she soon discovered to be exceedingly precarious. The Provost had not, indeed, committed him to close custody, as Claud Halcro had anticipated, recollecting, perhaps, the favourable circumstances under which he had surrendered himself, and loath, till the moment of the last necessity, altogether to break faith with him. But although left apparently at large, he was strictly watched by persons well armed and appointed for the purpose, who had directions to detain him by force, if he attempted to pass certain narrow precincts which were allotted to him. He was quartered in a strong room within what is called the King's Castle, and at night his chamber door was locked on the outside, and a sufficient guard mounted to prevent his escape. He therefore enjoyed only the degree of liberty which the cat, in her cruel sport, is sometimes pleased to permit to the mouse which she has clutched ; and yet, such was the terror of the resources, the courage, and ferocity of the pirate Captain, that the Provost was blamed by the Collector, and many other sage citizens of Kirkwall, for permitting him to be at large upon any conditions.

It may be well believed, that, under such circumstances, Cleveland had no desire to seek any place of public resort, conscious that he was the object of a mixed feeling of curiosity and terror. His favourite place of exercise, therefore, was the external aisles of the Cathedral of Saint Magnus, of which the eastern end alone is fitted up for public worship. This solemn old edifice, having escaped the ravage which attended the first convulsions of the Reformation, still retains some appearance of episcopal dignity. This place of worship is separated by a screen from the nave and western limb of the cross, and the whole is preserved in a state of cleanliness and decency, which might be well proposed as an example to the proud piles of Westminster and St. Paul's.

It was in this exterior part of the Cathedral that Cleveland was permitted to walk, the rather that his guards, by watching the single open entrance, had the means, with very little inconvenience to themselves, of preventing any possible attempt at escape. The place itself was well suited to his melancholy circumstances. The lofty and vaulted roof rises upon ranges of Saxon pillars, of massive size, four of which, still larger than the rest, once supported the lofty spire, which, long since destroyed by accident, has been rebuilt upon a disproportioned and truncated plan. The light is admitted at the eastern end through a lofty, well proportioned, and richly ornamented Gothic window, and the pavement is covered with inscriptions, in different languages, distinguishing the graves of noble Orcadians, who have at different times been deposited within the sacred precincts.

Here walked Cleveland, musing over the events of a misspent life, which, it seemed probable, might be brought to a violent and shameful close, while he was yet in the prime of youth.—"With these dead," he said, looking on the pavement, "shall I soon be numbered—but no holy man will speak a blessing ; no friendly hand register an inscription ; no proud descendant sculpture armorial bearings over the grave of the pirate Cleveland. My whitening bones will swing in the gibbet irons, on some wild beach or lonely cape, that will be esteemed fatal and accursed for my sake. The old mariner, as he passes the Sound, will shake his head, and tell of my name and actions, as a warning to his younger comrades.— But, Minna ! Minna ! what will be thy thoughts when the news reaches thee ?—Would to God the tidings were drowned in the deepest whirlpool betwixt Kirkwall and Burgh Westra, ere they came to her ear !—and oh ! would to Heaven that we had never met, since we never can meet again !"

He lifted up his eyes as he spoke, and Minna Troil stood before him. Her face was pale, and her hair dishevelled ; but her look was composed and firm, with its usual expression of high-minded melancholy. She was still shrouded in the large mantle which she had assumed on leaving the vessel. Cleveland's first emotion was astonishment ; his next was joy, not unmixed with awe. He would have exclaimed—he would have thrown himself at her feet—but she imposed at once silence and composure on him, by raising her finger, and saying, in a low but commanding accent,— "Be cautious—we are observed—there are men without—they let me enter with difficulty. I dare not remain long—they would think—they might believe—O Cleveland ! I have hazarded everything to save you !"

"To save me ?—Alas ! poor Minna !" answered Cleveland, "to save me is impossible.—Enough that I have seen you once more, were it but to say, for ever farewell !"

"We must, indeed say farewell," said Minna ; "for fate and your guilt have divided us for ever.—Cleveland, I have seen your associates—need I tell you more—need I say, that I know now what a pirate is ?"

"You have been in the ruffians' power !" said Cleveland, with a start of agony—"Did they presume"—

"Cleveland," replied Minna, "they presumed nothing—your name was a spell over them. By the power of that spell over these ferocious banditti, and by that alone, I was reminded of the qualities I once thought my Cleveland's !"

"Yes," said Cleveland, proudly, "my name has and shall have power over them, when they are at the wildest ; and, had they harmed you by one rude word, they should have found—Yet what do I rave about—I am a prisoner !"

"You shall be so no longer," said Minna—"Your safety—the safety of my dear father—all demand your instant freedom. I have formed a scheme for your liberty, which, boldly executed, cannot fail. The light is fading without—muffle yourself in my cloak, and you will easily pass the guards—I have given them the means of carousing, and they are deeply engaged. Haste to the Loch of Stennis, and hide yourself till day dawns, then make a smoke on the point, where the land, stretching into the lake on each side, divides it nearly in two at the Bridge of Broisgar. Your vessel, which lies not far distant, will send a boat ashore.—Do not hesitate an instant."

"But you, Minna !—Should this wild scheme succeed," said Cleveland, "what is to become of you ?"

"For my share in your escape," answered the maiden, "the honesty of my own intention will vindicate me in the sight of Heaven ; and the safety of my father, whose fate depends on yours, will be my excuse to man."

In a few words, she gave him the history of their capture and its consequences. Cleveland cast up his eyes and raised his hands to

Heaven, in thankfulness for the escape of the sisters from his evil companions, and then hastily added,—"But you are right, Minna ; I must fly at all rates—for your father's sake, I must fly.—Here, then, we part—yet not, I trust, for ever."

"For ever !" answered a voice, that sounded as from a sepulchral vault.

They started, looked around them, and then gazed on each other. It seemed as if the echoes of the building had returned Cleveland's last words, but the pronunciation was too emphatically accented.

"Yes, for ever !" said Norna of the Fitful Head, stepping forward from behind one of the massive Saxon pillars which support the roof of the Cathedral. "Here meet the crimson foot and the crimson hand. Well for both that the wound is healed whence that crimson was derived—well for both, but best for him who shed it.—Here, then, you meet—and meet for the last time !"

"Not so," said Cleveland, as if about to take Minna's hand ; "to separate me from Minna, while I have life, must be the work of herself alone."

"Away !" said Norna, stepping betwixt them, "away with such idle folly !—Nourish no vain dreams of future meetings—you part here, and you part for ever. The hawk pairs not with the dove ; guilt matches not with innocence.—Minna Troil, you look for the last time on this bold and criminal man—Cleveland, you behold Minna for the last time !"

"And dream you," said Cleveland indignantly, "that your mummery imposes on me, and that I am among the fools that see more than trick in your pretended art ?"

"Forbear, Cleveland, forbear ?" said Minna, her hereditary awe of Norna augmented by the circumstance of her sudden appearance. "Oh, forbear ?—she is powerful—she is but too powerful.—And do you, O Norna, remember my father's safety is linked with Cleveland's."

"And it is well for Cleveland that I do remember it," replied the Pythoness—"and that, for the sake of one, I am here to aid both. You, with your childish purpose of passing one of his bulk and stature under the disguise of a few paltry folds of wadmaal—what would your device have procured him but instant restraint with bolt and shackle ?—I will save him—I will place him in security on board his bark. But let him renounce these shores for ever, and carry elsewhere the terrors of his sable flag, and his yet blacker name ; for if the sun rises twice, and finds him still at anchor, his blood be on his own head.—Ay, look to each other—look the last look that I permit to frail affection—and say, if you *can* say it, Farewell for ever."

"Obey her," stammered Minna ; "remonstrate not, but obey her."

Cleveland, grasping her hand, and kissing it ardently, said, but so low that she only could hear it, "Farewell, Minna, but *not* for ever."

"And now, maiden, begone," said Norna, "and leave the rest to the Reimkennar."

"One word more," said Minna, "and I obey you. Tell me but if I have caught aright your meaning—is Mordaunt Mertoun safe and recovered ?"

"Recovered and safe," said Norna ; "else woe to the hand that shed his blood !"

Minna slowly sought the door of the Cathedral, and turned back from time to time to look at the shadowy form of Norna, and the stately and military figure of Cleveland, as they stood together in the deepening gloom of the ancient Cathedral. When she looked back a second time, they were in motion, and Cleveland followed the matron, as, with a slow and solemn step, she glided towards one of the side aisles. When Minna looked back a third time their figures were no longer visible. She collected herself, and walked on to the eastern door by which she had entered, and listened for an instant to the guard who talked together on the outside.

"The Zetland girl stays a long time with this pirate fellow," said one. "I wish they have not more to speak about than the ransom of her father."

"Ay, truly," answered another, "the wenches will have more sympathy with a handsome young pirate, that an old bedridden burgher."

Their discourse was here interrupted by her of whom they were speaking ; and, as if taken in the manner, they pulled off their hats, made their awkward obeisances, and looked not a little embarrassed and confused.

Minna returned to the house where she lodged, much affected, yet, on the whole, pleased with the result of her expedition, which seemed to put her father out of danger, and assured her at once of the escape of Cleveland, and of the safety of young Mordaunt. She hastened to communicate both pieces of intelligence to Brenda, who joined her in thankfulness to Heaven, and was herself wellnigh persuaded to believe in Norna's supernatural pretensions, so much was she pleased with the manner in which they had been employed. Some time was spent in exchanging their mutual congratulations, and mingling tears of hope, mixed with apprehension ; when, at a late hour in the evening, they were interrupted by Claud Halcro, who, full of a fidgeting sort of importance, not unmingled with fear, came to acquaint them, that the prisoner, Cleveland, had disappeared from the Cathedral, in which he had been permitted to walk, and that the Provost, having been informed that Minna was accessary to his flight, was coming, in a mighty quandary, to make inquiry into the circumstances.

When the worthy Magistrate arrived, Minna did not conceal from him her own wish that Cleveland should make his escape, as the only means which she saw of redeeming her father from imminent danger. But that she had any actual acccession to his flight, she positively denied ; and stated, "that she had parted from Cleveland in the Cathedral, more than two hours since, and then left him in company with a third person, whose name she did not conceive herself obliged to communicate."

"It is not needful, Miss Minna Troil," answered Provost Torfe ; "for, although no person but this Captain Cleveland and yourself was seen to enter the Kirk of Saint Magnus this day, we know well enough your cousin, old Ulla Troil, whom, you Zetlanders call Norna of Fitful Head, has been cruising up and down, upon sea and land, and air, for what I know in boats and on ponies, and it may be on broomsticks ; and here has been her dumb Drow, too, coming and going, and playing the spy on every one—and a good spy he is, for he can hear every thing, and tells nothing again, unless to his mistress. And we know, besides, that she can enter the Kirk when all the doors are fast, and has been seen there more than once, God save us from the Evil One !—and so, without farther questions asked, I conclude it was old Norna whom you left in the Kirk with this slashing blade—and, if so, they may catch them again that can.— I cannot but say, however, pretty Mistress Minna, that you Zetland folks seem to forget both law and gospel, when you use the help of witchcraft to fetch delinquents out of a legal prison ; and the least that you, or your cousin, or your father, can do, is to use influence with this wild fellow to go away as soon as possible, without hurting the town or trade, and then there will be little harm in what has chanced ; for, Heaven knows, I did not seek the poor lad's life, so I could get my hands free of him without blame ; and far less did I wish, that, through his imprisonment, any harm should come to worthy Magnus Troil of Burgh Westra."

"I see where the shoe pinches you, Mr. Provost," said Claud Halcro, "and I am sure I can answer for my friend Mr. Troil, as well as for myself, that we will say and do all in our power with this man, Captain Cleveland, to make him leave the coast directly."

"And I," said Minna, "am so convinced that what you recommend is best for all parties, that my sister and I will set off early to-morrow morning to the House of Stennis, if Mr. Halcro will give us his escort, to receive my father when he comes ashore, that we may acquaint him with our wish, and to use every influence to induce this unhappy man to leave the country."

Provost Torfe looked upon her with some surprise. "It is not every young woman," he said,"would wish to move eight miles nearer to a band of pirates."

"We run no risk," said Claud Halcro, interfering. "The House of Stennis is strong ; and my cousin, whom it belongs to, has men and arms within it. The young ladies are as safe there as in Kirkwall ; and much good may arise from an early communication between Magnus Troil and his daughters. And happy am I to see, that in your case, my good old friend,—as glorious John says,—

—After much debate,
The man prevails above the magistrate.

The Provost smiled, nodded his head, and indicated, as far as he thought he could do with decency, how happy he should be if the Fortune's Favourite, and her disorderly crew, would leave Orkney without further interference, or violence on either side. He could not authorise their being supplied from the shore, he said ; but, either for fear or favour, they were certain to get provisions at Stromness. This pacific magistrate then took leave of Halcro and the two ladies, who proposed, the next morning, to transfer their residence to the House of

Stennis, situated upon the banks of the salt-water lake of the same name, and about four miles by water from the Road of Stromness, where the Rover's vessel was lying.

CHAPTER THIRTY-EIGHTH

Fly, Fleance, fly !—Thou mayest escape.

MACBETH

IT was one branch of the various arts by which Norna endeavoured to maintain her pretensions to supernatural powers, that she made herself familiarly and practically acquainted with all the secret passes and recesses, whether natural or artificial, which she could hear of, whether by tradition or otherwise, and was, by such knowledge, often enabled to perform feats which were otherwise unaccountable. Thus, when she escaped from the tabernacle at Burgh Westra, it was by a sliding board which covered a secret passage in the wall, known to none but herself and Magnus, who, she was well assured, would not betray her. The profusion, also, with which she lavished a considerable income, otherwise of no use to her, enabled her to procure the earliest intelligence respecting whatever she desired to know, and, at the same time, to secure all other assistance necessary to carry her plans into effect. Cleveland, upon the present occasion, had reason to admire both her sagacity and her resources.

Upon her applying a little forcible pressure, a door which was concealed under some rich wooden sculpture in the screen which divides the eastern aisle from the rest of the Catherdral, opened, and disclosed a dark narrow winding passage, into which she entered, telling Cleveland, in a whisper, to follow, and be sure he shut the door behind him. He obeyed, and followed her in darkness and silence, sometimes descending steps, of the number of which she always apprised him, sometimes ascending, and often turning at short angles. The air was more free than he could have expected, the passage being ventilated at different parts by unseen and ingeniously contrived spiracles, which communicated with the open air. At length their long course ended, by Norna drawing aside a sliding panel, which, opening behind a wooden, or box-bed, as it is called in Scotland, admitted them into an ancient, but very mean apartment, having a latticed window and a groined roof. The furniture was much dilapidated ; and its only ornaments were, on the one side of the wall, a garland of faded ribbons, such as are used to decorate whale-vessels ; and on the other, an escutcheon, bearing an Earl's arms and coronet, surrounded with the usual emblems of mortality. The mattock and spade, which lay in one corner, together with the appearance of an old man, who, in a rusty black coat, and slouched hat, sat reading by a table, announced that they were in the habitation of the church-beadle, or sexton, and in the presence of that respectable functionary.

When his attention was attracted by the noise of the sliding panel, he arose, and testifying much respect, but no surprise, took his shadowy hat from his thin grey locks, and stood uncovered in the presence of Norna with an air of profound humility.

"Be faithful," said Norna to the old man, "and beware you show not any living mortal the secret path to the Sanctuary."

The old man bowed in token of obedience and of thanks, for she put money in his hand as she spoke. With a faltering voice, he expressed his hope that she would remember his son, who was on the Greenland voyage, that he might return fortunate and safe, as he had done last year, when he brought back the garland, pointing to that upon the wall.

"My cauldron shall boil, and my rhyme shall be said, in his behalf," answered Norna. "Waits Pacolet without with the horses ?"

The old Sexton assented, and the Pythoness, commanding Cleveland to follow her, went through a back door of the apartment into a small garden, corresponding, in its desolate appearance, to the habitation they had just quitted. The low and broken wall easily permitted them to pass into another and larger garden, though not much better kept, and a gate, which was upon the latch, let them into a long and winding lane, through which, Norna having whispered to her companion that it was the only dangerous place on their road, they walked with a hasty pace. It was now nearly dark, and the inhabitants of the poor dwellings, on either hand, had betaken themselves to their houses. They saw only one woman, who was looking from her door, but blessed herself and retired into her house with precipitation, when she saw the tall figure of Norna stalk past her with long strides. The lane conducted them into the country, where the dumb dwarf waited with three horses, ensconced behind the wall of a deserted shed. On one of these Norna instantly seated herself, Cleveland mounted another, and, followed by Pacolet on the third, they moved sharply on through the darkness ; the active and spirited animals on which they rode being of a breed rather taller than those reared in Zetland.

After more than an hour's smart riding, in which Norna acted as guide, they stopped before a hovel, so utterly desolate in appearance, that it resembled rather a cattle-shed than a cottage.

"Here you must remain till dawn, when your signal can be seen from your vessel," said Norna, consigning the horses to the care of Pacolet, and leading the way into the wretched hovel, which she presently illuminated by lighting the small iron lamp which she usually carried along with her. "It is a poor," she said, "but a safe place of refuge ; for were we pursued hither, the earth would yawn and admit us into its recesses ere you were taken. For know that this ground is sacred to the gods of old Valhalla.—And now say, man of mischief and of blood, are you friend or foe to Norna, the sole priestess of these disowned deities ?"

"How is it possible for me to be your enemy ?" said Cleveland.— "Common gratitude"—

"Common gratitude," said Norna, interrupting him, "is a common word—and words are the common pay which fools accept at the hands of knaves ; but Norna must be requited by actions—by sacrifices."

"Well, mother, name your request."

"That you never seek to see Minna Troil again, and that you leave this coast in twenty-four hours," answered Norna.

"It is impossible," said the Captain ; " I cannot be soon enough found in the sea-stores which the sloop must have."

"You can. I will take care you are fully supplied ; and Caithness and the Hebrides are not far distant—you can depart if you will."

"And why should I," said Cleveland, "if I will not ?"

"Because your stay endangers others," said Norna, "and will prove your own destruction. Hear me with attention. From the first moment I saw you lying senseless on the sand beneath the cliffs of Sumburgh, I read that in your countenance which linked you with me, and those who were dear to me ; but whether for good or evil, was hidden from mine eyes. I aided in saving your life, in preserving your property. I aided in doing so, the very youth whom you have crossed in his dearest affections—crossed by tale-bearing slander."

"*I* slander Mertoun !" exclaimed the Captin. "By Heaven, I scarce mentioned his name at Burgh Westra, if it is that which you mean. The peddling fellow Bryce, meaning, I believe, to be my friend, because he found something could be made by me, did, I have since heard, carry tattle, or truth, I know not which, to the old man, which was confirmed by the report of the whole island. But, for me, I scarce thought of him as a rival ; else, I had taken a more honourable way to rid myself of him."

"Was the point of your double-edged knife, directed to the bosom of an unarmed man, intended to carve out that more honourable way ?" said Norna, sternly.

Cleveland was conscience-struck, and remained silent for an instant, ere he replied, "There, indeed, I was wrong ; but he is, I thank Heaven, recovered, and welcome to an honourable satisfaction."

"Cleveland," said the Pythoness, "no ! The fiend who employs you as his implement is powerful ; but with me he shall not strive. You are of that temperament which the dark Influences desire as the tools of their agency ; bold, haughty , and undaunted, unrestrained by principle, and having only in its room a wild sense of indomitable pride, which such men call honour. Such you are, and as such your course through life has been onward and unrestrained, bloody and tempestuous. By me, however, it shall be controlled," she concluded, stretching out her staff, as if in the attitude of determined authority—"ay, even although the demon who presides over it should even now arise in his terrors."

Cleveland laughed scornfully. "Good mother," he said, "reserve such language for the rude sailor that implores you to bestow on him fair wind, or the poor fisherman that asks success to his nets and lines. I have been long inaccessible both to fear and to superstition. Call forth your demon, if you command one, and place him before me. The man that has spent years in company with incarnate devils, can scarce dread the presence of a disembodied fiend."

This was said with a careless and desperate bitterness of spirit, which proved too powerfully energetic even for the delusions of Norna's insanity ; and it was with a hollow and tremulous voice that she asked

Cleveland—"For what, then, do you hold me, if you deny the power that I have bought so dearly ?"

"You have wisdom, mother," said Cleveland ; "at least you have art, and art is power. I hold you for one who knows how to steer upon the current of events, but I deny your power to change its course. Do not, therefore, waste words in quoting terrors for which I have no feeling, but tell me at once, wherefore you would have me depart ?"

"Because I will have you see Minna no more," answered Norna—"Because Minna is the destined bride of him whom men call Mordaunt Mertoun—Because if you depart not within twenty-four hours, utter destruction awaits you. In these plain words there is no metaphysical delusion—Answer me as plainly."

"In as plain words, then," answered Cleveland, "I will *not* leave these islands—not, at least, till I have seen Minna Troil ; and never shall your Mordaunt possess her while I live."

"Hear him," said Morna—"hear a mortal man spurn at the means of prolonging his life !—hear a sinful—a most sinful being, refuse the time which fate yet affords for repentance, and for the salvation of an immortal soul !—Behold him how he stands erect, bold and confident in his youthful strength and courage ! My eyes, unused to tears—even my eyes, which have so little cause to weep for him, are blinded with sorrow, to think what so fair a form will be ere the second sun set !"

"Mother," said Cleveland, firmly, yet with some touch of sorrow in his voice, "I in part understand your threats. You know more than we do of the course of the Halcyon—perhaps have the means (for I acknowledge you have shown wonderful skill of combination in such affairs) of directing her cruise our way. Be it so,—I will not depart from my purpose for that risk. If the frigate comes hither, we have still our shoal water to trust to ; and I think they will scarce cut us out with boats, as if we were a Spanish xebeck. I am therefore resolved I will hoist once more the flag under which I have cruised, avail ourselves of the thousand chances which have helped us in greater odds, and, at the worst, fight the vessel to the very last ; and, when mortal man can do no more, it is but snapping a pistol in the powder-room, and, as we have lived, so will we die."

There was a dead pause as Cleveland ended ; and it was broken by his resuming a softer tone—"You have heard my answer, mother ; let us debate it no farther, but part in peace. I would willingly leave you a remembrance, that you may not forget a poor fellow to whom your services have been useful, and who parts with you in no unkindness, however unfriendly you are to his dearest interests.—Nay, do not shun to accept such a trifle," he said, forcing upon Norna the little silver enchased box which had been once the subject of strife betwixt Mertoun and him ; "it is not for the sake of the metal, which I know you value not, but simply as a memorial that you have met him of whom many a strange tale will hereafter be told in the seas which he has traversed."

"I accept your gift," said Norna, "in token that, if I have in aught been accessary to your fate, it was as the involuntary and grieving agent of

314

other powers. Well did you say we direct not the current of the events which hurry us forward, and render our utmost efforts unavailing ; even as the wells of Tuftiloe* can wheel the stoutest vessel round and round, in despite of either sail or steerage.—Pacolet !" she exclaimed, in a louder voice, "what, ho ! Pacolet !"

A large stone, which lay at the side of the wall of the hovel fell as she spoke, and to Cleveland's surprise, if not somewhat to his fear, the misshapen form of the dwarf was seen, like some overgrown reptile, extricating himself out of a subterranean passage, the entrance to which the stone had covered.

Norna, as if impressed by what Cleveland had said on the subject of her supernatural pretensions, was so far from endeavouring to avail herself of this opportunity to enforce them, that she hastened to explain the phenomenon he had witnessed.

"Such passages," she said, "to which the entrances are carefully concealed, are frequently found in these islands—the places of retreat of the ancient inhabitants, where they sought refuge from the rage of the Normans, the pirates of that day. It was that you might avail yourself of this, in case of need, that I brought you hither. Should you observe signs of pursuit, you may either lurk in the bowels of the earth until it has passed by, or escape, if you will, through the farther entrance near the lake, by which Pacolet entered but now.—And now farewell ! Think on what I have said ; for as sure as you now move and breathe a living man, so surely is your doom fixed and sealed, unless,within four-and-twenty hours, you have doubled the Burgh Head."

"Farewell, mother !" said Cleveland, as she departed, bending a look upon him, in which, as he could perceive by the lamp, sorrow was mingled with displeasure.

The interview, which thus concluded, left a strong effect even upon the mind of Cleveland, accustomed as he was to imminent dangers and to hairbreadth escapes. He in vain attempted to shake off the impression left by the words of Norna, which he felt the more powerful, because they were in a great measure divested of her wonted mystical tone, which he contemned. A thousand times he regretted that he had from time to time delayed the resolution, which he had long adopted, to quit his dreadful and dangerous trade ; and as often he firmly determined, that, could he but see Minna Troil once more, were it but for a last farewell, he would leave the sloop, as soon as his comrades were extricated from their perilous situation, endeavour to obtain the benefit of the King's pardon, and distinguish himself, if possible, in some more honourable course of warfare.

This resolution, to which he again and again pledged himself, had at length a sedative effect on his mental perturbation, and, wrapt in his cloak, he enjoyed, for a time, that imperfect repose which exhausted nature demands as her tribute, even from those who are situated on the

* A *well*, in the language of those seas, denotes one of the whirlpools, or circular eddies, which wheel and boil with astonishing strength and are very dangerous. Hence the distinction, in old English, betwixt *wells* and *waves*, the latter signifying the direct onward course of the tide, and the former the smooth, glassy, oily-looking whirlpools, whose strength seems to the eye almost irresistible.

verge of the most imminent danger. But, how far soever the guilty may satisfy his own mind, and stupify the feelings of remorse, by such a conditional repentance, we may well question whether it is not, in the sight of Heaven, rather a presumptuous aggravation, than an expiation of his sins.

When Cleveland awoke, the grey dawn was already mingling with the twilight of an Orcadian night. He found himself on the verge of a beautiful sheet of water, which, close by the place where he had rested, was nearly divided by two tongues of land that approach each other from the opposing sides of the lake, and are in some degree united by the Bridge of Broisgar, a long causeway, containing openings to permit the flow and reflux of the tide. Behind him, and fronting to the bridge, stood that remarkable semicircle of huge upright stones, which has no rival in Britain, excepting the inimitable monument at Stonehenge. These immense blocks of stone, all of them above twelve feet, and several being even fourteen or fifteen feet in height, stood around the pirate in the grey light of the dawning, like the phantom forms of antediluvian giants, who, shrouded in the habiliments of the dead, came to revisit, by this pale light, the earth which they had plagued by their oppression and polluted by their sins, till they brought down upon it the vengeance of long-suffering Heaven.*

Cleveland was less interested by this singular monument of antiquity, than by the distant view of Stromness, which he could as yet scarce discover. He lost no time in striking a light, by the assistance of one of his pistols, and some wet fern supplied him with the fuel sufficient to make the appointed signal. It had been earnestly watched for on board the sloop ; for Goffe's incapacity became daily more apparent ; and even his most steady adherents agreed that it would be best to submit to Cleveland's command till they got back to the West Indies.

Bunce, who came with the boat to bring off his favourite commander, danced, cursed, shouted, and spouted for joy, when he saw him once more at freedom. "They had already," he said, "made some progress in victualling the sloop, and they might have made more, but for that drunken old swab Goffe, who minded nothing but splicing the main-brace."

The boat's crew were inspired with the same enthusiasm, and rowed so hard, that, although the tide was against them, and the air of wind failed, they soon placed Cleveland once more on the quarter-deck of the vessel which it was his misfortune to command.

The first exercise of the Captain's power was to make known to Magnus Troil that he was at full freedom to depart—that he was willing to make him any compensation in his power, for the interruption of his voyage to Kirkwall ; and that Captain Cleveland was desirous, if agreeable to Mr. Troil, to pay his respects to him on board his brig—thank him for former favours, and apologise for the circumstances attending his detention.

To Bunce, who, as the most civilised of the crew, Cleveland had intrusted this message, the old plain-dealing Udaller made the following

* Note U. Standing Stones of Stennis.

answer:—"Tell your Captain that I should be glad to think he had never stopped any one upon the high sea, save such as have suffered as little as I have. Say, too, that if we are to continue friends, we shall be most so at a distance ; for I like the sound of his cannon-balls as little by sea, as he would like the whistle of a bullet by land from my rifle-gun. Say, in a word that I am sorry I was mistaken in him, and that he would have done better to have reserved for the Spaniard the usage he is bestowing on his countrymen."

"And so that is your message, old Snapcholerick ?" said Bunce—"Now stap my vitals if I have not a mind to do your errand for you over the left shoulder, and teach you more respect for gentlemen of fortune ! But I won't, and chiefly for the sake of your two pretty wenches, not to mention my old friend Claud Halcro, the very visage of whom brought back all the old days of scene-shifting and candle-snuffing. So good morrow to you, Gaffer Seal's-cap, and all is said that need pass between us."

No sooner did the boat put off with the pirates, who left the brig, and now returned to their own vessel, than Magnus, in order to avoid reposing unnecessary confidence in the honour of these gentlemen of fortune, as they called themselves, got his brig under way ; and, the wind coming favourably round, and increasing as the sun rose, he crowded all sail for Scalpa-flow, intending there to disembark and go by land to Kirkwall, where he expected to meet his daughters and his friend Claud Halcro.

CHAPTER THIRTY-NINTH

Now, Emma, now the last reflection make,
What thou wouldst follow, what thou must forsake.
By our ill-omen'd stars and adverse Heaven,
No middle object to thy choice is given.
HENRY AND EMMA

THE sun was high in heaven ; the boats were busily fetching off from the shore the promised supply of provisions and water, which, as many fishing-skiffs were employed in the service, were got on board with unexpected speed, and stowed away by the crew of the sloop, with equal despatch. All worked with good will ; for all, save Cleveland himself, were weary of a coast, where every moment increased their danger, and where, which they esteemed a worse misfortune, there was no booty to be won. Bunce and Derrick took the immediate direction of this duty, while Cleveland, walking the deck alone, and in silence, only interfered from time to time, to give some order which circumstances required, and then relapsed into his own sad reflections.

There are two sorts of men whom situations of guilt, and terror, and commotion, bring forward as prominent agents. The first are spirits so naturally moulded and fitted for deeds of horror, that they stalk forth

317

from their lurking-places like actual demons, to work in their native element, as the hideous apparition of the Bearded Man came forth at Versailles, on the memorable 5th October 1789, the delighted executioner of the victims delivered up to him by a bloodthirsty rabble. But Cleveland belonged to the second class of these unfortunate beings, who are involved in evil rather by the concurrence of external circumstances than by natural inclination, being, indeed, one in whom his first engaging in this lawless mode of life, as the follower of his father, nay, perhaps, even his pursuing it as his father's avenger, carried with it something of mitigation and apology;—one also who often considered his guilty situation with horror, and had made repeated, though ineffectual efforts, to escape from it.

Such thoughts of remorse were now rolling in his mind, and he may be forgiven if recollections of Minna mingled with and aided them. He looked around, too, on his mates, and, profligate and hardened as he knew them to be, he could not think of their paying the penalty of his obstinacy. "We shall be ready to sail with the ebb tide," he said to himself—"why should I endanger these men, by detaining them till the hour of danger, predicted by that singular woman, shall arrive ? Her intelligence, howsoever acquired, has been always strangely accurate ; and her warning was as solemn as if a mother were to apprise an erring son of his crimes, and of his approaching punishment. Besides, what chance is there that I can again see Minna ? She is at Kirkwall, doubtless, and to hold my course thither would be to steer right upon the rocks. No, I will not endanger these poor fellows—I will sail with the ebb tide. On the desolate Hebrides, or on the north-west coast of Ireland, I will leave the vessel, and return hither in some disguise—yet, why should I return, since it will perhaps be only to see Minna the bride of Mordaunt ? No—let the vessel sail with this ebb tide without me. I will abide and take my fate."

His meditations were here interrupted by Jack Bunce, who, hailing him noble Captain, said they were ready to sail when he pleased.

"When *you* please, Bunce ; for I shall leave the command with you, and go ashore at Stromness," said Cleveland.

"You shall do no such matter, by Heaven !" answered Bunce. "The command with me, truly ! and how the devil am I to get the crew to obey me ? Why, even Dick Fletcher rides rusty on me now and then. You know well enough that without you, we shall be all at each other's throats in half-an-hour ; and, if you desert us, what a rope's end does it signify whether we are destroyed by the king's cruisers, or by each other ? Come, come, noble Captain, there are black-eyed girls enough in the world, but where will you find so tight a sea-boat as the little Favourite here, manned as she is with a set of tearing lads,

Fit to disturb the peace of all the world,
And rule it when 'tis wildest ?

"You are a precious fool, Jack Bunce," said Cleveland, half angry, and, in despite of himself, half diverted by the false tones and exaggerated gesture of the stage-struck pirate.

"It may be so, noble Captain," answered Bunce, "and it may be that I have my comrades in my folly. Here are you, now, going to play All for Love, and the World well Lost, and yet you cannot bear a harmless bounce in blank verse—Well, I can talk prose for the matter, for I have news to boot."

"Well, prithee deliver them (to speak thy own cant) like a man of this world."

"The Stromness fishers will accept nothing for their provisions and trouble," said Bunce—"there is a wonder for you !"

"And for what reason, I pray ?" said Cleveland ; "it is the first time I have ever heard of cash being refused at a seaport."

"True—they commonly lay the charges on as thick as if they were caulking. But here is the matter. The owner of the brig yonder, the father of your fair Imoinda, stands paymaster, by way of thanks for the civility with which we treated his daughters, and that we may not meet our due, as he calls it, on these shores."

"It is like the frank-hearted old Udaller !" said Cleveland ; "but is he then at Stromness ? I thought he was to have crossed the island for Kirkwall."

"He did so purpose," said Bunce ; "but more folks than King Duncan change the course of their voyage. He was no sooner ashore than he was met with by a meddling old witch of these parts, who has her finger in every man's pie, and by her counsel he changed his purpose of going to Kirkwall, and lies at anchor for the present in yonder white house, that you may see with your glass up the lake yonder. I am told the old woman clubbed also to pay for the sloop's stores. Why she should shell out the boards I cannot conceive an idea, except that she is said to be a witch, and may befriend us as so many devils."

"But who told you all this ?" said Cleveland, without using his spy-glass, or seeming so much interested in the news as his comrade had expected.

"Why," replied Bunce, "I made a trip ashore this morning to the village, and had a can with an old acquaintance, who had been sent by Master Troil to look after matters, and I fished it all out of him, and more too, than I am desirous of telling you, noble Captain."

"And who is your intelligencer ?" said Cleveland ; "has he got no name ?"

"Why, he is an old, fiddling, foppish acquaintance of mine, called Halcro, if you must know," said Bunce.

"Halcro !" echoed Cleveland, his eyes sparkling with surprise—"Claud Halcro !—why, he went ashore at Inganess with Minna and her sister—Where are they ?"

"Why, that is just what I did not want to tell you," replied the confidant—"yet hang me if I can help it, for I cannot baulk a fine situation.—That start had a fine effect—Oh, ay, and the spy-glass is turned on the House of Stennis *now* ?—Well, yonder they are, it must be confessed—indifferently well guarded too. Some of the old witch's people are come over from that mountain of an island—Hoy, as they call it; and the old gentleman has got some fellows under arms himself. But what of all that, noble Captain ?—give you but the word, and we snap up the wenches to-night—clap them under hatches—man the capstern by day-break—up top-sails—and sail with the morning tide."

"You sicken me with your villany," said Cleveland, turning away from him.

"Umph !—villany, and sicken you !" said Bunce—"Now, pray, what have I said but what has been done a thousand times by gentlemen of fortune like ourselves ?"

"Mention it not again," said Cleveland ; then took a turn along the deck, in deep meditation, and, coming back to Bunce, took him by the hand, and said, "Jack, I will see her once more."

"With all my heart," said Bunce, sullenly.

"Once more will I see her, and it may be to abjure at her feet this cursed trade, and expiate my offences"—

"At the gallows !" said Bunce, completing the sentence—"With all my heart !—confess and be hanged is a most reverend proverb."

"Nay—but, dear Jack !" said Cleveland.

"Dear Jack !" answered Bunce, in the same sullen tone—"a dear sight you have been to dear Jack. But hold your own course—I have done with caring for you for ever—I should but sicken you with my villanous counsels."

"Now must I soothe this silly fellow as if he were a spoiled child," said Cleveland, speaking at Bunce, but not to him ; "and yet he has sense enough, and bravery enough, too ; and one would think, kindness enough to know that men don't pick their words during a gale of wind."

"Why, that's true, Clement," said Bunce, "and there is my hand upon it—And, now I think upon't, you shall have your last interview, for it's out of my line to prevent a parting scene ; and what signifies a tide—we can sail by to-morrow's ebb as well as by this."

Cleveland sighed, for Norna's prediction rushed on his mind ; but the opportunity of a last meeting with Minna was too tempting to be resigned either for presentiment or prediction.

"I will go presently ashore to the place where they all are," said Bunce ; "and the payment of these stores shall serve me for a pretext ; and I will carry any letters or message from you to Minna with the dexterity of a valet de chambre."

"But they have armed men—you may be in danger," said Cleveland.

"Not a whit—not a whit," replied Bunce. "I protected the wenches when they were in my power ; I warrant their father will neither wrong me, nor see me wronged."

"You say true," said Cleveland ; "it is not in his nature. I will instantly write a note to Minna." And he ran down to the cabin for that purpose, where he wasted much paper, ere, with a trembling hand, and throbbing heart, he achieved such a letter as he hoped might prevail on Minna to permit him a farewell meeting on the succeeding morning.

His adherent, Bunce, in the meanwhile, sought out Fletcher, of whose support to second any motion whatever, he accounted himself perfectly sure ; and followed by this trusty satellite, he intruded himself on the awful presence of Hawkins the boatswain, and Derrick the quarter-master, who were ragaling themselves with a can of rumbo, after the fatiguing duty of the day.

"Here comes he can tell us," said Derrick.—"So, Master Lieutenant, for so we must call you now, I think, let us have a peep into your counsels— When will the anchor be a-trip?"

"When it pleases Heaven, Master Quarter-master," answered Bunce, "for I know no more than the stern-post."

"Why, d——n my buttons," said Derrick, "do we not weigh this tide?"

"Or to-morrow's tide, at farthest?" said the Boatswain—"Why, what have we been slaving the whole company for, to get all these stores aboard?"

"Gentlemen," said Bunce, "you are to know that Cupid has laid our Captain on board, carried the vessel, and nailed down his wits under hatches."

"What sort of play-stuff is all this?" said the Boatswain, gruffly. "If you have anything to tell us, say it in a word, like a man."

"Howsomdever," said Fletcher, "I always think Jack Bunce speaks like a man, and acts like man too—and so, d'ye see"—

"Hold your peace, dear Dick; best of the bullybacks, be silent," said Bunce—"Gentlemen, in one word, the Captain is in love."

"Why, now, only think of that!" said the Boatswain; "not but that I have been in love as often as any man, when the ship was laid up."

"Well, but," continued Bunce, "Captain Cleveland is in love—Yes— Prince Volscius is in love; and, though that's the cue for laughing on the stage, it is no laughing matter here. He expects to meet the girl to-morrow, for the last time; and that, we all know, leads to another meeting, and another, and so on till the Halcyon is down on us, and then we may look for more kicks than halfpence."

"By ——" said the Boatswain, with a sounding oath, "we'll have a mutiny, and not allow him to go ashore,—eh, Derrick?"

"And the best way, too," said Derrick.

"What d'ye think of it, Jack Bunce?" said Fletcher, in whose ears this counsel sounded very sagely, but who still bent a wistful look upon his companion.

"Why, look ye, gentlemen," said Bunce, "I will mutiny none, and stap my vitals if any of you shall!"

"Why, then, I won't, for one," said Fletcher; "but what are we to do since howsomdever"—

"Stopper your jaw, Dick, will you?" said Bunce.—"Now, Boatswain, I am partly of your mind, that the Captain must be brought to reason by a little wholesome force. But you all know he has the spirit of a lion, and will do nothing unless he is allowed to hold on his own course. Well, I'll go ashore and make this appointment. The girl comes to the rendezvous in the morning, and the Captain goes ashore—we take a good boat's crew with us, to row, against tide and current, and we will be ready at the signal, to jump ashore and bring off the Captain and the girl, whether they will or no. The pet-child will not quarrel with us, since we bring off his whirligig alongst with him; and if he is still fractious, why we will

321

weigh anchor without his orders, and let him come to his senses at leisure, and know his friends another time."

"Why, this has a face with it, Master Derrick," said Hawkins.

"Jack Bunce is always right," said Fletcher ; "howsomdever, the Captain will shoot some of us, that is certain."

"Hold your jaw, Dick," said Bunce ; "pray, who the devil cares, do you think, whether you are shot or hanged ?"

"Why, it don't much argufy for the matter of that," replied Dick ; "howsomdever"—

"Be quiet, I tell you," said his inexorable patron, "and hear me out.— We will take him at unawares, so that he shall neither have time to use cutlass nor pops ; and I myself, for the dear love I bear him, will be the first to lay him on his back. There is a nice tight-going bit of a pinnace, that is a consort of this chase of the Captain's—if I have an opportunity, I'll snap her up on my own account."

"Yes, yes," said Derrick ; "let you alone for keeping on the look-out for your own comforts."

"Faith, nay," said Bunce, "I only snatch at them when they come fairly in my way, or are purchased by dint of my own wit ; and none of you could nave fallen on such a plan as this. We shall have the Captain with us, head, hand, and heart, and all, besides making a scene fit to finish a comedy. So I will go ashore to make the appointment, and do you possess some of the gentlemen who are still sober, and fit to be trusted with the knowledge of our intentions."

Bunce, with his friend Fletcher, departed accordingly, and the two veteran pirates remained looking at each other in silence, until the Boatswain spoke at last. "Blow me, Derrick, if I like these two daffadandilly young fellows ; they are not the true breed. Why, they are no more like the rovers I have known, than this sloop is to a first-rate. Why, there was old Sharpe that read prayers to his ship's company every Sunday, what would he have said to have heard it proposed to bring two wenches on board ?"

"And what would tough old Black Beard have said," answered his companion, "if they had expected to keep them to themselves ? They deserve to be made to walk the plank for their impudence ; or to be tied back to back and set a-diving, and I care not how soon."

"Ay, but who is to command the ship, then ?" said Hawkins.

"Why, what ails you at old Goffe ?" answered Derrick.

"Why, he has sucked the monkey so long and so often," said the Boatswain, "that the best of him is buffed. He is little better then an old woman when he is sober, and he is roaring mad when he is drunk—we have had enough of Goffe."

"Why, then, what d'ye say to yourself, or to me, Boatswain ?" demanded the Quarter-master. "I am content to toss up for it."

"Rot it, no," answered the Boatswain, after a moment's consideration ; "if we were within reach of the trade-winds, we might either of us make a shift ; but it will take all Cleveland's navigation to get us there ; and so, I think, there is nothing like Bunce's project for the present. Hark, he calls for the boat—I must go on deck and have her lowered for his honour, d——n his eyes."

The boat was lowered accordingly, made its voyage up the lake with safety, and landed Bunce within a few hundred yards of the old mansion-house of Stennis. Upon arriving in front of the house, he found that hasty measure had been taken to put it in a state of defence, the lower windows being barricaded, with places left for use of musketry, and a ship-gun being placed so as to command the entrance, which was besides guarded by two sentinels. Bunce demanded admission at the gate, which was briefly and unceremoniously refused to him with an exhortation to him, at the same time, to be gone about his business before worse came of it. As he continued, however, importunately to insist on seeing some one of the family, and stated his business to be of the most urgent nature, Claud Halcro at length appeared, and, with more peevishness than belonged to his usual manner, that admirer of glorious John expostulated with his acquaintance upon his pertinacious folly.

"You are," he said, "like foolish moths fluttering about a candle, which is sure at last to consume you."

"And you," said Bunce, "are a set of stingless drones, whom we can smoke out of your defences at our pleasure, with half-a-dozen of hand-grenades."

"Smoke a fool's head !" said Halcro ; "take my advice, and mind your own matters, or there will be those upon you will smoke you to purpose. Either be gone, or tell me in two words what you want ; for you are like to receive no welcome here save from a blunderbuss. We are men enough of ourselves ; and here is young Mordaunt Mertoun come from Hoy, whom your Captain so nearly murdered."

"Tush, man," siad Bunce, "he did but let out a little malapert blood."

"We want no such phlebotomy here," said Claud Halcro ; "and, besides, your patient turns out to be nearer allied to us than either you or we thought of ; so you may think how little welcome the Captain or any of his crew are like to be here."

"Well : but what if I bring money for the stores sent on board ?"

"Keep it till it is asked of you," said Halcro. "There are two bad paymasters—he that pays too soon, and he that does not pay at all."

"Well, then, let me at least give our thanks to the donor, " said Bunce.

"Keep them too, till they are asked for," answered the poet.

"So this is all the welcome I have of you for old acquaintance' sake ?" said Bunce.

"Why, what can I do for you, Master Altamont ?" said Halcro, somewhat moved.—"If young Mordaunt had had his own will, he would have welcomed you with 'the red Burgundy, Number a thousand.' For God's sake begone, else the stage direction will be, Enter guard, and seize Altamont."

"I will not give you the trouble," said Bunce, "but will make my exit instantly.—Stay a moment—I had almost forgot that I have a slip of paper for the tallest of your girls there—Minna, ay, Minna is her name. It is a farewell from Captain Cleveland—you cannot refuse to give it her."

"Ah, poor fellow !" said Halcro—"I comprehend—I comprehend—Farewell, fair Armida—

> Mid pikes, and 'mid bullets, 'mid tempest and fire,
> The danger is less than in hopeless desire.

Tell me but this—is there poetry in it ?"

"Chokeful to the seal, with song, sonnet, and elegy," answered Bunce ; "but let her have it cautiously and secretly."

"Tush man !—teach me to deliver a billet-doux !—me, who have been in the Wits' Coffee-house, and have seen all the toasts of the Kit-Cat Club !—Minna shall have it, then, for old acquaintance' sake, Mr. Altamont, and for your Captain's sake, too, who has less of the core of devil about him, than his trade requires. There can be no harm in a farewell letter."

"Farewell, then, old boy, for ever and a day !" said Bunce ; and seizing the poet's hand, gave it so hearty a gripe, that he left him roaring and shaking his fist, like a dog when a hot cinder has fallen on his foot.

Leaving the rover to return on board the vessel, we remain with the family of Magnus Troil, assembled at their kinsman's mansion of Stennis, where they maintained a constant and careful watch against surprise.

Mordaunt Mertoun had been received with much kindness by Magnus Troil, when he came to his assistance, with a small party of Norna's dependants, placed by her under his command. The Udaller was easily satisfied that the reports instilled into his ears by the Yagger, zealous to augment his favour towards his more profitable customer, Cleveland, by diminishing that of Mertoun, were without foundation. They had, indeed, been confirmed by the good Lady Glowrowrum, and by common fame, both of whom were pleased to represent Mordaunt Mertoun as an arrogant pretender to the favour of the sisters of Burgh Westra, who only hesitated, sultan-like, on whom he should bestow the handkerchief. But common fame, Magnus considered, was a common liar, and he was sometimes disposed (where scandal was concerned) to regard the good Lady Glowrowrum as rather an uncommon specimen of the same genus. He therefore received Mordaunt once more into full favour, listened with much surprise to the claim which Norna laid to the young man's duty, and with no less interest to her intention of surrendering to him the considerabale property which she had inherited from her father. Nay, it is even probable that, though he gave no immediate answer to her hints concerning a union betwixt his eldest daughter and her heir, he might think such an alliance recommended, as well by the young man's personal merits, as by the chance it gave of reuniting the very large estate which had been divided betwixt his own father and that of Norna. At all events, the Udaller received his young friend with much kindness, and he and the proprietor of the mansion joined in intrusting to him, as the youngest and most active of the party, the charge of commanding the night-watch, and relieving the sentinels around the House of Stennis.

CHAPTER FORTIETH

Of an outlawe, this is the lawe—
That men him take and bind,
Without pitie hang'd to be,
And waive with the wind.
THE BALLAD OF THE NUT-BROWN MAID

MORDAUNT had caused the sentinels who had been on duty since midnight to be relieved ere the peep of day, and having given directions that the guard should be again changed at sunrise, he had retired to a small parlour, and, placing his arms beside him, was slumbering in an easy-chair, when he felt himself pulled by the watch-cloak in which he was enveloped.

"Is it sunrise," said he, "already ?" as, starting up, he discovered the first beams lying level upon the horizon.

"Mordaunt !" said a voice, every note of which thrilled to his heart.

He turned his eyes on the speaker, and Brenda Troil, to his joyful astonishment, stood before him. As he was about to address her eagerly, he was checked by observing the signs of sorrow and discomposure in her pale cheeks, trembling lips, and brimful eyes.

"Mordaunt," she said, "you must do Minna and me a favour—you must allow us to leave the house quietly, and without alarming any one, in order to go as far as the Standing Stones of Stennis."

"What freak can this be, dearest Brenda ?" said Mordaunt, much amazed at the request—"some Orcadian observance of superstition, perhaps ; but the time is too dangerous, and my charge from your father too strict, that I should permit you to pass without his consent. Consider, dearest Brenda, I am a soldier on duty, and must obey orders."

"Mordaunt," said Brenda, "this is no jesting matter—Minna's reason, nay, Minna's life, depends on your giving us this permission."

"And for what purpose ?" said Mordaunt ; "let me at least know that."

"For a wild and a desperate purpose," replied Brenda—"It is that she may meet Cleveland."

"Cleveland !" said Mordaunt—"Should the villain come ashore, he shall be welcomed with a shower of rifle-balls. Let me within a hundred yards of him," he added, grasping his piece, "and all the mischief he has done me shall be balanced with an ounce bullet !"

"His death will drive Minna frantic," said Brenda ; "and him who injures Minna, Brenda will never again look upon."

"This is madness—raving madness !" said Mordaunt—"Consider your honour—consider your duty."

"I can consider nothing but Minna's danger," said Brenda, breaking

325

into a flood of tears ; "her former illness was nothing to the state she has been in all night. She holds in her hand his letter, written in characters of fire, rather than of ink, imploring her to see him for a last farewell, as she would save a mortal body and an immortal soul ; pledging himself for her safety ; and declaring no power shall force him from the coast till he has seen her.—You *must* let us pass."

"It is impossible !" replied Mordaunt, in great perplexity—"This ruffian has imprecations enough, doubtless, at his fingers' ends—but what better pledge has he to offer ?—I cannot permit Minna to go."

"I suppose," said Brenda, somewhat reproachfully, while she dried her tears, yet still continued sobbing, "that there is something in what Norna spoke of betwixt Minna and you ; and that you are too jealous of this poor wretch, to allow him even to speak with her an instant before his departure."

"You are unjust," said Mordaunt, hurt, and yet somewhat flattered by her suspicions,—"you are as unjust as you are imprudent. You know—you cannot but know—that Minna is chiefly dear to me as *your* sister. Tell me, Brenda—and tell me truly—if I aid you in this folly, have you no suspicion of the Pirate's faith ?"

"No, none," said Brenda ; "if I had any, do you think I would urge you thus ? He is wild and unhappy, but I think we may in this trust him."

"Is the appointed place the Standing Stones, and the time daybreak ?" again demanded Mordaunt.

"It is, and the time is come," said Brenda,—"for Heaven's sake let us depart !"

"I will myself," said Mordaunt, "relieve the sentinel at the front door for a few minutes, and suffer you to pass.—You will not protract this interview, so full of danger ?"

"We will not," said Brenda ; "and you, on your part, will not avail yourself of this unhappy man's venturing hither, to harm or to seize him ?"

"Rely on my honour," said Mordaunt—"He shall have no harm, unless he offers any."

"Then I go to call my sister," said Brenda, and quickly left the apartment.

Mordaunt considered the matter for an instant, and then, going to the sentinel at the front door, he desired him to run instantly to the main-guard, and order the whole to turn out with their arms—to see the order obeyed, and to return when they were in readiness. Meantime, he himself, he said, would remain upon the post.

During the interval of the sentinel's absence, the front door was slowly opened, and Minna and Brenda appeared, muffled in their mantles. The former leaned on her sister, and kept her face bent on the ground as one who felt ashamed of the step she was about to take. Brenda also passed her lover in silence, but threw back upon him a look of gratitude and affection, which doubled, if possible, his anxiety for their safety.

The sisters in the meanwhile passed out of sight of the house ; when Minna, whose step, till that time, had been faint and feeble, began to erect her person, and to walk with a pace so firm and so swift, that Brenda, who had some difficulty to keep up with her, could not forbear remonstrating on the imprudence of hurrying her spirits, and exhausting her force, by such unnecessary haste.

"Fear not, my dearest sister," said Minna ; "the spirit which I now feel will and must sustain me through the dreadful interview. I could not but move with a drooping head, and a dejected pace, while I was in view of one who must necessarily deem me deserving of his pity, or his scorn. But you know, my dearest Brenda, and Mordaunt shall also know, that the love I bore to that unhappy man was as pure as the rays of that sun, that is now reflected on the waves. And I dare attest that glorious sun, and yonder blue heaven, to bear me witness, that, but to urge him to change his unhappy course of life, I had not, for all the temptations this round world holds, ever consented to see him more."

As she spoke thus, in a tone which afforded much confidence to Brenda, the sisters attained the summit of a rising ground, whence they commanded a full view of the Orcadian Stonehenge, consisting of a huge circle and semicircle of the Standing Stones, as they are called, which already glimmered a greyish white in the rising sun, and projected far to the westward their long gigantic shadows. At another time the scene would have operated powerfully on the imaginative mind of Minna, and interested the curiosity at least of her sensitive sister. But, at this moment, neither was at leisure to receive the impressions which this stupendous monument of antiquity is so well calculated to impress on the feelings of those who behold it ; for they saw in the lower lake, beneath what is termed the Bridge of Broisgar, a boat well manned and armed, which had disembarked one of its crew, who advanced alone, and wrapped in a naval cloak, towards that monumental circle which they themselves were about to reach from another quarter.

"They are many, and they are armed," said the startled Brenda, in a whisper to her sister.

"It is for precaution's sake," answered Minna, "which, alas ! their condition renders but too necessary. Fear no treachery from him—that, at least, is not his vice."

As she spoke, or shortly afterwards, she attained the centre of the circle, on which, in the midst of the tall erect pillars of rude stone that are raised around, lies one flat and prostrate, supported by short stone pillars, of which some relics are still visible, that had once served, perhaps, the purpose of an altar.

"Here," she said, "in heathen times (if we may believe legends, which have cost me but too dear) our ancestors offered sacrifices to heathen deities—and here will I, from my soul, renounce, abjure, and offer up to a better and a more merciful God than was known to them, the vain ideas with which my youthful imagination has been seduced."

She stood by the prostrate table of stone, and saw Cleveland advance towards her, with a timid pace and a downcast look, as different from his usual character and bearing, as Minna's high air and lofty demeanour, and calm contemplative posture, were distant from those of the love-lorn and broken-hearted maiden, whose weight had almost borne down the support of her sister as she left the House of Stennis. If the belief of those is true, who assign these singular monuments exclusively to the Druids, Minna might have seemed the Haxa or high priestess of the order, from whom some champion of the tribe expected inauguration. Or if we hold the circles of Gothic and Scandinavian origin, she might have seemed a descended Vision of Freya, the spouse of the Thundering Deity, before whom some bold Sea King or Champion bent with an awe, which no mere mortal terror could have inflicted upon him. Brenda, overwhelmed with inexpressible fear and doubt, remained a pace or two behind, anxiously observing the motions of Cleveland, and attending to nothing around, save to him and to her sister. Cleveland approached within two yards of Minna, and bent his head to the ground. There was a dead pause, until Minna said, in a firm but melancholy tone, "Unhappy man, why didst thou seek this aggravation of our woe ? Depart in peace, and may Heaven direct thee to a better course than that which thy life has yet held !"

"Heaven will not aid me," said Cleveland, "excepting by your voice. I came hither rude and wild, scarce knowing that my trade, my desperate trade, was more criminal in the sight of man or of Heaven than that of those privateers whom your law acknowledges. I was bred in it, and, but for the wishes you have encouraged me to form, I should have perhaps died in it, desperate and impenitent. Oh, do not throw me from you ! let me do something to redeem what I have done amiss, and do not leave your own work half-finished !"

"Cleveland," said Minna, "I will not reproach you with abusing my inexperience, or with availing yourself of those delusions which the credulity of early youth had flung around me, and which led me to confound your fatal course of life with the deeds of our ancient heroes. Alas ! when I saw your followers, that illusion was no more !—but I do not upbraid you with its having existed. Go, Cleveland ; detach yourself from those miserable wretches with whom you are associated, and believe me, that if Heaven yet grants you the means of distinguishing your name by one good or glorious action, there are eyes left in these lonely islands, that will weep as much for joy, as—as—they must now do for sorrow."

"And is this all ?" said Cleveland ; "and may not I hope, that if I extricate myself from my present associates—if I can gain my pardon by being as bold in the right, as I have been too often in the wrong cause— if , after a term, I care not now long—but still a term which may have an end, I can boast of having redeemed my fame—may I not—may I not hope that Minna may forgive what my God and my country shall have pardoned ?"

"Never, Cleveland, never," said Minna, with the utmost firmness ; "on this spot we part, and part for ever, and part without longer indulgence. Think of me as of one dead, if you continue as you now are ; but if, which may Heaven grant, you change your fatal course, think of me then as one, whose morning and evening prayers will be for your happiness, though she has lost her own.—Farewell, Cleveland !"

He kneeled, overpowered by his own bitter feelings, to take the hand which she held out to him, and in that instant, his confidant Bunce, starting from behind one of the large upright pillars, his eyes wet with tears, exclaimed—

"Never saw such a parting scene on any stage ! But I'll be d——d if you make your exit as you expect !"

And so saying, ere Cleveland could employ either remonstrance or resistance, and indeed before he could get upon his feet, he easily secured him by pulling him down on his back, so that two or three of the boat's crew seized him by the arms and legs, and began to hurry him towards the lake. Minna and Brenda shrieked and attempted to fly ; but Derrick snatched up the former with as much ease as a falcon pounces on a pigeon, while Bunce, with an oath or two which were intended to be of a consolatory nature, seized on Brenda ; and the whole party, with two or three of the other pirates, who, stealing from the water-side, had accompanied them on the ambuscade, began hastily to run towards the boat, which was left in charge of two of their number. Their course, however, was unexpectedly interrupted, and their criminal purpose entirely frustrated.

When Mordaunt Mertoun had turned out his guard in arms, it was with the natural purpose of watching over the safety of the two sisters. They had accordingly closely observed the motions of the pirates, and when they saw so many of them leave the boat and steal towards the place of rendezvous assigned to Cleveland, they naturally suspected treachery, and by cover of an old hollow way or trench, which perhaps had anciently been connected with the monumental circle, they had thrown themselves unperceived between the pirates and their boat. At the cries of the sisters, they started up and placed themselves in the way of the ruffians, presenting their pieces, which, notwithstanding, they dared not fire, for fear of hurting the young ladies, secured as they were in the rude grasp of the marauders. Mordaunt, however, advanced with the speed of a wild deer on Bunce, who, loath to quit his prey, yet unable to defend himself otherwise, turned to this side and that alternately, exposing Brenda to the blows which Mordaunt offered at him. This defence, however, proved in vain against a youth, possessed of the lightest foot and most active hand ever known in Zetland, and after a feint or two, Mordaunt brought the pirate to the ground with a stroke from the butt of the carabine, which he dared not use otherwise. At the same time firearms were discharged on either side by those who were liable to no such cause of forbearance, and the pirates who had hold of Cleveland, dropped him, naturally enough, to provide for their own defence or retreat. But they only added to the numbers of their enemies ; for Cleveland perceiving Minna in the arms of Derrick, snatched her from the ruffian with one hand, and with the other shot him dead on the spot. Two or three more of the pirates fell or were taken, the rest fled to their boat, pushed off, then turned their broadside to the shore, and fired repeatedly on the Orcadian party, which they returned, with little injury on either side. Meanwhile Mordaunt having first seen that the sisters were at liberty and in full flight towards the house, advanced on Cleveland with his cutlass drawn. The pirate presented a pistol, and calling out at the same time,—"Mordaunt, I never missed my aim," he fired into the air, and threw it into the lake ; then drew his cutlass, brandished it round his head, and flung that also, as far as his arm could send it, in the same direction. yet such was the universal belief of his personal strength and resources, that Mordaunt still used precaution, as, advancing on Cleveland, he asked if he surrendered ?

"I surrender to no man," said the Pirate captain ; "but you may see I have thrown away my weapons."

He was immediately seized by some of the Orcadians, without his offering any resistance ; but the instant interference of Mordaunt prevented his being roughly treated or bound. The victors conducted him to a well-secured upper apartment in the House of Stennis, and placed a sentinel at the door. Bunce and Fletcher, both of whom had been stretched on the field during the skirmish, were lodged in the same chamber ; and two prisoners who appeared of lower rank, were confined in a vault belonging to the mansion.

Without pretending to describe the joy of Magnus Troil, who, when awakened by a noise and firing, found his daughters safe, and his enemy a prisoner, we shall only say, it was so great, that he forgot, for the time at least, to inquire what circumstances were those which had placed them in danger ; and that he hugged Mordaunt to his breast a thousand times, as their preserver ; and swore as often by the bones of his sainted namesake, that if he had a thousand daughters, so tight a lad, and so true a friend, should have the choice of them, let Lady Glowrowrum say what she would.

A very different scene was passing in the prison-chamber of the unfortunate Cleveland and his associates. The Captain sat by the window, his eyes bent on the prospect of the sea which it presented, and was seemingly so intent on it, as to be insensible of the presence of the others. Jack Bunce stood meditating some ends of verse, in order to make his advances towards a reconciliation with Cleveland ; for he began to be sensible, from the consequences, that the part he had played towards his Captain, however well intended, was neither lucky in its issue, nor likely to be taken. His admirer and adherent Fletcher lay half asleep it seemed, on a truckle-bed in the room, without the least attempt to interfere in the conversation which ensued.

"Nay, but speak to me, Clement," said the penitent Lieutenant, "if it be but to swear at me for my stupidity.—

'What ! not an oath ?—Nay, then, the world goes hard,
If Clifford cannot spare his friends an oath.'

"I prithee peace, and be gone !" said Cleveland ; "I have one bosom friend left yet, and you will make me bestow its contents on you, or on myself."

"I have it," said Bunce, "I have it !" and on he went in the vein of Jaffier—

' Then, by the hell I merit, I'll not leave thee,
Till to thyself at least thou'rt reconciled,
However thy resentment deal with me !'

330

"I pray you once more to be silent," said Cleveland—"Is it not enough that you have undone me with your treachery, but you must stun me with your silly buffoonery ?—I would not have believed *you* would have lifted a finger against me, Jack, of any man or devil in yonder unhappy ship."

"Who I ?" exclaimed Bunce, "I lift a finger against you !—and if I did it was in pure love, and to make you the happiest fellow that ever trod a deck, with your mistress beside you, and fifty fine fellows at your command. Here is Dick Fletcher can bear witness I did all for the best, if he would but speak, instead of lolloping there like a Dutch dogger laid up to be careened.—Get up, Dick, and speak for me, won't you ?"

"Why, yes, Jack Bunce," answered Fletcher, raising himself with difficulty and speaking feebly, "I will if I can—and I always knew you spoke and did for the best—but howsomdever, d'ye see, it has turned out for the worst for me this time, for I am bleeding to death, I think."

"You cannot be such an ass ?" said Jack Bunce, springing to his assistance, as did Cleveland. But human aid came too late—he sank back on the bed, and, turning on his face, expired without a groan.

"I always thought him a d——d fool," said Bunce, as he wiped a tear from his eye, "but never such a consummate idiot as to hop the perch so sillily. I have lost the best follower"—and again wiped his eye.

Cleveland looked on the dead body, the rugged features of which had remained unaltered by the death-pang—"A bull-dog," he said, "of the British breed, and, with a better counsellor, would have been a better man."

"You may say that of some other folks, too, Captain, if you are minded to do them justice," said Bunce.

"I may indeed, and especially of yourself," said Cleveland in reply.

"Why then, say, *Jack, I forgive you*," said Bunce ; "it's but a short word, and soon spoken."

"I forgive you from all my soul, Jack," said Cleveland, who had resumed his situation at the window ; "and the rather that your folly is of little consequence—the morning is come that must bring ruin on us all."

"What ! you are thinking of the old woman's prophecy you spoke of ?" said Bunce.

"It will be soon accomplished," answered Cleveland. "Come hither ; what do you take yon large square-rigged vessel for, that you see doubling the headland on the east, and opening the Bay of Stromness ?"

"Why, I can't make her well out," said Bunce, "but yonder is old Goffe takes her for a West Indiaman loaded with rum and sugar I suppose, for d——n me if he does not slip cable, and stand out to her !"

"Instead of running into the shoal-water, which was his only safety," said Cleveland.—"The fool ! the dotard ! the drivelling drunken idiot !—he will get his flip hot enough ; for yon is the Halcyon—See, she hoists her colours and fires a broadside ! and there will soon be an end of the Fortune's Favourite ! I only hope they will fight her to the last plank. The Boatswain used to be stanch enough, and so is Goffe, though an incarnate demon.—Now she shoots away, with all the sail she can spread, and that shows some sense."

331

"Up goes the Jolly Hodge, the old black flag, with the death's head and hour-glass, and that shows some spunk," added his comrade.

"The hour-glass is turned for us, Jack, for this bout—our sand is running fast.—Fire away yet, my roving lads ! The deep sea or the blue sky, rather than a rope and a yard-arm."

There was a moment of anxious and dead silence : the sloop, though hard pressed, maintaining still a running fight, and the frigate continuing in full chase, but scarce returning a shot. At length the vessels neared each other, so as to show that the man-of-war intended to board the sloop, instead of sinking her, probably to secure the plunder which might be in the pirate vessel.

"Now, Goffe—now, Boatswain !" exclaimed Cleveland, in an ecstasy of impatience, and as if they could have heard his commands, "stand by sheets and tacks—rake her with a broadside, when you are under her bows, then about ship, and go off on the other tack like a wild-goose. The sails shiver—the helm's a-lee—Ah !—deep-sea sink the lubbers !—they miss stays, and the frigate runs them aboard !"

Accordingly the various manœuvres of the chase had brought them so near, that Cleveland, with his spy-glass, could see the man-of-war's-men boarding by the yards and bowsprits in irresistible numbers, their naked cutlasses flashing in the sun, when, at that critical moment, both ships were enveloped in a cloud of thick black smoke, which suddenly arose on board the captured pirate.

"Exeunt omnes," said Bunce, with clasped hands.

"There went the Fortune's Favourite, ship and crew," said Cleveland, at the same instant.

But the smoke, immediately clearing away, showed that the damage had only been partial, and that, from want of a sufficient quantity of powder, the pirates had failed in their desperate attempt to blow up their vessel with the Halcyon.

Shortly after the action was over, Captain Weatherport of the Halcyon sent an officer and a party of marines to the House of Stennis, to demand from the little garrison the pirate seamen who were their prisoners, and, in particular, Cleveland and Bunce, who acted as Captain and Lieutenant of the gang.

This was a demand which was not to be resisted, though Magnus Troil could have wished sincerely that the roof under which he lived had been allowed as an asylum at least to Cleveland. But the officer's orders were peremptory ; and he added, it was Captain Weatherport's intention to land the other prisoners, and send the whole, with a sufficient escort, across the island to Kirkwall, in order to undergo an examination there before the civil authorities, previous to their being sent off to London for trial at the High Court of Admiralty. Magnus could therefore only intercede for good usage to Cleveland, and that he might not be stripped or plundered, which the officer, struck by his good mien, and compassionating his situation, readily promised. The honest Udaller would have said something in the way of comfort to Cleveland himself, but he could not find words to express it, and shook his head.

"Old friend," said Cleveland, "you may have much to complain of—

yet you pity instead of exulting over me—for the sake of you and yours, I will never harm human being more. Take this from me—my last hope, but my last temptation also"—he drew from his bosom a pocket-pistol, and gave it to Magnus Troil. "Remember me to—But no—let every one forget me.—I am your prisoner, sir," said he to the officer.

"And I also," said poor Bunce ; and putting on a theatrical countenance, he ranted, with no very perceptible faltering in his tone, the words of Pierre—

> Captain, you should be a gentleman of honour,
> Keep off the rabble, that I may have room
> To entertain my fate, and die with decency.

CHAPTER FORTY-FIRST

Joy, joy, in London now !
SOUTHEY

THE news of the capture of the Rover reached Kirkwall about an hour before noon, and filled all men with wonder and with joy. Little business was that day done at the Fair, whilst people of all ages and occupations streamed from the place to see the prisoners as they were marched towards Kirkwall, and to triumph in the different appearance which they now bore, from that which they had formerly exhibited when ranting, swaggering, and bullying in the streets of that town. The bayonets of the marines were soon seen to glisten in the sun, and then came on the melancholy troop of captives, handcuffed two and two together. Their finery had been partly torn from them by their captors, partly hung in rags about them ; many were wounded and covered with blood, many blackened and scorched with the explosion, by which a few of the most desperate had in vain striven to blow up the vessel. Most of them seemed sullen and impenitent, some were more becomingly affected with their condition, and a few braved it out, and sung the same ribald songs to which they had made the streets of Kirkwall ring when they were in their frolics.

The Boatswain and Goffe, coupled together, exhaused themselves in threats and imprecations against each other ; the former charging Goffe with want of seamanship, and the latter alleging that the Boatswain had prevented him from firing the powder that was stowed forward, and sending them all to the other world together. Last came Cleveland and Bunce, who were permitted to walk unshackled ; the decent melancholy, yet resolved manner of the former, contrasting strongly with the stage strut and swagger which poor Jack thought it fitting to assume, in order to conceal some less dignified emotions. The former was looked upon with compassion, the latter with a mixture of scorn and pity ; while most of the others inspired horror, and even fear, by their looks and their language.

333

There was one individual in Kirkwall who was far from hastening to see the sight which attracted all eyes, that he was not even aware of the event which agitated the town. This was the elder Mertoun, whose residence Kirkwall had been for two or three days, part of which had been spent in attending to some judicial proceedings, undertaken at the instance of the Procurator-Fiscal, against that grave professor Bryce-Snailsfoot. In consequence of an inquisition into the proceedings of this worthy trader, Cleveland's chest, with his papers and other matters therein contained, had been restored to Mertoun, as the lawful custodier thereof, until the right owner should be in a situation to establish his right to them. Mertoun was at first desirous to throw back upon Justice the charge which she was disposed to intrust with him ; but on perusing one or two of the papers he hastily changed his mind—in broken words requested the Magistrate to let the chest be sent to his lodgings, and hastening homeward, bolted himself into the room, to consider and digest the singular information which chance had thus conveyed to him, and which increased, in a tenfold degree, his impatience for an interview with the mysterious Norna of the Fitful Head.

It may be remembered that she had required of him, when they met in the churchyard of Saint Ninian, to attend in the outer aisle of the cathedral of Saint Magnus, at the hour of noon, on the fifth day of the Fair of Saint Olla, there to meet a person by whom the fate of Mordaunt would be explained to him.—"It must be herself," he said ; "and that I should see her at this moment is indispensable. How to find her sooner I know not ; and better lose a few hours even in this exigence than offend her by a premature attempt to force myself on her presence."

Long, therefore, before noon—long before the town of Kirkwall was agitated by the news of the events on the other side of the island, the elder Mertoun was pacing the deserted aisle of the cathedral, awaiting, with agonising eagerness, the expected communication from Norna. The bell tolled twelve—no door opened—no one was seen to enter the cathedral ; but the last sounds had not ceased to reverberate through the vaulted roof, when, gliding from one of the interior side aisles, Norna stood before him. Mertoun, indifferent to the apparent mystery of her sudden approach (with the secret of which the reader is acquainted), went up to her at once, with the earnest ejaculation—"Ulla—Ulla Troil—aid me to save our unhappy boy !"

"To Ulla Troil," said Norna, "I answer not—I gave that name to the winds on the night that cost me a father."

"Speak not of that night of horror," said Mertoun ; "we have need of our reason—let us not think on recollections which may destroy it ; but aid me, if thou canst, to save our unfortunate child !"

"Vaughan," answered Norna, "he is already saved—long since saved ; think you a mother's hand—and that of such a mother as I am—would await your crawling, tardy, ineffectual assistance ? No, Vaughan—I make myself known to you but to show my triumph over you—it is the only revenge which the powerful Norna permits herself to take for the wrongs of Ulla Troil."

"Have you indeed saved him—saved him from the murderous crew ?"

said Mertoun or Vaughan—"speak !—and speak truth !—I will believe everything—all you would require me to assent to !—prove to me only he is escaped and safe !"

"Escaped and safe by my means," said Norna—"safe, and in assurance of an honoured and happy alliance. Yes, great unbeliever !—yes, wise and self-opinioned infidel !—these were the works of Norna ! I knew you many a year since ; but never had I made myself known to you, save with the triumphant consciousness of having controlled the destiny that threatened my son. All combined against him—planets which threatened drowning—combinations which menaced blood—but my skill was superior to all.—I arranged—I combined—I found means—I made them— each disaster has been averted ;—and what infidel on earth, or stubborn demon beyond the bounds of earth, shall hereafter deny my power ?"

The wild ecstasy with which she spoke so much resembled triumphant insanity, that Mertoun answered—"Were your pretensions less lofty, and your speech more plain, I should be better assured of my son's safety."

"Doubt on, vain sceptic !" said Norna—"And yet know, that not only is our son safe, but vengeance is mine, though I sought it not—vengeance on the powerful implement of the darker Influences by whom my schemes were so often thwarted, and even the life of my son endangered—Yes, take it as a guarantee of the truth of my speech, that Cleveland—the pirate Cleveland—even now enters Kirkwall as a prisoner, and will soon expiate with his life the having shed blood which is of kin to Norna's."

"Who didst thou say was prisoner ?" exclaimed Mertoun, with a voice of thunder—"*Who*, woman, didst thou say should expiate his crimes with his life ?"

"Cleveland—the pirate Cleveland !" answered Norna ; "and by me, whose counsel he scorned, he has been permitted to meet his fate."

"Thou most wretched of women !" said Mertoun, speaking from between his clenched teeth—"thou hast slain thy son as well as thy father !"

"My son !—what son ?—what mean you ?—Mordaunt is your son—your only son !" exclaimed Norna—"is he not ?—tell me quickly—is he not ?"

"Mordaunt is indeed *my* son," said Mertoun—"the laws, at least, gave him to me as such—But, O unhappy Ulla ! Cleveland is your son as well as mine—blood of our blood, bone of our bone ; and if you have given him to death, I will end my wretched life along with him !"

"Stay—hold—stop, Vaughan !" said Norna ; "I am not yet overcome— prove but to me the truth of what you say, I would find help, if I should evoke hell !—But prove your words, else believe them I cannot."

"*Thou* help ? wretched, overweening woman !—in what have thy combinations and thy stratagems—the legerdemain of lunacy—the mere quackery of insanity—in what have these involved thee ?—and yet I will speak to thee as reasonable—nay, I will admit thee as powerful—Hear, then, Ulla, the proofs which you demand, and find a remedy if thou canst:—

"When I fled from Orkney," he continued, after a long pause—"it is now five-and-twenty years since—I bore with me the unhappy offspring to whom you had given light. It was sent to me by one of your kinswomen, with an account of your illness, which was soon followed by a generally received belief of your death. It avails not to tell in what misery I left Europe. I found refuge in Hispaniola, wherein a fair young Spaniard undertook the task of comforter. I married her—she became mother of the youth called Mordaunt Mertoun."

"You married her !" said Norna, in a tone of deep reproach.

"I did, Ulla," answered Mertoun ; "but you avenged. She proved faithless, and her infidelity left me in doubts whether the child she bore had a right to call me father—But I also was avenged."

"You murdered her !" said Norna, with a dreadful shriek.

"I did that," said Mertoun, without more a direct reply, "which made an instant flight from Hispaniola necessary. Your son I carried with me to Tortuga, where we had a small settlement. Mordaunt Vaughan, my son by marriage, about three or four years younger, was residing in Port Royal for the advantages of an English education. I resolved never to see him again, but I continued to support him. Our settlement was plundered by the Spaniards when Clement was about fifteen—Want came to aid despair and troubled conscience. I became a corsair, and involved Clement in the same desperate trade. His skill and bravery, though then a mere boy, gained him a separate command ; and after a lapse of two or three years, while we were on different cruises, my crew rose on me, and left me for dead on the beach of one of the Bermudas. I recovered, however, and my first inquiries, after a tedious illness, were after Clement. He, I heard, had been also marooned by a rebellious crew, and put ashore on a desert islet, to perish with want—I believed he had so perished."

"And what assures you that he did not ? said Ulla ; "or how comes this Cleveland to be identified with Vaughan ?"

"To change a name is common with such adventurers," answered Mertoun, "and Clement had apparently found that of Vaughan had become too notorious—and this change, in his case, prevented me from hearing any tidings of him. It was then that remorse seized me, and that, detesting all nature, but especially the sex to which Louisa belonged, I resolved to do penance in the wild islands of Zetland for the rest of my life. To subject myself to fasts and to the scourge was the advice of the holy Catholic priests whom I consulted. But I devised a nobler penance—I determined to bring with me the unhappy boy Mordaunt, and to keep always before me the living memorial of my misery and my guilt. I have done so, and I have thought over both till reason has often trembled on her throne. And now, to drive me to utter madness, my Clement—my own, my undoubted son, revives from the dead to be consigned to an infamous death by the machinations of his own mother !"

"Away, away !" said Norna, with a laugh, when she had heard the story to an end ; "this is a legend framed by the old corsair, to interest my aid in favour of a guilty comrade. How could I mistake Mordaunt for my son, their ages being so different ?"

"The dark complexion and manly stature may have done much," said Basil Mertoun ; "strong imagination must have done the rest."

"But give me proofs—give me proofs that this Cleveland is my son, and, believe me, this sun shall sooner sink in the east, than they shall have power to harm a hair of his head."

"These papers, these journals," said Mertoun, offering the pocket-book.

"I cannot read them," she said, after an effort, "my brain is dizzy."

"Clement had also tokens which you may remember, but they must have become the booty of his captors. He had a silver box with a Runic inscription, with which, in far other days, you presented me—a golden chaplet."

"A box !" said Norna, hastily ; "Cleveland gave me one but a day since—I have never looked at it till now."

Eagerly she pulled it out—eagerly examined the legend around the lid, and as eagerly exclaimed—"They may now indeed call me Reimkennar, for by this rhyme I know myself murderess of my son, as well as of my father !"

The conviction of the strong delusion under which she had laboured, was so overwhelming, that she sunk down at the foot of one of the pillars—Mertoun shouted for help, though in despair of receiving any ; the sexton, however, entered, and, hopeless of all assistance from Norna, the distracted father rushed out, to learn, if possible the fate of his son.

CHAPTER FORTY-SECOND

Go, some of you, cry a reprieve !
BEGGAR'S OPERA

CAPTAIN WEATHERPORT had, before this time, reached Kirkwall in person, and was received with great joy and thankfulness by the Magistrates, who had assembled in council for the purpose. The Provost, in particular, expressed himself delighted with the providential arrival of the Halcyon, at the very conjuncture when the Pirate could not escape her. The Captain looked a little surprised, and said—"For that, sir, you may thank the information you yourself supplied."

"That I supplied !" said the Provost, somewhat astonished.

"Yes, sir," answered Captain Weatherport, "I understand you to be George Torfe, Chief Magistrate of Kirkwall, who subscribes this letter."

The astonished Provost took the letter addressed to Captain Weatherport of the Halcyon, stating the arrival, force, etc., of the pirates' vessel ; but adding, that they had heard of the Halcyon being on the coast, and that they were on their guard and ready to baffle her, by going among the shoals, and through the islands and holms, where the frigate could not easily follow ; and at the worst, they were desperate enough to propose running the sloop ashore and blowing her up, by which much

337

booty and treasure would be lost to the captors. The letter, therefore, suggested, that the Halcyon should cruise betwixt Duncansbay Head and Cape Wrath, for two or three days, to relieve the pirates of the alarm her neighbourhood occasioned, and lull them into security, the more especially as the letter-writer knew it to be their intention, if the frigate left the coast, to go into Stromness Bay, and there put their guns ashore for some necessary repairs, or even for careening their vessel, if they could find means. The letter concluded by assuring Captain Weatherport, that, if he could bring his frigate into Stromness Bay on the morning of the 24th of August, he would have a good bargain of the pirates—if sooner, he was not unlikely to miss them.

"This letter is not of my writing or subscribing, Captain Weatherport," said the Provost ; "nor would I have ventured to advise any delay in your coming hither."

The Captain was surprised in his turn. "All I know is that it reached me when I was in the Bay of Thurso, and that I gave the boat's crew that brought it five dollars for crossing the Pentland Firth in very rough weather. They had a dumb dwarf as cockswain, the ugliest urchin my eyes ever opened upon. I give you much credit for the accuracy of your intelligence, Mr. Provost."

"It is as lucky as it is," said the Provost ; "yet I question whether the writer of this letter would not rather that you had found the nest cold and the bird flown."

So saying, he handed the letter to Magnus Troil, who returned it with a smile, but without any observation, aware, doubtless, with the sagacious reader, that Norna had her own reasons for calculating with accuracy on the date of the Halcyon's arrival.

Without puzzling himself farther concerning a circumstance which seemed inexplicable, the Captain requested that the examinations might proceed ; and Cleveland and Altamont, as he chose to be called, were brought up the first of the pirate crew, on the charge of having acted as Captain and Lieutenant. They had just commenced the examination, when, after some expostulation with the officers who kept the door, Basil Mertoun burst into the apartment and exclaimed, "Take the old victim for the young one !—I am Basil Vaughan, too well known on the windward station—take my life, and spare my son's !"

All were astonished, and none more than Magnus Troil, who hastily explained to the Magistrates and Captain Weatherport, that this gentleman had been living peaceably and honestly on the Mainland of Zetland for many years.

"In that case," said the Captain, "I wash my hands of the poor man, for he is safe, under two proclamations of mercy ; and, by my soul, when I see them, the father and his offspring, hanging on each other's neck, I wish I could say as much for the son."

"But how is it—how can it be ?" said the Provost: "we always called the old man Mertoun, and the young, Cleveland, and now it seems they are both named Vaughan."

"Vaughan," answered Magnus, "is a name which I have some reason

338

to remember : and, from what I have lately heard from my cousin Norna, that old man has a right to bear it."

"And, I trust, the young man also," said the Captain, who had been looking over a memorandum. "Listen to me a moment," added he, addressing the younger Vaughan, whom we have hitherto called Cleveland. "Hark you, sir, your name is said to be Clement Vaughan—are you the same, who, then a mere boy, commanded a party of rovers, who, about eight or nine years ago, pillaged a Spanish village called Quempoa, on the Spanish Main, with the purpose of seizing some treasure ?"

"It will avail me nothing to deny it," answered the prisoner.

"No," said Captain Weatherport, "but it may do you service to admit it.—Well, the muleteers escaped with the treasure, while you were engaged in protecting, at the hazard of your own life, the honour of two Spanish ladies against the brutality of your followers. Do you remember any thing of this ?"

"I am sure *I* do," said Jack Bunce ; "for our Captain here was marooned for his gallantry, and I narrowly escaped flogging and pickling for having taken his part."

"When these points are established," said Captain Weatherport, "Vaughan's life is safe—the women he saved were persons of quality, daughters to the governor of the province, and application was long since made, by the grateful Spaniard, to our government, for favour to be shown to their preserver. I had special orders about Clement Vaughan, when I had a commission for cruising upon the pirates, in the West Indies, six or seven years since. But Vaughan was gone then as a name amongst them ; and I heard enough of Cleveland in his room. However, Captain, be you Cleveland or Vaughan, I think that, as the Quempoa hero, I can assure you a free pardon when you arrive in London."

Cleveland bowed, and the blood mounted to his face. Mertoun fell on his knees, and exhausted himself in thanksgiving to Heaven. They were removed, amidst the sympathising sobs of the spectators.

"And now, good Master Lieutenant, what have you got to say for yourself ? said Captain Weatherport to the ci-devant Roscius.

"Why, little or nothing, please your honour ; only that I wish your honour could find my name in that book of mercy you have in your hand ; for I stood by Captain Clement Vaughan in that Quempoa business."

"You call yourself Frederick Altamont ? said Captain Weatherport. "I can see no such name here ; one John Bounce, or Bunce, the lady put on her tablets."

"Why, that is me—that is I myself, Captain—I can prove it ; and I am determined, though the sound be something plebeian, rather to live Jack Bunce, than to hang as Frederick Altamont."

"In that case," said the Captain, "I can give you some hopes as John Bunce."

"Thank your noble worship !" shouted Bunce ; then changing his tone, he said, "Ah, since an alias has such virtue, poor Dick Fletcher might have come off as Timothy Tugmutton ; but howsomdever d'ye see, to use his own phrase"—

"Away with the Lieutenant," said the Captain, "and bring forward Goffe and the other fellows ; there will be ropes reeved for some of them, I think." And this prediction promised to be amply fulfilled, so strong was the proof which was brought against them.

The Halcyon was accordingly ordered round to carry the whole prisoners to London, for which she set sail in the course of two days.

During the time that the unfortunate Cleveland remained at Kirkwall, he was treated with civility by the Captain of the Halcyon ; and the kindness of his old acquaintance, Magnus Troil, who knew in secret how closely he was allied to his blood, pressed on him accommodations of every kind, more than he could be prevailed on to accept.

Norna, whose interest in the unhappy prisoner was still more deep, was at this time unable to express it. The sexton had found her lying on the pavement in a swoon, and when she recovered, her mind for the time had totally lost its equipoise, and it became necessary to place her under the restraint of watchful attendants.

Of the sisters of Burgh Westra, Cleveland only heard that they remained ill, in consequence of the fright to which they had been subjected, until the evening before the Halcyon sailed, when he received, by a private conveyance, the following billet:—"Farewell, Cleveland—we part for ever, and it is right that we should—Be virtuous and be happy. The delusions which a solitary education and limited acquaintance with the modern world had spread around me, are gone and dissipated for ever. But in you, I am sure, I have been thus far free from error—that you are one to whom good is naturally more attractive than evil, and whom only necessity, example, and habit, have forced into your late course of life. Think of me as one who no longer exists, unless you should become as much the object of general praise, as now of general reproach ; and then think of me as one who will rejoice in your reviving fame, though she must never see you more !"—The note was signed M. T. ; and Cleveland, with a deep emotion, which he testified even by tears, read it an hundred times over, and then clasped it to his bosom.

Mordaunt Mertoun heard by letter from his father, but in a very different style. Basil bade him farewell for ever, and acquitted him henceforward of the duties of a son, as one on whom he, notwithstanding the exertions of many years, had found himself unable to bestow the affections of a parent. The letter informed him of a recess in the old house of Yarlshof, in which the writer had deposited a considerable quantity of specie and of treasure, which he desired Mordaunt to use as his own. "You need not fear," the letters bore, "either that you lay yourself under obligation to me, or that you are sharing the spoils of piracy. What is now given over to you, is almost entirely the property of your deceased mother, Louisa Gonzago, and is yours by every right. Let us forgive each other," was the conclusion, "as they who must meet no more."—And they never met more ; for the elder Mertoun, against whom no charge was ever preferred, disappeared after the fate

340

of Cleveland was determined, and was generally believed to have retired into a foreign convent.

The fate of Cleveland will be most briefly expressed in a letter, which Minna received within two months after the Halcyon left Kirkwall. The family were then assembled at Burgh Westra, and Mordaunt was a member of it for the time, the good Udaller thinking he could never sufficiently repay the activity which he had shown in the defence of his daughters. Norna, then beginning to recover from her temporary alienation of mind, was a guest in the family, and Minna, who was sedulous in her attention upon this unfortunate victim of mental delusion, was seated with her, watching each symptom of returning reason, when the letter we allude to was placed in her hands.

"Minna," it said—"dearest Minna!—farewell, and for ever! Believe me, I never meant you wrong—never. From the moment I came to know you, I resolved to detach myself from my hateful comrades, and had framed a thousand schemes, which have proved as vain as they deserved to be—for why, or how, should the fate of her that is so lovely, pure, and innocent be involved with that of one so guilty?—Of these dreams I will speak no more. The stern reality of my situation is much milder than I either expected or deserved; and the little good I did has outweighed, in the minds of honourable and merciful judges, much that was evil and criminal. I have not only been exempted from the ignominious death to which several of my compeers are sentenced; but Captain Weatherport, about once more to sail for the Spanish Main, under the apprehension of an immediate war with that country, has generously solicited and obtained permission to employ me, and two or three more of my less guilty associates, in the same service—a measure recommended to himself by his own generous compassion and to others by our knowledge of the coast, and of local circumstances, which, by whatever means acquired, we now hope to use for the service of our country. Minna, you will hear my name pronounced with honour, or you will never hear it again. If virtue can give happiness, I need not wish it to you, for it is yours already.—Farewell, Minna."

Minna wept so bitterly over this letter, that it attracted the attention of the convalescent Norna. She snatched it from the hand of her kinswoman, and read it over at first with the confused air of one to whom it conveyed no intelligence—then with a dawn of recollection—then with a burst of mingled joy and grief, in which she dropped it from her hand. Minna snatched it up, and retired with her treasure to her own apartment.

From that time Norna appeared to assume a different character. Her dress was changed to one of a more simple and less imposing appearance. Her dwarf was dismissed, with ample provision for his future comfort. She showed no desire of resuming her erratic life; and directed her observatory, as it might be called, on Fitful Head, to be dismantled. She refused the name of Norna, and would only be addressed by her real appellation of Ulla Troil. But the most important change remained behind. Formerly, from the dreadful dictates of spiritual despair, arising out of the circumstances of her father's death, she seemed to have considered herself as an outcast from divine grace ; besides that, enveloped in the vain occult sciences which she pretended to practise, her study, like that of Chaucer's physician, had been "but little in the Bible." Now, the sacred volume was seldom laid aside ; and, to the poor ignorant people who came as formerly to invoke her power over the elements, she only replied—"*The winds are in the hollow of His hand.*"— Her conversion was not, perhaps, altogether rational ; for this, the state of a mind disordered by such a complication of horrid incidents, probably prevented. But it seemed to be sincere, and was certainly useful. She appeared deeply to repent of her former presumptuous attempts to interfere with the course of human events, superintended as they are by far higher powers, and expressed bitter compunction when such her former pretensions were in any manner recalled to her memory. She still showed a partiality to Mordaunt, though, perhaps, arising chiefly from habit ; nor was it easy to know how much or how little she remembered of the complicated events in which she had been connected. When she died, which was about four years after the events we have commemorated, it was found that, at the special and earnest request of Minna Troil, she had conveyed her very considerable property to Brenda. A clause in her will specially directed, that all the books, implements of her laboratory, and other things connected with her former studies, should be commmitted to the flames.

About two years before Norna's death, Brenda was wedded to Mordaunt Mertoun. It was some time before old Magnus Troil, with all his affection for his daughter, and all his partiality for Mordaunt, was able frankly to reconcile himself to this match. But Mordaunt's accomplishments were peculiarly to the Udaller's taste, and the old man felt the impossibility of supplying his place in his family so absolutely, that at length his Norse blood gave way to the natural feeling of the heart, and he comforted his pride while he looked around him, and saw what he considered as the encroachments of the Scottish gentry upon the COUNTRY (so Zetland is fondly termed by its inhabitants), that as well "his daughter married the son of an English pirate, as of a Scottish thief," in scornful allusion to the Highland and Border families, to whom Zetland owes many respectable landholders ; but whose ancestors were generally esteemed more renowned for ancient family and high courage than for accurately regarding the trifling distinctions of *meum* and *tuum*. The jovial old man lived to the extremity of human life, with the happy prospect of a numerous succession in the family of his younger daughter ; and having his board cheered alternately by the minstrelsy of Claud Halcro, and enlightened by the lucubrations of Mr. Triptolemus Yellowley, who, laying aside his high pretensions, was, when he became better acquainted with the manners of the islanders, and remembered the various misadventures which had attended his premature attempts at reformation, an honest and useful representative of his principal, and never so happy as when he could escape from the spare commons of his sister Barbara, to the genial table of the Udaller. Barbara's temper also was much softened by the unexpected restoration of the horn of silver coins (the property of Norna), which she had concealed in the mansion of old Stourburgh, for achieving some of her mysterious plans, but which she now restored to those by whom it had been accidentally discovered, with an intimation, however, that it would again disappear unless a reasonable portion was expended on the sustenance of the family, a precaution to which Tronda Dronsdaughter (probably an agent of Norna's) owed her escape from a slow and wasting death by inanition.

Mordaunt and Brenda were as happy as our mortal condition permits us to be. They admired and loved each other—enjoyed easy circumstances—had duties to discharge which they did not neglect ; and, clear in conscience as light of heart, laughed, sung, danced, daffed the world aside, and bid it pass.

But Minna—the high-minded and imaginative Minna—she, gifted with such depth of feeling and enthusiasm, yet doomed to see both blighted in early youth, because, with the inexperience of a disposition equally romantic and ignorant, she had built the fabric of her happiness on a quicksand instead of a rock,—was she, could she be happy ? Reader, she *was* happy ; for, whatever may be alleged to the contrary by the sceptic and the scorner, to each duty performed, there is assigned a degree of mental peace and high consciousness of honourable exertion, corresponding to the difficulty of the task accomplished. That rest of the body which succeeds to hard and industrious toil, is not to be compared to the repose which the spirit enjoys under similar circumstances. Her resignation, however, and the constant attention which she paid to her father, her sister, the afflicted Norna, and to all who had claims on her, were neither Minna's sole nor her most precious source of comfort. Like Norna, but under a more regulated judgment, she learned to exchange the visions of wild enthusiasm which had exerted and misled her imagination, for a truer and purer connection with the world beyond us, than could be learned from the sagas of heathen bards, or the visions of later rhymers. To this she owed the support by which she was enabled, after various accounts of the honourable and gallant conduct of Cleveland, to read with resignation, and even with a sense of comfort, mingled with sorrow, that he had at length fallen, leading the way in a gallant and honourable enterprise, which was successfully accomplished by those companions to whom his determined bravery had opened the road. Bunce, his fantastic follower in good, as formerly in evil, transmitted an account to Minna of this melancholy event in terms which showed that, though his head was weak, his heart had not been utterly corrupted by the lawless life which he had for some time led, or at least that it had been amended by the change ; and that he himself had gained credit and promotion in the same action, seemed to be of little consequence to him, compared with the loss of his old captain and comrade.* Minna read the intelligence, and thanked

* We have been able to learn nothing with certainty of Bunce's fate ; but our friend, Dr. Dryasdust, believes he may be identified with an old gentleman, who, in the beginning of the reign of George I, attended the Rose Coffee-house regularly, went to the theatre every night, told mercilessly long stories about the Spanish Main, controlled reckonings, bullied waiters, and was generally known by the name of Captain Bounce.

Heaven, even while the eyes which she lifted up were streaming with tears, that the death of Cleveland had been in the bed of honour ; nay, she even had the courage to add to her gratitude, that he had been snatched from a situation of temptation ere circumstances had overcome his new-born virtue ; and so strongly did this reflection operate, that her life, after the immediate pain of this event had passed away, seemed not only as resigned, but even more cheerful than before. Her thoughts, however, were detached from the world, and only visited it, with an interest like that which guardian spirits take for their charge, in behalf of those friends with whom she lived in love, or of the poor whom she could serve and comfort. Thus passed her life, enjoying, from all who approached her, an affection, enhanced by reverence ; insomuch, that when her friends sorrowed for her death, which arrived at a late period of her existence, they were comforted by the fond reflection, that the humanity which she then laid down, was the only circumstance which had placed her, in the words of Scripture, "a little lower than the angels!"

Drawn by C. Fielding, from a sketch by the Marchioness of Stafford.

Engraved by Edw. Finden

The Hill of Hoy

NOTES TO THE PIRATE

— ◆ —

NOTE A, p. 3.—WILLIAM ERSKINE OF KINEDDER.

William Erskine of Kinedder, son of an Episcopal minister in Perthshire, was educated for the legal profession, and passed advocate 3d July 1790. He was appointed Sheriff-Depute of Orkney 6th June 1809, and in that capacity was accompanied by Scott in the Lighthouse voyage round the coast. He was raised to the bench, and took his seat as Lord Kinedder, 29th January 1822. Unfortunately, he did not long enjoy this honour, as he died, unexpectedly, on the 14th of August following, to the great grief of Sir Walter, who at this very time was wholly occupied with the arrangements connected with George IV's visit to Edinburgh. Lord Kinedder, to whom Scott had from boyhood been deeply attached, was a most amiable and accomplished man.

In 1788, when the Ode on the Popular Superstitions of the Highlands was first published (which the Wartons thought superior to the other works of Collins, but which Dr. Johnson says, "no search has yet found"), Mr. Erskine wrote several supplementary stanzas, intended to commemorate some Scottish superstitions omitted by Collins. These verses first appeared in the *Edinburgh Magazine* for April 1788.

NOTE B, p. 13.—PLANTIE CRUIVE.

A patch of ground for vegetables. The liberal custom of the country permits any person, who has occasion for such a convenience, to select out of the unenclosed moorland a small patch, which he surrounds with a dry-stone wall, and cultivates as a kail-yard, till he exhausts the soil with cropping, and then he deserts it, and encloses another. This liberty is so far from inferring an invasion of the right of proprietor and tenant, that the last degree of contempt is inferred of an avaricious man, when a Zetlander says, he would not hold a *plantie cruive* of him.

NOTE C, p. 18.—NORSE FRAGMENTS.

Mr Baikie of Tankerness, a most respectable inhabitant of Kirkwall, and an Orkney proprietor, assured me of the following curious fact :—

A clergyman, who was not long deceased, remembered well when some remnants of the Norse were still spoken in the island called North Ronaldshaw. When Gray's Ode, entitled the "Fatal Sisters," was first published, or at least first reached that remote island, the reverend gentleman had the well-judged curiosity to read it to some of the old persons of the isle, as a poem which regarded the history of their own country. They listened with great attention to the preliminary stanzas :—

> Now the storm begins to lour,
>   Haste the loom of hell prepare ;
> Iron sleet of arrowy shower
>   Hurtles in the darken'd air.

But when they heard a verse or two more, they interrupted the reader, telling him they knew the song well in the Norse language, and had often sung it to him when he asked them for an old song. They called it the Magicians, or the Enchantresses. It would have been singular news to the elegant translator, when executing his version from the text of Bartholine, to have learned that the Norse original was still preserved by tradition in a remote corner of the British dominions. The circumstance will probably justify what is said in the text concerning the traditions of the inhabitants of those remote isles, at the beginning of the eighteenth century.

Even yet, though the Norse language is entirely disused, except in so far as particular words and phrases are still retained, these fishers of the Ultima Thule are a generation much attached to these ancient legends. Of this the Author learned a singular instance.

About twenty years ago, a missionary clergyman had taken the resolution of traversing those wild islands, where he supposed there might be a lack of religious instruction, which he believed himself capable of supplying. After being some days at sea in an open boat, he arrived at North Ronaldshaw, where his appearance excited great speculation. He was a very little man, dark complexioned, and from the fatigue he had sustained, in removing from one island to another, he appeared before them ill-dressed and unshaved ; so that the inhabitants set him down as one of the Ancient Picts, or, as they called them with the usual strong guttural, Peghts. How they might have received the poor preacher in this character, was at least dubious ; and the schoolmaster of the parish, who had given quarters to the fatigued traveller, set off to consult with Mr. Stevenson, the able and ingenious engineer of the Scottish Lighthouse Service, who chanced to be on the island. As his skill and knowledge were in the highest repute, it was conceived that Mr. S. could decide at once whether the stranger was a Peght, or ought to be treated as such. Mr. S. was so good-natured as to attend the summons, with the view of rendering the preacher some service. The poor missionary, who had watched for three nights, was now fast asleep, little dreaming what odious suspicions were current respecting him. The inhabitants were assembled round the door. Mr. S., understanding the traveller's condition, declined disturbing him, upon which the islanders produced a pair of very little uncouth-looking boots, with prodigiously thick soles, and appealed to him whether it was possible such articles of raiment could belong to any one but a Peght. Mr. S., finding the prejudices of the natives so strong, was induced to enter the sleeping apartment of the traveller, and was surprised to recognise in the supposed Peght a person whom he had known in his worldly profession of an Edinburgh shopkeeper, before he had assumed his present profession. Of course, he was enabled to refute all suspicions of Peghtism.

346

I have said, in the text, that the wondrous tales told by Pontoppidan, the Archbishop of Upsal, still find believers in the Northern Archipelago. It is in vain they are cancelled even in the later editions of Guthrie's Grammar, of which instructive work they used to form the chapter far most attractive to juvenile readers. But the same causes which probably gave birth to the legends concerning mermaids, sea-snakes, krakens, and other marvellous inhabitants of the Northern Ocean, are still afloat in those climates where they took their rise. They had their origin probably from the eagerness of curiosity manifested by our elegant poetess, Mrs. Hemans :

> What hid'st thou in thy treasure-caves and cells,
> Thou ever-sounding and mysterious Sea ?

The additional mystic gloom which rests on these northern billows for half the year, joined to the imperfect glance obtained of occasional objects, encourage the timid or the fanciful to give way to imagination, and frequently to shape out a distinct story from some object half seen and imperfectly examined. Thus, some years since, a large object was seen in the beautiful Bay of Scalloway in Zetland, so much in vulgar opinion resembling the kraken, that though it might be distinguished for several days, if the exchange of darkness to twilight can be termed so, yet the hardy boatmen shuddered to approach it, for fear of being drawn down by the suction supposed to attend its sinking. It was probably the hull of some vessel which had foundered at sea.

The belief in mermaids, so fanciful and pleasing in itself, is ever and anon refreshed by a strange tale from the remote shores of some solitary islet.

The author heard a mariner of some reputation in his class vouch for having seen the celebrated sea-serpent. It appeared, so far as could be guessed, to be about a hundred feet long, with the wild mane and fiery eyes which old writers ascribe to the monster ; but it is not unlikely the spectator might, in the doubtful light, be deceived by the appearance of a good Norway log floating on the waves. I have only to add, that the remains of an animal, supposed to belong to this latter species, were driven on shore in the Zetland Isles, within the recollection of man. Part of the bones were sent to London, and pronounced by Sir Joseph Banks to be those of a basking shark ; yet it would seem that an animal so well known ought to have been immediately distinguished by the northern fishermen.

NOTE E, p. 60.—SALE OF WINDS.

The King of Sweden, the same Eric quoted by Mordaunt, "was," says Olaus Magnus, "in his time held second to none in the magical art ; and he was so familiar with the evil spirits whom he worshipped, that what way soever he turned his cap, the wind would presently blow that way. For this he was called Windy-cap."—*Historia de Gentibus Septentrionalibus. Romæ*, 1555. It is well known that the Laplanders drive a profitable trade in selling *winds*, but it is perhaps less notorious, that within these few years such a commodity might be purchased on British ground, where it was likely to be in great request. At the village of Stromness, on the Orkney main island, called Pomona, lived, in 1814, an aged dame, called Bessie Millie, who helped out her subsistence by selling favourable winds to mariners. He was a venturous master of a vessel who left the roadstead of Stromness without paying his offering to propitiate Bessie Millie ; her fee was extremely moderate, being exactly sixpence, for which, as she explained herself, she boiled her kettle and gave the bark advantage of her prayers, for she disclaimed all unlawful arts. The wind thus petitioned for was sure, she said, to arrive, though sometimes the mariners had to wait some time for it. The woman's dwelling and appearance were not unbecoming her pretensions ; her house, which was only accessible by a series of dirty and precipitous lanes, and for exposure might have been the abode of Eolus himself, in whose commodities the inhabitant dealt. She herself was, as she told us, nearly one hundred years old, withered and dried up like a mummy. A clay-coloured kerchief, folded round her head, corresponded in colour to her corpse-like complexion. Two light-blue eyes that gleamed with a lustre like that of insanity, an utterance of astonishing rapidity, a nose and chin that almost met together, and a ghastly expression of cunning, gave her the effect of Hecaté. She remembered Gow the pirate, who had been a native of these islands, in which he closed his career, as mentioned in the preface. Such was Bessie Millie, to whom the mariners paid a sort of tribute, with a feeling betwixt jest and earnest.

Note F, p. 65.—Reluctance to save Drowning Men.

It is remarkable, that in an archipelago where so many persons must be necessarily endangered by the waves, so strange and inhuman a maxim should have ingrafted itself upon the minds of a people otherwise kind, moral, and hospitable. But all with whom I have spoken agree, that it was almost general in the beginning of the eighteenth century, and was with difficulty weeded out by the sedulous intructions of the clergy, and the rigorous injunctions of the proprietors. There is little doubt it had been originally introduced as an excuse for suffering those who attempted to escape from the wreck to perish unassisted, so that, there being no survivor, she might be considered as lawful plunder. A story was told me, I hope an untrue one, that a vessel having got ashore among the breakers on one of the remote Zetland islands, five or six men, the whole or greater part of the unfortunate crew, endeavoured to land by assistance of a hawser, which they had secured to a rock ; the inhabitants were assembled, and looked on with some uncertainty, till an old man said, "Sire, if these men come ashore, the additional mouths will eat all the meal we have in store for winter ; and how are we to get more ?" A young fellow, moved with this argument, struck the rope asunder with his axe, and all the poor wretches were immersed among the breakers, and perished.

The ancient Zetlander looked upon the sea as the provider of his living, not only by the plenty produced by the fishings, but by the spoil of wrecks. Some particular islands have fallen off very considerably in their rent, since the Commissioners of the Lighthouses have ordered lights on the Isle of Sanda and the Pentland Skerries. A gentleman, familiar with those seas, expressed surprise at seeing the farmer of one of the isles in a boat with a very old pair of sails. "Had it been His will"—said the man, with an affected deference to Providence, very inconsistent with the sentiment of his speech—"Had it been *His* will that light had not been placed yonder, I would have had enough of new sails last winter."

NOTE H, p. 84.—THE DROWS.

The Drows, or Trows, the legitimate successors of the northern *duergar*, and somewhat allied to the fairies, reside, like them, in the interior of green hills and caverns, and are most powerful at midnight. They are curious artificers in iron, as well as in the precious metals, and are sometimes propitious to mortals, but more frequently capricious and malevolent. Among the common people of Zetland, their existence still forms an article of universal belief. In the neighbouring isles of Feroe, they are called Foddenskencand, or subterranean people ; and Lucas Jacobson Debes, well acquainted with their nature, assures us that they inhabit those places which are polluted with the effusion of blood, or the practice of any crying sin. They have a government, which seems to be monarchical.

NOTE I, p. 95.—ZETLAND CORN-MILLS.

There is certainly something very extraordinary to a stranger in Zetland corn-mills. They are of the smallest possible size ; the wheel which drives them is horizontal, and the cogs are turned diagonally to the water. The beam itself stands upright, and is inserted in a stone quern of the old-fashioned construction, which it turns round, and thus performs its duty. Had Robinson Crusoe ever been in Zetland, he would have had no difficulty in contriving a machine for grinding corn in his desert island. These mills are thatched over in a little hovel, which has much the air of a pig-sty. There may be five hundred such mills on one island, not capable any one of them of grinding above a sackful of corn at a time.

NOTE J, p. 125.—SIR JOHN URRY.

Here, as afterwards remarked in the text, the Zetlander's memory deceived him grossly. Sir John Urry, a brave soldier of fortune, was at that time in Montrose's army, and made prisoner along with him. He had changed so often that the mistake is pardonable. After the action, he was executed by the Covenanters ; and

> Wind-changing Warwick then could change no more.

Strachan commanded the body by which Montrose was routed.

The Sword-Dance is celebrated in general terms by Olaus Magnus. He seems to have considered it as peculiar to the Norwegians, from whom it may have passed to the Orkneymen and Zetlanders, with other northern customs.

Of their Dancing in Arms

"Moreover, the northern Goths and Swedes had another sport to exercise youth withall, that they will dance and skip amongst naked swords and dangerous weapons : And this they do after the manner of masters of defence, as they are taught from their youth by skilful teachers, that dance before them, and sing to it. And this play is showed especially about Shrovetide, called in Italian *Mascherarum*. For, before carnivals, all the youth dance for eight days together, holding their swords up, but within the scabbards, for three times turning about ; and then they do it with their naked swords lifted up. After this, turning more moderately, taking the points and pummels one of the other, they change ranks, and place themselves in an triagonal figure, and this they call *Rosam ;* and presently they dissolve it by drawing back their swords and lifting them up, that upon every one's head there may be made a square Rosa, and then by a most nimbly whisking their swords about collaterally, they quickly leap back, and end the sport, which they guide with pipes or songs, or both together ; first by a more heavy, then by a more vehement, and lastly, by a most vehement dancing. But this speculation is scarce to be understood but by those who look on, how comely and decent it is, when at one word, or one commanding, the whole armed multitude is directed to fall to fight, and clergymen may exercise themselves, and mingle themselves among others at this sport, because it is all guided by most wise reason."

To the Primate's account of the sword-dance, I am able to add the words sung or chanted, on occasion of this dance, as it is still performed in Papa Stour, a remote island of Zetland, where alone the custom keeps its ground. It is, it will be observed by antiquaries, a species of play or mystery, in which the Seven Champions of Christendom make their appearance, as in the interlude presented in "All's Well that Ends Well." This dramatic curiosity was most kindly procured for my use by Dr. Scott of Halsar Hospital, son of my friend Mr. Scott of Melbie, Zetland. Dr. Hibbert has, in his description of the Zetland Islands, given an account of the sword-dance, but somewhat less full than the following :—

Words used as a prelude to the Sword-Dance, a Danish or Norwegian Ballet, composed some centuries ago, and preserved in Papa Stour, Shetland.

(*Enter* Master, *in the character of* St. George.)

Brave gentles all within this boor,†
If ye delight in any sport,
Come see me dance upon this floor,
Which to you all shall yield comfort.
Then shall I dance in such a sort,
As possible I may or can ;
You, minstrel man, play me a Porte,††
That I on this floor may prove a man.
(*He bows, and dances in a line.*)
Now have I danced with heart and hand,
Brave gentles all, as you may see,
For I have been tried in many a land,
As yet the truth can testify ;
In England, Scotland, Ireland, France,
Italy, and Spain,
Have I been tried with that good
sword of steel.
(*Draws, and flourishes.*)
Yet, I deny that ever a man did make
me yield ;
For in my body there is strength,
As by my manhood may be seen ;
And I, with that good sword of
length,
Have oftentimes in perils been,
And over champions I was king.
And by the strength of this right
hand,
Once on a day I kill'd fifteen,
And left them dead upon the land.
Therefore, brave minstrel, do not
care,
But play to me a Porte most light,
That I no longer do forbear,
But dance in all these gentles' sight ;
Although my strength makes you
abased,
Brave gentles all, be not afraid,
For here are six champions, with me,
staid,
All by my manhood I have raised.
(*He dances.*)
Since I have danced, I think it best
To call my brethren in your sight,
That I may have a little rest,
And they may dance with all their
might ;

With heart and hand as they are
knights,
And shake their sword of steel so
bright,
And show their main strength on this
floor,
For we shall have another bout
Before we pass out of this boor,
Therefore, brave minstrel, do not care
To play to me a Porte most light,
That I no longer do forbear,
But dance in all these gentles' sight.
(*He dances, and then introduces his
knights as under.*)
Stout James of Spain, both tried and
stour§
Thine acts are known full well
indeed ;
And champion Dennis, a French
knight,
Who stout and bold is to be seen ;
And David, a Welshman born,
Who is come of noble blood ;
And Patrick also, who blew the horn,
An Irish knight amongst the wood.
Of Italy, brave Anthony the good,
And Andrew of Scotland King ;
St. George of England, brave indeed,
Who to the Jews wrought muckle
tinte.∫
Away with this !—Let us come to
sport,
Since that ye have a mind to war,
Since that ye have this bargain
sought,
Come let us flight and do not fear.
Therefore, brave minstrel, do not care
To play to me a Porte most light,
That I no longer do forbear,
But dance in all these gentles' sight.
(*He dances, and advances to* James
of Spain.)
Stout James of Spain, both tried and
stour,
Thine acts are known full well
indeed,
Present thyself within our sight,
Without either fear or dread.
Count not for favour or for feid,
Since of thy acts thou hast been sure ;
Brave James of Spain, I will thee lead,

---

* So placed in the old MS.
† *Boor*—so spelt to accord with vulgar pronunciation of the word *bower.*
†† *Porte*—so spelt in the original. The word is known as indicating a piece of music on the bagpipe, to which ancient instrument, which is of Scandinavian origin, the sword-dance may have been originally composed.
§ *Stour*—great.
∫ *Muckle tinte*—much loss or harm ; so in MS.

To prove thy manhood on this floor.
(JAMES *dances*.)
Brave champion Dennis, a French knight,
Who stout and bold is to be seen,
Present thyself here in our sight,
Thou brave French knight,
Who bold hast been ;
Since thou such valliant acts hast done,
Come let us see some of them now
With courtesy, thou brave French knight,
Draw out thy sword of noble hue.
(DENNIS *dances, while the others retire to a side*.)
Brave David a bow must string, and with awe
Set up a wand upon a stand,
And that brave David will cleave in twa.*
(DAVID *dances solus*.)
Here is, I think, an Irish knight,
Who does not fear, or does not fright,
To prove thyself a valiant man,

As thou hast done full often bright ;
Brave Ptrick, dance, if thou can.
(*He dances*.)
Thou stout Italian, come thou here ;
Thy name is Anthony, most stout ;
Draw out thy sword that is most clear,
And do thou flight without any doubt ;
Thy leg thou shake, thy neck thou lout,†
And show some courtesy on this floor,
For we shall have another bout,
Before we pass out of this boor.
Thou kindly Scotsman, come thou here ;
Thy name is Andrew of Fair Scotland ;
Draw out thy sword that is most clear,
Fight for thy king with thy right hand ;
And aye as long as thou canst stand,
Fight for thy king with all thy heart ;
And then, for to confirm his band,
Make all his enemies for to smart.
(*He dances*.)—(*Music begins*.)

FIGUIR.‡

"The six stand in rank with their swords reclining on their shoulders. The Master (St. George) dances, and then strikes the sword of James of Spain, who follows George, then dances, strikes the sword of Dennis, who follows behind James. In like manner the rest—the music playing—swords as before. After the six are brought out of rank, they and the Master form a circle, and hold the swords point and hilt. This circle is danced round twice. The whole, headed by the Master, pass under the swords held in a vaulted manner. They jump over the swords. This naturally places the swords across, which they disentangle by passing under their right sword. They take up the seven swords, and form a circle, in which they dance round.

"The Master runs under the sword opposite, which he jumps over backwards. The others do the same. He then passes under the right-hand sword, which the others follow, in which position they dance, until commanded by the Master, when they form into a circle, and dance round as before. They then jump over the right-hand sword, by which means their backs are to the circle, and their hands across their backs. They dance round in that form until the Master calls, 'Loose,' when they pass under the right sword, and are in a perfect circle.

"The Master lays down his sword, and lays hold of the point of James's sword. He then turns himself, James, and the others, into a clew. When so formed, he passes under out of the midst of the circle ; the others follow ; they vault as before. After several other evolutions, they

* Something is evidently amiss or omitted here. David probably exhibited some feat of archery.
† *Lout*—to bend or bow down, pronounced *loot*, as *doubt* is *doot* in Scotland.
‡ *Figuir*—so spelt in MS.

352

throw themselves into a circle, with their arms across the breast. They afterwards form such figures as to form a shield of their swords, and the shield is so compact that the master and his knights dance alternately with this shield upon their heads. It is then laid down upon the floor. Each knight lays hold of their former points and hilts with their hands across, which disentangle by figuirs directly contrary to those that formed the shield. This finishes the Ballet.

EPILOGUE

Mars does rule, he bends his brows,
He makes us all agast ;[*]
After the few hours that we stay here,
Venus will rule at last.
Farewell, farewell, brave gentles all,
That herein do remain,
I wish you health and happiness
Till we return again.   [*Exeunt.*

The manuscript from which the above was copied was transcribed from *a very old one,* by Mr. William Henderson jun. of Papa Stour, in Zetland. Mr. Henderson's copy is not dated, but bears his own signature, and from various circumstances, it is known to have been written about the year 1788.

NOTE L, p. 160.—THE DWARFIE STONE.

This is one of the wonders of the Orkney Islands, though it has been rather undervalued by their late historian, Mr. Barry. The island of Hoy rises abruptly, starting as it were out of the sea, which is contrary to the gentle and flat character of the other Isles of Orkney. It consists of a mountain, having different eminences or peaks. It is very steep, furrowed with ravines, and placed so as to catch the mists of the Western Ocean, and has a noble and picturesque effect from all points of view. The highest peak is divided from another eminence, called the Ward Hill, by a long swampy valley full of peat-bogs. Upon the slope of this last hill, and just where the principal mountain of Hoy opens into a hollow swamp, or corri, lies what is called the Dwarfie Stone. It is a great fragment of sandstone, composing one solid mass, which has long since been detached from a belt of the same materials, cresting the eminence above the spot where it now lies, and which has slid down till it reached its present situation. The rock is about seven feet high, twenty-two feet long, and seventeen feet broad. The upper end of it is hollowed by iron tools, of which the marks are evident, into a sort of apartment, containing two beds of stone, with a passage between them. The uppermost and largest bed is five feet eight inches long, by two feet broad, which was supposed to be used by the dwarf himself ; the lower couch is shorter, and rounded off, instead of being squared at the corners. There is an entrance of about three feet and a half square, and a stone lies before it calculated to fit the opening. A sort of skylight

[*] *Agast*—so spelt in MS.

353

window gives light to the apartment. We can only guess at the purpose of this monument, and different ideas have been suggested. Some have supposed it the work of some travelling mason ; but the *cui bono* would remain to be accounted for. The Rev. Mr. Barry conjectures it to be a hermit's cell ; but it displays no symbol of Christianity, and the door opens to the westward. The Orcadian traditions allege the work to be that of a dwarf, to whom they ascribe supernatural powers and a malevolent disposition, the attributes of that race in Norse mythology. Whoever inhabited this singular den certainly enjoyed

Pillow cold and sheets not warm.

I observed, that commencing just opposite to the Dwarfie Stone, and extending in a line to the sea-beach, there are a number of small barrows, or cairns, which seem to connect the stone with a very large cairn where we landed. This curious monument may therefore have been intended as a temple of some kind to the northern Dii Manes, to which the cairns might direct worshippers.

NOTE M, p. 160.—CARBUNCLE ON THE WARD HILL.

"At the west end of this stone (*i.e.* the Dwarfie Stone) stands an exceeding high mountain of a steep ascent, called the Ward Hill of Hoy, near the top of which, in the months of May, June and July, about midnight, is seen something that shines and sparkles admirably, and which is often seen a great way off. It hath shined more brightly before than it does now, and though many have climbed up the hill and attempted to search for it, yet they could find nothing. The vulgar talk of it as some enchanted carbuncle, but I take it rather to be some water sliding down the face of some smooth rock, which, when the sun, at such a time, shines upon, the reflection causeth that admirable splendour."—Dr. WALLACE'S *Description of the Islands of Orkney*, 8vo, Lond., 1700, p. 52.

NOTE N, p. 181.—FORTUNE-TELLING RHYMES.

The Author has in chapter xx supposed that a very ancient northern custom, used by those who were accounted soothsaying women, might have survived, though in jest rather than earnest, among the Zetlanders, their descendants. The following original account of such a scene will show the ancient importance and consequence of such a prophetic character as was assumed by Norna :—

"There lived in the same territory (Greenland) a woman named Thorbiorga, who was a prophetess, and called the Little Vola (or fatal sister), the only one of nine sisters who survived. Thorbiorga during the winter used to frequent the festivities of the season, invited by those who were desirous of learning their own fortune, and the future events which impended. Torquil being a man of consequence in this country, it fell to his lot to inquire how long the dearth was to endure with which the country was then afflicted ; he therefore invited the prophetess to his house, having made liberal preparation, as was the custom, for receiving

354

a guest of such consequence. The seat of the soothsayer was placed in an eminent situation, and covered with pillows filled with the softest eider down. In the evening she arrived, together with a person who had been sent to meet her, and show her the way to Torquil's habitation. She was attired as follows :— She had a sky-blue tunic, having the front ornamented with gems from the top to the bottom, and wore around her throat a necklace of glass beads.* Her head-gear was of black lambskin, the lining being the fur of a white wild cat. She leant on a staff, having a ball at the top.† The staff was ornamented with brass, and the ball or globe with gems or pebbles. She wore a Hunland (or Hungarian) girdle, to which was attached a large pouch, in which she kept her magical implements. Her shoes were of sealskin, dressed with the hair outside, and secured by long and thick straps, fastened by brazen clasps. She wore gloves of the wild cat's skin with the fur in-most. As this venerable person entered the hall, all saluted her with due respect. But she only returned the compliments of such as were agreeable to her. Torquil conducted her with reverence to the seat prepared for her, and requested she would purify the apartment and company assembled by casting her eyes over them. She was by no means sparing of her words. The table being at length covered, such viands were placed before Thorbiorga as suited her character of a soothsayer. These were a preparation of goat's milk and a mess composed of the hearts of various animals ; the prophetess made use of a brazen spoon and a pointless knife, the handle of which was composed of a whale's tooth, and ornamented with two rings of brass. The table being removed, Torquil addressed Thorbiorga, requesting her opinion of his house and guests, at the same time intimating the subjects on which he and the company were desirous to consult her.

"Thorbiorga replied, it was impossible for her to answer their inquiries until she had slept a night under his roof. The next morning, therefore, the magical apparatus necessary for her own purpose was prepared, and she then inquired, as a necessary part of the ceremony, whether there was any female present who could sing a magical song called *Vardlokur*. When no songstress such as she desired could be found, Gudrida, the daughter of Torquil, replied, 'I am no sorceress or soothsayer : but my nurse, Haldisa, taught me, when in Iceland, a song called *Vardlokur*.'—'Then thou knowest more than I was aware of,' said Torquil. 'But as I am Christian,' continued Gudrida, 'I consider these rites as matters which it is unlawful to promote, and the song itself as unlawful.'—'Nevertheless,' answered the soothsayer, 'thou mayest help us in this matter without any harm to thy religion, since the task must remain with Torquil to provide everything necessary for the present purpose.' Torquil also earnestly entreated Gudrida till she consented to grant his request. The females then surrounded Thorbiorga, who took her place on a sort of elevated stage; Gudrida then sung the magic song, with a voice so sweet and tuneful, as to excel anything that had been

* We may suppose the beads to have been of the potent adderstone, to which so many virtues were ascribed.

† Like those anciently borne by porters at the gates of distinguished persons as a badge of office.

355

heard by any present. The soothsayer, delighted with the melody, returned thanks to the singer, and then said, 'Much I have now learned of dearth and disease approaching the country, and many things are now clear to me which before were hidden as well from me as others. Our present dearth of substance shall not long endure for the present, and plenty will in the spring succeed to scarcity. The contagious diseases, also, with which the country has been for some time afflicted, will in a short time take their departure. To thee, Gudrida, I can, in recompense for thy assistance on this occasion, announce a fortune of higher import than any one could have conjectured. You shall be married to a man of name here in Greenland ; but you shall not long enjoy that union ; for your fate recalls you to Iceland, where you shall become mother of a numerous and honourable family, which shall be enlightened by a luminous ray of good fortune. So, my daughter, wishing thee health, I bid thee farewell.' The prophetess, having afterwards given answers to all queries which were put to her, either by Torquil or his guests, departed to show her skill at another festival to which she had been invited for that purpose. But all which she presaged, either concerning the public or individuals, came truly to pass."

The above narrative is taken from the Saga of Erick Randa, as quoted by the learned Bartholine in his curious work. He mentions similar instances, particularly of one Heida, celebrated for her predictions, who attended festivals, for the purpose, as a modern Scotsman might say, of *spaeing* fortunes, with a gallant *tail* or retinue of thirty male and fifteen female attendants.—See *De Causis Contemptœ a Danis adhue Gentilibus Mortis*, lib. iii cap. 4 [Hafniæ, 1689, 4to].

NOTE O, p. 182.— ZETLAND FISHERMEN.

Dr. Edmonston, the ingenious author of *A View of the Ancient and Present State of the Zetland Islands*, has placed this part of the subject in an interesting light. "It is truly painful to witness the anxiety and distress which the wives of these poor men suffer on the approach of a storm. Regardless of fatigue, they leave their homes and fly to the spot where they expect their husbands to land, or ascend the summit of a rock, to look out for them on the bosom of the deep. Should they get the glimpse of a sail, they watch, with trembling solicitude, its alternate rise and disappearance on the waves ; and though often tranquillised by the safe arrival of the objects of their search, yet it sometimes is their lot 'to hail the bark that never can return.' Subject to the influence of a variable climate, and engaged on a sea naturally tempestuous, with rapid currents, scarcely a season passes over without the occurrence of some fatal accident or hairbreadth escape."—*View, etc., of the Zetland Islands*, vol. I. p. 238. Many interesting particulars respecting the fisheries and agriculture of Zetland, as well as its antiquities, may be found in the work we have quoted.

NOTE P, p. 188.—PROMISE OF ODIN

Although the Father of Scandinavian mythology has been as a deity long forgotten in the archipelago, which was once a very small part of his realm, yet even at this day his name continues to be occasionally attested as security for a promise.

It is curious to observe that the rites with which such attestations are still made in Orkney correspond to those of the ancient Northmen. It appears from several authorities that in the Norse ritual, when an oath was imposed, he by whom it was pledged passed his hand, while pronouncing it, through a massive ring of silver kept for that purpose.* In like manner, two persons, generally lovers, desirous to take the promise of Odin, which they considered as peculiarly binding, joined hands through a circular hole in a sacrificial stone, which lies in the Orcadian Stonehenge, called the Circle of Stennis, of which we shall speak more hereafter. The ceremony is now confined to the troth-plighting of the lower classes, but at an earlier period may be supposed to have influenced a character like Minna in the higher ranks.

NOTE Q, p. 224.—PICTISH BURGH.

The Pictish Burgh, a fort which Norna is supposed to have converted into her dwelling-house, has been fully described in the Notes upon Ivanhoe, vol. ix p. 477, of this edition. An account of the celebrated Castle of Mousa is there given, to afford an opportunity of comparing it with the Saxon Castle of Coningsburgh. It should, however, have been mentioned, that the Castle of Mousa underwent considerable repairs at a comparatively recent period. Accordingly, Torfæus assures us that even this ancient pigeon-house, composed of dry stones, was fortification enough, not indeed to hold out a ten years' siege, like Troy in similar circumstances, but to wear out the patience of the besiegers. Erland, the son of Harold the Fairspoken, had carried off a beautiful women, the mother of a Norwegian earl, also called Harold, and sheltered himself with his fair prize in the Castle of Mousa. Earl Harold followed with an army, and, finding the place too strong for assault, endeavoured to reduce it by famine ; but such was the length of the siege, that the offended Earl found it necessary to listen to a treaty of accommodation, and agreed that his mother's honour should be restored by marriage. This transaction took place in the beginning of the thirteenth century, in the reign of William the Lion of Scotland.† It is probable that the improvements adopted by Erland on this occasion, were those which finished the parapet of the Castle, by making it project outwards, so that the tower of Mousa rather resembles the figure of a dicebox, whereas others of the same kind have the form of a truncated cone. It is easy to see how the projection of the highest parapet would render the defence more easy and effectual. [In 1859, the Society of Antiquaries exerted themselves in effecting repairs on the Tower, which give promise of permanency.]

NOTE R, p. 246.—ANTIQUE COINS FOUND IN ZETLAND.

While these sheets were passing through the press, I received a letter from an honourable and learned friend, containing the following

* See the Eyrbiggia Saga.
† See Thorm. *Torfœi Orcades*, p. 131.

passage, relating to a discovery in Zetland :—"Within a few weeks, the workmen taking up the foundation of an old wall, came on a hearthstone, under which they found a horn, surrounded with massive silver rings, like bracelets, and filled with coins of the Heptarchy, in perfect preservation. The place of finding is within a very short distance of the supposed residence of Norna of the Fitful Head."—Thus one of the very improbable fictions of the tale is verified by a singular coincidence.

Note S, p. 273.—CHARACTER OF NORNA.

The character of Norna is meant to be an instance of that singular kind of insanity, during which the patient, while she or he retains much subtlety and address for the power of imposing upon others, is still more ingenious in endeavouring to impose upon themselves. Indeed, maniacs of this kind may be often observed to possess a sort of double character, in one of which they are the being whom their distempered imagination shapes out, and in the other, their own natural self, as seen to exist by other people. This species of double consciousness makes wild work with the patient's imagination, and judiciously used, is perhaps a frequent means of restoring sanity of intellect. Exterior circumstances striking the senses, often have a powerful effect in undermining or battering the airy castles which the disorder had excited.

A late medical gentleman, my particular friend, told me the case of a lunatic patient confined in the Edinburgh Infirmary. He was so far happy that his mental alienation was of a gay and pleasant character, giving a kind of joyous explanation to all that came in contact with him. He considered the large house, numerous servants, etc., of the hospital, as all matters of state and consequence belonging to his own personal establishement, and had no doubt of his own wealth and grandeur. One thing alone puzzled this man of wealth. Although he was provided with first-rate cook and proper assistants, although his table was regularly supplied with every delicacy of the season, yet he confessed to my friend, that, by some uncommon depravity of the palate, everthing he ate *tasted of porridge*. This peculiarity, of course, arose from the poor man being fed upon nothing else, and because his stomach was not so easily deceived as his other senses.

NOTE T, p. 274.—BIRDS OF PREY.

So favourable a retreat does the island of Hoy afford for birds of prey, that instances of their ravages, which seldom occur in other parts of the country, are not unusual there. An individual was living in Orkney not long since, whom, while a child in its swaddling clothes, an eagle actually transported to its nest in the hill of Hoy. Happily the eyry being known, and the bird instantly pursued, the child was found uninjured, playing with the young eagles. A story of a more ludicrous transportation was told me by the reverend clergyman who is minister of the island. Hearing one day a strange grunting, he suspected his servants had permitted a sow and pigs, which were tenants of his farmyard, to get among his barley crop. Having in vain looked for the transgressors upon solid earth, he at length cast his eyes upwards, when he discovered one of the litter in the talons of a large eagle, which was soaring away with the unfortunate pig (squeaking all the while with terror) towards her nest in the crest of Hoy.

NOTE U, p. 316.—THE STANDING STONES OF STENNIS.

The Standing Stones of Stennis, as by a little pleonasm this remarkable monument is termed, furnishes an irresistible refutation of the opinion of such antiquaries as hold that the circles usually called Druidical were peculiar to that race of priests. There is every reason to believe, that the custom was as prevalent in Scandinavia as in Gaul or Britain, and as common to the mythology of Odin as to Druidical superstition. There is every reason to think, that the Druids never occupied any part of the Orkneys, and tradition, as well as history, ascribes the Stones of Stennis to the Scandinavians. Two large sheets of water, communicating with the sea, are connected by a causeway, with openings permitting the tide to rise and recede, which is called the Bridge of Broisgar. Upon the eastern tongue of land appear the Standing Stones, arranged in the form of a half-circle, or rather a horse-shoe, the height of the pillars being fifteen feet and upwards. Within this circle lies a stone, probably sacrificial. One of the pillars, a little to the westward, is perforated with a circular hole, through which loving couples are wont to join hands when they take the *Promise of Odin*, as had been repeatedly mentioned in the text. The enclosure is surrounded by barrows, and on the opposite isthmus, advancing towards the Bridge of Broisgar, there is another monument of Standing Stones, which, in this case, is completely circular. They are less in size than those on the eastern side of the lake, their height running only from ten or twelve to fourteen feet. This western circle is surrounded by a deep trench drawn on the outside of the pillars ; and I remarked four tumuli, or mounds of earth, regularly disposed around it. Stonehenge excels this Orcadian monument ; but that of Stennis is, I conceive, the only one in Britain which can be said to approach it in consequence. All the northern nations marked by those huge enclosures the places of popular meeting, either for religious worship or the transaction of public business of a temporal nature. The *Northern Popular Antiquities* contain, in an abstract of the Eyrbiggia Saga, a particular account of the manner in which the Helga Fels, or Holy Rock, was set apart by the Pontiff Thorolf for solemn occasions.

I need only add, that, different from the monument on Salisbury Plain, the stones which were used in the Orcadian circle seemed to have been raised from a quarry upon the spot, of which the marks are visible.

GLOSSARY TO THE PIRATE

– ◆ –

A', all.
ABOON, above.
AE, one.
AIGRE, sour.
AIK, oak.
AIRN, iron.
ALOW, ablaze.
ANGUS, Forfarshire.
AROINT, avaunt.
AVER, a cart-horse.
AWMOUS, alms.

BACK-SPAULD, back part of the shoulder.
BAILIE, a magistrate.
BAIRN, a child.
BEE-SKEP, bee-hive.
BERN, a child.
BICKER, a wooden dish.
BIGGIN, building.
BLAND, a drink made from butter-milk.
BLATE, bashful.
BLURT, to burst, out-speaking.
BOLE, a small aperture.
BONALLY, a parting drink.
BONNIE-WALLIES, gewgaws.
BOOBIE, a dunce.
BOWIE, wooden dish for milk.
BRAID, broad.
BRAWS, fine clothes.
BREEKLESS, wanting the breeches.

CALLANT, a lad.
CARLINE, a witch.
CATERAN, a Highland robber.
CAUSEYED SYVER, causewayed sewer.
CHAPMAN, a small merchant, or pedlar.

CHIELD, a fellow.
CLASHES AND CLAVERS, scandal and nonsense.
CLAVER, gossip, scandal.
CLOG, a billet of wood.
COAL-HEUGH, coal pit.
COG, a wooden bowl.
COGFU', a bowlful.
COUP, to barter.
CRAIG, a crag.
CRAIG, the neck.
CREEL, a basket ; IN A CREEL, foolish.
CROWDIE, meal and water.
CUMMER, neighbour, gossip.
CUSSER, a stallion.
COWP, to upset.

DAFFIN, larking.
DAFT, crazy.
DAIKER, to work or walk in a lazy, irresolute way.
DEAD THRAW, the last agony.
DEFTLY, handsomely.
DEIL, devil.
DIE, a toy.
DING, knock.
DIVOT, thin turf used for roofing cottages.
DOUR, stubborn.
DOWLAS, a strong linen cloth.
DOWIE, dark.
DRAMMOCK, meal soaked in water.
DUDS, rags.
DUNT, to knock.

EEN, eyes.
EMBAYE, enclose.

FA', fall.
FACTOR, a land steward.

360

FARCIE ON HIS FACE, a malediction.

FASH, trouble.

FERLIES MAKE FOOLS FAIN, wonders make fools eager.

FEY-FOLK, fated or unfortunate folk.

FIFISH, crazy, eccentric.

FLICHTER, to flutter or tremble.

FLOTSUM and JETSUM (*legal*), what has been floated ashore from a wreck.

FORBY, besides.

FORPIT, the fourth part of a peck measure.

FOWD, the judge who formerly presided over the court of Orkney and Shetland.

FREIT, a charm or superstition.

GABERLUNZIE, a beggar.

GAED, went.

GANE, gone.

GAR, to oblige or force.

GATE, way, or mode.

GANGREL, vagrant.

GEAR, property.

GEY MONY, a good many.

GIE, give.

GILLS, the jaws.

GIN, if.

GLAMOUR, fascination or charm.

GLEBE, land belonging to the parsonage.

GLOWER, to gaze.

GOWK, a fool.

GOWPEN, as much as can be held in both hands when placed together.

GRAIP, a grip or stable-fork.

GREW, to shiver.

GRIST, mill-fee payable in kind.

GUDE SAIN ! God bless us !

GUDEMAN and GUDEWIFE, the heads of the house.

GUISARD, a mummer.

GYRE-CARLINE, hobgoblin.

HAENA, have not.

HALD, hold.

HALLENSHAKER, a vagabond or beggar.

HALSE, the throat.

HAND-QUERN, hand-mill.

HAPPER, a seed-trough in a mill.

HARRIE, to rob.

HASP, a hank of yarn.

HAUD, hold.

HJALTLAND, the old name for Shetland, supposed to have been derived from Hialti, a Norse Viking.

HINNY, honey.

HIRPLE, to hobble.

HIRSEL, to move or slide down.

HOUSEWIFESKEP, housewifery.

HOUT ! tut !

HAVINGS, behaviour.

HOWFF, a retreat or meeting-place.

ILL-FA'RD, ill-favoured.

ILKA, each.

IN A CREEL, foolish.

INFANG and OUTFANG, right of trying thieves.

JOUGS, an instrument for securing criminals at the pillory.

KALE-POT, large pot for boiling broth.

KAILYARD, cabbage garden.

KIEMPIE, a Norse champion.

KIST, a chest.

KITTLE, ticklish.

KNAVESHIP, dues payable to the mill servants.

LAIR, learning.

LAVE, the remainder.

LAWRIGHT-MAN, the judge of weights and measures.

LAWTING, Shetland Court of Judicature.

LISPUND, thirty pounds avoirdupois.

LOCK, a small quantity.
LUG, the ear.
LUM, a chimney.

MAIN, to moan.
MAIR, more.
MASKING-FAT, a mashing-vat.
MAUN, must.
MEARNS, Kincardineshire.
MELTITH, food, a meal.
MUCKLE, much.
MY CERTIE ! my faith !

NACKET, a portable refreshment
or luncheon.
NAPERY, linen.
NATHELESS, nevertheless.
NEIST, next.
NIEVEFU', a handful.
NOWT, black cattle.

OUT-TAKEN, except.
OVERLAY, a cravat.
OWSEN, oxen.

PARTAN, a crab.
PELTRIE, trash.
PIT, put.
PLANT-A-CRUIVE, small
enclosure for growing
vegetables.
PUIR, poor.
PUND SCOTS, 1s. 8d. sterling.

QUERN, hand-mill.

RANDY, a scold.
RAPE, rope.
RANZELMAN, a sort of constable
or petty magistrate.
REDDING-KAME, a dressing-
comb.
REEK, smoke.
RITT, a scratch or incision.
ROKELAY, a short cloak.
ROOSE THE FORD, judge of the
ford.
ROTTON, a rat.

SAIN, to bless.
SAIR, sore.

SANDIE-LAVROCK, the sea-lark.
SAUNT, saint.
SAUT, salt.
SCART, scratch ; also a sea-fowl.
SCOURIE, a young gull.
SCOWRIE, shabby, mean.
SEALGH, a seal.
SHARNEY-PEAT, fuel made of
cow's dung.
SHELTIE, a Shetland pony.
SHOGH, *Gaelic*, there.
SIC, such.
SICCAR, sure, easy.
SILLOCK, a young coal-fish or
cod.
SILLER, money.
SKELPING, galloping.
SKEP, a hive.
SKIO, a hut.
SKIRL, scream.
SKUDLER, master of the
ceremonies.
SLAP, a gap or pass.
SLOCKEN, to quench.
SNACK, a hasty meal.
SNECK, the latch of the door.
SONSY, stout and handsome.
SORNER, one who lives upon his
friends.
SOUGH, a sigh.
SPAED, foretold.
SPEER, inquire.
SPREICHERIE, movables.
SPUNK, fire, a match.
STITHY, an anvil.
STREEK, stretch.
STRIDDLE, to straddle.
SUCKEN, mill-dues.
SULD, should.
SUMPH, a lubbery fellow.
SYNE, ago, since.
SYVER, a sewer or drain.

TAEN, taken.
THAIRM, catgut.
THEGITHER, together.
THIGGER, a dependant, a
beggar.

THIRL, the obligation on a tenant to have his flour ground at a certain mill.

THOLE, endure.

THRAWART, perverse, athwart.

TITTIE, little sister.

TOOM, empty.

TOY, a sort of mutch hanging over the shoulders.

TRINDLE, to trundle.

TROCK, to bargain or do business.

TROW, a spirit or elf believed in by the Norse.

UDALLER, a landholder by right of long succession.

ULZIE, oil.

UMQUHILE, the late.

UNCO, particularly.

UNHALSED, unhailed or saluted.

VIFDA, dried beef.

VIVERS, victuals.

VOE, an inlet of the sea.

WADMAAL, woollen cloth made in Shetland.

WARLOCK, witch.

WAUR, worse.

WHEEN, a few.

WHITTLE, a knife.

WHITTIE-WHATTIE, shuffling or wheedling.

WHOMLED, turned over.

WOWF, crazy.

YAGGER, a travelling merchant, or pedlar.

YARFA, a fibrous kind of peat.

YARN WINDLE, a winding instrument.

YARTA or YARTO, my dear (from the Icelandic *Hiarta*, the heart).

YELLOCHED, yelled.

YESTREEN, yesterday.

YETT, a gate.